Sara
CRAVEN

HIS RELUCTANT BRIDE

C000059773

THE *Sara* CRAVEN
COLLECTION

August 2016

September 2016

October 2016

November 2016

Sara
CRAVEN
HIS RELUCTANT BRIDE

MILLS &
BOON

All rights reserved including the right of reproduction in whole or in part in any form. This edition is published by arrangement with Harlequin Books S.A.

This is a work of fiction. Names, characters, places, locations and incidents are purely fictional and bear no relationship to any real life individuals, living or dead, or to any actual places, business establishments, locations, events or incidents. Any resemblance is entirely coincidental.

This book is sold subject to the condition that it shall not, by way of trade or otherwise, be lent, resold, hired out or otherwise circulated without the prior consent of the publisher in any form of binding or cover other than that in which it is published and without a similar condition including this condition being imposed on the subsequent purchaser.

® and TM are trademarks owned and used by the trademark owner and/or its licensee. Trademarks marked with ® are registered with the United Kingdom Patent Office and/or the Office for Harmonisation in the Internal Market and in other countries.

First Published in Great Britain 2016
By Mills & Boon, an imprint of HarperCollins*Publishers*
1 London Bridge Street, London, SE1 9GF

HIS RELUCTANT BRIDE © 2016 Harlequin Books S.A.

The Marchese's Love-Child © 2004 Sara Craven
The Count's Blackmail Bargain © 2005 Sara Craven
In the Millionaire's Possession © 2005 Sara Craven

ISBN: 978-0-263-92240-0

09-1016

Our policy is to use papers that are natural, renewable and recyclable products and made from wood grown in sustainable forests.
The logging and manufacturing processes conform to the legal environmental regulations of the country of origin.

Printed and bound in Spain
by CPI, Barcelona

THE MARCHESE'S
LOVE-CHILD

Former journalist **Sara Craven** published her first novel 'Garden of Dreams' for Mills & Boon in 1975. Apart from her writing (naturally!) her passions include reading, bridge, Italian cities, Greek islands, the French language and countryside, and her rescue Jack Russell/cross Button. She has appeared on several TV quiz shows and in 1997 became UK TV Mastermind champion. She lives near her family in Warwickshire – Shakespeare country.

CHAPTER ONE

'YOU'RE going back to Italy?' There was outrage in Lily Fairfax's voice as she turned on her daughter. Anger too. 'Oh, I don't believe it. You can't—you mustn't.'

Polly Fairfax sighed soundlessly. 'Mother, I'm escorting an elderly lady to Naples, where she'll be met by her family, upon which—I catch the next flight home. I'll be gone for a few hours at most. Hardly *Mission Impossible*.'

'You said you'd never return there,' her mother said. 'You swore it.'

'Yes, I know,' Polly acknowledged wearily. 'But that was three years ago. And circumstances change. This is a work assignment, and there's no one else to do it. Since Safe Hands was featured on that holiday programme, we've been snowed under with requests.' She adopted a persuasive tone. 'And you enjoyed seeing me on television—you know you did.' She added a smile. 'So you can't complain if I'm in demand as a consequence.'

Mrs Fairfax wasn't pacified. 'Is this why this woman—this Contessa Whatsit wants you? Because you've been on television?'

Polly laughed. 'I shouldn't think so for a moment. She's far too grand to bother with anything so vulgar. And her name's the Contessa Barsoli.'

Her mother dismissed that impatiently. 'I didn't think you liked her very much.'

Polly shrugged. 'I don't particularly. She's been a total pain the whole week I've been with her. And I'm damned sure she doesn't care for me either,' she added musingly. 'She always looks at me as if I'm a slug in her salad. Believe me, I shan't be tempted to linger.'

'Then why did she choose you?'

'The devil she knows, perhaps.' Polly shrugged again. 'As opposed to some stranger. Anyway, she needs someone to see to her luggage, and make sure she's got all her documentation. Which is where Safe Hands comes in, of course.'

7

She leaned forward. 'To be honest, Mum, I don't know how much longer I can go on turning down jobs in Italy, just because of something that happened three years ago. I like my job, and I want to hang on to it. But Mrs Terence is running a business here, not an agency for people who've been crossed in love.'

'It was,' her mother reminded her tightly, 'rather more than that.'

'Whatever.' Polly bit her lip. 'But I can't pick and choose my clients, and I think Mrs T has made all the allowances over Italy that she's going to. So I have to treat it as just another destination from now on.'

'And what about Charlie?' Mrs Fairfax demanded fiercely. 'What's going to happen to him while you're gadding off?'

It hardly seemed to Polly that enduring another twenty-four hours in the company of a disdainful Italian autocrat counted as 'gadding'.

And her mother had never objected to her role as child-minder before, even when Polly was absent on other, much longer trips. In fact she'd declared that Charlie's presence had given her a new lease of life.

She looked out of the window to where her cheerful two-year-old was trotting about after his grandfather, picking up hedge clippings.

She said slowly, 'I thought he would stay with you, as usual.'

There were bright spots of colour in her mother's face. 'But it's not usual—is it? You're deliberately defying my wishes—yet again. I was totally against your taking that job in Sorrento three years ago, and how right I was. You came slinking home pregnant by some local Casanova, who didn't want to know about you any more. Can you deny it?'

'To be fair, Sandro had no more idea that I was expecting a baby than I did myself,' Polly said levelly. 'Although I agree it would have made no difference if he had known. But that's all in the past. I've—rebuilt my life, and he'll have moved on too.' She paused. 'All the same, I promise not to go within ten miles of Sorrento, if that will make you feel better.'

'I'd feel better if you didn't go at all,' her mother returned sharply. 'But if it really is just a day trip, I suppose I can't stop you.'

'You'll hardly know I've gone,' Polly assured her. 'Thanks, Mum.' She gave her a swift hug. 'You're a star.'

'I'm an idiot,' Lily Fairfax retorted, but she sounded slightly mollified. 'Are you going to stay for supper? I've made one of my steak pies.'

'It's good of you, darling,' said Polly, mentally bracing herself for another battle. 'But we must get back. I have this trip to prepare for.'

Mrs Fairfax gave her a tragic look. 'But I've got Charlie's favourite ice-cream for dessert. He'll be so disappointed.'

Only because you've already told him, Polly thought without pleasure.

Aloud, she said, 'You really mustn't spoil him like that.'

Her mother pouted. 'It's a sad thing if I can't give my only grandchild the occasional treat.' She paused. 'Why not leave him here—if you're going to be busy this evening?' she coaxed. 'It'll save you time in the morning if you have a plane to catch.'

'It's a kind thought.' Polly tried to sound positive. 'But I really look forward to my evenings with Charlie, Mum. I—I see so little of him.'

'Well, that's something your father and I wanted to discuss with you,' her mother said with sudden briskness. 'There's a lot of unused space in this house, and if we were to extend over the garage, it would make a really nice flat for you both. And it would mean so much less disruption for Charlie.'

She emptied the carrots she'd been scraping into a pan. 'We've had some preliminary plans drawn up, and, if you stayed, we could look at them over supper perhaps.'

Polly supposed, heart sinking, that she should have seen it coming—but she hadn't. Oh, God, she thought, is this the day from hell, or what?

She said quietly, 'Mum, I do have a flat already.'

'An attic,' her mother dismissed with a sniff, 'with a room hardly bigger than a cupboard for Charlie. Here, he'd have room to run about, plus a routine he's accustomed to. And we're in the catchment area for a good primary school, when the time comes,' she added. 'I think it's the perfect solution to all sorts of problems.'

My main problem, Polly thought wearily, is prising Charlie out of this house at the end of the working day. Of staking a claim in my own child. She'd seen trouble looming when her own former bedroom was extensively redecorated and refitted for Charlie, despite her protest that he wouldn't use it sufficiently to justify the expense.

Her mother must have had this in mind from the first.

She rallied herself, trying to speak reasonably. 'But I need my independence. I'm used to it.'

'Is that what you call the way you live? You're a single mother, my girl. A statistic. And this glamorous job of yours is little better than slavery—running around all over the place at the beck and call of people with more money than sense. And where did it lead? To you making a fool of yourself with some foreigner, and ruining your life.' She snorted. 'Well, don't come to me for help if you mess up your life a second time.'

Polly's head went back in shock. She said unsteadily, 'That is *so* unfair. I made a mistake, and I've paid for it. But I still intend to live my life on my own terms, and I hope you can accept that.'

Mrs Fairfax's face was flushed. 'I can certainly see you're determined to have your own way, regardless of Charlie's wellbeing.' She sent her daughter a fulminating glance. 'And now I suppose you'll take him with you, just to make your point.'

'No,' Polly said reluctantly. 'I won't do that—this time. But I think you have to accept that I do have a point.'

'Perhaps you'd send Charlie indoors as you leave.' Her mother opened a carton of new potatoes and began to wash them. 'He's getting absolutely filthy out there, and I'd like him to calm down before he eats.'

'Fine.' Polly allowed herself a small, taut smile. 'I'll pass the message on.'

As she went into the garden, Charlie headed for her gleefully, strewing twigs and leaves behind him. Polly bent to enfold him, the breath catching in her throat as she inhaled his unique baby scent. Thinking again, with a pang, how beautiful he was. And how painfully, searingly like his father...

Her mother had never wanted to know any details about his paternity, referring to Sandro solely as 'that foreigner'. The fact that Charlie, with his curly black hair, olive skin and long-lashed eyes the colour of deep topaz, was also clearly a Mediterranean to his fingertips seemed to have eluded her notice.

But it was the details that only Polly could recognise that brought her heart into her mouth, like the first time her son had looked at her with that wrenchingly familiar slow, slanting smile. His baby features were starting to change too, and she could see that he was going to have Sandro's high-bridged nose one day, and the same straight brows.

It would be like living with a mirror image before too long, Polly told herself, thinking forlornly that nature played cruel tricks at times. Why couldn't Charlie have inherited her own pale blonde hair and green eyes?

She smoothed the hair back from his damp forehead. 'Gran wants you to go inside, darling,' she whispered. 'You're sleeping here tonight. Won't that be fun?'

Her father came to join them, his brows lifting at her words. 'Will it, my love?' His voice was neutral, but the glance he sent her was searching.

'Yes.' Polly cleared her throat, watching Charlie scamper towards the house. 'It—it seems a shame to uproot him, when I have to start work early tomorrow.'

'Yes.' He paused. 'She means it all for the best, you know, Poll,' he told her quietly.

'He's my child, Dad.' Polly shook her head. 'I have to have an opinion on what's best for him, too. And that doesn't include moving back here.'

'I know that,' her father said gently. 'But I'm also aware how hard it must be raising a child without any kind of support from his father—and I'm not simply talking about the economics of it.'

He sighed. 'You were so precious to me, I can't imagine a man not wanting to involve himself with his own flesh and blood.'

Polly's lips moved in a wintry little smile. 'He didn't want to know, Dad—about either of us. It was best to leave it that way.'

'Yes, love,' he said. 'So you told me. But that hasn't stopped me from worrying—or your mother either.' He gave her a swift hug. 'Take care.'

Polly's thoughts were troubled as she rode home on the bus alone. Her mother's attempts to totally monopolise her grandson was becoming a seriously tricky situation, and she wasn't sure she had sufficient wisdom to resolve it.

The last thing she wanted was for Charlie to become a battleground, but even a mild suggestion that she should enrol him at a local nursery for a few hours a week so that he could mix with other children had provoked such an injured reception from Mrs Fairfax that she hadn't dared raise the subject again.

Her mother's hostile attitude to her work was a different thing.

Safe Hands had proved the job of her dreams, and she knew, without conceit, that she was good at it.

The people who made use of the company were mainly female and usually elderly, people who needed someone young, relatively strong and capable to deal with their luggage, guide them through airports and escort them safely round unfamiliar foreign cities.

Polly was the youngest of Mrs Terence's employees, but she had a gift for languages, and her brief career as a holiday rep had taught her patience and tolerance to add to her natural sense of humour—qualities she soon found she needed in abundance.

She knew how to diffuse potentially explosive situations with overseas Customs, find restaurants that were sympathetic to delicate digestions, hotels in peaceful locations that were also picturesque, and shops prepared to deliver purchases to hotels, or post them on to addresses abroad. She could also discover which art galleries and museums were prepared to arrange quiet private tours for small groups.

And she never showed even a trace of irritation with even the most high-handed behaviour from her charges.

After all, she was being paid for acceding to their whims and fancies, and part of her skill was in making them forget that was how she earned her living, and persuading them that she was there for the sheer pleasure of their company.

But with the Contessa Barsoli, it had been a struggle from day one.

Polly had long accepted that not all her clients would like her, but she did need them to trust her, and, from the start, her senses had detected an inflexible wariness, bordering on hostility at times, in the *contessa*'s attitude which she was at a loss to account for.

Whatever the reason, there had never been any real warmth between them, so Polly had been genuinely astonished to hear that the *contessa* had specifically requested her services again for the homeward leg of her journey to southern Italy, and was prepared to pay her a generous cash bonus too.

Surprised—but also alarmed enough to ask herself if the money was really worth the damage to her nervous system.

Her previous visit—the first and last—had left her scarred—and scared. And there was no way she'd have dared risk a return, if there'd been the slightest chance she might encounter Sandro again. But the odds against such a meeting must run into millions to one. But irrational as it might seem, even the remotest possibility still had the power to make her tremble.

They said time was a great healer, but the wound Sandro had dealt her was still agonisingly raw.

She'd tried so hard to block out the memories of that summer in Sorrento three years ago. The summer she thought she'd fallen in love, and believed she was loved in return. But the images she'd hoped were safely locked away forever had broken free, and were running wild in her brain again.

Her room, she thought, wincing, during the hours of siesta, the shutters closed against the beat of the sun, and only the languid whirr of the ceiling fan and their own ragged breathing to break the silence.

And Sandro's voice murmuring soft, husky words of passion, his hands and mouth exploring her naked body with sensuous delight. The heated surge of his body into hers at the moment of possession.

She had lived for those shadowed, rapturous afternoons, and warm, moonlit nights, which made the pain of his ultimate betrayal even more intense.

What a gullible little fool I was, Polly thought with self-derision. And I can't say I wasn't warned. The other reps said that he was just looking for some easy summer sex, and cautioned me to be careful, but I wouldn't listen because I knew better.

I knew that he loved me, and that when the summer was over we were going to be married. I was convinced of it—because he'd said so.

I thought it was that innocent—that simple. I should have realised that he wasn't what he seemed. He told me he worked at one of the big hotels, but he always had too much money to be just a waiter or a barman. And these jobs were usually taken by younger men, anyway, while Sandro was thirty at least.

I knew from the first that there were depths to him that belied the seaside Romeo tag—and that the latent power I always sensed in him was part of his attraction for me.

But I liked the fact that he was something of an enigma. That there were questions about him still to be answered. I thought I would have the rest of my life to find out the truth.

Yes, I was a fool, but it never once occurred to me that I could be in any real danger. That there was another darker side to his life, far away from the sunlight and whispered promises.

Not until he got bored with me. Not until his friend arrived—the man in the designer suit with the smile that never reached his eyes. The man who came to tell me that it was all over, and to suggest, smiling suavely and icily, that it would be better for my health to get out of Sorrento, and away from Italy altogether.

The man who told me that I'd become an inconvenience, and that it would be much safer for me to quit my job and go back to England.

And that I should never try to contact Sandro, or come back to Italy again—ever.

In return for which I was to receive the equivalent of fifty thousand pounds.

Polly shuddered. Even now the memory made her shake inside. But what had crucified her then, and still hurt today, was that Sandro hadn't had the guts to come to her himself—to tell her in person that it was finished between them. And why...

She'd rejected his money with anger and contempt, unable to believe that he could insult her like that. Ordered his confederate out of her room.

But, all the same, she'd obeyed and left, because she was too heartbroken—and also too frightened to stay. She didn't know what Sandro could be involved with to afford a bribe of that size—and she didn't want to know. But something had reached out from the shadows around him, which had touched her life, and destroyed her hope of happiness.

She had been at home for several weeks before it dawned on her that she was pregnant—a knowledge born slowly from grief, bewilderment and unbelievable loneliness. At first she'd told herself that it could not be true—that they'd always been so careful—except for one night when their frantic, heated need for each other had outweighed caution.

And that, she had realised, stunned, must have been when it happened. Another blow to deepen the agony of pain and betrayal. Yet, although the prospect of single-motherhood had filled her with dread, she'd never once considered the obvious alternative and sought an abortion.

Her mother had thought of it, of course. Had urged her to do it, too, cajoling one minute, threatening the next. Railing at Polly for her stupidity, and for bringing shame on the family. Swearing that she would have nothing further to do with her daughter or the baby if the pregnancy went ahead. A resolution that had lasted no longer than an indrawn breath from the moment she had seen her newborn grandson.

Charlie had instantly taken the place of the son she'd always longed for. And there'd never been any question about who was going to look after him when Polly recovered and went back to work.

But, as Polly ruefully acknowledged, the arrangement had become a two-edged sword. Over the months, she seemed to have been sidelined into playing an elder sister's role to Charlie. Any slight wail, bump or graze brought her mother running, leaving Polly to watch helplessly while Mrs Fairfax hugged and comforted him. And that was not good.

She had to admit that her mother had not been too wide of the mark when she'd described Polly's flat as an attic. It had a reasonable-sized main room, a basic bathroom and a minuscule kitchen opening out of it, plus Charlie's cubby-hole. Polly herself slept on the sofa bed in the living room.

But she couldn't deny it was a weary climb up steep and badly lit stairs to reach her front door, especially when she was encumbered with Charlie, his bag of necessities and his buggy, which she didn't dare leave in the entrance hall in case it was stolen.

Once inside, she kept her home space clean and uncluttered, the walls painted in cool aqua. Most of the furniture had been acquired at auction sales, including the sofa bed, for which she'd bought a new cover in an Aztec print of deep blue, crimson and gold.

It wasn't flash, but the rent was reasonable, and she always felt the place offered comfort and a welcome as she went in.

And tonight she was in sore need of both.

It was a warm evening, so she unlocked the living-room window and pushed up the lower sash, sinking down onto the wooden seat beneath. There was some cold chicken and salad in the fridge, and it would be a moment's work to put a potato to bake in her second-hand microwave.

But she was in no hurry to complete her supper preparations. She felt tired and anxious—and more than a little disheartened. It seemed strange not to hear the clatter of Charlie's feet on the stripped boards as he trotted about, or his incessant and often unintelligible chatter.

She missed, too, his sudden, unsteady gallop to her arms. That most of all, she thought, her throat tightening.

I should have brought him home, she told herself restlessly, and not let myself be out-manoeuvred like that.

She felt, she realised, totally unsettled, for all kinds of reasons, so maybe this would be a good time to review her life, and see if she needed to make some changes.

And, first and foremost, she needed to be able to spend more time with Charlie.

When she began working again, after he was born, Safe Hands had seemed ideal, more of a career choice than an ordinary job. Having her cake, and eating it—or so she'd thought then.

She had been able to go on with the travelling she loved, and, as well as her salary, the majority of the clients paid her a cash bonus as well. Even at London prices, she could afford to live, and provide Charlie with what he needed, although there was never much left over for extras.

But his needs were changing, and so, she realised, were hers.

For one thing, it wasn't essential to work, or even live, in London. In fact, it would be sheer relief to be able to say goodbye to those stifling journeys on the underground and buses.

She could move to a totally different area altogether, away from the south-east of England. Deliberately select a place where it would be cheaper to live, and find a job in local tourism. Something strictly nine-to-five, with no time away from home, so that she could spend her leisure hours with her son.

During the day she'd need a minder for him, of course. There was no way out of that. But she'd look for someone young and lively, caring for other children too, so that Charlie would have playmates. Maybe, in time, she could even get a foot on the housing ladder—find somewhere small and manageable, hopefully with a garden. Something she would never be able to afford in London.

She would miss this flat, she thought, sighing, and it would be a wrench leaving Safe Hands but reason was telling her it would be for the best.

I have, she thought, to make a life for us both. For Charlie and myself. I need to build a proper relationship with him. And I can't do that if we stay here. Because I won't be allowed to.

But she wasn't delusional enough to think she could strike out on her own without a struggle, she told herself, wrinkling her nose. Her mother would fight her every step of the way, coming up with every possible reason why she should not do this thing—and a few impossible ones, too.

And when she saw Polly could not be moved, she would be very bitter. There might even be an open breach between them.

But that won't last forever, she thought. Whatever Mum thinks of me, she'll still want to maintain contact with Charlie.

She got to her feet. She would eat now, and when supper was over she'd use her laptop to go internet-exploring, looking at house prices in different parts of the country. Now that she'd made up her mind, there was no time to be lost.

Strange, she thought, how I can suddenly be so sure of that.

Yet the pressure on her to accept the Italian assignment must have contributed to her decision. It had left her feeling uneasy—and awoken too many bad memories.

A clean break with the past was what she needed. New job—new home—new friends.

She would never be able to forget, of course, that Sandro was Charlie's father. But in time, it might begin to hurt less. And she might even be able to stop being afraid. One day.

'See Naples and die, eh?' The man in the adjoining seat emphasised the originality of his remark with a slight dig in Polly's ribs, as their plane descended towards Capodichino Airport. 'That's what they say, isn't it?'

Polly gritted her teeth as she gave a wintry smile in acknowledgement.

But I don't care what 'they' say, she told herself fiercely. Naples is going to be my jumping-off point for a whole new life. And I plan to live every moment of it.

She couldn't say she'd enjoyed the flight. The *contessa* might need her physical assistance, but she certainly hadn't wanted her company. Which was why she was seated in first class, while Polly herself was in economy, with a neighbour who considered her presence his personal bonus.

Never mind, she thought. In a few moments I'll never have to see him again, or the *contessa* either.

She'd sipped mineral water throughout the flight, in spite of her fellow traveller's unceasing efforts to buy her what he called a proper drink. And the irony was that she'd have welcomed some alcohol, to dispel the shaky chill which had settled in the pit of her stomach. The closer they had got to their destination, their progress cheerfully marked by the captain, the more nervous she'd become.

I shan't relax until I'm safely back in Britain, she thought.

On the surface, she was calmness itself. She was wearing the company uniform of a slim-fitting, button-through dress in navy linen, with the distinctive silver brooch showing a pair of clasped hands pinned to her left shoulder. Her pale hair was in a loose knot on top of her head, and she wore her usual dusting of powder, and soft pink lipstick.

As they touched down, and the plane began to taxi to its stand, Polly reached under the seat, and extracted the navy leather satchel which held the travel documents and a few basic necessities in case of delay. Her client, she was sure, would have an eagle eye for the slightest lapse in efficiency.

Her companion nudged her again. 'Dangerous city, they say,' he whispered. 'If you're on your own tonight, I'd be happy to show you around.'

'Tonight,' she told him, 'I intend to be back in London.' And left him gaping.

Contessa Barsoli was a tall woman, rake-thin, with immaculately coiffed white hair and still handsome in a chilly way. A member of the cabin staff was permitted to help her descend the aircraft steps while Polly followed, instinctively lifting her face to the brilliant warmth of the southern sun.

Once inside the terminal, she found her charge a chair, retrieved her luggage and guided her through the formalities.

'There has been a small change of plan,' the older woman informed her abruptly. 'I am too tired to undertake a long car journey down to the Campania, so my cousin has arranged a suite for me at the Grand Hotel Neapolitana. You will accompany me there.'

Polly knew resignedly that she shouldn't be surprised. Most of the arrangements she'd made for the *contessa* during her stay in Britain had been subject to alteration, usually at the last moment. Why should this time be any different?

But this wasn't just irritating, she reminded herself, schooling her expression. It was seriously inconvenient. She had a return flight to catch, and the *contessa* knew it.

'Do you wish me to get us a taxi?' she asked quietly. If she could find a driver who knew a few short cuts through Naples' crowded streets, she might still be in with a chance.

'A taxi?' The *contessa* made it sound like a tumbrel. 'My cousin has sent a car and chauffeur for us. Oblige me by finding him.'

That was easily achieved. Transferring the *contessa* and her luggage to the roomy depths of the limousine was a completely different matter. The lady liked to take her time, oblivious to Polly's simmering frustration as the minutes ticked past.

The traffic was a nightmare, and when they did reach the hotel at last, Polly accepted that she probably wouldn't make it back to the airport in time for her flight.

I haven't a prayer, she told herself resignedly. It'll take me half an hour to get her to the lift.

But to her astonishment, the *contessa* suddenly became quite sprightly. She conducted her own registration at the desk, waving Polly regally away, and made no fuss about the prompt unloading of her luggage.

An under-manager escorted her, bowing, to the lift, where Polly caught up with her.

She said awkwardly, 'I need to say goodbye now, *contessa*, if I'm to get my flight.'

She got a severe look. 'But I wish you to accompany me to the suite, *signorina*. I have ordered coffee and *biscotti* to be served there. Besides,' she added, seeing that Polly was on the verge of protest, 'there is still the question of the money I offered you. I do not conduct such transactions in the foyers of hotels. If you want to be paid, you will come with me now.'

Groaning silently, Polly stood beside her as the lift made its way upward. They emerged onto a crimson-carpeted corridor, opposite a heavily carved door.

The under-manager produced a key with a flourish, and unlocked the door, and, still bowing, showed them ceremoniously into the suite.

Polly found herself in a large drawing room, shaded by the shutters which had been drawn over the long windows to combat the force of the mid-June sunlight. She had a confused impression of brocaded sofas and fresh flowers in elaborate arrangements, their scent hanging languidly in the air.

And realised suddenly that the room wasn't empty as she'd first thought. Because someone was there—someone standing by the windows, his figure silhouetted against the slatted light. Someone tall, lean and unforgettably—terrifyingly—familiar.

Even before he spoke, Polly knew who he was. Then his voice, low-pitched and faintly husky, reached her, and there was no longer room for any doubt. Or any hope, either.

He said, 'Paola *mia*. So, you have come to me at last.'

He moved—came away from the window, and walked towards her with that long, lithe stride she would have known anywhere, his shadow falling across the floor as he approached.

She tried to speak—to say his name, but her trembling mouth could not obey her and shape the word.

Because this could not be happening. Sandro could not be here, in this room, waiting for her.

As he reached her, she cried out and flung up her bare and unavailing hands in a desperate effort to keep him at bay. Only to find the shadows crowding round her, welcoming her, as she slid helplessly downwards into the dark whirl of oblivion.

CHAPTER TWO

AWARENESS returned slowly, accompanied by an acrid smell that filled her nose and mouth with its bitterness, making her cough and mutter a feeble protest.

She lay very still, fighting against a feeling of nausea, hardly daring to open her eyes. Her senses told her that she was cushioned on satiny softness, and that she was not alone. That in the real world behind her closed eyelids, there was movement—people talking. And the heavy noise of traffic.

She propped herself dizzily on one elbow, and looked around her. She was lying in the middle of a vast bed, covered in deep gold embroidered silk. She was shoeless, she realised, and the top buttons of her dress had been unfastened.

The first person she saw was the *contessa*, as she stepped back, replacing the stopper in a small bottle. Smelling salts, Polly thought, dazedly. The older woman always insisted on having some handy in case travel motion upset her.

And, standing in silence a few yards away, was Sandro, head bent, his face in profile.

Not a figment of her imagination, as she'd hoped, but a nightmare that lived and breathed, and would not go away.

And not the laughing, dishevelled lover, wearing frayed shorts and an old T-shirt, and badly in need of a haircut, that she'd once known and desired so passionately, but that other, hidden man whose identity she'd never even suspected as she lay in his arms.

This other Sandro wore a dark suit that had clearly emanated from a great Italian fashion house. The dark curling hair had been tamed, to some extent at least, and there wasn't a trace of stubble, designer or otherwise, on what she could see of the hard, tanned face, only a faint breath of some expensive cologne hanging in the air.

His immaculate white shirt set off a sombre silk tie, and a thin platinum watch encircled his wrist.

Whatever path he'd chosen to follow, it had clearly brought him serious money, Polly thought, anger and pain tightening her throat. And she didn't want to contemplate how it might have been obtained. Who said crime didn't pay?

Nor was he staying silent out of weakness, or any sense of guilt. Instinct told her that. He was simply exercising restraint. Under the stillness, Polly could sense his power—and the furious burn of his anger, rigorously reined in. Could feel the violence of his emotions in the pulse of her blood and deep within her bones, just as she'd once known the naked imprint of his skin on hers, and the intimate heat of his possession.

As if, she thought with a sudden sick helplessness, she lived within his flesh. Part of him. As she had once been.

Now that the impossible had happened, and she was face to face with him again, she was shocked by the intensity of her physical reaction to him. Ashamed too.

She had to make herself remember the cruel brutality of his rejection. The cynical attempt to buy her off, and the explicit threat that had accompanied it.

She needed to remind herself of the abyss of pain and loneliness that had consumed her after she'd fled from Italy. And, most important of all, she had to get out of here, and fast.

She sat upright, lifting a hand to her head as the room swayed about her.

The movement riveted everyone's attention, and Sandro took a hasty step forward, pausing when Polly flinched away from him involuntarily, his mouth hardening in an icy sneer.

'No,' he said. 'It is not pretty. You should have been prepared in advance, perhaps. Warned what to expect.'

As he came closer, Polly saw his face clearly for the first time. Saw the jagged scar that had torn its way from the corner of his eye, across the high cheekbone and halfway to his jaw.

For a brief moment she was stunned, as shocked as if she had seen some great work of art deliberately defaced.

He looked older too, and there was a weariness in the topaz eyes that had once glowed into hers.

Oh, God, she thought, swallowing. He thinks that I find him repulsive, and that's why I turned away just now.

A pang of something like anguish twisted inside her, then she took a deep breath, hardening herself against a compassion he did not need or deserve.

Let him think what he wanted, she thought. He'd chosen his life, and however rich and powerful he'd become he'd clearly paid violently for his wealth. And she'd been fortunate to escape when she did, and keep her own wounds hidden. That was all there was to be said.

She looked away from him. 'I don't understand.' Her voice was small and strained. 'What am I doing here? What—happened?'

'You fainted, *signorina*.' It was the *contessa* who answered her. 'At my cousin's feet.'

'Your cousin?' Polly repeated the words dazedly, her mind wincing away from the image the older woman's words conjured up of herself, unconscious, helpless. She shook her head, immediately wishing that she hadn't. 'Is that supposed to be some kind of joke?'

The *contessa* drew herself up, her brows lifting in hauteur. 'I do not understand you, *signorina*. There is no joke, I assure you. Alessandro is the son of my husband's late cousin. Indeed, his only child.'

'No,' Polly whispered. 'He can't be. It's not possible.'

'I am not accustomed to having my word doubted, Signorina Fairfax.' The *contessa*'s tone was frigid. She paused. 'But you are not yourself, so allowances must be made.' She handed Polly a glass of water. 'Drink this, if you please. And I will ask for some food to be brought. You will feel better when you have eaten something.'

'Thank you, but no.' Polly put down the empty glass and moved to the edge of the bed, putting her feet to the floor. She was still feeling shaky, but self-preservation was more important than any temporary weakness.

She'd fainted—something she'd never done in her life before, and a betraying sign of vulnerability that she could ill afford.

She spoke more strongly, lifting her chin. 'I would much prefer to leave. Right now. I have a flight to catch.'

'You are not very gracious, Paola *mia*.' Sandro's voice was soft, but there was a note in it that made her quiver. 'Especially when I have had you brought all the way from England just to see you again.'

Had you brought... The words echoed in her head, menacing her.

'Then you've wasted your time, *signore*.' Was that how you

addressed the supposed cousin of an Italian countess? Polly had
no idea, and didn't much care. 'Because I have no wish to
see you.'

There was a bitter irony in this, she thought. This was supposed
to be the first day of her new life, and instead she seemed to have
walked into a trap.

Ironic, inexplicable—and dangerous too, she realised, a shiver
chilling her spine.

The *contessa* had deliberately set her up, it seemed. So she must
be in Sandro's power in some way. But however scaring that was,
it couldn't be allowed to matter, Polly reminded herself swiftly.
She didn't know what was going on here, nor did she want to
know. The most important thing, now, was to distance herself, and
quickly.

'"*Signore*"?' Sandro questioned, his mouth twisting. 'Isn't that
a little formal—for us, *bella mia*?'

Her pulses quickened at the endearment, putting her instantly
on the defensive.

'To me this is a formal occasion,' she said tautly. 'I'm working—escorting the *contessa*. And there is no "us",' she added.
'There never was.'

'You don't think so?' The topaz eyes were watchful. 'Then I
shall have to jog your memory, *cara*.'

'I can remember everything I need to, thanks.' Polly spoke
fiercely. 'And it doesn't change a thing. You and I have nothing
to say to each other. Not now. Not ever again.' She took a deep
breath. 'And now I wish to leave.'

Sandro shook his head slowly. 'You are mistaken, *carissima*.'
His voice was soft. 'There is a great deal to be said. Or else I
would not be here. But perhaps it would be better if we spoke
alone.'

He turned to the *contessa*. 'Would you excuse us, Zia Antonia?'
His tone was coolly courteous. 'I think Signorina Fairfax and I
should continue our conversation in private.'

'No.' Polly flung the word at him, aware that her voice was
shaking. That her body was trembling too. 'I won't stay here—
and you can't make me.'

He looked at her, his mouth relaxing into a faint smile. 'You
don't think so, Paola *mia*? But you're so wrong.'

'*Contessa!*' Polly appealed as the older woman moved towards the door. 'You had no right to do this. Don't leave me alone—please.'

The *contessa* gave her a thin smile. 'You require a chaperone?' she queried. 'But surely it is a little late for that?' She paused, allowing her words to sting, then turned to Sandro. 'However, Alessandro, Signorina Fairfax might feel more at ease if you conducted this interview in the *salotto*. A suggestion, merely.'

'I bow to your superior wisdom.' Sandro spoke briskly.

Before Polly could register what he intended, and take evasive action, he had stepped forward, scooping her up into his arms as if she were a child. She tried to hit him, but he controlled her flailing hands, tucking her arms against her body with insulting ease.

'Be still,' he told her. 'Unless, of course, you would prefer to remain here.' He glanced significantly back at the bed.

'No, I would not.' She glared up into the dark, ruined face. 'But I can walk.'

'When you are shaking like a leaf? I think not.'

In spite of her continuing struggles, Sandro carried her back into the now deserted drawing room. The *contessa* had disappeared, Polly realised with a stab of panic, and, although neither of them were her company of choice, it meant that she and Sandro were now alone. Which was far worse...

'This was easier when you were unconscious,' he commented as he walked across the room with her. 'Although I think you have lost a little weight since our last meeting, Paola *mia*.'

'Put me down.' Polly was almost choking with rage, mingled with the shock of finding herself in such intimately close proximity to him. 'Put me down, damn you.'

'As you wish.' He lifted a shoulder nonchalantly, and dropped her onto one of the sofas flanking the fireplace. She lay, winded and gasping, staring up at him.

'You bastard,' she said unevenly, and he clicked his tongue in reproach as he seated himself on the sofa opposite.

'What a name to call the man you are going to marry.'

'Marry?' The word strangled in her throat. Polly struggled to sit up, pulling down the navy dress which had ridden up round her thighs. 'You must be insane.'

He shrugged. 'I once asked you to be my wife. You agreed.' He watched as she fumbled to re-fasten the buttons he'd undone, his lips slanting into faint amusement. Looking so like Charlie that she almost cried out. 'That makes us *fidanzato*. Or am I wrong?'

'You're wrong,' she bit back at him, infuriated at her own awkwardness, and at the pain he still had the power to cause her. 'Totally and completely mistaken. And you know it, as well as I do, so let's stop playing games.'

'Is that what we're doing?' Sandro shrugged again. 'I had not realised. Perhaps you would explain the rules to me.'

'Not rules,' she said. 'But laws. Laws that exist to deal with someone like you.'

'*Dio,*' he said. 'So you think our government interests itself in a man's reunion with his woman? How enlightened of them.'

'Enlightened enough to lock you up for harassment,' Polly said angrily. 'And I am not your woman.'

He grinned at her, making her realise that the scar had done little to diminish the powerful sexual charisma he'd always been able to exert, which was as basic a part of him as the breath he drew. He was lounging on the sofa opposite, jacket discarded and tie loosened, his long legs thrust out in front of him, totally at his ease. Enjoying, she thought bitterly, his control of the situation. While she remained shaken and on edge, unable to comprehend what was happening. Or why. Especially why...

'No? Perhaps we should have stayed in the bedroom after all, *cara mia*, and continued the argument there.' The topaz eyes held a familiar glint.

'You dare to lay a hand on me again,' Polly said, through gritted teeth, 'and I'll go straight to the police—have you charged.'

'With what offence? The attempted seduction of my future bride?' He shook his head regretfully. 'A girl who once spent a summer as my lover. I don't think they would take you seriously, *carissima*.'

'No,' she said. 'I expect they have to do what you want—like the *contessa*. And where is she, by the way?'

'On her way back to Comadora, where she lives.'

'But she was supposed to be staying here.'

He shook his head. 'No, Paola *mia*. I reserved the suite for myself.' He smiled at her. 'And for you to share with me.'

'If this is a joke,' Polly said, recovering herself from a stunned silence, 'I don't find it remotely funny.'

'And nor do I,' Sandro said with sudden curtness. 'This is no game, believe me. I am entirely serious.' He paused. 'Do you wish to test my determination?'

He hadn't moved, but suddenly Polly found herself remembering the strength of the arms that had held her. Recognised the implacable will that challenged her from his gaze and the sudden hardening of the mobile, sensuous mouth which had once stopped her heart with its caresses.

She bit her lip, painfully. 'No.'

'You begin to show sense at last,' he approved softly.

'Not,' she said, 'when I agreed to come to Italy today. That was really stupid of me.'

'You must not blame Zia Antonia,' he said. 'She shares your disapproval of my methods.' He shrugged. 'But if you and I had not met again tonight, then it would have been at some other time, in some other place. Or did you think I would simply allow you to vanish?'

She said coldly, 'Yes, of course. In fact, I counted on it.'

His head came up sharply, and she saw the sudden tensing of his lean body. 'You were so glad to be rid of me?'

You dare to say that—to me? After what you did?

The words trembled on the tip of her tongue, but she fought them back. He must never know how she'd felt in those dazed, agonised weeks following his rejection. How she'd ached for him, drowning in bewilderment and pain. Pride had to keep her silent now. Except in defiance.

She shrugged in her turn. 'Do you doubt it?' she retorted. 'After all, when it's over, it's over,' she added with deliberate *sang-froid*.

'You may think that, *mia cara*.' His voice slowed to a drawl. 'I do not have to agree.'

She looked down at her hands, clamped together in her lap. 'Tell me something,' she said in a low voice. 'How did you find me?'

'I was at a conference on tourism. A video was shown of a British company which looks after single travellers. You were its star, *cara mia*. I was—most impressed.'

Polly groaned inwardly. Her one and only television appearance, she thought, that her mother had been so proud of. It had never occurred to her that it might be shown outside the UK.

She said coldly, 'And you were suddenly overwhelmed by nostalgia, I suppose.'

'If so,' Sandro said with equal chill, 'I would have sighed sentimentally and got on with my life. But it reminded me that there are issues still unresolved between us.' He paused. 'As you must know, also.'

She moistened her dry lips with the tip of her tongue. 'I need to say something. To tell you that—I've never talked about you. Never discussed anything that happened between us. And I wouldn't—I give you my word...'

He stared at her, frowning. 'You wished to wipe me from your memory? Pretend I had never existed? But why?'

She swallowed, her throat tightening. *Because it hurt too much to remember,* she thought.

'Once I discovered your—your background,' she said, 'I realised it was—necessary. The only way...'

His gaze became incredulous. 'It disturbed you to find that I was rich. You'd have preferred me to be a waiter, existing on tips?' He gave a short laugh. *'Dio mio.'*

Polly sat up very straight. She said coldly, 'It was the way you'd acquired your money that I found—unacceptable. And your—connections,' she added bravely, controlling a shiver as she remembered the man who had confronted her. The scorn and menace he'd exuded.

'Unbelievable,' he said slowly. 'But if you expect me to apologise for my family, Paola, you will wait a long time.' The look he sent her was hard—unrelenting. 'I am what I am, and nothing can change that. Nor would I wish it to.'

He was silent for a moment. *'Certamente,* I hoped—at one time—that you would find it possible to live in my world. Understand how it works, and accept its limitations.'

But you soon changed your mind about that, Polly thought painfully. In fact, once you realised that I'd never be suitable, you were willing to pay a small fortune to get me out of your life altogether—and I should be grateful for that. Relieved that you sent me away, and saved me from an impossible moral dilemma. Prevented me from making a choice I might have hated myself for later, when I was sane again...

And knowing that has to be my salvation now. Has to...

She said stiltedly, 'That could—never have happened. It was better—safer for us to part.'

'You think so?' He drew a harsh breath. 'Then how is it I have been unable to forget you, Paola *mia*, no matter how hard I have tried? Or how many other women there have been in my life since you?'

She lifted her chin, resisting the sudden anguish that stabbed her. 'Am I supposed to feel flattered?'

'You ask me about your emotions?' Sandro asked derisively. 'What did I ever know about your thoughts—your feelings? I saw what I wished to see—believed what I needed to believe.'

He shook his head. '*Madonna*, how many times in these long months I have wished I could simply—dismiss you from my mind.' He paused. 'Forget you as easily as you have rejected the memory of me.'

Oh, God, Polly thought numbly, how little you know...

She tried to speak evenly. 'Life doesn't remain static. It moves on—and we have to go with it.'

'Do you go alone?' Sandro enquired, almost negligently studying his fingernails. 'Or do you have company on your journey?'

Polly tensed. 'That,' she said, 'is no concern of yours.'

'Then let us make it my concern,' he said softly. 'Because I wish to know the truth. Do you live alone?'

The question seemed to hang in the air between them while her mind ran in frantic circles, looking for a way out.

Useless to go on telling him it was none of his business. That would not deter him. On the other hand, it would be a humiliation to admit that since him, there had been no one in her life. That she existed in self-imposed celibacy.

She could invent a lover, but she'd always been a terrible liar, and the risk of him seeing through her story was too great.

And then, as if a light had dawned, she realised there was no need for invention after all.

Polly lifted her chin, and faced him. 'No,' she said, very clearly. 'I don't live alone.'

It was no more than the truth, she thought. And it might just set her free...

Sandro was very still suddenly, little golden fires leaping in his eyes as his gaze met hers. He said, 'And, naturally, your companion is male?' He watched her swift, jerky nod.

There was another silence, then he said harshly, 'Do you love him?'

Unbidden, an image of Charlie's small sleeping face invaded

her mind, and her mouth curved involuntarily, instinctively into tenderness.

'Yes,' she said. 'And I always will.'

As soon as she spoke the words, she knew they were a mistake. That she'd snatched at a means of escape from him, without fully considering the consequences. And that she could have gone too far.

'You dare to tell me that?' His voice crackled with suppressed anger.

Her heart jolted nervously, but she knew that she had to finish what she'd started. That she had no other choice.

She tilted her chin defiantly. 'What did you expect? That I'd stay single in memory of you? Like you remained celibate for me?' she added scornfully. 'Dream on—please.'

Sandro's eyes were fixed on her, a slow flame burning in their depths. 'And how long has he been part of your life? The truth.'

She touched the tip of her tongue to her dry lips. 'Two years—or so.'

'So,' he said slowly. 'You went from my arms to his.' His gaze went over her, measuring and contemptuous. 'I see you wear no ring.'

She swallowed. 'That's my own choice.'

'And have you whispered the same promises to him that you once made to me?' His voice was quiet. Compelling.

She hesitated, choosing her words with care. 'He knows that I'll—always be there for him.'

'How touching,' Sandro said softly. 'Yet you left him to come to Italy.' His sudden smile was cool. Dangerous. 'And to me.'

'I believed I was working for the *contessa*,' Polly returned fiercely, trying to conceal the fact that she was shaking inside, nearing the edge of panic. 'I had no idea that she could be a relation of yours—or that you were even in the region. If I'd known, I wouldn't be here.'

She flung back her head. 'So, how did you persuade her to do your dirty work? Bribery—or blackmail?'

His mouth thinned. 'You are not amusing, *carissima*. Be very careful.'

'Why?' she challenged recklessly. 'I already know the lengths you're prepared to go to—when there's something you want.'

Or when you've stopped wanting...

You sent me away, she thought. *So why are you here now, tormenting me like this—reviving all these unwanted memories?*

Her throat ached suddenly at the thought of them. But that was a weakness she couldn't afford, because the room seemed to be shrinking, the walls closing in, diminishing the space between them. A space she needed to maintain at all costs.

'I wonder if that's true.' Sandro's voice was quiet—reflective. 'Perhaps you don't know me as well as you think.'

'Well,' she said, 'that hardly matters any more.' She paused. 'And I don't think there's much point in continuing this discussion either.'

His smile twisted. 'Then we agree on something at last.'

'So, if you can tell me where to find my shoes and jacket, I'll go.'

'Back to him? Your *innamorato*?'

'Back to my life,' Polly said, lifting her chin. 'In which you have no part, *signore*.'

'I can hardly argue with that,' Sandro shrugged. 'You will find your belongings in the bedroom, Paola *mia*.'

He did not, she noticed, offer to fetch them for her, as the Sandro she'd once known would have done.

Don't fool yourself, she thought as she trod, barefoot, into the bedroom and paused, looking around her. As he said—you never really knew him at all.

Her jacket and bag were on a small sofa by the window, her shoes arranged neatly beneath it. As she reached them she was aware of a sound behind her, and turned.

Sandro had followed her, she realised, her heart missing a beat. She hadn't been aware of his approach, because he too had discarded his shoes. But the noise she'd heard was the sound of the door closing behind him, shutting them in together.

And now he was leaning back against its panels, watching her with hooded eyes, his expression cool and purposeful as, with one hand, he began to unfasten the buttons on his shirt.

Polly felt the breath catch in her throat. With a supreme effort, she controlled her voice, keeping it steady. 'Another game, *signore*?'

'No game at all, *signorina*.' Cynically, he echoed her formality. 'As I am sure you know perfectly well.'

She had picked up her bag, and was holding it so tightly that the strap cut into her fingers. 'I—I don't know what you're talking about.'

Sandro tutted. 'Now you're being dishonest, *bella mia*, but I expected that.' He allowed his discarded shirt to drop to the floor, and began to walk towards her.

She swallowed. 'I think you must be going crazy.'

'Possibly,' he said with sudden harshness. 'And I want to be sane again.' He halted, the topaz eyes blazing at her. 'You are under my skin, Paola. In my blood, like a fever that refuses to be healed. And that is no longer acceptable to me. So, I plan to cure myself of you once and for all—and in the only possible way.'

'No.' She stared back at him, her appalled heart thudding frantically. 'No, Sandro. You can't do this. I—I won't let you.'

'You really believe you have a choice?' He gave a short laugh. 'I know better.'

She backed away until her retreat was cut off by the wall behind her. Until he reached her.

'Please, Sandro,' she whispered. 'Please let me go.'

He laughed again, touching a finger to her trembling lips, before outlining the curve of her jaw, and stroking down the delicate line of her throat to the neckline of her dress.

'Once I have finished with you, *carissima*,' he drawled insolently, 'you are free to go anywhere you wish.'

'Do you want me to hate you?' Her voice pleaded with him.

'I thought you already did.' Almost casually, he detached her bag from her grasp and tossed it to one side, his brows snapping together as he saw the marks on her skin.

He lifted both her hands to his lips, letting them move caressingly on the redness the leather strap had left.

'I had almost forgotten how easily you bruise.' His voice was low and husky. 'I shall have to be careful.'

Her whole body shivered at the touch of his mouth on her flesh, the aching, delirious memories it evoked. And the promise of further, dangerous delights in his whispered words.

A promise she could not allow him to keep.

She snatched her hands from his grip, and pushed violently at the bare, tanned wall of his chest, catching him off balance. As Sandro was forced into a step backwards, she dodged past, running for the door.

With no shoes and no money, she was going nowhere, but if

she could just get out of this bedroom it might be possible to reason with him—deflect him from his apparent purpose.

She flung herself at the door handle, twisted it one way, then the other, trying to drag the door open, but it wouldn't budge an inch, and she realised with horror that he must have locked it too—and taken the key.

'Trying to escape again.' His voice was sardonic, his hands hard on her shoulders as he swung her relentlessly to face him. 'Not this time, *bella mia*.' His smile mocked her. 'Not, at least, until you have said a proper goodbye to me.'

'Sandro.' Her voice cracked. 'You can't do this. You must let me go...'

'Back to your lover? Surely he can spare me a little of your time and attention first. After all, he has reaped the benefit of our previous association, wouldn't you say?' He paused. 'And, naturally, I am intrigued to know if your repertoire has increased since then.'

Her face was white, her eyes like emerald hollows, as she stared up at him, her skin seared by his words.

She said chokingly, 'You bastard.'

'If you insist on calling me bad names,' Sandro said softly, 'I have no option but to stop you speaking at all.' And his mouth came down hard on hers.

She tried to struggle—to pull away from him, so that she could talk to him—appeal, even on the edge, to his better nature. Tell him that his actions were an outrage—a crime. But what did that matter to someone who lived his life outside the law anyway? her reeling mind demanded.

Her efforts were in vain. The arm that held her had muscles of steel. At the same time, his free hand was loosening the dishevelled knot of her hair, his fingers twisting in its silky strands to hold her still for the ravishment of his kiss.

Her breasts were crushed against his naked chest. She could feel the warmth of his skin penetrating her thin dress. Felt the heat surge in her own body to meet it.

She heard herself moan faintly in anguished protest—pleading that this man, to whom she'd once given her innocence, would not now take her by force.

But Sandro used the slight parting of her lips for his own advantage, deepening the intimacy of his kiss with sensual intensity as his tongue invaded the moist sweetness of her mouth.

No sign now of the tenderness with which he'd caressed her fingers only moments ago. Just the urgency of a need too powerful to be denied any longer.

A fever in the blood, he'd called it, she thought in a kind of despair, her starved body craving him in turn. And how was it possible that she could feel like this? That she could want him so desperately in return?

When at last he raised his head, the scar on his face was livid against the fierce burn of colour along his taut cheekbones.

He said, 'Take off your dress,' his voice hoarse, shaken. And when he saw her hesitate, 'Or do you wish me to tear it off you?'

'No.' She sounded small and breathless. 'I—I'll do it.' She turned away from him, as her shaking fingers fought with the buttons. When half of them were loose, she pushed the navy linen from her shoulders, freeing her arms from the sleeves as she did so, and letting the dress fall to the floor.

She faced him slowly, her arms crossed defensively across her body, trying to conceal the scraps of white broderie anglaise that were now her only covering.

'But how delicious,' he said, softly. 'Bought for your lover?'

Polly shook her hair back from her face. 'I dress to please myself.'

'Ah,' he said. 'And now you will undress to please me. *Per favore*,' he added silkily.

She could hear nothing but the wild drumming of her own pulses, and the tear of her ragged breathing. See nothing but the heated flare of hunger in his eyes. A hunger without gentleness, demanding to be appeased.

And his hands reaching for her—like some ruthless hawk about to seize his prey.

Not like this, she thought in anguish. Oh, dear God, not like this. Not to lie naked in his arms and be taken—enjoyed for one night alone. To be used, however skilfully, just so that he could get her out of his system, only to find herself discarded all over again when his need for her was finally assuaged. And to be forced to go through all that suffering a second time—unappeased.

It was unthinkable—unbearable.

Her voice shook. 'Sandro—please—don't hurt me...'

She paused, knowing she was on the edge of complete self-betrayal here. Realising too that she must not let him see that he still had the power to inflict more misery on her.

The sudden silence was total. He was completely still, apart from a muscle which moved swiftly, convulsively in his throat.

When at last he spoke, his voice was hoarse. '*Dio mio*, you think that I'm going to rape you? That I might be capable of such a thing?' He shook his head. 'How could you believe that? It is an insult to everything we have ever been to each other.'

He lifted his hand, and touched the scar. 'This has only altered my face, Paola. It has not turned me into a monster.'

'I—I didn't mean...' Polly began, then bit her lip. This was a misunderstanding that she could not put right—not without the kind of explanation she was desperate to avoid, she told herself wretchedly.

'*Basta,*' Sandro said sharply. 'Enough.' He bent and retrieved his shirt from the floor, dragging it on with swift, jerky movements.

'Now dress yourself and go,' he instructed icily. 'And be quick. Otherwise I might lose all self-respect, and justify your low opinion of me. Punish you in the way you deserve,' he added grimly.

He went to the door, unlocked it, then turned.

'Remember this, *mia bella*.' His voice grated across her taut nerve-endings, just as his contemptuous gaze flayed her skin. 'Even if I had taken you there on the floor like the *sciattona* you are, it would still not have been rape.' He smiled at her with insolent certainty. 'You know it as well as I do, so do not fool yourself.

'Now, get out of my sight,' he added curtly, and left, slamming the door behind him.

CHAPTER THREE

SHE had missed her plane, but eventually managed to catch the last flight of the evening, thanks to a no-show.

Her escape from the hotel had been easier than she could have hoped. She had dressed quickly, her shaking hands fumbling so badly with the buttons on her dress that she had to begin again.

Then she'd wasted precious moments listening tautly at the door for some sound from the room beyond. Dreading that Sandro might be waiting there for her, still angry and possibly vengeful.

But when she had finally risked taking a look, the room was completely deserted, and she left on the run. The hotel commissionaire had summoned a cab for her, allotting her dishevelled state a discreetly impassive glance.

She had prowled around the airport, her eyes everywhere. Terrified that he might change his mind, and come to find her. To prevent her from leaving. Even when she presented her boarding card, she was half expecting his hand to reach over her shoulder and take it from her.

When the plane finally took off, she was almost sick with relief. She ordered a double brandy from the stewardess, and fell asleep before she'd drunk half of it.

She took a cab from the airport to her flat, unlocking the door and falling inside in the same movement. There was a strange empty chill about the place that she had never experienced before, that seemed to match the cold hollow inside her.

A voice in her head whispered, 'You're safe—you're safe...' But somehow she couldn't believe it. She even found herself picking her way in the darkness to her living-room window, and drawing the curtains before she switched on the lights.

Then she sank down on the sofa, and tried to stop trembling.

I didn't suspect a thing, she thought. To me, the *contessa* was simply another very demanding client, nothing more—but it was all a trick.

She had to be deeply in Sandro's power to agree to something

36

like that, Polly told herself, and shivered as she remembered how nearly she'd surrendered to that power herself.

Oh, God, she thought. He only had to touch me...

But it had always been like that. From the first time his hand had taken hers as they walked together, her body had responded with wild yearning to his touch. She had hungered and thirsted for his mouth on hers—for the brush of his fingers over her ardent flesh. For the ultimate mystery of his body joined to hers.

Sandro had enraptured her every sense, and she had mistaken that for love. And he had cynically allowed that—had said the words she wanted to hear—whispered the promises that would keep her enthralled until he chose to leave her.

She'd been just one more girl in his bed, easily discarded, instantly replaced. Except that he'd caught a fleeting glimpse of her on television and discovered, for some inexplicable reason, that he still wanted her.

Sandro Domenico, she thought painfully. A man rich enough to pay for his whims, and powerful enough to pull the strings that would satisfy them.

And yet he'd let her go, outraged at the idea that he could rape her physically, but too arrogant to realise he'd already done far worse damage to her emotionally.

Still, it was over now, and she had nothing more to fear. She'd insulted his sense of honour, such as it was, and he would never come near her again.

In fact, she'd got off comparatively lightly, she told herself. Yes, she was bruised by his anger and disgust, but she'd recover from that—given time. And her future held plenty of that.

In some ways, it all seemed like a bad dream—some torment dredged up from the depths of her unconscious. But the faint lingering tenderness of her lips forced her to face reality.

Wincing, she touched her mouth with her fingertips, telling herself that it could all have been so much worse. That at this moment, she might have been in his bed, and in his arms, with a whole new cycle of heartbreak and regret to endure.

For all she knew he could be married to someone 'suitable'. A dynastic union from the criminal network he belonged to, she thought with a pang.

But she—she was all right, she rallied herself. She'd had a narrow escape, that was all.

Just the same, her vague plans for a change of location had become a firm resolve as a result of the past twenty-four hours.

She and Charlie would move, somewhere anonymous and preferably far away. And, to ensure she could never be so easily traced again, she'd find out the legal implications of changing her name.

Drastic measures, she thought, but, in view of her recent scare, perfectly justified.

She stripped in her tiny bathroom, putting her clothing in the laundry basket, then took a shower, scrubbing herself from top to toe, and even shampooing her hair to make sure she erased every trace of him.

She only wished she could wash away the memories of the heated pressure of his mouth, and the familiar, arousing scent of his skin just as easily.

Dear God, she thought, towelling her hair with more than necessary vigour, that is—frighteningly pathetic.

She put on her cotton housecoat, belting it securely round her slim waist, and trailed into the kitchen.

She needed a hot drink, but not with the additional stimulus of caffeine. She'd have enough trouble sleeping as it was through what little was left of the night.

No, she'd have a herbal tea instead, she decided. A *tisana* at bedtime was a habit she'd acquired in Italy. One of the good ones, she amended wryly.

While the kettle was boiling, she wandered back into the living room, and, for reasons she couldn't properly explain, crossed to the window, and pulled back the edge of the curtain slightly.

The road below seemed empty, or was there an added density among the shadows opposite, in a gateway just out of the range of the street light?

No, she thought, hurriedly letting the curtain fall back into place. It was simply her imagination. Sandro had traced her through her work, simply and easily, so there was no need for him to compile a complete dossier on her.

Because if he'd done so, he'd have realised at once that her 'live-in lover' was pure invention, and told her so. And he'd have known, too, about Charlie...

She turned her head, staring at the chest of drawers, and the framed photograph that occupied pride of place. Charlie, on his second birthday. His father's image smiling at her.

Sandro's out of your life, she told herself feverishly. He's gone.

Nevertheless, on the way back to the kitchen, Polly found herself taking Charlie's portrait off the chest, and stowing it in the top drawer instead.

Better, she thought, safe than sorry, and shivered again.

Polly slept badly, in spite of her *tisana*. When morning came, she telephoned Safe Hands, said quite truthfully that she felt like death, then crawled back into bed and slept until lunchtime.

She woke with a start, thinking of Charlie. Why was she wasting time, when she could have the bonus of a whole afternoon in his company without the distractions of shopping and housework?

She rang her mother's house but there was no reply, so she left a message on the answering machine to say she would be over to collect him in an hour.

She took a quick shower, then dressed in a casual blue denim skirt, topping it with a crisp white cotton shirt, and sliding her feet into flat brown leather sandals. She brushed her hair back from her face and secured it at the nape of her neck with a silver barette, and hung small blue enamel cornflowers on delicate silver chains from her earlobes.

She had some work to do with the blusher and concealer she kept for emergencies, or her mother would guess something was wrong. And Polly had enough bad news to give her without mentioning Sandro's shock reappearance in her life.

But that was all over, so there was no need to cause her further distress, she told herself firmly, applying her lipstick and attempting an experimental smile which, somehow, turned into a wry grimace.

Positive thinking, she adjured herself, and, grabbing her bag, she left.

The house seemed unusually quiet when she let herself in, and Polly paused, frowning a little. Surely her mother hadn't taken Charlie out somewhere, she thought, groaning inwardly. Was this the latest move in the battle of wits between them? She hoped not.

She kept her voice deliberately cheerful. 'Mum—Dad—are you there?'

'We're in the living room.' It was her mother's voice, high-pitched and strained.

Her frown deepening, Polly pushed open the door and walked in.

It wasn't a particularly large room, and her instant impression was that it had shrunk still further in some strange way.

The first person she saw was her mother, sitting in the chair beside the empty fireplace, her face a mask of tension, and Charlie clasped tightly on her lap.

The second was a complete stranger, stockily built with black hair and olive skin, who rose politely from the sofa at her entrance.

And the third, unbelievably, was Sandro, standing silently in the window alcove, as if he had been carved out of granite.

For a moment the room seemed to reel around her, then she steadied herself, her hands clenching into fists, her nails scoring her palms. She was *not*, under any circumstances, going to faint again.

She said hoarsely, 'What the *hell* are you doing here?'

'Is it not obvious?' The topaz eyes were as fierce as a leopard's, and as dangerous. His voice was ice. 'I have come for my son. And please do not try to deny his parentage,' he added bitingly. 'Because no court in the world would believe you. He is my image.' He paused. 'But I warn you that I am prepared to undergo DNA testing to prove paternity, if it becomes necessary.'

Polly stared at him, her stomach churning, her heart pounding against her ribs. 'You must be mad.'

'I was.' His smile was grim. 'Before I discovered quite what a treacherous little bitch you are, Paola *mia*. But now I am sane again, and I want my child.'

Her low voice shook. 'Over my dead body.'

He said softly, 'The way I feel at this moment, that could easily be arranged. Do not provoke me any further.'

'He's going to take him away from us,' her mother wailed suddenly. 'Take him to Italy. I'll never see him again.'

Horror caught Polly by the throat. She turned on Sandro. 'You can't do that.'

'And what is there to stop me?' His glance challenged her.

'It—it's kidnapping,' Polly flung at him. She took a breath. 'Although I suppose that's an everyday occurrence in your world.'

And it was more common than she wanted to admit in her own,

she thought numbly. There'd been numerous headlines in the papers over the past few years where children had been snatched and taken abroad by a parent. They called them 'tug of love' babies...

She looked with scorn at the other man, who had got quietly to his feet. 'And what are you—another of his tame thugs?'

His brows rose. 'My name is Alberto Molena, *signorina*, and I am a lawyer. I act for the *marchese* in this matter.'

.Polly gave him a scornful glance. 'Don't you mean you're his *consigliere*?' she queried with distaste.

He paused, sending Sandro a surprised look. 'May I suggest that you sit down, Signorina Fairfax, and remain calm? It would be better too if the little boy was taken to another room. I think he's becoming frightened.'

'I have a better suggestion,' Polly flared. 'Why don't you and your dubious client get out of here, and leave us alone?'

His tone was still quiet, still courteous. 'I'm afraid that isn't possible. You must understand that your child is the first-born son, and thus the heir of the Marchese Valessi, and that he intends to apply through the courts for sole custody of the boy. Although you will be permitted proper access, naturally.'

He looked at Charlie, who was round-eyed, his knuckles pushed into his mouth. 'But, believe me, it would be better if the little boy was spared any more upset from this discussion. We have a trained nanny waiting to look after him.'

He walked to the door and called. A pleasant-faced girl in a smart maroon uniform came in and removed Charlie gently but firmly from his grandmother's almost frenzied grasp, talking to him softly as she carried him out of the room.

'Where's she taking him?' Polly demanded shakily.

'Into the garden,' the lawyer told her, adding less reassuringly, 'For the time being.'

She swallowed convulsively, turning to the silent man by the window. 'Sandro.' Her voice was pleading, all pride forgotten. 'Please don't do this. Don't try to take him away from me.'

'I have already been deprived of the first two years of his life,' he returned implacably. 'There will be no more separation.' His lip curled. 'How remiss of you, *cara mia*, not to inform me of his existence. Even last night, when we talked so intimately about your living arrangements, you said nothing—gave no hint that you had borne me a child. Did you really think you could keep him hidden forever?'

She moistened her dry lips. 'How—how did you find out?'

He shrugged. 'I employed an agency to trace you. They suggested broadening the scope of their enquiries.' His voice was expressionless. 'I received their full report last night after you left. It made fascinating reading.'

She stared down at the carpet. 'So there was someone watching me when I got back,' she said almost inaudibly.

'Can you wonder?' Sandro returned contemptuously. 'I have a beautiful son, Paola, and you deliberately barred me from his life. You preferred to struggle alone than ask me for help—or give me the joy of knowing I was a father.' His gaze was cold, level. 'How can such a thing be forgiven?'

'It was over between us.' Polly lifted her chin. 'What did you expect me to do—beg?'

'I think,' he said softly, 'that is something you may have to learn for the future.'

There was a silence. Polly could hear her mother weeping softly.

'No court in the world,' she said huskily, 'would take a baby away from his mother.'

'Yet it is his grandmother who has the care of him each day.' His tone was harsh. 'I was watching when you came into the room, and he did not try to go to you. Is he even aware that you are his mother?'

Polly gasped, and her head went back as if he had slapped her.

She said unsteadily, 'I go out to work to support us both. As the *contessa* has probably told you, the hours can be long and difficult. But I needed the money, so I had no choice.'

'Yes,' he said, his voice quiet and cold. 'You did. You could have chosen me. All that was needed was one word—one sign.'

There was an odd intensity in his voice, which startled and bewildered her. And also rekindled her anger.

He talks, she thought, as if I deserted him.

A sudden noise from her mother—something between a sigh and a groan—distracted her, and she went over and sat on the arm of her chair, putting an arm round her shoulders.

Oh, God, she thought. To think I was going to tell her that I was taking Charlie away. But how could I have guessed this was going to happen?

'It's going to be all right, Mum,' she said softly. 'I promise.'

'How can it be?' Mrs Fairfax demanded, almost hysterically. 'He's going to take my little treasure to Italy, and I can't bear it.' She reared up from Polly's sheltering arm, glaring venomously at Sandro, who was regarding her with narrowed eyes, his mouth hard and set. 'How dare you come here, ruining our lives like this?' she stormed. 'Get out of my house. And never come back.'

'You are not the only one to suffer, *signora*.' His tone was almost dismissive. He looked at Polly. 'But it would be better for my son to be looked after by someone else until the custody hearing. The nanny I have engaged will move in with you.'

'She can't,' Polly told him curtly. 'My flat is far too small for that.'

He shrugged. 'Then you will be found somewhere else to live.'

'I don't want that,' she said raggedly. 'I don't want anything from you. I just need you to go, and leave us in peace.'

'The *marchese* is being generous, Signorina Fairfax,' Alberto Molena intervened unexpectedly. 'He could ask for the child to be transferred to the care of a temporary guardian while the custody issue is decided.'

'And, of course, he's so sure he'll get custody.' Polly got to her feet, her eyes blazing. 'So bloody arrogant and all-conquering. But what court's going to hand over a baby to someone with his criminal connections? And I'll make sure they know all about his underworld background,' she added defiantly. 'Whatever the cost.'

There was a stunned silence. Then Sandro muttered, *'Dio mio,'* and turned sharply, walking back to the window, his fists clenched at his sides.

Signor Molena's voice was hushed. 'I think you're making a grave mistake, *signorina*. Since the death of his father, the *marchese* has become head of an old and much respected family in southern Italy, and chairman of a business empire with strong interests in the tourist industry among other things.'

He spread his hands almost helplessly. 'You must surely have heard of the Comadora chain of hotels? They are internationally famous.'

'Yes.' Polly had to force suddenly numbed lips to form the words. Her shocked gaze went from his embarrassed face to Sandro's rigid back. 'Yes, I know about them.'

Signor Molena paused, awkwardly. 'And *marchese* means

"marquis" in your language. It is an aristocratic title, not what you seem to think.' He shook his head. 'To suggest that any member of the Valessi family has ever been linked with criminal elements would be a serious slander if it were not so laughable.'

Polly had never felt less like laughing in her entire life. If she'd been cold before, she was now consumed in an agony of burning humiliation, blushing from her feet to the top of her head.

She wrapped her arms defensively round her body. 'I—I'm sorry,' she mumbled.

Behind her, her mother moaned faintly, and sank back in her chair.

Sandro turned slowly and studied them both reflectively. When he spoke his voice was calm but there was no sign of softening in his attitude.

'That is what you thought?' he asked. 'What you really believed, in spite of everything? It almost defies belief. Almost,' he added quietly, 'but not quite. And it explains a great deal.'

He paused. 'I understand from the *signora*, your mother, that your father is at his office. Perhaps he could be fetched. I do not think that she should be alone.'

Polly shook herself into action. 'Yes—yes, I'll telephone him. And her doctor...' She went out into the hall, standing helplessly for a moment as she tried to remember the number. Realising her mind was a blank.

Sandro followed, closing the door of the living room behind him.

She didn't look at him, doggedly turning the leaves of the directory. 'What—what will happen now?'

'The legal process will begin. But for tonight you may take Carlino to sleep at your *appartamento*.'

'Thank you,' she said with irony.

'The *bambinaia*, whose name is Julie Cole, will accompany you to put him to bed,' he went on, as if she hadn't spoken. 'Then she will return in the morning at seven o'clock to take care of him.'

He spoke as if he was conducting a board meeting, Polly thought incredulously, rather than trying to destroy her life.

She said, 'We could all stay here, perhaps. There's—plenty of room.'

'No,' he said. 'This is not an environment I want for my son.'

Why? she wanted to cry. Because it's an ordinary suburban

house rather than a *palazzo*? Just as I was an ordinary girl, and therefore not deemed as a suitable candidate to become your *marchesa*?

She could see now why it had been so important to pay her off, in order to get rid of her. There was too much at stake dynastically to allow a mistake like herself to enter the equation.

The old pain was back like a knife twisting inside her. A pain that her pride forbade her to let him see. So she would never ask the question 'Why did you leave me?' because she now knew the answer to that, beyond all doubt.

Besides, it would expose the fact that she cared, and that he still had the power to hurt her. And she needed that to remain her secret, and her solitary torment.

Besides, at the moment she was faced with all the suffering she could handle.

Unless she could divert him from his purpose somehow, she thought. Unless...

She picked up the phone irresolutely, then put it down again. She said quickly, before her courage ran out, 'Sandro, it doesn't have to be like this. Surely we could work something out. Share custody in some way.'

His mouth thinned. 'I am expected to trust you? When you have deliberately kept our child from me and even claimed to have a lover to sustain the deception? How much do you think your word is worth?'

Polly swallowed. 'I don't blame you for being angry.'

'Mille grazie.' His tone was sardonic.

'And maybe doing my best to be Charlie's mother hasn't been good enough,' she went on, bravely. 'But he doesn't know you at all, and if he was just whisked off to another country among strangers, however well-meaning, he'd be disorientated—scared. He—he's shy with people at first.'

'A trait he shares with you, *mia bella,* if memory serves,' Sandro drawled with cool mockery.

She remembered too. Recalled how gentle and considerate he had been that first time in bed together. How he'd coaxed her out of her clothes and her initial inhibitions.

She flushed hotly and angrily. 'May we cut out the personal reminiscences?' she requested curtly.

He shrugged. 'It is difficult to see how. Making a child together is an intensely personal matter.' He paused. 'And by the time I take Carlino to Italy, we will be well acquainted with each other. I guarantee that. And my own old nurse, Dorotea, will be waiting to look after him. The transition will not be too hard.'

But it will be agony for me, she thought, her throat tightening convulsively. First I lost you, and now you're trying to take Charlie away. And already I feel as if I'm dying inside.

She said tonelessly, 'I'd better make those calls.'

He inclined his head courteously, and went past her, and out into the garden.

Presently, distant but gleeful, Charlie's laughter came to her on the light summer wind, and she stood, staring in front of her unseeingly, her teeth sunk so deeply into her lower lip that she could taste blood.

She wanted to hate Julie Cole, but it was impossible. She was too kind, too tactful, and she thought that Charlie was heaven on legs.

And if she knew that her job was more for security than enjoyment, she kept that to herself.

The creamy scrambled eggs she made for supper were good too, and Charlie loved the triangles of buttered toast that went with them, although Polly could barely force her portion past the sick, scared lump in her throat.

She had wanted to wait at the house to talk to her father, or perhaps just put her head down on his shoulder and cry out her fear, but suddenly there was a car and driver at the gate, and Sandro was insisting quietly but implacably that she should take Charlie home.

She'd begun a protest, but Sandro had simply looked at her, his brows lifted haughtily, questioningly, and the words seemed to stutter and die on her lips.

'You begin to learn,' he had approved coldly.

She had been shaken to find him carrying Charlie down to the car in his arms, and found herself hoping that the little boy would have one of his infrequent tantrums, kicking, screaming and reaching for her as proof that no one else would do.

He didn't; nor did he burst into tears when Sandro had gently but firmly removed his thumb from his mouth.

She had said defensively, 'He doesn't really do that any more. Only when he's tired—or frightened.'

'All the more reason, then, to take him home,' Sandro had retorted unarguably.

She could only imagine the kind of scene that would erupt once her father returned, and her mother had some solid support.

'I'll make your father sell the house,' she'd hissed at Polly as she was leaving. 'Marquis or not, I'm going to fight this man through every court in the land.'

Polly sighed silently. She really doesn't know what she's up against, she thought unhappily. And I'm only just beginning to find out, too.

Only twenty-four hours ago or less, she'd been planning for her life to change, but not to this extreme, catastrophic extent. She'd seen a period of struggle ahead, but never the bleak desert of loneliness that now threatened her.

'He may not win,' she thought. And only realised she'd spoken aloud when Julie said, 'Are you all right, Miss Fairfax?'

Polly jumped, then mustered an attempt at a smile. 'Yes, fine,' she lied.

Julie studied her dubiously. 'I saw some white wine in the fridge while I was getting the eggs. Why don't you sit down and put your feet up, while I do the dishes, and then I'll bring you a glass?'

I don't want a glass, thought Polly. I want a bottle, a cellar, a whole vineyard. I want the edges of my pain blurred, and to be able to stop thinking.

She cleared her throat. 'I know Sandro—the *marchese*— instructed you to put Charlie to bed, but I'd really like to do it myself, if you wouldn't mind.'

'Sure, Miss Fairfax.' Was that compassion in the other girl's voice? 'Anything you say.'

Charlie was tired, and more than a little grumpy, especially when he realised his usual playtime in the bath was going to be curtailed. By the time she'd wrestled him into his pyjamas, Polly felt limp, and close to tears.

'Let me take him.' Julie spoke gently behind her. 'You look all in.'

Polly submitted, standing in his doorway, while her grizzling son was tucked in deftly and firmly.

He'll never settle, she told herself with a kind of sour triumph, only to be confounded when he was fast asleep within five minutes.

She stood at the side of the cot, watching the fan of dark lashes on his cheek, and the small mouth pursed in slumber. She ached to snatch him up and hold him. To run with him into the night to a place where they would never be found.

But she was crying for the moon, and she knew it. Even if there was such a place, she hadn't enough money to go on the run, or enough skill to outwit Sandro for long. And she couldn't afford to provoke his wrath again. She needed to reason with him—to persuade—even to plead, if she had to. Besides, on a purely practical level, instinct warned her that if she attempted to leave, whoever waited in the shadows opposite would step out and prevent her from going.

She sank down onto the floor, and leaned her head against the bars of the cot, listening to Charlie's soft, even breathing. And thinking of all the nights of silence that could be waiting for her.

When she finally returned to the other room, she discovered gratefully that the sofa bed had been opened and made up for the night, and the glass of wine was waiting with a note that said, 'See you in the morning. J.'

She took a first sip, then carried the wine into the bathroom, and began to half fill the tub with warm water, softened by a handful of foaming bath oil. No shower tonight, she told herself. She wanted to relax completely.

She took off her clothes and slid with a sigh into the scented water, reaching for her wineglass.

It would help her sleep, she thought. And tomorrow, when she was more rested, things might seem better. After all, she knew now the worst that could happen to her, and there must be a way of dealing with it that would not leave her utterly bereft.

She leaned back, resting her head on the rim of the bath, and closing her eyes.

Yes, tomorrow she would make plans. Find out if she qualified for legal aid, and get herself a lawyer of her own. Someone who would negotiate with Sandro on her behalf, and allow her to maintain some kind of distance from him.

I really need to do that, she thought. To stay calm—and aloof. I can fight him better that way.

And at that moment, as if he were some demon she'd conjured

up from her own private hell, she heard his voice, low, mocking and far too close at hand.

'Falling asleep in the bath, *mia bella*? That will never do. Surely you don't wish Carlino to become motherless so soon?'

CHAPTER FOUR

POLLY started violently, giving a strangled cry of alarm as the glass jerked and the wine spilled everywhere.

She looked round and saw Sandro leaning in the doorway, watching her with cool amusement.

She tried to sit up, remembered just in time that there weren't enough bubbles to cover her, slipped on the oily surface, and was nearly submerged. She grabbed the rim of the bath, gasping in rage, and saw Sandro walking towards her.

'Keep away from me.' Her voice rose in panic.

'I am coming to rescue your glass, nothing more,' he countered silkily. 'If it breaks, you could hurt yourself badly.' He took it from her hand. 'Besides, how shameful if I had to tell people that the mother of my child drowned while drunk,' he added, his mouth slanting into a grin.

'Just keep me out of your conversations,' Polly said hotly, aware she was blushing under his unashamed scrutiny. 'How the hell did you get in here?'

'I told Julie not to lock the door when she left.'

'You did what?' Polly almost wailed. 'Oh, God, how could you? You realise what she'll think?'

He shrugged. 'I am not particularly concerned.' He gave her a dry look. 'Anyway, I imagine one look at Carlino told her all that she needs to know. We cannot hide that we once had a relationship.'

'Yes,' she said. 'With the emphasis on the ''once''. But not now, and not ever again, so will you please get out of here? Before I call the police,' she added for good measure.

Sandro shook his head reprovingly. 'Your skills as a hostess seem sadly lacking, *cara mia*. Perhaps you feel at a disadvantage for some reason?'

'Or maybe I prefer company I actually invited here,' Polly threw back at him. 'And you'll never be on any guest-list of mine.'

'You entertain much, do you—in this box? I'm sure you find

50

the sofa that turns into a bed a convenience—for visitors who linger.'

'This is my home,' she said. 'And I assure you it caters for all my needs.' She paused. 'Now I'd like you to go.'

Quite apart from anything else, it was uncomfortable and undignified crouching below the rim of the bath like this. And the water was getting colder by the minute, she thought angrily.

His brows lifted. 'Without knowing why I am here? Aren't you a little curious, Paola *mia*?'

'I can't think of one good reason for you to inflict yourself on me again,' she told him raggedly. 'Can't you understand you're the last person I want to see?' She sent him a hostile glance. 'Unless you've come to tell me that you've had a change of heart, and you've decided not to proceed with the custody application.'

'No,' Sandro said gently. 'I have not. I simply felt that we should talk together in private. Maybe even in peace. Who knows?'

'I know.' Her voice was stormy. 'And we have nothing to discuss. You want to rob me of my son? I'm going to fight you every step of the way. And my parents will be behind me.'

'No.' Sandro inclined his head almost regretfully. 'They will not.' He raised the glass he was still holding. 'Now, I am going to pour you some more wine. I think you are going to need it.'

He allowed her to absorb that, then continued. 'So, I suggest you stop trying to hide in that inadequate bath, and join me in the other room.' He took a towel from the rail and tossed it to her, then walked out, closing the door behind him.

Polly scrambled to her feet, holding the towel defensively against her as she stepped out gingerly onto the mat. She began to dry herself with hasty, clumsy hands, keeping an apprehensive eye on the door in case Sandro chose to return.

Not that she could do much about it even if he did, she thought, grimacing. And it was ridiculous, anyway, behaving like some Victorian virgin in front of a man who'd seen her naked so many times before. Someone who'd kissed and caressed every inch of the bare skin she was now so anxious to conceal.

Instead of this burning self-consciousness, she should have pretended it didn't matter. Demonstrated her complete and utter indifference to his presence whether she was dressed or undressed.

Fine in theory, she thought. But much trickier in practice.

Especially if Sandro had interpreted her apparent sang-froid as provocation...

Her mouth felt suddenly dry, forcing her to abandon that train of thought for one just as disturbing. What was that comment about her parents meant to imply? What had been said in her absence—and, dear God, what pressure had been brought to bear?

She needed to find out, and quickly.

She looked down at the small pile of clothing she'd discarded earlier. Common sense suggested she should put it back on. Use it as part of the armour her instinct assured her that she was going to need.

But in the end, she opted for the elderly cotton robe hanging on the back of the door. It was plain and prim, without an ounce of seduction in its unrevealing lines, she thought, fastening the sash in a tight double bow. Her equivalent of a security blanket, perhaps.

Then, drawing a deep breath, she squared her shoulders and marched defiantly into the living room, only to halt, disconcerted, when she found it deserted.

The door to Charlie's room was ajar, however, and she ran, stumbling slightly on the skirts of her robe, and pushed it open.

Sandro's back was to the door, but he was bending over Charlie's cot, his hands reaching down, and she felt her heart miss a beat. Was he planning to snatch her baby while he thought she was safely in the bathroom?

'What are you doing in here?' she hissed. 'Don't touch him. Don't dare.'

Sandro straightened, and turned. 'I saw this on the floor.' He held up a small brown teddy bear. 'I was replacing it.' He paused. 'And I came in simply to watch my son sleep. A pleasure that has been denied me for the past two years,' he added coldly.

'And which you want to deny me permanently,' Polly flung at him, tight-lipped.

His smile was wintry. 'Just as you would have done to me, *mia cara*, if fate had not intervened,' he returned unanswerably.

He held the door, allowing her to precede him back into the living room.

He looked round him, his expression disparaging. 'And this is where you have allowed him to spend the beginning of his life? In this *conigliera*?'

'And what precisely does that mean?'

'A hutch,' he said. 'For rabbits.'

She bit her lip. The room did seem to have shrunk suddenly, or was it just the effect of Sandro's presence? And the bed being open and made up didn't help either. In fact it was a serious embarrassment.

'It was all I could afford at the time,' she said. 'And it works,' she added defiantly, thinking of the hours she'd spent painting the walls, and stripping and stencilling the small chest of drawers which held Charlie's things, and which just fitted into his room. He gave no credit, either, she thought bitterly, for the way she kept the place neat and spotless.

'One word from you,' he said harshly, 'one hint that you were *incinta*, and it would all have changed. My son would have come into the world at Comadora, in the bed where I was born, and my father and grandfather before me.' He took her by the shoulder, whirling her to face him. His voice was passionate. '*Dio*, Paola, why did you not tell me? How could you let me exist without knowing?'

'Because we were no longer together.' She freed herself from his grasp. 'I made a decision that my baby was going to be part of my life only, and that I wanted nothing from you.' She paused. 'Didn't I make that clear enough at the time?'

'More than clear.' His mouth twisted. 'What I could not understand was—why.' He frowned. 'You could not have truly believed I was Mafioso. That is impossible—*assurdo*.'

'Why not? It was evident there were things you hadn't told me,' Polly countered. 'Things you didn't want me to know.' She shrugged. 'What was I supposed to think?'

'Not, perhaps, to give me the benefit of the doubt?'

'No,' she said. 'Any more than you decided to tell me the truth. And I expect we both had our reasons.'

'*Sì,*' Sandro said quietly. 'But I also have regrets, which you do not seem to share.'

'You're wrong.' She looked down at the floor. 'I wish very much that I had never met you.'

'Unfortunately for us both, the situation cannot be changed.' His voice was a drawl. He picked up her refilled glass from the chest of drawers and handed it to her. 'Shall we drink to our mistakes?'

Polly realised she was holding the glass as if it might explode. 'This isn't a social occasion,' she reminded him tautly. 'You said you came here to talk.'

'And I would do so,' he said, 'if I thought you were in any mood to listen.' He paused. 'I had better fortune with your parents.'

Polly stiffened. 'What have you been saying to them? If you've threatened them...'

He gave her a weary look. 'With what? A cattle prod, perhaps?' His mouth curled. 'Once again, you are allowing your imagination to run away with you, *mia cara*.'

She flushed. 'You're trying to tell me they gave up without a fight. I don't believe it.'

'Your mother, I think, would have gone to any lengths to thwart me,' he said. 'Your father, however, was more reasonable.'

'He thinks I should simply hand Charlie over to you?' Her voice broke on a little sob. 'Oh, how could he?'

'No, he knows that even if he made the kind of sacrifices your mother was demanding, he would still not have the financial resources for a lengthy court battle.' His smile was brief and hard. 'Especially if it took place in Italy,' he added softly.

The colour deepened in her face. 'You'll go to any lengths—pull any dirty trick to win, won't you?' she accused in a stifled voice.

Sandro shrugged. 'I see little point in losing, *bella mia*,' he returned. 'But I am prepared to offer a draw—a negotiated settlement.'

She stared at him. 'Would it mean that Charlie stayed with me?'

'That would depend on you,' he said. 'Carlino is coming to Italy with me. As my son, he needs to learn about his heritage. I am merely inviting you to accompany him.'

'As what? Some kind of glorified nanny?' she demanded. She shook her head. 'I think I'd rather have my day in court.'

'He already has a nanny,' Sandro told her evenly. 'And another waiting in Italy to love him. But what he really needs is the stability of both parents in his life. So, Paola *mia*, I am asking you once again, as I did three years ago, to be my wife.'

For a long, dazed moment Polly was too shaken to speak.

At last, she said huskily, 'Is this some grotesque joke?'

'No,' he said. 'We are, if you remember, already engaged to each other,' he added cynically.

Her breathing quickened. 'Was I really supposed to believe that—that nonsense? I—I don't think so. And whatever happened between us, it was all over a long time ago, and you know it. You can't simply revive it—on a whim.'

'Very well, then,' Sandro returned equably. 'Let us forget it ever took place. Pretend that, for the first time, I am making you an offer of marriage, Paola *mia*.'

She shook her head. 'But you don't—you can't want to marry me.'

'I have no particular desire to be married at all,' he retorted. 'But there are good reasons why I should sacrifice my freedom.'

'Your freedom?' Polly almost choked. 'What about mine?'

He looked around him. 'You call this liberty? Working long hours. Living in little more than one room? I don't think so.'

'I could always sue you for child support.' She drew a breath. 'That would improve my circumstances by a hundred per cent.'

'But I am already offering to support our child—as the Marchese Valessi,' he said silkily. 'Besides, our marriage would remove any possible objections to Carlino's right to inherit when the time comes, and it would mean that his well-being and nurture becomes the concern of us both from day to day.' He paused. 'I suggest it as a practical alternative to a custody battle.'

'Which I might win,' she said swiftly.

'You might, but could you fight the appeal which would follow?' Sandro countered. 'Or the appeal against the appeal?' His smile was chilly. 'The case might last for years.'

'Or until I run out of money, of course,' she said bitterly. 'You don't need a cattle prod, *signore*.'

His brows lifted. 'You regard marriage to me as some kind of torture, *signorina*?' he asked softly. 'Then perhaps I should make something clear to you at once. What I am offering is only a matter of form. A way of legalising the situation between us. But it would not be a love match. Too much has taken place for that. We would share nothing more than a roof, if that is what concerns you.'

He gave her a level look. 'I accept now that any feelings we had for each other belong in the past. That we are different people, and we have both moved on.'

'You say that now.' Her voice was husky. 'Yet only last night you told me I was still in your blood.'

'But a lot has happened since then,' Sandro said harshly. 'And my feelings towards you have naturally changed as a result.' He paused. 'Now our child remains the only issue between us, and his ultimate welfare should be our sole consideration. You agree with that, I hope?'

Polly nodded numbly.

'Bene,' he said briskly. 'In return, I promise that your life as the Marchesa Valessi will be as easy as I can make it. You will be made a suitable allowance, and asked occasionally to act as my hostess.' His smile was hard. 'But you may spend your nights alone.'

She swallowed. 'And—you?'

'I hardly think that concerns you,' he said coldly. 'However, I will ensure that any liaisons I have are conducted discreetly.'

She bit her lip. 'As ours was?'

'Davvero,' he nodded. 'Precisely.'

She said with difficulty, 'And what about me—if I met someone?'

His brows lifted. 'I should require you to behave with equal discretion. I would tolerate no open scandal in my family.'

He paused. 'So what is your answer, Paola? Will you be my wife?'

'I don't know what to say.' Concealed by the skirts of her robe, her hands were clenched painfully into fists. 'I mean—you might want more children at some point.'

'I have a son to safeguard the inheritance. That was always my priority in such matters. As to the rest...' He shrugged again. 'I have cousins, both married with *bambini*. At times my house seems full of children. Although that, of course, will be good for Carlino,' he added thoughtfully. 'He does not talk as well as he should, and he hardly knows how to kick a ball. That must change.'

Polly's lips parted in sheer outrage. 'How—dare you? Last week you didn't even know you were a father. Now you're a bloody expert on child-rearing.'

'I made no such claim,' Sandro returned mildly. 'But Julie had concerns which she mentioned to me.'

'Then she had no right,' Polly flared. 'Charlie's absolutely beautiful, and he can do all kinds of things,' she added hotly, burying the memory of various clashes she'd had with her mother on that very subject.

'And could do far more, I suspect.' Sandro's smile was cold, 'if he was allowed to—and once keeping his clothes clean from every speck of dust is no longer a major priority.' He allowed her to absorb that, then went on, 'Can he swim?'

She reddened, still stung by his last comment, but honestly unable to refute it. He hadn't missed much during his first encounter with her mother, she thought ruefully.

'No, not yet,' she said in a subdued voice. 'I meant to take him to the local baths, but weekends are always so busy.'

'It's not a problem,' he said. He smiled at her for the first time that night without edge, the sudden unforced charm making the breath catch in her throat. 'I shall enjoy teaching him myself in our own pool.'

She caught her lower lip in her teeth, struggling to regain her equilibrium. Trying to disregard the image his words had presented. 'Yes—I suppose...'

'So,' he said, after a pause, 'shall we settle this thing now? Will you marry me, and come to Italy with our son?'

'I don't seem to have much of a choice,' she said in a low voice.

Something unreadable came and went in his face. 'And if you could choose? What then?'

'I would wish to be as far from you,' she said passionately, 'as it's possible to get.'

His head went back, and his eyes narrowed. 'Well, do not despair, *bella mia*,' he drawled scornfully. 'My home at Comadora is large, a *palazzo*, with thick walls, and many rooms. You should be able to avoid me easily.'

'Thank you,' she said huskily.

'Tonight, however, you will not be so fortunate,' he added.

She stiffened. 'What are you talking about?'

'I intend to spend the night here.'

She gasped. 'But—but you can't...' She tried not to look at the all too obtrusive sofa bed. 'There's no room.'

'It will be cramped,' he agreed. He took off his jacket, and began to loosen his tie. 'But it is only for one night.'

She said in a choked voice, 'You promised me—you swore this wouldn't happen. Oh, why did I think I could trust you?'

'The boot is on the other foot, *cara mia*.' He began unhurriedly to unfasten his shirt. 'I do not trust *you*. Who knows what you might be tempted to do, if you were left alone?

'But I have no intention of breaking my word,' he added. 'This armchair looks comfortable enough, so I shall use that.' His smile grazed her skin. 'And you can have that *congegno* quite undisturbed. I hope you sleep well.'

He draped his shirt over the back of the chair, sat down and removed his shoes and socks, while Polly watched in growing alarm. But when he stood up, his hands going to the waistband of his trousers, she intervened.

'Kindly stop right there,' she said grittily.

'You have some problem?'

'Yes.' Her green eyes were stormy. 'Of course I do.'

'Then deal with it.' He unzipped his trousers, stepped out of them, then placed them, folded, with the rest of his clothes. He was wearing brief silk shorts, and the rest of him was smooth tanned skin. For one burning moment of self-betrayal she found herself remembering the taste of him, and felt her body clench in uncontrollable excitement.

'Why, Paola, you are blushing,' he jeered softly. 'But not even to spare you will I sleep in my clothes. And you were not always such a prude,' he added drily. He indicated his shorts derisively. 'These, as you know, are a concession. But if the sight of me is still too much, you could always close your eyes.' He paused. 'Have you a towel I can use?'

Dry-mouthed, she muttered acquiescence, and went to the chest of drawers. As she reached for a towel, she uncovered Charlie's photograph.

'What is that?' Sandro came to her side, and took it from the drawer. He studied it for a moment, brows lifted, then turned to her. 'Is this where you usually keep it?'

'No,' she admitted reluctantly.

'You hid it,' he asked, incredulously. 'In case I came here?'

'Think whatever you wish,' she flung at him. 'I don't give a damn.'

He set the photograph carefully on top of the chest of drawers. 'And you wonder why I do not trust you,' he said silkily. He rescued the towel from her nerveless hand and went into the bathroom, closing the door behind him.

For a moment she stood irresolutely, trying to decide what to do. She could hardly go to bed in her robe, without exciting the kind of comment from him she most wished to avoid. And what nightgowns she possessed were far too thin and revealing.

However...

Polly knelt, opening the bottom drawer of the chest, searching with feverish fingers. There were some oddments of winter clothing here, she knew. Among them...

She drew out the pyjamas with a sigh of relief. They were worn out, washed out, and she'd never liked them, but they were good old-fashioned winceyette, and they covered her from her throat down to her feet.

She was just fastening the last button on the mandarin-style jacket when Sandro returned, and stopped dead at the sight of her.

'Santa Madonna,' he breathed, with a kind of fascinated horror. 'No wonder you sleep alone. I think I shall have to choose your trousseau myself, particularly the *biancheria intima.*'

'Thank you,' Polly returned icily. 'But I prefer to pick my own lingerie. And if you don't like the way I look, you can close your eyes too,' she added triumphantly.

'That is one solution,' he admitted musingly. 'But I can think of others that I would enjoy more.' He saw her blench, and grinned. 'Calm down, *cara mia.* I intend to keep my word. But sometimes to cover too much can be a mistake, because it excites the imagination.' He paused. 'I suppose a spare blanket is too much to hope for.'

She wanted to scream at him that she hoped he caught galloping pneumonia and died alone in a ditch. Instead she heard herself say unwillingly, 'Yes, there is one.'

She fetched it from the corner cupboard, pale blue and still in its wrappings. 'I bought it for Charlie,' she told him, gruffly. 'For when he moves into a bed instead of his cot.'

There was a silence. 'Then I am doubly grateful,' he said quite gently. 'Because this is a sacrifice for you. And I will make sure it goes with us to his new home.'

For a moment, there was a note in his voice that made her want to cry. She turned away hurriedly, and got into bed, pulling the covers over her, the metal base creaking its usual protest as she settled herself.

'*Dio*,' Sandro muttered. 'And that—atrocity will remain here.'

Well, she wasn't going to argue about that, Polly thought wearily. Aloud, she said, past the constriction in her throat, 'Will you turn the light off, please? When you're ready.'

'I am ready now.'

She lay, eyes tight shut, as he went past her, and the room was plunged into darkness. Waited for him to return to the chair.

Instead, she was aware of him standing beside her. He said quietly, 'Paola, do you ever wish you could turn back the clock? Wipe out what has been?'

'No,' she said. 'Because I know it's impossible, and I prefer to deal with reality.'

He sighed. 'Then could we not declare a truce for this one night? Be together for old times' sake?'

She wanted so badly to yield. To reach up and draw him down to her. She was starving for him, her body quivering with need, aching for him. Reminding her that she'd never shared a room with him before without eventually falling asleep in his arms in the drugged sweetness of sensual exhaustion.

But if she surrendered, she would be lost forever. And if she resisted, as she knew she must, at least she would retain what remained of her pride. Which might be all she had left to sustain her in the weeks, months, even years ahead.

'Even if I was in the mood for casual sex,' she said stonily, 'you gave me your word.' And paused. 'Besides, you flatter yourself, *signore*,' she added, coolly and distinctly. 'The old times weren't that special.'

She heard his swift intake of breath, and flinched, knowing she had gone too far. Waiting for a retribution which seemed inevitable.

But there was nothing.

She felt rather than heard the moment he moved away. Listened, all her senses tingling, as he wrapped himself in the blanket. Then, in the heavy silence which followed, she turned her face into the single pillow, and lay like a dead thing.

It had never occurred to her that she would sleep. She was too aware of his even breathing only a few feet away, demonstrating quite clearly, she realised, that her rejection couldn't have weighed too heavily with him after all.

She sighed silently, searching for a cool place on the pillow. She needed to look calm and rested in the morning, not wan and heavy-eyed.

Because Sandro must not be allowed to think that he still mattered to her.

That was what she needed to remember above all. Anything else would be a disaster, because, as those few moments in the darkness had proved all over again, it was going to be difficult to remain immune to the devastating allure of his sexuality.

But that, she thought, had always been her downfall from their first meeting. She had been too much in love, too blinded by the passion and glamour of him to ask the right questions and demand answers that made sense.

Her first major surprise had been his brilliant command of English, but when she'd asked him about it he'd simply said he'd had good teachers.

Polly had wondered, with a pang, whether he meant other women, and decided not to probe any further. Now she suspected that he'd gone to school in England, and probably university too, either here or in America.

He'd told her too that he worked at the Grand Hotel Comadora, but she'd never gone there to see him because its sheer expensive exclusivity discouraged casual visitors. The entrances were controlled by security guards, and the staff were subject to strict rules, so she'd stayed away. Otherwise she'd have soon found out that he wasn't simply an employee, but the owner. And that had been the last thing he wanted her to know.

Her own *naïveté* made her cringe now. The way she'd trusted him with all her small, loving dreams of their future.

'I'd like a tiny house,' she told him once. 'In one of the villages high above the sea, with a terraced garden, and its own lemon tree.'

'Mm.' He'd stroked her hair back from her love-flushed face with gentle fingers. 'And will you make me *limoncello* from our tree?'

He was talking about the lethally potent liqueur that was brewed locally, and she'd laughed.

'Well, I could try.'

God, what a fool she'd been, and how he must have been secretly amused at her, knowing full well that he was going to dump her once their warm, rapturous summer together was over.

He'd found himself an inexperienced virgin, and cynically turned her into an instrument for his pleasure.

I bet he couldn't believe his own luck. I must have been the perfect mistress, she thought, wincing. Easily duped, and ecstatically wanton. He didn't even have to kiss me. The sound of his voice—the warmth of his skin as he stood next to me were enough.

And, as she'd discovered tonight, they still were.

So how was she going to deal with the bleak sterility of the future that awaited her in Italy? A wife who was not a wife, she thought, living in a house that would never be her home. Her only link with Sandro, the child he had made in her body. A child, at the same time, who had driven them further apart than any years or miles could have done.

Sandro blamed her for keeping her pregnancy from him, but what else could she have done when she'd been dismissed so summarily from his life? And the accompanying threat might have been veiled, but it was real enough to have kept her from Italy ever since. Or until yesterday, at least.

And that had been all his own doing.

And now amazingly she was going to return to the Campania at his side. Somehow, she was going to have to learn to be his *marchesa*. To sit at his table, wearing the clothes and probably the jewellery he provided. To be pleasant to his family, and welcoming to his guests. And never by word, look or gesture let anyone suspect that she was bleeding slowly to death.

She supposed there would be compensations. She knew there would be heartbreak. And she was scared.

Scared of the inevitable isolation that awaited her—the power he still exerted over her trembling senses—and the ever-present danger of self-betrayal.

She needed to work on her anger—her bitterness at his desertion. They would protect her. Build a barrier that not all his sensual expertise could breach. That was the way she must go.

All the same, she found her mind drifting wistfully back to the tiny dream house and its lemon tree, and she saw herself walking beneath it with Sandro, her hand in his, as the sun glinted through the leaves.

And though her mouth smiled, there were tears on her face as she finally fell asleep.

CHAPTER FIVE

SHE was weighed down, sinking into the depths of a dark and bottomless sea, unable to move or save herself.

Polly opened her eyes, gasping, to the familiar surroundings of the flat, bathed in early-morning light through the thin curtains, but the sensation of being pinned down persisted. Even increased.

Slowly, and with foreboding, she turned her head, and saw that Sandro was lying next to her, on top of the covers. The blue blanket was thrown lightly over him, and, she realised incredulously, Charlie's small pyjamaed form was also present, sprawled across his father's bare chest, his dark head tucked into the curve of his shoulder. Both of them were fast asleep.

For a moment Polly was transfixed by this unexpected tableau. And deep within her, she felt such a stir of tenderness that she almost cried out.

She swallowed deeply, reclaiming her self-control. Reminding herself that she would have to get accustomed to seeing them together, although not in such intimate circumstances. And, at the same time, knowing a pang of jealousy that Charlie, usually awkward with strangers, should have capitulated so readily. She overcame an impulse to snatch him back.

Slowly and stealthily, she began to ease her way towards the edge of the bed. It was still early, but her need for coffee was evenly matched with her desire to extract herself from a difficult situation.

Besides, she wanted both Charlie and herself to be ready by the time Julie arrived.

Julie, she thought, her mouth tightening, who was going to get a piece of her mind. And yet was that really fair to the girl, who'd only been doing the job she was hired for?

Yes, she had concerns, but so had Polly. She'd been worried about her mother's apparent resolve to keep Charlie a baby for as long as possible, and therefore more dependent than he should be at his age. Mrs Fairfax had lavished presents on 'my little prince' and 'Gran's sweet little man', most of them in the form of expensive clothing which she fussed to keep pristine. Even helping his grandfather to gather up hedge clippings seemed to be on the forbidden list, Polly recalled wryly. Hardly any wonder that Charlie didn't shine at outdoor activities.

And he was lazy about feeding himself, and doing simple tasks that Polly set him, probably because he was used to having everything done for him at other times.

I knew there were problems, she admitted as she slid with infinite care from under the covers, but at the same time I wanted to avoid another confrontation with my mother. So I have only myself to blame.

She stood up, then paused, suddenly aware of movement behind her. Stiffening as Sandro's voice said a husky, '*Buongiorno*'.

'Good morning.' She didn't look at him. 'I was going to make coffee—if you'd like some. I—I don't have espresso,' she added stiltedly.

'Coffee would be good,' he said. 'If I can free myself sufficiently to drink it.' She could hear the smile in his voice, and bit her lip.

'Shall I put him back in his cot?' she asked.

'Why disturb him for no cause?'

'Perhaps I should ask you the same thing.' Polly stared down at the floor. 'What is he doing here?'

'He was crying,' Sandro said shortly. 'He wanted a drink, which I gave him. Should I have left him thirsty?'

'He'd have needed changing too.' God, she thought, she sounded so carping—like a miserable shrew.

'I even managed that,' he returned. 'After a struggle. Although I do not guarantee my handiwork,' he added drily.

'You did that?' Polly turned then, staring down at him.

'But of course. He was uncomfortable.'

'Well—thank you for that,' Polly said reluctantly. She shook her head. 'I can't understand why I didn't hear him myself. I always do...'

'You were dead to the world.' His voice gentled a little. 'You did not even scream "rape" when I joined you on the bed. Perhaps you sensed Carlino was there to act as chaperone.'

'Maybe so,' she agreed stiffly.

'A friend warned me that when you have a child, the concept

of "three in a bed" takes on a new meaning,' he went on. 'I now know what he means.'

Polly looked away, her mouth tightening, and he sighed. 'That was a joke.'

'An inappropriate one,' she said, hating the primness in her voice. 'I'll get the coffee now. And—thanks again for helping with Charlie.'

'It was my pleasure,' he said, his voice faintly weary.

By the time she returned, Charlie had woken and was in a grizzly mood.

'You are sour in the mornings, *figlio mio*,' Sandro told him. He slanted a faint grin at Polly. 'Like your *mammina*.'

She sipped the strong, scalding brew she'd made. 'I'm sorry.' Her voice was defensive. 'But this isn't easy for me.'

'Or for me, *cara mia*,' he said. 'Or for me.'

He swallowed his own coffee with the complete disregard for its temperature that she remembered so well, then rose, swinging Charlie up into his arms. 'Come, my little grumbler. Come and take a bath with Papa and see if it improves your temper.' He glanced at Polly. 'You have no objections, I hope.'

'No,' she said. 'None.'

She occupied herself with stripping the bed and turning it back into a sofa, while attempting to ignore the noise of splashing and Charlie's gleeful squeals coming from the bathroom. Trying hard, too, not to feel envious and even slightly dejected, because that would get her nowhere.

Her path might have been chosen for her, but she had to follow it, whatever the cost.

What would happen next? she wondered. She supposed she would have to see Mrs Terence and tell her that Safe Hands would be losing her earlier than planned.

And she would have to visit her parents and break the news to them too—a situation which had all the makings of a Class A nightmare.

And if Sandro was serious about moving her into a larger flat, and so far he seemed to have meant everything he said, then she would have to pack.

She wandered into the tiny kitchen and poured herself some orange juice. She felt as if she needed all the vitamins she could get.

It was as if her life had been invaded by a sudden whirlwind, all her plans and certainties swept away.

And at some point she would have to stand beside Sandro in a church or registry office, and listen to him making promises he had no intention of keeping as he put his ring on her finger.

Three years ago, all my dreams were of marrying him, she thought unhappily. And now it's happening at last, but not in a way I could ever have hoped. Because I'm being offered the façade of a marriage, without its fulfillment. And, for Charlie's sake, I have to find some way—to endure.

She rinsed out her glass and put it on the draining board.

What was the old saying? she wondered drearily. Be careful what you wish for, in case your wish comes true?

Well, she had wished so hard to be Sandro's wife—once.

She gave a small wretched sigh, then went into Charlie's room to choose his clothes for the day, and that was where Sandro found her a few minutes later. He was fully dressed, while Charlie, capering beside him, was in a towel draped like a Roman toga.

'Do you have a mop, or a cloth, perhaps? I need to dry the bathroom floor.' Sandro's tone was faintly rueful.

'It doesn't matter,' Polly said too brightly. 'I'll clear up when I have my own bath.' She paused. 'You seemed to be having fun together,' she went on with an effort. 'Somehow—he's not shy with you.'

'Why should he be?' Sandro lifted a hand and touched his scarred cheek. 'Did you think, perhaps, that this would terrify him—make him run away from me screaming, and force me to think again?' he added sardonically.

'No—oh, no,' Polly stammered. 'But he can be tricky with people he's only just met. But not you.'

Sandro shrugged. 'Blood calling to blood, perhaps.'

'Yes,' she said. 'That must be it.'

He was watching her. He said quietly, 'Paola, I am not trying to take your place. You will always be his mother. But he needs us both.'

Her throat closed. She nodded, unable to speak, her hands restlessly folding and unfolding a little T-shirt.

His hand closed on her shoulder. His touch was gentle, but she felt its resonance through her blood and bone.

'Go and dress yourself,' he directed quietly. 'I will see to our son.'

She didn't want his kindness, his consideration, Polly thought wildly as she fled. She needed antagonism to feed her anger—her determination to stay aloof from him at all costs. To blank out forever the memories of those days and nights when her universe had narrowed to one room, and the bed where she lay in his arms.

She needed to hate him.

The state of the bathroom was a spur to that, of course. It looked as if it had been hit by a tidal wave, and it took ten minutes' hard graft with a mop and bucket, and a roll of paper towels, to render it usable again.

But even then the recollection of Charlie's crows of delight diffused her resentment.

And it occurred to her, too, that next time Sandro chose to play submarines or whatever with his son it would be someone else's task to do the clearing up after them.

It was clear that her life was going to change at all levels, not just the strictly personal. And would she be able to cope?

Although she would not be Sandro's wife in the accepted sense, she would have some practical role to play in his life, and maybe she should ask to have it defined.

She sighed. So many things she needed to know—not least how he'd acquired the scar on his face. Her own assumptions had been totally and embarrassingly wrong, of course, but she'd been offered no other explanation for an injury that must have gone dangerously deep.

She could only suppose that Sandro found the circumstances surrounding it too difficult and painful to discuss. So what could possibly have happened, and could she ever persuade him to talk about it?

Then there was his family. It seemed that he had other cousins apart from the *contessa*. How much did they know about her existence? she wondered. And what would they feel about her arrival—an interloper with a child?

Polly sighed again. She was just beginning to realise there were problems she hadn't even imagined awaiting her in Campania.

When she emerged from the bathroom, freshly attired in jeans and a pale blue shirt, she found Sandro standing by the window with

Charlie in his arms, apparently having a murmured conversation about the traffic in the street below.

'Have you pointed out the security men watching the flat?' Polly asked caustically.

'I sent them away last night,' Sandro told her, unfazed. 'From now on, *cara*, I shall be watching you myself.' He paused, watching the swift rush of colour to her face. 'So, what are your plans for the day?'

'Principally, giving up my job, and trying to calm my mother.' Polly thrust her hands into the pockets of her jeans in an effort at nonchalance. 'She's probably looking for a hit man right now to take you out of the equation.'

'What a pity I am not Mafioso as you thought,' he murmured. 'I could perhaps have suggested someone.'

Polly's mouth tightened. 'I suppose I should also start packing—if you really intend to move us out of here. Or was that simply a threat?'

'I do intend it,' he said. 'And as quickly as possible. But do not bring too much, *cara*. I plan to provide you and Carlino with everything you need, including new wardrobes.'

She lifted her chin. 'And I prefer to choose my own things.'

He looked her up and down, brows raised. 'Of which those are a sample?'

'There was a time,' Polly said, 'when you would have found these clothes perfectly acceptable.'

'But then we are neither of us the same people,' he said, gently. 'Are we, Paola?'

'No,' she said. 'We're not. And, as a matter of interest, who was the Sandro Domenico you once claimed to be?'

'You are interested?' His brows lifted mockingly. 'A step forward, perhaps. Domenico was the name of my late father, and was given to me as a second name at my christening. I used it when I did not wish to reveal my true identity.'

'Of course,' she said. 'Why didn't I guess?'

'So, will you allow me to make reparation for that, and accept that I wish to show my gratitude to you for agreeing to marry me, and how better than with a *corredo di sposa*?'

'I don't want your gratitude,' she said stonily. 'Or a trousseau of designer dresses. Just the space you promised me.'

'Does that exclude you from having lunch with me at my hotel—the Grand Capital? There are things we need to discuss.'

Polly bit her lip. 'If I must.'

Sandro shrugged. 'You overwhelm me,' he told her drily. 'Shall we say one o'clock in the bar?'

'Lunch in a restaurant?' Polly gave her angelically smiling son a dubious glance. 'I'm not sure Charlie could manage that.'

'He does not have to,' Sandro said briskly. 'I have arranged for him to spend some time with friends of mine, Teresa and Ernesto Bacchi, so we can talk without distraction.'

Polly drew a swift breath. 'That's very arbitrary,' she said mutinously. 'I might not like these friends of yours.'

'Well, you will meet them later today, so you can judge for yourself,' he said, shrugging.

'And it might upset Charlie, too.'

'I doubt that,' he said. 'They have twins his age. And he is more adaptable than you think.' Sandro smoothed the little boy's hair back from his forehead. 'Tell Mammina,' he whispered. He pointed to himself. 'Who am I?'

'Papa,' Charlie said promptly, and hid his face on his father's shoulder.

Polly made herself laugh and applaud. How easily Sandro had won him over, she thought. But why should she wonder at that?

Before he'd even spoken to her that first day in Sorrento, she'd been aware of the intensity of his gaze, her own mouth curving shyly—involuntarily—in response to his smile. Her heart had thudded in anticipation of the moment when he would come to her side.

Dear God, she thought wearily. She'd been seduced with just a look. A number-one, first-class pushover.

She turned away blindly, murmuring about finding her bag, and then the door buzzer sounded to announce Julie's arrival.

She'd decided it would be hypocritical to have a battle with the nanny over concerns that she actually shared, so she greeted her with a polite word, and smile instead.

She took herself into the kitchen to make more coffee while Julie received her instructions for the day.

At the moment Sandro ruled, and there was nothing she could do about it, she thought, leaning against the cramped work surface while she waited for the kettle to boil.

She was still inwardly reeling from the shock of his return, and its traumatic aftermath, but her confusion wouldn't last forever. Soon, she would be back in control of herself, and she'd make damned sure that more of a partnership was established over Charlie's parenting than existed at the moment.

Something that might be easier once she was officially Sandro's wife—and one of the few advantages of the forthcoming marriage, she thought painfully.

When she returned to the living room, Sandro came over to her, having relinquished Charlie to his nanny.

'I must go,' he said. He took out his wallet, and extracted what seemed to be an obscene amount of money, which he placed next to Charlie's photograph on the chest of drawers. 'For taxis,' he said. 'Tomorrow there will be a car and driver for your use.'

'Public transport has always been perfectly adequate,' Polly informed him loftily, conveniently forgetting how often she had cursed its delays and overcrowding.

Sandro shrugged. 'Then spend it as you wish,' he said. 'In this, at least, the choice is yours.'

Ignoring her mutinous glance, he took her hand and bowed over it.

'I will not kiss you, *bella mia*,' he said softly. He lifted her imprisoned fingers, drawing them lightly over his unshaven chin, the topaz eyes meeting hers in open challenge. 'I would not wish to mark your exquisite skin.'

Polly mumbled something incoherent, and withdrew her hand from his with more haste than courtesy, aware that Julie, in spite of her training, was watching open-mouthed.

And probably thinking every inch of me is grazed to the bone, she thought, cringing inwardly.

If you only knew, she told the other girl silently. If you only—truly—knew...

And found herself sighing under her breath.

She handed in her notice at Safe Hands, aware that she was causing a slight shock wave, but unable to explain or defend her decision. Far too tricky, she thought.

And then, of course, she had her parents to face.

She'd expected her mother to be instantly on the attack when she arrived at the family home, but Mrs Fairfax was upstairs, lying on her bed with the curtains drawn. The look she gave Polly was subdued, almost listless.

'So, he's persuaded you,' she said heavily. 'I supposed he would. A man like that. I—we didn't realise what we were taking on.'

Polly took her mother's cold hand in hers. 'It won't be so bad,' she said, wondering which of them she was trying to convince. 'And Italy's such a beautiful country. You'll be able to come and visit as often as you like. I'm sure Sandro will want that,' she added, mentally crossing her fingers.

'Crumbs from the rich man's table,' her mother said with a harsh laugh. 'How could I ever have imagined it would end like this—that he'd come to find you?'

'She'll be all right,' her father told Polly comfortingly as they went downstairs. 'I'm going to take her down to Cornwall for a few days. She loves it there, but we haven't been able to go recently.'

'No.' Polly bit her lip. 'Because you've been too busy looking after Charlie. Maybe the break will do her good—stop her brooding.' She hesitated. 'Dad—about the wedding—when it happens...'

'You want us to stay away?'

She shook her head vehemently. 'I'm counting on you to give me away, but how is Mum going to feel about it?'

'Let's cross that bridge when we come to it,' he said gently. He gave her a searching look. 'Sweetheart—tell me something.'

'If I can.'

'Charlie's father,' he said. 'Was it just a temporary fling, or did you really care about him?'

She looked away. 'I—cared,' she said in a low voice. 'But I discovered that—he didn't.'

'Well, at least he's trying to put things right now, no matter what your mother says.' He gave an awkward chuckle. 'Even asked my permission, which threw me.' He put his hand on her shoulder. 'It won't be easy, I know, but maybe you could try meeting him halfway?'

But he would have to want that too, she thought. *And he doesn't. Besides, how can I meet him anywhere when I don't even know who he is? And never did...*

She suppressed a sigh, and her little smile was wintry. 'Perhaps that's a bridge I have to cross.' She kissed his cheek. 'Good luck with Cornwall. I'll be in touch.'

She didn't want to be late for lunch, so she reluctantly spent some of Sandro's money on a taxi after all.

She hadn't changed into anything more formal for their meeting, just added her favourite pair of earrings—the tiny enamelled cornflowers on delicate silver chains. But she began to wish she had dressed more smartly as she walked across the Grand Capital's marble foyer, skirting the fountain and the groups of elegant women who'd gathered there to chat before lunch.

Sandro was already sitting at the bar when Polly entered. He was laughing at something the barman had said, and she hesitated, almost stunned, as the full force of his attraction hit her once more like a punch in the throat.

Nor was she the only one, she realised, recovering her breath. Women were sending him predatory looks from all over the room. No change there, then, she thought drily, remembering the same reaction every time she'd walked down a street with him in Sorrento.

And the scar on his cheek had not detracted from his appeal in any way. On the contrary, thought Polly, he looked like some Renaissance swordsman injured in a duel.

At that moment, he looked round and saw her. He slid off the stool, coming across to her, his mouth curling in faint cynicism as he registered her instant tension.

'*Cara,*' he said softly, and took her hand. 'So you have decided to join me. I could not be sure. But I am delighted.' He leaned towards her, his gaze travelling to her mouth, and Polly flinched, freeing her fingers from his grasp.

'Still no kiss?' His tone was mocking. 'Even though I have learned my lesson from this morning, and shaved more closely in anticipation?'

'I don't consider that any particular inducement,' Polly responded stonily. 'I've agreed to marry you, and I see no need for any—embellishments.'

'Now, there we disagree. I see I shall have to teach you the difference between public and private behaviour, my reluctant bride.' He smiled as he spoke, and only Polly was aware of the ice in his voice. 'But we will discuss that later.'

He took her to a corner table, and signalled to a hovering waiter. 'What would you like to drink. Is it still Campari and soda?'

More unwanted memories, she thought, biting her lip. She said coolly, 'Just a mineral water, please.'

'Last night you drank white wine.'

'Today I need to keep a clear head.'

He gave her a thoughtful look, then turned to the waiter. 'Mineral water, *per favore*,' he directed. 'For both of us.'

The waiter departed, leaving a silence behind him that Sandro was the first to break.

'Have you had a productive morning?' he asked.

'I suppose so.' Polly gave a slight shrug. 'I resigned from my job, and visited my parents, who are planning a holiday in Cornwall.'

'I have not been idle either,' he said. 'The legal requirements for our marriage are being fast-tracked, so I have decided it would be best if you moved here to my suite until the wedding.'

'I—move in with you?' she repeated blankly. 'What are you talking about?'

'Finding a flat to rent for such a short time could be a problem,' he explained. His mouth curled slightly. 'But do not be too disturbed, *cara*. The suite has two large bedrooms.'

She said in a hollow voice, 'There are three of us. Four with Julie.'

'The *bambinaia* will work only in the daytime. At night, we will care for Carlino ourselves. You have been doing that since he was born,' he added. 'So it is scarcely a hardship. He can decide whose room he shares each evening.' He gave her a cool smile. 'An excellent arrangement, don't you think?'

Her voice shook. 'You don't want to know what I think.'

'Probably not,' he agreed drily. 'But you will not be forced to endure my company for too long. We shall leave for Italy and Comadora immediately after our wedding, and, once there, I will do my best to keep out of your way. In view of my work commitments, it should not be too difficult.'

Polly gave him a pleading look. 'Can't we do a deal over this? As it's only for a short time, couldn't Charlie and I stay at the flat?'

'Unfortunately that is impossible.' His hand closed over hers, his thumb stroking her soft palm, sending tiny tremors through her senses which she was unable to ignore or control. 'You see, *carissima*, I need you near to me,' he whispered huskily. 'Especially at night. Just in case you decided to try and escape me after all.'

At that moment, the waiter arrived back with their drinks, and a colleague came hurrying with menus and a wine list.

Polly withdrew her hand from his clasp, not trusting herself to speak, longing for a sliver of ice long and sharp enough to pierce her tormentor to the heart.

She took refuge behind her menu while she regained her equilibrium.

Last night had been bad enough, she thought broodingly. She'd never envisaged having to move in with him, but she realised now that she'd been naïve. There were probably plenty of other options, but his will was paramount, and he was letting her know it.

Yet he'd been so different once; gentle, humorous, patient—and adoring, or so she'd believed.

Now, she thought, wretchedness gnawing at her, it seemed that treacherous, deceitful and arrogant were more accurate descriptions.

He'd simply played the part of the sincere lover, as a ploy to keep her in his bed, trusting and eager, all summer long.

Yet, while she knew this, how was it possible that his lightest touch still had the power to stir her to the depths of her being, reigniting needs and longing that should be dead?

It was madness, and she needed to become sane again, or her existence, even on the outskirts of his life, would become intolerable.

She'd never felt less hungry in her life, but she knew she should eat something, so decided on consommé and chicken in wine sauce to follow. Fuel, she thought, for the next battle.

'So,' Sandro said when they were alone again, 'you will stay here with me, and no more arguments?'

She nodded abruptly, and he smiled at her. 'I am charmed by your obedience,' he told her, and raised his glass. 'Shall we drink to marital harmony?'

'No,' Polly said grittily, 'thank you. Not even in water.'

'*Che peccato,*' he said lightly. 'What a shame. Then, instead, let us drink to your earrings.' He put a hand out as if to touch one of the little cornflowers, and Polly shrank back.

He stared at her, his brows snapping together. When he spoke, his voice crackled with anger. 'Tell me, Paola, do you intend to cringe each time I come near you?'

'Isn't that the whole point?' she demanded huskily. 'I don't want you near me. You've promised to keep your distance, but can I believe you?'

'And how can I make you see that some contact between us is inevitable, and that you must accept it?' he asked coldly. 'I am letting it be known among my family and friends that we are reunited lovers.'

She said thickly, 'You can't expect me to go along with that. Not after everything that's happened...'

'I do expect it,' he said harshly. 'In fact, I insist on it. There is bound to be talk—even scandal—when our marriage, and our child, become public knowledge. I wish to minimise that for Carlino's sake. Make people believe that we were victims of fate who have been given a second chance together.'

She gave him a scornful look. 'That is such hypocrisy.'

'You would prefer to have the whole truth broadcast?' His voice bit. 'I can tell you my cousin Emilio would be delighted. He publishes a whole range of cheap gossip magazines, exposing secrets that the rich and famous would prefer to remain hidden.

'Until yesterday, he considered himself my heir, and will not be pleased to find himself demoted,' he added cuttingly. 'If he finds out that ours is simply a marriage of convenience, then our sleeping arrangements will be headline news in every trashy publication he puts on the streets. Is that what you want?'

'Oh, God.' Polly put down her glass. 'He couldn't, surely.'

'Think again,' he said. 'We have never liked each other, so he would do it and revel in it. So I prefer to safeguard my pride and my privacy, *cara mia*. And you would be well advised to co-operate too, unless you wish to feature as a discarded mistress—and the unwanted wife that Alessandro Valessi threw out of his bed. Is that what you choose?'

'No,' she said, staring down at the table. 'I—I don't want that.'

'Then play your part, and stop behaving as if I were a leper,' he told her. 'Because it bores me.' He paused. 'It also makes me wonder,' he added softly, 'what you would do if, some night, I—tested your resolve. *Capisce?*'

'Yes.' Her voice was a thread.

'Bene.' He gave her a swift, hard smile. 'Now let us go, happily united, into lunch.'

CHAPTER SIX

SHE walked into the restaurant beside him, moving like an automaton. His hand was under her arm as if she was in custody, as they followed the head waiter to yet another corner table.

'They have a new chef here,' Sandro told her as he took his place beside her. His sleeve, she realised, was only a few inches from her bare arm. Altogether too close for comfort. 'And the food is said to be very good,' he added.

'You seem to know a lot about it,' she said. 'Is this hotel part of the Comadora chain, by any chance?'

'We acquired it six months ago.'

'I see.' She played nervously with the cutlery. 'Will—will you tell me something?'

His gaze sharpened. 'If I can,' he said, after a pause.

'When we first met—why didn't you tell me who you really were? Why did you let me think you were simply a minor hotel employee?'

'Because that is exactly what I was,' he said. 'I had been travelling round all the hotels in the group to learn the trade, working in every department, so I could see what shape they were in.

'Traditionally my family has always been involved in agriculture and banking. The hotels were acquired in the nineteenth century by one of my ancestors who is said to have won them in a poker game.

'When my father inherited them, he wanted to get rid of them. He had no interest in tourism. But I felt differently. I thought managing the chain—updating and improving it—would be more interesting than citrus fruit and olive oil, or sitting in some air-conditioned office in Rome.

'So I was working incognito, and compiling a report that I hoped would convince my father to keep the hotels and invest in them.'

'But I wasn't involved with any hotels,' Polly protested. 'I

77

worked for an independent tour company. You could have told me the truth.'

He said quietly, 'Paola, as the Valessi heir, I brought a lot of baggage with me. We are a wealthy family, and there had been women in my life whose sole priority was my money. I had become—wary.'

He spread his hands. 'You had no idea who I was, and yet you wanted me—for myself. For Sandro Domenico. I found that— irresistible. Can you understand that?'

'I understand.' There was a constriction in her throat. 'But your money must have been useful when you needed to be rid of— someone.'

His mouth hardened. 'Yes,' he said. 'In the end, it usually came down to—money.' He paused. 'Is that all you want to ask?'

'No.' She shook her head. 'I have a hundred questions. But I'm not sure you'd be prepared to answer them all.'

'No?' He sent her a meditative look. 'Try me.'

She took a deep breath. 'Well—the scar on your cheek. I was wondering how that happened.'

'I was in an accident,' he said expressionlessly. 'In the hills above Comadora. My car left the road on a bend and plunged into a ravine. I was thrown clear, but badly injured. My life was saved by a local man who found me, and administered some rough first aid before the ambulance got to me.'

It was a bald recital of the facts—something he'd clearly done many times before. He spoke as if it no longer had the power to affect him, but Polly could sense the tension in him.

She stared down at the immaculate white tablecloth. She said quietly, 'You were—lucky.'

You could have died, she thought, the breath catching in her throat. You could have been killed so easily. And I—I might never have known just how much I had to mourn.

'Yes,' he agreed. 'Fortunate, indeed.' His eyes were hooded as he looked at her. 'Do you require further details?'

Oh, God, Polly thought. I know what I have to ask—but I don't want to hear the answer.

She took a deep breath. She said, 'When did it happen? Was anyone else involved—in the crash?'

'Three years ago. I had a passenger,' he said levelly. 'A girl called Bianca DiMario. She—did not get clear.'

Polly stared at him, aware of the sudden chill spreading through her veins. She said hoarsely, 'That's—terrible.'

She wanted to stop there—to ask nothing more. But that was impossible, of course.

I have to go on, she thought, steeling herself. I—I have to know.

'You—you were close? You knew her well?' *She was a casual acquaintance? You were just giving her a lift? Please say that's all it was—please...*

'I had known her for most of my life,' he said quietly. 'She came to live at the *palazzo* with her aunt, the *contessa*, at my father's invitation. Bianca's parents were both dead, and the *contessa* was a widow who had been left with little money.

'My father had a strong sense of family, and he considered it a duty and an honour to care for them both.' He paused. 'Bianca was also intended to be the next Marchesa Valessi,' he added, evenly. 'The announcement of our engagement had been planned for the week after the accident.'

Polly was reduced to stricken silence as the pain returned, twisting inside her. She could see so clearly now why he'd had to get rid of her with such indecent haste—and offered such a high price to achieve that.

She'd become an embarrassment, she thought. Their affair an insult to his future wife.

She bent her head. 'I—I'm sorry,' she said huskily. 'It must have been utterly ghastly—to lose the girl you were going to marry in such a way.'

'Yes,' he said. 'It was the worst time of my life. Something I cannot let myself forget.' His faint smile was grim. 'So I keep the scar to remind me how I was robbed forever of my chance of happiness.'

How can I listen to this? she asked herself imploringly. How can I let him hurt me all over again? She wanted to throw herself at him, hitting him with her fists, and screaming that she mattered too.

She wanted to weep until she had no tears left.

With a supreme effort, she mastered herself.

'The accident,' she said. 'Does anyone know what caused it?' How could she speak normally—discuss this terrible thing when she was falling apart inside? When she had to face all over again that everything he'd ever said to her—promised her—had been a lie?

Sandro shrugged. 'The inquiry found a burst tyre on my car, so I was—exonerated. But I still have to live with the memory.'

And I, Polly thought, shall have to live with your betrayal of me—and I don't know if I can do that. I think you may be asking the impossible.

She met his gaze. 'Bigamy,' she said clearly. 'Is that another Valessi family tradition? Because you seem to have been engaged to two women at one time.'

He sighed harshly. 'I should never have let things go so far, and I know it.' His mouth twisted. 'Believe me, I have been well punished for my silence.'

'Bianca.' She forced herself to say the name. 'Did she—know about me?'

A muscle moved beside his mouth. 'Yes.' One small, uncompromising word.

'I see,' she said. She was silent for a moment. 'So—I was the only fool.'

'No,' he said. 'I meant to tell you everything. To explain, and ask you to forgive me. But then the crash came, and after that—everything changed.' His smile was icy. 'As you know.'

'Yes,' Polly said almost inaudibly. She paused. 'It must have been awful for the *contessa* too—to lose her niece.' She forced a smile. 'No wonder she doesn't like me.'

He sighed again. 'Paola *mia*, Bianca has been dead for three years. Zia Antonia has to accept that.'

'And she still lives at the *palazzo*—in spite of it all?'

'Of course,' he said. 'I could hardly ask her to leave. Besides, I am often away, and she currently manages the house and estate for me.'

'So she's bound to have constant reminders of Bianca.' Polly hesitated. 'And three years isn't all that long—when you care deeply for someone.' She took a breath. 'After all, you must think about her too.'

She saw his face harden, his hand lift as if to touch his scarred cheek, then fall again.

'*Sì*,' he said harshly. 'I think about her. And three years can seem an eternity.'

I asked for that, Polly thought wretchedly. A self-inflicted wound.

She said in a low voice, 'I'm sorry. I shouldn't have pried.'

'You had to know,' he said. 'And I wished to explain. But up to now, you have shown no curiosity about the past.' His mouth twisted. 'Who knows? I might have spent all these years in the Regina Coeli prison for robbery with violence.' He put his hand briefly over hers. 'So, is there nothing else you wish to ask me?'

For a moment, she thought she detected a note of pleading in his voice. But that was ridiculous. Sandro had never pleaded in his life.

And there were questions teeming in her brain, falling over themselves to escape. But she knew she could not bear to hear the answers. The news about Bianca had been as much as she could take today.

She shook her head. 'There's nothing I need to know. After all, it's not as if ours will be a real marriage. It's just an arrangement, for Charlie's sake. So, it's better if we can keep our lives separate—and private.'

He was silent for a moment, then he inclined his head almost wryly. 'As you wish.'

The food when it came was delicious, but Polly might as well have been chewing sawdust. She had to force every mouthful past the tightness in her throat, helped down by the Orvieto Classico he'd chosen. Because she couldn't allow Sandro to glimpse her inner agony.

He broke my heart once, she thought. I can't allow him to do that again. Especially when I know that he could—all too easily. And she sighed quietly.

When the largely silent meal was finally over, Polly found her next ordeal was accompanying Sandro up to the penthouse to inspect her temporary home.

She'd hoped she would find some insoluble problem with the accommodation, but the bright, airy rooms with their masses of fresh flowers seemed just about perfect.

To her unspoken relief, the bedrooms were well apart, facing each other from opposite sides of the large and luxurious drawing room. And each had its own bathroom, so she could hardly complain about a lack of privacy.

'Will you be comfortable here?' he asked, watching her prowl around. 'I hope it has everything you want.'

'Everything,' she said. 'Except the freedom to make decisions, and live my own life.'

'A trifle, surely.' Sandro's tone was solemn, but his eyes were glinting in sudden amusement. 'When the cage you occupy is so beautifully gilded. Also unlocked.' He produced a key from his pocket. 'For your bedroom door,' he said. 'In case I walk in my sleep.'

Her heart missed a beat, but she spoke lightly. 'You'd soon wake up when Charlie started yelling.' She glanced at her watch. 'When are we picking him up from your friends? Time's moving on, and I still have to go back to the flat and pack our things.'

'I have arranged for two of the girls from Administration here to do that for you,' Sandro said calmly, meeting her fulminating gaze head-on. 'I told them to bring the minimum. I will have the remainder suitably disposed of.'

'My God,' she said furiously. 'You take a lot upon yourself. Is this part of your campaign to force me to buy new clothes?'

He smiled at her. 'No, I am relying on Teresa to do that,' he said. 'She cannot wait to take you shopping.'

'I can buy my own damned things,' Polly threw at him. 'And I don't need a minder.'

'I hope she will be much more than that,' he told her with a trace of chill. 'Her husband is one of my greatest friends, and I was best man at their wedding. They have been—good to me in return.'

He paused. 'You are going to a new life, Paola, with its own demands. As my wife, you will be expected to patronise Italian designers. How many do you know? What formal clothes will you need? How many dinner dresses—how many ballgowns?

'This is a world Teresa knows, and you can trust her advice.' He paused. 'She can also help you in another way. Before she married Ernesto, she worked as a linguist. So you may practice speaking Italian to her. Start to regain your former fluency.'

Her face warmed suddenly as she recalled precisely how that proficiency had been acquired during those long, hot afternoons a lifetime ago. The things he had whispered to her as she lay in his arms—and taught her to say to him in return.

She was suddenly aware that he was watching her, observing

the play of embarrassed colour on her skin, before he added softly and cynically, 'But with a rather different vocabulary, *carissima*.'

She said with deliberate coldness, 'Do you have any other orders for me?'

He was unfazed. 'If I think of any, I will let you know.'

'How nice it must be,' she said, 'to always get your own way. Think about it.' She ticked off on her fingers. 'You need an heir—you have one ready-made. You require somewhere convenient to keep us—and you own a hotel with a vacant suite. You don't wish to be married—and you find a wife who doesn't want to be anywhere near you either. You're ahead on all points.'

'Am I, *bella mia*?' His tone was cordial. 'How interesting that you should think so. But perhaps you should refrain from mentioning my good fortune to Teresa and Ernesto. They might not agree with you.'

He paused. 'One more thing before we go to meet them.' He reached into the inside pocket of his jacket and extracted a small velvet box.

As he opened it, Polly drew an unsteady breath at the coruscating fire from the enormous diamond it contained.

'Give me you hand.' It was a command, not a request, but she still hesitated.

'Surely—this isn't necessary...'

'On the contrary, it is essential,' Sandro contradicted her. 'So—*per favore...*'

Mutely, reluctantly, she allowed him to slide the ring onto her finger. A moment, she thought in anguish, that she'd imagined so many times during the summer of their love. But not like this. Never like this.

Her voice shook slightly. 'It's—beautiful.'

At the same time its dazzling brilliance seemed almost alien on her workaday hand, she thought, making her feel like some latter-day Cinderella.

But Sandro was no Prince Charming, she reminded herself soberly. And his diamond was altogether too magnificent a symbol of the cold, sterile bargain they had made with each other.

As if Sandro had read her thoughts, he said quietly, 'You will soon accustom yourself to wearing it.'

She bent her head. 'Along with everything else, it seems.'

'There will be compensations,' he told her. 'Tomorrow I shall open a bank account for you.'

She shook her head almost violently. 'I don't want that.'

'Dio mio.' His voice was weary. 'Paola, do you have to fight me each step of the way? Do you wish our child to be brought up in a battlefield?'

She looked away. 'No, of course not.'

'Then please try and accept the arrangements that must be made.'

'I can—try,' she said unsteadily. 'But it's not easy when your whole world has suddenly been—turned upside down.'

'You think you are alone in that?' There was a note of harsh derision in his voice. 'I too am obliged to make—adjustments.'

'But you don't have to.' She faced him with new determination, hands clenched at her sides. 'I—I understand that you need to see Charlie, to spend time with him, and I swear I'll co-operate in any way over this. But why tie yourself to an unwanted marriage when you could meet someone to love—someone who knows how to be a *marchesa*?' She paused. 'Someone the *contessa* might even approve of.'

'You think that is an essential quality in my bride?' His mouth twisted.

'I think that, otherwise, there'll be problems,' Polly said flatly. 'You must see that. After all, she runs your home—and she'll see me as an interloper. A poor substitute for the girl she loved.'

'Then she too will have to adjust.' His voice hardened. 'Believe this, Paola. My son will grow up in my home with the knowledge that his mother is my wife. Nothing else will do—either for him, or for the world at large.'

He walked to the door, and held it open. 'Now begin to play your part. My friends expect to meet a girl happily reunited with her lover—so pretend,' he added flatly. *'Avanti.'*

The serial killer was on the move, and the heroine was alone in her apartment, with a thunderstorm growling overhead. Any minute now she was going to run herself a bath or take a shower, Polly thought wearily, because that was what always happened.

I need, she thought, blanking out the television screen with one terse click of the remote control, to be distracted, not irritated.

She also wanted to relax—but her inner tensions were not so easily dispelled.

Besides, she could do without artificial horrors. Her mind was full enough already of disturbing sounds and images—bleached rock in the blazing sun, the squeal of tyres, the screech of brakes and wrenched metal. A girl screaming in fright, and then an even more terrifying silence, with Sandro lying unconscious and bleeding under a pitiless sky.

Perhaps this was why she was still up and restless, when common sense suggested she should be in bed, with Charlie fast asleep in his cot near by. She'd wondered if he would react badly to his new surroundings, but he'd settled with little more than a token protest.

Perhaps I should be more like him, Polly thought with a grimace. Learn to deal with six impossible things before breakfast.

However, liking Teresa and Ernesto had not proved impossible at all. She was tall, and slim as a wand, with long dark hair and laughing eyes. And although she was the epitome of chic, that did not stop her indulging in a rough-and-tumble on the floor with Charlie and the twins.

Ernesto was quieter, with a plain, kind face, observing his wife and children with doting fondness through his silver-rimmed glasses.

In other circumstances, Polly would have loved to have them as friends. As it was, she felt a total fraud. And sitting next to Sandro on one of the deeply cushioned sofas in their drawing room, with his arm draped casually round her shoulders, had proved unnervingly difficult.

Blissfully married herself, Teresa, left alone with Polly, had made it clear that she thought Sandro was glamorous and sexy beyond belief, in spite of his scarred face, and that she was assisting at the romance of the century.

And even if I told her that marrying Sandro was simply a rubber stamp on a legal arrangement I want no part of, Polly thought sadly, she wouldn't believe me.

'Ah, but shopping will be such fun, *cara*,' Teresa had told her buoyantly. 'Particularly as Alessandro has put no limit on our spending,' she added with glee.

And although she must have been brimming with curiosity

about Sandro and Polly's former relationship, she nobly refrained from asking questions that her guest might find difficult to answer.

There had been only one awkward moment, when Teresa had been admiring Polly's engagement ring. 'A diamond?' she exclaimed. 'But I thought...' She encountered a swift glance from Ernesto, and hastily went on, 'I thought, as your bride has green eyes, you would have chosen an emerald for her. Or do you believe they are unlucky? Some people do, I think. And a diamond is forever, no?'

Sandro had smiled lazily. 'Forever,' he agreed.

But Polly found herself wondering what Teresa had meant to say.

'So, was that such a hardship?' he'd asked as their chauffeur-driven car took them back to the hotel, with Charlie bouncing between them.

'No,' she admitted. 'They were lovely. I hate making fools of them like this.'

He gave her a dry look. 'Do not underestimate Teresa, *cara*. She is a shrewd lady.'

Is she? Polly thought. Yet she clearly thinks Sandro and I will be having an intimate dinner for two in our suite, followed by a rapturous night in each other's arms. How wrong can anyone be?

'Then I'll take care to be extra-careful,' she said. She paused. 'Why did she query my engagement ring being a diamond?'

'You noticed.' Sandro gave a shrug. 'She would expect you to wear the Valessi ruby, which is traditionally passed to each bride.'

'But not to me.'

'No,' he said, his mouth hardening. 'It was found in the wreckage of the car. My father had it buried with Bianca.'

'I see.' She swallowed. 'Well, that's—understandable.' She paused, desperate for a change of subject. 'I—I wonder if the box containing my life has been delivered yet?'

He looked at her thoughtfully. 'That has made you angry,' he said. 'Which was not my intention. I thought I had simply relieved you of a tedious job.'

'It would have been,' she admitted. She forced a smile. 'I'm just accustomed to my independence.'

'Then it may please you to know that you will not be burdened with my presence at dinner tonight,' he told her drily. 'I am going out. Would you prefer to dine in the suite, or go down to the restaurant?'

'I'll stay in the suite. It will be better for Charlie.'

'As you wish. I will arrange for Room Service to bring you a menu.'

Polly wondered where he was planning to spend the evening, but knew she could never ask. Because she did not have the right. This was the life she had agreed to for Charlie's sake. A life of silences. No questions asked, or information volunteered. A life where to be blind and deaf might be a positive advantage.

'I shall come to say goodnight to Carlino before I leave,' he added. 'If you permit, of course.'

'I can hardly prevent you.'

'You have a key to your room,' he reminded her. 'There could be a locked door between us.'

Yes, Polly had thought, her mouth drying. But would that really keep you out, if you wanted to come in?

Remembering that now, she got up with a shiver, and, walking over to the long glass doors which opened on to the balcony, she pushed them open and stepped out into the sultry night, tightening the sash on the towelling robe as she did so.

Her elderly, much-loved cotton dressing gown had not survived the Great Pack, so she'd had to use the one hanging on the bathroom door in its plastic cover. She missed her old robe badly. She'd had it for years—even taken it to Italy with her, when she worked for the travel company, and now it was gone. Like a symbol of her old life, she thought sadly.

But at least they'd brought Charlie's blue blanket—and the brown teddy bear, both of them now adorning his cot. She would have to find something else to comfort herself with.

How peaceful everything looked in the moonlight, she thought, leaning on the stone balustrade. How normal. And how deceptive appearances could be.

She would not be welcome at Comadora, and she knew it. The *contessa* would be bound to resent her savagely, but at least she knew she had not imagined the older woman's hostility to her.

It was probable that Bianca had confided her hurt over Sandro's affair to her aunt. And now the *contessa* had to watch the hated mistress elevated to wife.

I'd hate me too, she thought soberly. But it's still going to be a problem.

She turned restlessly to go back inside, and cannoned into Sandro, who had come, silent and completely unsuspected, to stand behind her.

She recoiled with a little cry, and immediately his hands gripped her arms to steady her.

'Forgive me,' he said quietly. 'I did not mean to startle you.'

She freed herself, her heart thudding. 'I—I didn't expect to see you.'

His brows lifted. 'You thought I would celebrate our *fidanzamento* by staying out all night,' he asked ironically.

Polly lifted her chin. 'Even if you did,' she said, 'it would be no concern of mine. Do whatever you want.'

'You are giving me permission to stray, *cara mia*?' Sandro drawled. 'How enlightened of you, but totally unnecessary. Because I shall, indeed, do as I please.' He paused. 'I thought you would be in bed.'

'I'm just going,' she said hastily.

She wanted to escape. With his arrival, the night was suddenly too warm and the balcony too enclosed as if the balustrade and surrounding walls had shrunk inwards.

And Sandro was too close to her, almost but not quite touching. She felt a bead of sweat trickle between her breasts, and dug her nails into the palms of her hands.

'Then before you do, perhaps you will allow me to steal another look at my son.'

'Of course,' Polly said, edging past him into the living room. 'And he's my son too,' she added over her shoulder.

'I have not forgotten,' he said. 'What were you doing out there, Paola? Gazing at the moon?'

'Just—thinking.' She paused, looking down at the floor. 'Will—will the *contessa* be returning for the wedding?'

'No,' he said. 'She will remain at the *palazzo* to make sure everything is ready for our arrival.'

'And afterwards?'

He paused. 'She will stay, at least until you are ready to take over the running of the household.'

'Or even longer?' She still did not look at him.

'Perhaps.' He sighed. 'Paola, my father promised her a home.

Out of respect for his memory, I cannot honourably deprive her of it, unless she wishes to go, no matter what has happened.' He paused. 'I hope you can accept that.'

'It seems I shall have to.' *And more easily than she will ever accept me...*

She turned and walked into her dimly lit bedroom. Sandro followed, and stood by the cot, an expression of such tenderness on his face that her heart turned over.

She thought, Once he looked at me like that, and winced at the wave of desolation that swept over her. Ridiculous reaction, she told herself fiercely. Unforgivable, too.

She went back to the door and waited, her arms hugged defensively round her body.

Sandro looked at her meditatively on his way past to the living room.

'Yes?' She felt suddenly nervous, and her voice was more challenging than she intended. 'You have something to say?'

'Our son,' he said quietly. 'How curious to think we should have made a child between us, when, now, you cannot even bear to stand next to me.' His voice changed suddenly—became low, almost urgent. 'How can this have happened, Paola *mia*? Why are you so scared to be alone with me? So frightened that I may touch you?'

'I'm not scared,' Polly began, but he cut across her.

'Do not lie to me.' There was a hard intensity in his tone. 'You were a virgin when you came to me, yet, even then, you never held back. From that first moment, you were so warm—so willing in my arms that I thought my heart would burst with the joy of you.'

Oh, God, she thought wildly. *Oh, dear God...*

She could feel the slow burn of heat rising within her at his words, at the memories they engendered, and had to fight to keep her voice deliberately cool and clear.

'But that,' she said, 'was when I was in love with you. It—makes—quite a difference.'

Her words seemed to drop like stones into the sudden well of silence between them. The air seemed full of a terrible stillness that reached out into a bleak eternity.

Polly felt her body quiver with tension. She had provided the lightning flash, and now she was waiting for the anger of the storm to break.

But when he spoke, his voice was calm. 'Of course,' he said. 'You are right. It—changes everything. I am obliged to you for the reminder. *Grazie* and goodnight.'

She was aware of him moving, turning away. Then, a moment later, she heard his own door open and close, and knew she was alone. And safe again.

Her held breath escaped her on a long, trembling sigh.

She'd had a lucky escape and she knew it. Now all she had to deal with was the deep ache of traitorous longing that throbbed inside her.

But she could cope, she told herself, shivering. She had things to do. Clothes to buy. Italian lessons to learn. Long days with Charlie to enjoy for the first time since he was a baby.

So much to keep her busy and banish all those long-forbidden thoughts, and desires. And, for her own sake, she should make a start at once. Telephone Teresa in the morning. Make a list of all the books she'd not had time to read. She could even have parcels of them, she thought, sent to her in Italy. She might even book for a theatre matinée, now that she had a nanny. Go to the cinema. Something. Anything.

While, at the same time, she underwent the painful process of turning herself into some stranger—the Marchesa Valessi. The wife that no one wanted—least of all Sandro himself.

CHAPTER SEVEN

'So,' TERESA said, 'in two days you will be married. It is exciting, no?'

'Wonderful,' Polly agreed in a hollow voice.

She didn't feel like a bride, she thought, staring at herself in the mirror, although the hugely expensive cream linen dress which Teresa had persuaded her to buy, and which would take her on to the airport and her new life after the ceremony, was beautifully cut and clung to her slenderness as if it adored her, managing to be stunning and practical at the same time. While her high-heeled strappy shoes were to die for.

It wasn't just the usual trappings of tulle and chiffon that were missing, she thought. It was radiance she lacked.

And at any moment, Teresa would be ordering her to relax, because otherwise the tension in her body would spoil the perfect line of her dress. But the other girl would never understand in a million years that this was not merely bridal nerves, but sheer, blind panic.

Since their confrontation on her first night in the hotel Sandro had taken her at her word and left her strictly to her own devices, except when they were with Teresa and Ernesto, when he continued to play the part of the charming, attentive bridegroom.

On the other occasions when they encountered each other, he was polite but aloof. But these were rare. Except for the sacrosanct hours he devoted to Charlie, he spent very little time at the hotel.

Well, she could not fault him for obeying her wishes, she thought. But she alone knew that she was lonely, and that her sense of isolation would only increase once she reached Comadora.

'Now take the dress off and hang it away,' Teresa cautioned. 'Sandro must not see you in it before the wedding.' She paused. 'Is all well with you, Paola? You are quiet today.'

Polly stepped out of the dress, and slipped it onto a padded hanger. 'Well, for one thing, there's Julie.'

'Oh?' Teresa's eyes twinkled. 'Has she fallen in love with Alessandro?'

'No, of course not,' Polly said. 'At least, I don't think so.'

Teresa giggled. 'They all do. I had a nanny from Australia when the twins were born, and each time Alessandro came into the house she would go pink—like a carnation—and refuse to speak for hours.'

Polly's brows lifted. 'And how did he react?'

'*Ahime*, he did not even notice.' Teresa shrugged. 'It is endearing how little vanity he has in such matters.'

'Well, his arrogance in other ways more than compensates for that,' Polly said crisply, zipping herself into a pretty blue shift dress.

'You would not think so if you had known his father, the Marchese Domenico,' said Teresa. 'Now, there was a supreme autocrat. And of course that old witch he brought to the house after his wife died encouraged him to think he could do no wrong. She and Bianca, her secret weapon.'

Polly put her wedding dress away in the wardrobe. She said, 'What was she like—Bianca? Was she beautiful?'

'An angel.' Teresa waved a languid hand. 'A dove. Submissive and so sweet. I longed to bite her and see if there was honey in her veins instead of blood. And taught by nuns,' she added darkly. 'She wore her purity like a sword—every inch of her being saved for the marriage bed.'

She sighed. 'No wonder Alessandro looked for amusement elsewhere.' She stopped dead, clapping a hand over her mouth, looking at Polly in round-eyed horror. '*Dio*, Paola. My mouth will be my death. Forgive me—please.'

Polly sat down at her dressing table, and ran a comb through her hair. She said quietly, 'There's nothing to forgive. I'm really under no illusion about Sandro—or myself.'

'*Cara*,' Teresa shot off the bed where she'd been sprawling, and came to kneel beside Polly. 'Listen to me. Ernesto—myself—every friend Sandro has—we are so happy that you are together. And that you have given him a son that he adores. Let the past rest. It does not matter.'

'Bianca died,' Polly said. 'That makes it matter.'

'You think he wished to marry her?' Teresa demanded. 'No, and no. It was the *contessa*, who saw to it that Bianca had the old *marchese* twisted round her little finger. With Sandro, he was always harsh, but Bianca was his sweetheart, his darling child. And Bianca wanted Alessandro.'

'Yet you say they weren't lovers.'

Teresa gave her a worldly look. 'But whose choice was that? Ernesto, who has known Alessandro since they were children, told me that she used to watch him constantly—try always to be near him. He said—forgive me, this is not nice, and Ernesto is never unkind—that she was like a bitch on heat.' She shrugged. 'And for her, he was unattainable.'

'Then why did he agree to marry her?'

'His parents' marriage had been an arranged one,' Teresa said. 'It was made clear to him what was expected of him in turn. And perhaps he felt it was a way to please his father at last. He was only twelve when his mother died, and after that his relationship with the *marchese* became even more troubled. And Sandro was wild when he was younger,' she added candidly.

She gave Polly a serious look. 'But you can understand, *cara*, why his relationship with Carlino is so important to him. Why he wishes to make his own son feel loved and secure.'

'Yes,' Polly said quietly. 'I can—see that.'

Teresa got to her feet, brushing the creases from her skirt. 'But you were telling me of Julie. There is some problem?'

'She's having some time off this afternoon to go for a job interview.' Polly sighed. 'Apparently, she's only on a temporary contract with us, which lasts until we get to Italy and then Sandro's staff take over, and she flies back. I—I'm going to miss her badly, and so will Charlie. And she's someone I can talk to in my own language.'

'Then ask him if you may keep her on.' Teresa shrugged. 'It is quite simple.' She gave Polly a wicked grin. 'I am sure that you can persuade him, *cara*. Do as I do. Wait until you are in bed, and you have made him very happy. He will give you anything. And the rest of the servants will be pacified when they have your other *bambini* to care for.'

Polly's blush deepened painfully, but she made herself speak lightly. 'That's the kind of cunning plan I like.'

The way things were between them, he was more likely to fire Julie instantly, she thought ruefully when Teresa had gone. But she could always ask, although it wouldn't be in the way the other girl had suggested.

Not that she had the opportunity for the rest of the day. In the afternoon, she went to visit her parents in a last-ditch effort to get them to come to the wedding.

But Mrs Fairfax, still in her dressing gown and looking pale and wan, was adamant, insisting she wasn't well enough to go, and needed her husband with her in case of emergency.

And she alarmed Charlie by hugging him too tightly, and weeping.

Polly got back to the hotel feeling as if she'd been run down by a train, her only comfort her father's quiet, 'She'll come round, sweetheart. She just needs time.'

Sandro was out, and, although she planned to tackle him about Julie on his return, he was still missing by the time she eventually admitted defeat and went to bed.

He was spending the eve of his wedding with Teresa and Ernesto, who were going to act as their witnesses, so she would just have to catch him first thing in the morning before he left, she told herself.

Charlie had already been collected by Julie, and taken down to the dining room for breakfast, when she woke, so she had the bathroom to herself.

She bathed and put on one of her new dresses—primrose silk with a scooped neck, and slightly flared skirt. Nailing her colours to the mast, she thought with faint defiance as she crossed the drawing room to his door.

'*Avanti.*' The response to her knock was cool and casual, and Polly, drawing a deep breath, opened the door and went in.

The curtains were drawn back, filling the room with sunlight, and Sandro was in bed, lying back against the piled-up pillows, reading a newspaper and drinking coffee from the breakfast trolley beside him. His skin looked like mahogany against the pristine dazzle of the white bed linen.

He glanced up, his brows snapping together as he saw her.

'*Buongiorno,*' he murmured after a pause. 'You will forgive me if I do not get up,' he added, indicating the sheet draped over his hips which was quite clearly his only covering. 'Would you like coffee?'

'No, thank you.' Polly shifted uneasily from one foot to the other, praying she would not blush, and wondering if it was possible to look at someone without actually seeing them. And certainly without staring. And particularly without feeling that treacherous excitement slowly uncurling inside her. 'I've had breakfast.'

'How virtuous of you, *cara*,' he drawled. 'They bring an extra cup each morning, presumably because they hope I will eventually get lucky. I think I shall have to tell them to stop.' He refilled his own cup. 'So—to what do I owe this extraordinary pleasure?'

Polly gritted her teeth. 'I—I've come to ask you a favour.'

His brows rose. 'You fascinate me, *bella mia*. Especially when you choose my bedroom to make your request.'

'Well, don't read anything into that,' Polly said shortly. 'It's just that I seem to see so little of you these days.'

Sandro moved, stretching slowly and indolently, letting the concealing sheet slip a little. 'You are seeing enough of me this morning, *carissima*,' he drawled. 'Or do you want more?'

She glared at him. 'No.'

'You disappoint me,' he murmured. 'But if it is not my body, I presume it is money. How much do you want?'

'Money?' Polly repeated in bewilderment. 'Of course it isn't. I haven't spent half the allowance you made me.'

'I would not grudge more.' Folding his arms behind his head, Sandro studied her through half-closed eyes, frankly absorbing the cling of the silk to her body, a faint smile curving his mouth. 'You seem to be spending it wisely.'

She flushed under his scrutiny. 'Thank you—I think.'

'*Prego.*' He continued to watch her. 'I hope you do not wish me to persuade your mother to attend the wedding. I should hate to disappoint you.'

She bit her lip. 'No. I've accepted that it's a lost cause. Besides, she wouldn't listen to you. You—you seem to make her nervous.'

'*Mi dispiace,*' he returned without any real sign of regret. 'I seem to have the same effect on you, *cara mia*. So—what is it?'

She swallowed. 'I'd like Julie to stay in Italy with us, and go on looking after Charlie—please.'

Sandro moved slightly, adjusting the sheet to a more respectable level. He sent her a meditative look.

He said, 'Paola, I have a houseful of staff who are dancing for joy at the prospect of looking after the future *marchese*. He will not lack for attention, I promise you.'

'No,' she said. 'But he's used to Julie, and he likes her. Anyway, the others will speak Italian to him, and he might feel lost at first.' She hesitated. 'And I like Julie too, and I can talk to her in English. In spite of Teresa's coaching, I'm going to feel pretty isolated.'

'*Davvero?*' His tone was sardonic. 'You do not feel that you could talk to me, perhaps?'

That was what Teresa had said, she thought, biting her lip again. She looked at the floor. 'That isn't very likely,' she said constrictedly. 'After all, we're not marrying for any kind of companionship, but for Charlie's sake.'

'Does one rule out the other?' He was frowning slightly.

'I think it has to,' Polly countered, with a touch of desperation. 'And after all, you—you won't always be there,' she added, feeling dejectedly that she was losing the argument. 'You have your work—your own life to lead.'

'No,' he said, quietly. 'That is true.' He shrugged a naked shoulder. '*Va bene.* If that is what you want, I agree.'

'Oh.' Polly found herself blinking. 'Well—thank you.'

'Is that all? I am disappointed.' The topaz eyes glinted at her. 'I was hoping for a more—tangible expression of gratitude.'

Polly stiffened. 'I don't think I understand.'

'And I think you do.' He smiled at her, and held out a hand in invitation. 'Is one kiss too much to ask?'

She wanted to tell him to go to hell, but there was too much riding on this transaction.

She said coldly, 'You're not as generous as I thought.'

'And nor are you, *carissima*,' he said gently. 'Which is why I have so far asked for so little. Besides, you will have to kiss me tomorrow at the wedding. It is tradition.' His smile widened. 'And you certainly need the practice.'

There was a taut silence, then Polly trod awkwardly to the side of the bed. Ignoring his proffered hand, she bent to brush his cheek with swift, unyielding lips.

But before she could straighten, Sandro had grasped her wrists in an unbreakable hold, and she was being drawn inexorably downwards, losing her balance in the process. She found she was being turned skilfully, so that she was lying across his body, the outrage in her eyes meeting the mockery in his. Mockery mingled with something altogether more disturbing. Something that, in spite of herself, every pulse in her body leapt to meet.

He said softly, 'But I will not settle for as little as that, Paola *mia.*'

And her instinctive cry of protest was stifled by the warmth of his mouth on hers.

He kissed her deeply and thoroughly, holding her imprisoned in one arm, while his other hand twined in her hair to hold her still, defeating any attempt she might make to struggle. Forcing her to endure the sensuous and unashamedly possessive invasion of his tongue, as his mouth moved on hers in sheer and unashamed enticement.

Robbing her, she realised numbly, of any real desire to fight him. Awakening very different memories—and longings.

The heat of the sun pouring through the window—the unforgettable scent of his naked skin—the pressure of his lithe, muscular body against hers sent the last three years rolling back, and they were lovers again, their bodies aching and melting to be joined together in the ultimate intimacy, yet deliberately holding back to prolong the sweetness of the final moments.

He had always wooed her with kisses, she remembered dazedly, arousing her with a patient, passionate tenderness that splintered her control, and sent her reason spinning, so that she clung to him mutely imploring his possession.

Why else had she been unable to see that bringing her to eager, quivering acquiescence was the work of a practised seducer?

Yet even now, it seemed, she was unable to resist him, or the sensual magic of his lips.

When he lifted his head she was breathless, her heart thudding unevenly against her ribcage—which he must have known, because his hand had moved and was gently cupping her breast, his thumb stroking her hardening nipple to a rapturous peak through the silk of her dress.

He looked down at her, his eyes glittering and intent, asking a question which she was too scared and confused to answer. She only knew that if he kissed her again, she would be lost. And as he bent to her once more, a soft moan, half-fear, half-yearning, parted her lips.

And then, swiftly and shockingly, it was over, as the telephone beside the bed suddenly rang, its stridency shattering the heated intensity within the room like a fist through a pane of glass.

Sandro swore softly and fluently, but his hold on her relaxed, and she forced herself out of his embrace and off the bed, and ran to the door.

She flew across the intervening space, snatching at the door handle to her own bedroom, but as she did so it opened anyway, and she half fell into the room beyond.

As she struggled to recover her balance, there was a cry of 'Mammina' and Charlie, looking angelic, came scampering towards her from the bathroom, with Julie close behind.

'He had a little accident with his cereal this morning,' she told Polly, trying to look severe. 'I've just had to change his top and trousers. You wouldn't believe how far he can spread one small bowl.'

As Polly bent to him, fighting for calm, the door opposite was flung wide, and Sandro came striding towards them, his face like thunder, tying the belt of a robe he'd clearly thrown on as an afterthought.

Polly scooped Charlie up in her arms, and turned to face him defensively.

He halted, staring at her, his ominous frown deepening. He said in Italian, 'We need to talk, you and I. Now.'

'There's nothing to talk about,' Polly said, nervously aware that Julie had vanished with discreet haste back into the bathroom. She reverted to her own language. 'I should have known I couldn't trust you.'

His mouth twisted contemptuously. 'No,' he said. 'I think, my beautiful hypocrite, that you realised you could not trust yourself. It is that simple. So why, for once in your life, can't you be honest?'

He took a step towards her, and she recoiled, still clutching Charlie, who was beginning to wriggle. She said hoarsely, 'Don't touch me. Don't dare to come near me. You—you promised to leave me alone.'

'That will be my pleasure,' Sandro hit back. 'Now, be silent. You are frightening our son.' Charlie was squirming round, his lip trembling, holding out his arms to his father, and Sandro took him from her, soothing the little boy quietly.

He said, 'He will spend the day with me. I will telephone to say when he may be collected.' He carried him back to his own room, where he turned and looked back at Polly, his eyes icy with warning.

He said too softly, 'And, as long as you live, *signorina*, never—never again use our child as a barrier between us.'

The door closed behind them both, leaving Polly shaking and alone in the middle of the room.

'Are you all right, Miss Fairfax?' Julie was regarding her anxiously from the doorway.

Polly mustered her reserves. 'Yes,' she lied. 'Fine. A—a misunderstanding, that's all.'

'I thought at first that the *marchese* had come to give you the good news,' Julie said. 'He spoke to me as I was going off duty yesterday evening, and suggested that I should go to Italy as well, to help Charlie to settle in. Isn't that great? I was going to tell you myself, first thing, only his lordship there did his trick with the cereal.'

Polly's hands slowly curled into fists. He knew, she thought, fury uncurling inside her. He knew exactly what I was going to ask, and used it against me. A ploy to get me into bed with him. And—dear God—I was almost fool enough to fall for it. To give in.

'Miss Fairfax?' Julie was looking puzzled. 'I thought you'd be pleased.'

'Yes,' Polly said, summoning a hurried smile. 'I'm delighted. That's—absolutely wonderful. Just what we both wanted.'

She paused. 'And Charlie's spending the day with his father, so you have some free time to go and pack for the Campania. Mind you take a couple of bikinis too,' she added over-brightly. 'Apparently the *palazzo* has a pool.'

Julie's face lit up. 'Well—if you don't mind...'

When the other girl had gone, Polly walked over to one of the sofas and sat for a long time, with her face buried in her hands.

She was angry, but her anger was mixed with guilt too. It was wrong of her to use Charlie like that, but the truth was she hadn't dared allow Sandro to touch her again. Or come within a yard of her, for that matter.

As it was, she felt sick with shame at how easily he'd drawn a response from her. And how her unfulfilled body now felt torn apart by frustration. Like the first time he had made love to her, she thought wretchedly, when she'd been wild for him, his caresses exciting her to the point of desperation. When, at last, he'd entered her, her body had been molten with need, and there'd been no pain.

Just a rapturous sense of total completion, she thought wretchedly. And what she'd believed was utter love.

I know better now, she told herself, her mind raw. I know he was just using me for sex—nothing more, but that's something I'll learn to live with.

But I can't let it happen ever again—and I won't.

She hadn't taken his money, she thought harshly. Nor would she accept the false coin of his lovemaking, no matter what the cost to her as a woman. And no matter how she might ache for him, as she did now.

The next day, she married Sandro in a ceremony so brief she could hardly believe it was legal. As they were pronounced man and wife, and he turned to her, she closed her eyes, bracing herself for the promised kiss, only to feel his lips brush her cheek swiftly and coldly.

As she stepped back she glimpsed Teresa and Ernesto exchanging astonished glances, and moved to them to be hugged with real warmth. Teresa drew her to one side. 'A little gift, *cara*,' she whispered, handing her a flat parcel, wrapped in silver tissue with violet ribbons. 'Do not open it now. Wait until tonight.'

Polly forced a smile of thanks, and put the package in the soft leather shoulder bag which served as her hand luggage.

There were no problems on the flight itself. Polly had never travelled first class before, and sitting in comfort, being served champagne, at least gave a veneer of celebration to the day's proceedings.

Charlie chatted in wonder about 'big planes', gave an imitation of a jumbo jet taking off, then fell asleep, but he awoke grouchily when they reached Naples, and the subsequent journey soon disintegrated into nightmare.

Polly discovered, dismayed, that her son did not enjoy travelling by car, even an air-conditioned limousine, and that he was constantly and miserably sick throughout the trip.

Every few miles they were forced to stop, so that Charlie could be cleaned up and comforted, and eventually Julie, who'd borne the brunt of the little boy's misery, was sent to sit in the passenger seat beside the chauffeur, and Sandro took her place, cradling Charlie on his lap and talking to him gently.

'Why not give him back to me?' Polly suggested, aware that her linen dress was already ruined. 'I'm worried that he'll spoil your beautiful suit,' she added awkwardly.

He gave her a look of faint impatience. *'Che importa?'* he demanded, and Polly subsided, biting her lip and turning to look out of the window.

Up till now, she'd been totally unaware of the scenery she was passing through, all her attention given to Charlie's woes. But now she had a breathing space to take in the reality of her surroundings. The road they were travelling had been carved out of the rock-face which towered above them. On the other side was the eternal blue of the Mediterranean, serene today, reflecting the cloudless sky. And straight ahead, nestling in the curve of the bay, a cluster of terracotta roofs round a boat-studded marina.

Beyond it, a rocky promontory jutted into the sea, dominated by a large rectangular building with faded pink walls, made even more imposing by the tower at each of its corners.

She did not need Sandro's quiet 'Comadora at last' to recognise that this place, more a fortress than a palace, was to be her home, and Charlie's inheritance.

She said, 'It—it looks a little daunting.'

'That would have been the intention, when it was built,' he agreed drily. 'This coast was often attacked by pirates.'

'Yes,' she said, her tone subdued. 'That was part of the local history I had to learn when I was here—before.' She hesitated. 'I suppose I must learn not to mention that.'

'Perche?' His brows lifted. 'Why should you think so?'

She said stiffly, 'I didn't think you'd want your family to know that your wife used to be a travel rep.'

'Why, Paola,' he said softly, 'what a snob you are.'

Polly bit her lip. 'How did you explain why I was back in your life? It might be better if I knew.'

He shrugged. 'After the crash, I suffered memory problems for a while, something they all know. Once I recovered fully, you had disappeared, and it took time for me to find you.' He looked at her over Charlie's sleeping head, his smile mocking. 'And now we are together again—united in bliss forever.'

Polly drew a breath. 'Your restored memory seems to have been pretty selective.'

'You have a better version?'

'No,' she admitted unwillingly. 'But no one's ever going to believe that we're—blissfully happy.'

'Then pretend, *cara mia*.' There was a sudden hard note in his voice. 'Pretend like you did three summers ago, when you let me believe you found pleasure in bed with me.'

'Sandro—please...' She felt her face warm, and turned away hurriedly, her body clenching in swift, intimate yearning.

That jibe of hers, uttered purely in self-defence that first night at the flat, seemed to have hit a nerve, she thought unhappily. But it didn't mean anything. After all, no man liked to have his expertise as a lover challenged.

'Do I embarrass you?' he asked coldly. 'My regrets.'

There was a silence, then he said, 'Will you tell me something, Paola? When you went back to England, did you already know that you were carrying my child?'

'No,' she said. 'No, I didn't.'

'Ah,' Sandro said quietly.

The car turned in between tall wrought-iron gates, and negotiated the long winding drive which ended in a paved courtyard before the main entrance to the *palazzo*.

It was bright with flowers in long stone troughs, and in the middle was a fountain sending a slender, glittering spire of water into the air.

Thank God, Polly thought as the car drew up. Peace at last. She stretched, moving her aching shoulders, longing for a bath and a change of clothing, hopefully with a cold drink included somewhere too.

The car bringing their luggage would have arrived ages ago, she thought.

It seemed that if she was going to be unhappy, at least it would be in comfort. But for now, that thought brought no solace at all.

The massive arched double doors opened, and a man, short and balding, dressed in an immaculate grey linen jacket came hurrying across the courtyard to meet them, looking anxious.

He looks like the bearer of bad news, thought Polly. Perhaps there's been another accident and our luggage is all at the bottom of the Mediterranean.

Clearly Sandro was concerned, because he deposited Charlie on her lap and got out.

The little man, hands waving, launched himself into some kind of diatribe, and Polly watched Sandro's expression change from disbelief to a kind of cold fury, and he turned away, lifting clenched fists towards the sky.

When he came back to the car, he was stony-faced as he opened Polly's door.

'The *contessa*,' he said, 'has decided to surprise us with a welcome party, and has filled the *palazzo* with members of my family, including my cousin Emilio,' he added with a snap. 'Tonight, Teodoro tells me, there will be a formal dinner, followed by a reception for some of the local people.'

'Oh, God, no.' Polly looked down in horror at her stained and rumpled dress. 'I can't meet people like this. Is there no other entrance we could use?'

'There are many,' he said. 'But the Marchesa Valessi does not sneak into her house through a back door. Give me Carlino, and we will face them all together.'

Stomach churning, she obeyed, pulling her dress straight and pushing shaking fingers through her dishevelled hair.

Then Sandro's hand closed round hers, firmly and inflexibly, and she began to walk beside him towards the doorway of the *palazzo*. As they reached it, she lifted her chin and straightened her shoulders, and was aware of his swift approving glance.

She was fleetingly aware of a hall hung with tapestries, and a wide stone staircase leading up to a gallery. A clamour of voices abruptly stilled.

People watching her, eyes filled with avid curiosity or open disapproval, a few smiling. And, for a moment, she almost froze.

Then Charlie lifted his head from his father's shoulder, and looked at all the strange faces around him. In a second his expression had changed from bewilderment to alarm, and he uttered a loud howl of distress, and began to sob.

Polly felt the atmosphere in the great hall change instantly. Censure was replaced by sympathy, and the marked silence that had greeted them changed to murmurs of, 'Poor little one, he is tired,' and, 'He is a true Valessi, that one.'

The crowd parted, and a small, plump woman, her hair heavily streaked with grey, came bustling through. Arms outstretched, voice lovingly scolding, she took Charlie from his father's arms and, beckoning imperiously to the wilting Julie to follow, disappeared just as rapidly, the sobbing Charlie held securely against the high bib of her starched apron.

'That was Dorotea,' Sandro said quietly, his taut mouth relaxing into a faint smile. 'Don't worry, Paola, she has a magic touch. Carlino will be bathed, changed, fed and in a good mood before he knows what is happening. And Julie also,' he added drily.

Lucky them, Polly thought, and groaned inwardly as the crowd parted again for the *contessa*.

'*Caro* Alessandro.' She embraced him formally. 'Welcome home. As you see, your family could not wait to meet your beautiful wife.'

'I am overwhelmed,' Sandro said politely. 'But I wish you had allowed Teodoro to give me advance warning of your plans.'

She gave a tinkling laugh. 'But then there would have been no surprise.'

'No,' he said. 'That is precisely what I mean.'

He looked about him. 'I am delighted to welcome you all,' he began. 'But as you can see we have had a bad journey with a sick child, and my wife is exhausted. She will meet you all when she has rested.' He turned to Polly. 'Go with Zia Antonia, *carissima*, and I will join you presently.'

Polly was aware of an absurd impulse to cling to his hand. 'Don't leave me with her,' she wanted to say. Instead she forced a smile and nodded, and followed the *contessa*'s upright figure towards the stairs.

From the gallery, they seemed to traverse a maze of passages until they arrived at last at another pair of double doors, elaborately carved.

The *contessa* flung them open and motioned Polly to precede her. 'This is where you are to sleep,' she said.

Polly paused, drawing a deep breath. She had never imagined occupying such a room, she thought dazedly. It was vast and very old, its ceiling beamed, and the walls decorated with exquisite frescos.

It was dominated by one enormous canopied bed, with crimson

brocade curtains and a magnificent bedspread in the same colour, quilted in gold thread, but little other furniture.

'That door is to the bathroom.' The *contessa* pointed a manicured hand. 'I think you will find all you need.' And the sooner the better, her tone of voice seemed to indicate. 'The other leads to the dressing room, where your clothes have been unpacked for you.' She paused. 'Would you like some tea to be brought to you?'

'That would be kind.' Polly hesitated. 'If it's not too much trouble—as you have all these other guests, I mean.'

'How can it be a difficulty?' The thin lips wore a vinegary smile. 'After all, *cara* Paola, you are the mistress of the house now, and your wish is our command.' She indicated a thick golden rope. 'Pull the bell, if you wish for the services of a maid to help you dress. Or perhaps your husband will prefer to assist you himself— as this is your *luna di miele*.'

'I can manage,' Polly said quietly, conscious of the faint sneer in the older woman's voice, and the swift pang of alarm that her words engendered. 'But I would like to make sure my son is all right, and I don't know where the nursery is.'

'I will instruct Dorotea to take you to him later.' She looked Polly up and down with faint disdain. 'Now, I recommend that you do as Alessandro suggests, and take some rest. After all, this will be your wedding night, officially at least,' she added, with another silvery laugh, and left the room, closing the door behind her.

Left to herself, Polly walked over to the long windows and opened the shutters. She knelt on the embrasure, lifting her face to the heavy golden warmth of the late afternoon.

If the *contessa* had deliberately plotted to present her at her worst, she could not have done a better job, she thought bitterly. But there was no way the older woman could have known how badly Charlie would react to the long journey from the airport.

I wish I could stay here, she thought, because I think I've already got *'null points'* from the jury downstairs.

Instead, she had to put on one of the evening dresses Teresa had made her buy, and play her unwanted role as *marchesa* with whatever style and grace she could summon. And undo, if possible, that first unfortunate impression.

And talking of Teresa... Polly fetched her shoulder bag, and retrieved the parcel it contained. As she undid the ribbons, the tissue parted to reveal a cascade of the finest black lace.

Polly's eyes widened as she examined it. It was a nightgown, she realised, low-necked, split to the thigh on one side, and almost transparent. Provocation at its most exquisite. An expensive, daring tease.

Any girl who wore it would feel irresistibly sexy. And any man who saw it couldn't fail to be aroused.

It seemed clear that Teresa had sensed the tensions in her relationship with Sandro, and decided the honeymoon could need a kick-start.

As Sandro said, you're shrewd, Polly addressed her friend silently, bundling the delicate fabric back into its wrappings, and wondering where she could hide it. But this time you've misread the situation badly.

She left the package on the bed for the time being, and went to investigate the bathroom. The room itself probably dated from the Renaissance, she thought, but the plumbing was strictly twenty-first century, and luxurious in the extreme.

The walls were tiled in shades of blue, interspersed with mother-of-pearl, which gave the impression that the room was under shimmering water.

There was a deep sunken bath, and a capacious shower cubicle in the shape of a hexagon, with a pretty gilded roof.

Thankfully Polly slipped out of her clothes, and stepped behind its glass panels. There was a corner shelf holding toiletries, and she chose some scented foam, lathering her body sensuously. The jet was powerful, but reviving, and she twisted and turned under it, feeling some of the tensions of the day seeping away.

She dried herself slowly, her body refreshed and glowing, then took another bath sheet from the pile and wound it round herself, sarong-style, securing it just above her breasts.

If only her tea was waiting, she thought, opening the bathroom door, then, however briefly, life might be perfect.

She walked into the bedroom, and stopped dead, lips parted in shock, and her heart beating an alarmed tattoo.

Because Sandro was there, stretched out across the bed, his coat and tie discarded, and his shirt unbuttoned to the waist.

'Ciao, bella,' he said softly, his eyes lingering on her bare shoulders in undisguised appreciation. 'You look wonderful, and smell delicious,' he went on. 'And now there is this.' He held up the black nightgown with a soft whistle. 'Perhaps marriage may have its compensations after all.'

And as she watched, transfixed, he lifted himself lithely off the bed, and began to walk towards her, the black lace draped over his arm.

CHAPTER EIGHT

POLLY took a step backwards. She said hoarsely, 'What are you doing here?'

'I want to take a shower,' he said. 'I decided you would probably not wish me to join you, so—I waited.'

She took a breath. 'How—considerate.' Her voice stung. 'Perhaps you'd be even kinder and go to your own room, and use your own shower. I'd like my privacy.'

'So would I, *cara*, but we are both to be disappointed. Thanks to Zia Antonia, all the rooms in the *palazzo* are occupied by other people and will remain so for tomorrow—the day after—who knows?' He paused. 'Also you are under a misapprehension. This is my room—and my shower.'

He paused to allow her to digest that, his mouth twisting in sardonic amusement at her shocked expression.

'The accommodation intended for you is currently taken by my aunt Vittoria, a pious widow with a hearing problem,' he went on. 'She does not like to share either. Also, she snores, which, as you know, I do not.'

He smiled at her. 'But she is certainly leaving tomorrow, so you will only have one night to endure in my company,' he added lightly.

She stared at him, her hands nervously adjusting the towel. 'You really imagine I'm actually going to sleep here—with you?' Her voice rose stormily. 'You must be mad. I can't—I *won't*...'

'You will certainly spend the night with me,' he interrupted, a harsh note in his voice. 'I cannot predict whether or not you will sleep. That is not my concern.'

'Then what does concern you?' She glared at him. 'Certainly not keeping your word.'

He flung exasperated hands at the ceiling. '*Dio*—you think I planned this? That I have deliberately filled my house with a pack of gossiping relatives, including my cousin Emilio, may he rot in

108

hell,' he added with real bite, 'just so that I can trick you into bed with me?'

He gave her a scornful look. 'You overestimate your charms, *bella mia*. You will stay here tonight, without fuss or further argument, for the sake of appearances, because it is our wedding night, and because we have no choice in the matter.

'But let me attempt to allay your obvious fears,' he went on cuttingly. Clasping her wrist, he strode back to the bed, with Polly stumbling after him, tripping on the edge of her towel. He dragged back the satin coverlet, dislodging the huge lace-trimmed pillows to reveal a substantial bolster. 'That,' he said, pointing contemptuously, 'placed down the middle of the bed, should deter my frenzy of desire for you. I hope you are reassured.'

He paused. 'May I remind you, Paola, you agreed to co-operate in presenting our marriage as a conventional one.'

'Yes.' Polly bit her lip. 'But—I didn't realise then what could be involved.'

His smile was thin. 'Well, do not worry too much, *carissima*. There are enough willing women in the world. I see no need to force someone so clearly reluctant.'

He held up the nightgown. 'Although your prudishness hardly matches your choice of nightwear. Why buy a garment so seductive, if you do not wish to be seduced?'

'I didn't buy it,' Polly said stonily. 'It was a present from Teresa.'

'Indeed,' he murmured. 'I never guessed she was such a romantic. Or such an optimist,' he added, his mouth curving in genuine amusement.

'Don't tear it,' he told her mockingly, as Polly made an unavailing attempt to snatch it from him. 'That is a privilege I might prefer to reserve for myself.'

She glared at him. 'Not in this lifetime,' she said defiantly.

'And certainly not unless I wish to do so,' he reminded her softly. 'However, for now, I shall have to console myself with imagining how it might look if you wore it, *bella mia*.' He gave it a last, meditative glance. 'Like a shadow falling across moonlight,' he said quietly, and tossed it to her. 'I must write to Teresa and thank her,' he added with a swift grin, as he straightened the bedclothes.

'And I,' she said coldly, 'shall not.' She swallowed. 'I would like to get dressed now, please.'

His brows lifted, as he scanned the slipping towel. 'You want assistance?'

'No.' She managed just in time to avoid stamping her bare foot on the tiled floor. 'Just some privacy.' She shook her head. 'Oh, can't you see how impossible this all is?'

'I can only see that I shall have to stop teasing you, *cara mia*,' he said with unexpected gentleness. 'Get dressed if you wish, but there is no need for you to face the inquisition downstairs, unless you want to do so. And it is a long time until dinner, when you will be expected to make an appearance, so why not rest quietly here until then? I promise you will not be disturbed,' he added levelly. 'By anyone.'

As she hesitated there was a knock on the door, and a small, round-faced girl came in carrying a tray with Polly's tea. She stopped, her mouth forming into an embarrassed 'o'.

'*Mi scusi, excellenza,*' she stammered. 'I thought the *marchesa* was alone.'

Sandro smiled at her. 'Come here and meet your new mistress, Rafaella.' He turned to Polly. 'I have arranged for this child to become your personal maid, *cara mia*. She is the granddaughter of an old friend, so be kind to her.'

Polly, about to flatly deny any need of a personal maid, saw the girl's eager face, and subsided.

'Once you have had your tea,' Sandro went on, 'I hope she can persuade you to sleep for a while, even if I cannot,' he added wryly. 'And I shall ask her to return at eight to help you to dress for dinner.'

Polly nodded resginedly. 'Thank you. Darling,' she added as an afterthought, and saw his lips twitch before he turned away, heading for the bathroom.

Rafaella set the tray down on one of the old ornamental tables that flanked the bed, then flew to the dressing room, returning with a dark blue satin robe, which Polly awkwardly exchanged for the towel.

'*Parli inglese?*' she asked as the girl folded back the coverlet to the foot of the bed, and plumped up the pillows.

Her face lit up. '*Sì, vossignoria.* I worked for an English family, *au pair*, for two years. I learn much.'

'Yet you came back to work at the *palazzo*?'

Rafaella nodded vigorously. 'It is an honour for me, and for my grandfather, who asked for this post for me, when his *signoria* wished to reward him.'

'Reward him?' Polly queried.

'It was my grandfather who found the *marchese* when his car crashed into the ravine,' Rafaella explained. 'He saw it happen, and ran to help. At first he thought his *signoria* was dead, because he did not move, and there was so much blood, but then he could feel his pulse and knew that he lived, so my grandfather went to the car to rescue the lady.' She shrugged. 'But it was too late.'

Polly winced. 'It must have been a horrible experience for him.'

'*Sì, vossignoria*. He spoke about it to the inquiry, and also to his *signoria* when he was in hospital, but never since. There is too much pain in such memories.'

She bent to retrieve the discarded bath sheet, then straightened, beaming. 'So it is good that the *marchese* is now happy again.'

'Yes.' Polly realised with acute embarrassment that the girl was holding up the black lace nightgown, which must have been entangled in the folds of the towel. 'I—I suppose so.'

She tried to concentrate on her tea, and ignore Rafaella's stifled giggle as she carried the nightdress off to the dressing room.

No doubt the rumour mill at the *palazzo* would soon be in full swing, she thought, swallowing. But at least it would support the idea that this was a real marriage, which would please Sandro.

She put down her cup and turned on her side, shutting her eyes determinedly, and, presently, she heard Rafaella's quiet departure.

It would be good to relax, she thought, burrowing her cheek into the lavender-scented pillow. To recover from the stress and strain of the past days and weeks, and re-focus on this extraordinary new life, to which, for good or ill, she now belonged.

Thanks to the *contessa*, it was proving a more difficult start than she'd anticipated, she told herself, sighing.

For one thing, and in spite of the closed bathroom door, she could clearly hear the sound of the shower, reviving all kinds of past associations, and she pressed her hands over her ears, in an attempt to shut them out.

She didn't want to remember those other times when Sandro had been showering, and she'd joined him, their bodies slippery under the torrent of water, her mouth fierce on his skin, his arms strong as he lifted her against him, filling her with the renewed urgency of his desire.

But the memories were too strong, too potent to be dismissed, and for a moment, as her body melted in recollection, she was pierced once more with the temptation to abandon all pride and go to him.

But it would pass, she thought. It had to. Because she would not be drawn again into the web of sensuality where she'd been trapped before. It was just a moment of weakness because she was tired—so very tired...

And gradually, the distant rush of water became a lullaby that, against all odds, soothed her to sleep.

She had never really dressed for dinner before, Polly thought as she sat in front of the mirror, watching Rafaella apply the finishing touches to her hair. The other girl had drawn the shining strands into a loose knot on top of Polly's head, softening the look with a few loose tendrils that were allowed to curl against her face, and the nape of her neck.

Her dress was a sleek column of black silk, long-sleeved, with a neckline that discreetly revealed the first swell of her breasts, and gave her skin the sheen of a pearl.

She'd kept her make-up deliberately muted, faintly emphasising the green of her eyes, and curving her mouth with a soft rose lustre.

Whatever her inward inadequacies, this time she would at least look the part of the Marchesa Valessi, she thought.

She had hoped that Sandro would be beside her again, to guide her through her second entrance, but Rafaella had told her that he had changed for dinner and rejoined his guests while she still slept.

So, she'd have to brave them all alone.

Sighing under her breath, she rose. 'Rafaella, I'd like to say goodnight to my son before dinner. Can you take me to the nursery, *per favore*?'

'*Sì, vossignoria.* Of course.'

'And that "*vossignoria*" is a terrible mouthful,' Polly went on. 'Maybe we could change it. What did you call your last boss?'

Rafaella looked a little startled. '*Signora*, sometimes, but usually *madame*.'

Polly smiled at her. 'Then that will be fine with me, too.'

'But I was instructed, *vossignoria*, by the *contessa*.'

'And now you're getting further instructions from me,' Polly advised her crisply. 'From now on it's *madame*, and that's final.'

'As you say, *madame*.' Rafaella's agreement was subdued.

Polly was expecting another maze of passages, but the nursery turned out to be only round a corner, and up a flight of stairs.

It wouldn't have been far for Dorotea to come, she thought as she opened the door and walked in.

She found herself in a spacious room lined with cupboards. There was a table in the middle, and a young girl was tidying up, placing toys in a large wicker basket.

Her jaw dropped as Polly entered in a rustle of silk, and she hurried over to a half-open door on the other side of the room, and said something in a low voice. A moment later, Dorotea joined them. She inclined her head stiffly to Polly, then turned to Rafaella and launched herself into a flood of half-whispered Italian, complete with gestures.

Rafaella looked at Polly with an awkward shrug. 'She regrets, *madame*, but your son is asleep. She was not expecting a visit from you. She understood that your duties to your guests came first.'

'Nothing comes before my little boy,' Polly said quietly. 'And I thought it was arranged that she would come and fetch me once he was settled. I have been waiting.'

She paused. 'Clearly, there has been some misunderstanding tonight, but explain to her, please, that we will speak in the morning about Carlino's future routine. And now I would like to kiss my son goodnight.'

Dorotea listened to Rafaella's translation, but it brought no lightening of her expression. And she stood unwillingly aside to give Polly access to the night nursery.

A nightlight in a holder shaped like a shell was burning near his cot, and Charlie was lying on his back, his arms flung wide, his breathing soft and regular.

Polly stood looking down at him, then bent and brushed a strand of hair back from his face with gentle fingers. At the same time she became aware that Dorotea, who'd been watching from the doorway, arms folded across her bosom, was bobbing a kind of curtsy and muttering a deferential *'Excellenza'* as she backed out of the room. And she realised that Sandro had come to join her.

She had never seen him in dinner jacket and black tie before, and the breath caught in her throat, because this new formality conferred its own kind of magnificence. It also set him at a distance, which was all to the good, she told herself.

She summoned a smile. *'Buonasera.* I came to say goodnight. Maybe even goodbye, just in case they tear me to pieces downstairs.'

'They will not do that. They are all eager to meet you.'

She looked back at the cot. 'How—how beautiful,' she said, softly. 'Don't you think so?'

'Sì,' he agreed quietly. 'Beautiful indeed.' And she realised that he was looking at her, and turned away as she felt her body quiver in instinctive response, walking past him into the now-deserted day nursery.

He followed. 'But I did not come simply to see Carlino,' he went on. 'I have something for you, *cara mia.'* His hands touched her shoulders, halting her, and Polly felt the slide of something metallic against her throat, and glanced down.

The necklace was nearly an inch wide, a flat, delicate network of gold, studded with the blue-white fire of diamonds. She touched it with a wondering hand. 'Sandro—it's lovely. But there's no need for this.'

'I am permitted to give you a wedding present,' he told her drily.

'I—suppose.' She shook her head. 'But I feel dreadful because I have nothing for you.'

'You don't think so?'

He turned her slowly to face him, then bent towards her, and she felt his lips rest softly, briefly on her forehead. She had not expected that, and his intense gentleness made her tremble.

'My beloved girl,' he whispered. 'You are here with me at last.'

The sudden flash of light from the doorway was a harsh, unbearable intrusion. Stunned and dazzled, Polly pulled free, looking round wildly. 'What was that?'

'My cousin Emilio,' Sandro said with a shrug. 'Armed with a camera, and searching for some moment of intimacy between us to thrill his readers.'

She stared at him. 'You *knew* he was there?'

'I was aware he had followed me upstairs,' he said. 'And guessed his motive. I think we provided what he wanted,' he added, casually. 'And you did well, Paola *mia*. You almost convinced me.'

Hurt slashed at her like a razor. Just for a moment, she'd believed him—believed the tenderness of his kiss.

She said colourlessly, 'I'm starting to learn—at last.'

She paused, taking a steadying breath. 'And while I'm on a roll, why don't you take me downstairs and present me to your family? Because I'm ready.'

'And no more only children,' Zia Vittoria boomed authoritatively. 'In Alessandro's case, it was understandable. His mother was a delicate creature, and no one expected too much, but you seem to be a healthy young woman, and Alessandro's first born is a fine child, in spite of his irregular birth. I commend you,' she added graciously.

Polly, seated at her side, with her smile nailed on, murmured something grateful, and wondered what the penalty might be for strangling a deaf Italian dowager. She was aware of sympathetic smiles around the room, and a swift glance, brimming with unholy mirth, from Sandro.

I should have known it was going too well, she thought grimly.

Dinner in the tapestry-hung banqueting hall had been a splendid occasion. She had sat opposite her husband at the end of a long candlelit table shining with exquisite silver and crystal, and been formally welcomed to the family by Sandro's ancient great-uncle Filippo. Her health had been drunk with every course served, and her neighbours had vied with each other to talk to her, delighted when she'd attempted to reply in Italian. Only the *contessa* had stayed aloof from the talk and laughter round the table, sitting like a marble statue, her mouth set in a thin, unamused smile.

At the reception which followed, Polly had been presented to various local dignitaries, and invited to serve on several charity committees. Sandro, standing at her side, his arm lightly encircling her waist, explained with great charm that, with a young child, his wife's time was limited, but she would consider all proposals in due course.

After which the visitors left expressing their good wishes for

the happiness of the *marchese* and his bride, and Polly had felt
able to relax a little. Until, that was, she'd found herself summoned
by Zia Vittoria, and subjected to an inquisition on her background,
upbringing and education in a voice that was probably audible in
the marina, even before she tackled Polly's suitability to add to
the Valessi dynasty.

When the good lady was finally distracted by the offer of more
champagne, Polly seized the opportunity to escape. It was a warm
night, and the long windows of the *salotto* had been opened. Polly
slipped through the filmy drapes, and out onto the terrace, drawing
a shaky breath of relief when she found herself alone.

The air was still, and the sky heavy with stars, just as she remembered. Even before she met Sandro, she had always loved the
Italian nights, so relaxed and sensuous.

Polly moved to the edge of the terrace, and leaned on the stone
balustrade, inhaling the faint scents that rose from the unseen garden below. Tomorrow, she would explore the *palazzo*'s grounds
with Charlie—find the swimming pool perhaps. Take hold of this
new life with both hands, and make it work somehow.

As she stared into the darkness, she suddenly became aware of
another scent, more pungent and less romantic than the hidden
flowers. The smell of a cigar.

She turned abruptly, and saw a man standing a few yards away
from her. He was of medium height, and verging towards the
plump. Handsome, too, apart from the small, petulant mouth beneath his thin black moustache. And well-pleased with himself,
instinct told her.

She met his bold, appraising stare, her chin lifted haughtily.

'Forgive this intrusion, *marchesa*.' His English was good, if
heavily accented. 'But I could not wait any longer to meet my
cousin's bride. My name is Emilio Corzi.'

'I think we've encountered each other already, *signore*.' Polly
paused. 'Earlier this evening—in my son's nursery.'

He laughed, unabashed. 'I hope I did not offend, but the moment was irresistible, if surprising. Not unlike yourself,
vossignoria,' he added softly. 'I have been watching you with
interest, and you have much more charm and style than I was led
to believe.'

'Really?' Polly raised her eyebrows. 'I don't need to ask who
was doing the leading.'

'You are right, of course.' Emilio Corzi sighed. 'Poor Antonia Barsoli. She has never recovered from the death of that unfortunate girl, Bianca. It must be hard for her to see someone set in her place, especially when Alessandro swore after the accident that he would never marry.' He paused. 'Although she has less reason to be bitter than I have.'

'Ah.' Polly gave him a level look. 'You mean the loss of your inheritance.'

He sighed elaborately. 'It is unfortunately true. His late father had two brothers and a sister, my mother, who produced ten children between them, all girls except for myself, and I was the youngest of three. Alessandro, of course, was an only child, and I dare say too much was expected of him, at too early an age.'

Polly knew she should walk away, but against her better instincts, she lingered.

'Why do you say that?'

'Relations between him and his father were always strained.' Emilio drew reflectively on his cigar. 'And became worse once his mother was no longer there to act as mediator. As you know, she died when he was twelve.' He looked at her, brows raised. 'Or did you know?'

'Of course.' Polly lifted her chin.

'I could not be certain,' he said. 'There are so many areas of his life about which he is silent. Although I am sure he has his reasons.'

'Probably because he doesn't want the details splashed all over your magazines,' Polly suggested shortly.

'But he wrongs me, my dear cousin.' Emilio's tone was plaintive. 'I have not made capital out of his forbidden affair with you—or his secret love-child. I am treating it as a romantic story with a happy ending. My family loyalty is real.' He paused. 'I have not even expressed my doubts in public over the mystery of Bianca DiMario's death. Or not yet anyway.'

'Mystery?' Polly repeated. 'What are you talking about? It was a tragic accident.'

'That was the decision of the inquiry, certainly. But I am fascinated by the reticence of the only witness who was called—Giacomo Raboni.' He smiled at her. 'But after all, his family have served the Valessi faithfully for generations. Who knows what someone less partisan might have said?'

Polly stiffened. 'That is—a disgusting implication. There was a burst tyre on the car. These things happen.'

'But the inquiry was held so quickly,' Emilio countered. 'While Alessandro was still seriously ill in hospital, and unable to give evidence. But perhaps they thought he never would,' he added swiftly. 'It was still possible that he would end his days in a wheel-chair, and that there might be permanent brain damage.'

He shrugged. 'But in the end he suffered only some temporary amnesia, and he made a full recovery—to everyone's enormous relief,' he added piously.

'Yes,' Polly said stonily. 'I bet you were thrilled to bits.' She was leaning back against the balustrade, shaking like a leaf, her stomach churning, as she thought of Sandro trapped, perhaps, in a helpless body. Unable even to understand, maybe, that he had fathered a child, let alone hold him or love him.

'But even when he was well again, he was never questioned about that afternoon in the mountains,' Emilio said softly. 'The advantage, I suppose, of being the son of a rich and influential man. And there was much sympathy, too, for my uncle Domenico, who had lost a young girl he cherished as a daughter. So, many questions were left unanswered.'

'Such as?' she demanded curtly.

'What did Giacomo Raboni know, but not speak about? I know he was well rewarded at the time by my uncle. And now, I find, his granddaughter has been given a position of prestige as your personal maid.'

She said hoarsely, 'But gratitude is quite natural. Sandro told me that Giacomo had saved his life. That's quite a service.'

He shrugged. 'I think his silence has been a greater one. And they say too that generosity is often prompted by a guilty con-science.' He lowered his voice conspiratorially. 'Have you ever wondered whether the scar on your husband's cheek might be the mark of Cain?'

'I think you've said enough.' Her tone was ice. 'You're supposed to be Sandro's guest. It would be better if you left.'

He tutted reproachfully. 'You are harsh, my dear Paola. And your loyalty to Alessandro is misplaced, believe me. I am simply trying to be your friend, and one day you may need me.'

'I can't imagine that,' she returned curtly.

'But then did you foresee finding yourself Marchesa Valessi, with Alessandro's diamonds on your hand and circling your throat? I note he has not given you the jewels that have been in the Valessi family for centuries, but these trinkets are valuable enough.'

'Thank you,' Polly said grittily. 'I'll tell him you approve.'

'Oh, no,' he said. 'I do not think you will discuss our conversation with him at all.' He paused. 'So, what will you do when the little Carlo becomes his legal heir, and Alessandro tires of playing husband, and wants you out of his life a second time?'

Shock was like bile in her throat. 'What the hell do you mean?'

He sighed. 'I hoped you would be honest at least. Your days and nights with my cousin are numbered, and you know it. He has never wished to be married. Not to the unfortunate Bianca. Not to you. No one woman will ever fill his need for variety.' His lip curled. 'Do you wish to know the name of his mistress in Rome?'

'That,' she said huskily, 'is it. Go, please. Just pack and—get out.'

There was sudden venom in his voice. 'Did you make him sign a pre-nuptial agreement, or will he make you settle for the same paltry sum as last time's parting price before he sends you home? If so, you may be glad to turn to me. I would pay you well for a personal view of your association with him.'

'You,' Polly said, steadying her voice, 'are completely vile.'

'And he, Paola *cara*, is totally ruthless, as you must know, else why are you here?' He made her a little bow. 'I will leave you to your solitary contemplation. We shall meet again—once you have learned sense.'

He turned and walked along the terrace, disappearing from view into the darkness.

Polly found she was gasping for breath. She stood, a hand pressed to her throat as she fought for self-control.

She could not stay out here on the terrace forever. Soon, now, she would have to go back inside, and she needed at least the appearance of serenity to fool the sharp eyes that would be watching her.

All the vicious things Emilio had said to her were tumbling around in her head. She might tell herself they were ludicrous, vindictive lies of a disappointed man, but in some ways they seemed like the confirmation of all her worst nightmares.

What had really happened the day Sandro's car went into the ravine? Rafaella had told her that her grandfather refused to speak about it. What had he seen—or heard—that prompted him to silence?

Somehow or other, she thought, I'm going to have to ask him— and make him tell me the truth. Because I need to know.

As for Emilio's comments about her marriage... A little shiver ran through her. He was probably right about that. After all, it was only a means to an end, as Sandro had made clear. And once he had Charlie established as his heir, why would he bother to keep her around? Especially when he had other interests?

Do you wish to know the name of his mistress in Rome?

The words ate at her like some corrosive acid.

The fact that there was another woman in his life had not stopped him trying to seduce her back into his bed, she thought, hurt and anger warring inside her. 'A fever in the blood' he'd once called it. And once the fever had been quenched, what then? Had he expected her to be so much in thrall to him that she was compliantly prepared to share him with his Roman beauty?

She bit her lip so hard that she tasted blood. I can't think about that, she told herself desperately. I dare not go there...

But there was another problem, too, that she had to confront. Was it just Emilio or did other members of the family know that he'd tried to pay her off three years before? If so, that was the ultimate humiliation, and she wanted to run somewhere and hide, away from the smiles and sneers that would accompany such knowledge.

But most of all, she wanted to hide from Sandro. And instead she was obliged to go upstairs, and get into one side of the extravagantly wide bed she had to share with him tonight. And be expected to sleep.

Oh, God, she thought, her fists clenching convulsively. It's all such a charade. Such total hypocrisy.

And if I had any guts, I'd get Charlie, and make a run for it back to England, and see how Sandro deals with a scandal like that.

But, realistically, how far would she get? She was here in this— fortress in a foreign country, where he had power, and she had none. Even the money in the bank account he'd opened for her had been transferred to Italy.

She was helpless—and she was suddenly afraid too.

'So, here you are.' Sandro was walking across the terrace towards her. 'What are you doing out here alone?'

She swallowed slowly and deeply, aware of the frantic thud of her heart at the sight of him.

'I needed some fresh air.' She forced herself to sound light and cool. 'Pretending to be pleasant is hard work, and every actress needs an interval.'

'Is it really so hard to meet such goodwill halfway?' he asked unsmilingly.

'I think it exists for Charlie, not myself,' she returned curtly. 'I'm your wife by accident not design, and they must know that.'

He said drily, 'In the eyes of most of my family, you are not yet my wife at all. I am being given embarrassingly broad hints that I should take you upstairs without further delay and rectify the matter.'

'Oh, God.' Polly pressed her hands to her burning cheeks.

'I am truly sorry, *cara mia*.' His voice was suddenly gentle. 'I never meant you to be subjected to this. We had better face them.'

'Very well.' Ignoring his outstretched hand, she walked stiffly beside him towards the open windows of the *salotto*.

'I can give you ten minutes' privacy,' he added quietly. 'But no longer, or Zia Vittoria will be demanding to know why I am not with you, doing my duty by the next generation.'

Her throat muscles felt paralysed, but she managed a husky, 'Thank you.'

In spite of her tacit resistance, Sandro slid an arm round her waist, holding her against his side, as they went into the brightness of the room and paused to meet the laughter and faint cheers that awaited them.

Then she felt his lips touch her hot cheek, as he whispered, 'Go now, *bella mia*.'

The door seemed a million miles away, especially when she had to reach it through a sea of broad grins and openly voiced encouragement. She was aware that people were swarming after her into the hall, watching her walk up the stairs.

She glanced back once, and saw Sandro standing a little apart from them all. He was unsmiling, his eyes bleak, as he looked at her, raising the glass he was holding in a cynical toast. Then he drained the contents in one jerky movement, and went back into the *salotto*.

Leaving Polly to go on, feeling more alone than she had ever done in her life before.

CHAPTER NINE

THE bedroom was empty, but it was prepared and waiting for her. And, she thought, her senses tautening, for him.

Lamps on tall wrought-iron stands were burning on either side of the bed. The coverlet had been removed and the white lace-edged sheets turned down and scattered with crimson rose petals.

And, she supposed, inevitably, the black lace nightdress was draped across the bed in readiness too.

Well, that she could deal with, she thought, folding it with quick, feverish hands into a tiny parcel of fabric. She went into the dressing room, and stowed it away in her wardrobe in the pocket of a linen jacket against the moment when she could dispose of it for good and all. Otherwise it was going to haunt her.

She also needed an alternative to wear, she thought, rummaging through the exquisitely arranged contents of her lingerie drawer. She decided on a plain ivory satin nightgown, cut on the bias, its neckline square across her breasts, and supported by shoestring straps.

Discreet enough to be an evening dress, she thought as she slipped it over her head after showering briefly in the bathroom. Especially with the diamonds still glittering round her neck. Where they would have to remain, as the clasp resisted all her efforts to unfasten it.

Sighing, Polly shook her hair loose, ran a swift brush through it, and went back into the bedroom.

She was aware the minutes had been ticking past, but she'd still hoped she might be granted a little more leeway than Sandro had suggested. Prayed that it might be possible to be in bed, pretending to be asleep before he came to join her.

But her hopes were dashed, because Sandro was there already, dinner jacket removed and black tie loosened, walking towards the bed. He turned, surveying her without expression as she hesitated in the doorway.

He said, 'Do you not think you are a little overdressed, *bella mia*?'

Her heart skipped. 'What are you talking about?'

His mouth twisted. 'I was referring to the diamonds, naturally.'

She lifted her chin. 'I couldn't unfasten them—and Rafaella wasn't here.'

'She would not risk her life by intruding.' He beckoned. 'Come to me.'

She went slowly towards him, waiting, head bent, while he dealt with the clasp, his touch brisk and impersonal.

'Take it.' He dropped the necklace into her hand.

She said, 'But shouldn't you have it?'

'It was a gift, Paola,' he said shortly. 'Not a loan.'

'I meant—wouldn't it be better in a safe...somewhere?'

'There is a place in the dressing room for your jewellery. Rafaella will show you in the morning.' Sandro turned back to the bed, and began brushing away the rose petals. One of them drifted to Polly's feet, and she bent and retrieved it, stroking the velvety surface with her fingertips.

She said, 'Someone has taken a lot of trouble. Perhaps you were right about the goodwill.'

'The wedding night of a *marchese* and his bride is always a great occasion.' Sandro dragged out the bolster from under the pillows, and arranged it down the centre of the bed. 'How fortunate they will never know the truth,' he added sardonically.

'There,' he said, when he had finished. 'Will that make you feel safe?'

'Yes,' Polly said stiltedly. 'Yes—thank you.'

He walked away towards the dressing room, and Polly switched off her lamp and got hastily into bed. She slid her necklace under the pillow, then lay down, her back turned rigidly towards the bolster. The scent of the roses still lingered beguilingly, and she buried her face in the pillow, breathing in the perfume, and relishing the coolness of the linen against the warmth of her skin.

When at last she heard Sandro returning, she burrowed further down under the sheet, closing her eyes so tightly that coloured lights danced behind her lids.

She sensed that the other lamp had been extinguished, then heard the rustle of silk as he discarded his robe, and the faint dip of the bed as he took his place on the far side of the bolster.

There was a silence, then he said, 'Paola, you are permitted to stop acting when we are alone together. And I know you are not asleep.'

She turned reluctantly, and looked at him over her shoulder. In the shadows of the room, she could see the outline of him, leaning on the bolster, watching her, but she was unable to read the expression on his face.

She kept her voice cool. 'But I'd like to be. This has been one hell of a day.'

'Crowned, I imagine, by your meeting with my cousin Emilio,' he drawled. 'Where did you encounter him?'

Polly, unprepared for the question, hunched a shoulder. 'He happened to be on the terrace while I was there,' she said evasively.

'Emilio does not "happen" to be anywhere, *cara*,' he said drily. 'His locations are always intentional.' He paused. 'Did you share a pleasant conversation?'

'No,' she said. 'Not particularly. I hope he isn't a frequent visitor.'

'I believe he comes mainly to see Zia Antonia,' he said. 'Usually when I am not here. As he is leaving early in the morning, he has asked me to pass on a message to you.'

Polly shifted uncomfortably. 'Oh?'

'He sends you his homage,' Sandro went on silkily. 'And hopes that tonight will provide you with wonderful memories for the rest of your life.'

She punched the pillow with unnecessary vigour, and lay down again. 'Well, neither of us are likely to forget it,' she said shortly.

'That is true,' he said. 'But I am surprised to find you on a level of such intimacy with Emilio.'

'I'm not,' she returned heatedly. 'He's a loathsome little worm, and I'm amazed that someone hasn't dealt with him by now.'

'They have tried,' Sandro said drily. 'He has been pushed off a balcony in Lucca, and thrown into the Grand Canal in Venice. And he was nearly the victim of a drive-by shooting in Rome, but it seems that was a case of mistaken identity.'

Polly was surprised into a giggle. 'What a shame.'

'As you say,' he agreed solemnly. 'But, in a way, he can be pitied. For years he has been waiting confidently for me to break my neck on the polo field, be caught in an avalanche or drown while sailing. The car crash must have made him feel that his dream could come true at last.

'Yet here I am with a wife and a son, and his hopes of the Valessi inheritance are finally dashed.'

She put up a hand to her pillow, hugging it closer. Her voice was faintly muffled. 'Is that why you were so determined to take Charlie? To put Emilio out of the running?'

'It played its part. But I wanted him for his own sake, too.' His voice sharpened. 'Paola, you cannot doubt that, surely.'

'No,' she said. 'I—know you did.'

It was almost her only certainty, she thought. Emilio's vile insinuations were still turning like a weary treadmill in her brain, reminding her yet again just how tenuous her position was. And how easily she might lose everything in the world that mattered to her.

And in spite of the warmth of the night, she gave the slightest shiver.

He noticed instantly. 'Are you cold? Do you wish for a blanket?'

'It's not that.' She sat up, making a little helpless gesture. 'I— I just don't know what I'm doing here—why I let myself do this. I don't understand what's happening.'

He was silent for a moment, then he said wearily, a trace of something like bitterness in his voice, 'Currently, you and I, *cara mia*, are about to spend a very long and tedious night together. When it is over, we will see what tomorrow brings, and hope that it is better. Now, sleep.'

He turned away, and lay down with his back to her, and, after a pause, she did the same.

Time passed, and became an hour—then another. Polly found herself lying on the furthermost edge of the bed, listening to Sandro's quiet, regular breathing, scared to move or even sigh in case she disturbed him.

She felt physically and emotionally exhausted, but her brain would not let her rest. She was plagued by images that hurt and bewildered her, images of fear and isolation, but she found them impossible to dismiss, however much she wanted to let go, and allow herself to drift away into sleep.

At one point, she seemed to be standing at one end of a long tree-lined avenue, watching Sandro, who was ahead of her, walking away with long, rapid strides. And she knew with total frightened certainty that if she allowed him to reach the end of the avenue, that he would be gone forever. She tried to call out, to summon him back, but her voice emerged as a cracked whisper.

Yet somehow he seemed to hear, because he stopped and looked back, and she began to run to him, stumbling a little, her legs like leaden weights.

She said his name again, and ran into his arms, and they closed round her, so warm and so safe that the icy chill deep inside her began to dissolve away as he held her.

And she thought, This is a dream. I'm dreaming... And knew that she did not want to wake, and face reality again.

When she eventually opened her eyes the following day, that same feeling of security still lingered, and she felt relaxed and strangely at peace.

The first thing she saw was that the bolster was back in its normal place, and that the bed beside her was empty. She was completely alone, too, with only the whirr of the ceiling fan to disturb the hush of the room. Sandro had gone.

Well, she thought, I should be grateful for that.

She sat up, pushing her hair back from her face. It was very hot, she realised, and the shutters at the windows were closed to exclude the molten gold of the sun. At some moment in the night, she'd kicked away the covering sheet, but her satin nightdress was clinging damply to her body.

She glanced at her watch, and gasped. No wonder the temperature was soaring—the morning was nearly over. She felt as if she'd slept for a hundred years, and that, if she left this room, she would find the passages choked with cobwebs.

And, as if on cue, there was a knock on the door and Rafaella came in carrying a tray.

'*Buongiorno*, madam.' Her smile was wide and cheerful.

Polly spread her hands helplessly. 'It's almost afternoon!' she exclaimed. 'Why did no one wake me?'

'The *marchese* said that you needed to sleep, and should not be disturbed,' Rafaella returned demurely, her eyes straying to the tray she had just placed on the bed.

Polly followed her gaze, and saw that in addition to the orange juice, the fresh rolls, the dish of honey, the bowl of grapes and the silver coffee pot, there was a red rose lying across the snowy tray cloth, and a folded note beside it.

Swallowing, she reached for it. It said simply, '*Grazie, mi amore,*' and was signed with his name.

Polly realised she was blushing to the roots of her hair, and hurriedly crushed the paper in her hand. Everyone in the *palazzo*, she thought, would know about his message by now, and the remembered passion implied in its words.

It was simply another brick in the wall of pretence around their marriage, and she knew it, but that didn't make it any easier to take.

She had also seen the faintly puzzled glance that the girl had sent the ivory nightgown.

Maybe I should have left the black one shredded on the floor, she thought ruefully. Silenced any lingering doubts that way.

She cleared her throat. 'Where—where is the *marchese*?'

'He has been bidding goodbye to his guests, madam. Now he has gone down to the port with his son and the *bambinaia*.' She beamed. 'The little Carlo wished for ice-cream, I think.'

'His father has a short memory,' Polly commented crisply. 'Charlie, ice-cream and a car ride could be a lethal combination.'

'Ah, no, *signora*. The *marchese* was also ill on journeys when he was a *bambino*, and Dorotea has her own special remedy,' Rafaella reassured her cheerfully. 'Shall I pour *signora*'s coffee?'

Dorotea? Polly thought, as she sipped the strong brew. Then where was Julie?

'The *maggiordomo*, Teodoro, sends his respects to *vossignoria*,' Rafaella reported when she returned from running Polly's bath. 'The *marchese* has instructed him to show you the *palazzo*, and he awaits your convenience.'

'Oh,' Polly said, slowly. 'Well, please thank him for me. It will be my pleasure.' She paused, spreading a roll with honey. 'I was also thinking, Rafaella, that I would really like to meet your grandfather.' She made her tone casual. 'Thank him for all he did for the *marchese*. Could you arrange that for me?'

'It would be his honour, *signora*,' Rafaella's dark eyes shone. 'But at the moment he is away, visiting my sister in Salerno, who is expecting her first child. When he returns, perhaps?'

'That would be fine,' Polly agreed. 'I'll hold you to it.'

An hour later, bathed and dressed in a knee-length white skirt and a sleeveless navy top, she made her way to the nursery, hoping that Charlie might be back. Instead, she found Julie sitting alone at the big table, listlessly leafing through the pages of a magazine.

'Oh.' Polly checked at the sight of her. 'So you didn't go to the port.'

Julie sighed. 'Dorotea may not speak much English, but she made it plain I wasn't wanted,' she said wryly. 'Instead, I've been cleaning out these already spotless cupboards.'

Polly frowned. 'Doesn't she realise you're here to be with Charlie?'

'That's the problem. Apparently there's only one way to look after his excellency's son, and it's not the way I do it. And the Contessa Barsoli was here earlier, asking when I planned to go home.' She looked squarely at Polly. 'I think my coming here was a big mistake.'

Polly forced a smile. 'I'm hardly the flavour of the month with them either. I was only just allowed to say goodnight to him yesterday,' she added candidly, then paused. 'But please hang in there, Julie. I'm sure things can only get better.' And mentally crossed her fingers.

Teodoro was waiting in the hall for her, still looking anxious, but his face cleared a little when Polly spoke to him in his own language. Overall, she thought afterwards, the tour of the *palazzo* went well, although there were too many rooms, too many glorious works of art on the walls, too many priceless tapestries, statues and ceramics on display to be assimilated all at once. And most of the furniture in everyday use would have graced any museum. Becoming familiar with it all would be a life's work. And her days here were limited.

If she had a criticism, she thought, it would be that it all seemed incredibly formal and curiously lifeless. Everything appeared to have its own place, which it had occupied for centuries.

The exception was Sandro's study, and the small office which adjoined it, staffed by a severe woman with glasses called Signora Corboni. This was where the work was done, Polly surmised, surveying the computers and fax machine, and metal filing cabinets, but even here the past intruded in the shape of a massive antique desk.

And she had never seen so many fireplaces. Every room seemed to have one, and the largest often had two. But there was no central heating, so logs would be burned to dispel the chill and damp of an Italian winter.

There was only one door locked against her. The room, Teodoro told her with faint embarrassment, occupied by the *contessa*. And Polly smiled and shrugged to indicate that there was no problem— that the *contessa* was an elderly woman entitled to her privacy.

Teodoro had clearly been keeping the best until last, flinging the final door open with a flourish. 'And this, *vossignoria*, this is all for you.'

It was far from the largest room she'd been shown, yet her flat in England would probably have fitted into it quite comfortably. And comfort was the theme, with a carpeted floor, two deeply cushioned sofas covered in a blue and cream floral design flanking the stone hearth, and matching curtains hanging at the large window.

'Oh.' Polly knelt on the window seat, looking down over a sloping riot of dark green trees and shrubs to the azure sea beyond. 'Oh, how lovely.'

Teodoro beamed in satisfaction, and began to point out the other amenities, which included a television set, a state-of-the-art music centre with a rack of CDs, and a tall case stocked with the latest English fiction and non-fiction titles.

There were no old masters on the walls, but some delightful water-colours. There were roses filling the air with scent on a side-table, and the ornaments, although undoubtedly valuable, had clearly been selected for their charm.

'This was the favoured room of the *marchese*'s late mother, may God grant her peace,' Teodoro said, crossing himself devoutly. 'Messere Alessandro ordered it to be specially prepared for you. He wished you to have somewhere quiet and private for yourself alone, to sit and read, perhaps, or play music.'

And be out of his way? Polly wondered wryly. But, whatever Sandro's motives, she couldn't deny her pleasure in the room, or fail to appreciate the thought that had gone into it.

She said quietly, 'That's—very kind of him.'

He nodded, pleased. He indicated the telephone standing on a small, elegant writing desk. 'If you wish to make a call, our switchboard will connect you. And if there is anything else *vossignoria* requires, be gracious enough to pull the bell by the fireplace.'

After that there were more practical matters to be dealt with. There were food stores and the wine cellars to be inspected, plus the laundry and the bakery to be visited.

The *palazzo* was a little world of its own, she thought, and pretty much self-sufficient, probably dating from the days when it was regularly besieged by its enemies.

Not a lot of change there, she thought ironically as she refused lunch, but gratefully accepted Teodoro's offer of iced lemonade served on the terrace.

She had just seated herself in a cushioned chair under the shade of a sun umbrella when Sandro appeared, walking up the steps from the garden.

He was wearing shorts, and an unbuttoned cotton shirt, his feet thrust into canvas shoes, and was carrying an excited Charlie on his shoulders.

'*Ciao.*' His greeting was casual, but the look he sent her was curiously watchful. 'Did you sleep well?'

She forced a smile. 'Better than I could have hoped. And you?'

He said laconically, 'I survived.' And lowered Charlie down to the flags.

The little boy came rushing to Polly. 'Mammina, I went in a boat, with *big* sails.' Waving arms indicated a vast expanse of canvas. 'And a man give me a fish all of my own. Doro says I can eat it for supper.'

Polly sent Sandro a surprised look. 'What's this?'

'I took him to meet an old friend of mine, called Alfredo.' Sandro poured himself some lemonade. 'When I was a young boy, I used to escape whenever I could down to the port, and Fredo would take me fishing with him. A pleasure I would like Carlino to share.'

'But he can't swim,' Polly protested. 'Supposing the boat had capsized?'

Sandro shrugged, his face hardening. 'Supposing we had all been abducted by aliens?' he countered impatiently. 'And I intend to give him his first swimming lesson later today, after siesta.' He paused. 'Perhaps you would like to come and make sure his life is not endangered again.'

She said stiffly, 'I suppose you think I'm making a fuss about nothing.'

'Yes,' he said, 'if you think I would allow harm to come to one hair on his head.'

Biting her lip, she turned back to Charlie and gave him a big hug. 'So, tell me about your fish, darling. What colour is it?'

He gave it frowning thought, then, 'Fish-coloured,' he decided.

Sandro's lips twitched. '*Avanti,*' he said. 'Let us go and find Doro, *figlio mio*. It is time you had a rest.'

'Let me take him,' Polly said quickly. 'To Julie.'

'But I am already going upstairs,' he said. 'So there is no need for you to do so. Unless, of course, you wish to share the siesta with me,' he added with touch of mockery.

'Thank you,' Polly acknowledged, stonily. 'But no.'

His mouth twisted. 'You seemed to find it enjoyable once.'

'Perhaps,' she said. 'But I really don't need to be constantly reminded of my mistakes—especially those in the distant past.'

'Last night is not so distant, *cara*,' he said softly. 'And you slept happily in my arms for most of it.'

Polly put her glass down very carefully. 'What are you talking about?'

'Think about it,' he advised, then swung Charlie onto his hip and went indoors, leaving her staring after him, alarm clenching like a fist inside her.

He was teasing her, Polly told herself, pacing backwards and forwards across her living room. For reasons of his own, he enjoyed needling her—seeing how far he could push her before the explosion came. That was all it was. She was sure of it.

And yet—and yet...

She couldn't forget that curious feeling of well-being that had surrounded her when she'd awoken that morning. How rested she'd felt. How completely relaxed.

And remembered, too, those times when they were lovers that he'd joined her in bed when she was already asleep, and she'd woken to find herself wrapped in his arms, her head tucked into the curve of his shoulder, and her lips against his skin. And, smiling, had slept again.

There was a strange familiarity about it all.

Oh, no, she groaned silently. Please—no...

And, all too soon now, she had to face him again, she thought glumly. She couldn't hide away anywhere, so the only thing she could do was bluff it out. Pretend that nothing had happened, which might even be true, and never refer to it again.

She was halfway to the door, when it opened abruptly and the *contessa* came in.

So much for privacy, Polly thought wryly.

She said, politely, '*Buongiorno, contessa*. Is there something I can do?'

The older woman stared around her for a long moment, then turned back to Polly, smiling stiffly. 'On the contrary, dear Paola. I came to make sure that you had everything you wanted—in your new domain.'

She gave the room another sharp, appraising look. 'I confess I have not visited it since Alessandro gave orders for its total renovation. I—I find it painful to see the changes, indeed I can barely recognise it, but I know I must not be a foolish old woman.'

Polly said quietly, 'I don't think anyone would ever see you in that light, *contessa*.' She paused. 'Were you very close to Sandro's mother? I didn't know.'

'Close to Maddalena?' the older woman queried sharply. 'I knew her, of course, but we were never on intimate terms. No, I was speaking of my cherished Bianca, who was also given this room by Alessandro's father as her personal retreat. She loved it here.' She sighed deeply. 'Now every trace of her has gone, even the portrait of her that my cousin Domenico had painted.' She paused, and a note of steel entered her voice. 'I am astonished that your husband should have so little regard for his father's wishes.'

'I'm sorry you feel like that,' Polly said, caught at a loss. 'Maybe you should take up the matter with Sandro himself.'

'My poor Bianca.' The *contessa* swept on regardless. 'How much she loved him—and what she endured for his sake. And how soon she is forgotten.' And she sighed again.

'I'm sure that's not true,' Polly told her quietly. 'I know he has the greatest respect for her memory, *contessa*.'

'Dear child, you are kind to say so. But the evidence makes that so hard to believe. She was such an innocent, and her only sin was to love Alessandro too much. And because of that—she died.'

She shook her head with the appearance of someone labouring under more sorrow than anger.

'He drove too fast—always. And that terrible day, he was in a temper—a wicked, dangerous rage. He had quarrelled with his father, so Bianca followed him, like the angel she was—insisted on going in the car with him to reason with him. To persuade him to return and make peace with his father.'

Her voice broke a little. 'Only for her, there was no return. He was too angry—too reckless to judge the bend correctly, and the car went into the ravine.

'He was never made to answer for what he had done, of course. His own injuries saved him from possible charges.

'But it is guilt he feels, my dear Paola—not respect—and that is why he has had every remnant of my poor Bianca's presence removed—even her portrait.'

She paused, looking keenly at Polly, who was standing with her arms wrapped round her body in an instinctive gesture of defence. 'I am sorry if I grieve you, but it is as well you should know the truth.'

Polly said quietly, 'I am sure my husband blames himself just as much as you could wish, *contessa*.'

The older woman's tone was almost purring. 'But call me Zia Antonia, I beg you. We cannot be strangers. Your position in this house is hardly an enviable one,' she added. 'Alessandro is so—unpredictable, and I fear you may find yourself much neglected. I hope that when problems arise, you will know you can always turn to me.'

'Thank you,' Polly said. 'I—I'm very grateful.' *Or am I?* she asked herself silently as she watched the *contessa* walk to the door, bestow another thin, honeyed smile and leave. *It's like feeling obligated to a cobra that's already bitten you once.*

But the *contessa*'s words had left her shaking inside. She was clearly implying that Sandro was guilty of manslaughter at the very least.

This, coupled with Emilio's comments about a possible cover-up at the official inquiry, painted a frightening picture, and one Polly did not even want to contemplate.

If he had been recklessly speeding and made a fatal error of judgement which caused the accident, then surely he had been well-punished for it. *The mark of Cain,* she thought, and shud-dered.

But, at the same time, the power of the Valessi family was being highlighted for her in an awesome way, she realised unhappily.

Money was waved, and things happened. A girl who could prove a nuisance was dismissed back to her own country. An eyewitness to a car crash was persuaded to doctor his account of the tragedy to protect the heir to a dynasty. An expensive court action was threatened, and that same heir acquired a wife and child.

He would have hated the scandal of a court appearance, she thought. If I'd listened to my mother and stood up to him, maybe he'd have backed off. And I would not be here now, torn apart by doubts. Tormented equally by my fears and longings.

She looked down at the glow of the diamond on her hand. A symbol of a fever in the blood? she wondered. Or a cold flame that would consume her utterly, reducing her to ashes? As it might have destroyed Bianca three years earlier, she thought, and shiv-ered.

And once she had gone, would she be so easily forgotten too?

There was a tap on the door, and Teodoro appeared.

'Please excuse me.' He inclined his head respectfully. 'But the *marchese* is asking for you to join him at the swimming pool. I should be happy to show you the way, *marchesa*, if you will accompany me.'

'Yes,' she said, and took a deep breath. 'Yes, of course.'

She got slowly to her feet, pushing her hair back with a me-chanical gesture. Life went on, and whatever her mental turmoil, it seemed she was required to join Sandro, and needed to obey the summons. Accept the situation that had been forced upon her, she thought, and all its implications.

Because, after all, what other choice did she have?

And, straightening her shoulders, she reluctantly allowed Teodoro to escort her from the room, and out into the sunlight.

CHAPTER TEN

THE pool was an oval turquoise set in creamy marble, created, Polly guessed, out of a former sunken garden and reached by a series of shallow steps, which wound their way downwards through banks of flowering shrubs. And where Teodoro left her to make the rest of her way alone.

As she descended, she saw that the pool was surrounded by a broad sun-terrace with cushioned loungers and parasols, and, at the far end, there was a flamboyant piece of statuary, depicting some sea god surrounded by leaping dolphins.

And with equal flamboyance, a large inflatable duck with a coy smile and long eyelashes was bobbing quietly at the pool's shallow end.

Sandro was stretched out under one of the umbrellas, reading. He was wearing a pair of brief black trunks, which set off his lithe, bronzed body in a way that made her heart skip a momentary beat. His only other covering was the pair of designer sunglasses which he removed at her approach.

'Ciao.' He surveyed her with a faint frown. 'Are you all right?'

'Never better,' Polly lied too brightly. She looked around her. 'What—what a wonderful spot this is. And so peaceful.'

'I think the peace will be broken when Dorotea arrives with Carlino,' he said drily.

'Dorotea?' Polly asked, her own brows creasing, seating herself on an adjoining lounger. 'Why not Julie?'

He shrugged. 'Perhaps she is still learning her way about—or tired from the events of yesterday.'

'Yes,' she said. 'Perhaps.' She hesitated. 'I should apologise for my failure to join you this morning, and say goodbye to your guests. I hope no one was offended.'

'I explained you needed your rest,' he said. 'They understood completely.'

Faint colour invaded her face. 'Oh, I expect you made sure of that.'

136

'It was hardly a lie,' he said. 'You did not sleep well, because you were clearly troubled by bad dreams. Otherwise, why would you have spoken my name and reached for me, as you did?'

Her flush deepened. She said coldly, 'I wasn't aware of it, believe me. And I've had nightmares before,' she added.

'Not,' he said softly, 'when you have been in bed with me, *carissima*.'

She bit her lip. 'Perhaps not. But there was no need for any— intervention on your part.'

'Well,' he said lightly, picking up his book again, 'it will not occur again. From tonight, you will sleep alone, *bella mia*. I have given the necessary orders.'

'Thank you,' she said. 'My own bedroom as well as a personal living room. What luxury.' She paused. 'But can I ask not to be allocated another shrine to Bianca?'

His gaze sharpened. 'What are you talking about?'

'Your cousin Antonia visited me earlier. She was upset about the changes you'd made to your mother's room—especially the removal of Bianca's portrait.'

'I will tell Teodoro to rescue it from storage,' he said. 'And hang it in her own suite, if it means so much to her. But she already maintains a shrine to Bianca,' he added coldly. 'It is on the mountain road at the place where the car went over. There is a photograph, with a candle burning in front of it, and fresh flowers which she places there regularly. I am sure she would show it to you, if you asked.'

She said, 'I'll bear it in mind.' She paused. 'Not that it matters, but don't your servants find it a little strange that we're having separate rooms?'

'They are not paid to question my decisions,' he drawled. 'And they will not find it so extraordinary. My parents and grandparents had the same arrangements, and probably every generation of my family before that.

'And you are also under a misapprehension,' he added. 'You will not be moving. You will continue to sleep in the master bedroom, which is quite free of any connection with Bianca.' His tone was expressionless. 'As far as I know, she never entered it.'

She said uncertainly, 'But surely that's your room, and you should keep it.' She tried to smile. 'After all, you're very much the master here.'

'I can sleep anywhere,' he said. 'And besides, I shall be away from the *palazzo* a great deal.'

'You will?' She looked at him uncertainly.

'*Naturalamente.* My work involves a great deal of travelling, and this trip has been planned for a long time.' He slanted a look at her. 'If circumstances were different, I would take you with me, *cara.* But I cannot guarantee there will always be convenient bolsters in our accommodation.'

'Not that they seem to make much difference to you,' she flashed.

He hunched an indifferent shoulder. 'I held you, Paola, while you slept, and because you seemed to need comfort. If you wish me to apologise for that,' he added deliberately, 'you will wait forever.'

He looked her over. 'You are not dressed for swimming. You do not intend to join your son in the pool for the first time?'

She bit her lip. 'I didn't bring any swimwear with me. I—I suppose Teresa thought there was no need...that I would buy something when I got here.'

'It's not a problem.' He pointed to the pair of changing cabins that stood on the opposite side of the pool. 'You will find a selection there. I hope there will be something to your taste.'

'Or yours anyway,' she returned coolly.

He picked up his book. 'Then keep your clothes on,' he said with cool indifference, 'if you do not want to swim. And also if you do not care about the disappointment to Carlino,' he added silkily, offering the killer blow.

Oh, but she did want to swim. The sun seemed to be pouring its full intensity into this secluded marble bowl, and she could feel the sweat trickling down her body. The thought of cool water against her skin was irresistible.

She said, 'I care very much, and you know it. I—I'll go and change.'

Feeling self-conscious, she crossed to the women's cabin, but a swift glance backwards revealed that Sandro was absorbed in his book again.

The swimwear was displayed in a cupboard, a whole row of bikinis on padded hangers. There was one in black, and the rest were in a range of clear, pretty colours. To her surprise, all of them were in her size, and, even more astonishing, none of them were nearly as revealing as they might have been.

The violet bikini she eventually picked had sleek, simple lines, with cups that lifted and enhanced her breasts without undue exposure, and briefs that discreetly skimmed her hip bones. She slipped on the gauzy jacket that matched it, and slid her feet into white canvas mules before venturing outside again.

Sandro watched her walk towards him, his face enigmatic. 'I am glad at least one met with your approval,' he commented.

'They were all—lovely.' She hesitated. 'And not what I'd expected you to choose for your ladies.'

Sandro sighed, and put down his book. 'I chose them for you, Paola, this morning at the marina. You, and no one else,' he told her with a touch of harshness. 'This is my home, and I have never invited my ''ladies'', as you call them, here for poolside orgies, whatever you may believe.

'Finally, you are my wife,' he added cuttingly. 'And, in theory, I am permitted to see you in private in any state of undress I wish. In public, however, I prefer a certain decorum. Do I make myself clear?'

She bent her head. 'Perfectly. It's all down to appearances again.'

His smile was cynical. 'Of course, *cara mia*. Because appearances are all we have. So accustom yourself, as I am doing.'

He paused. 'And now try to smile, because here comes our son.'

Against all the odds, thought Polly as she pulled herself out of the water and reached for a towel, the session in the pool had turned out to be one of the happiest times she could remember in her life.

To her surprise, Charlie, his armbands securely in place, had taken to the water as if he belonged in it, and his wide-eyed enjoyment of this new environment had prompted a more relaxed response from herself as well. They played with a ball in the shallow end, and after some rowdy splashing games Polly steered her son carefully round the pool on the back of the duck, as he squealed with delight. Afterwards, she watched and encouraged as Charlie, under Sandro's patient guidance, managed his first uncertain swimming strokes.

It was, however, apparent that Sandro was strictly avoiding any but the most fleeting physical contact with herself, which created a few moments of awkwardness.

The only other drawback was the presence of Dorotea, who sat with her knitting at the poolside, uttering faint cries of alarm at intervals, in the apparent belief that Charlie was about to be allowed to drown by his negligent and uncaring parents.

If she really found it all so nerve-racking, why on earth hadn't she let Julie, who had swimming and life-saving qualifications, bring him down to the pool instead? Polly wondered with faint irritation.

As it was, Dorotea could not wait to get her charge out of the water and towelled down, as she clucked over him.

My mother all over again, Polly thought wryly. And something I shall have to watch.

Charlie was furious to discover that the inflatable duck would not be permitted to accompany him back to the *palazzo* or sleep with him that night, and threatened a tantrum. But Sandro diverted this by reminding the little boy that he was to have his special fish for supper, and that the duck might steal it from him. Besides, he added, improvising rapidly, the duck would also miss his pool, and keep them all awake during the night with his homesick quacking.

Polly, vigorously rubbing her dripping hair, watched Charlie depart, his hand in Dorotea's.

She glanced across at Sandro, who was also drying himself. She said on impulse, 'He's going to miss you terribly while you're away.'

'This time it is unavoidable, but it will not be for long,' Sandro said. 'And next time he will not miss me at all, because I shall take him with me.'

Polly folded the towel she'd been using with immense care.

She said, 'I'm sorry. What are you saying? Because I don't think I quite understand.'

'It is perfectly simple, *cara*,' he drawled. 'My next trip is a much shorter one, and I intend Carlino to accompany me.'

Polly looked at him, stupefied. 'But he's only a baby,' she whispered.

'He will not be asked to make any boardroom decisions.' Sandro tossed his towel aside and sat down on the lounger, raking back the tousled dark hair.

'It's still ludicrous,' she protested. 'You—you can't take him away.'

He smiled faintly. 'And who is going to stop me? You, *bella mia*?' He shook his head. 'I don't think so.'

She took a deep breath. 'Why are you doing this?'

'Because I love his company,' he said. 'And I wish to strengthen the bond between us, now that it has been established.'

'But I've never been without him for more than a night,' Polly said desperately.

'Then you are fortunate,' he said with sudden harshness. 'I have already missed too much of his life, and I do not mean him to grow up a stranger to me, as I was to my own father for so long.'

She went over and knelt beside him, her hands gripping his arms. 'Sandro.' Her tone was pleading. 'Don't do this to me, please. Or to him. He's too young.'

His face expressionless, he freed himself gently but inexorably from her clasp.

'My mind is made up,' he said. 'He would be travelling with me tomorrow, but my arrangements are already made.'

'Including a trip to Rome, no doubt.' The words were out before she could stop them.

His brows lifted. 'Rome, yes,' he said, with faint mockery. 'That is unmissable, of course. Afterwards—Milan, Florence, Turin and Venice. The next time will involve a simpler route.'

She stayed on her knees, looking up at him. She said huskily, 'Let me go with you.'

For a long moment he was silent, then very slowly and with infinite care his finger traced the curve of her breast above the cling of the soaked bikini cup, then slid under the strap, pulling it down without haste from her shoulder.

He said quietly, the topaz eyes intent and watchful, 'But when do you offer your company, *carissima*? In a few weeks with Carlino? Or tomorrow—alone—with me? On a honeymoon?'

The vivid sunlight seemed to enclose them both in a golden breathless cloud, where she could hear nothing but the trembling hurry of her own heart. Feel nothing but the burn of his touch on her cool, damp skin. See in his eyes the urgency of another, deeper question that she dared not answer.

She longed to tell him 'Yes', she realised dazedly, and with shame.

Because she knew that tiny tendrils of sensation were uncurling at his touch, arousing potent memories of her nakedness explored and exquisitely enjoyed. Igniting the urgent need to yield herself once more to the pleasure of his hands and mouth. To lose herself, trembling, in the totality of his powerful masculinity. A woman reunited with the only man she had ever known. Ever wanted.

Her nipples ached to be free of their flimsy covering and offered to the balm of his tongue.

She wanted to give up the struggle, and surrender. To forget the unhappiness of the past, and abandon the remnants of her pride to the passionate delight of the moment.

Instead she snatched, drowning, at the last vestige of sanity and self-respect she possessed. Because a moment in time was all he might have to give her. And she could not bear to be taken and then discarded once again on a whim.

Especially when he had just made it more than clear that it was only their child he wanted and valued.

He said softly, 'Paola, I need you to answer me.'

'I'm sure you know already,' she said. 'It has to be—Charlie, and always will be.'

Hand miraculously steady, she hitched her bikini strap back into place, and got to her feet.

'After all, a business trip is scarcely a honeymoon, *excellenza*,' she went on with forced lightness. 'And, as you say, your arrangements for tomorrow are already made—including some I am sure you would not wish to alter. And for which I would be—surplus to requirements.'

Tell me it's not true, her heart cried out to him silently. Say that you want me, and only me. That you love me. Beg me—just once—please—please...

But: 'How understanding you are, *cara*,' he drawled. 'The perfect wife for a man who does not wish to be married.'

'I wish,' she said, 'that I could pay you the same compliment. Say that you're the ideal husband for a reluctant wife.' She paused. 'And now perhaps you will excuse me?'

She turned away, walking to the changing pavilion, but before she had gone three yards Sandro was beside her, swinging her round to face him.

'Tell me one thing.' His voice was soft and savage. 'Who will you reach for in the nights ahead, when the bad dreams come?'

She tore herself free. 'No one,' she answered hoarsely. 'A lesson I should have learned three years ago, because all my bad dreams are about you, *signore.*' She paused. 'Now let me go.'

His mouth curled. 'With pleasure, my sweet wife. Enjoy your freedom, because it is all you will have from me.'

He went back to his lounger, and lay there face downwards, and motionless, pillowing his head on his folded arms.

Suddenly, getting back to the *palazzo* seemed a safer option than retrieving her clothes, and Polly found herself going up the stone steps two at a time, as a voice in her head whispered breathlessly, It's over—finished—done with.

And wishing with all her heart that she could feel relief, instead of the desolation that stalked her like a shadow through the late-afternoon sun.

The *palazzo* without its master was a different proposition altogether, and Polly became aware of that within forty-eight hours of Sandro's departure.

Following the afternoon at the pool, he had not joined her for dinner, informing her through a bewildered Teodoro that he had an engagement in town. And the next morning he was gone almost before the sun was up, so there was no opportunity to say goodbye.

Polly gathered from Rafaella that a courteous reluctance to disturb her through his early departure had been used to explain his move to another bedroom. She also realised, almost at once, that the excuse had fooled nobody, and that being regarded as the *marchese*'s unwanted bride was not an enviable situation to be in.

How else to explain the none-too-subtle shift in attitude by the rest of the household almost as soon as Sandro had gone? The thinly veiled hostility she'd encountered in the nursery seemed to have spread through the *palazzo* like a miasma.

The food she was served was often cold, her attempts to speak Italian were ignored, her bell left unanswered, and once, in a mirror, she'd caught a glimpse of one of the maids making the sign to ward off the evil eye behind her back.

It was no comfort to realise that Julie was faring even worse. She saw hardly anything of Charlie, being designated instead to hand-wash and iron all his clothes, and even his bedding, in between scouring the nursery itself.

And when Polly told Dorotea firmly that this had to stop, and Charlie's things must be sent to the laundry, so that Julie could bring the little boy down to the pool each afternoon, she was met with shrugs and looks of incomprehension.

And each time Polly herself entered the nursery, she could feel the resentment in the air.

Even Rafaella seemed oddly subdued, and it was hard to get a smile out of her.

Perhaps she resents working for someone who's a *marchesa* only in name, and a second-class citizen in reality, Polly thought wryly.

But it wasn't just the attitude of the staff that she found difficult to take. It was missing Sandro.

She thought of him all the time, found herself listening for his step, and the sound of his voice. She had no idea when he was to return, and there was no one she could ask.

Least of all himself, she acknowledged, even though he telephoned the *palazzo* each day to speak to Charlie. On the occasions when he asked to speak to her too, their exchanges were cool and stilted.

Strangers, she thought achingly. With nothing to say to each other.

But even living a separate existence under his roof was preferable to his continuing absence, she thought. And her imagination worked overtime in picturing where he was, and what he might be doing. And with whom...

The nights were the worst. In spite of the summer heat, the vast bed she occupied seemed as wide and chilly as a winter ocean, and sleep was a deep pit of loneliness which swallowed her up, then released her, restless and unrefreshed when morning came. And often, when she woke, her face was wet with tears.

She wished with all her heart that she'd been the one to move out. Everything that belonged to him had been scrupulously removed, but it had made little difference. His presence still seemed to linger, invisible but potent.

He had been gone nearly a fortnight when Polly received a pleasant surprise—a flying visit from Teresa, Ernesto and the twins, who had come to visit his parents in Naples.

They were clearly stunned to discover Sandro's absence, but quickly concealed their shock under a flood of chatter and laughter.

Polly knew that Teresa would have picked up immediately on her wan face and shadowed eyes, but that good manners would keep her from asking awkward questions.

But when Ernesto was down at the pool with the children, and Polly was alone with Teresa in her living room, she did confide in the other girl about her staff problems, and saw her frown.

'Your Italian is good,' she said. 'And will become better with practice. So, there should be no misunderstandings—especially with Dorotea. She has worked at the *palazzo* longer than anyone, and is devoted to the Valessi family. You are the mother of Alessandro's heir, so she should be your greatest supporter.' She patted Polly's hand. 'I will go and ask for some coffee and almond cakes to be brought, and see what I can find out.'

When she returned, her face was solemn. 'They believe they are going to lose their jobs,' she said. 'That you intend to replace them all with your own servants from England, and that Julie is only the first of many.'

'But that's complete nonsense.' Polly stared at her, aghast. 'I haven't got any servants in England, for heaven's sake. And Julie's here on a strictly temporary basis. In fact, I'm surprised she hasn't walked out already.'

She shook her head. 'And even if I wanted to make changes— which I don't—Sandro would never allow it. Surely they know that?'

Teresa shrugged. 'They know only that he is a man with a new bride,' she commented drily. 'And that you have powers of persuasion with him that they lack.'

She hesitated. 'Dorotea has been the most deeply hurt. She believes you think her too elderly to have charge of Carlino, and too old-fashioned in her ways, and that is why she will be the first to be replaced.'

'No wonder it's like walking into a brick wall whenever I go near the nursery,' Polly said bitterly. 'Oh, God, how can this have happened?'

Teresa chose her words carefully. 'It is clear to me, Paola, that these rumours have been started by someone with authority, whose word they feel they can trust. I think you have an enemy, *cara*,' she added gently.

Polly had been staring at the floor, but now her head came up sharply. 'Don't tell me,' she said with sudden grimness. 'The *contessa*.'

'It seems so. She has offered to be their champion, and fight their cause with you. No doubt she is already telling them that you are intransigent, and will make no concessions.

'You need to do something, Paola, before they walk out,' she added candidly, 'and Alessandro returns to find his house deserted.'

'Perhaps I'm the one who should leave,' Polly said in a low, unhappy voice. 'I'm clearly out of my depth here. I thought they just despised me because I didn't know how to be a *marchesa*.'

'But you have one great advantage over any lies that Antonia Barsoli tells,' Teresa said quietly. 'You are Alessandro's chosen wife, and they love him.' She smiled encouragingly at Polly. 'Make it clear their jobs are not threatened, and fill that big nursery with more babies for Dorotea to cherish, and they will love you too.'

Easier said than done, Polly thought, forcing a smile of agreement. On both counts.

She was smiling again when she waved them off a few hours later, but she felt bleak as she went slowly back indoors. For a while, she'd been let off the hook, and allowed to put her troubles aside to enjoy their company.

Now her temporary reprieve was over, and her problems were crowding round again. But at least she now knew what she was up against, she thought. And Teresa's advice had been practical as well as bracing, so she had a plan of action too.

It had done her so much good to have them here, and she'd extracted a serious promise from them to come for a proper visit later in the summer. If, of course, she was still here, she amended with a pang.

However, just for a few hours, she hadn't felt quite so isolated, and she missed them all badly now that they'd gone back to Naples.

Nor was she the only one.

Charlie, Julie reported ruefully, had screamed blue murder when he realised the twins were leaving, and had subsequently cried himself to sleep.

'He really needs other children to play with on a regular basis,' she added, with a swift sideways glance at Polly, who flushed, guessing that the other girl was thinking in terms of brothers and sisters for him.

Clearly, because she was part of the opposition, any gossip about the separate rooms had passed her by completely.

Perhaps, as time went on, she would establish some kind of social life, Polly thought, trying to be hopeful, and meet other young mothers whose children could provide Charlie with companionship.

Meanwhile, she would simply have to go on enduring all these none-too-subtle hints, she told herself and sighed.

The next morning dawned overcast and heavy, with even a hint of thunder in the air.

Good day for starting a different kind of storm, perhaps, Polly thought as she drank the tea that Rafaella had brought to her bedroom.

As the girl emerged from the dressing room with the pale blue linen trousers and matching jersey top that she'd been asked to fetch, Polly gave her a quick smile.

'Has your grandfather come back yet from Salerno?' she asked. 'Because I'd still like to talk to him.'

'I have not forgotten, *madame*.' There was a faintly evasive note in Rafaella's voice. 'I will ask again.' She paused. 'Shall I run your bath now?'

'Yes—please.'

Polly took another reflective sip of tea. It sounded as if Giacomo had already been approached and returned a negative response, she thought, troubled. Which seemed to suggest that he might well have something to hide over Sandro's accident.

For good or ill, I need to know, she told herself.

In the mail that was brought to her living room later that morning was a postcard from Cornwall. 'Just like old times,' ran the message. 'Keep well. Be happy.' The handwriting was her father's, but her mother had signed it too, she noticed thankfully.

She took out the notes that she'd made the previous day with Teresa's help, and read them through several times, committing them to memory, before she put them in the empty grate and set fire to them.

Then she rang for Teodoro. 'Will you tell all the staff that I wish to see them in the *salotto* at three o'clock?' she instructed quietly. 'And I mean everyone.'

'Even Dorotea? The little Carlino is upset because he cannot swim today, and she plans to take him out in the car this afternoon.'

'Certainly Dorotea,' Polly said crisply. 'Julie can look after my son.'

'*Sì, Vossignoria.*' He hesitated, studying her with worried eyes. 'Is there some problem?'

She smiled at him. 'Nothing that can't be fixed, I hope. Three p.m., then.'

Teodoro had done his work well, because the *salotto* seemed full of people when Polly entered.

She had decided not to change into more formal clothes, because that might look as if she was trying too hard. Instead, she had simply combed her hair and applied some colour to her lips.

She stood in front of them all, her back to the open door, and spoke slowly using the Italian phrases that Teresa had written down for her. 'I have called you here today to clear up a serious misunderstanding. Some of you may have heard a rumour that I plan to take your jobs from you, and have you dismissed from the *palazzo*. I wish to set your minds at rest, and assure you that there is no truth in this story, and I cannot understand where it has come from, or why it has been spread in this malicious way.'

She heard faint gasps from her audience, but went quietly on. 'I am sorry that none of you felt able to come to me and ask if it was true, but we are to a large extent still strangers to each other. I intend to change that, and take on much of the everyday management of the household myself.'

More gasps, and louder.

'One thing I must make clear at once,' she continued, raising her voice a little above the whispering that had also broken out. 'In the last few weeks, the life of my little boy has changed completely. He has a new environment to learn, and a new language, too.'

She paused. 'Julie, who came with us from England, is not simply a *bambinaia*, but a friend who is helping him come to terms with all these puzzling changes. But it was always the plan of the *marchese* that Dorotea, who cherished him in childhood, should ultimately take full charge of his son in turn. And this is my wish, also.'

She looked directly at Dorotea, who was staring back, her mouth working, and her hands twisting in her white apron.

'My husband, the *marchese*, has a demanding career,' Polly continued. 'And I wish him to have a peaceful and well-run home to return to. I hope we can work together to achieve this, but anyone who cannot accept my regime is, of course, free to leave.'

She smiled around her, keeping it positive. Letting them see she expected their co-operation. 'Although, naturally, I hope you will all stay. And that you will bring any future difficulties straight to me. Because I am the mistress of the house.'

But it appeared she had lost them, because nearly all eyes were looking past her to the door behind.

And then she heard Sandro's voice, cool and slightly mocking. '*Bravo, marchesa.* I am impressed.'

She swung round, her heart thumping, and saw him, leaning against the massive doorframe, watching her steadily with a smile that did not reach his eyes.

CHAPTER ELEVEN

THE almost agonised leap of her heart at the sight of him stilled and died. She checked the impulsive step towards him she'd been about to take, waiting rigidly instead for him to come to her side.

As he did, his cool gaze sweeping the room, his hand lightly clasping her shoulder. 'So,' he said, 'I suggest that anyone wishing to remain in our employ gets back to work—*subito.*'

Polly had never seen a room empty so quickly or silently.

'Teodoro,' Sandro added as the majordomo approached, 'be good enough to bring us coffee—in the *marchesa*'s own living room, I think, if you permit, *cara mia*?'

As if she had any real choice in the matter, thought Polly, finding herself led gently but firmly by the hand to the room in question.

Sandro waved Polly to one of the sofas, and seated himself opposite, long legs stretched out in front of him as he loosened his tie. He looked tired, she thought, and he needed a shave.

She looked down at her clasped hands. 'I wasn't expecting to see you.'

'I did not anticipate returning so soon.'

She cleared her throat. 'Did—did you have a successful trip?'

'So far,' he said. 'Unfortunately, it was curtailed before I reached Rome.'

'Oh.' She felt a stab of fierce pleasure. 'Why was that?'

'Because last night I received a telephone call from Teresa and Ernesto telling me that you had problems here, and might need me.'

She looked at him, stunned. So, they knew where to find you, she thought, biting her lip. And I didn't.

'Therefore, I came to you at once,' he went on. 'Only to find you coping admirably alone.'

She said, 'It's kind of them to be so concerned, but they've already been of great help. They—they shouldn't have dragged

150

you into this. Interrupted your trip.' She shrugged. 'Really, it was all pretty trivial. A storm in a teacup.'

His mouth twisted. 'If it is like the storm outside, Paola *mia*,' he said as a sudden flash of lightning illuminated the room, followed almost at once by a reverberating clap of thunder, 'then it may get worse before it is better.'

He paused. 'So, has your rallying call halted the revolution, *cara*?' he asked softly. 'Or are there still matters to be dealt with?'

She met his gaze with as much composure as she could muster. 'I think it's—settled.'

'Ah,' he said. 'Then Zia Antonia is at this moment packing her bags.'

She swallowed. 'No, of course not. I—I couldn't do that.'

'But you are the mistress here,' he said. 'I heard you say so.'

'Yes.' Her hands tightened on each other almost painfully. 'But perhaps I was presuming too much.'

'Or not enough,' he returned drily. 'While I have been away, I have had time to think, and I realise that the situation here cannot be allowed to continue.'

Before she could even ask what he meant, the door was flung open and the *contessa* came in, all smiles.

'*Caro* Alessandro.' He rose at her entrance, and she reached up to embrace him. 'But what a wonderful surprise for us all. I should have been here to greet you, but I was resting in my room. This weather—so dreadful. I shall be fortunate to avoid a migraine.'

She turned to Polly, a reproving note in her voice. 'But, my dear child, you have ordered no refreshment for your husband on his return. A little remiss of you, if you will forgive me for saying so.'

'I am sure she will do so,' Sandro said quietly. 'And coffee is being brought, so do not concern yourself.'

The *contessa*'s tone became steel covered by honey. 'But I must express my anxieties, my dearest cousin. Your household is in my charge after all, and yet my maid had to inform me of your arrival.' She tutted smilingly. 'She also informs me that our dear Paola summoned all the staff to a meeting a little while ago, to harangue them on the subject of loyalty. If she had issues to raise on that or any other matter, then surely she should have come to me first.'

The smile she bestowed on Polly was pure acid. 'One must make allowances for your inexperience, dear girl. You are not accustomed to dealing with servants, of course. But, in future, there is certainly no need to indulge in such...ludicrous histrionics—or to send for your husband, while he is away on important business, and involve him in a purely domestic matter.

'I hope Alessandro is not too angry with you,' she added on a teasing note that set Polly's teeth on edge.

'I am not angry at all,' Sandro corrected her courteously. 'And nor did Paola send for me. I had other reasons for my return.' He moved across to Polly and put his arm round her, drawing her close to his side.

'I felt, you understand, that I had left my bride alone for too long, and could not bear to spend another night away from her. A very different domestic matter,' he said softly.

Polly looked down at the floor, aware that every drop of blood in her veins had moved to her face and was tingling there.

The *contessa*'s little laugh was husk-dry. 'Why, Alessandro, how marriage has tamed you,' she said. 'You have become quite a romantic, *caro mio*.' She paused theatrically. '*Dio mio*. Tell me that I have not intruded on a private moment.'

Sandro smiled back at her. 'Not,' he said softly, 'while the key for that door remains unaccountably missing. Perhaps you would have the goodness to search for it again.'

Just open, Polly told the floor silently. Just open and swallow me—please.

'In fact,' Sandro went on remorselessly, 'you may bring my wife all the keys. She can hardly embark upon her new duties without them.'

The delicate blusher that the *contessa* wore was suddenly like a stain on her white face. Her drawn breath was a hiss.

'You intend *her* to manage the *palazzo*. A girl from nowhere, without family or position? A girl for whom you sacrificed my Bianca, and broke your father's heart? And whose only accomplishment has been to bear your bastard?'

Her strident laugh broke in the middle. 'Are you insane? You see for yourself that she cannot handle your servants. And who will ever accept her?'

'I have,' Sandro said with deadly quietness. 'Nothing else is necessary.' He paused. 'Ever since Paola came here you have attempted to undermine her, but each time she has proved to be more than your equal. Today was one such moment. Nor will I allow her to endure your insults any longer.'

He looked at the older woman, his mouth hard and set. 'My father offered you a home, and I acceded to his wishes and permitted you to remain, setting convenience against my better judgement. But my tolerance is now exhausted.'

'No,' she said hoarsely. 'No, Alessandro. You cannot do this.'

He went on as if she had not spoken. 'Out of respect for my father, I shall provide you with a house. I shall also consult with my lawyer on a suitable supplement to your income. But you must and will leave Comadora.'

'But I helped you find her.' Her fingers were twisting together like claws. 'I searched for this—*sciattona* in England because you still wanted her.'

'No, *contessa*,' Sandro said softly, 'you discovered somehow that I wished to find her, and told Emilio. What did you do, I wonder? Listen at a door? Read my correspondence?' He shook his head. 'It would not be the first time.

'And Emilio sent you to England on his own behalf, hoping to buy lurid details of my affair with Paola, and discredit me at last.' He shrugged. 'But, unluckily for both of you, I guessed what you were doing, and found her first. So you had to pretend you had been working for me all the time.'

His mouth twisted. 'How galling that must have been. How much had Emilio offered for your services?'

Her thin body was as taut as a wire. 'I would have done it for nothing,' she spat back. 'How could I have known you would forget everything that was due to your name, and marry your discarded whore?'

There was a terrible silence. Polly turned away, feeling sick, her hands pressed to her burning face. Sandro walked to the fireplace and reached for the bell rope, but as he did so there was a knock on the door, and Teodoro came in with the tray of coffee.

He checked instinctively, his glance darting from one to another, but Sandro beckoned him forward. 'Please escort the *contessa* to her room,' he said. 'She is unwell. Call her doctor, and tell her maid to stay with her.'

Teodoro set the tray on a side-table, and offered the *contessa* a deferential arm which she ignored, walking slowly and stiffly to the door. Where she turned.

'You will be sorry for this.' Her tone sounded almost conversational. 'In the past I have argued against Emilio's wish to have the inquiry into Bianca's death reopened. But no longer. This time, *marchese*, you will appear and answer for what you did. And your loyal accomplice, Giacomo Raboni, will be made to tell all he knows—in public. Emilio will see to that.'

Another lightning flash lit up the room. In its momentary glare, Sandro's face looked carved from granite, the scar livid against his cheek.

He said, 'If he hopes to buy Giacomo, he is wasting his time.'

The *contessa* shrugged. 'Everyone has their price, my dear cousin,' she said softly. She sent Polly a malevolent glance. 'Including, if you remember, the little gold-digger you call your wife. Where will she be, I wonder, when you come out of jail?'

Teodoro, his face rigid with shock, seemed to grow another six inches in height. He took the *contessa*'s arm without gentleness and hustled her from the room.

The thunder roared again, and rain began to fall, huge, heavy drops beating a tattoo on the terrace, and hurling themselves in gusts against the window.

Polly sank down on one of the sofas, because her legs would no longer support her. Resting her elbows on her knees, she buried her face in her hands and waited for the shaking to stop.

Eventually she became aware that Sandro had come to sit beside her, and she raised her head and looked at him.

She said in a small, quiet voice, 'That was so—terrible.'

'I am sorry, Paola.' He spoke gently. 'You should not have had to endure that. I did not realise she was so near the edge.' His hand covered hers and she realised he was trembling a little too.

She said on a rush, 'I—I should go up to the nursery. Charlie may be frightened of the storm.'

'In a moment,' he said. 'But stay with me now. We need to talk.'

'Yes.' She ran the tip of her tongue round her dry mouth. 'I— I suppose we must.' She paused. 'I always knew the *contessa* didn't like me,' she said slowly. 'But—it was more than that. It was hatred. Not just for me—but also for you.'

His mouth tightened. 'Until now, I only saw the bitterness, and thought I understood. When she came here twenty years ago, I think she believed that my father would eventually offer her marriage. Only he had no such intention. His relationship with my mother had brought happiness to neither, and, after her death, he was content with an occasional discreet liaison.

'When Antonia saw she had nothing to hope for from him, she diverted all that fierce energy into preparing Bianca as a bride for me. Perhaps she felt her own thwarted dreams would be fulfilled by the next generation. But it was not the usual matchmaking that older women sometimes indulge in. Even as young as I was, and as careless, I sensed there was something wrong. Something obsessive—and dark. Just as I felt...' He paused. 'Well, that is not important. Let me say that I began to spend as little time as possible at Comadora.'

'But why did your father go along with her scheme if he saw how you felt?'

Sandro hesitated. 'He saw marriage as a business arrangement, not a matter of emotion,' he told her slowly. 'Also I believe he felt guilty, so his encouragement was a form of recompense to Antonia for having disappointed her so deeply himself.'

Polly thought of the portrait of the late *marchese* which hung at the top of the stairs, remembering the harsh lines of the dark face beneath the grizzled hair, the thin mouth and piercing eyes that she felt followed her as she passed. Not a man, she thought, who looked as if he ever suffered from remorse, and she repressed a shiver.

'When the accident happened to Bianca, the *contessa* must have felt as if she'd died herself,' she said quietly. 'Perhaps we shouldn't blame her too harshly. Especially...' She stopped hurriedly, aware that she'd been about to say *when there are so many questions over what really happened.*

'Especially?' Sandro had noticed her hesitation.

She said, 'Especially when you have lost someone that you love so much.' She remembered the weeks after her return to England. The greyness of her life as one bleak day followed another. The nights she'd spent in bitter weeping, her eyes and throat raw with grief and bewilderment. Her stunned sense of isolation, caught as she was between her mother's anger and her father's disappointment.

'She'll feel as if she's in an abyss,' she went on, half to herself. 'With no way out, and no one to turn to. Facing an eternity of emptiness.'

Her own turning point had come when she'd felt the first faint flutter of her baby moving inside her, she realised. And from somewhere she'd found the strength to reclaim her life and sanity.

If there hadn't been Charlie, she thought, I could have ended up like the *contessa*, corroded with anger and bitterness.

He said with faint grimness, 'Almost you persuade me, *cara*, but not quite. She cannot remain here.'

'But you can't make her go,' Polly said passionately. 'Can't you see she means what she says? She and Emilio will rake up everything that happened three years ago and use it against you. You know that they will.'

He was very still suddenly. And when he moved, it was to release her hand.

He said quietly, almost conversationally, 'You speak, *cara*, as if I had something to fear. Is that what you think?'

'How do I know what to think?' The loss of the gentle clasp of his fingers round hers made her feel suddenly bereft. 'All I hear is that the inquiry wasn't told everything. That Rafaella's grandfather, who found you, is sworn to secrecy. My God, you've just admitted as much.' She swallowed. 'So I have to believe you have something to hide—and that the *contessa* and your vile cousin will move heaven and earth to uncover it. And once these things start, who knows where they can lead?'

'Clearly you imagine they could lead to prison,' Sandro drawled. 'Unless I decide instead to submit to blackmail. Neither option has much appeal, *bella mia*. And I would not be much of a man if I were to choose either of them without a fight.

'But then you do not have a very high opinion of me, anyway,' he added with a shrug. 'Is that why you have been trying to persuade Giacomo to meet you through Rafaella? And why you have had no success?

'Unfortunately for you, whenever an attempt is made to contact him, he immediately informs my lawyers, and they tell me. And that, my loving wife, is one of the other reasons I decided to make an early return, to suggest that you waste no more time on these fruitless enquiries.

'But then, what does it really matter?' He got to his feet, stretching lithely. 'Except that I am once again the villain,' he added mockingly. 'But that is something I shall have to live with.'

He paused. 'And now I am going to shower and change,' he

went on. 'Under the circumstances, I shall dine in the town tonight. I would not wish to spoil your appetite by forcing you to eat with a murderer.'

'I never said that,' Polly protested. 'I never would.'

His smile was grim. 'But I swear it must have crossed your mind, *mi adorata*. And the knowledge of that might turn my stomach too.'

As he strode to the door, she said huskily, 'Sandro—please. I just need to know the truth.'

'Truth,' he echoed contemptuously. 'It is just a word, Paola, like so many others. Like love, for example, and loyalty. Like honour and faith. Just words to be used and forgotten, as we will eventually forget today ever existed.' He inclined his head curtly, and was gone.

Polly sat staring at the closed door. She knew she should go after him, pour out all her doubts and fears—all her confused emotions. Make him listen. Make him, somehow, understand.

He had clearly expected her to trust him without question, but how was that possible when she was still dealing with the nightmare of the past, and his betrayal?

We both loved him, she thought wretchedly. Both Bianca, and myself. And he wanted neither of us. The only difference is that I survived, and she didn't. The margin is that small.

And I still love him, no matter what he does, or what he is. And I know now that beyond logic, beyond reason, I always shall, because I can't help myself. He's part of me—my flesh, my blood, the pulse of my heart. Because, in spite of everything, I only feel safe with his arms around me.

And, like the *contessa*, that's a tragedy I have somehow to endure.

She gave a long, shaking sigh. The abyss was back, it seemed, and deeper than ever. And with as little hope for escape.

After a while she got up wearily, and went to the table where the forgotten coffee waited. It was still hot, and it provided her momentarily with the jolt she needed.

She and Sandro might be a million miles apart, but upstairs was a child who might need her.

When she reached the nursery she paused, taking a deep breath before she went in. If she walked into the usual wall of resentment, she wasn't sure she could bear it.

Dorotea was there, seated in one of the big rocking chairs that flanked the hearth, knitting busily, while opposite her sat Julie with Charlie on her lap, fast asleep.

The older woman looked up at Polly hovering in the doorway, and her plump face creased into an equally hesitant smile.

She got to her feet, indicating respectfully that Polly should take her seat, then signalled to Julie to transfer the little boy to his mother's arms.

This safely achieved, Dorotea stood for a moment, and patted Polly awkwardly on the shoulder as Charlie murmured drowsily and pushed his small round head against the familiar curve of her breast. *'Bene,'* she said. 'Is good now, *vossignoria, sì?'*

'Sì,' Polly agreed, her throat tightening. 'This—is good.'

Dorotea beckoned to Julie, and they both disappeared into the night nursery, leaving Polly alone with her child. Leaning back, eyes half closed, she listened to the storm retreating over the hills. Just the act of holding Charlie quietly seemed to offer a kind of peace amid the turmoil of emotions that assailed her.

Whatever Sandro might feel about her, she told herself, whatever darkness there might be inside him, his love for Charlie was unqualified and beyond doubt, and she could cling to that. Because even if her husband never smiled at her again—never touched her—their son remained an indissoluble link between them.

She was suddenly aware she was no longer alone, and, glancing round, saw Sandro standing in the doorway, watching her, his mouth hard, the dark brows drawn together.

She wanted to speak, but what could she say? Tell him that as long as they were together, nothing else mattered? But they were not together, and how could they ever be, when there was so much to divide them?

Unless you came to me now, she thought, her heart in her eyes as she looked back at him. Unless you held us—your wife, and your child. And if you would promise to try and love me a little as you love him. Then I wouldn't care about anything else.

Surely—*surely* he could feel the yearning in her, the unassuaged and aching need, and show her a little mercy—couldn't he?

But just as her lips pleadingly framed his name, he turned away and left as silently as he'd appeared.

And Polly sat where she was, forcing back the tears that were bitter in her throat, because she could not allow Charlie to wake and find her crying.

She spent a restless, unhappy night, and woke late the following morning, to the sunlight and an incongruously flawless sky.

'*Buongiorno, madame.*' Rafaella appeared with coffee as if on signal. 'It is so beautiful today with no storm.' She beamed at Polly. 'The *marchese* asks if you will honour him by joining him at breakfast. And wishes you to know that Signor Molena will be there also.'

'Molena?' Polly queried, feeling the name should mean something.

'His *signore*'s *avoccato*,' Rafaella explained.

'Oh,' Polly said in a hollow voice, recalling that terrible afternoon at her mother's house. 'The lawyer. I—I remember.'

'*Sì*, the lawyer.' Rafaella said the word with care, and smiled again. 'Today, *vossignoria* is to meet with my grandfather,' she added with real excitement. 'His excellency has said so.'

Polly stared at her. 'Your grandfather?' she said slowly. 'Are you serious?'

'*Certamente, madame.*' The girl paused. 'Also the *contessa* goes with you,' she added more hesitantly.

'I see.' Polly digested that apprehensively, not understanding at all. 'Is she—well enough?'

She had questioned Teodoro haltingly about the *contessa*'s condition the previous evening, and been told that the doctor had paid her a lengthy visit, and administered a sedative. Also that a nurse would be coming to spend the night, and that a transfer to a private clinic the next day was also being considered.

Polly, wincing inwardly, had given him a quiet word of thanks.

But if the *contessa* was well enough to go out, maybe a less rigorous solution would be found, she thought.

She popped into the nursery on her way downstairs to kiss Charlie good morning, and wished she could have lingered there forever.

When she finally reached the door of the *sala da pranzo*, she had to force herself to open the door and go in.

'Good morning, *cara*,' Sandro rose politely. 'You remember Alberto, of course.'

'It is a pleasure to see you again, *marchesa*.' Signor Molena bowed politely, and she murmured something in reply.

Why was he there? she wondered as she helped herself to a slice of cold ham she would never eat, and poured some coffee. Had he been summoned to tell her that her brief, ill-starred marriage was over?

She sat pushing the meat round her plate, while the two men talked quietly, their faces slightly troubled.

But the coffee put heart into her, and when Sandro said abruptly, 'If you have finished breakfast, Paola, we will go,' she was able to rise to her feet with a semblance of composure.

There were two cars parked in front of the house, and Polly saw that the *contessa* was being helped into the second of them by a brisk-looking woman in a white uniform.

The older woman looked bent and ill, and for an instant Polly quailed. Then she felt her arm taken firmly, and Sandro was guiding her towards the leading car.

She hung back, looking up into his face, searching in vain for some sign of softening.

'Sandro,' she whispered. 'Please—we don't have to do this.'

'Yes,' he said quietly, 'we do, *cara mia*.'

'But it's none of my business—I see that now. And I'm sorry— so sorry to have interfered.'

'It is too late to draw back,' he told her harshly. 'Only the truth will do for my cousin, and for you, it seems. This is what you wanted, and this is what you will get. So, *andiamo*. Let's go.'

She sat rigidly beside him in the back of the car, her hands clenched together, as Signor Molena took his place beside the chauffeur, and the cars began to move forward.

And above the whisper of tyres on gravel, she could hear a small voice in her head repeating 'Too late' over and over again, and she was afraid.

CHAPTER TWELVE

THE dusty road in front of them climbed steeply and endlessly. They had passed through several tiny villages where the main streets were passable by only one vehicle at a time, but all signs of habitation were now behind them.

Polly had gone down to the town and visited the marina several times, but this was the first time she had been driven up into the mountains behind Comadora, and she was too tense to take real stock of her surroundings.

After the rain, the air was clear, and the creamy stone of the jagged crags, heavily veined in shades of grey and green, seemed close enough to touch. It was a landscape of scrub and thorn, stabbed in places with the darkness of cedars. Above it a solitary bird wheeled, watchful and predatory.

She found she was shivering slightly, and broke the silence. 'Is this the road to Sorrento?'

'One of them.' He did not look at her, and she could see his hand was clenched on his thigh.

I've made him do this, she thought bleakly. Made him confront whatever demons are waiting in this desolate place, and he'll never forgive me.

They had been travelling for about ten more minutes when the chauffeur began to slow down. The car rounded a sharp bend, and Polly gasped soundlessly as she saw that immediately beyond it the ground fell away, and she was looking down into a deep gorge with a glimmer of water far below.

They pulled over to the rough verge on the opposite side of the narrow road, and stopped.

Sandro turned to Polly, his face expressionless. 'Come,' he said, 'if you wish to see.'

After the fuss she'd made, she thought wretchedly, she could hardly tell him it was the last thing she wanted, so she followed him out into the sunlight. In spite of the heat, she felt cold.

Sandro's face was rigid, the slash of the scar prominent against

161

his dark skin. Alberto Molena came to his side, talking softly, encouragingly, and eventually he nodded curtly and they crossed the road together, and stood looking down into the depths below.

She did not go with them. Her eyes had detected a flash further along the road, as if the sunlight was being reflected back from glass. She could see a smudge of colour too, and guessed this was the shrine that Sandro had mentioned.

There was nothing unique about it. Polly knew that they were seen all over the Mediterranean where bad accidents had occurred. But none of the others had carried any meaning for her.

Slowly, almost reluctantly, she went to face one of her own demons. Bianca had indeed been a beautiful girl, her face heart-shaped, and her eyes dark and dreaming. The only jarring note was struck by a set, almost hard look about the mouth, but Polly supposed she could not be blamed for that.

Knowing the man you love feels nothing for you in return can do that to you, she thought sadly.

Also in the elaborate frame was a small plaster figure of a saint, with an unlit votive light in front of it, and a vase of slightly wilted flowers.

She heard a step, and, glancing round, saw the *contessa* approaching, leaning heavily on a cane.

'Get away from here.' The older woman's voice was harsh, almost metallic. 'You are not fit to breathe the same air that she did.'

She turned and stared malevolently at Sandro, standing motionless on the edge of the drop, only yards away. Polly's heart missed a beat, and she was just about to cry a warning when they were joined by the nurse, who took the *contessa*'s arm gently but firmly, murmuring to her in a soothing tone.

Polly crossed the road and stood at Sandro's side. She said in a low voice, 'Coming here may have been a bad idea. I think your cousin's getting agitated.'

'She has been here many times before,' he said stonily. 'Unlike myself.'

She looked at him, shocked. 'Is this the first time—since the crash?'

'The first, and I hope the only time. We came here solely to meet Giacomo Raboni, so that you could see what happened at this place through his eyes.' Sandro paused. 'He speaks little

English, but Alberto will translate for you—if you can trust his accuracy,' he added with a touch of bitterness.

'Yes,' she said, 'of course I can.'

She looked down. Just below the edge, the ground, littered with rocks and boulders of all sizes, sloped steeply away for about a hundred yards before reaching a kind of rim, beyond which it disappeared into infinity.

The kind of drop, she thought, that nightmares were made of, and shuddered.

She said, 'Will Signor Raboni be long? I'd like to get away from here.'

'It has always been a bad place,' Sandro told her quietly. 'But it is part of the truth which is so important to you.' He paused. 'And you will not be detained here much longer. Giacomo is coming now.'

She heard a rattle of stones behind her and turned. A man was coming down the hill, half walking, half sliding, an elderly dog scrabbling beside him.

Giacomo Raboni was of medium height, and stout, wearing ancient flannel trousers, a collarless shirt and a cap pulled on over curling white hair. He had a mouth that looked as if it preferred to smile. But for now, his expression was faintly grim.

He gave the *contessa* a measuring look, then turned his head and spat with great accuracy, just missing the dog. Then he turned shrewd dark eyes on Polly, telling her without words that she wasn't the subject of his whole-hearted approbation either.

He took Sandro's offered hand and shook it warmly. He said gruffly, 'You should not be here, *excellenza*. Why not let the dead girl sleep?'

Sandro's voice was harsh. 'Because, my old friend, she still poisons my life as she did when she was alive.' He paused. 'You agreed to keep silent to protect the living, and spare them more grief. But my father can no longer be hurt by what you saw, and the Contessa Barsoli has tried to use your silence to damage me, and my marriage, so she is no longer worthy of my consideration.'

He threw back his head. 'But my wife is a different matter, so it is time to speak, if you please, and tell her what happened here. And slowly, so that Signor Molena can tell her what is said.'

Giacomo Raboni gave a reluctant nod. He said, 'I had been on the hill that day, looking at my goats. A neighbour had told me that two of them seemed sick. As I came down the track, I heard the sound of a car. As it came round the corner, I recognised it as the car which belonged to the Signore Alessandro. But it was being driven strangely, swerving from side to side, and I could see why. There was a passenger beside him—a girl, but not in the passenger seat, you understand. She was leaning towards him—clinging to him, it seemed.'

He stared at the brink, frowning. 'At first I thought it was love play between them, and that they were fools, bringing their games to such a dangerous road. Then I realised that the *marchese* was not embracing her, but struggling, trying to push her away, and control the car too.'

He turned his head and looked steadily at Polly. 'At that moment, *vossignoria*, I knew that your husband was fighting for his life. Because she was not reaching for him, but trying to grab the wheel. I think, also, she went for his eyes, because he flung up an arm to defend himself, and in that instant she turned the car towards the edge of the cliff.'

'Oh, God,' Polly said numbly. 'Oh, no.'

'As it went over, I heard her scream something. Then there was the sound of the crash, and I ran.

'I saw that the car had hit a rock, but glanced off it and continued down. It had reached the brink, but there it ran into a dead tree so it could go no further.

'But the *marchese* had somehow been thrown clear. I climbed down to him and realised he was badly injured. There was much blood and his pulse was weak.'

He paused. 'I realised too that the girl was still in the vehicle, and that the engine was running. The tree was a spindly thing, old and brittle, with shallow roots. It could not hold the car for much longer, so the *signorina* was inches from death.

'I went down to her, careful not to fall myself. The driver's door was open, and she was lying across the seat. She too was terribly injured, but I reached in to her, tried to take her hands to pull her free before the tree gave way.

'I spoke to her—called her Signorina Bianca, but she seemed barely conscious, and it was plain she did not know who I was. In her pain, she looked at me with eyes that saw nothing, and whispered something.

'She thought she was speaking to the *marchese*—that he was

with her still, and she repeated the same words she had used before.'

His own voice was hushed with the horror of it. 'She said, "If I cannot have you then no one will." And with her last movement, she put her foot on the accelerator and sent the car over the edge.'

Polly stood rigidly, her hands pressed to her mouth. Then the *contessa*'s hoarse voice broke the silence. 'You're lying,' she accused, her face twisted. 'The *marchese* has paid you to say these terrible things.'

He drew himself up with immense dignity. 'The *marchese* has paid me with nothing but his regard. All this I would have said at the inquiry, but he knew the distress it would give his father, who loved the Signorina Bianca and was already a sick man. For his sake and no other, we allowed it to become an accident. And, for the honour of the Valessi, I have kept my silence until now.'

His voice became deeper, more resonant. 'But I, Giacomo Raboni, I tell you that the Signorina Bianca tried to murder the Signore Alessandro. And I saw it all.'

There was a terrible keening noise from the *contessa*, who had sunk to her knees in the dust.

'No,' she was moaning. 'It cannot be true. Not my angel—my beautiful dove. She never harmed anyone—or anything in her life.'

'No,' Sandro said, harshly. 'That is the real lie. There were stories about her—rumours of cruelty from the moment she came to Comadora. A dog that belonged to one of the grooms tied up in the sun and left to die without water or food because it left paw-marks on her skirt. The pony my father bought for her which threw her, and mysteriously broke its leg in its stall soon after.

'And the convent school she attended. Did you know that the superior asked my father to remove her? Or how much he had to give to the chapel-restoration fund for her to be permitted to remain? He insisted of course that the nuns were mistaken.'

He shook his head. 'All I knew was that she'd repelled me from the first. And nothing my father could have said or done would have persuaded me to make her my wife.'

The *contessa* was weeping noisily. 'It cannot be true. She would never have harmed you. In spite of your cruelty and indifference, she loved you. You know that.'

He said grimly, 'I knew that she was obsessed by me. And that she was determined to become the Marchesa Valessi. Between you, you forced me away from my family home, and drove a wedge between my father and myself. Unforgivable things were done at your instigation.'

'No,' she moaned. 'No, Alessandro.'

Polly said softly, 'Sandro—she's in real pain. No more, please.'

He looked at her sombrely, then went reluctantly to the *contessa*, and lifted her to her feet. He said more gently, 'Just the same, I would have spared you this knowledge, as I did my father, if you had not started your insidious campaign against my wife— the whispers at the party you organised with such kindness, the rumours among the staff, all stemming from you.

'But Paola emerged triumphantly from each trap you set for her. How that must have galled you. But it is all over now. There are no more secrets, unless you choose to keep from Emilio what you have heard today. Can you imagine what a feast he would make of it—what the headlines would say about your beloved Bianca?'

A shudder went through her. She looked up at him, her face suddenly a hundred years old. 'I shall say nothing,' she told him dully. 'All I can ask, Alessandro, is a little kindness.'

'There is the house on Capri,' he said. 'You have always liked it there. Alberto will examine your financial circumstances and make suitable arrangements for your comfort. Now he will escort you back to Comadora.'

She nodded with difficulty, then took his hand and kissed it.

Polly watched Signor Molena offer his arm, and lead her back to the car. Saw it turn carefully, then go back towards Comadora.

Leaving her, she thought, to travel alone with Sandro. She stole a glance at him, and saw that he was staring down at the crash site again, his eyes hooded, his face like a mask.

He said quietly, 'There is nothing there. No sign that anything ever happened.'

Only that scar, she thought. The one you will carry forever.

She wanted to go to him. To take his face in her hands, and kiss the harshness from his mouth. To offer him the healing warmth of her body.

But she didn't dare.

I made him face this, she thought. I made him remember the unthinkable—the grotesque. The fear and the pain. And how can he ever forgive that? How can he ever forgive me?

She swallowed. 'Sandro—shall we go home?'

'Home?' he queried ironically. 'You mean that huge empty house I visit sometimes, that stopped being home after the death of my mother?'

'But it could be again,' she said. 'It has to be—for Charlie.'

His sigh was small and bitter. 'Yes,' he said. 'At least I have my son.'

He walked away to where Giacomo Raboni waited. They spoke quietly for a moment or two, then embraced swiftly, and the old man, whistling to his dog, went back the way he had come.

On the journey home they sat, each in their separate corners, the silence between them total.

At last Polly could bear it no longer. She said, 'Is the chauffeur's glass partition soundproof?'

'Yes,' he said. 'Completely.'

She hesitated. 'Then may—may I ask you something?'

'If you wish.' His tone was not encouraging.

'What was Bianca doing in your car that day?'

'You imagine I invited her for a drive?' he asked bleakly. 'I had just had a bad interview with my father—one of the worst. He had done something I could not forgive, and I needed quickly to put it right. Bianca must have been listening at the door as she often did, because when I went out to the car she was there in the passenger seat, waiting for me.

'I told her to get out—that I had no time for her little power games—but she refused. I had no time to argue, and to put her bodily out of the car would have been distasteful, so I had to let her stay. Although I warned her that I was not returning, and she would have to make her own way back to Comadora alone.

'She began bragging to me almost at once about her power over my father. Said that I could run away, but in the end he would make me marry her or strip me of my inheritance. Leave me with an empty title. Then she became amorous—said she would give me pleasure in ways I had never had before. She even described some of them,' he added, his mouth curling in contempt.

'I was fool enough to let her see my disgust, and she began to get angry in a way I had never seen before. She began to talk about you—said filthy, obscene things, becoming more and more hysterical. Finally she was screaming at me that I belonged to her. That she would kill both of us rather than lose me to another girl. That was when she began trying to seize the wheel.

'Even then I did not realise she was serious, may God forgive me. I thought she was just being—Bianca. The one that only I seemed to see.'

He shook his head. 'I was shouting back at her—telling her I was going to throw her out of the car if she didn't stop.' His mouth tightened. 'That was when she attacked me with her nails, as Giacomo said. And the rest you know.'

Polly said in a small voice, 'Do you think she was mad?'

He shrugged. 'I have asked myself that a thousand times. If so, she hid it well with everyone but me.'

'Yes.' Polly swallowed. She said with a touch of desperation, 'Sandro, I'm so sorry—for everything.'

'There is no need,' he said. 'The *contessa* had nursed her delusions for too long, and it was time the truth was told. So do not blame yourself.'

He sounded kind but remote, and her heart sank.

But she mustered a smile. 'Thank you. That's generous.'

'Is it?' he asked, an odd note in his voice. 'But then, Paola, you ask for so little.'

And there was silence again.

Back at the *palazzo*, there was an air of shock that evening. The *contessa* had gone by private ambulance for a few days' rest at a clinic, and it was apparent that she would not be returning.

Alberto Molena stayed for dinner, and, although conversation was general over the meal, it was clear there were pressing matters to be discussed. So Polly was not surprised when courteous excuses were made over coffee, and the two men retired to Sandro's study, and remained closeted there.

Polly listened to music for a while in an effort to calm herself, then went upstairs to her room and sat by the window. She had plenty to think about. Questions that still remained unanswered, but which could be more complex than she'd believed.

Sandro had been on his way back to Sorrento when the accident had happened, she thought. And he'd spoken of some 'unforgivable' action of his father. What had the old *marchese* done to prompt such a reaction? she asked herself.

And why was Sandro coming to her, if he intended to end their affair? It made no sense. Especially as Bianca was clearly convinced that their relationship was still a threat to her, and Sandro had not denied it during their fatal quarrel.

The man who had visited her, scaring her with his oblique threats and offering her money to leave—who had sent him? Was it really Sandro, as she'd always believed? For the past three years, she'd looked on it as the agonising proof of his cruel betrayal. Now, suddenly, that certainty was shaken to its foundations.

I have to know, she thought. I have to put the last missing pieces in place—even if I don't get the answers I want, and all my worst fears are confirmed. But I can't just barge in, asking questions.

Somehow, she knew, she had to bridge the distance between them. And there was one sure way to do that, she thought, warm colour rising to her face.

How did they manage these things in the old days? she wondered, sending the huge bed a speculative look. Did the then *marchese* announce over dinner that he would be visiting his wife later? Or did the *marchesa* send a note to her husband, requesting the pleasure of his company in bed? Or was there simply a look— a smile—any of the covert signals that lovers had always used?

Whatever, she didn't think any of that would work in her own situation. Maybe the direct approach would be best.

She went into the dressing room, and retrieved the black lace nightgown from her jacket pocket, before taking a long scented bath.

A shadow over moonlight, he'd once called it, she thought, looking at herself in the mirror, and the most blatant evidence of her wishes that she could ask for.

She put on a satin robe in case she encountered a lurking servant, and made her way, barefoot, to his room.

She drew a deep, steadying breath, then knocked swiftly and went in. Sandro was there. He was in bed. And he was alone.

In fact he was propped up by pillows, frowning over a sheaf of papers he was reading. He glanced up at her entrance, his expression changing to total astonishment.

'Paola? What is it? Is there something wrong?'

She'd planned what to say, but the words were sliding round in her brain. 'It's Charlie,' she blurted out at last.

He sat up. 'Is he ill?' he demanded, his voice sharpening in alarm.

'No,' she said. 'As far as I know, he's fast asleep. But he's lonely. He was so happy when the twins were here, and he really needs children near his own age around him.'

She swallowed, her fingers nervously playing with the sash of her robe. She said, 'You said I never asked for anything. So—I was thinking—maybe he should have brothers and sisters.'

She stole a glance at him under her lashes, hoping for some reaction, but she was disappointed. Sandro's face was expressionless.

'Indeed?' he said politely, after a pause. 'So what do you suggest—adoption, or some scientific trick in a laboratory?'

She hadn't expected that either. 'No, of course not.' She made a small helpless gesture. 'I thought that you—that I...'

She ran out of words, so she slipped off the robe and let it drop to the floor, allowing him to assimilate the full effect of the cobweb of lace that was the only covering for her nakedness.

He looked at her very slowly, his hooded gaze travelling over her from head to foot.

He said quietly, 'Are you really so desperate for another child? Then take that thing off and come here.'

She'd thought he would get out of bed, and come to her. That he'd tear the gown from her with his own hands as he'd once suggested.

But she obeyed him, quickly, almost nervously sliding under the sheet he'd turned back for her. Knowing with a kind of sick certainty that this was not going according to any plan of hers.

He pushed the papers to the floor and turned to her, the topaz eyes sombre as he looked down at her.

Once he kisses me, she thought desperately, it will be all right. I can make it all right...

But Sandro did not kiss her. His hands slid down her body in an almost perfunctory caress, then moved under her flanks, lifting her towards him. She was already aroused, wildly receptive to even the prospect of his possession, so there was no physical barrier to his invasion of her body, which was wordless, clinical and immediate.

And as she lay beneath him, stunned, it was apparent that it was also going to be over very quickly. He cried out once, harshly, and she felt the scalding heat of his climax. Then he rolled away from her and lay, his chest heaving as he recovered his breath, one arm across his eyes.

When he spoke his voice was muffled. 'I hope I have performed my duties as stud satisfactorily, *marchesa*. I trust, also, that your wish for conception will be granted, as I would not wish to undergo this experience a second time.'

'Is that—that all you have to say to me?' The husky words were forced from her dry throat. Her bewildered, unsatisfied body was aching for the fulfillment he had never before denied her. Burning for him to *love* her.

'No,' he said, '*cara mia*.' He made the endearment sound like an insult. 'I could think of much more, but you would not wish to hear it, believe me. And now perhaps you will leave me to sleep.'

She was dying inside, but somehow she managed to reach her robe, and huddle it round her before she fled.

Too late, she thought, her heart thudding, as she almost fell into her own room and slammed the door shut behind her. He had told her it was too late as they left the house that morning. But she hadn't understood. Or had she just been deliberately blind and deaf?

Now comprehension had finally dawned, and with it a heartbreak that threatened to destroy her utterly. And she pressed herself against the unyielding hardness of the heavy door, and let the fierce agony of tears have their way with her.

CHAPTER THIRTEEN

POLLY got into the rear of the limousine, placing the bouquet of flowers she'd been given on the seat beside her, then leaned forward to wave a smiling farewell to the women who'd thronged out of the restaurant to see her depart.

As the car threaded its way through the narrow streets crowded with tourists, she leaned back and closed her eyes, kicking off her high-heeled sandals and wriggling her toes, the nails enamelled in an elegant pale pink to match her fingers.

Teresa had advised her well, she thought, looking down at the deep blue of her silk suit. Whatever else might be wrong with her life, at least she dressed well.

Today she had been the guest of honour at a charity luncheon in aid of a local children's home, and she'd made a small speech at the end of it in her increasingly fluent Italian, and been warmly applauded.

She took lessons several times a week with a retired schoolmaster, who lived with his plump, cheerful wife in a small white-painted villa on the edge of town. Usually they sat under an awning on the patio, and when work was finished the *signora* would serve coffee with tiny almond *biscotti*, often accompanied by a glass of her home-made *limoncello*.

The first time it had been offered, Polly had felt wrenched in half, remembering with vivid poignancy how Sandro had once teased her about making the delicious citrus liqueur for him. But she had smiled gallantly, and praised it extravagantly, to the delight of her hostess.

But then smiling radiantly, and behaving with grace and modesty, were all part of the public persona she was establishing. A façade behind which she could hide the lonely, heartsick girl that she was in reality.

It was almost three weeks since her humiliated flight from Sandro's bedroom. And it had taken every ounce of courage she

172

possessed to face him the next day, instead of staying in her room, pleading a headache.

And when they had finally met, she was able, somehow, to match his cool politeness with her own. She had even found herself painfully wondering what had happened to the nightgown she'd left on the floor, but she did not mention the subject.

Which was how it still was, she thought, her mouth twisting. Nothing was ever mentioned. She and Sandro were like satellites, pursuing their separate orbits round the small, beloved moon that was Charlie.

By mutual, if tacit, consent, they were never alone together. She went down to the swimming pool with their son only in the mornings, when she knew Sandro would be working in his study, or out. And she was thankful that he respected her privacy. The thought of being caught by him in a bikini, or any other form of undress, made her shrivel inside.

And in the afternoons, after siesta, she remained in the shade of the terrace so that he could have Charlie to himself.

The little boy could swim like a fish now, and he was also learning, under his father's supervision, to ride the pony that was kept at one of the farms.

Although Sandro was not always at Comadora. She was kept abreast of his schedule by Signora Corboni, who was not nearly as dour as she looked, and who presented her with a printed list of his engagements each week, including the occasions when he would be away from the *palazzo*. Polly knew this was only so that she could make the appropriate domestic arrangements, and not because Sandro wished her to keep track of him. And she could not help noticing painfully that two of these absences had been spent in Rome.

But with each day that passed, she found she was learning more and more about her new life, and becoming absorbed into the established routine at the *palazzo*.

For instance, she had soon discovered that Sandro had far more than a hotel chain and the family's banking and corporate interests to occupy him. The Valessi estate owned acres of olive and citrus orchards, together with vineyards, and even a small quarry. In addition, the farms produced enough fruit and vegetables to supply most of the local tourist facilities.

When Sandro was at home, many of the lunches at the *palazzo* were working affairs, where she was expected to act as hostess, and, although she did not understand all that was being discussed, she picked up enough to take an intelligent interest. And invariably she was rewarded by a brief, formal word of thanks from Sandro as their guests departed.

She knew that was probably just for the sake of appearances, but it was a crumb of comfort to be cherished, all the same.

On the downside, there'd been a few moments of nightmare embarrassment the previous week when she'd felt obliged to seek him out and tell him that there would be no baby after all.

Sandro had been at his desk, making notes in the margin of some report, and his pen had stilled momentarily. Then he'd said with remote courtesy, 'My regrets for your disappointment,' and returned to his report.

And she had turned and left the study, and gone to talk to the cook. Because life went on, and people had to be fed and welcomed, even if she felt she was breaking up emotionally.

So, she told herself with bitter self-mockery as the car turned onto the long hill that led up to the *palazzo*, I shall become known for my good works—and Charlie, poor babe, will remain an only child.

Hardly enough to fill her days, she thought with a stifled sigh. While she could not even bear to contemplate the long, restless, driven nights that were already her torment.

She knew that most of the people who saw her in her chauffeur-driven car and designer clothes thought that she had nothing else in her life to wish for.

Only Polly knew that the Valessi family now had another closely guarded secret—her total estrangement from the only man she had ever loved.

On arrival at the *palazzo* she went straight up to her room, where Rafaella was waiting for her. She took Polly's flowers to place in water, and waited for her to change out of the suit, so she could restore it to its usual pristine condition.

Polly took a quick shower and changed into a jade-green halter-necked sun-dress, which was cool and decorous at the same time. Then she collected her sunblock, and the book she was reading, and made her way towards the stairs and her intended destination of the terrace.

She was halfway down the wide sweep, when she heard a man's

voice in the entrance hall below, and hesitated, finding herself oddly reluctant to proceed any further. For one thing, this was not the usual time of day for visitors, she told herself. For another— there was something disturbingly familiar about the visitor's smooth tone, as if he was someone she should recognise.

Moving cautiously to the balustrade, she leaned over and looked down.

She saw him at once, talking to Teodoro. A tall, well-dressed man with a smile that seemed to have been painted on his thin mouth. As he spoke he was hunching his shoulders, spreading his hands to emphasise a point, and always that smile—quite unforgettable and still with the power to scare her even three years on.

She would have known him anywhere, she thought. It was the man who'd told her to leave Sorrento—and who'd offered her Sandro's pay-off. And who was now here at the *palazzo*.

Suddenly her stomach was churning, and she lifted a hand to her mouth to stifle her startled cry of recognition. And as she did so the bottle of sunblock fell, and rolled down the stairs.

Both men turned and looked up at her, so her planned retreat was impossible. Cursing her clumsiness, she made herself walk down the rest of the stairs, moving slowly and gracefully, steadying her breathing with an effort. Teodoro had retrieved her sunblock, and returned it to her with a respectful bow. Polly thanked him mechanically, knowing that the other man's flat dark eyes were devouring her.

'So,' he said in English. 'The charming Signorina Fairfax. Or should I say—the Marchesa Valessi? An honour I had not anticipated.' The smile widened. 'Your ladies' luncheon was expected to last longer, I think.'

The significance of that was not lost on her. I'm not supposed to be here, she thought, stiffening.

She turned to Teodoro. 'Does this person have business here?' she asked in Italian, with an assumption of coolness.

'*Sì, vossignoria.* He had an appointment with the *marchese*, but his *excellency* has not yet returned from his own lunch engagement.'

'You do not ask why I am here,' the other man intervened mockingly. 'But perhaps, *marchesa*, you already suspect the nature of my business with your husband. After all, it would not be the first time.'

Polly lifted her chin. 'My husband sees a great many people, I do not question his business with them—or his choice of associate.'

Teodoro was regarding her round-eyed, having never heard his mistress speak so dismissively to a visitor before.

She looked stonily back at him. 'Please show the *marchese*'s— guest to the *salotto*.'

'I already know my way,' he said. 'But I thank you for your graciousness.' He paused. 'Would a cold drink be possible?'

Polly said, 'Will you see to it, *per favore*, Teodoro?' She walked away, her head high, but she was quaking inside, and a block of ice seemed to have settled in the pit of her stomach.

The terrace was altogether too accessible from the *salotto*, she realised, so she walked down into the gardens, finding a secluded stone bench under a flowering hedge, and sinking onto it.

So it was true after all, she thought with desolation, her hands clasping the edge of the bench so tightly that her knuckles turned white. He had been working for Sandro after all, and any lingering hopes that she might have misread the situation were stone dead.

And now he had returned, which could only mean that Sandro had decided to put an end, once and for all, to the tragic farce their marriage had become. And with unbelievable cruelty, he'd summoned his stooge, all over again, to conduct the negotiations and offer her a final settlement.

Go away and keep quiet, would be the ultimatum once more, as it had been three years ago.

But this time there was Charlie to put into the equation, and the kind of deal she might be offered made her feel sick with fear.

He would stay in Italy, of course, because this was a battle she could not fight without weapons. All she could hope for was to be allowed to spend time with him on some regular basis. Surely Sandro would permit that, and not send her off into some kind of limbo of isolation and misery.

The *contessa*, she knew, was now installed in the house on Capri, with a nurse-companion. Was similar accommodation being planned for her somewhere? They said, she thought numbly, that Ischia was very beautiful...

She heard someone moaning, and realised that the low, desperate sound was coming from her own lips.

Had Sandro decided it was time for her to be finally dismissed from his life when she'd told him that she was not pregnant by that brief, soulless coupling a few weeks earlier?

But what difference did it make? she asked herself, wrapping her arms round her shivering body. Even if she was expecting another child, it would only win her a temporary reprieve at best.

She rose, and began to pace up and down the flagged walk, suddenly unable to keep still. Needing to do something—anything—while her raging, unhappy mind tried to find its focus. A way forward into a future that was no future at all.

But she would not wait meekly to be told, she thought with sudden determination. If it killed her, she would take matters into her own hands and leave with some kind of dignity.

And she would take nothing from him except the right to see Charlie. That, surely, he could not deny her...

The *salotto* was empty when she returned to the *palazzo*, and Teodoro was just coming from the direction of Sandro's study, having presumably delivered the unwelcome guest to his host.

He gave her a wary look, and she couldn't blame him. She'd behaved with an outstanding lack of hospitality, and she probably looked like a madwoman.

She laid a detaining hand on his sleeve. 'Teodoro, so silly of me. I've forgotten the name of my husband's visitor.'

His expression changed to astonishment. 'It is Signor Ginaldi, *vossignoria*. The *avvocato* from Salerno.'

'Of course,' she said. *'Grazie.'*

A lawyer, she thought. Why hadn't she guessed? Sandro was bound to have more than one. There was Alberto Molena, the acceptable, trustworthy face of the law, and, in the shadows, this other to do his dirty work.

She forced a smile. 'Will you be good enough to tell me when he's gone? I—I need to talk to the *marchese.'*

'Of course, *vossignoria.'* He paused. 'And a package came for you earlier, which I have placed in your living room.'

A package, Polly thought. She wasn't expecting to receive anything. And surely it couldn't be divorce papers already? Wasn't there some minimum time for a marriage to exist before it could be legally dissolved? Maybe this was another point for Sandro to consult his shady lawyer about—whether the process could be hurried on in some way.

She closed the living-room door, and stood looking round her.

My room, she thought, her throat tightening. Created specially for me. But why—when he must have already known I would not be staying? Why pretend that he cared—even this much?

The package was lying on a side-table, a large padded envelope addressed to her in her mother's handwriting. Polly picked it up, frowning a little, weighing it in her hand. This was the first direct communication she'd received from Mrs Fairfax since she'd arrived in Italy.

She'd written to both her parents, of course, and she telephoned several times a week, but conversation with her mother was still faintly stilted, and confined to strictly neutral subjects.

Oh, God, she thought, wincing. What would her mother say when she came back without Charlie? Her father had said only last week that she seemed to be recovering from her depression, but this latest blow was bound to have a profound effect on her.

And what consolation can I possibly offer? she wondered.

She sat down and opened the envelope. A sheet of folded notepaper fell out, followed by another package, wrapped in plastic and heavily taped.

Her mother had written,

Dearest Polly,

This is not an easy thing for me to tell you, but it has to be done. After you came back from Italy three years ago, these letters began arriving, sent on by the travel company you used to work for.

I realised, of course, that they must be from *him*, and I opened the first ones and read them. My excuse was that I saw how unhappy he'd made you, and I didn't want him to cause more misery and disruption in your life. But that wasn't all of it. It was obvious that he wanted you to come back, and I knew I couldn't bear to part with you or the baby you were expecting. I told myself that I had a right to see my grandchild born. That he'd had his chance, and blown it, as people say these days.

The letters continued coming for months. I meant to burn them because you seemed to have accepted the situation and settled down. And I didn't want your father to find out about them either, because I knew he'd say I must hand them over.

When your husband came here, one of the first things he asked was why he'd never received a reply to any of them. I tried to tell him that we hadn't received any letters, but I can't be a very good liar because he guessed immediately. He was terribly angry, and very bitter, but I begged him not to tell you, because I was afraid you would never forgive me. And he eventually agreed he would say nothing to you if I didn't fight him for Charlie. It was the hardest thing I've ever had to do, but I see now I deserved it.

Some of the letters were heartbreaking, Polly, and I had to stop reading them, but I had no right, even so, to keep them from you. There were things in them that you needed to know. And maybe you still do, because I can tell from your voice that you're not as happy as you make out.

While we were in Cornwall I told your father everything, and he was very shocked. He said I had to make things right between you both, and that is what I'm trying to do now.

He has forgiven me, bless him, and I hope so much, darling, that you'll feel able to do the same one day. And your husband too, perhaps.

Darling, I'm so truly sorry.

Your loving mother.

Polly snatched up the packet and began to tear it open, her carefully manicured nails snapping as she wrestled with the tape, until she reached the bundle of airmail envelopes inside.

About five of them had been opened, in all, but each of the letters had been carefully inscribed by her mother with the date it had been received.

The first one began abruptly,

Paola,
I have to tell you that I am in hospital in Naples. I have been in a bad car crash, and will have to remain here for several more weeks. There is an English nurse working here on an exchange, and she is writing this for me, because I can do very little for myself, except lie here and think. And my thoughts are not happy. I have known for some time that you have left Sorrento, and no

one will tell me where you have gone. But the company you
worked for has said it will forward this to you, so I can only hope
it will reach you.

Forgive me for not writing before, my dearest love, but when I
first recovered consciousness I could remember little of what had
happened. However my memory has slowly returned, and with it
came you, my blessed girl.

The specialists also feared that I had damaged my back so severely
that I might never be able to walk again, and I knew I could not
keep you to your promise of marriage if I was to spend the rest
of my life in a wheelchair.

I know now that I shall make a full recovery, but it will take time,
which would pass more quickly if you were with me. Please write
or call me, and come to me soon.

Your Alessandro.

'Oh, dear God,' Polly whispered. She slid off the sofa onto her
knees, the flimsy blue envelopes cascading round her.

The next one was in his own shaky handwriting.

My darling, why have I not heard from you? If it is the money
that my father gave you to leave, I promise it does not matter to
me. I know how ruthless he can be, and how confused and miserable he must have made you. It was the last thing he told me
before the accident, and we quarrelled terribly. I swore to him that
if he had truly forced you to leave, I would never see him or speak
to him again. And that I would find you wherever you had gone,
and make you my wife.

In the letters that followed he told her his real identity, and all
about Bianca, and the accident, holding nothing back, she discovered with incredulity. He wrote,

It has been decided that for the sake of the family name, none of this should be made public. Also my father is very sick, and any more shocks could kill him. He has asked me to forgive him for sending you away, and we are better friends than we were. I hope you can forgive him too, as he accepts now that I shall always love you, and is ready to welcome you as a daughter.

He ended, 'My dear love, this silence from you is more than I can bear.'

'Sandro,' Polly whispered, tears pouring down her face. 'Oh, *Sandro*.'

She tore open more envelopes, scanning the increasingly desperate words.

'My face was torn by a piece of rock,' he told her at one point. 'The doctors say I should have plastic surgery, but I know that if you were only here to kiss me, I would be healed.'

And later:

I think of you night and day, my sweet one, and pray for you to come back to me, but God doesn't seem to hear me. If you no longer want me, be merciful and tell me so. With each day that passes, it becomes more difficult to hope.

And eventually the desperation faded, and the anger and bitterness began. And the reproaches.

I see now that you never loved me. That my father was right when he said that you had found out somehow who I was, and decided to make money from your knowledge. You should have held out for a better price, Paola. The lovely body you gave me was worth far more than that pittance.

And at last:

My father has died, may God give him peace, and I am now the Marquis Valessi. I am also enough of a fool to still want you. Even now, if you came to me, I would take you, although not as my wife. And if the thought of my scarring revolts you, you can always close your eyes, and think of the financial rewards.
But I shall not ask again.

'Yet you did,' Polly wept aloud, rocking backwards and forwards on her knees. 'In spite of everything, you came to find me. Oh, God, if I'd known—if I'd only known…'

She suddenly heard the unwelcome sound of the door opening. She looked round, her eyes blurred with tears, and saw Sandro in the doorway, staring at her, his lips parted in shock.

If she'd been humiliated the other night, it seemed nothing to what she felt now. She'd intended to walk out of the *palazzo*, and his life, with her head high, commanding his grudging respect if nothing else.

But, at this terrible moment, Polly knew exactly what she looked like. Because she did not cry prettily. Her face would be blubbered with tears, her nose running and her damp hair plastered to her forehead. And when she sobbed out loud, her mouth looked like a frog's.

'What the hell are you doing here?' She choked on the words.

'Teodoro said you were asking for me.' There was no harshness in his voice, or arrogance. He sounded uncertain—bewildered.

'But I was coming to you, not you to me.' She glared at him, and actually hiccuped as she did so. 'So will you please get out?'

But instead, he walked towards her. Sank to his knees beside her, his hands framing her wet, snuffling, desperate face.

'Paola,' he said gently. 'What is it?'

She tried to think of a lie, but somehow, with his eyes looking tenderly and gravely into hers, only the truth would do.

'You loved me,' she burst out, her voice breaking. She gestured wildly at the scattered letters. 'You really loved me, and I never knew,' she ended on a little wail.

'I loved you the first moment I saw you.' He produced an exquisite linen square, and began to dry her white, unhappy face. 'You know that.' As he moved he heard the rustle of paper under his knee, and glanced down. His brows snapped together. 'Where did you get these?' he demanded abruptly.

'My mother sent them. She wanted me to know how you'd really felt after I left. And that you hadn't sent me away—only it's too late—too late.' And she began to sob again.

'*Mi amore*,' he said softly. '*Mi adorata*. What are you talking about?'

'You're going to send me away,' Polly said wildly. 'You're going to ask that man to tell me—to get rid of me. I—I saw him earlier, waiting for you. Waiting for his orders. But from you, this time, not your father.'

She tried to swallow. 'And I'll go—really. I won't make a fuss, I promise—except that I'm doing that already, I suppose, but you weren't meant to see me like this, so it doesn't count.'

'Paola,' he said, cutting through her confused ramblings. 'My beloved, my angel. How can I send you away? It would cut the heart out of my body.'

'But I saw him,' she gulped. 'The lawyer—your lawyer, who threatened me and tried to pay me that money. And you think I took it.' She began to grope for the appropriate letter. 'But I didn't.'

'I know you did not,' he said quietly, capturing her hands and holding them in both of his. 'As he has just been persuaded to admit. He deceived my father, and he deceived me. And he has never been my lawyer. He is simply a creature of the *contessa*'s that my father used once as an intermediary. You need never think of him again.'

'But what happened to the money?' She stared at him.

'I believe that he and the *contessa* divided it between them,' he said drily. 'Alberto has found unexplained funds deposited to her credit around that time.'

'The *contessa* a thief?' Polly took his handkerchief and blew her nose. 'Surely not.'

He shrugged. 'For years, Teodoro has suspected her of—er—creative accountancy with the *palazzo*'s finances. But forget her too,' he added firmly. 'And tell me why you have been crying.'

She bent her head. 'Because you were alone and in pain all those months, and I didn't know.'

'How could you,' he said, 'when you did not get my letters?' He paused. 'Would you have come to me if you had known?'

'Yes,' she said, and tried to smile. 'Even if I'd had to walk all the way over broken glass.'

He said softly, 'My sweet, my beautiful girl.'

She kept staring at the floor. 'That's not true,' she said gruffly. 'When I cry I look like a frog.'

'Do you?' There was the breath of a smile in his voice. He bent and kissed her lightly and tenderly on the lips. 'Then now you are a princess again. And I will try very hard to give you no more cause for grief.'

He got lithely to his feet, pulling her up with him, then seated himself on the sofa with her on his knee, held close in his arms.

He looked deeply into her eyes. 'Paola, is it true? Do you love me?'

'I never stopped,' she admitted shakily. 'Although God knows I tried.'

'I cannot blame you for that,' Sandro said ruefully. 'I tried hard myself, but it was impossible. And I knew that despite anything you might do, I was condemned to love you always, until death, and beyond. So, at last, I came to find you.'

She smoothed the collar of his shirt, not looking at him directly. 'But what about your mistress in Rome? Your vile cousin Emilio told me about her.'

'That was over a long time ago,' he said, adding grimly, 'As Emilio well knows.' He hesitated. 'But she was not the only one, *cara*. See, I confess everything, but it was a time when I thought you were lost to me forever. My father had just died, and my life was hell. But all it taught me was that you were my only love, and always would be.'

She looked up into the dark face, her eyes questioning. 'Then why—*why*—that other night...?'

He was silent for a moment, then he said slowly, 'Because I was angry, and I wanted you very badly. That is a dangerous combination in a man, *cara mia*.

'When I saw you standing there, I thought paradise was mine at last. I looked at you, longing for you to tell me that you loved me—or at least that you desired me. One kiss—a touch of your hand—and I would have been yours.

'But you spoke only of Carlino—his happiness, his need for a playmate, as if that mattered more, somehow, than you being in my arms, a woman with her man.

'It was as if my being exonerated of Bianca's death had convinced you that I was a suitable candidate for fatherhood again. I felt as if I was some tame stud, to be used only when required. And that my needs and emotions were immaterial.

'And frankly I found that unbearable—an insult to my manhood, and everything I felt for you. But I was also scared that anger might get the better of me, and I would lose all control and treat you in a way we could both regret for the rest of our lives.

'So I told myself, *Bene*—if that is all she wants, it is all she shall have. Until afterwards, when I saw your wounded eyes.' He drew her closer repentantly. 'I was afraid that I had hurt you too much—driven you away forever.'

'But I'd been scared too,' she whispered. 'In case you rejected me. I knew how much you loved Charlie, and thought he might prove a link between us. A way to approach you.'

'And do you know why I love him so?' Sandro asked quietly. 'Because he reminds me of you, when we first met—so innocent, so trusting, so unstinting in affection. And he wanted to be with me, even though I was being shunned by you.'

Polly sighed. 'And I thought you only wanted him. That I was just here on sufferance.'

His mouth twisted. 'More suffering than sufferance, I think, *bella mia*. Living with you has been heaven and hell. Heaven to hear the sound of your voice, see your smile, breathe, sometimes, the fragrance of your skin—your hair.

'But hell to be aware of all these things, and yet be denied the right to hold you in my arms at night.

'I should have told you. I came back early from that trip principally because I could not bear to be apart from you another day.'

'I dared not believe you,' she said. 'I couldn't risk having my heart broken a second time.'

He said softly, 'So, are you prepared to take that risk now, *carissima*? To be my wife, and face whatever our lives bring at my side?'

'Yes.' She smiled into his eyes. 'I'm ready to do that, *caro mio*. My dear love.'

He carried her in his arms out of the room, and up the broad sweep of the staircase.

'So much for public decorum,' she teased breathlessly.

'At least you are still wearing your clothes.' His answering grin was as mischievous as a boy's.

But when they were alone and the door was not merely closed but locked, Polly saw the stark hunger in his eyes, and knew a fleeting moment of fear, in case he demanded more than she had the power to give.

Then his hands descended on her bare shoulders, and her body exploded wildly in the sheer shock of recognition. And of overwhelming, aching need.

He bent his head, and his lips parted hers deeply and sensuously. His arms tightened round her, crushing her breasts fiercely against his hard chest.

When the long kiss ended, they were both breathless. Then he reached for her again. They undressed each other, swiftly, almost frantically, tearing at buttons and zips, ripping recalcitrant fabric away. And the years of separation faded into oblivion as Polly lay naked in his arms at last in the sunlit warmth of the afternoon.

Their mouths feverishly explored the familiarity of flesh and bone, seeking unforgotten pleasures, reviving the shuddering sweetness of touch, their voices whispering—urging.

His tongue was liquid fire against her taut nipples, his fingers like silk as they found the molten, eager core of her and lingered, creating their own exquisite torment.

'Do you remember?' he murmured against her lips. 'The things you once said to me?'

'I've forgotten nothing.' Her voice was a husky purr.

'Then say them now.' He whispered, as his body slid into hers with one powerful thrust. He was not gentle, but she did not wish him to be so. His claim on her was as total as her surrender to him, and she gloried in it, her body arching against him, drawing him ever more deeply into the moist heat of her. Closing round the pulsating length of him, and making him groan with pleasure. And all the time, her lips whispered against his skin, until time ceased to exist, and her voice splintered hoarsely into rapture. Speech was impossible, overtaken by her incoherent, delirious cries of delight.

And, as he came in his turn, Sandro cried out her name as if it had been dragged from the very depths of his being.

Afterwards, they lay wrapped together, sated and languid. 'Am I forgiven?' he whispered.

'For the other night?' She stretched herself against him bonelessly, smiling against his shoulder. 'Far too early to tell, *excellenza*.'

'*Dio mio*. You have other penances in mind?'

'Enough to last for the rest of our lives.' Polly sighed luxuriously. 'And only an hour ago, I thought I would never be happy again.'

'I always hoped, *mi adorata*,' Sandro said drowsily. 'Even when it seemed all hope was gone.'

'Now we have something better than hope,' she told him gently. 'We have each other. Forever.' And she pressed her lips tenderly to his scarred cheek.

THE COUNT'S
BLACKMAIL
BARGAIN

CHAPTER ONE

IT WAS a warm, golden morning in Rome, so how in the name of God was the city in the apparent grip of a small earthquake?

The noble Conte Alessio Ramontella lifted his aching head from the pillow, and, groaning faintly from the effort, attempted to focus his eyes. True, the bed looked like a disaster area, but the room was not moving, and the severe pounding, which he'd assumed was the noise of buildings collapsing nearby, seemed to be coming instead from the direction of his bedroom door.

And the agitated shouting he could hear was not emanating from some buried victim either, but could be recognised as the voice of his manservant Giorgio urging him to wake up.

Using small, economical movements that would not disturb the blonde, naked beauty still slumbering beside him, or increase the pressure from his hangover, Alessio got up from the bed, and extracted his robe from the tangle of discarded clothing on the floor, before treading across the marble-tiled floor to the door.

He pulled the garment round him, and opened the door an inch or two.

'This is not a working day,' he informed the anxious face outside. 'Am I to be allowed no peace?'

'Forgive me, *Eccellenza*.' Giorgio wrung his hands. 'For the world I would not have disturbed you. But it is your aunt, the Signora Vicente.'

There was an ominous pause, then: 'Here?' Alessio bit out the word.

'On her way,' Giorgio admitted nervously. 'She telephoned to announce her intention to visit you.'

Alessio swore softly. 'Didn't you have enough wit to say I was away?' he demanded.

'Of course, *Eccellenza*.' Giorgio spoke with real sorrow. 'But regrettably she did not believe me.'

Alessio swore again more fluently. 'How long have I got?'

'That will depend on the traffic, *signore*, but I think we must count in minutes.' He added reproachfully, 'I have been knocking and knocking...'

With another groan, Alessio forced himself into action. 'Get a cab for my guest,' he ordered. 'Tell the driver to come to the rear entrance, and to be quick about it. This is an emergency. Then prepare coffee for the *Signora*, and some of the little almond biscuits that she likes.'

He shut the door, and went back to the bed, his hangover eclipsed by more pressing concerns. He looked down at all the smooth, tanned loveliness displayed for his delectation, and his mouth tightened.

Dio, what a fool he'd been to break his own cardinal rule, and allow her to stay the night.

I must have been more drunk than I thought, he told himself cynically, then bent over her, giving one rounded shoulder a firm shake.

Impossibly long lashes lifted slowly, and she gave him a sleepy smile. 'Alessio, *tesoro mio*, why aren't you still in bed?' She reached up, twining coaxing arms round his neck to draw him down to her, but he swiftly detached the clinging hands and stepped back.

'Vittoria, you have to go, and quickly too.'

She pouted charmingly. 'But how ungallant of you, *caro*. I told you, Fabrizio is visiting his witch of a mother, and will not be back until this evening at the earliest. So we have all the time in the world.'

'An enchanting thought,' Alessio said levelly. 'But, sadly, there is no time to pursue it.'

She stretched voluptuously, her smile widening. 'But how can I leave, *mi amore*, when I have nothing to wear? You won all my clothes at cards last night, so what am I to do? It was, after all, a debt of honour,' she added throatily.

Alessio tried to control his growing impatience. 'Consider it cancelled. I cheated.'

She hunched a shoulder. 'Then you will have to fetch my clothes for me—from the *salotto* where I took them off. Unless you wish me to win them back, during another game of cards.'

This, thought Alessio, was not the time to be sultry.

His smile was almost a snarl. 'And how, precisely, *bella mia*, will you explain your presence, also your state of undress, to my aunt Lucrezia, who counts Fabrizio's mother among her closest cronies?'

Vittoria gave a startled cry and sat up, belatedly grabbing at the sheet. '*Madonna*—you cannot mean it. Promise me she is not here?'

'Not quite, but due imminently,' Alessio warned, his tone grim.

'*Dio mio.*' Her voice was a wail. 'Alessio—do something. I must get out of here. You have to save me.'

There was another knock at the door, which opened a crack to admit Giorgio's discreet arm holding out a handful of female clothing. His voice was urgent. 'The taxi has arrived, *Eccellenza.*'

'*Un momento.*' Alessio strode over and took the clothes, tossing them deftly to Vittoria who was already running frantically to the bathroom, her nakedness suddenly ungainly.

He paused, watching her disappear, then gave a mental shrug. Last night she'd been an entertaining and inventive companion, but daylight and danger had dissipated her appeal. There would be no more cards, or any other games with the beautiful Vittoria Montecorvo. In fact, he thought, frowning, it might be wiser, for the future, to avoid discontented wives altogether. The only real advantage of such affairs was not being expected to propose marriage, he told himself cynically.

He retrieved his underwear from the pile of discarded evening clothes beside the bed, then went into his dressing room, finding and shrugging on a pair of cream denim trousers and a black polo shirt. As he emerged, thrusting his bare feet into loafers, Vittoria was waiting, dressed but distraught.

'Alessio.' She hurled herself at him. 'When shall I see you again?'

The honest reply would be, 'Never,' but that would also be unkind.

'Perhaps this narrow escape is a warning to us, *cara mia*,' he returned guardedly. 'We shall have to be very careful.'

'But I am not sure I can bear it.' Her voice throbbed a little. 'Not now that we have found each other, *angelo mio*.'

Alessio suppressed a cynical smile. He knew who his predecessor had been. Was sure that his successor was already lined up. Vittoria was a rich man's beautiful daughter married to another rich man, who was all too easy to fool.

She was spoiled, predatory and bored, as, indeed, he was himself.

Maybe that had been the initial attraction between them, he thought, with an inner grimace. Like calling to like.

Suddenly he felt jaded and restless. The heat of Rome, the noise of the traffic seemed to press upon him, stifling him. He found himself thinking of windswept crags where clouds drifted. He longed to breathe the dark, earthy scents of the forests that clothed the lower slopes, and wake in the night to moonlit silence.

He needed, he thought, to distance himself.

And he could have all that, and more. After all, he was overdue for a vacation. Some re-scheduling at the bank, and he could be gone, he told himself as Vittoria pressed herself against him, murmuring seductively.

He wanted her out of the *appartamento*, too, he thought grimly, and realised he would have felt the same even if he hadn't been threatened by a visit from his aunt.

Gently but firmly, he edged her out of the bedroom, and along the wide passage to where Giorgio was waiting, his face expressionless, just as the entrance bell jangled discordantly at the other end of the flat.

'I'll get that. You take the *signora* to her cab.' Alessio freed himself from the clutching, crimson-tipped fingers, murmuring that of course he would think of her, would call her—but only if he felt it was safe.

He paused to watch her leaving, her parting glance both suspicious and disconsolate, then drew a deep breath of thanksgiving, raking the hair she'd so playfully dishevelled back from his face with impatient fingers.

The bell rang again, imperative in its summons, and Alessio knew he could hardly delay his response any longer. Sighing, he went to confront the enemy at the gates.

'Zia Lucrezia,' he greeted the tall, grey-haired woman waiting on his doorstep, her elegant shoe beating a tattoo against the stone. 'What a charming surprise.'

Her glance was minatory as she swept past him. 'Don't be a hypocrite, Alessio. It does not become you. I was not expecting to be welcome.' She paused for a moment, listening to the distant sound of a car starting up, and the rear door closing with a clang. 'Ah, so your other visitor has safely made her escape,' she added with a sour smile. 'I regret spoiling your plans for the day, nephew.'

He said gently, 'I rarely make plans, my dear aunt. I prefer to wait and see what delights the day offers.' He escorted her into the *salotto*, one swift, sweeping glance assuring him that it had been restored to its usual pristine condition. The tell-tale wineglasses had been removed, together with the empty bottles, and the *grappa* that had followed had also been put away. As had the scattered cards from last night's impromptu session of strip poker.

And the windows to the balcony stood innocently open to admit the morning sun, and dispel any lingering traces of alcohol fumes, and Vittoria's rather heavy perfume.

Making a mental note to increase Giorgio's salary, he conducted the Signora to a sofa, and seated himself in the chair opposite.

'To what do I owe the pleasure of seeing you, Zia Lucrezia?'

She was silent for a moment, then she said curtly, 'I wish to speak to you about Paolo.'

He looked across at her in frank surprise. Giorgio's arrival with the tall silver pot of coffee, and the ensuing ritual of pouring the coffee and handing the tiny sweet biscuits, gave him a chance to gather his thoughts.

When they were alone again, he said softly, 'You amaze me, *cara Zia*. I am hardly in a position to offer advice. You have always allowed me to understand that my example to your only son is an abomination.'

'Don't pretend to be a fool,' the Signora said shortly. 'Of course, I don't want advice.' She hesitated again. 'However, I do find that I need your practical assistance in a small matter.'

Alessio swallowed some coffee. 'I hope this is not a request to transfer Paolo back to Rome. I gather he is making progress in London.'

'That,' said Paolo's mother glacially, 'is a matter of opinion. And, anyway, he is returning to Rome quite soon, to spend his vacation with me.'

Alessio's eyes narrowed slightly. 'The idea doesn't appeal to you? Yet I remember you complaining to me when we met at Princess Dorelli's reception that you didn't see him often enough.'

There was another, longer silence, then the Signora said, as if the words were being wrung out of her, 'He is not coming alone.'

Alessio shrugged. 'Well, why should he?' he countered. 'Let me remind you, dear aunt, that my cousin is no longer a boy.'

'Precisely.' The Signora poured herself more coffee. 'He is old enough, in fact, to be a husband. And let me remind *you*, Alessio, that it has always been the intention of both families that Paolo should marry Beatrice Manzone.'

Alessio's brows snapped together. 'I know there was some such plan when they were children,' he admitted slowly. 'But now—now they are adults, and—things change. People change.'

She looked back at him stonily. 'Except for you, it seems, my dear nephew. You remain—unregenerate, with your boats and your fast cars. With your gambling and your womanising.'

He said gently, '*Mea culpa*, Zia Lucrezia, but we are not here to discuss my manifold faults.' He paused. 'So, Paolo has a girl-friend. It's hardly a mortal sin, and, anyway, to my certain knowledge, she is not the first. He will probably have many more before he decides to settle down. So, what is the problem?'

'Signor Manzone is an old friend,' said the Signora. 'Naturally, he wishes his daughter's future to be settled. And soon.'

'And is this what Beatrice herself wants?'

'She and my Paolo grew up together. She has adored him all her life.'

Alessio shrugged again. 'Then maybe she'll be prepared to wait until he has finished sowing his wild oats,' he returned indifferently.

'Hmm.' The Signora's tone was icy. 'Then it is fortunate she is not waiting for you.'

'Fortunate for us both,' Alessio said gently. 'The Signorina Manzone is infinitely too sweet for my taste.'

'I am relieved to hear it. I did not know you bothered to discriminate between one foolish young woman and the next.'

As so often when he talked to his aunt, Alessio could feel his jaw clenching. He kept his voice even. 'Perhaps you should remember, *Zia*, that my father, your own brother, was far from a saint until he married my mother. Nonna Ramontella often told me she wore out her knees, praying for him.' *And for you,* he added silently.

'What a pity your grandmother is no longer here to perform the same service for you.' There was a pause, and, when she spoke again, the Signora's voice was slightly less acerbic. 'But we should not quarrel, Alessio. Your life is your own, whereas Paolo has—obligations, which he must be made to recognise. Therefore this—*relazione amorosa* of his must end, *quanta prima tanto meglio.*'

Alessio frowned again. 'But sooner may not be better for Paolo,' he pointed out. 'They may be genuinely in love. After all, this is the twenty-first century, not the fifteenth.'

The Signora waved a dismissive hand. 'The girl is completely unsuitable. Some English *sciattona* that he met in a bar in

London,' she added with distaste. 'From what I have gleaned from my fool of a son, she has neither family nor money.'

'Whereas Beatrice Manzone has both, of course,' Alessio said drily. 'Especially money.'

'That may not weigh with you,' the Signora said with angry energy. 'But it matters very much to Paolo.'

'Unless I break my neck playing polo,' Alessio drawled. 'Which would make him my heir, of course. My preoccupation with dangerous sports should please you, Zia Lucrezia. It opens up all kinds of possibilities.'

She gave him a fulminating look. 'Which we need not consider. You will, of course, remember in due course what you owe to your family, and provide yourself with a wife and family.

'As matters stand, you are the chairman of the Arleschi Bank. He is only an employee. He cannot afford to marry some pretty nobody.'

'So, she's pretty,' Alessio mused. 'But then she would have to be, if she has no money. And Paolo has Ramontella blood in his veins, so she may even be a beauty—this...?'

'Laura,' the Signora articulated coldly. 'Laura Mason.'

'Laura.' He repeated the name softly. 'The name of the girl that Petrarch saw in church and loved for the rest of his life.' He grinned at his aunt. 'I hope that isn't an omen.'

'Well,' the Signora said softly, 'I depend on you, my dear Alessio, to make certain it is not.'

'You expect me to preach to my cousin about family duty?' He laughed. 'I don't think he'd listen.'

'I wish you to do more than talk. I wish you to bring Paolo's little romance to an end.'

His brows lifted. 'And how am I supposed to do that?'

'Quite easily, *caro mio*.' She gave him a flat smile. 'You will seduce her, and make sure he knows of it.'

Alessio came out of his chair in one lithe, angry movement. 'Are you insane?'

'I am simply being practical,' his aunt returned. 'Requesting that you put your dubious talents with women to some useful purpose.'

'Useful!' He was almost choking on his rage. '*Dio mio*, how dare you insult me by suggesting such a thing? Imagine that I would be willing even for one moment...' He flung away from her. Walked to the window, gazed down into the street below with unseeing eyes, then turned back, his face inimical. 'No,' he said. 'And again—no. Never.'

'You disappoint me,' the Signora said almost blandly. 'I hoped you would regard it as—an interesting challenge.'

'On the contrary,' he said. 'I am disgusted—nauseated by such a proposal.' He took a deep breath. 'And from you of all people. You—astound me.'

She regarded him calmly. 'What exactly are your objections?'

He spread his hands in baffled fury. 'Where shall I begin? The girl is a complete stranger to me.'

'But so, at first, are all the women who share your bed.' She paused. 'For example, *mio caro*, how long have you known Vittoria Montecorvo, whose hasty departure just now I almost interrupted?'

Their eyes met, locked in a long taut, silence. Eventually, he said, 'I did not realise you took such a close interest in my personal life.'

'Under normal circumstances, I would not, I assure you. But in this instance, I need your—co-operation.'

Alessio said slowly, 'At any moment, I am going to wake up, and find this is all a bad dream.' He came back to his chair. Sat. 'I have other objections. Do you wish to hear them?'

'As you wish.'

He leaned forward, the dark face intense. 'This romance of Paolo's may just be a passing fancy. Why not let it run its course?'

'Because Federico Manzone wishes my son's engagement to Beatrice to be made official. Any more delay would displease him.'

'And would that be such a disaster?'

'Yes,' his aunt said. 'It would. I have entered into certain—accommodations with Signor Manzone, on the strict understanding that this marriage would soon be taking place. Repayment would be—highly inconvenient.'

'*Santa Maria.*' Alessio slammed a clenched fist into the palm of his other hand. Of course, he thought. He should have guessed as much.

The Signora's late husband had come from an old but relatively impoverished family, but, in spite of that, her spending habits had always been legendary. He could remember stern family conferences on the subject when he was a boy.

And age, it seemed, had not taught her discretion.

Groaning inwardly, he said, 'Then why not allow me to settle these debts for you, and let Paolo live his life?'

There was a sudden gleam of humour in her still-handsome face. 'I am not a welcome client at the bank, Alessio, so are you inviting me to become your private pensioner? Your poor father would turn in his grave. Besides, the lawyers would never allow it. And Federico has assured me very discreetly that, once our families are joined, he will make permanent arrangements for me. He is all generosity.'

'Then why not change the plan?' Alessio said with sudden inspiration. 'You're a widow. He's a widower. Why don't you marry him yourself, and let the next generation find their own way to happiness?'

'As you yourself are doing?' The acid was back. 'Perhaps we could have a double wedding, *mio caro*. I am sure honour will demand you ask the lovely Vittoria to be your wife, when her husband divorces her for adultery. After all, it will make a hideous scandal.'

Their glances met again and clashed, steel against steel.

He said steadily, 'I was not aware that Fabrizio had any such plans for Vittoria.'

'Not yet, certainly,' the Signora said silkily. 'But if he or my good friend Camilla, his mother, should discover in some unfortunate way that you have planted horns on him, then that might change.'

Eventually, Alessio sighed, lifting a shoulder in a resigned shrug. 'I have seriously underestimated you, Zia Lucrezia. I did not realise how totally unscrupulous you could be.'

'A family trait,' said the Signora. 'But desperate situations call for desperate measures.'

'But, you must still consider this,' Alessio went on. 'Even if his affair with the English girl is terminated, there is no guarantee that Paolo will marry Beatrice. He may still choose to look elsewhere. He might even find another rich girl. How will you prevent that?' He gave her a thin smile. 'Or have you some scheme to blackmail him into co-operation too?'

'You speak as if he has never cared for Beatrice.' His aunt spoke calmly. 'This is not true. And, once his disillusion with his English fancy is complete, I know he will realise where his best interests lie, and turn to her again. And they will be happy together. I am sure of it.'

Alessio sent her a look of pure exasperation. 'How simple you make it sound. You pull the strings, and the puppets dance. But there are still things you have not taken into account. For one thing, how will I meet this girl?'

'I have thought of that. I shall tell Paolo that I have workmen at my house in Tuscany putting in a new heating system, so cannot receive guests. Instead, I have accepted a kind invitation from you for us all to stay at the Villa Diana.'

He snorted. 'And he will believe you?'

She shrugged. 'He has no choice. And I shall make sure you have the opportunity to be alone with the girl. The rest is up to you.' She paused. 'You may not even be called on to make the ultimate sacrifice, *caro*. It might be enough for Paolo to discover you kissing her.'

He said patiently, 'Zia Lucrezia, has it occurred to you that this—Laura—may be truly in love with Paolo, and nothing will persuade her to even a marginal betrayal?'

He paused, his mouth twisting. 'Besides, and more importantly, you have overlooked the fact that she may not find me attractive.'

'*Caro* Alessio,' the Signora purred. 'Let us have no false modesty. It has been often said that if you had smiled at Juliet, she would have left Romeo. Like your other deluded victims, Laura will find you irresistible.'

'*Davvero?*' Alessio asked ironically. 'I hope she slaps my face.' He looked down at his hand, studying the crest on the signet ring he wore. 'And afterwards—if I succeed in this contemptible ploy? I would not blame Paolo if he refused to speak to me again.'

'At first, perhaps, he may be resentful. But in time, he will thank you.' She rose. 'They will be arriving next week. I hope this will not be a problem for you?'

He got to his feet too, his mouth curling. He walked over to her, took her hand and bowed over it. 'I shall count the hours.'

'Sarcasm, *mio caro*, does not become you.' She studied him for a moment. 'Like your father, Alessio, you are formidable when you are angry.' She patted his cheek. 'I hope you're in a better mood when you finally encounter this English girl, or I shall almost feel sorry for her.'

He gave her a hard, unsmiling look. 'Don't concern yourself for her, Zia Lucrezia. I will do my best to send her home with a beautiful memory.'

'Ah,' she said. 'Now I really do feel sorry for her.' And was gone.

Alone, Alessio went to a side table, and poured himself a whisky. He rarely drank in the daytime, but this was like no other day since the beginning of the world.

What the devil was Paolo thinking of—bringing his little *ragazza* within a hundred miles of his mother? If he gave a damn about her, he would keep them well apart.

And if I had an atom of decency, Alessio thought grimly, I would call him, and say so.

But he couldn't risk it. Zia Lucrezia had more than her full share of the Ramontella ruthlessness, as he should have remembered, and would not hesitate to carry out her veiled threat about his ill-advised interlude with Vittoria. And the fall-out would, as she'd predicted, be both unpleasant and spectacular.

Laura, he repeated to himself meditatively. Well, at least she had a charming name. If she had a body to match, then his task might not seem so impossible.

He raised his glass. '*Salute*, Laura,' he said with cynical emphasis. '*E buona fortuna.*' He added softly, 'I think you will need it.'

CHAPTER TWO

'WELL, it all sounds iffy to me,' said Gaynor. 'Think about it. You've cancelled your South of France holiday with Steve because you didn't like the sleeping arrangements, yet now you're off to Italy with someone you hardly know. It doesn't make any sense.'

Laura sighed. 'Not when you put it like that, certainly. But it truly isn't what you think. I'm getting a free trip to Tuscany for two weeks, plus a cash bonus, and all I have to do is look as if I'm madly in love.'

'It can't be that simple,' Gaynor said darkly. 'Nothing ever is. I mean, have you ever *been* madly in love? You certainly weren't with Steve or you wouldn't have quibbled about sharing a room with him,' she added candidly.

Laura flushed. 'I suppose I thought I was—or that I might be, given time. After all, we've only been seeing each other for two months. Hardly a basis for that kind of commitment.'

'Well, not everyone would agree with you there,' Gaynor said drily.

'I know.' Laura paused in her packing to sigh again. 'I'm a freak—a throwback. I admit it. But if and when I have sex with a man, I want it to be based on love and respect, and a shared future. Not because double rooms are cheaper than singles.'

'And what kind of room is this Paolo Vicente offering?'

'All very respectable,' Laura assured her, tucking her only swimsuit into a corner of her case. 'We'll be staying with his mother at her country house, and she's a total dragon, it seems. Paolo says she'll probably lock me in at night.'

'And she has no idea that you're practically strangers?'

'No, that's the whole point. She's pushing him hard to get engaged to a girl he's known all his life, and he won't. He says

18

she's more like his younger sister than a future wife, and that I'm going to be his declaration of independence. A way of telling his mother that he's his own man, and quite capable of picking a bride for himself.'

'Isn't that like showing a red rag to a bull? Do you *want* to be caught in the middle of two warring factions?'

'I won't be. Paolo says, at worst, she'll treat me with icy politeness. And he's promised I won't see that much of her—that he'll take me out and about as much as possible.' Laura paused. 'It could even be fun,' she added doubtfully.

'Ever the optimist,' muttered Gaynor. 'How the hell did you ever become part of this gruesome twosome?'

Laura sighed again. 'He works for the Arleschi Bank. We pitched for their PR work a few weeks ago, and Carl took me along to the presentation. Paolo was there. Then, a fortnight ago, he came into the wine bar, and we recognised each other.' She wrinkled her nose. 'I'd just split with Steve, so I was feeling down, and Paolo was clearly fed up too. He stayed on after closing time, and we had a drink together, and started talking.

'He wanted to know why I was moonlighting in a wine bar when I was working for Harman Grace, so I told him about Mum being a widow, and Toby winning that scholarship to public school, but always needing extra stuff for school, plus this field trip in October.

'Then Paolo got very bitter about his mother, and the way she was trying to tie him down with this Beatrice. And, somehow, over a few glasses of wine, the whole scheme evolved.'

She shook her head. 'At first, I thought it was just the wine talking, but when he came back the following night to hammer out the details I discovered he was deadly serious. I also realised that the extra cash he was offering would pay for Toby's field trip, and compensate Steve for the extra hotel charges he's been emailing me about incessantly.'

'Charming,' said Gaynor.

Laura pulled a face. 'Well, I did let him down over the holiday, so I suppose he's entitled to feel sore.

'However, when push came to shove, I honestly couldn't afford to turn Paolo down.' She sounded faintly dispirited, then rallied. 'And, anyway, I've always wanted to go to Italy. Also it may be my last chance of a proper holiday, before I seriously start saving towards the Flat Fund.'

'I've already begun.' Gaynor gave a disparaging glance around the cramped bedsit, a mirror-image of her own across the landing. 'There's an ugly rumour that Ma Hughes is all set to raise the rents again. If we don't find our own place soon, we won't be able to afford to move out. And Rachel from work is definitely interested in joining us,' she added buoyantly. 'Apparently, living at home is driving her crazy.'

She got up from the bed, collecting up their used coffee-cups. On her way to the communal kitchenette, she paused at the door. 'Honey, you are sure you can trust this Paolo? He won't suddenly develop wandering hands when you're on your own with him?'

Laura laughed. 'I'm sure he won't. He likes voluptuous brunettes, so I'm really not his type, and he certainly isn't mine,' she added decisively. 'Although I admit he's good-looking. Besides, I have his mother as chaperon, don't forget. And he tells me she strongly disapproves of open displays of affection, so all I really have to do is flutter my eyelashes occasionally.'

Laura gave a brisk nod. 'No, this is basically a business arrangement, and that's fine with me.'

Her smile widened. 'And I get to see Tuscany at last. Who could ask for more?'

But as the plane began its descent towards Rome's Leonardo da Vinci Airport she did not feel quite so euphoric about the situation, although she could not have fully explained why.

She had met up with Paolo the previous night to talk over final details for the trip.

'If we're dating each other, then you need to know something about me, *cara*, and my family,' he explained with perfect reason.

She'd already gathered that he occupied a fairly junior position at the bank's London branch. What she hadn't expected to hear was that he was related to the Italian aristocrat who was the Arleschi chairman.

'We are the poor side of the family,' he explained. He was smiling, but there was a touch of something like peevishness in his voice. 'Which is why my mother is so eager for me to marry Beatrice, of course. Her father is a very wealthy man, and she is his only child.'

'Of course,' Laura echoed. Who are these people? she wondered in frank amazement. And just what planet do they inhabit?

She thought of her mother struggling to make ends meet. Of herself, spending long evenings in the wine bar so that she could help towards her shy, clever brother having the marvellous education he deserved.

When Paolo used the term 'poor' so airily, he had no idea what it really meant.

Her throat tightened. She'd treated herself to some new clothes for the abortive French holiday, but they were all chain-store bought, with not a designer label among them.

She was going to stick out like the proverbial sore thumb in this exclusive little world she was about to join, however briefly. So, could she really make anyone believe that she and Paolo were seriously involved?

But perhaps this was precisely why he had chosen her, she thought unhappily. Because she was so screamingly unsuitable. Maybe this would provide exactly the leverage Paolo needed to escape from this enforced marriage.

'Anyone,' his mother might say, throwing up her hands in horrified surrender. 'Anyone but her!'

Well, she could live with that, because Paolo, in spite of his smoothly handsome looks and august connections, held no appeal for her. In fact, Laura decided critically, she wouldn't have him if he came served on toast with a garnish.

He was arrogant, she thought, and altogether too pleased with himself, and, although no one should be forced to marry someone they didn't love, on balance her sympathies lay with his would-be fiancée.

'I must insist on one thing,' she said. 'No mention of Harman Grace.'

'As you wish.' He shrugged. 'But why? They are a good company. You have nothing to be ashamed of by working for them.'

'I know that. But we're now the bank's official PR company in London. Your cousin must know that, and he'll recognise the name if it's mentioned. He may not appreciate the fact that you're supposedly dating someone who's almost an employee.'

'Don't disturb yourself, *cara*. I am nothing more than an employee myself. Besides, the chances of your meeting my cousin Alessio are slim. But Harman Grace shall remain a secret between us, if that's what you want.'

'Yes,' she said. 'I really do. Thank you.'

She was astonished to find that they were flying first class, proving that poverty was only relative, she thought grimly, declining the champagne she was automatically offered.

A couple of glasses of wine had got her into this mess. So, from now on she intended to keep a cool head.

She was also faintly disconcerted by Paolo's attempts to flirt with her. He kept bending towards her, his voice low and almost intimate as he spoke. And she didn't like his persistent touching either—her hair, her shoulder, the sleeve of her linen jacket.

Oh, God, she thought uneasily. Don't tell me Gaynor was right about him all along.

She was aware, with embarrassment, that the cabin staff were watching them, exchanging knowing looks.

'What are you doing?' she muttered, pulling her hand away as he tried to kiss each of her fingers.

He shrugged, not in the least discomposed. 'For every performance, there must be a rehearsal, no?'

'Definitely no,' Laura said tartly.

She was also disappointed to hear there'd been a slight change of plan. That instead of hiring a car at the airport and driving straight to Tuscany, they were first to join the Signora Vicente at her Rome apartment.

'But for how long?' she queried.

Paolo was unconcerned. 'Does it matter? It will give you a

chance to see *my* city before we bury ourselves in the country-side,' he told her. He gave a satisfied smile. 'Also, my mother employs a driver and a car for her journeys, so we shall travel in comfort.'

Laura felt she had no option but to force a smile of agreement. It's his trip, she thought resignedly. I'm just the hired help.

The Signora's residence was in the Aventine district, which Paolo told her was one of the city's more peaceful locations with many gardens and trees.

She occupied the first floor of a grand mansion, standing in its own grounds, and Laura took a deep, calming breath as they mounted the wide flight of marble stairs.

You've got your passport in your bag, she reminded herself silently. Also, your return ticket. All you have to do, if you really can't hack this, is turn and run.

When they reached the imposing double doors, Paolo rang the bell, and Laura swallowed as he took her hand in his with a reassuring nod.

It's only a couple of weeks, she thought. Not the rest of my life.

The door was opened by a plump elderly maid, who beamed at Paolo, ignoring Laura completely, then burst into a flood of incomprehensible Italian.

Laura found herself in a windowless hall, its only illumination coming from a central chandelier apparently equipped with low-wattage bulbs. The floor was tiled in dark marble, and a few pieces of heavy antique furniture and some oil paintings in ornate frames did little to lighten the atmosphere.

Then the maid flung open the door to the *salotto*, and sunlight struggled out, accompanied by a small hairy dog, yapping furiously and snarling round their ankles.

'Quiet, Caio,' Paolo ordered, and the dog backed off, although it continued its high-pitched barking, and growling. Laura liked dogs, and usually got on with them, but something told her that Caio was more likely to take a chunk out of her ankle than respond to any overtures she might make.

Paolo led her into the room. 'Call off your hound, *Mamma*,' he said. 'Or my Laura will think she is not welcome.'

'But I am always ready to receive your friends, *figlio mio*.' The Signora rose from a brocaded sofa, and offered her hand.

She was a tall woman, Laura saw, and had been handsome once rather than a beauty. But time had thinned her face and narrowed her mouth, and this, together with her piercing dark eyes, made her formidable. She wore black, and there were pearls round her neck, and in her ears.

'Signorina Mason, is it not so?' Her smile was vinegary as she absorbed Laura's shy response. 'You would like some tea, I think. Is that not the English habit?'

Laura lifted her chin. 'Now that I'm here, *signora*, perhaps I should learn a few Italian customs instead.'

The elegantly plucked brows lifted. 'You will hardly be here long enough to make it worthwhile, *signorina*—but as you wish.' She rang a bell for the maid, ordered coffee and cakes, then beckoned Paolo to join her on the sofa.

This, thought Laura, taking the seat opposite that she'd been waved towards, is going to be uphill all the way. And she was still inwardly flinching from 'my Laura'.

It was a beautiful room, high-ceilinged and well proportioned, but massively over-furnished for her taste. There were too many groups of hard-looking chairs, she thought, taking a covert glance around. And far too many spindly-legged tables crowded with knick-knacks. The windows were huge, and she longed to drag open the tall shutters that half-masked them and let in some proper light. But she supposed that would fade the draperies, and the expensive rugs on the parquet floor.

'I have some news for you, *mio caro*,' the Signora announced, after the maid had served coffee and some tiny, but frantically rich chocolate cakes. 'And also for the *signorina*, your companion. I regret that I cannot after all entertain you at my country home. It is occupied by workmen—so tedious, but unavoidable.'

Laura froze, her cup halfway to her lips. Were they going to spend the whole two weeks in this apartment? Oh, God, she thought, surely not. It might seem spacious enough, but she suspected that even a few days with the Signora would make it seem totally claustrophobic.

Paolo was looking less than pleased. 'But you knew we were coming, *Mamma*. And I promised Laura that she should see Tuscany.'

'Another time, perhaps,' the Signora said smoothly. 'This time she will have to be content with a corner of Umbria.' Her expression was bland. 'Your cousin Alessio has offered us the use of the Villa Diana at Besavoro.'

There was an astonished pause, then Paolo said slowly, 'Why should he do that?'

'*Mio caro.*' The Signora's voice held a hint of reproof. 'We are members of his family. His only living relatives.'

Paolo shrugged. 'Even so, it is not like him to be so obliging,' he countered. 'And, anyway, Besavoro is at the end of the world.' He spread his hands. 'Also, the Villa Diana is halfway up a mountain on the way to nowhere. It is hardly an adequate substitute.'

'I think Signorina Mason will find it charming.' Again the smile that did not reach her eyes. 'And not overrun by her own countrymen.' She turned to Laura. 'I understand that Tuscany has come to be known as Chiantishire. So amusing.'

'Has it?' Laura enquired with wooden untruthfulness. 'I didn't know.' Dear God, she thought. I'm going to be staying at a house owned by the chairman of the Arleschi Bank. This can't be happening.

'And Umbria is very beautiful,' the Signora continued. 'They call it the green heart of Italy, and there are many places to visit—Assisi—Perugia—San Sepulcro, the birthplace of the great Rafael. You will be spoiled for choice, *signorina*.'

Paolo cast a glance at the decorated ceiling. 'You call it a choice, *Mamma*?' he demanded. 'To risk our lives up and down that deathtrap of a road every time we want to go anywhere?'

He shook his head. 'If anything happens to my cousin Alessio, and I inherit, then the Villa Diana will be for sale the next day.'

There was another lengthier pause. Then: 'You must forgive my son, *signorina*,' the Signora said silkily. 'In the heat of the moment, he does not always speak with wisdom. And, even if it is a little remote, the house is charming.'

'And Alessio?' Paolo demanded petulantly, clearly resenting the rebuke. 'At least he can't mean to use the house himself, if we are there. Or he never has in the past.' He snorted. 'Probably off chasing some skirt.'

'Dear boy, the offer was made, and I was glad to accept. I did not enquire into his own plans.'

Laura had been listening with a kind of horrified fascination. She thought, I should not be hearing this.

Aloud, she said quietly, 'Paolo—isn't there somewhere else we could stay? A hotel, perhaps.'

'In the height of the tourist season?' Paolo returned derisively. 'We would be fortunate to find a cellar. No, it will have to be my cousin's villa. And at least it will be cooler in the hills,' he added moodily. 'When do we leave?'

'I thought tomorrow,' said the Signora. She rose. 'You must be tired after the flight, Signorina Mason. I shall ask Maria to show you your room so that you may rest a little.'

And so you can give your son your unvarnished opinion of his latest acquisition, thought Laura. But then this was only what she'd been led to expect, she reminded herself. She supposed she should be grateful that the Signora hadn't made a hysterical scene and ordered her out of the apartment.

The bedroom allocated to her was on the small side, and the bed was narrow, and not particularly comfortable. She had been shown the bathroom—a daunting affair in marble the colour of rare beef, but she was glad to find that the still-unsmiling Maria had supplied a jug of hot water and a matching basin for the washstand in her room.

She took off her shoes and dress, and had a refreshing wash. The soap was scented with lavender, and she thought with faint self-derision that it was the first friendly thing she'd discovered so far in Rome.

She dried herself with the rather harsh linen towel, then stretched out on top of the bed with a sigh.

The regrets she'd experienced on the plane were multiplying

with every moment that passed. Back in London, Paolo had persuaded her that it would be easy. A spot of acting performed against a backdrop of some of Europe's most beautiful scenery. Almost a game, he'd argued. And she'd be paid for it.

Well, she was fast coming to the conclusion that no amount of cash was worth the hassle that the next two weeks seemed to promise. Although most of her concerns about Paolo's future behaviour were largely laid to rest. The Signora, she thought with wry amusement, would prove a more than adequate chaperon. And if she had been in love with him, she'd have been faced with a frustrating time.

Her head was beginning to ache, and she reached down to her bag by the side of the bed for the small pack of painkillers she'd included at the last minute, and the bottle of mineral water she'd bought at the airport. It was lukewarm now, but better than nothing, she thought as she swallowed a couple of the tablets, then turned onto her side, resolutely closing her eyes.

The deed was done. She was in Italy, even if it wasn't turning out to be a dream come true.

Whatever, she thought wearily. There was no turning back now.

Dinner that night was not an easy occasion. Paolo had announced plans to take Laura out for a meal, but the Signora had pointed out with steely insistence that this would be unwise, as they would be making an early start in the morning to avoid travelling in the full heat of the day.

So they ate in the formal dining room, at a table that would have accommodated three times their number with room to spare. It did not make for a relaxed atmosphere, and conversation was so stilted that Laura wished Paolo and his mother would just speak Italian to each other, and leave her out of the situation.

She realised, of course, that she was being grilled. Remembered too that she and Paolo had agreed to keep her actual personal details to a minimum. As far as the Signora was concerned, she was a girl who shared a flat with several others, and who enjoyed a good time. Someone, she hinted with a touch of coyness, who had not allowed for the sudden entry of Mr Right into her life. And she sent Paolo a languishing look.

And whatever slights and unpleasantness might come her way, Laura knew she would always treasure the memory of the expression on the august lady's face as she absorbed that.

She had rehearsed the invented story of how and when she and Paolo had met so often that she was word-perfect. After all, she needed to give the impression that theirs was an established relationship of at least two months' standing, which deserved to be taken seriously, and might be ready to move on to the next stage.

For Steve, she thought with wry regret, substitute Paolo.

She even managed to turn some of the Signora's more probing queries into her background back on themselves by ingenuously asking what Paolo had been like as a small boy, and whether there were any childhood photographs of him that she could see.

She had to admit the food was delicious, although she'd had little appetite for it. And when dinner was over they returned to the *salotto*, and listened to music by Monteverdi.

And that, thought Laura, was by far the most pleasant part of the evening, not just because her late father had loved the same composer, but because conversation was kept to a minimum.

She was just beginning to relax when the Signora announced in a tone that did not welcome opposition that it was time to retire for the night.

Paolo wished her a very correct goodnight outside the *salotto*, but when Laura, dressing-gown clad, returned from the bathroom, she found him waiting in her room.

She checked uneasily. 'What are you doing here?'

'I wished to speak to you in private.' The grin he sent her was triumphant. 'You are completely brilliant, *carissima. Dio mio*, you almost convinced me. And *Mamma* is in such a fury.' He shook his head. 'I have just overheard her on the telephone, and she was *incandescente*. She must be speaking to her old friend Camilla Montecorvo, because she mentioned the name Vittoria several times.'

'Does that mean something?' Laura felt suddenly tired, and more than a little bewildered.

'Vittoria is the *nuora*—the daughter-in-law—of Signora Montecorvo,' Paolo explained, his grin widening. 'She causes big problems, and *Mamma* has heard all about them. Always, she has been the one to give advice to Camilla. But now it is her turn to complain,' he added gleefully. 'And she insists that her friend must listen, and help her.'

He almost hugged himself. 'It is all going as I hoped.'

'I wish I could say the same.' Laura bit her lip.

'You are regretting Tuscany?' Paolo shrugged. 'It was an unwelcome surprise for me also. And Alessio has other houses he could have lent *Mamma* that are not as remote as Besavoro,' he added, grimacing. 'For instance, he has a place near Sorrento where he keeps his boat, but no doubt he will be using that himself. He would not choose to stay anywhere near *Mamma*, so calm yourself on that point.'

'You're not a very close family,' Laura commented.

'Alessio likes to go his own way. *Mamma* tries to interfere.' He shrugged again. 'Maybe he is hoping she will stray too far from the house, and be eaten by the wolves.'

Laura stared at him. 'You mean there are such things..actually running wild?' Her tone held a hollow note.

'Yes, and they are on the increase. And there are bears too.' He laughed at her expression. 'But they are mainly found in the national parks, and I promise you that they prefer orchards and beehives to humans.'

'How—reassuring.' Laura took a deep breath. 'But it's not just disappointment over Tuscany, Paolo. Or the thought of moving to some Italian safari park either.'

She gave him a steady look. 'We shouldn't have started this. If your mother's so genuinely upset, it isn't a game any longer. I feel we should rethink.'

'For me, it has never been a game.' Paolo smote himself on the chest. 'For me—it is my life! I need my mother to know that my future is my own affair, and that I will not be dictated to by her or anyone. And that I am not going to marry Beatrice

Manzone.' He lowered his voice. Made it coaxing. 'Laura—you promised you would help me. We have an agreement together. And it is going well. Just two weeks—that is all. Then you will be free. You will have had your Italian vacation, and also been paid. This is so easy for you.'

He dropped a hand on her shoulder, making her move restively. 'After all,' he went on persuasively, 'what can possibly happen in two short weeks? Tell me that.' He smiled at her, then moved to the door. 'I tell you there is nothing to worry about.' His voice was warm—reassuring. 'Nothing in the world.'

CHAPTER THREE

LAURA did not sleep well that night. She was constantly tossing and turning, disturbed by a series of fleeting, uneasy dreams. Or, she wondered as daylight imposed itself at last, was she simply troubled by finding herself under the roof of a woman who cordially detested her—and with no reprieve in sight?

It was no particular surprise to find that the early start to Besavoro did not transpire. The car arrived punctually with Giacomo, its uniformed chauffeur, and there the matter rested while the Signora, after a leisurely breakfast, issued a stream of contradictory orders, made telephone calls, and wrote a number of last minute notes to friends.

Laura had discovered to her dismay that Caio was to accompany them and more time was wasted while Maria hunted the apartment for the special collar and lead he wore on holiday, and the new cushioned basket specially bought for the trip.

By the time the luggage was finally put in the car, Paolo looked as if he was about to become a basket case himself, Laura thought without particular sympathy.

It was one of the most luxurious vehicles she'd ever travelled in, but, seated in the back with the Signora and her dog in the opposite corner, she found it impossible to relax.

She'd expected another barrage of questions, and steeled herself to fend them off, but it didn't happen. The Signora seemed lost in thought, and, apart from lifting his lip in the occasional silent snarl if Laura glanced at him, Caio seemed equally detached.

There were numerous stops along the way—comfort breaks for Caio featuring frequently. But there were also pauses to buy coffee, chilled mineral water, and, once, some excellent rolls crammed with ham and cheese, at the busy roadside service stations. The Signora did not deign to leave the car on these occasions, but Laura was glad to stretch her legs in spite of the heat outside the air-conditioned car.

Her back was beginning to ache with the tension of trying to remain unobtrusive, she realised wryly.

She'd chosen her thinnest outfit for the journey—a loose-fitting dress in fine cream cotton with cap sleeves and a modestly square neckline. She wore low-heeled tan sandals, and a broad brimmed linen hat that could be rolled up in her bag when she was in the car. Apart from the obligatory sunblock, she'd put nothing on her face but a shading of mascara on her lashes, and a touch of light coral lustre to her mouth.

She tried to comfort herself with the reflection that the Signora might loathe her, but she couldn't truthfully complain about her appearance. Still it seemed small consolation.

The car didn't really need air conditioning, she thought ruefully. Paolo's mother could have lowered the temperature to arctic proportions with one look. And the cost of her brother's school trip was rising by the minute. He'd better enjoy it, that's all, she muttered under her breath.

But as they drove into Umbria she found herself succumbing to the sheer beauty of the scenery around her, all other considerations taking second place. Everywhere she looked seemed to be composed of endless shades of green, and every hilltop seemed crowned with its own little town, clinging precariously to its rocky crag.

Half an hour later they reached Besavoro, which seemed to be hardly more than a large village on the bank of a river, which Paolo told her was a tributary of the Tiber. The central point was the square, where houses and shops huddled round a tall, ornate church. There was a market taking place, and the cramped space had to be negotiated with care.

Once free of the village, they began to climb quite steeply, taking a narrow road up the side of the valley. They passed the occasional house, but generally it was rugged terrain with a steep rocky incline leading up to heavy woodland on one side, and, on the other, protected only by a low wall, a stomach-churning drop down to the clustering roofs, and the river, now reduced to a silver thread, below them.

She remembered Paolo's comment about a death trap, and suppressed a shiver, thankful that Giacomo was such a good driver.

'We are nearly there, *signorina*.' To her surprise, Laura found herself being addressed by the Signora. The older woman was even smiling faintly. 'No doubt you are eager to see where you will be spending your little vacation. I hope it lives up to your expectations.'

Any overture, however slight, was welcome, and Laura responded. 'Has the house been in the family long?' she enquired politely.

'For generations, although it has been altered and extended over the years. At one time, it is said to have been a hermitage, a solitary place where monks who had sinned were sent to do penance.'

'I know how they feel,' Paolo commented over his shoulder. 'I am astonished that Alessio should waste even an hour in such a place. He has certainly never repented of anything in his life.'

His mother shrugged. 'He spent much of his childhood here. Perhaps it has happy memories for him.'

'He was never a child,' said Paolo. 'And his past is what happened yesterday—no more.' He leaned forward. 'Look, Laura *mia*. You can see the house now, if you look down a little through the trees.'

She caught a glimpse of pale rose stonework, and faded terracotta tiles, and caught her breath in sudden magic.

It was like an enchanted place, sleeping among the trees, she thought, and she was coming to break the spell. And she smiled to herself, knowing she was being utterly absurd.

Impossible to miss the sound of an approaching car in the clear air, Alessio thought. His unwanted guests were arriving.

Sighing irritably, he swung himself off the sun lounger, and reached for the elderly pair of white tennis shorts lying on the marble tiles beside him, reluctantly dragging them on. For the past few days, he'd revelled in freedom and isolation. Basked in his ability to swim in the pool and sunbathe beside it naked, knowing that Guillermo and Emilia who ran the villa for him would never intrude on his privacy.

Now his solitude had ended.

He thrust his feet into battered espadrilles, and began walking up through the terraced gardens to the house.

Up to the last minute, he'd prayed that this nightmare would never happen. That Paolo and his *ragazza* would quarrel, or that Zia Lucrezia would love her as a daughter on sight, and withdraw her objections. Anything—anything that would let him off this terrible hook.

But her phone call the previous night had destroyed any such hopes. She'd been almost hysterical, he remembered with distaste, railing that the girl was nothing more than a gold-digging tart, coarse and obvious, a woman of the lowest class. But clever in a crude way because she obviously intended to trap into marriage her poor Paolo, who did not realise the danger he was in.

At the same time, she'd made it very clear that her threat to expose his fleeting affair with Vittoria, if he did not keep his word, was all too real.

'I want the English girl destroyed,' she had hissed at him. 'Nothing less will do.'

Alessio had been tempted to reply that he would prefer to destroy Vittoria, who was proving embarrassingly tenacious, bombarding him with phone calls and little notes, apparently unaware that her voluptuously passionate body in no way compensated for her nuisance value.

If she continued to behave with such indiscretion, Fabrizio and his mother might well smell a rat, without any intervention from Zia Lucrezia, he told himself grimly.

He'd been thankful to escape from Rome, and Vittoria's constant badgering, to this private hideaway where he could remain *incomunicabile*. He hoped that, during his absence, she would find some other willing target for her libido, or he might ultimately have to be brutal with her. A thought that gave him no pleasure whatsoever.

And now he was faced with another, worse calamity. This

unknown, unwanted girl that he had somehow to entice from Paolo's bed into his own. Probably, he decided, after he'd deliberately made himself very, very drunk...

If I emerge alive from this mess, I shall take a vow of celibacy, he thought moodily.

Guillermo was already opening the heavy wooden entrance door, and Emilia was hovering anxiously. He knew that his instructions would have been minutely carried out, and that the arrangements and the food would be perfect. But visitors at the villa were still a rarity, and the servants were more accustomed to their employer's own brand of casual relaxation. Zia Lucrezia's presence would prove taxing for all of them.

He stepped out of the shadowy hall into the sunlight. The car had halted a few feet away, and the chauffeur was helping the Signora to alight, while Caio yapped crossly from her arms.

But Alessio's attention was immediately on the girl, standing quietly, a little apart, looking up at the house. His first reaction was that she was not his type—or Paolo's, for that matter, and he found this faintly bewildering. In fact she fitted none of the preconceived images his aunt's fulminations had engendered, he thought critically as he observed her. Nearly as tall as Paolo himself, with clear, pale skin, a cloud of russet hair reaching to her shoulders, eyes like smoke, and a sweet, blunt-cornered mouth.

Not a conventional beauty—but curiously beguiling all the same.

Probably too slim, he mused, although the cheap dress she was wearing was singularly unrevealing.

And then, as if in answer to some silent wish, a faint breeze from the hills behind them blew the thin material back against her body, moulding it against the small, high breasts, the slight concavity of her stomach, the faintly rounded thighs, and long, slender legs.

Alessio, astonished, felt the breath catch suddenly in his throat, and, in spite of himself, he found his body stirring with frank and unexpected anticipation.

I've changed my mind, he thought in instant self-mockery. I

shan't get drunk after all. On the contrary, I think this *ragazza* deserves nothing less than my complete and sober attention.

He became aware that the Signora was approaching, her eyes studying him with disfavour.

'Is this how you dress to receive your visitors, Alessio?'

He took her hand, bowing over it. His smile glinted coldly at her. 'Ten minutes ago, Zia Lucrezia, I was not dressed at all. This is a concession.' He eyed Caio grimly. 'And you have brought your dog, I see. I hope he has learned better manners since our last encounter.' He looked past her to his cousin. 'Ah, Paolo, *come stai*?'

Paolo stared at him suspiciously. 'What are you doing here?'

Alessio gave him a look of mild surprise. 'It is my house, which makes me your host. Naturally, I wish to be here to attend to your comfort.'

'You are not usually so concerned,' Paolo muttered.

Alessio grinned at him. 'No? Then perhaps I have seen the error of my ways. And the house has enough rooms for us all. You will not be required to share with me, cousin,' he added blandly, then looked at the girl as if he had just noticed her. 'And the name of your charming companion?' Deliberately, he kept his voice polite rather than enthusiastic, noting the nervousness in the grey eyes under their dark fringe of lashes.

Paolo took her hand defensively. 'This is Signorina Laura Mason, who has come with me from London. Laura, may I present my cousin, the Count Alessio Ramontella.'

He saw that she did not meet his gaze, but looked down instead at the flagstoned courtyard. 'How do you do, *signore*?' Her voice was quiet and clear.

'Allow me to welcome you to my home, *signorina*.' He inclined his head with formal courtesy, then led the way into the house. 'Emilia, please show the ladies where they are to sleep. And the dog. Guillermo, will you take my cousin to his room?'

As he was turning away Paolo grabbed his arm. 'What is this?' he hissed. 'Where are you putting Laura?'

'In the room next to your mother's—at her request.' Alessio shrugged. 'I am sorry if you are disappointed, but you also know that she would never permit you to sleep with your girlfriend under any roof that she was sharing. Besides, if you even approach that part of the house, that little hairy rat of your *mamma's* will hear and start yapping.' His grin was laced with faint malice. 'Like the old monks, you will have to practise chastity.'

'A lesson you have yet to learn,' Paolo returned sourly.

'In general, perhaps, but I have never brought a woman here,' Alessio told him softly.

'Talking of which,' Paolo said, 'what do you think of my little English *inamorata*?'

'Do you need my opinion?' Alessio gave him a steady look. 'If she satisfies you, cousin, that should be enough.' He paused. 'Although usually you like them with more...' He demonstrated with his hands.

'*Sì*,' Paolo agreed lasciviously. 'But this girl has—hidden depths, if you take my meaning.' And he laughed.

It occurred to Alessio that he had never particularly liked his cousin, and at this moment it would give him great pleasure to smack him in the mouth.

Instead he invited him to make himself at home, and went off to his own room to shower and change.

Laura felt dazed as she followed Emilia and the Signora along a series of passages. The Villa Diana was a single-storey building, and it seemed to ramble on forever in a leisurely way. But she was in no mood to take real stock of her surroundings. Not yet.

That, she thought with disbelief, *that* was the Count Ramontella, the august head of the Arleschi Bank? That half-naked individual with the unruly mane of curling black hair, and the five o'clock shadow?

She'd assumed, when she first saw him, that he must be the caretaker, or the gardener.

She'd expected an older, staider version of Paolo, conventionally good-looking with a figure that would incline to plumpness in middle age. But the Count was fully six feet tall, with a lean, muscular golden-skinned body that she'd had every opportunity to admire. The shorts he'd been wearing, slung low on his narrow hips, just erred on the right side of decency, she thought, her face warming slightly at the recollection.

And he was nowhere near middle life—hardly more than in his early thirties, if she was any judge. Not, she supposed, that she was.

As for the rest of him—well, his face was more striking than handsome, with a high-bridged beak of a nose, a frankly cynical mouth, and eyes as dark as midnight that looked at the world with bored indifference from under their heavy lids. Or at least, she amended, that was the way he'd looked at her.

And he wasn't his aunt's greatest admirer either, as Paolo had suggested. She hadn't understood their brief exchange, but she'd detected a certain amount of snip, all the same.

But, if that was how he felt about his visitors, why was he here, when he wasn't expected and it was clear that he had better places to go? It seemed to make no sense.

Whatever, she could not imagine him being pleased to find he was entertaining a very minor cog from his London branch's PR machine. All the more reason, she told herself, for her connection with Harman Grace to remain a closely guarded secret. So—she'd continue to be the girl Paolo had met in a bar, and let his noble relative pick the bones out of that.

But her troubled musings ceased when Emilia, a comfortably built woman with a beaming smile, flung open a door with a triumphant, *'Ecco, signorina,'* indicating that this was her bedroom.

Laura took a step inside, and looked round, her eyes widening with delight. It couldn't have presented a greater contrast to the opulent and cluttered apartment where she'd stayed yesterday. For one thing, it was double the size of the room she'd occupied there, she realised, with a floor tiled in a soft pink marble, while the white plaster walls still bore traces of ancient frescos, which she would examine at her leisure.

But that was the only suggestion of the villa's age. For the present day, there was a queen-sized bed, prettily hung with filmy white curtains, which also graced the shuttered windows. A chest of drawers, a clothes cupboard, and a night table comprised the rest of the furniture, and a door led to a compact but luxurious shower room, tiled in the same shade of pink. The only other additions to the bedroom were a lamp beside the bed, and a bowl of roses on the chest.

She turned to Emilia. 'Perfect,' she said, smiling. And, managing to ignore Signora Vicente's disdainful glance, *'Perfetto.'*

When she was alone, she went over to the window, and pulled it wide. It opened, she saw, onto a three-sided courtyard, bordered by a narrow colonnade, like a medieval cloister, and she stepped through, gazing around her. There was a small fountain in the centre of the paved area, with a battered cherub pouring water from a shell into a shallow pool, while beside it stood a stone bench.

Directly ahead of her, Laura saw, the courtyard itself opened out into the sunlit grass and flowers of the garden beyond, and from somewhere not too far away she could hear the cooing of doves.

But it wasn't all peace and tranquillity, she realised wryly. From even closer at hand, she could hear the raised autocratic tones of the Signora, mingled with Emilia's quieter replies.

A salutary reminder that this little piece of Eden also had its serpents, not to mention wolves and bears, she thought, gazing up at the thickly forested slopes that brooded above her.

Suddenly, she felt tired, sticky and a little dispirited. She'd seen that there were towels and a range of toiletries waiting in the shower room, so decided she might as well make use of them.

She stood under the powerful jet of warm water, lathering her skin luxuriously with soap that smelt of lilies, feeling as if her anxieties were draining away with the suds and she were being somehow reborn, refreshed and invigorated.

Most of the towels were linen, but there were a couple of fluffy bath sheets as well, and when she was dry she wound herself in one of them, and trailed back into the bedroom.

While she'd been occupied, her case had arrived and was waiting on the bed, so she busied herself with unpacking. She hadn't brought nearly enough, she thought, viewing the results with disfavour, and very little that was smart or formal enough for someone who found herself staying with a count at his private villa.

The outfit that had survived with the fewest creases was a wrap-around dress in a silver-grey silky material, and she decided to try and create a good impression by wearing it for dinner that night.

She had a solitary credit card, kept for emergencies, and maybe she could persuade Paolo to risk the road from hell on a trip to Perugia, so that she could supplement her wardrobe a little.

Whatever she wore, the Signora would sneer, and she accepted that. But for reasons she could not explain, or even admit to, she did not want Count Ramontella looking at her with equal disdain.

She wanted him to accept the fiction that she and Paolo were an item. Perhaps to acknowledge, in some way she hadn't worked out yet, that she was an eligible bride for his cousin, and welcome her as such.

And pigs might fly, she thought morosely.

In the meantime, she wasn't sure what to do next. The whole villa seemed enveloped in sleepy heat. There was even silence from the adjoining room, the only sound being the faint soothing splash of the fountain.

Laura felt she could hardly blunder about exploring her new surroundings, alone and uninvited, in case she committed some kind of social *faux pas*.

So, she decided, she was probably better off remaining where she was until summoned.

She was just about to stretch out on the bed with her book when there was a knock at the door.

Paolo, she thought instantly, wishing she were wearing something more reliable than a big towel. But when she cautiously opened the door, and peeped round it, she found Emilia waiting with a tray.

Beaming, the older woman informed her in halting English that His Excellency thought the *signorina* might need some refreshment after her journey, then placed the tray in her hands and departed.

Laura carried the tray over to the bed and set it down with

care. It held a teapot, with a dish of lemon slices, a plate of tiny crustless sandwiches containing some kind of pâté, and a bowl of golden cherries faintly flushed with crimson.

It was a kindness she had not anticipated, she thought with faint bewilderment. In fact the Count Ramontella seemed positively full of surprises.

But perhaps she was reading too much into this. Clearly his hospitality was primarily aimed at his aunt, and she'd been included as an afterthought.

Because her host didn't seem like a man who went in for random acts of kindness, Laura thought, remembering uneasily the faint curl of that beautifully moulded mouth.

So, she might as well make the most of this one, while it was on offer.

She ate every scrap of the delicious sandwiches with two cups of tea, then lay back with a contented sigh, savouring the cherries as she read. Later, she dozed for a while.

When she eventually awoke, the sun was much lower in the sky, and shadows were beginning to creep across the courtyard outside.

She donned a lacy bra and briefs, then sat down to make up her face with rather more care than usual, before giving her glossy fall of russet hair a vigorous brushing and fastening silver hoops in her ears. Finally, she sprayed her skin with the fresh, light scent she used, then slipped into the chosen dress, winding its sash round her slender waist and fastening it in a bow.

She'd brought one pair of flattish evening sandals in a neutral pewter shade—light years away from the glamorous shoes with their dizzyingly high heels that Italy was famous for. But even if she'd possessed such a pair, she wouldn't have been able to wear them, she conceded regretfully, because that would have made her slightly taller than Paolo, who was sensitive about his height.

Count Ramontella, of course, had no such concerns, she thought. The highest heels in the world would only have raised her to a level with his chin. And God only knew why such a thing had even occurred to her.

It was time she concentrated on Paolo, and the task she'd agreed to perform.

She let herself out of her bedroom, and started down the passage, trying to retrace her earlier steps. She had more time to observe her surroundings now, and she realised that the whole place was a series of courtyards, some completely enclosed, each of them marked by its own fountain, or piece of statuary.

And a good job too, because it's like a labyrinth, she thought, hesitating, totally at a loss, as the passage she was negotiating crossed another. To her relief, the white-coated manservant who had been at the entrance when they'd arrived appeared from nowhere, and indicated politely that she should follow him.

The room she was shown to was enormous, its focal point a huge stone fireplace surmounted by a coat of arms. It was also empty, and Laura hesitated in the doorway, feeling dwarfed by her surroundings, and a little isolated too.

Obviously, she had left her room much too early. The Italians, she recalled, were apt to dine later than people did in England, but she decided to stay where she was rather than attempt that maze of passages again.

She saw with interest that, in here, some restoration work had been done to the frescoed walls, and wandered round, taking a closer, fascinated look and speculating on their age. There were various hunting scenes, and, more peacefully, an outdoor feast with music and dancing, and the style of dress suggested the sixteenth century.

At the far end of the room, large floor-length windows stood open, leading out to a terrace from which a flight of steps descended, leading down to further gardens below.

Once again, furniture in the *salotto* had been kept to a minimum—a few massive sofas, their dimensions reduced by the proportions of the room, and a long, heavily carved sideboard were the main features. Also, more unusually, a grand piano.

It was open and, intrigued, Laura crossed to it and sat down on the stool, running her fingers gently over the keys, listening to its lovely, mellow sound.

She gave a small sigh. So many sad things had followed her

father's death, and the loss of her own much-loved piano was only one of them.

She tried a quiet chord or two, then, emboldened by the fact that she was still alone, launched herself into a modern lullaby that she had once studied as an exam piece.

Perhaps because it had always been a favourite of hers, she got through it without too much faltering, and sighed again as she played the final plangent notes, lost in her own nostalgic world.

She started violently as the music died to be replaced with the sound of someone clapping. She turned swiftly and apprehensively towards the doorway.

'*Bravo,*' said the Count Ramontella, and walked slowly across the room towards her.

CHAPTER FOUR

'OH CHRISTMAS,' Laura muttered under her breath, aware that she was blushing. 'I'm so sorry, *signore*. I didn't realise...' She swallowed. 'I had no right—no right at all...'

'*Nonsenso*. That was charming.' He came to lean against the corner of the piano, the dark eyes watching her coolly. He was totally transformed, she thought, having shaved, and combed his hair neatly back from his face. And he was wearing slim-fitting black trousers, which emphasised his long legs, offset by a snowy shirt, open at the throat, and topped by a crimson brocaded waistcoat, which he had chosen to leave unbuttoned.

He looked, Laura thought, swallowing again, casually magnificent.

'At last my decision to keep it in tune is justified,' he went on. 'It has not been played, I believe, since my mother died.'

'Oh, God, that makes everything worse.' She shook her head wretchedly. 'I must apologise again. This was—is—such an unforgivable intrusion.'

'But I do not agree,' he said. 'I think it delightful. Won't you play something else?'

'Oh, no.' She got up hastily, her embarrassment increasing, and was halted, the hem of her dress snagged on the protruding corner of the piano stool. 'Damn,' she added, jerking at the fabric, trying to release herself.

'*Sta' quieto,*' the Count commanded. 'Keep still, or you will tear it.' He dropped gracefully to one knee beside her, and deftly set her free.

She looked down at the floor. 'Thank you.'

'It is nothing.' He rose to his feet, glancing around him. 'What have you done with Paolo?'

'I—I haven't seen him since we arrived.'

44

'*Davvero?*' His brows lifted. 'I hope he is not neglecting you.' He sent her a faint smile. 'If so, you may be glad of the piano to provide you with entertainment.'

'Oh, no,' she said quickly. 'He isn't neglectful. Not at all.' She paused. 'Perhaps his mother wanted to talk to him.'

'If so, I think her revolting little dog would have told us all.' He was silent for a moment. 'Tell me, did you enjoy your afternoon tea?'

Her eyes flew to his dark face. 'You—really arranged that? That was very kind.'

He shrugged. 'We tend to have the evening meal later than you are used to in England. I did not wish you to faint with hunger.' He smiled at her pleasantly. 'You will soon become accustomed to Italian time.'

'I'll certainly try,' she said. 'But you can't make many adjustments in two weeks.'

His smile widened slightly. 'On the contrary, I think a great deal can change very quickly.' He walked over to the sideboard. 'May I get you a drink? I intend to have a whisky.'

'I'm fine—really.' She wasn't. Her throat felt as dry as a bone, and had done ever since she'd seen him standing there.

'There is orange juice,' he went on as if she hadn't spoken. 'Have you tried it with campari?'

'Well—no.'

'Then do so now.' He mixed the drink, and brought it to her. Touched his glass to hers. '*Salute.*'

'*Grazie,*' Laura said rather stiffly.

'*Prego.*' This time his smile was a grin. 'Tell me, *signorina*, are you always this tense?'

She sipped her drink, liking the way the sweetness of the juice blended with the bitterness of the campari. She said, haltingly, 'Not always, but this is a difficult situation for me.' She took a breath. 'You must be wondering, *signore*, what I'm doing here.'

'You came with my cousin,' he said. 'It is no secret.'

She took a deep breath. 'So, you must also know that his mother is not pleased about my presence.'

He drank some whisky, his eyes hooded. 'I do not concern

myself in my aunt's affairs, *signorina*.' He paused, and she saw that slight curl of the mouth again. 'At least, not unless they are forced upon my notice.'

She said rather forlornly, 'Just as I have been—haven't I?'

'Perhaps,' he said. 'But, believe me, *signorina*, now that we have met, I expect nothing but pleasure from your visit.' Before she could prevent him, he took her hand and raised it to his lips, kissing it lightly and swiftly.

The dark gaze glinted at her as he released her. 'Would it help you relax if we were a little less formal with each other? My name is Alessio, and I know that yours is Laura.'

She was aware that the colour had stormed back into her face. She said a little breathlessly, 'I think your aunt might object.'

His tone was silky. 'Then let us agree to leave her to her own devices, *si*?'

'Yes,' she said. 'If you're quite sure.'

'I am certain.' He paused. 'Shall we take our drinks onto the terrace? It is pleasant there in the evenings.'

Laura followed reluctantly. She hadn't bargained for this, she thought uneasily. She'd expected Paolo to be hovering constantly, acting as a barrier between her and his family.

There was a table on the terrace, and comfortable cushioned chairs. Alessio held one for her courteously, then took the adjoining seat. There was a silence, and Laura took a nervous sip of her drink.

'You and Paolo aren't very alike—for cousins,' she ventured at last.

'No,' Alessio said, contemplating his whisky. 'There is very little resemblance between us. Physically, I believe he favours his late father.'

'I see.' She hesitated, then said in a small wooden voice, 'His mother, the Signora, is a very—striking woman.'

'She has a forceful personality, certainly,' he said drily. 'I understand that, when she was young, she was also considered a great beauty.' He leaned back in his chair. 'Tell me, Laura, how did you meet my cousin?'

'I work in a wine bar,' she said. 'He was one of the customers.'

'Ah,' he said. 'So you are not always as shy as you are with me.'

'But then,' she returned, 'I wasn't expecting to meet you, *signore*.'

'You have forgotten,' he said. 'We agreed it would be Alessio.'

No, she thought. I haven't forgotten a thing. I'm not ready to be on first-name terms—or any terms at all—with someone like you.

There was a loud sneeze from inside the *salotto*, and Paolo emerged, flourishing a large handkerchief. '*Maledizione*, I am getting a cold,' he said peevishly. 'Some germ on the plane, *indubbiamente*.'

Laura decided this was her cue. 'Darling.' She got up and went to his side, sliding her arm through his. 'How horrid for you. Summer colds are always the worst.'

For a second, he looked at her as if he'd forgotten who she was, then he pulled himself together, kissing her rather awkwardly on the cheek. 'Well, I must take care not to pass it on to you, *carissima. Che peccato*, eh? What a pity.' He slid an arm round her, his fingers deliberately brushing the underside of her breast.

Laura, nailing on a smile, longed to pull away and kick him where it hurt. Alessio drank some more whisky, his face expressionless.

If she'd hoped that the arrival of his mother a short while later would impose some constraint upon Paolo, Laura was doomed to disappointment. He'd drawn his chair close beside hers at the table, and appeared glued to her side, his hand stroking her arm and shoulder possessively, his lips never far from her ear, her hair, or her cheek, nibbling little caresses that she found positively repellent.

She knew, of course, that the Signora was watching, her mouth drawn into a tight line, because that was the purpose of the exercise. And there was nothing she could do about it. But she was also sharply aware that the Count was sending them the odd meditative glance, and this, for some reason, she found even more disturbing than the older woman's furious scrutiny.

She found she was silently repeating, 'Think of the money. Think of the money,' over and over again like a mantra, but it was not producing the desired calming effect, and she was thankful to her heart when dinner was finally announced, and Paolo reluctantly had to relinquish his hold.

The dining room was a long, low-ceilinged room, with a wonderful painted ceiling depicting some Bacchanalian revel, with people wearing bunches of grapes instead of clothes.

The scene below was much more decorous, the polished table gleaming with silver and crystal in the light of several elaborate candelabra. Alessio sat at the head of the table, with his aunt facing him at its foot, and Laura was seated halfway down, opposite Paolo, the width of the table putting her beyond the reach of any more amorous overtures.

Not that he seemed in the mood any longer. Instead he kept sighing, blowing his nose, and occasionally putting a hand to his forehead, as if checking his own temperature.

In spite of her concerns, Laura found she was really hungry, and tucked into the wild mushroom risotto, the veal in a rich wine sauce, and the creamy almond-flavoured dessert that she was offered with a good appetite. But she was far more sparing with the wine that Guillermo tried to pour into her glass, recognising that she needed to keep her wits about her.

Conversation was kept to general topics, and conducted in English. The Signora tried a few times to switch to Italian, but was forestalled by the Count, who silkily reminded her that she was overlooking the presence of their guest, so that she was forced to subside, glaring.

The meal was almost over when Paolo dropped his bombshell. '*Mamma*—the ring that my grandmother left me, which you keep in the safe at the *appartamento*. You will give it to me when we return to Rome, if you please?'

The ensuing silence was electric. Laura kept her eyes fixed on her plate. Oh, God, she wailed inwardly. What possessed him to say that—and why didn't he warn me?

Whatever she herself might think of the Signora, and no matter what disagreement over the future Paolo might be engaged in with her, the older woman was still his mother—and he was deliberately taunting her. Pushing his supposed relationship to new limits.

She thought, biting her lip, This is so wrong...

'It is a valuable piece of jewellery,' the Signora said at last, her voice shaking a little. 'It needs to be kept in security. But of course, *figlio mio*, it is for you to decide.'

'And I have done so.' Paolo sent her a bland smile. 'It is time it was in my keeping.'

Laura put down her spoon, unable to eat another mouthful. Across the candle flames, she sent Paolo a condemnatory look.

After that the conversation flagged, and she was thankful when the Count suggested that they have coffee in the *salotto*.

It was served black and very strong in small cups.

'*Grappa* for the *signorina*.' Guillermo proffered a tiny glass of colourless liquid, and she glanced across at Paolo, whose expression was so smug she could have slapped him.

'What is *grappa*?' she asked.

'A kind of brandy,' he said. 'Good for the digestion.'

For medicinal purposes only, Laura thought, raising the glass to her lips. She took one cautious sip, and nearly choked, eyes streaming.

'My God,' she said when she could speak, accepting the glass of mineral water that Alessio handed her. 'How strong is that?'

'About ninety-per-cent proof,' he told her, amused. 'You have never drunk it before?'

'No,' she said with feeling. 'I would definitely have remembered.'

The Count looked at his cousin. 'Paolo, you have neglected Laura's education.'

Paolo stopped mopping his face long enough to leer. '*Al contrario*, my dear Alessio, I've been concentrating on the things that matter.'

Alessio gave him a thoughtful look, but made no comment, while Laura sat, her face burning, wishing the floor would open.

The Signora, who had been sitting like a stone statue in a corner of the sofa, abruptly announced her intention of watching television, which, Laura discovered, was housed in a large carved cabinet in the corner of the room. It was some kind of current affairs programme, which she was unable to follow, so her interest soon waned.

Instead, she watched the chess game now in progress between the two men. She was no expert, but it was soon obvious that Paolo had got himself into an impossible position.

'I feel too ill to play,' he said peevishly as he resigned. 'I shall tell Emilia to make a *tisana* and bring it to my bedroom.'

He pushed back his chair and got up, kissing Laura on the cheek. 'Goodnight, *carissima*. If I sleep now, I shall be well tomorrow, so that we can spend some time alone together, and I can show you my beautiful country. Starting maybe with Assisi, hmm?'

Laura forced a smile, and murmured that it would be wonderful.

He kissed his mother's hand, ignored the basilisk glance she sent him, and disappeared.

Alessio moved the pieces back to the starting point and looked up at Laura. 'Would you like to challenge the winner?' he asked.

'After the way you dealt with Paolo, I don't think so.' Her tone was rueful. 'You need my young brother. He was school chess champion when he was six.'

'Your brother?' the Signora suddenly interrupted. 'I thought you were an only child, *signorina*.'

Laura realised too late that was what she'd agreed with Paolo. Not just an only child, but an orphan too. It would save them many problems if she was without family, he'd decreed. And she'd just blown it.

Which meant she would have to warn him first thing tomorrow about her unguarded words.

In the meantime: 'Is that the impression I gave, *signora*?' She made herself speak lightly. 'It was probably wishful thinking.' She paused. 'And now, perhaps you'll excuse me, too. It's been a long day, and I still have to negotiate the maze back to my room.'

Alessio rose. 'Permit me,' he said. He walked to the fireplace and tugged at the bell-pull that hung there. A moment later, Guillermo appeared, his face enquiring. 'The *signorina* is ready to retire. Please escort her,' he directed quietly.

Laura was still suddenly, aware of an odd disappointment. Then: 'Thank you,' she said stiltedly. 'And—goodnight.'

Alessio watched in silence as she followed Guillermo from the room.

As soon as they had gone the Signora was on her feet with a hiss of impatience. 'Are you mad? Why did you not take her to her room yourself? It was your chance to be alone with the little fool.'

His mouth tightened in the knowledge he had been sorely tempted to do exactly that, and had deliberately resisted the impulse. 'I know what I am doing,' he told her curtly. 'Or do you want her to take fright, and scuttle off to Paolo for sanctuary?'

'Take fright?' she echoed contemptuously. 'That one? What are you talking about?'

Alessio sighed. 'I merely wish to point out that she does not seem a girl one would pick up in a bar. I am—surprised.'

She gave a harsh laugh. 'So that look of mock innocence has deceived you, my worldly nephew, as it has my poor boy.' She spread her hand. 'Can you doubt how besotted he is with her? To ask for Nonna Caterina's ring so brazenly. The ring I planned for him to give to Beatrice. I could not believe it.'

'Neither, I think, could she,' Alessio said drily. 'Are you really so sure they are in love, or does he simply wish to sell the ring to pay off his gambling debts?'

'Love?' She almost spat the word, ignoring his jibe. 'What does that mean? She is attracted by my son's background—his position in the world. She believes he is also wealthy.'

'Then show her his bank statements,' Alessio said coldly. 'That will cure her, and save me a great deal of trouble.'

'But it will not cure him. You saw him this evening. He could not keep his hands off her.'

'So it would seem,' Alessio agreed slowly. 'It is as well, perhaps, that they are sleeping at opposite ends of the house.'

'You have forgotten this sightseeing tour tomorrow.' The Signora frowned. 'No doubt they will go only as far as the nearest hotel willing to rent them a room for a few hours.'

Alessio felt his mouth twist with sudden and profound distaste at the image her words conjured up, and denounced himself with silent savagery for being a hypocrite.

He said icily, 'Then I suggest, my dear aunt, that you too develop a sudden interest in the local attractions. You have not, after all, seen the Giotto frescos in the basilica at Assisi since their restoration. Go with them, and act as chaperon, if you think it is necessary. And take the dog with you. Teach him to bite Paolo each time he touches the girl.'

'Oh, there is no reasoning with you when you are in this mood.' The Signora swept to the door. 'I will bid you goodnight.' She turned and gave him a measuring look. 'But our agreement still stands. Be in no doubt of that.'

When he was alone, Alessio walked over to the piano, and stood picking out a few notes with one finger, his face thoughtful. He found himself remembering the delicate flush that had warmed Laura's pale skin when she'd looked up and seen him watching and listening in the doorway. Recalled even more acutely how her clean fragrance had assailed his senses as he'd knelt beside her to free her skirt.

The dress had been a beguiling one altogether, he thought. In other circumstances it would have been so simple to release the sash, and let it fall apart, revealing the warm sweetness beneath the silvery folds. So enticing to touch her as he wished, and feel her smooth skin under his mouth.

He found himself smiling, wondering if she would blush as deeply when she was aroused.

Not a wise thought to take to bed with you, he told himself wryly as he began to turn off the lights in the room. And he must be insane to indulge in this kind of adolescent fantasy about a girl he needed to keep, coolly and clinically, on the far edge of his life. But, then, only a fool would have allowed himself to be caught in this kind of trap in the first place.

And found he was sighing with unexpected bitterness as he walked to the door.

It was a long time before Laura fell asleep that night. She was tired, but aware of too many disturbing vibrations in the house to be able to relax completely. And her one recurring thought was that she was no longer sure she could go on with this charade, which was becoming far too complicated.

And, she suspected, unmanageable.

What was Paolo going to demand she did next? she asked herself, exasperated. Actually become engaged to him?

Once she'd got him to herself tomorrow, she would be able to talk to him seriously, she thought with determination. Persuade him that things had gone far enough, and his mother had been given sufficient shocks to last a lifetime. Surely the Signora must be convinced by now that her plan to marry him off was dead in the water—especially after that stunt he'd pulled at dinner, she thought grimly. They didn't need to take any more risks.

Now, somehow, she had to persuade him to take her away from the Villa Diana. Or, if she was really honest, separate her from its owner.

In spite of the heat, she found herself shivering.

She had been following Guillermo through the passages when it had suddenly hit her just how much she'd been hoping that the Count himself would offer to accompany her.

And how many kinds of madness was that? she asked herself with a kind of despair.

She'd been in his company for only a few hours, and already her awareness of him was threatening to spin out of control.

For God's sake, grow up, she told herself wearily, giving the pillows a thump.

Yes, there'd been times when the courtesy she knew he'd have shown to any guest under his roof had seemed to slip into kindness, but that could have been an attempt to make amends for his aunt's unfailing rudeness. And she'd be fooling herself if she thought otherwise, even for a moment.

The Arleschi Bank was considered a model of its kind, keenly efficient, highly respected, and superbly profitable, which was why Harman Grace were so keen to represent it. And it was clear that the bank's chairman played a key role in its achievements.

Count Alessio Ramontella lived in the full radiance of the sun, Laura thought, whereas she occupied some small, cold planet on the outmost edge of the solar system. That was the way it was, and always would be. And it was her bad luck that their paths had ever been forced to cross.

She closed her eyes against the memory of his smile, its sudden brilliance turning the rather ruthless lines of his mouth to charm and humour. She tried to forget, too, the warmth of that swift brush of his lips on her hand, and the way even that most fleeting of touches had pierced her to the bone.

It occurred to her that if Steve's kisses had carried even a fraction of the same shattering charge, he'd probably have been a happy man at this very moment, and Paolo would have had to look elsewhere for a partner in his scam.

I really need to get away from here, she told herself, moving restlessly, feeling the fine linen sheet that covered her grazing her skin as if it were raw. And soon.

It could be managed, of course, and quite easily. Paolo could pretend to take her on the visit to Tuscany they'd originally planned. Once they were alone, who would ever know if she slipped away and took an early flight back to London? And as long as Paolo kept a low profile, he could spend his vacation time exactly as he wished.

It wasn't what she wanted—it saddened her that she wouldn't see Florence or any of the region's other proud cities—but it was clear that she could no longer trust Paolo. And it was a way of dealing with a problem that was threatening to snowball into a crisis, entirely through her own stupidity.

Not that she could ever tell Paolo that. This was another truth that would have to be suppressed.

And he never wanted to come here in the first place, she thought. So he can hardly complain if I say I want to leave.

She turned over, burying her face determinedly in the pillow. And if her sleep was haunted by dreams, they did not linger to be remembered in the morning.

The determination, however, persisted, stronger than ever, and Laura sang softly to herself as she showered and dressed in a blue denim skirt and a sleeveless white top.

It was another glorious day, with the sun already burning off the faint haze around the tops of the hills. Probably her last day in Italy, she thought, and she would make the most of every minute.

She and Paolo would sort everything on the trip to Assisi, and by tomorrow they could be out of here, and life could return to normal again.

She would even learn to laugh about the last couple of days. Make a good story out of the Signora. Tell Gaynor, 'Hey, I met a man who was the ultimate sex on a stick, and fabulously wealthy too.' Let it all sound like fun, without a moment of self-doubt, she thought as she brushed her hair.

She had taken careful note of the route to the main part of the house the previous night, and found the dining room without difficulty, only to discover that it was deserted with no sign of food.

They eat dinner late, maybe breakfast is the same, she thought, slightly nonplussed. As she was wandering back into the entrance hall she was swooped on by Emilia, who led her firmly into the *salotto* and indicated that she should go out onto the terrace.

She emerged cautiously and paused in dismay, because Alessio was there alone, seated at the table, which was now covered by a white cloth. A few feet away, in the shade, a large trolley was stationed, and she saw that it held a platter with ham on the bone, together with a dish of cheese, a basket of bread rolls and a bowl of fruit. A pot of coffee was keeping warm on a heater.

'Buon giorno.' He had seen her, and, putting down the news-

paper he was reading, rose to his feet, depriving her of the chance to retreat back into the villa. 'You rested well?'

'Yes—thank you.' Reluctantly, she took the seat he indicated and unfolded her napkin, glancing at the table. 'Only two places?' Her brow furrowed. 'Where are the others?'

'They are breakfasting in their rooms,' Alessio told her. 'My aunt, because she prefers it. Paolo, because he is too ill to leave his bed,' he added sardonically.

'Too ill?' Laura echoed, taking the glass of chilled peach juice he'd poured for her. 'What do you mean?'

He shrugged. 'His cold. It has become infinitely worse. His mother is most concerned. Every lemon we possess is being squeezed to make drinks for him, and she has commandeered every painkiller in the house.'

'Oh.' Laura digested this, her dismay deepening by the second. She had not bargained for this development. She said, 'Perhaps I'd better go to him, too. See how he is, and if I can help.'

'A word of advice, *bella mia*,' Alessio said lazily. 'A wolf, a bear and my aunt Lucrezia—never come between any of them and their cubs. So, stay where you are, and eat. You will be much safer, I promise you.'

He got to his feet, lithe in cream denim trousers and a black polo shirt, and went to the trolley. 'May I bring you some of this excellent ham?'

'Thank you.' She watched him carve several slices off the bone with deft precision. As he placed the plate in front of her she said, 'Maybe he'll feel better later on, and be able to get up. We're supposed to be going to Assisi.'

'Paolo will be going nowhere for the foreseeable future,' Alessio said calmly. 'Unless his mother insists on my summoning a helicopter to take him to the nearest hospital, of course.'

'He has a cold in the head.' Laura's mouth tightened. 'It's hardly terminal.'

'It would be inadvisable to say so in front of Zia Lucrezia.' Alessio ate a forkful of ham. 'Not that we will see much of her either,' he added meditatively. 'Her time will be taken up with nursing the invalid, smoothing his pillow, reading aloud to him, and bullying my poor Emilia into creating little delicacies to tempt his failing appetite.'

Laura finished her peach juice, and set down the glass. She said slowly, 'You're really serious about this.'

'No, but my aunt is. However,' he added silkily, 'I gather that, with rest and quiet, the prognosis is generally favourable.'

In spite of her private concerns, Laura found herself laughing. 'It's just so absurd. All this fuss about a cold.'

'Ah, but it is the areas of fuss that matter in marriage, I am told,' Alessio said blandly. 'It is best to discover what they are before the ceremony, and you have now been given a valuable insight into Paolo's concerns about his health.'

He watched with interest as Laura began to cut her ham into small, careful squares.

'You plan to marry my cousin, of course?' he added after a pause.

Her eyes flew warily to his face. 'I—I think...I mean—there's nothing formal. Not yet.'

'But you are travelling with him in order to meet his family. And last night it seemed certain,' he said. 'For the Vicentes, as for the Ramontellas, the giving of a ring—particularly an heirloom—is a serious thing. A declaration of irrevocable intent. One man, one woman bound in love for the rest of their lives.'

'Oh.' She swallowed. 'I didn't know that. He—didn't tell me.'

'And now you must wait until he recovers from this trying cold,' Alessio agreed, adding briskly, 'Would you like coffee, or shall I tell Emilia to bring you tea?'

Her mind had gone into overdrive, and she had to drag herself back to the present moment. 'Oh—coffee would be fine.'

She took the cup he brought her with a murmur of thanks.

'You seem a little upset,' he commented as he resumed his seat. 'May I know the problem?'

'It's nothing, really.' She bit her lip. 'Just that I feel a bit useless and in the way with Paolo being ill.' She tried to smile. 'I shan't know what to do with myself.'

'Then I suggest you relax.' He pointed to the steps. 'They lead down to the swimming pool, a pleasant place to sunbathe—and dream about the future, perhaps.'

He smiled at her. 'And try not to worry too much about Paolo,' he advised lightly. 'He has about six colds a year. You will have plenty of opportunity to nurse him, I promise.'

She put down her cup, staring at him suspiciously. 'You're making fun of me.'

'Well, a little, perhaps.' The smile widened into a grin. 'Teasing you is almost irresistible, believe me.'

He pushed away his plate and sat back in his chair, regarding her. 'But allow me to make amends. I have to go out presently on a matter of business in the village. But if you came with me, we could combine it with pleasure by driving on to Assisi. There is much to see there, and a good restaurant where we can have lunch. Would you like that?'

There was a tingling silence. Laura's look of uncertainty deepened.

She said, 'You—you're offering to take me to Assisi.' To her discomfiture, she felt herself beginning to blush. 'That—that's very kind of you, *signore*, and I—I'm grateful. But I couldn't put you to all that trouble—not possibly.'

'But it would be no trouble,' he said. '*Al contrario*, I would find it delightful.' He paused deliberately. 'But I notice that you still have a problem calling me by my given name, so perhaps you feel you cannot yet trust me enough to spend a day alone with me.'

Or perhaps it is yourself you do not trust, *bella mia*, he added silently, watching the colour flare in her face. And if so—you are mine.

'N-no,' she stammered. 'Oh, no. It's not that—not that at all.' She cast around frantically for an excuse—any excuse. 'You see—it's Paolo. The Assisi trip was his idea, and maybe I should wait until he's better, and we can go together. I—I don't want to hurt his feelings. Can you understand that?'

'Of course,' he said. 'I understand perfectly, believe me.' More than you think or wish, my sweet one, he added under his breath.

He sighed with mock reproach. 'However, I am distressed that my shattered hopes do not concern you. Now that is cruel. But if I cannot persuade you, so be it.'

And when the time comes, he thought as he pushed back his chair and rose to his feet, some day—some night soon—then I will make you come to me. Because you are going to want me so much that you will offer yourself, my shy, lovely girl. Make no mistake about that. And I will take everything you have to give, and more.

Aloud, he said, '*Arriverderci*, Laura.' His smile was pleasant—even slightly impersonal as he looked down at her. 'Enjoy your solitude while you can,' he added softly.

And he walked away, humming gently under his breath, while Laura stared after him, still floundering in her own confusion.

CHAPTER FIVE

LAURA finished applying sun lotion to her arms and legs, and lay back in the shade of the big striped umbrella with a little sigh of contentment. Contrary to her own expectations, she was enjoying her solitude. The pool area occupied an extended hollow at the foot of the gardens, offering a welcome haven of tranquillity, with its marble tiles surrounding a large rectangle of turquoise water, and overlooked by terraced banks of flowering shrubs.

It was sheltered and very private, and, apart from birdsong and the hum of insects, it was also wonderfully quiet.

She put on her sunglasses and applied herself to taking an intelligent interest in her book, but the heroine's ill-starred attempts to pursue entirely the wrong man struggled to hold her attention, and at last she put the thing down, sighing impatiently.

In view of her current circumstances, it wasn't the ideal plot to engage her, she thought ruefully. In fact, *War and Peace* might have been a more appropriate choice. Especially as she'd just been totally routed by the enemy.

She'd managed to waylay a harassed Emilia, asking politely if she'd find out when it would be convenient for her to visit Paolo. But the reply conveyed back from the Signora was unequivocal. Paolo had a high fever but was now sleeping, so could not be disturbed.

If I were genuinely in love with him, I'd be chewing my nails to the quick by now, Laura thought indignantly.

But it was clear she had to start practising patience, and hope that, when his temperature eventually went down, Paolo would demand to see her instead.

She sighed. God, what a situation to be in, and all her own stupid doing, too. Why hadn't she remembered there was no such thing as a free lunch?

But the deep indolent heat was already soothing her, encouraging her to close her eyes and relax. Reminding her that it was pointless to fret, because, for the time being at least, she was no longer in control of her own destiny.

Che sera, sera, she thought drowsily, removing her sunglasses and nestling further into the soft cushions of the lounger. Whatever will be, will be. Isn't that what they say? So I may as well go with the flow. Especially as I don't seem to have much of a choice.

She closed her eyes. Oh, Paolo. She sent the silent plea winging passionately to the villa. For heaven's sake get well quickly, and get me out of here.

Alessio parked the Jeep in front of the house, and swung himself out of the driving seat. He needed, he thought as he strode indoors, a long cold drink, and a swim.

What he did not require was the sudden appearance of his aunt, as if she'd been lying in wait for him.

'Where have you been?' she demanded, and he checked resignedly.

'Down to the village. Luca Donini asked me to talk to his father—persuade him not to spend another winter in that hut of his.'

'He asked you?' Her brows lifted haughtily. 'But how can this concern you? Sometimes, Alessio, I think you forget your position.'

He gave her a long, hard look. 'Yes, Zia Lucrezia,' he drawled. 'Sometimes, I do, as the events of the past few weeks have unhappily proved. But Besavoro is my village, and the concerns of my friends there are mine too.'

She snorted impatiently. 'You did not take the girl with you?'

He shrugged. 'I invited her, but she refused me.'

She glared at him. 'That is bad. You cannot be trying.'

'No,' he said. 'It is better than I expected after such a short time.' His smile was cold. 'But do not ask me to explain.'

She changed tack. 'You should have told me you were going

to the village. You could have gone to the pharmacy for my poor
boy. Last night he was delirious—talking nonsense in his sleep.'

'It is probably a habit of his,' Alessio commented curtly. 'Why
not ask his *innamorata*?'

She gave him a furious look, and swept back to her nursing
duties.

Alessio proceeded moodily to his room. The jibe had been
almost irresistible, but he regretted it. There'd been no need to
remind himself that Laura and Paolo had been enjoying an intimate relationship prior to their arrival in Italy. Because he knew
it only too well already.

But what he could not explain was why he found it so galling.
After all, he thought, he had never felt jealous or possessive about
any of his previous involvements. For him, sex was usually just
another appetite to be enjoyably and mutually satisfied. And there
was nothing to be gained by jealousy or speculation over other
lovers.

He'd awaited Laura's arrival at the villa with a sense of blazing
resentment, even though he knew he had only himself to blame
for his predicament, and, instead, found himself instantly intrigued by her. From that, it had only been a brief step to desire.
And he strongly suspected this would have happened if he'd met
her somewhere far from his aunt's interference.

He remembered, with distaste, icily promising to send her
home with a beautiful memory. Now he wasn't sure he'd send
her back at all. Certainly not immediately, he thought, frowning
as he stripped and found a pair of brief black swimming trunks.

Maybe he'd whisk her away somewhere—the Seychelles or
the Maldives, perhaps, or the Bahamas—for a few weeks of exotic pampering, with a quick trip to Milan first, of course, to
reinvent her wardrobe. Buy her the kind of clothes he would
enjoy removing.

And on that enticing thought he collected a towel and his sunglasses, and went down to the pool to find her.

He found her peacefully asleep, the long lashes curling on her
cheek, her head turned slightly to one side. The sun had moved
round, leaving one ankle and foot out in the open, vulnerable to

its direct rays, and he reached up to make a slight adjustment to the parasol.

Having done so, he did not move away immediately, but stood for a moment, looking down at her. In the simple dark green one-piece swimsuit, her slender body looked like the stem of a flower, her hair crowning it like an exotic corolla of russet petals.

A single strand lay across her cheek, and he was tempted to smooth it back, but knew he could not risk so intimate a gesture.

Because he wanted her so fiercely, so unequivocally, it was like a blow in the guts. However, now was not yet the moment, so he would have to practise unaccustomed restraint, he reminded himself grimly.

Swallowing, he turned away, tossing his towel and sunglasses onto an adjoining lounger, then walked to the edge of the pool and dived in, his body cutting the water as cleanly as a knife.

Dimly, Laura heard the splash and came awake, lifting herself onto one elbow as she looked around her, faintly disorientated.

Then her eyes went to the pool, and the tanned body sliding with powerful grace through the water, and her mind cleared, with an instantaneous nervous lurch of the stomach.

Stealthily, she watched him complete another two lengths of the pool, then turn towards the side. She retrieved her sunglasses and slid them on, then grabbed her book, holding it in front of her like a barrier as Alessio lifted himself lithely out of the water and walked towards her, his body gleaming, sleek as a seal, in the sunlight.

'*Ciao.*' His smile was casual as he began to blot the moisture from his skin with his towel.

'Hello,' she responded hesitantly, not looking at him directly. Those trunks, she thought, her mouth drying, were even briefer than his shorts had been. She hurried into speech. 'You—you're back early. Did you settle all your business?'

'Not as I wished.' He grimaced. 'I had a battle of wills with a stubborn old man and lost.'

'Well,' she said. 'That can't happen too often.'

'It does with Fredo.' His face relaxed into a grin. 'He cannot forget that his son and I grew up together, and that he was almost a second father to me when my parents were away. He even took his belt to Luca and myself with complete impartiality when we behaved badly, and likes to remind me of it when he can.'

He shrugged. 'But he also showed us every track and trail in the forest, and taught us to use them safely. He even took me on my first wild boar hunt.'

'So why are you disagreeing now? Not that it's any of my business,' she added hastily.

'It's no secret. Even when his wife was alive, he did not like life in town, so when she died he moved up to a hut on the mountain to look after his goats there. He has been there ever since, and Luca worries that he is getting too old for such a life. He wants his father to live with him, but Fredo says his daughter-in-law is a bad cook, and has a tongue as sharp as a viper's bite, and I could not argue with that.'

'Absolutely not,' she agreed solemnly. 'A double whammy, no less.'

He laughed. 'As you say, *bella mia*. But the campaign is not over yet.'

'You don't give up easily.'

'I do not give up at all.'

He spread his towel on the lounger and stretched out, nodding at the book she was still clutching. 'Is it good?'

'The jacket says it's a best-seller.'

'Ah,' he said, softly. 'But what does Laura say?'

'That the jury's still out, but the verdict will probably be guilty. Murder by cliché.' She sighed. 'However, it's all I brought with me, so I have to make it last.'

'There are English books in my library up at the villa,' he said. 'Some classics, and some modern. You are welcome to borrow them. Ask Emilia to show you where they are.'

'Thank you, that's—very kind.' Her brows lifted in surprise. 'Is that why your English is so incredibly good—because you read a lot?'

'I learned English as a second language at school,' he said. 'And attended university in Britain and America.' His grin teased her. 'And it is fortunate that I did, as your Italian is so minimal.'

'But my French isn't bad,' she defended herself. 'If I'd gone on the holiday I originally planned, I'd have shone.'

'Ah,' he said. 'And what holiday was that?'

She was suddenly still, cursing herself under her breath. She'd let her tongue run away with her again. 'I thought of the Riviera,' she said. 'But then I met Paolo—and changed my mind, of course.'

'Of course.' She thought she detected a note of irony in his voice.

'Perhaps you should have stuck to plan A,' he went on. 'Then you would have avoided a meeting with Zia Lucrezia.'

'Indeed,' she said lightly. 'And Paolo might not have caught a cold.'

'Not with you to keep him warm, I am sure,' he said softly, and watched with satisfaction as the inevitable blush rose in her face. 'Have you been to see him?'

'I tried,' she admitted. 'But his mother wouldn't allow it. Apparently he's running a temperature.'

'Which you might raise to lethal limits.' He paused. 'And she may have a point,' he added silkily. 'But would you like me to speak to her for you—persuade her to see reason?'

'Would you?' she asked doubtfully. 'But why?'

'Who am I to stand in the way of love?' He shrugged a negligent shoulder, and Laura tried to ignore the resultant ripple of muscle.

Abruptly, she said, 'Do you know Beatrice Manzone?'

'I have met her,' he said. 'Why do you ask?'

'I was wondering what she was like.'

The dark gaze narrowed. 'What does Paolo say?'

She bit her lip. 'That she's rich.'

'A little harsh,' he said. 'She is also pretty and docile.' He grinned faintly. 'And cloying, like an overdose of honey. Quite unlike you, *mia cara*.'

She bit her lip. 'I wasn't looking for comparisons.'

'Then what do you want? Reassurance?' There was a sudden crispness in his tone. 'You should look to Paolo for that. And according to him, the Manzone girl is history.'

'His mother doesn't seem to think so.'

There was an odd silence, then he said, '*Mia bella*, if you and Paolo want each other, then what else matters?' He swung himself off the lounger, as if suddenly impatient. 'And now it is time we went up to the house for some lunch.'

Once again only two places had been set for the meal, which, this time, was being served in the coolness of the dining room. And her seat, Laura observed uneasily, had been moved up the table to within touching distance of his. It made serving the food more convenient, but at the same time it seemed as if she was constantly being thrust into close proximity with him—suddenly an honoured guest rather than an unwanted visitor—and she found this disturbing for all kinds of reasons.

But in spite of her mental reservations, her morning in the fresh air had certainly sharpened her appetite, and she ate her way through a bowl of vegetable soup, and a substantial helping of pasta. But her eyes widened in genuine shock when Guillermo carried the next course—a dish of cod baked with potatoes and parmesan—to the table.

'More food?' She shook her head. 'I don't believe it.'

Alessio looked amused. 'And there is still cheese and dessert to follow. You are going to be an Italian's wife, Laura. You must learn to eat well in the middle of the day.'

'But how can anyone do any work after all this?'

'No one does.' Alessio handed her a plate of food. 'Has Paolo not introduced you to the charms of the siesta?' He kept his voice light with an effort, knowing fiercely that he wanted to be the one to share with her those quiet, shuttered afternoon hours. To sleep with her wrapped in his arms, then wake to make slow, lazy love.

'We rest and work later when it is cooler,' he added, refilling her glass with wine.

'I think Paolo is used to London hours now,' she said, looking down at her plate.

'But he will not always work there, you understand.' He gave her a meditative look. 'How would you like living in Turin—or Milan?'

'I haven't thought about it.'

'Or,' he said slowly, 'it might even be Rome.'

She said, 'Oh, I expect I'd adjust—somehow.'

Except, she thought, that it will never happen, and began to make herself eat.

She wished with sudden desperation that she could confide in him. Tell him exactly why she was here, and how Paolo had persuaded her into this charade.

But there was no guarantee that he would understand, and he might not appreciate being made a fool of, and having his hospitality abused in such a way.

And although he and his aunt were plainly not on the best of terms, he might disapprove of the older woman being deliberately deceived.

Besides, and more importantly, thought Laura, it would render her even more vulnerable where he was concerned, and she could not afford that.

She'd come this far, she told herself rather wanly. She might as well go on to the bitter end—whenever that might be.

His voice broke across her reverie. 'What are you thinking?'

Quickly she forced a smile. Spoke eagerly. 'Oh, just how good it will be to see Paolo again. We don't seem to have been alone together for ages.' She managed a note of anxiety. 'You really do think you'll be able to persuade your aunt?'

'Yes,' Alessio said quietly, after a pause. 'Yes, I do.'

And they ate the rest of the meal in silence.

Siestas were probably fine in theory, thought Laura. In practice, they didn't seem to work quite so well. Or not for her, anyway.

She lay staring up at the ceiling fan, listening to its soft swish as it rotated, and decided she had never felt so wide awake. She needed something to occupy her.

Her book was finished, its ending as predictable as the rest of the story, and she had no wish to lie about thinking. Because her mind only seemed to drift in one direction—towards the emotional minefield presided over by the Count Alessio Ramontella.

And it was ludicrous—pathetic—to allow herself to think about a man who, a week ago, had been only a name on the paperwork from the Arleschi Bank's head office. A distant figurehead, and nothing more.

And no matter how attractive he might be, that was how he would always remain—remote. No part of any world that she lived in, except for these few dreamlike, unforgettable days.

Except that she had to forget them—and pretty damned quickly too—as soon as she returned to England, if not before.

She slid off the bed. She'd have a shower, she decided, and wash her hair. She'd brought no dryer with her, but twenty minutes or so with a hairbrush in the courtyard's afternoon sun would serve the same purpose.

Ten minutes later, demurely wrapped in the primly pretty white cotton robe she'd brought with her, and her hair swathed into a towel, she opened the shutters and stepped outside into the heated shimmer of the day.

She was greeted immediately with a torrent of yapping as Caio, who was lying in the shade of the stone bench, rose to condemn her intrusion.

Laura halted in faint dismay. Up to now, although he was in the adjoining room, he hadn't disturbed her too much with his barking. But she'd assumed that the Signora had taken him with her to the other end of the house to share her sick room vigil. She certainly hadn't bargained for finding him here in sole and aggressive occupation.

'Good dog,' she said without conviction. 'Look, I just want to get my hair dry. There's enough room for us both. Don't give me a hard time, now.'

Still barking, he advanced towards her, then almost jerked to a halt, and she realised he was actually tied to the bench. And, next to where he'd been lying, there was a dish with some dry-looking food on it, and, what was worse, an empty water bowl.

'Oh, for heaven's sake.' She spoke aloud in real anger. Caio would never feature on any 'favourite pets' list of hers, but he deserved better than to be left tied up and thirsty.

She moved round to the other end of the bench, out of the range of his display of sharp teeth, and grabbed the bowl. She took it back to her bathroom, and filled it to the brim with cold water.

When she reappeared, Caio had retreated back under the bench. He growled at her approach, but his heart clearly wasn't in it, and the beady, suspicious eyes were fixed on the bowl. She put it on the ground, then, to demonstrate that the suspicion was mutual, used her hairbrush to push the water near enough for the tethered dog to reach it. He gave a slight whimper, then plunged his muzzle into the bowl, filling the silence with the sound of his frantic lapping.

When he'd finished every drop, he raised his head and looked at her in unmistakable appeal.

I could lose a hand here, Laura thought, but Caio made no attempt to snap as she retrieved the bowl and refilled it for him.

'You poor little devil,' she said gently as he drank again. 'I bet she's forgotten all about you.'

The leash used to tie him was a long one, but Laura realised that it had become twined round the leg of the bench, reducing his freedom considerably.

She could, she thought, untangle it, if he'd let her. But would he allow her close enough to unclip the leash from his collar, without doing her some damage?

Well, she could but try. She certainly couldn't leave him here like this. She could remember hearing once that looking dogs in the eye made them more aggressive, so she seated herself at the far end of the bench, and moved towards him by degrees. When she was in his space, she clenched her hand into a fist and offered it to him, trying to be confident about it, and talking to him quietly at the same time. His initial sniff was reluctant, but he didn't bite, and she tried stroking his head, which he permitted warily.

'You may be spoiled and obnoxious,' she told him, 'but I don't think you have much of a life.'

She slid her fingers down to the ruff of hair round his neck and found his collar. As she released the clip Caio made a sound between a bark and a whimper, and was gone, making for the open space of the garden beyond the courtyard. And after that, presumably, the world.

'Oh, God,' Laura muttered, jumping to her feet and running after him, stumbling a little over the hem of her robe.

What the hell would she do if she couldn't find him? And what was she going to say to the Signora, anyway? She'd be accused of interfering, which was true, and coming back with a counter-accusation of animal negligence, however justified, wouldn't remedy the situation.

She had no idea how extensive the villa's grounds were, or if they were even secure. Supposing he got out onto the mountain itself, and a wolf found him before she could?

This is what happens when you try to be a canine Samaritan, she thought breathlessly as she reached the courtyard entrance, only to find herself almost cannoning into Alessio, who was approaching from the opposite direction with a squirming Caio tucked firmly under his arm.

'Oh, you found him,' she exclaimed. 'Thank heaven for that.'

'I almost fell over him,' he told her tersely. 'Where has he come from?'

'He was tied to the bench over there. I was trying to make him more comfortable, and he just—took off. I was terrified that I wouldn't be able to find him.'

'He was out here—in this heat?' Alessio's tone was incredulous, with the beginnings of anger. He glanced at the bench. 'At least he had water.' He looked at Laura again, more closely. 'Or did he?'

She sighed. 'Well, he has now, and that's what matters.' She was suddenly searingly conscious of the fact that she was wearing nothing but a thin robe, and that her damp hair was hanging on her shoulders. 'I—I'll leave him with you, shall I?' she added, beginning to back away.

'One moment,' he said. 'What made you come out here at this time?'

'I couldn't sleep. I thought I'd wash my hair, and dry it in the sun.' She forced a smile. 'As you see.'

His brows lifted. 'A rather primitive solution, don't you think? Why didn't you ring the bell for Emilia? She would have found you an electric dryer.'

'I felt she had enough on her plate without running around after me. And it is siesta time, after all.' She paused. 'So, why are you here, come to that?'

'I could not sleep either.' He glanced down at Caio, who returned him a baleful look. 'Under the circumstances, that was fortunate.'

'Just in time to spoil his bid for freedom, poor little mutt.' She offered the dog her hand again, and found her fingers being licked by his small rough tongue.

'You seem to have made a friend, *bella mia*.' Alessio sounded amused. 'My aunt will have another reason for jealousy.' He scratched the top of Caio's head. 'And I thought the whole world was his enemy.'

'He'll think so too, if we tie him up to that bench again,' Laura said ruefully.

'Then we will not do so. I will put him in my aunt's room instead, with his water. His basket is there, anyway, and he will be cooler,' he added, frowning. 'I cannot imagine why she would leave him anywhere else.' He sighed. 'Another topic for discussion that will displease her.'

'Another?'

'I have yet to raise the subject of your visit to Paolo.'

'Oh, please,' Laura said awkwardly. 'I've been thinking about that, and maybe I shouldn't persist. If she's so adamant, it will only cause problems.'

He said gently, 'But that is nonsense, Laura *mia*. Of course you must see your lover. Your visit can do nothing but good, I am sure.' His gaze travelled over her, from the high, frilled neck of her robe, down to her bare insteps, and she felt every inch of concealed skin tingle under his lingering regard. Felt an odd heat burgeoning inside her, which had nothing to do with the warmth of the day.

He smiled at her. 'And I will ask Emilia to bring you the hair-dryer,' he added softly, then turned away.

Laura regained the sanctuary of her room, aware that her breathing had quickened out of all proportion.

She closed the shutters behind her, then, on impulse, decided to fasten the small iron bar that locked them. It had clearly not been used for some time because it resisted, finally falling into place with a bang that resounded in the quiet of the afternoon like a pistol shot.

She could only hope Alessio hadn't heard it, because he'd be bound to put two and two together. And the last thing she needed was for him to think that he made her nervous in any way.

Because she had nothing to fear from him, and she was flattering herself to think otherwise.

Someone like Alessio Ramontella would live on a diet of film stars and heiresses, she told herself, pushing her damp hair back from her face with despondent fingers. And if he's kind to me, it's because he recognises I'm out of my depth, and feels sorry for me.

And as long as I remember that, I'm in no danger. No danger at all.

Her reunion with the dying Paolo was scheduled to take place before dinner. A note signed 'Ramontella' informing her of the arrangement had been brought to her by Emilia, along with the promised hair-dryer.

He'd certainly wasted no time over the matter, Laura thought as she followed Guillermo over to the other side of the villa. All she had to do now was pretend to be suitably eager.

She'd dressed for the occasion, putting on her other decent dress, a slim fitting blue shift, sleeveless and scoop-necked. Trying to upgrade it with a handful of silver chains and a matching bracelet.

She'd painted her fingernails and toenails a soft coral, and used a toning lustre on her mouth, emphasising her grey eyes with shadow and kohl.

The kind of effort a girl would make for her lover, she hoped.

She found herself in a long passageway, looking out onto yet another courtyard. The fountain here was larger, she saw, pausing, and a much more elaborate affair, crowned by the statue of a woman crafted in marble. She stood on tiptoe, as if about to take flight, hair and scanty draperies flying behind her, and a bow in her hand, gazing out across the tumbling water that fell from the rock at her feet.

'The goddess Diana for whom the villa is named, *signorina*,' Guillermo, who had halted too, told her in his halting English. 'Very beautiful, *sì*?'

'Very,' Laura agreed with less than total certainty as she studied the remote, almost inhuman face. The virgin huntress, she thought, who unleashed her hounds on any man unwise enough to look at her, and who had the cold moon as her symbol.

And not the obvious choice of deity for someone as overtly warm-blooded as Alessio Ramontella. Her dogs would have torn him to pieces on sight.

She looked down the passage to the tall double doors at the end. 'Is that Signor Paolo's room?'

'But no, *signorina*.' He sounded almost shocked. 'That is the suite of His Excellency. The *signore*, his cousin, is here.' He turned briskly to the left, down another much shorter corridor, and halted, knocking at a door.

It was flung open immediately, and the Signora swept out, her eyes raking Laura with an expression of pure malevolence.

'You may have ten minutes,' she snapped. 'No more. My son needs rest.'

What does she think? Laura asked herself ironically as she entered. That I'm planning to jump his bones?

The shutters were closed and the drapes were drawn too, so the room, which smelled strongly of something like camphorated oil, was lit only by a lamp at the side of the bed.

Paolo was lying, eyes closed, propped up by pillows. He was wearing maroon pyjamas, which made him look sallow, Laura thought. Or maybe it was the effect of the lamplight.

She pulled up a chair, and sat beside the bed. 'Hi,' she said gently. 'How are you feeling?'

'Terrible.' His voice was hoarse and pettish, and the eyes he turned on her were bloodshot and watering. 'Not well enough to talk, but Alessio insisted. I had to listen to him arguing with my mother, and my headache returned. What is it you want?'

'I don't want anything.' She bit her lip. 'Paolo, we're supposed to be crazy about each other, remember? It would seem really weird if I didn't ask for you.' She hesitated. 'I think your cousin feels that I'm stuck here in a kind of vacuum, and feels sorry for me.'

'He would do better to concentrate his compassion on me,' Paolo said sullenly. 'He refuses to call a doctor, although he knows that I have had a weak chest since childhood, and my mother fears this cold may settle there.' He gave a hollow cough as if to prove his point. 'He said he would prefer to summon a vet to examine Caio, and he and my mother quarrelled again.'

Laura sighed. 'I'm sorry if you're having a difficult time, but you're not the only one.' She leaned forward. 'Paolo, I'm finding it really hard to cope with being the uninvited guest round here. I need you to support me—take off some of the pressure.' She paused. 'How long, do you think, before you're well enough to get up and join the real world again?'

'When *Mamma* considers I am out of danger, and not before,' he said, with something of a snap. 'She alone knows how ill I am. She has been wonderful to me—a saint in her patience and care.' He sneezed violently, and lay back, dabbing his nose with a bunch of tissues. 'And my health is more important than your convenience,' he added in a muffled voice.

She got to her feet. She said crisply, 'Actually, it's your own convenience that's being served here. You seem to be overlooking that. But if you'd rather I kept my distance, that's fine with me.'

'I did not mean that,' he said, his tone marginally more conciliatory. 'Of course I wish you to continue to play your part, now more than ever. I shall tell *Mamma* that you must visit me each day—to aid my recovery. That I cannot live without you,' he added with sudden inspiration.

Her mouth tightened. 'No need to go to those lengths, perhaps. But at least it will give me a purpose for staying on.'

'And you can go sightseeing, even if I am not with you,' he went on. 'I shall tell *Mamma* to put Giacomo and the car at your service at once.' He coughed again. 'But now I have talked enough, and my throat is hurting. I need to sleep to become well, you understand.'

'Yes,' she said. 'Of course.' She moved to the door. 'Well— I'll see you tomorrow.'

Outside, she leaned against the wall and drew a deep breath. The daily visits would be a rod for her back, but, to balance that, being able to use the car was an unexpected lifeline.

It offered her a means of escape from the enclosed world of the villa, she thought, and, more vitally, meant that she would no longer be thrown into the company of Alessio Ramontella.

And that was just what she wanted, she told herself. Wasn't it?

CHAPTER SIX

EXCEPT, of course, it had all been too good to be true. As she should probably have known, Laura thought wryly.

Several long days had passed since Paolo had airily promised her the use of the car, and yet she was still confined to the villa and its grounds, with no release in sight.

Naturally, it was the Signora who had applied the veto. Paolo was still far from well, she'd pronounced ominously, and, if there was an emergency, then the car would be needed.

'If you had wished to explore Umbria, *signorina*, then perhaps you should have accepted my nephew's generous invitation,' she'd added, making Laura wonder how she'd come by that particular snippet of information.

But it was an invitation that, signally, had not been repeated, although she often heard the noise of the Jeep driving away.

And far from them being thrown together, after that first day, the Count seemed to have chosen deliberately to remain aloof from her.

He'd finished his breakfast and gone by the time she appeared each morning, but he continued to join her at dinner, although the conversation between them seemed polite and oddly formal compared with their earlier exchanges. And afterwards, he excused himself quickly and courteously, so that she was left strictly to her own devices.

So perhaps he too had sensed the danger of being over-friendly. And, having brought about her reunion with Paolo in spite of his aunt's disapproval, considered his duty done.

She should have found the new regime far less disturbing, and easier to cope with, but somehow it wasn't.

Even in his absence, she was still conscious of him, as if his presence had invaded every stone of the villa's walls. She found

76

she was waiting for his return—listening for his footsteps, and the sound of his voice.

And worst of all was seeing his face in the darkness as she fought restlessly for sleep each night.

The evening meal, she acknowledged wretchedly, was now the highlight of her day, in spite of its new restrictions.

It was an attitude she'd have condemned as ludicrous in anyone else, and she knew it.

And if someone had warned her that she would feel like this, one day, about a man that she hardly even knew, she would not have believed them.

Yet it was happening to her—twenty-first-century Laura. She was trapped, held helpless by the sheer force of her own untried emotions. By feelings that were as old as eternity.

She'd soon discovered that he was not simply on vacation at the villa when she'd made herself take up his invitation to borrow something to read. His library, she saw, was not merely shelved out with books from floor to ceiling, but its vast antique desk was also home to a state-of-the-art computer system, which explained why he was closeted there for much of the time he spent at the villa.

Though not, of course, when she'd paid her visit. It had been Emilia who had waited benignly while she'd made her selection. She had just been hesitating over a couple of modern thrillers, when, to her surprise, she had come on a complete set of Jane Austen, and her choice had been made. She'd glanced through them, appreciating the beautiful leather bindings, then decided on *Mansfield Park*, which she hadn't read since her school days.

The name Valentina Ramontella was inscribed on the flyleaf in an elegant sloping hand, and Emilia, in answer to her tentative enquiry, had told her, with a sigh, that this had been the name of His Excellency's beloved mother, and these books her particular property.

'I see.' Laura touched the signature gently with her forefinger. 'Well, please assure the Count I'll take great care of it.'

However tenuous, it was almost a connection between them, she thought as she took the book away.

But, although the hours seemed strangely empty in Alessio's absence, she was not entirely without companionship as one day stretched endlessly into the next.

Because, to her infinite surprise, Caio had attached himself to her. He was no longer kept in the courtyard, but she'd come across a reluctant Guillermo taking him for a walk in the garden, on the express orders of his master, he'd told her glumly. Seeing his face, and listening to the little dog's excited whimpers as he'd strained on the leash to reach her, Laura had volunteered to take over this daily duty—if the Signora agreed.

Even more surprisingly, permission had been ungraciously granted. And, after a couple of days, Caio trotted beside her so obediently, she dispensed with the leash altogether.

He sometimes accompanied her down to the pool, lying under her sun lounger, and sat beside her in the *salotto* in the evenings as she flexed her rusty fingering on some of the Beethoven sonatas she'd found in bound volumes inside the piano stool. At mealtimes, apart from dinner, he was stationed unobtrusively under her chair, and he'd even joined her on the bed for siesta on a couple of occasions, she admitted guiltily.

'I see you have acquired a bodyguard,' was Alessio's only comment when he encountered them together once, delivered with a faint curl of the mouth.

Watching him walk away, she scooped Caio defensively into her arms. 'We're just a couple of pariahs here,' she murmured to him, and he licked her chin almost wistfully.

But she never took Caio to Paolo's room, instinct telling this would be too much for the Signora, who had no idea of the scope of her pet's defection to the enemy.

And I don't want her to know, Laura thought grimly. I'm unpopular enough already. I don't want to be accused of pinching her dog.

On his own admission, Paolo's cold symptoms had all but vanished, but he refused to leave his room on the grounds that he was still suffering with his chest.

Laura realised that her impatience with him and her ambiguous situation was growing rapidly and would soon reach snapping point.

These ten-minute stilted visits each evening wouldn't convince anyone that they were sharing a grand passion, she thought with exasperated derision. And if the Signora was listening at the door, she'd be justified in wagering her diamonds that she'd soon have Beatrice Manzone as a daughter-in-law.

But: 'You worry too much,' was Paolo's casual response to her concern.

Well, if he was satisfied, then why should she quibble? she thought with an inward shrug. He was the paying customer, after all. And found herself grimacing at the thought.

But as she left his room that evening the Signora was waiting for her, her lips stretched in the vinegary smile first encountered in Rome. Still, any calibre of smile was a welcome surprise, Laura thought, tension rising within her.

She was astonished to be told that, as Giacomo would be driving to the village the next morning to collect some special medicine from the pharmacy, she was free to accompany him there, if she wished.

'You may have some small errands, *signorina*.' The older woman's shrug emphasised their trifling quality. 'But the medicine is needed, so you will not be able to remain for long.'

Well, it was better than nothing, Laura thought, offering a polite word of thanks instead of the cartwheel she felt like turning. In fact, it was almost a 'get out of jail' card.

Saved, she thought, with relief. Saved from cabin fever, and, hopefully, other obsessions too.

She'd have time to buy some postcards at least—let her family know she was still alive. And Gaynor, too, would be waiting to hear from her.

In the morning, she was ready well before the designated time, anxious that Giacomo would have no excuse to set off without her. She still couldn't understand why the Signora should suddenly be so obliging, and couldn't help wondering if the older woman was playing some strange game of cat and mouse with her.

But that makes no sense, she adjured herself impatiently. Don't start getting paranoid.

Seated in the front, Laura kept her eyes fixed firmly ahead as the car negotiated the winding road down to the valley, avoiding any chance glimpse of the mind-aching drop on one side, and praying that they would meet no other vehicles coming from the opposite direction.

She only realised when the descent was completed that she'd been holding her breath most of the time.

Giacomo drove straight to the main square, and parked near the church. Pointing to the hands on his watch, he conveyed that she had fifteen minutes only to spend in Besavoro, and Laura nodded in resigned acceptance.

Well, that was the deal, she told herself philosophically as she set off. And she would just have to make the most of it.

She soon realised that Besavoro was in reality a small town, and not what she thought of as a village at all. The square was lined with shops, selling every sort of food, as well as wine, olive oil, hardware and clothing. It all had a busy, purposeful air, without a designer boutique or gift shop in sight.

But the little news agency she came to sold a few postcards, featuring mainly Assisi and the Majella national park, and she bought four, deciding to send one to Carl, her immediate boss at Harman Grace as well.

No one in the shop spoke English, but with great goodwill the correct stamps for Britain were offered, and her change was counted carefully into her hand.

A few doors away was a bar with tables on the pavement, and Laura took a seat, ordering a coffee and a bottle of mineral water.

She glanced across the square, checking the car, and then, carefully, her watch, before starting to write her cards.

At the same time she was aware that people were checking her, not rudely, but with open interest. English tourists were clearly a rarity here, she realised, turning her own attention back to the task in hand.

She was sorely tempted to put, 'Having ghastly time. Glad you're not here,' but knew that would involve her in impossible explanations on her return. Better, she decided, to stick to the usual anodyne messages. To Gaynor alone could she eventually reveal the grisly truth, and wait for her to say, 'I told you so,' she thought ruefully.

Although there were things about her stay at the villa that she wasn't prepared to talk about—ever. Not even to Gaynor.

Now all she needed was a postbox, she thought, rifling through her small phrase book for the exact wording. On the other hand it was probably quicker and easier to ask Giacomo.

She slipped her pen back into her bag, and felt for her purse, looking again towards the church as she did so.

But where the car had stood only minutes before, there was an empty space.

Laura shot to her feet with a stifled cry of dismay. It couldn't have gone, she thought wildly. There were still minutes to spare. And if Giacomo had just looked across the square he'd have seen her. So why hadn't he come across to her—or sounded his horn even? Why—simply drive off?

The bar owner came dashing out, clearly worried that she was about to do a runner, his voice raised in protest.

Laura pointed. 'My lift—it's vanished. I—I'm stranded.'

The owner spread his hands in total incomprehension, talking excitedly. She became aware that people were pausing—staring. Beginning to ask questions. Hemming her in as they did so. Making her uncomfortably aware of her sudden isolation, in a strange country, and unable to speak a word of the language.

Then, suddenly, across the increasing hubbub, cut a drawl she recognised. '*Ciao, bella mia.* Having problems?'

Alessio had come through the small crowd, which had obediently parted for him, and was standing just a couple of feet away, watching her from behind dark glasses, hands on hips. The shorts he was wearing today were marginally more decent than the first pair she'd seen him in, but his dark blue shirt was unbuttoned almost to the waist.

And if she was pleased to see him, she was determined that he wasn't going to know it.

She faced him furiously. 'Actually—yes. The damned car's

gone without me.' She almost stamped her foot, but decided against it. 'Oh, God, I don't believe it.' She bit her lip. 'I suppose this is your aunt's idea—to make me walk back up that hill, in the hope I'll die of heatstroke.'

He grinned. 'Calm yourself, Laura. This time Zia Lucrezia is innocent. I told Giacomo to return to the villa.'

'But why?' She stared at him. 'There was no need. We had a perfectly good arrangement...'

Alessio shrugged. 'I felt you needed a break. Also, that Besavoro deserved more than just fifteen minutes of your time. Was I so wrong?'

'Well, no,' she conceded without pleasure.

'Good,' he approved lazily. 'And when you have completed your sightseeing, I will drive you back in the Jeep.'

Laura suddenly realised that public interest in her activities had snowballed since the Count's arrival. The fascinated circle gathering around them was now three deep.

She said stiffly, 'I thought I'd made it clear. I don't want you to put yourself to any trouble on my behalf.'

'There is no trouble—except perhaps with Luigi here.' He indicated the gaping bar owner. 'So, why don't you sit down and finish your drink before he has a fit, hmm?'

He turned to the nearest onlooker, and said something softly. As if a switch had been pressed, the crowd began to melt unobtrusively away.

Such is power, Laura thought mutinously as she obeyed. She watched him drop into the chair opposite, stretching long tanned legs out in front of him as he ordered another cappuccino for Laura, and an espresso for himself from Luigi.

He'd caught her totally on the back foot, she thought. And she resented that swift painful thud of the heart that his unexpected appearance had engendered. Especially when he'd practically ignored her for the past week.

But I should want to be ignored, she thought. I should want to be totally ostracised by him. Because it's safer that way...

'Please do not let me interrupt.' He nodded to the small pile of cards. 'Finish your correspondence.'

'I already have done.' She smiled over-brightly. 'Just touching base with family and friends.'

'Ah,' he said. 'The family that, according to my aunt, does not exist.'

Laura groaned inwardly. Paolo had reacted with ill temper to her confession that she'd deviated from the party line.

She made herself shrug. 'I can't imagine where she got that idea. Perhaps it suited her better to believe that I was a penniless orphan.'

'Which, of course, you are not.'

'Well, the penniless bit is fairly accurate. It's been a real struggle for my mother since my father died. I'm just glad I've got a decent job, so that I can help.'

The dark brows lifted. 'Does working in a wine bar pay so well? I did not know.'

But that's not the day job. The words hovered on her lips, but, thankfully, remained unspoken.

Oh, God, she thought, hastily marshalling her thoughts. I've goofed again.

She met his sardonic gaze. 'It's a busy place, *signore*, and the tips are good.'

'Ah,' he said softly. He glanced around him. 'So, what are your impressions of Besavoro?'

'It's larger than I thought, and much older. I didn't think I would catch more than a glimpse of it, of course.'

'I thought you would be pleased that I sent Giacomo away for another reason,' he said, leaning back in his chair, and pushing his sunglasses up onto his forehead. 'It will mean that Paolo will get his medicine more quickly, and maybe return to your arms, *subito*, a man restored.'

'I doubt it.' She looked down at the table. 'He seems set for the duration.' She hesitated. 'Has he always fussed about his health like this? I mean—he's simply got a cold.'

'Why, Laura,' he said softly. 'How hard you are. For a man, no cold is ever simple.'

'Well, I can't imagine you going to bed for a week.'

'No?' His smile was wicked. The dark eyes seemed to graze

her body. 'Then perhaps you need to extend the scope of your imagination, *mia cara*.'

I am not—*not* going to blush, Laura told herself silently. And I don't care how much he winds me up.

She looked back at him squarely, 'I meant—with some minor ailment, *signore*.'

'Perhaps not.' He shrugged. 'But my temper becomes so evil, I am sure those around me wish I would retire to my room—and stay there until I can be civil again.'

He paused while Luigi placed the coffees in front of them. 'But I have to admit that Paolo was a sickly child, and I think his mother plays on this, by pampering him, and making him believe every cough and sneeze is a serious threat. It is her way of retaining some hold on him.'

'I'm sure of it,' Laura said roundly. 'I suspect Beatrice Manzone has had a lucky escape.' And could have bitten her tongue out again as Alessio's gaze sharpened.

'*Davvero?*' he queried softly. 'A curious point of view to have about your *innamorato*, perhaps.'

'I meant,' Laura said hastily, in a bid to retrieve the situation, 'that I shan't be as submissive—or as easy to manipulate—as she would have been.'

'*Credo,*' he murmured, his mouth twisting. 'I believe you, *mia cara*. You have that touch of red in your hair that spells danger.'

He picked up his cup. 'Now, drink your coffee, and I will take you to see the church,' he added more briskly. 'There is a Madonna and Child behind the high altar that some people say was painted by Raphael.'

'But you don't agree?' Laura welcomed the change of direction.

He considered, frowning a little. 'I think it is more likely to have been one of his pupils. For one thing, it is unsigned, and Raphael liked to leave his mark. For another, Besavoro is too unimportant to appeal to an artist of his ambition. And lastly the Virgin does not resemble Raphael's favourite mistress, whom he is said to have used as his chief model, even for the Sistine Madonna.'

'Wow,' Laura said, relaxing into a smile. 'How very sacrilegious of him.'

He grinned back at her. 'I prefer to think—what proof of his passion.' He gave a faint shrug. 'But ours is still a beautiful painting, and can be treasured as such.'

He drank the rest of his coffee, and stood up, indicating the postcards. 'You wish me to post these? Before we visit the church?'

'Well, yes.' She hesitated. 'But you don't have to come with me, *signore*. After all, I can hardly get lost. And I know how busy you are. I'm sure you have plenty of other things to do.'

'Perhaps,' he said. 'But today, *mia cara*, I shall devote to you.' His smile glinted. 'Or did you think I had forgotten about you these past days?'

'I—I didn't think anything at all,' she denied hurriedly.

'I am disappointed,' he said lightly. 'I hoped you might have missed me a little.'

'Then maybe you should remember something.' She lifted her chin. 'I came to Besavoro with your cousin, *signore*.'

'Ah,' Alessio said softly. 'But that is so fatally easy to forget, Laura *mia*.'

And he walked off across the square.

The interior of the church was dim, and fragrant with incense. It felt cool, too, after the burning heat of the square outside.

There were a number of small streets, narrow and cobbled, opening off the square, their houses facing each other so closely that people could have leaned from the upper-storey windows and touched, and Laura explored them all.

The shuttered windows suggested a feeling of intimacy, she thought. A sense of busy lives lived in private. And the flowers that spilled everywhere from troughs and window boxes added to Besavoro's peace and charm.

'So,' Alessio said as they paused for some water at a drinking fountain before visiting the church. 'Do you like my town?'

'It's enchanting,' Laura returned with perfect sincerity, smiling inwardly at his casual use of the possessive. The lord, she thought, with his fiefdom. 'A little gem.'

'*Sì,*' he agreed. 'And now I will show you another. *Avanti.*'

Laura trod quietly up the aisle of the church, aware of Alessio following silently. The altar itself was elaborate with gold leaf, but she hardly gave it a second glance. Because, above it, the painting glowed like a jewel, creating its own light.

The girl in it was very young, her hair uncovered, her blue cloak thrown back. She held the child proudly high in her arms, her gaze steadfast, and almost defiant, as if challenging the world to throw the first stone.

Laura caught her breath. She turned to Alessio, eyes shining, her hand going out to him involuntarily. 'It's—wonderful.'

'Yes,' he returned quietly, his fingers closing round hers. 'Each time I see it, I find myself—amazed.'

They stood in silence for a few minutes longer, then, as if by tacit consent, turned and began to walk around the shadowy church, halting briefly at each shrine with its attendant bank of burning candles.

Laura knew she should free her hand, but his warm grasp seemed unthreatening enough. And she certainly didn't want to make something out of nothing, especially in a church, so she allowed her fingers to remain quietly in his.

But as they emerged into the sunshine he let her go anyway. Presumably, thought Laura, the Count Ramontella didn't wish 'his' citizens to see him walking hand in hand with a girl.

Or not my kind of girl, certainly, she amended silently.

She'd expected to be driven straight back to the villa, but to her uneasy surprise Alessio took another road altogether, climbing the other side of the valley.

'Where are we going?' she asked.

'There's a view I wish to show you,' he said. 'It belongs to a *trattoria*, so we can enjoy it over lunch.'

'But aren't we expected back at the villa?'

'You are so keen to return?' He slanted a smile at her. 'You think, maybe, that Paolo's medicine has already worked its magic?'

'No,' she said stiffly. 'Just wondering what your aunt will think.'

'It is only lunch,' he said. The smile lingered—hardened a little. 'And I do not think she will have any objection—or none that need trouble either of us.'

The *trattoria* was a former farmhouse, extensively renovated only a couple of years earlier. Among the improvements had been a long wide terrace, with a thatched roof to provide shade, which overlooked the valley.

Their welcome was warm, but also, Laura noticed, respectful, and they were conducted to a table at the front of the terrace. Menus were produced and they were offered an *aperitivo*.

Laura found herself leaning beside Alessio on the parapet of the broad stone wall, holding a glass of white wine, and looking down onto an endless sea of green, distantly punctuated by the blue ribbon of the river and the dusty thread of the road.

On the edge of her vision, she could see the finger of stone that was Besavoro's *campanile* rising from the terracotta roofs around it.

Higher up, the crags looked almost opalescent in the shimmer of the noonday sun, while on the opposite side of the valley, almost hidden by the clustering forest, she could just make out the sprawl of greyish pink stone that formed the Villa Diana.

She said softly, 'It's—unbelievable. Thank you for showing it to me.'

'The pleasure is mine,' he returned. 'It is a very small world, this valley, but important to me.'

She played with the stem of her glass. 'Yet you must have so many worlds, *signore*.'

'And some I prefer to others.' He paused. 'So, where is your world, Laura? The real one?'

Her tone was stilted. 'London, I guess—for the time being anyway. My work is there.'

'But surely you could work anywhere you wished? Wine bars are not confined to your capital. But I suppose you wish to remain for Paolo's sake.'

She had a sudden longing to tell him the truth. To turn to him and say, 'Actually I work for the PR company your bank has just hired. The wine bar is moonlighting, and Harman Grace would probably have a fit if they knew. Nor am I involved with Paolo. He's renting me as his pretend girlfriend to convince his mother that he won't marry Beatrice Manzone.'

But she couldn't say any such thing, of course, because she'd given Paolo her word.

Instead she said, 'Also, I'm flat-hunting with some friends. We all want to move on from our current grotty bedsits, especially Gaynor and myself, so we thought we'd pool our resources.'

'Does Paolo approve of this plan?' Alessio traced the shape of one of the parapet's flat stones with his finger. 'Won't he wish you to live with him?'

She bit her lip. 'Perhaps—ultimately. I—I don't know. It's too soon for that kind of decision.'

'But this holiday could have been the first step towards it.' There was an odd, almost harsh note in his voice. 'My poor Laura. If so, how cruel to keep you in separate rooms, as I have done.'

She forced a smile. 'Not really. The Signora would have had a fit and I—I might have caught Paolo's cold.'

His mouth twisted. 'A practical thought, *carissima*.' He straightened. 'Now, shall we decide what to eat?'

A pretty, smiling girl, who turned out to be the owner's wife, brought a bowl of olive oil to their table, and a platter of bread to dip into it. The cooking, Alessio explained, was being done by her husband. Then came a dish of Parma ham, accompanied by a bewildering array of sausages, which was followed up by wild boar pâté.

The main course was chicken, simply roasted and bursting with flavour, all of it washed down with a jug of smoky red wine, made, Alessio told her, from the family's own vineyard in Tuscany.

But Laura demurred at the idea of dessert or cheese, raising laughing hands in protest.

'They'll be charging me excess weight on the flight home at this rate.'

Alessio drank some wine, the dark eyes watching her over the top of his glass. 'Maybe you need to gain a little,' he said. 'A man likes to know that he has his woman in his arms. He does not wish her to slip through his fingers like water. Has Paolo never told you so?'

She looked down at the table. 'Not in so many words. And I don't think it's a very fashionable point of view, not in London, anyway.'

The mention of Paolo's name brought her down to earth with a jolt. It had been such a wonderful meal. She'd felt elated—euphoric even—here, above the tops of the trees.

I could reach up a hand, she thought, and touch the sky.

And this, she knew, was entirely because of the man seated across the table from her. The man who somehow had the power to make her forget everything—including the sole reason that had brought her to Italy in the first place.

Stupid, she castigated herself. Eternally, ridiculously stupid to hanker after what she could never have in a thousand years.

Because there was far more than just a table dividing them, and she needed to remember that in her remaining days at the Villa Diana.

Apart from anything else, they'd been acquainted with each other for only a week, which was a long time in politics, but in no other sense.

So how was it that she felt she'd known him all her life? she asked herself, and sighed inwardly. That, of course, was the secret of his success—especially with women.

And her best plan was to escape while she could, and before she managed to make an even bigger fool of herself than she had already.

She was like a tiny planet, she thought, circling the sun, when any slight change in orbit could draw her to self-destruction. Burning up for all eternity.

That cannot happen, she told herself. And I won't let it.

He said, 'A moment ago, you were here with me. Now you have gone.' He leaned forward, his expression quizzical.

'"When, Madonna, will you ever drop that veil you wear in shade and sun?"'

She looked back at him startled. 'I don't understand.'

'I was quoting,' he said. 'From Petrarch—one of his sonnets to Laura. My own translation. It seemed—appropriate.'

She tried to speak lightly. 'You amaze me, *signore*. I never thought I'd hear you speaking poetry.'

He shrugged. 'But I'm sure you could recite from Shakespeare, if I asked you. Am I supposed to have less education?'

'No,' she said quickly. 'No, of course not. I'm sorry. After all, we're strangers. I shouldn't make any assumptions about you.'

He paused. 'Besides, the question is a valid one. Because you also disappear behind a veil sometimes, so that I cannot tell what you're thinking.'

She laughed rather weakly. 'I'm—relieved to hear it.'

'So I shall ask a direct question. What are you hiding, Laura?'

Her fingers twined together in her lap. 'I think as well as a good education, *signore*, you have a vivid imagination.'

He studied her for a moment, his mouth wry. 'And you still will not call me Alessio.'

'Because I don't think it's necessary,' she retorted. 'Or even very wise, you being who you are. Not just a count, but Chairman of the Arleschi Bank.'

'You could not put that out of your mind for a while?'

'No.' Her fingers tightened round each other. 'That's not possible. Besides, I'll be gone soon, anyway.'

'But you forget, *signorina*,' he said silkily. 'You are to become a member of my family. We shall be cousins.'

She paused for a heartbeat. 'Well, when we are,' she said, 'I'll think again about your name.' She gave him a bright smile. 'And now will you take me back to the villa, please? Paolo may need me,' she added for good measure.

As he rose to his feet he was laughing. 'Well, run while you may, my little hypocrite,' he told her mockingly. 'But remember this: you cannot hide—or not for ever.' His fingers stroked her face from the high cheekbone to the corner of her mouth, then he turned and walked away across the terrace to the restaurant's main door, leaving Laura to stare uneasily after him, her heart and mind locked into a combat that offered no prospect of peace. And which, she suddenly knew, could prove mortal.

But only to me, she whispered to herself in swift anguish. Only to me...

CHAPTER SEVEN

THE return journey was conducted mainly in silence. Laura was occupied with her own troubling thoughts, while Alessio was reviewing the events of the morning with a sense of quiet satisfaction.

She had missed him, he thought. Everything—including all the things she had not said—had betrayed it. So his ploy of keeping aloof from her had succeeded. And, now, she was desperately trying to reinforce her own barricades against him.

But it won't work, *carissima*, he told her silently.

After he'd got rid of Giacomo that morning, he'd stood for a while, watching her from the other side of the square.

She might not have the flamboyant looks of a woman like Vittoria, but her unselfconscious absorption as she wrote gave an impression of peace and charm that he had never encountered before.

And her hair had been truly glorious in the sunlight, the colour of English leaves in autumn. He'd found himself suddenly longing to see it spread across his pillow, so that he could run his fingers through its soft masses and breathe their fragrance.

Also, he'd noted, with additional pleasure, she was again wearing the dress that had so fired his imagination at their first meeting.

And soon, he thought, as he turned the Jeep onto the road up to the villa—soon his fantasies would all be realised.

Not that it would be easy, he mentally amended with sudden restiveness. She might have let him take her hand for a while without protest, but, in many ways, she still continued to elude him, and not just in the physical sense either.

Her relationship with his cousin was certainly an enigma. He didn't particularly share his aunt's opinion that the pair were in love and planning immediate marriage. But then, he admitted, he'd hardly seen them together. Although, that first evening, he'd observed that the little Laura had not seemed to relish her lover's advances. But that might have been because she preferred privacy for such exchanges, and not a family dinner.

Well, privacy she should have, he promised himself, smiling inwardly, and his entire undivided attention as well.

However, he still wondered if, given time, the whole Paolo affair might have withered and died of its own accord, and without Zia Lucrezia's interference.

Not that he'd been able to convince her of that, although he had tried. She'd simply snapped that she could not afford to be patient, and that Paolo's engagement to the Manzone girl must be concluded without further delay.

She'd added contemptuously that the English girl was nothing more than a money-grubbing trollop who deserved to be sent packing in disgrace for attempting to connect herself, even distantly, to the Ramontella family.

'And your part in all this should have been played by now,' she added angrily. 'You should have spent more time with the little fool.'

'I know what I'm doing,' he returned coldly. 'Precisely because the girl is far from a fool, or any of the other names you choose to call her.'

How, in the name of God, could he feel so protective, he asked himself ruefully, afterwards, when he might be planning the possible ruin of Laura's life? If, indeed, it turned out that she cared for Paolo after all.

But on one thing he was totally determined. When he took her, it would be out of their mutual desire alone, and not to placate his aunt. That, he told himself, would be the least of his considerations.

He could salve his conscience to that extent.

And, if humanly possible, it would happen well away from the Villa Diana, and Zia Lucrezia's inevitable and frankly indecent gloating.

Because he needed to make very sure that Laura would never know how they'd been manipulated into each other's arms.

Although that was no longer strictly true—or not for him, anyway, he reminded himself wryly. On his side, at least, the need was genuine, and had been so almost from the first. She was the one who required the persuasion.

Staying away from her over the past few days had been sheer torment, he admitted, to his own reluctant surprise. She had been constantly in the forefront of his mind, waking and sleeping, while his entire body ached intolerably for her too.

He was not accustomed, he acknowledged sardonically, to waiting for a woman. In his world, it was not often that he found it necessary. And it would make her ultimate surrender even more enjoyable.

He cast a lightning sideways glance at her, and saw that her hands were clenched tightly in her lap.

He said lightly, 'Is it the road or my driving that so alarms you, Laura?'

She turned her head, forcing a smile. 'It's the road, although I'm trying to get used to it. We don't have so many death-defying drops in East Anglia, where I come from.'

'Try not to worry too much, *mia bella*.' His tone was dry. 'Believe that I have a vested interest in staying alive.'

There was a movement at the side of the road ahead, and Alessio leaned forward, his gaze sharpening as a stocky, white-haired man wearing overalls came into view, carrying a tall cane shaped like a shepherd's crook. 'Ah,' he said, half to himself. 'Fredo.' He drew the Jeep into the side of the road, and stopped. 'Will you forgive me, *cara*, if I speak to him again about moving down to Besavoro? He has been avoiding me, I think.'

Laura sat in the Jeep and watched with some amusement. The old man stood like a rock, leaning on his cane, occasionally moving his head in quiet negation as Alessio prowled round in front of him talking rapidly in his own language, his hands gesturing urgently in clear appeal.

When at last he paused for breath, the old man reached up and clapped him on the shoulder, his wrinkled face breaking into a smile. Then they talked together for a few more minutes before Fredo turned away, making his slow way up a track on the hillside, and Alessio came back to the Jeep, frowning.

'Still no luck?' she asked.

'He makes his own goats seem reasonable.' He started the engine. 'Also, he says that the weather is going to change. That we shall have storms,' he added, his frown deepening.

Laura looked up at the cloudless sky. 'It doesn't seem like it,' she objected.

'Fredo is rarely wrong about these things. But it will not be for a day—perhaps two.' He slanted a smile at her. 'So make the most of the sun while you can.'

'I've been doing just that.' She paused. 'In fact,' she went on hesitantly, 'I was—concerned in case I'd kept you away from the pool. If you preferred to have it to yourself. Because I've noticed that you—you haven't been swimming for a while.'

'I swim every day,' he said. 'But very early. Before breakfast, when there is no one else about, but that is not through any wish to avoid your company, *mia bella*, but because I like to swim naked.'

'Oh.' Laura swallowed. 'Oh, I—I understand. Of course.'

'Although,' he went on softly, 'you could always join me if you wished. The water feels wonderful at that time of day.'

'I'm sure it does,' Laura said woodenly, all sorts of forbidden images leaping to mind. 'But I think I'll stick to my own timetable. *Grazie*,' she added politely.

'*Prego,*' he returned, and she could hear the laughter in his voice.

Furiously aware that her face had warmed, Laura relapsed into a silence that lasted until their arrival at the villa.

As she left the Jeep she thanked Alessio for the lunch in the tone of a polite schoolgirl taking leave of a favourite uncle, and went off to her room, trying not to look as if she was escaping.

Her clothes were clinging to her in the heat, so she stripped quickly and took a cool shower. Then, she put on her robe and lay down on the bed, trying to relax. But her mind was still teeming with thoughts and impressions from the morning.

It was weird, she thought, that Alessio—the Count, she amended hastily—should just turn up like that, out of the blue. And even more disturbing that she should have enjoyed being with him quite so much.

She'd been unnerved too by his suggestion that she was hiding something. He might have dressed it up in poetic language about veils, she thought ruefully, but basically he was issuing a warning that he was on to her.

And in turn she would have to warn Paolo, on her evening visit, that his lordly cousin was growing suspicious.

She found herself sighing a little. These visits were becoming more problematic each time. Quite apart from his obsession about his cold, it was difficult to hold a conversation with someone she hardly knew, and with whom she barely had a thought in common, especially when she suspected his mother was listening at the door.

I wish all this had never happened, she told herself vehemently. That I'd never agreed to this ridiculous pretence. And, most of all, that I'd never come here and set eyes on Count Ramontella. Better for me that he'd just remained a name on a letterhead.

Easy to say, she thought, but did she really mean it? Would she truly have wanted to live her life without having experienced this frankly dangerous encounter? Without having felt the lure of his smile, or reacting to the teasing note in his voice? Without realising, dry-mouthed, that he had simply—entered the room?

No, she thought sadly. If I'm honest, I wouldn't have wanted to miss one precious moment with him. But now the situation's getting altogether trickier, and I really need to distance myself. Put the width of Europe between us, and become sane again.

It's safer that way, and I'm a safety-conscious girl. I have to be.

She sighed again. Alessio Ramontella was just a dream to take back with her to mundane reality, she thought wistfully. A private fantasy to lighten up her fairly staid existence. And that was all he ever would, or could be...

Until one day, when he would become nothing but a fading

memory. And she could relax, lower her guard, and get on with her own life.

Perhaps, in time, she might even convince herself that none of this had ever happened.

She sat up, swinging her legs to the floor. She was obviously not going to sleep, so she might take the Count's advice, and exploit the fine weather while it persisted.

She changed swiftly into her swimsuit, slipped on the filmy voile shirt she used as a cover-up, and went down to the pool.

As she reached the bottom of the steps she was disconcerted to see that she would not be alone that afternoon either. That Alessio was there before her, stretched out on a lounger, reading.

He seemed deeply absorbed, and Laura hesitated, wondering if she should turn quietly and make a strategic withdrawal before she was noticed. But it was already too late for that, because he was putting down his book and getting to his feet in one lithe movement, the sculpted mouth smiling faintly as he looked at her.

'So you came after all,' he said softly. 'I had begun to wonder.'

'I—I decided to take your friend at his word.' She paused. 'I hope I'm not disturbing you.'

He said lightly, 'Not in any way that you think, *mia cara*.' He moved a lounger into the shade of a parasol for her, and arranged the cushions.

'Thank you.' She felt self-conscious enough to have stood on one leg and sucked her thumb. And he'd placed her sunbed far too close to his own, she thought with misgiving. However, it seemed unwise to make any kind of fuss, so she walked across and sat down, forcing a smile as she looked up at him. 'Heavens, it's hotter than ever.'

'Yes.' Alessio glanced up at the mountains with a slight frown. 'I begin to think Fredo may be right.'

Laura reached down and retrieved his book, which had slipped off his lounger onto the marble tiles between them. 'Francesco Petrarca' was emblazoned in faded gilt letters across its leather cover.

'Reading more poetry about veiled ladies, *signore*?' She

handed it to him. Literature, she thought. Now there's a safe topic for conversation.

'There is much to read,' he said drily. 'The great Francesco made his Laura's name a song for twenty years.'

'How did they meet?'

'He saw her,' Alessio said, after a pause. 'Saw her one day, and fell in love for ever.'

'And did they live happily ever after?'

'They lived their own lives, but not together. She—belonged to another man.'

She made a thing of adjusting her sunglasses. She said lightly, 'Then maybe he shouldn't have allowed himself to fall in love.'

'Ah,' he said softly. 'But perhaps, Laura *mia*, he could not help himself. Listen.' He found a page, and read aloud. '"I was left defenceless against love's attack, with no barrier between my eyes and my heart."'

He put the book down. 'Is there a defence against love, I wonder?' The dark gaze seemed to bore into hers. 'What do you think, *bella mia*? Did Paolo travel straight from your eyes to your heart when you saw him first?'

No, she thought, pain twisting inside her. But you did—and now I'm lost for ever...

She made herself look back at him. 'Naturally there was—a connection. Why else would I be here?'

'Why indeed?' he said softly. He stretched slowly, effortlessly, making her numbly aware of every smooth ripple of muscle in his lean body. 'I am going to swim, Laura. Will you join me?'

'No,' she managed somehow. 'No, thank you.'

He smiled at her. 'You do not feel the necessity to cool off a little?'

'I'm a very poor swimmer,' she said. 'I don't like being out of my depth, and your pool has no shallow end.'

'Ah,' he said meditatively. 'Then why do you not allow me to teach you?'

There was a loaded silence, and Laura found she was biting her lip. 'That's—very kind,' she said, trying to keep her voice steady. 'But I couldn't—possibly—impose on you like that.'

'No imposition, *cara mia*.' His voice was a drawl. 'It would be my privilege, and my pleasure. Besides,' he added with faint reproof, 'everyone should be able to swim safely. Don't you agree?'

'I—I suppose so.' Except that we're not really talking about swimming, she thought wildly, and we both know it. So why— why are you doing this?

He said softly, 'But you are not convinced.' He walked to the far end of the pool, and dived in, swimming the whole length under water. He surfaced, shaking the water from his hair, and swam slowly to the edge, resting his arms on the tiled surround.

He beckoned. 'Laura, come to me.' He spoke quietly, but the imperative came over loud and clear. She realised, not for the first time, why he was a force to be reckoned with within the Arleschi Bank.

Reluctantly, she shed the voile shirt and walked over to the edge of the pool, reed-slender in her green swimsuit.

She said coolly, 'Do you always expect to be obeyed, *signore*?'

'Always.' The sun glistened on the dark hair as he looked up at her. He added softly, 'But I prefer compliance to submission, *signorina*.' He paused, allowing her to assimilate that, then smiled. 'Now sit on the edge,' he directed. 'Put your hands on my arms, and lower yourself into the water. I promise I will keep you safe.'

Her heart juddered. Oh, but it's too late, she thought. Much too late for that.

But she did as she was told, gasping as the coolness of the water made contact with her overheated skin, aware of Alessio's hands, firm as rocks, under her elbows.

'You can stand,' she accused breathlessly. 'But I can't reach. I'm treading water.'

'Then do so,' he said. 'You will come to no harm.' He added with faint amusement, 'And I can do nothing about the disparity in our heights, *bella mia*.'

He paused. 'You say you can swim a little?' And, when she

nodded without much conviction, 'The width of the pool, perhaps?'

'Possibly,' Laura said with dignity. She hesitated. 'But not without touching the bottom with my toe,' she conceded unwillingly.

He sighed. 'Then the true answer is no,' he commented austerely. 'So, we shall begin.'

It was one of the strangest hours of her life. If she'd imagined Alessio had lured her into the pool for his own dubious purposes, then she had to think again and quickly, because his whole attitude was brisk, almost impersonal. He really intended to teach her to swim, she realised in astonishment as she struggled to co-ordinate her arm and leg movements and her breathing, while his hand cupped her chin.

One of her problems, he told her, was her apparent reluctance to put her face in the water.

'What does it matter if your make-up is spoiled?' he said.

'I'm not wearing make-up,' she retorted, trying to catch her breath.

He slanted a faint grin at her. 'I know. Now let us try again.

'You lack confidence, no more than that, so you must learn to trust the water,' he directed eventually. 'Let it hold you, and do not fight it. Now, turn on your back and float for a while. I will support you.'

She did as she was bidden, feeling the dazzle of the sun on her closed eyelids.

She was not even aware of the moment he gently withdrew his hand from beneath her head until she heard him say, '*Brava*, Laura. You do well,' and realised he was no longer beside her.

Her eyes flew open in swift panic, to see him watching her from the side of the pool, and she floundered suddenly, coughing and spluttering. He reached her in a moment, and held her.

'You let go of me,' she gasped.

'About five minutes ago,' he told her drily. 'You stopped believing. That is all. But now, when you are ready, you will swim beside me across the pool, because you know you can. And remember to breathe,' he added sternly.

She gave him a mutinous look. *'Sì, signore.'*

But to her amazement she did it, and she felt almost euphoric with achievement when she found herself clinging to the opposite edge, catching her breath.

Alessio pulled himself out of the water, and stood for a moment, raking back his wet hair. Then he bent, sliding his hands under Laura's armpits, lifting her out to join him as if she were a featherweight.

'But I wanted to swim back,' she objected, smiling up at him as he put her down on the tiles.

'I think that is enough for the first time,' he said softly. He paused. 'After all, I do not wish to exhaust you.' His hands moved slowly to her shoulders. Remained there.

Laura was suddenly aware of a strange stillness as if the world had halted on its axis. Or was it just that her heart seemed to have stopped beating? He had told her to breathe, she thought confusedly, but it was impossible. Her throat was too tight.

In spite of the heat, she was shivering, an unfamiliar weakness penetrating the pit of her stomach.

He was looking down at her, she realised, watching her parted lips. He was smiling a little, but there was no laughter in the half-closed eyes, which studied her with frank intensity, as if mesmerised.

He bent towards her, and she thought, He's going to kiss me.

Deep within her, she felt a pang of yearning so acute that the stifled breath burst from her in a raw, shocked gasp. And with it came a kind of sanity as she realised exactly what she was inviting. And from whom...

She heard a voice she barely recognised as her own say raggedly, 'No—Alessio—please, no!'

The dark brows lifted wryly. He reached up, and framed her face with both hands, his thumbs stroking back the wet strands of hair behind her ears, then stroking gently along her cheekbones and down to the fragility of her jawline.

She felt him touch the corners of her quivering mouth, then the long fingers travelled down her throat to her shoulders again.

He said softly, 'No?'

He hooked a finger under the strap of her swimsuit, and drew it down, then bent, brushing his lips softly across the faint mark it had left on her skin.

Laura felt her whole body shudder in sudden heated delight at his touch. Knew, with dismay, that he would have recognised that too.

He said quietly, 'Laura, I have a house overlooking the sea near Sorrento. It is quiet, and very beautiful, and we could be there together in just a few hours.' His dark eyes met hers. 'So— are you still quite sure it is—no?' he asked.

Somehow, even at this stage, she had to retrieve the situation. Somehow...

She stepped back, out of range, lifting her chin in belated defiance. 'I'm—absolutely certain.' Fiercely, she jerked her strap back into place. 'And you—you—you have no right—no right at all to think—to assume...'

'I assume nothing, *carissima*.' He raised his hands in pretended surrender, his tone amused—rueful. 'But you cannot blame me for trying.'

'But I do blame you,' she flung back at him. 'And so would Paolo, if I decided to make trouble and tell him.' She swallowed. 'Do you think he'd be pleased to know you were—going behind his back like this?'

He shrugged. 'Paolo's feelings were never a consideration, I confess. I was far more concerned with my own pleasure, *bella mia*.' He smiled. 'And with yours,' he added softly.

She felt betraying colour swamp her face, but stood her ground. 'You still seem very sure of yourself, *signore*. I find that extraordinary.'

'Losing a battle,' he said, 'does not always alter the course of the war.' He paused. 'And you called me Alessio just now— while you were waiting for me to kiss you.'

Her flush deepened at this all-too-accurate assessment. She said through gritted teeth, 'The war, as you call it, is over. I shall tell Paolo I want to go back to England immediately. As soon as my flight can be rearranged.'

'And he may even agree,' he said. 'As long as it does not

interfere with his own plans. But if there are difficulties, do not hesitate to ask for my help.' He added silkily, 'I have some influence with the airline.'

Ignoring her outraged gasp, he walked across to his lounger, picked up the towel and began to dry himself with total unconcern. Laura snatched up her own things and headed for the steps.

'*Arrivederci.*' His voice followed her. 'Until later, *bellissima.*'

'Until hell freezes over,' she threw back breathlessly, over her shoulder, then forced her shaking legs to carry her up the steps and out of the sight and sound of him.

Alessio watched her go, caught between exultancy and irritation, with a heaped measure of sexual frustration thrown in.

He ached, he thought sombrely, like a moonstruck adolescent.

Stretching out on the lounger, he gazed up at the sky, questions rotating in his mind.

Why, in the name of God, had he let her walk away like that? He'd felt her trembling when he'd touched her. Why hadn't he pressed home his advantage—thrown the cushions on the ground, and drawn her down there with him, peeling the damp swimsuit from her body, and silencing her protests with kisses as he'd taken her, swiftly and simply?

Winning her as his woman, he thought, while he appeased the hunger that was tearing him apart.

Afterwards, he would have sent her to pack her things while he enjoyed another kind of satisfaction—the moment when he told Paolo, and his damnable mother, that he was taking Laura away with him. His mission accomplished in the best possible way.

Then, off to Sorrento to make plans—but for what? The rest of their lives? He frowned swiftly. He had never thought of any woman in those terms. But certainly the weeks to follow—maybe even the months.

At some point, they would have to return to Rome. It would be best, he decided, if he rented an apartment for her. A place without resonances, containing a bed that he'd shared with no one else.

But what was the point of thinking like this, he derided himself, when none of it had happened? When she'd rejected him, using Paolo's name like a shield, as she always did. And he'd let her go...

Dio, he could still taste the cool silkiness of her skin.

And now she wished to leave altogether—to go back to London. Well, so she might, and the sooner the better. Because he would follow.

In England, he could pursue her on his own terms, he thought. He'd have the freedom to date and spoil her exactly as he wished, until her resistance crumbled. And there would be no Zia Lucrezia to poison the well.

Yes, he thought with a sigh of anticipation. London was the perfect answer.

Unless... He sat up suddenly, mind and body reeling as if he'd been punched in the gut. Was it—could it be possible that he'd misjudged the situation completely? Might it be that she was genuinely in love with his weasel of a cousin after all? The idea made him nauseous.

Yet she'd wanted him very badly to kiss her. His experience with women left him in no doubt about that, while her own female instinct must have told her that, once she was in his arms, it would not stop at kissing.

She'd allowed Paolo to kiss her, of course, and all the other intimacies he dared not even contemplate, because they filled him with such blind, impotent rage that he longed to go up to the house, take his cousin from his sick bed, and put him in hospital instead.

He looked down at the book beside him, his mouth hardening. Ah, Francesco, he thought. Was that the image that haunted you every night—your Laura in her husband's arms?

He supposed in some twisted way he should be grateful to his aunt for persuading her malingering son that he was far more sick than he really was, and keeping the lovers apart. At least he didn't have the torment of knowing they were together under his roof.

Santa Madonna, he thought. Anyone might think I was jealous. But I have never been so in my whole life.

And I do not propose to start now, he added grimly.

No, he thought. He would not accept that Laura had any serious feelings for Paolo. Women in love carried their own protection like a heat-shield. No one existed in their private radiant universe but the beloved. Yet he'd been able to feel her awareness of him just as surely as if she'd put out her hand and touched his body.

So, maybe she really believed that, with Paolo, she would be marrying money—or at least where money was. The thought made him wince, but it now had to be faced and dealt with. Because it was clear that, living in one room and working in a bar, she was struggling near the bottom of the ladder.

And, if he was right, he thought cynically, then he would have to convince her that he would be a far more generous proposition than his cousin. That, financially, she would do much better as his mistress than as Paolo's wife.

A much pleasanter task, he resolved, would be to set himself to create for her such an intensity of physical delight that she would forget all other men in his arms. It occurred to him, wryly, that it was the least she deserved.

But what do I deserve? he asked himself quietly. And could find no answer.

'What is this? What are you saying?' Paolo's face was mottled with annoyance.

'I want to go home,' Laura repeated levelly. 'I—I'm totally in the way here, and it's becoming a serious embarrassment for me.'

'An embarrassment for which you will be well paid,' he snapped. He paused. 'But what you ask is not possible. My mother will become suspicious if you go home alone—think that we have quarrelled.'

'I fail to see how,' Laura said coldly. 'We haven't spent enough time together to have a row.'

He waved an impatient hand. 'I have worked too hard to convince her to fail now.' He thought for a moment. 'But we could leave earlier than planned, if we go together—in two or three days, perhaps.'

'Will you be well enough to travel?' Laura asked acidly, but her sarcasm was wasted.

He shrugged. 'We must hope. And *Mamma* intends me to take a little trip with her very soon, so we shall see.'

She said quietly, 'Paolo, I'm deadly serious about this, and I don't intend to wait indefinitely. In twenty-four hours, I'm looking for another flight.'

I can survive that long, she thought bleakly as she went to her room to change for dinner. But this time, I'll be the one adopting the avoidance tactics.

CHAPTER EIGHT

NOTHING happened. Nothing happened. The words echoed and re-echoed in Laura's head, matching the reluctant click of her heels on the tiled floor as she walked to the *salotto* that evening.

But even if that was true, she could hardly take credit for it, she acknowledged bitterly. Nor could she pretend otherwise for her own peace of mind. And she felt as guilty as if she and Paolo had been genuinely involved with each other.

She'd stayed in her room as long as possible, pacing restlessly up and down, frankly dreading the moment when she would have to face Alessio again.

She still seemed to feel his touch as if it were somehow in-grained in her. She'd been almost surprised, as she'd stood under the shower, not to find the actual marks of his fingers—the scar left by the graze of his lips on her skin.

But, invisible or not, they were there, she knew, and she would carry them for ever.

Guillermo was hovering almost anxiously in the hallway, em-phasising how late she'd left her arrival, and he sprang forward, beaming, to open the carved double doors to admit her to the *salotto*.

She squared her shoulders and walked in, braced—for what? Mockery—indifference? Or something infinitely more danger-ous...

And halted, her brows lifting in astonishment. Because she was not to be alone with Alessio as she'd feared after all. Paolo was there, reclining on a sofa, looking sullen, while the Signora oc-cupied a high-backed armchair nearby, her lips compressed as if annoyed about something.

And, alone by the open windows, looking out into the night, was Alessio, glass in hand.

All heads turned as Laura came forward, and she was immediately aware of an odd atmosphere in the silent room—a kind of angry tension. But she ignored it and went straight to Paolo, who rose sulkily to his feet at her approach.

'Darling,' she said. She reached up and kissed his cheek. 'You didn't say you were getting up for dinner. What a wonderful surprise.'

'Well, I shall not be able to take the time I need to recuperate, when you are in such a hurry to fly home,' he returned peevishly, making her long to kick him.

'Signorina Mason—at last you join us.' The Signora's smile glittered coldly at her. 'We were just talking about you. We have a small predicament, you understand.'

'I can't see what that could be. Paolo's well again.' Laura slid a hand through his arm as she faced the older woman, chin up. 'That's all that really matters.'

'Then I hope you are prepared to be gracious,' said the Signora, her smile a little fixed. 'Because tomorrow I must tear him away from you. We are to pay a visit to my dearest friend, and remain for lunch. She is not aware of your presence here, so I regret that you have not been included in her invitation. You will, I hope, forgive our absence.'

She turned her head towards Alessio, who looked back, his face expressionless.

'And now it seems that you will also be deserted by our host,' she went on, her voice faintly metallic. 'My nephew tells me he has business in Perugia tomorrow that cannot be postponed. We were—discussing the problem.'

Laura found herself torn between relief and a sense of desolation so profound that she was ashamed of herself. She dared not risk a glance in the direction of the tall young man standing in silence by the window.

Once again, it seemed, he was—letting her go.

'It's kind of you to be concerned, *signora*,' she returned with total insincerity. 'But I'm quite accustomed to my own company. Besides, His Excellency has already given me far too much of his time. And I have my packing to do. The time will pass in a flash.'

The Signora gave her a long look, then addressed herself to her nephew. 'Camilla tells me that her son, Fabrizio, will be joining us tomorrow, with his beautiful wife—I forget her name. Do you wish me to convey any message to them on your behalf?'

There was another tingling silence. Then: 'No,' Alessio said icily. 'I thank you.'

'Then let us dine,' said the Signora. 'I have quite an appetite. Come, *signorina*.'

On the way to the dining room, Alessio detained his cousin. 'Why in the name of God have you agreed to go to Trasimeno tomorrow?' he demanded in an undertone.

Paolo shrugged. '*Mamma* has suddenly become more amenable on the subject of my marriage plans. I felt she deserved a small concession. Besides,' he added, leering, 'you heard her say that tasty little plum Vittoria Montecorvo was going to be there. I thought I might try my chances with her.'

A single spark of unholy joy penetrated Alessio's inner darkness. 'Why not?' he drawled. 'Rumour says the lady is—receptive.' He paused. 'Although there is an obstacle, of course.'

'Obstacle?' Paolo stared at him, then laughed. 'You mean the husband? No problem there. He's a total fool.'

'I was thinking,' Alessio said levelly, 'of Signorina Mason.'

'Ah—yes.' Paolo looked shifty. 'But we are not married yet, and a man should be allowed his bachelor pleasures.'

'I could not agree more,' Alessio told him softly. 'I wish you luck, cousin.'

If Laura had thought the presence of other people at the table would make the situation easier, she soon realised her mistake.

Only the Signora, who seemed to have belatedly rediscovered the laws of hospitality and chattered almost vivaciously throughout dinner, appeared to enjoy the lengthy meal. Paolo was lost in some pleasant day-dream and hardly said a word, while Alessio's responses to his aunt's heavily playful remarks were crisp and monosyllabic.

Altogether, the atmosphere was tricky, and Laura, to her shame, found herself remembering almost nostalgically the meals she'd eaten alone with Alessio.

Don't even go there, she adjured herself severely as the ordeal drew to a close.

They returned to the *salotto* for coffee, and it occurred to her that she ought to talk to Paolo privately, and make certain that he'd taken seriously her insistence on going home. And that he intended to call the airline and change their flight as soon as he got back tomorrow.

She said with feigned brightness, 'Paolo, darling, why don't we have our coffee on the terrace? It's such a beautiful night and we can—enjoy the moonlight together.'

For a moment, she thought he was going to refuse, then comprehension dawned. 'But of course,' he said. 'What a wonderful idea.'

As she walked out through the windows she was aware of Alessio's enigmatic stare following her. She paused, realising that she was breathing much too fast, and went to lean on the balustrade as she tried to regain her composure.

If she was honest, she thought, looking up at the sky, it was far from being a lovely night. The air was hot and stifling, and there was a haze over the moon. Wasn't that supposed to be a sign of bad weather to come?

Then, as she waited she heard somewhere in the distance the long-drawn-out howl of an animal, an eerie sound that echoed round the hills, and made the fine hairs stand up on the nape of her neck.

Gasping, she turned and almost cannoned into Alessio, who was standing just behind her.

She recoiled violently. 'Oh, God, you startled me.' She swallowed. 'That noise—did you hear it?'

'It was a wolf, nothing more.' He put the cup of coffee he was carrying on the balustrade. 'They live in the forests, which is one of the reasons Fredo likes to stay up there too—to protect his goats. Didn't Paolo warn you about them?'

'Yes,' she said. 'He mentioned them.' She added coldly, 'But he failed to tell me that they don't all live in forests.'

Alessio winced elaborately. 'A little unjust, *bella mia*. According to the experts, wolves mate for life.'

'The four-legged kind, maybe.' She paused. 'I've never heard any of them before this evening. Why is that?'

'They are more vocal in the early spring, when they are breeding,' he explained. 'Perhaps, tonight, something has disturbed them.'

'Perhaps.' She looked past him towards the lights of the *salotto*. 'Where's Paolo?'

'His mother decided that the night air would be bad for his chest,' he said solemnly. 'And, as they have a journey tomorrow, she has persuaded him to have an early night.' He indicated the cup. 'So I brought your coffee to you.' He added, silkily, 'I regret your disappointment.'

'Paolo's health,' she said stonily, 'is far more important.'

The howl of the wolf came again, and she shivered. 'That's such a—lonely sound.'

'Maybe he is alone, and lonely.' Alessio faced her, leaning against the balustrade. 'A wolf occasionally does separate from the pack, and find that he does not wish to be solitary after all.'

'Well, I won't waste too much sympathy.' Laura kept her tone crisp. 'Wolves are predators, and I expect there are quite enough stray females about to prevent them becoming totally isolated. What do you think, *signore*?'

He grinned at her, unfazed. 'I think that I would very much like to put you across my knee, and spank you, *signorina*,' he drawled. 'But that, alas, would not be—politically correct. So I will leave you before you draw any more unflattering comparisons.'

And that, Laura thought bleakly, when he'd gone and she was left staring into the darkness, was probably our last exchange. I insulted him, and he threatened me with physical violence. Tomorrow he'll be in Perugia. The day after, I'll be on the plane to London. End of story.

And she looked up at the blurred moon, and realised unhappily that she felt like howling herself.

Laura made sure she was around in the morning to bid Paolo an openly fond farewell.

'As soon as you get back,' she whispered as she hugged him, 'you must phone the airline and change our flights. Please, Paolo. I—I can't stand it here much longer.'

'You are better off here than lunching with Camilla Montecorvo. She is a bigger dragon than my mother,' he returned morosely. 'And at least you will have the place to yourself while my cousin is in Perugia on this mysterious business of his.' He gave her a knowing look. 'If you ask me, he has a woman there, so he may not come back at all.' Then, more loudly, '*Arrivederci, carissima.* Hold me in your heart until I return.'

Breakfast, as usual, was served on the terrace, although Laura was not so sure this was a good idea. It was not a pleasant morning. The air was sultry, and there was no faint breeze to counteract it. Looking up, she saw that there were small clouds already gathering around the crests of the hills, and realised that Fredo's change in the weather was really on its way.

She thought, Everything's changing... and shivered.

She also noticed that two places had been set at the table.

'His Excellency comes soon,' Emilia told her. 'He swims.'

Yes, thought Laura, biting her lip, fighting the sudden image in her mind. He—told me.

For a moment she let herself wonder what would happen if she went down to the pool and joined him there.

'I've come for my swimming lesson,' she could say as she slid down into the water, and into his arms...

She shook herself mentally. She would never behave in such a way, not in a thousand years, so it was crazy even to think like that. And futile too.

A woman in Perugia, Paolo had said.

The lone wolf off hunting his prey, she thought. Looking for a mate.

And that, she told herself forcibly, her mind flinching, was definitely a no-go area. How the Count Ramontella chose to amuse himself was his own affair. And at least she had ensured that she would not be providing his entertainment, however shamefully tempting that might be.

At that moment Alessio arrived, striding up the steps from the pool, damp hair gleaming and a towel flung over his bare shoulder. He was even wearing, she saw, the same ancient white shorts as on the day of her arrival.

'*Buon giorno.*' He took the seat opposite, the dark gaze scanning her mockingly. 'You did not join me in the pool this morning.'

'I hardly think you expected me to,' Laura retorted coolly, refusing to think about how close a call it had been.

'I expect very little,' he said. 'In that way I am sometimes pleasantly surprised.' His eyes sharpened a little. 'I hope you slept well, but it does not seem so. You have shadows under your eyes.'

'I'm fine,' she said shortly, helping herself to orange juice. 'But I think the heat's beginning to get to me. I'll be glad to go home.'

'Yet for Paolo, this is home,' he reminded her softly. 'So maybe you should try to accustom yourself to our climate, hmm?'

She glanced back at the hills. 'At the moment it seems a little unpredictable.'

'Not at all,' he said. 'We are undoubtedly going to have a storm.' He poured himself some coffee. 'Are you afraid of thunder, Laura *mia*?'

'No, I don't think so.' She looked down at her plate. 'And sometimes a storm can—clear the air.'

'Or breed more storms.' He paused. 'Did you say a fond goodbye to your *innamorato* this morning?'

'He's going for lunch with friends,' she said. 'Not trekking in the Himalayas.'

'Both can be equally dangerous. I suspect that my aunt may have arranged for Beatrice Manzone to be present.' He paused. 'Does that disturb you?'

She kept her eyes fixed on her plate. 'Paolo is old enough to make his own decisions. I—I simply have to trust him to do that.'

'How admirable you are, *mia cara*.' His tone was sardonic. He finished his coffee in a single swallow, and rose. 'And now I too must leave you. But, unlike Paolo, you are in safe hands.' He gave her a tight-lipped smile. 'Guillermo and Emilia will look after you well.'

But when are you coming back? She thought it, but did not say it. Could not say it.

She watched him disappear into the house, and pushed her food away untouched as pain twisted inside her. There was so much, she thought, that she dared not let him see. So much that would still haunt her even when the width of Europe divided them—and when she herself was long forgotten.

It was going to be, she told herself unhappily, a very long day.

In fact, it seemed endless. She didn't even have Caio's company, as the Signora had chosen to reclaim him that morning, announcing imperiously that he would be accompanying them to Trasimeno. Laura had seen him struggling, his small face woebegone as he was carried inexorably to the car.

She spent some time by the pool, but soon gave it up as a bad job. The clouds had begun to gather in earnest, accompanied now by a strong, gusting wind, and even a few spots of rain, so she gathered up her things and returned to the villa.

She'd finished *Mansfield Park* so she went along to Alessio's library and returned it, borrowing *Pride and Prejudice* instead. She knew the story so well, she thought, that she could easily read it before it was time for her to leave.

She lingered for a while looking round the room. It seemed to vibrate with his presence. Any moment now, she thought, he would stride in, flinging himself into the high-backed leather chair behind the desk, and pulling the laptop computer towards him, the dark face absorbed.

The desk itself was immaculately tidy. Besides the laptop, it held only a tray containing a few sheets of the Arleschi Bank's headed notepaper, and that leather-bound copy of Petrarch's poetry that he'd been reading.

She opened the book at random, and tried to decipher some of the lines, but it was hopeless—rather like the love the poems described, she told herself wryly.

From the eyes to the heart, she thought, the words echoing sadly in her mind. How simple—and how fatal.

To Emilia's obvious concern, she opted to lunch only on soup and a salad. The working girl's diet, she reminded herself, her mouth twisting.

Elizabeth Bennett's clashes with Mr Darcy kept her occupied during the afternoon, but as evening approached Laura began to get restive. The skies were dark now, the menacing clouds like slate, and Emilia came bustling in to light the lamps, and also, she saw, with faint alarm, to bring in some branched candlesticks, which were placed strategically round the room, while Guillermo arrived with a basket of logs and proceeded to kindle a fire in the grate.

Laura was grateful for that, because the temperature had dropped quite significantly, and the crackling flames made the room feel cheerful.

But as time passed her worries deepened. Paolo knew she was relying on him to organise their departure, she thought, so surely he must return soon, especially with the deterioration in the weather.

She could see lightning flashes, and hear thunder rumbling round the hills, coming closer all the time. She remembered nervously that, in spite of her brave words at breakfast, she really didn't like storms at all. And this one looked as if it was going to be serious stuff.

It was raining heavily by now, the water drumming a ceaseless tattoo on the terrace outside. She dared not think what the road from Besavoro would be like, and her feeling of isolation began to prey on her.

Think about something else, she adjured herself as she went off to change for dinner, even though it seemed as if she'd be eating alone. Don't contemplate Alessio driving back from

Perugia in the Jeep, because he almost certainly won't be. He has every excuse now, always supposing he needed one, to stay the night there.

She put on the silver dress and stood for a moment, regarding herself with disfavour. Her wardrobe had been woefully inadequate for the purpose from day one, she thought. And it was only thanks to Emilia's efficient laundry service that she'd managed to survive.

As for this dress—well, she wouldn't care if she never saw it again.

By the time she got back to the *salotto*, the storm was even closer, and the lamps, she saw, were flickering ominously with every lightning flash.

And then, above the noise of the storm, she heard the distant sound of a vehicle, and a moment later Guillermo's voice raised in greeting.

Paolo, she thought with relief. At last. They'd made it.

She was halfway to the doors when they opened and she halted, her heart bumping, a shocked hand going to her throat.

She said hoarsely, 'I—I thought you were in Perugia.'

'I was,' Alessio said. He advanced into the room, rain glistening on his hair, shrugging off the trench coat he was wearing and throwing it carelessly across the back of a chair. 'But I did not think it was right for you to be alone here in these conditions, so I came back.' He gave her a mocking smile. 'You are allowed to be grateful.'

'I'm used to weather,' she returned, lifting her chin. 'In England we have loads of it.' She hesitated. 'I thought—I hoped Paolo had come back.'

He said lightly, 'I fear I have a disappointment for you. The servants took a call from my aunt two hours ago. In view of the weather, they have decided to remain at Trasimeno for the night. Or that is the story. So—you and I are alone, *bella mia*.'

And as he spoke all the lights went off. Laura cried out, and in a stride Alessio was beside her, taking her hands in his, drawing her towards him.

'Scared of the dark, *carissima*?' he asked softly.

'Not usually,' she said shakily. And far more scared of you, *signore*, she whispered under her breath. 'It's just—everything happening at once,' she added on a little gasp, tinglingly conscious of his proximity.

Don't let him know that it matters, she ordered herself sternly. For heaven's sake, act normally. And say something with no personal connotations, if that's possible.

She cleared her throat. 'Does the power always go off when there's a storm?'

'More often than I could wish. We have a generator for back-up at such times, but I prefer to keep it in reserve for real emergencies.' He paused. 'But Emilia does not like to cook with electricity, so at least dinner is safe.'

He let her go almost casually, and walked over to the fireplace, leaving Laura to breathe freely again. He took down a taper from the wide stone shelf above the hearth and lit it at the fire.

As he moved round the room each candle burst into light like a delicate golden blossom, and in spite of her misgivings Laura was charmed into an involuntary sigh of delight.

'You see.' He tossed the remains of the taper into the wide grate and smiled at her. 'Firelight and candle glow. Better, I think, than electricity.'

Not, she thought, aware that she was trembling inside, in these particular circumstances.

She steadied her voice. 'And certainly more in keeping with the age of the villa.'

Alessio inclined his head courteously. 'As you say.' He paused. 'May I get you a drink?'

'Just some mineral water, please.' Keep sane—keep sober.

His brows rose slightly, but he said nothing, bringing her exactly what she'd asked for and pouring a whisky for himself.

Laura sat on the edge of the sofa, gripping the crystal tumbler in one hand and nervously rearranging the folds of her skirt with the other.

Alessio added some more wood to the fire and straightened, dusting his hands. He sent her a considering look under his lashes, noting the tension in every line of her, and realising that he needed to ease the situation a little.

He said quietly, 'Laura, will you make me a promise?'

She looked up, startled, and instantly wary. 'I don't know. It—it would depend on what it was.'

'Nothing too difficult. I wish you to swear that when you are back in London you will go swimming at least once a week. You lack only confidence.'

'I suppose I could manage that,' she said slowly. 'There are some swimming baths quite near where I live.'

'Then there is no problem.' He added casually, 'Get Paolo to go with you.'

'Maybe,' she said, her mouth curving in such unexpected mischief that his heart missed a beat. 'If his health improves.'

He grinned back, shrugging. 'You can always hope, *carissima*.'

It had worked to some extent, he thought. She was no longer clinging to her glass as if it were a lifeline. But that strange intangible barrier that she'd built between them was still there.

Her reticence frankly bewildered him. He had once been forced to listen to Paolo's drunken boasting about his London conquests, and restraint had never featured as one of the qualities his cousin most favoured in a woman.

So what was he doing with this girl? His Laura, with her level smoky gaze and proud mouth? On her side, he supposed she might have been beguiled initially by Paolo's surface charm, but that must have been seriously eroded by the spoilt-child act of the past week.

And there was another factor that had been gnawing at him too. When he'd gone to post her cards that morning in Besavoro, he'd quickly noted down the names and addresses of the recipients, deciding they might prove useful for future reference. So who was the man Carl that she'd written to at Harman Grace, and what was their connection?

Could this whole trip with Paolo be simply a ploy to make her real lover jealous—provoke him into commitment, maybe? Was this what she was hiding behind that veil of cool containment?

No, he thought. I don't believe that—not in my heart. There's something else. And I have the whole night to find out what it is. To bring down the barrier and possess her utterly.

But first, he thought, he would have to get her to relax—to respond to him—to enjoy being teased a little. Perhaps tease him in return...

After all, he told himself with sudden cynicism, she would not be the first girl in the world to be coaxed into bed with laughter.

For one strange moment, he wished it were all over, and that she were joyously and passionately his, sitting beside him in the Jeep as they set off to some destination where his aunt's malice could not follow. Somewhere they could relax in the enjoyment of some mutual pleasure, he thought restlessly.

He longed, he realised, to fall asleep each night with her in his arms, and wake next to her each morning.

He wanted her as unequivocally and completely as he needed food and clothing. And he was going to wipe from his mind every vestige of the sordid bargain he'd been originally forced into by his aunt. From the moment he'd seen Laura, it had counted for nothing anyway.

But it could have been very different, he reminded himself grimly, so his amazing fortune was hardly deserved. And for a moment the thought made him disturbed and uneasy. And, he realised, almost fearful.

Pulling himself together, he picked up the nearest branch of candles and walked over to her, holding out his hand. 'Let us go into dinner,' he invited quietly.

Laura had made up her mind to plead a headache and go to her room directly after she'd eaten. But it was clearly ridiculous to express a wish for peace and quiet while the storm was still raging overhead, and might prompt Alessio to draw his own conclusions about her sudden need for seclusion. And that could be dangerous.

It was a strange meal. Conversation was necessarily sporadic. The flicker of the candles sent shadows dancing in the corners of the room, until they were eclipsed by the lightning flashes that illumined everything with a weird bluish glow. It seemed to Laura as if each crash of thunder was rolling without pause into the next, and it was difficult to concentrate on Emilia's delicious food when she was constantly jumping out of her skin. It was much easier, in fact, to drink the red wine that Alessio was pouring into her glass, and which made her feel marginally less nervous.

One particular thunderclap, however, seemed to go on for ever, with a long, rumbling roar that made the whole house shake.

Laura put down her spoon. 'Is—is that what an earthquake feels like?' she asked uneasily.

'Almost.' Alessio was frowning, but his gaze softened as he studied her small, pale face. 'My poor Laura,' he said. 'You came here expecting long, hot days and moonlit romantic nights, and instead—the storm of the century. But this house has withstood many storms, if that is any consolation. And it will survive this one too.'

'Yes,' she said. 'Yes, of course.' She bit her lip. 'But—I— I'm quite glad you decided not to stay in Perugia, *signore*.'

'Why, *mia bella*,' he said mockingly. 'What a confession. And I am also—pleased.'

She hesitated. 'Do you think it's this bad at Lake Trasimeno? They will be able to get back tomorrow? Paolo and I have all our travel arrangements to work out.'

He shrugged. 'As to that, I think we must—wait and see.'

'Maybe you could phone—and find out.' She tried not to sound as if she was pleading.

'Why, yes,' he said. 'If the telephone was still working. Guillermo tells me it went off not long after my aunt's call.'

'Oh, God.' She stared at him, unable to hide her shock and dismay. 'But you must have a cell phone, surely.'

'I have more than one, but there is no signal here. I regard that as one of the many pleasures of this house,' Alessio said, pouring more wine.

Lightning filled the room, and he smiled at her, his face a stranger's in the eerie light. 'So, for the time being, we are quite cut off, *mia cara*.' He paused. 'And there is nothing we can do about it,' he added softly.

CHAPTER NINE

THE fierce riot of the storm seemed suddenly to fade to some strange distance, leaving behind a silence that was almost tangible, and twice as scary.

Laura swallowed. 'Cut off?' she echoed. 'But we can't be.'

He shrugged again, almost laconically. 'It happens.'

'But how long are we going to be—stuck here like this?' she demanded defensively.

'Until the storm passes, and we can reassess the situation.'

She shook her head in disbelief. 'Don't you even care?'

'Why? There is nothing I can do, *mia cara*.' He smiled at her. 'So, I shall let you be agitated for both of us.'

Well, she could manage that—no problem, Laura thought grimly.

She picked up her glass, and drank again, aware that her hand was shaking, and hoping—praying—that he wouldn't notice in the uncertain light. She said huskily, 'There's the Jeep. We could—drive somewhere—some place with lights and a phone.'

'In this weather, on that road?' he queried softly. 'You are suddenly very brave, *mia bella*. Far braver than myself, I must tell you. So, do you wish me to give you the keys, because I am going nowhere.' He paused. 'You can drive?'

'I've passed my test,' she said guardedly.

His smile widened. 'Then the decision is yours. But you may feel it is safer to remain here.'

There was a silence, then Laura reluctantly nodded.

'*Bene*,' he approved lazily. 'And now I will make a deal with you, Laura *mia*. In the morning, when this weather has cleared, I will drive you anywhere you wish to go, but only if—tonight...' He paused again, deliberately allowing the silence to lengthen between them.

121

Laura's mouth felt suddenly dry. She said, 'What—what about tonight, *signore*? What are you asking?'

He said quietly, 'That you will again play the piano for me.'

'Play the piano?' Laura was genuinely taken aback. 'You're not serious.'

'I am most serious. You played the first night you were in my house. Why not the last? After all, you are going back to your own country. I may never have the opportunity to listen to you play again.'

Laura looked down at the table. 'I'd have thought that was a positive advantage.'

He clicked his tongue in reproof. 'And that is false modesty, *mia cara*. I have heard you practising each day. And once I found Emilia weeping in the hall, because your playing brought back memories of my mother for her also.'

'Oh, no.' Laura glanced up in dismay. 'Lord, I'm so sorry.'

'No need,' he said. 'They were happy tears. She loved my mother very much.' He rose. 'So, Laura *mia*, you will indulge me?'

Reluctantly, she followed him to the *salotto*, waiting while he carefully positioned more candelabra on top of the piano.

'There,' he said at last. 'Will that do?'

'Well, yes, I suppose...' She sat down at the keyboard, giving him a questioning look. 'What do you want me to play?'

'Something calming, I think.' Alessio sent a wry glance upwards as thunder rumbled ominously once more. 'That piece you have been practising, perhaps.'

'"Clair de Lune"?' She bit her lip. 'I'd almost forgotten it, and it's still not really up to performance standard.'

'But very beautiful,' he returned. He sat down in the corner of a sofa, stretching long legs in front of him. 'So—if you please?'

Swallowing nervously, she let her fingers touch the keys, searching out the first dreamy chords, only too conscious of the silent man, listening, and watching.

But, somehow, as she played her confidence grew with her concentration, and she found herself moving through the passionate middle section with barely a falter into the gentle, almost yearning clarity of the final passage. And silence.

Alessio rose and walked across to the piano, joining her on the long padded stool. He said softly, *'Grazie,'* and took her hand, raising it to his lips. He turned it gently, pressing his mouth to the leaping pulse in her wrist, then kissed the palm of her hand slowly and sensuously.

Her voice was suddenly a thread. 'Please—don't do that?'

He raised his head, the dark eyes smiling into hers. He said, 'I am not allowed to pay homage to your artistry—even when it has conquered the storm?'

The lightning was barely visible now, she realised, and the thunder only a distant growl.

'It—it does seem to have moved away.' She tried to retrieve her hand, and failed. 'Perhaps the electricity will come on again soon.'

'You don't like the candlelight?'

Laura hesitated. 'Oh, yes, but I wouldn't want to read by it, and I was really hoping to finish my book before tomorrow,' she added over-brightly, aware that his fingers were caressing hers, sending little tremors shivering down her spine. It seemed as if she could feel every thread in her dress touching her bare skin.

'Then we will have to think of some other form of entertainment that may be easier on the eyes.' Alessio paused. 'Do you play cards?'

She shrugged. 'The usual family games.'

'And poker?'

'I know the value of the various hands,' she said. 'But that's about all.'

'I could teach you.'

She stared at him. 'But don't you need more people?' she asked. 'Also it's a gambling game, and I—I haven't any money to lose.'

'It is possible to play for other things besides money, *carissima*. And one learns to make use of whatever is available. Sometimes that can be far more enjoyable than playing for mere cash.' He reached out, his fingers deftly detaching one of the small silver spheres on a chain that hung from her ear. He put it down on an ivory piano key, where it flashed in the candle flame. 'You see? Already you have something to stake.'

Strip poker, Laura thought numbly. Dear God, he's suggesting we should play strip poker...

She wrenched her hand away from his. 'Yes,' she said, her voice bitterly cold. 'And, no doubt, I'd have a great deal to lose, too. That's the problem with all your lessons, *signore*. They come at much too high a cost.'

He smiled at her, unruffled. 'How can you price the value of a new experience, *bella mia*?'

'Oh, you have an answer for everything—or you think you do.' She turned fiercely to face him. 'Why do you do this?' she demanded with sudden huskiness. 'Why do you—torment me like this?'

'Do I torment you, *mia cara*?' he countered harshly. One hand swept aside the silky fall of her hair to cup the nape of her neck, his thumb caressing the hollow beneath her ear, sending a sweet shiver along her nerve endings. 'Then why do you continue to deny what you know we both want?'

She could feel the heat rising in her body, the sudden, terrifying scald of yearning between her thighs, and was bitterly ashamed of her own weakness.

'I can't speak for you, *signore*,' she said, her voice shaking, 'but I just want to get out of here. Out of this house—this country—and back to where I belong. And nothing else.'

She paused, her chin lifting defiantly. 'And now that the storm's over, the telephone could be working again.'

He withdrew his hand with a faint sigh, letting one smooth russet strand of her hair slide lingeringly through his fingers. 'I think you are over-optimistic, Laura *mia*,' he told her drily.

'But could you find out for me—please? I really need to know the times of tomorrow's flights.'

He was her host, she thought with a kind of desperation. He couldn't—wouldn't—refuse her request, however stupid he might think it. She'd asked him to check something. Innate courtesy would take him from the room to do so.

And that would be her chance, she told herself feverishly. Because she needed to get away from him on a far more personal level—and tonight. The door to her room had a lock and key, she knew, and the window shutters had that bolt mechanism she'd used once before. She couldn't risk going through the house, of course, because he might intercept her, but she could cut across the gardens, and be safely locked in her room before he even realised she was missing.

Because she could not trust herself to be alone with him any longer. It was as simple and final as that. The necessity to go into his arms and feel his mouth on hers was an agony she had never experienced before. A consuming anguish she had not dreamed could exist.

And she dared not risk him touching her again. Not when the merest brush of his fingers could turn her to flame.

For a moment, she found herself thinking of Steve, and wondering if this was how he'd felt about her.

I hope not, she thought. I hope not with all my heart.

She watched Alessio walk to the door. Heard his footsteps receding, and his voice calling to Guillermo.

And then she ran across the room, tugging at the windows and their shutters to make a gap she could squeeze through.

She knew the route. She must have used it twenty times since her arrival. But always in the daytime. Never at night. And she had not bargained for the absolute darkness outside. The pretty ornamental lamps that dotted the grounds were out of commission, of course, but there wasn't a star showing, or even a faint glimmer of moonlight.

And, because the storm had passed over at last, she'd assumed the rain would have stopped too, but she was wrong. It was like walking into a wall of water, she thought, gasping.

Before she'd gone fifty yards she was completely drenched, her soaked dress clinging like a second skin, her feet slipping in her wet shoes, and her hair hanging in sodden rats' tails round her face.

She tried to peer through the darkness to get her bearings, but she could see nothing. She could only hope that she was going in the right direction—that somewhere ahead of her was the sanctuary she so desperately needed. She wanted to run, but her feet were sliding on the wet grass, and she was afraid of falling.

She was never sure of the precise moment when she realised that she was being followed. That Alessio was coming after her, running silently and surely in pursuit like a lone wolf from the hills.

She stumbled on, gasping, her heart pounding against her ribs, the words, 'No—please—no,' echoing their frantic rhythm in her brain.

But to no avail. He was suddenly beside her, taking her hand in an iron grasp and pulling her along with him as he ran, head bent.

She tried to drag herself free. 'Leave me alone...'

'*Idiota,*' he snarled breathlessly. 'Do you want me to carry you? *Avanti!*'

At last the sodden grass gave way to paving stones, and she saw a dim glow ahead of her and realised they must have reached her courtyard. Alessio dragged back the heavy glass doors, and pushed her inside ahead of him.

There were candles burning here too on the chest of drawers and the night table, and Emilia had also turned down the bed.

Laura stood, head bent, water running down her face and neck, and dripping off the hem of her skirt to form a forlorn puddle on the floor.

Alessio went past her into the bathroom, his sodden shirt adhering to his body like a second skin. He emerged, barefoot, carrying two towels, one of which he threw to her, using the other to rub his face and hair.

Laura stood motionless, the breath still raw in her lungs from that headlong dash. She held the towel against her in numb fingers, watching as he stripped off his shirt and began to dry his chest and arms. Her heart was beating wildly again, but for a very different reason.

He glanced up, and their eyes met. He said harshly, 'Don't just stand there, little fool. You are soaked to the skin, as I am. Take off your dress before you catch pneumonia.'

Her lips moved. 'I—can't...'

Alessio said something impatient and probably obscene under his breath, and walked over to her, his long fingers going swiftly and ruthlessly to work on the sash, which had tightened into a soggy and almost impenetrable knot. When it came free at last, he peeled the silver dress away from her body, and tossed it to the floor.

Laura made a small sound that might have been protest, but he ignored it anyway. He took the towel from her unresisting grasp and began to blot the chill dampness from her skin. Not gently. She gave an involuntary wince, and felt his touch soften a little. His expression, however, did not, even though the scraps of lace she was wearing were hardly a barrier to his dark gaze.

There was no sound in the room except their own ragged breathing. The shadows dancing on the walls seemed to reduce the room to half its size, closing them into the small area of light provided by the candles.

At last, Alessio threw the towel behind him, and stood looking down at her.

'So,' he said quietly. 'What in the name of God, Laura, did you think you were doing?'

'Running away.' Her voice was barely audible.

'Well, that is plain,' he said with sudden harshness. 'So eager to escape me, it seems, that you could not wait until tomorrow. That you were even prepared to risk damaging your health by this folly tonight. But why, Laura? Why did you do this?'

'You—know.'

'If I did,' he said, 'I would not ask. So, tell me.'

If there were words, she could not think of them. If there were arguments, she could not marshal them. There was her body's need roused to the brink of anguish by the rough movement of his hands on her skin as he'd dried her.

And there was candlelight and the waiting bed...

Oh, God, she thought with desperation. I want him so much. I never knew before—never realised that this could ever happen to me. And I—cannot turn back. Not now. I must have—this night.

Her throat was tight as she swallowed. As she lifted her hands and placed them on his shoulders, reaching up on tiptoe to kiss him shyly and rather clumsily on the mouth.

For a heartbeat, he was still, then his arms went round her, pinning her against him with a fierce hunger he made no attempt to disguise. He said her name quietly and huskily, then his lips took hers, exploring the soft, trembling contours with heated, passionate urgency, his heart lifting in exultation.

She was his, he thought, and she had offered herself as he'd once promised she would. Not that it mattered. The only essential was Laura herself—here at last, in his arms, her lips parting for him eagerly as their kisses deepened into sweet, feverish intimacy, allowing him to taste all the inner honey of her mouth.

He began to caress her, his fingers lightly stroking her throat and neck, then sliding the straps of her bra from her slender shoulders, so that when he found and unclipped its tiny hook the little garment simply fell away from her body. He caught his breath as he looked at her, his eyes heavy with desire, then pulled her closer, so that the tips of her small, perfect breasts grazed his bare chest with delicate eroticism.

He recaptured her mouth, burying his soft groan of pleasure in its moist fragrance, teasing her tongue with his as his hands continued their slow quest down her slim body.

When he reached the barrier of her briefs, he eased his fingers inside their lacy band, gently pushing them down from her hips to the floor.

He'd expected to feel her hands on him, discarding what remained of his clothing, wanting to uncover him in her turn, but, to his faint surprise, she made no such attempt. So he allowed himself a hurried moment to strip naked, before lifting her and putting her on the bed.

He followed her down, taking her in his arms, murmuring husky endearments, glorying in the cool enchantment of her quivering body against his.

He kissed her again, his hands cupping her breasts, stroking the nipples gently until they stood erect to his touch, his inward smile tender as he heard her small, startled sigh of pleasure. He bent his head and caressed the hard, rosy peaks with his mouth, the tip of his tongue drawing circles of sweet torment round the puckered flesh.

He was hotly, achingly aroused, but even in the extremity of his desire for her some remaining glimmer of sanity in his reeling mind warned him that, apart from her kisses, her response was more muted. That she still maintained some element of that reserve that had always intrigued him. Was it possible that, even now, when she was naked in his arms, she could be shy of him?

He wanted her to match him in passion—to be equally enraptured. He longed for the incitement of her hands and mouth on his body, which, so far, to his faint bewilderment, she'd withheld.

Was she scared, perhaps, of the moment when all thinking ceased and the last vestiges of control slipped away?

If so, he would have to be careful, because he could not lose her now.

Very gently, he began to kiss her body, caressing every shadowed curve, each smooth plane as the sweet woman-scent of her filled his nose and mouth.

He rested his cheek against her belly as his hand parted her thighs, finding the scalding moisture of her need.

He heard her gasp, her breathing suddenly frantic as her body arched involuntarily towards him in surrender to the sensuous pressure of his fingers. But he would offer her another kind of delight, he thought, smiling, as he bent to pleasure her with his mouth.

Yet suddenly she was no longer yielding. She was tense—even struggling a little, her hands tangling in his hair, trying to push him away.

'No—no—please.' Her voice was small, stifled. 'You mustn't—I can't...'

'Don't be afraid, *carissima*,' he whispered as he acceded reluctantly to this unexpected resistance. 'I will do nothing you don't like.' Or that I cannot persuade you to like, in time, *mi amore*.

Instead, his fingers sought her tiny hidden bud, stroking it rhythmically—delicately—while his mouth returned to her breast, suckling the engorged peak until she moaned in her throat.

'Touch me,' he breathed, starving for her. He took her hand and carried it to his body, clasping her fingers round his hardness while he moved over her, positioning himself between her thighs, waiting for her to guide him into her, to surrender to the first deep thrust that would make her his at last.

She was trembling violently, her movements almost awkward as she obeyed his silent demand, taking him to the heated threshold of her womanhood.

But as he began to enter her slowly, gently, prolonging the exquisite moment quite deliberately, he felt the sudden tension in her once again. Realised that the cry of pleasure he'd expected was one of pain instead, and that this time the resistance seemed to be physical.

'*Mi amore*—my sweet one,' he whispered urgently. 'Relax for me.'

And then he looked down into the wide frightened eyes, and he knew.

The hurting—the shock of that tearing pain—stopped almost as soon as it had begun. Laura, her fist pressed to her mouth, was aware of Alessio pulling back. Lifting himself away from her altogether.

She turned away too, curling into the foetal position, her startled body shaking uncontrollably.

She closed her eyes, but she couldn't shut out the sound of his harsh breathing as he fought for control. For an approximation of calm. The passing minutes seemed to stretch into eternity as she lay, waiting.

But for what?

Eventually, he said, 'Laura, look at me. Look at me, now.'

He was sitting up in the bed, the edge of the sheet pulled across his loins. His dark face was a stranger's as he looked at her.

He said, his voice flat, 'This was your first time with a man.' It was a statement, not a question, but he added sharply, 'Do not attempt to lie. I want the truth.'

'Yes.' The single word was a sob.

'You did not think to tell me?'

'I didn't know I needed to.' She bent her head wretchedly. 'It never occurred to me that it might—hurt...' She swallowed convulsively. 'I thought I could pretend—so that you wouldn't know that I hadn't—that I'd never...'

He said very wearily, *'Dio mio.'* There was a long silence, then she felt him stir, and braced herself for the inevitable question.

'Paolo,' he said quietly. 'You—and Paolo—you let me—you let everyone think that you were lovers. Why?'

'Paolo and I decided—to travel together. To see how it worked out.' Even now she had to try and keep the secret. 'Oh, God, I'm so sorry.'

'You have nothing to regret.' His voice was expressionless. 'The blame is mine entirely.'

She felt the mattress shift as he moved, looked up quickly to see him standing beside the bed, pulling on his clothes.

'Alessio.' She lifted herself onto her knees, reaching out a hand to him. 'Where are you going?'

'To my own room,' he said. 'Where else?'

'Please don't go,' she whispered. 'Don't leave me.'

'What you ask is impossible.' The back he kept turned to her was rigid, as if it had been forged out of steel.

She touched her tongue to her dry lips. Her voice was ragged. 'Alessio—please. What happened just now doesn't matter. I—I want you.'

'No,' he said. 'It ends here. And it should never have started. I had no right to—touch you.'

'But I gave you that right.'

'Then be glad I have the strength to leave you,' he said.

'Glad?' Laura echoed. 'How can I be—glad?'

'Because one day you will come to be married,' he said, the words torn harshly from his throat. 'And your innocence is a gift you should keep for your husband. He should have the joy of knowing he will be your first and only lover.'

He took a deep raw breath. 'It is far too—precious an offering to be wasted on someone like me.'

'Not just—someone,' she said in anguish. 'You, Alessio. You, and no one else.'

His need for her was a raw, aching wound, but he could not allow himself to weaken now. Because, one day, he needed to be able to forgive himself.

He bent and picked up his damp shirt from the floor, schooling his expression into cynicism.

'Your persistence forces me to be candid,' he drawled as he faced her. 'Forget the high-flown sentiments, *signorina*. The truth is that I was in the mood for a woman tonight, not an inexperienced girl.' He added coolly, 'Please believe that I have neither the time or the patience to teach you what you need to know in order to please me.'

He saw the stricken look in the grey eyes, and knew it was an image that would haunt him for the rest of his days.

He added, 'In the morning, we will deal with your departure. I am sure you have no wish to linger. Goodnight, *signorina*.' He inclined his head with cruel politeness, and left.

She watched the door close behind him, then looked down at herself with a kind of numb horror. It was the worst humiliation of her life—kneeling here naked—offering herself—pleading with a man who'd just made it brutally clear that he no longer desired her.

It had never occurred to her, she thought blankly, that losing her virginity would be anything but simple. She was a twenty-first-century girl, for God's sake, not some Victorian miss. And it seemed to her bewildered mind as if Alessio, in spite of what he'd just said, had been gentle. Yet, it had still hurt her in a way that she'd found it impossible to disguise.

But that, she thought wretchedly, was nothing compared with the aching agony of his subsequent rejection of her, both physically and emotionally. Her body still burned from its unfulfilled arousal.

Worst of all, she had almost, but thankfully not quite, told him, 'I love you.'

And in the morning she was going to have to face him somehow—with this nightmare between them. And she couldn't bear it—she couldn't...

With a little inarticulate cry, she dived under the covers, dragging them up to her throat, her whole body shaking uncontrollably as the first white-hot tears began to spill down her ashen face.

Alessio stood, shoulders slumped, one hand braced against the tiled wall of the shower, and his head bent against the remorseless cascade of cold water.

If he could manage somehow to numb his body, he thought starkly, then maybe he could also subdue his mind. But he knew already that would not be easy.

How many cold showers would it take to erase the memory of her eager mouth, her warm, slim body stretched beneath him in a surrender that should never have been required of her?

How could you not see? he accused himself savagely. You blind, criminal fool. How could you not realise that she was not merely shy, but totally inexperienced, when everything you did— everything she would not allow you to do—told you that more plainly than any words?

But that first sweet, awkward kiss offered of her own volition had wiped everything from his mind but the assuagement of his own need.

He paused and swore at himself. Was he actually daring to blame her, even marginally, when he had manoeuvred and manipulated her to a point when she had been no longer prepared to resist him?

The fact that his sense of honour had forced him to abandon the seduction in no way diminished his feelings of guilt.

He found himself remembering something his father had once said to him just as he'd been emerging from adolescence. 'Like most young men, you will find enough unscrupulous women in the world, Alessio, to cater for your pleasures. So, treat innocent girls with nothing but respect.' He'd added drily, 'Or until your intentions are entirely honourable.'

It had seemed wise advice, and until now he had followed it.

He had simply not dreamed that Laura could be still a virgin. At the same time, he was shamingly aware of a fierce, almost primitive joy to know that she had never given herself to Paolo.

But she did not belong to him either, he reminded himself with a kind of sick desolation. And, after that last act of necessary cruelty, she never would...

With a groan, he slid down the wall to the tiled floor of the shower, resting his forehead on his drawn-up knees, letting the water beat at him. He had done the right thing, he told himself. He had to believe that.

Yet, he had ignored his father's other piece of worldly wisdom, he realised with a flash of weary cynicism—that a gentleman should never leave the lady in his bed unsatisfied.

Well, his punishment and his penance would be to drive her to Rome tomorrow, and watch her walk away from him at the airport, through the baggage check and passport control, and out of his life.

'Laura,' he whispered. 'My Laura.' He had not cried since his father's funeral, but suddenly, at the sound of her name, he could taste tears, hot and acrid in his throat, and it took every scrap of control he possessed to stop him weeping like a child for his loss.

Swallowing, he lifted himself to his feet and turned off the shower. It was time to pull his life together, he commanded himself grimly, deciding, among other things, how he should deal with his aunt on her return. And, if she made good her threats, how he should handle the aftermath of her revelations.

I should have stood up to her at the start, he thought, his mouth tightening in cold anger as he reached for a towel. Told her to do her worst, then dismissed her from my life, together with Paolo.

But that I can still do, and I will.

It is the wrong that I have done Laura that can never be put right. And somehow I have to live with that for the rest of my days.

CHAPTER TEN

SHE'D cried herself to sleep, but Laura still found no rest. She spent the remainder of a troubled night, tossing and turning in the wide bed, looking for some sort of peace, but finding only wretchedness.

Alessio's hand on her shoulder, shaking her, and his voice telling her curtly to wake up just seemed part of another bad dream, until she opened unwilling eyes and saw him there, standing over her in the pallid daylight.

She snatched at the disarranged covers, dragging them almost frantically to the base of her throat, and saw a dark flush tinge his cheekbones and his mouth tighten to hardness as he registered what she was doing.

He was fully dressed, wearing jeans and a black polo shirt, but, as one swift glance under her lashes revealed, he was also unshaven and heavy-eyed, as if he too had found sleep elusive.

'What—what do you want?' She kept her voice as brusque as his own.

'There has been a serious problem,' he said. 'That noise we heard last night was, in fact, a landslip. Guillermo tried to get down to Besavoro earlier, and found the road to the valley completely blocked with rocks, trees and mud.'

'Blocked?' Laura repeated, her heart missing a beat. 'You mean—we can't get out?'

'Unfortunately, no.' He shrugged. 'But the emergency generator is now working, so you will have hot water, and electric light, which should make your stay more comfortable.'

'But how long am I to be kept here? I—I must get to the airport...'

'Heavy lifting equipment has been requested from Perugia,'

he told her expressionlessly, 'but it may not arrive until tomorrow at the earliest.'

'Not until then?' She digested the news with dismay. 'And how long will it take to clear the road after that?'

Alessio shrugged again. 'Who knows?'

'You don't seem very concerned that we're practically imprisoned here,' she accused, her voice unsteady.

'I regret the inconvenience,' he said icily, 'but at the moment I find Fredo a much greater worry. He is missing, and it is thought that his hut was in the path of the landslide.' He paused. 'I am going down to give what help I can.'

She bit her lip. 'I see—of course.' And as he turned away: 'Alessio, I—I'm really sorry.'

'Why?' At the door, he halted. The backward glance he sent her was unreadable. 'You do not know him.'

'No, but he's your friend, and he obviously means a great deal to you.' She added swiftly, 'I'd be sorry for anyone under the circumstances.' She hesitated. 'Is there anything I can do?'

His smile was faint and brief. 'Perhaps—if you know how to pray.' And was gone.

She lay, staring across the room at the closed door, her instinctive, 'Please take care,' still trembling, unspoken, on her lips. And quite rightly so, she told herself. To have indicated in any way that his well-being mattered to her would be dangerous madness.

So—it had happened, she thought. She had seen him, spoken to him, and somehow survived. She supposed the fact that he'd come to tell her there was an emergency had eased their meeting to a certain extent. It had had a purpose and an urgency that an embarrassed encounter across the breakfast table would have lacked.

But it also meant that she'd been deprived of her only shred of comfort in the entire situation—the knowledge that she was leaving. That she would not have to spend time alone with him, or pass another night in the vain pursuit of sleep under his roof.

All she wanted, quite simply, was to go far away, and try to forget the appalling humiliation of the past twelve hours. If that was, indeed, possible.

Yet now the trap had closed on her again, and she was caught. And there was literally nothing she could do about it except— endure.

It was a very small consolation to know that he would be equally reluctant to have her around after last night's wretched debacle.

Somehow, she reflected painfully, she must have given the impression that she possessed a level of sophistication that was beyond her. A willing female body ready to provide Alessio with the level of entertainment he expected from his sexual partners. Discarded when he realised the truth.

She would carry the stark cruelty of that for the rest of her life, like a scar, she thought.

She turned onto her stomach, burying her face in the pillow. So, when she'd opened her eyes just now and seen him there beside the bed, how was it possible that her body had stirred for one infinitesimal moment in hope and desire?

Because it had done so, she admitted painfully. It might be pathetic and shameful, but it was also quite undeniable.

Which meant that, even now, and in spite of everything, she— wanted him.

Dear God, she thought in angry self-derision, had the totality of his rejection taught her nothing?

Yet it might have been even worse if he'd persuaded her to go away with him. Made what amounted to a public statement of his desire for her, and then, almost in the next breath, dismissed her. At least, hidden away here at the Villa Diana, no one else would know of her humiliation.

She sat up, with sudden determination, pushing her hair back from her face. If she continued thinking along those lines, she could end up feeling grateful to him. And she wasn't.

But lying here, brooding, was no answer either. She had to get up and prepare for the rest of her life. Something that never had included Alessio Ramontella, and never would.

Somehow, she had to put this brief madness behind her, and become sane again.

And I can, she promised herself, lifting her chin with renewed pride. I can, and I will.

It was a strange day. The sky was still heavy with cloud, revealing the sun only in fitful bursts, yet at the same time it was stiflingly hot. The heavy air was filled with the almost jungle smell of wet earth and vegetation, and, although Guillermo had gone down and patiently cleaned out the pool, Laura was not tempted to spend much time out of doors.

In spite of her brave resolution, she found herself prowling round the house, restless and ill-at-ease, as if she were a caged animal.

Alessio did not return, and when Guillermo came back from taking midday food and wine down to those trying to clear some part of the landslide he could only say that Fredo had not yet been found, and the search was continuing.

She wanted to ask, 'Is the Count all right?' but bit back the words. This was not a question she had any reason or any right to ask.

She read the rest of her book and returned it, but did not allow herself to choose another, although *Emma* tempted her. On the one hand, she didn't want to think she might be around long enough to finish it. On the other, she hated the idea of leaving it half unread.

She spent some of her time exploring the house in greater detail, especially the older parts, examining the restoration work that had taken place on frescoed walls and painted ceilings. With a building of this age, careful renovation would always be needed, she thought. A labour of love that would last a lifetime.

And she could understand its attraction. The remoteness that aggravated Paolo had an appeal all its own. She could see how Alessio would regard it as a sanctuary—a much-needed retreat. What she couldn't figure so well was why someone, so very much of the world, should require such a place. Why he should ever want to escape.

But then the entire way the Count conducted his life was an enigma, she thought, or as far as she was concerned anyway. A mystery that had already caused her too much unhappiness, and which she could not afford to probe.

I have to begin to forget, she told herself. However hard that is. However long it takes.

As always, music was her solace. She had no idea when, if ever, she would have access to such a wonderful piano, but she was determined to make the most of it.

She found the book of Beethoven sonatas again, and glanced through them looking for those she'd learned to play in her younger days. She realised for the first time that there was an inscription inside the collection's embossed cover, and that even she could translate this brief message—'To my dearest Valentina from the husband who adores her. My love now and for ever.'

She turned the page swiftly, feeling with embarrassment that she should not have read the message—that she had somehow intruded on something private and precious.

She chose a page number totally at random, and, after loosening up with a few preliminary scales, began to practise.

It was only Emilia's quiet entry with another batch of candles that alerted her to the passage of time since she'd first sat down to play.

'Heavens.' Laura looked almost guiltily at her watch. 'It's nearly time to change for dinner. I didn't realise.' She paused. 'Has—has His Excellency come back yet?'

Emilia pursed her lips. 'No, *signorina*. But do not concern yourself,' she added encouragingly. 'He will return to you very soon.'

Laura was infuriated to find she was blushing again, and hotly, too. 'I just meant that we should maybe—hold dinner until he arrives.'

'But of course, *signorina*.' Emilia's smile was serene but also openly sceptical. Pull the other one, it seemed to advise drily. We are not blind, or deaf, Guillermo and I, and we have known Count Alessio all his life. So you cannot fool us—either of you.

But this time you're wrong, Laura wanted passionately to tell her. And I'm the one who was fooled.

Instead, she bent her head and concentrated on the passage she'd just stumbled over.

Alessio came home half an hour later, walking straight into the *salotto*. Laura glanced up, her hands stilling on the keys as she looked at him. His face was grey with weariness, and his clothes were heavily stained with mud and damp.

She swallowed. 'Did—did you find Fredo?'

'*Sì, alla fine.*' He walked to the drinks table and poured himself a whisky. 'We traced him because his dog was beside him barking.'

She gasped. 'Keeping the wolves away?' she asked huskily.

'Perhaps. It is all too possible.' He drank deeply, then brushed his knuckles across his mouth. 'Fredo is now in hospital, with a badly broken leg.' The words were hoarse and staccato. 'But he was also out all night, lying in that storm, and that is regarded as far more serious. Luca is with him, but his father has not yet regained consciousness.'

He did not tell her of the nightmare journey made by the search party, carrying the badly injured old man on an improvised stretcher across the side of the mountain unaffected by the landslide to the place on the road where the ambulance was waiting.

Nor did he say that the mental image of her face had gone with him every step of the way. That the sight of her now filled him with an illicit joy he could neither excuse nor condone.

Her voice was quiet. 'You said—we could try prayer.'

He walked slowly back and stood by the empty hearth, staring ahead of him. 'I have,' he said. 'I went to the church in Besavoro, and lit a candle.' His smile was twisted. 'I have not done that for a long time.'

As she looked at him Laura caught her breath. 'Your hands—they're bleeding.'

His own downward glance was indifferent. 'It is not important.'

'But you need to take care of them,' Laura insisted. 'Those cuts could easily become infected...'

Her voice tailed away as his brows lifted coldly.

'Your concern is touching, but unnecessary,' he said. 'I can look after myself.'

He spoke more brusquely than he'd intended, because he was fighting an impulse to go and kneel beside her, burying his face in her lap. He saw her flinch at his tone, and cursed himself savagely under his breath.

Yet it was for her own protection, he thought grimly. He dared not soften. He could not take the risk of going near her, or allow himself even the fleeting luxury of touch.

He finished the whisky and set down the glass. 'I had better bathe and change quickly,' he said, striving for a lighter tone. 'No storm will be as bad as Emilia's mood if her dinner is spoiled.'

Laura watched him go, then made her way slowly to her own room. She showered quickly, but made no attempt to dress afterwards. Instead, she sat on the edge of the bed in her cotton robe, staring into space, a prey to her own unhappy thoughts.

She was aroused from her reverie by a tap on the door, and Guillermo's voice telling her that dinner was served.

She got up quickly, and opened the door a fraction. 'I'm not very hungry tonight, Guillermo,' she said. 'I—I think it's the weather. It's so sultry. Will you—explain to His Excellency, please?'

Guillermo's face said plainly that he would prefer not to, and that his wife might also wish to know the reason for the *signorina* being absent, but he gave a small bow of reluctant acquiescence and departed.

But a few minutes later he was knocking again, and this time he presented her with a folded sheet of paper.

The words it contained were terse. 'Laura—do not force me to fetch you.' And it was signed 'Ramontella'.

'*Scusi, signorina.*' Guillermo spread his hands apologetically. 'I tried.'

'Yes,' she said. 'I'm sure you did. Tell the *signore* that I'll be there presently.'

The silver dress was out of bounds, and probably ruined anyway. She was sick of the sight of the blue shift, so she dressed almost defiantly in one of the few outfits she hadn't worn before—a pair of sage-green linen trousers, and a sage and white striped blouse, which buttoned severely to the throat.

Last night's rain hadn't done the pewter sandals any favours either, but they were all she had, so she slipped her feet into them and set off mutinously for the dining room.

Alessio was leaning on the back of his chair, waiting for her.

She lifted her chin, and met his gaze without flinching. She was trying to play it cool, but inside she was melting—dying. The day's wear and tear had been showered away, and, apart from a dressing on one hand, he looked his lean, dangerous self again.

He was wearing the usual black trousers and snowy shirt, and another of those amazing waistcoats—this time in black and gold.

Alessio's own first thought was that if she'd dressed deliberately to disguise her femininity, she had seriously miscalculated. The cut of the linen trousers only accentuated the slight curve of her hips and the length of her slim legs, while the wide waistband reduced her midriff to a hand's span. As he would have had pleasure in proving under different circumstances, he thought with a pang of longing.

And now that he had seen her naked, the prim lines of that blouse were nothing more than a tease. An incitement to remember the delicate beauty beneath.

He felt his heart thud suddenly and unevenly, and snatched at his control, straightening unsmilingly as she walked to the table and sat down.

'Prayer is one thing,' he said softly as she unfolded her napkin. 'Fasting, however, is quite unnecessary.'

She gave him a defiant look. 'I'm just not hungry.'

He shrugged as he took his own seat. 'And I do not care to eat alone,' he retorted. 'Besides, when the food arrives, your appetite will soon return.'

'Is that an order?' she inquired in a dulcet tone.

'No,' he said. 'Merely a prediction.'

She bit her lip, knowing that an icicle had more chance in hell than she had of turning up her nose at Emilia's cooking. 'I notice we're dining by candlelight again.'

'There is not much fuel for the generator,' Alessio returned casually. 'Guillermo wishes to conserve what is left.' His smile was swift and hard. 'Be assured it is not a prelude to romance, *signorina*.'

She met his gaze squarely. 'I never imagined it would be, *signore*.'

'But I understand that work to restore the electricity supply has already begun,' he went on. 'Also the telephones.'

'And the road?'

'I am promised that digging will commence at first light. As soon as there is a way through, you will be on your way to Rome. Does that content you?'

'Yes,' she said quietly. 'Of course.'

'*Bene,*' he commented sardonically. There was a silence, while his dark eyes dwelled on her thoughtfully, before he added, 'Believe me, *signorina*, I am doing all I can to hasten your departure.'

Laura stared down at the polished table. 'Yes,' she said, 'I do—believe it.' She swallowed past the sudden constriction in her throat. 'And I'm—sorry that you're being put to all this trouble, *signore*. I realise, of course, that I—I should never have come here.'

'Well, we can agree on that at least,' Alessio said with a touch of grimness. She thought she was being sent away for all the wrong reasons, he told himself painfully. But how could he possibly explain that he was, for once in his life, trying to do the right thing?

He could not, so maybe it was better to let matters rest as they were. To allow her to go away hurt and hating him—just as long as she did not turn to Paolo instead. The very idea sent a knife twisting inside him.

He found himself trying to hope that she would wait instead for someone decent and honourable who would treat her gently, and with tenderness, when the time came. But he knew that was sheer hypocrisy. That the thought of his Laura in any other man's arms was intolerable anguish, and would always be so.

It was a largely silent meal. Both of them, locked into their own unhappiness, ate just enough of her delicious food to appease Emilia, but without any real relish.

Afterwards, they went to the *salotto* for coffee, but more for convention's sake than a desire to endure more awkward time in each other's company. There were altogether too many no-go areas to avoid, and they both knew it.

Alessio, physically and mentally exhausted by the events of the past twelve hours, was tortured by his longing to have the right to go with Laura to her room, crawl into bed beside her and sleep the clock round in the comfort of her arms.

For her part, Laura felt as if she were suspended in some wretched limbo, waiting for a death sentence to be carried out, but not knowing when the blow might fall.

Everything that occurred tonight—each word, each action— might well be for the last time, she thought, and the knowledge that she would soon go from here and never see him again was almost destroying her.

I can't leave like this, she thought suddenly. Not when, even now, I want him so terribly. I know I don't have the experience he wants, but surely there must be something—*something*—I can do to capture his interest...

'May I offer you something with your coffee?' His tone was coolly formal, and Laura looked up with a start.

'Thank you,' she said. 'May I have *grappa*?'

His brows lifted. 'If that is what you wish.' He paused. 'I did not think you cared for it.'

Dutch courage, Laura thought, but did not say so.

'I certainly found it a shock the first time,' she said with assumed calm. 'But I'd like to—try again. If I may.'

Their eyes met in an odd tingling silence, then Alessio turned away abruptly, and went to the drinks table, returning with two glasses of the colourless spirit.

He handed her one and raised the other, his mouth twisting slightly. *'Salute.'*

She repeated the toast, and drank, hoping that her eyes wouldn't water or her nose bleed. That was hardly the impression she wanted to make.

She was sitting on one of the sofas, but Alessio had gone back to stand by the fireplace, she noticed—which was about as far away as it was possible to get without leaving the room. It was not a promising beginning.

Taking a deep breath, she swallowed the remainder of the *grappa* and held out her empty glass, trying for nonchalance. 'I think I'm developing a taste for this.'

'I do not advise it.' His tone was dry.

'It's my last night in Italy.' Her glance held a faint challenge. 'Maybe I should take a risk or two.'

His mouth tightened, but he refilled her glass without comment and brought it back to her.

As he turned away she said, 'Alessio...'

He looked down at her, frowning slightly. '*Cosa c'e?* What's the matter?'

'Last night, you asked me for a favour,' she said. 'You wanted me to play the piano for you.'

'I have not forgotten.'

'I was thinking that tonight it's my turn—to ask you for something.'

His sudden wariness was almost tangible.

'I am sorry to disappoint you,' he said with cool courtesy. 'But I do not, alas, play the piano.'

'No,' she said, feeling the swift thud of her heart against her ribcage. 'But you do play poker—and you offered to teach me—if you remember.' She took a breath. 'I would like to—take you up on that offer—please.'

He was very still. 'Yet, as you yourself pointed out, *signorina*, a poker school requires more people, and you have no money to lose. Nothing has changed.'

She said softly, 'Except I think you had a very different version in mind.' She detached one of her earrings and held it out to him on the palm of her hand. 'Isn't that so?'

'Perhaps.' The dark face looked as if it had been carved from stone, and his voice was as austere as an arctic wasteland. 'But it was a disgraceful—an unforgivable suggestion, which it shames me to think of, and I must ask you to forget that it was ever made. Also to excuse me. I wish you goodnight, *signorina.*'

He made her a slight, curt bow, and made to move away. She caught at the crisp sleeve of his shirt, detaining him, all pride gone, swept away by the starkness of her need.

Her voice was low, and shook a little. 'Alessio—please. Don't leave me. You—you made me think you wanted me. Wasn't it true?'

'Yes,' he said harshly. 'Or, true then, certainly. But—situations change, and now I wish you to go back to your own country, and get on with your life, as I must continue with mine. Tell yourself that you were never here—that this never happened. Forget me, as I shall forget you.' He released himself implacably from the clasp of her fingers.

'I recommend that you get some sleep,' he added, with chilling politeness. 'You have a long journey ahead of you when tomorrow comes.'

'Yes,' she said. 'And I'll make it without fuss—tomorrow. I swear it. I—I'll never even ask to see you again. But—oh, Alessio, won't you please give me—tonight?'

'I cannot do that.' His throat felt raw, and a heavy stone had lodged itself in his chest. 'And one day, Laura *mia*, you will be grateful to me. When you can look into the eyes of the man you love without shame.'

She watched him go, mind and body equally numb.

'The man you love,' she whispered, brokenly. 'The man you love. Is that really what you said to me? Oh, God, Alessio, if you only knew the terrible irony of that.'

And she buried her face in her hands, sitting motionless in the corner of the sofa, unconscious of the passage of time, until, one by one, the candles guttered and burned out.

Somehow, in the small hours, she got herself back to her own room, undressed and crept into bed, pulling the covers over the top of her head as if she wanted to hide from the coming day.

Or at least from the man she'd be forced to share it with. The man to whom she'd humbled herself for nothing.

No, she thought wretchedly. Not for nothing. For love.

Had he guessed? she wondered yet again. Had he realised that even this brief time in his company had been long enough for her to fall hopelessly, desperately in love with him? To build a pathetic fantasy where some kind of happy ending might be possible?

And was it the knowledge that he could break her heart, rather than his discovery of her inexperience, that had made him turn away from her?

He could hardly have expected such an outcome, after all. And it had clearly turned her from an amusing diversion into a potential nuisance.

And no amount of assurances on her part, or pleading, would convince him otherwise. She was now a serious embarrassment and he wanted her gone. That was totally clear.

I must have been mad, she thought, fighting back a dry sob. What part of 'no' did I not understand?

But that was history now. It had to be, whatever inner pain she was suffering. She would deal with that—somehow—when she was safely back in England.

There could not be long to wait. She would be on her way just as soon as a path to accommodate the Jeep was cleared through the debris. He'd told her that.

Now all that remained to her was to behave with as much dignity as she could still muster for the final hours of her stay at the villa.

And maybe Alessio would be merciful too, she thought unhappily, and leave her to her own devices.

Her packing was almost completed by first light. All that remained to go in the case were the robe she was still wearing and her toiletries.

It was going to be another very hot day, so she decided again to travel in the cream cotton dress, once more immaculately laundered by Emilia.

It's as well I'm leaving, she told herself, trying to wring some humour out of the situation. I could get thoroughly spoiled.

She opened the shutters and stepped out into the courtyard. The storm might never have happened, she thought, viewing the unclouded sky. Yet its aftermath still lingered in all kinds of ways.

It was still very early, and she doubted whether anyone else in the house was even stirring.

In the distance, coming to her through the clear air, she thought she could hear the sound of heavy machinery, but perhaps that was just wishful thinking. A longing to be able to leave the past behind and escape.

Except it might already be too late for that.

She felt suddenly very tired—and strangely defeated. She went slowly back into her room and lay down on top of the bed, stretching with a sigh.

After all, she told herself, she needed a sanctuary, and this was as good as any other. Alessio had no reason to come to this part of the house, and would certainly not be seeking her out deliberately, so she could feel relatively safe.

Presently, she would get showered and dressed, she thought, but not yet. Already the warmth of the sun spilling into the room was making her feel drowsy, and perhaps in sleep she might even find the peace that would be denied her in her waking hours.

So, almost gratefully, Laura closed her eyes, and allowed herself to drift away. But before she had taken more than three steps into the golden landscape before her, she became aware of a voice saying, *'Signorina!'*

She opened reluctant eyes to find Emilia bending over her. She sat up slowly. 'Is something wrong?'

'No—no,' Emilia assured her. 'But it is time to eat, *signorina*. Come.'

'I'm fine—really. I—I don't want any breakfast.'

'Breakfast?' The other woman's brows rose almost comically. 'But it is the *seconda colazione* that awaits you, *signorina*.'

'Lunch?' Laura queried in disbelief. This implied she'd been asleep for hours, when she knew she'd only just closed her eyes.

She peered at her watch, and gulped. 'My God, is it really that time already?'

'Sì—sì.' Emilia nodded vigorously, her face firm. 'The *signore* ordered that we should not disturb you from your rest, but you cannot sleep all day. You also need food.'

Laura hesitated. 'I—I have to get dressed first.'

'No need, *signorina*.' Emilia allowed herself a conspiratorial twinkle. 'No one here but you,' she added. 'The *signore* is at the *frana* speaking to engineers about how to make the road safe. He told me he will not come back until late, so you may eat in your *vestaglia*.'

'I see.' Laura got up from the bed, shaking out the crumpled skirts of her robe. He was doing her a kindness, she thought, and she should feel thankful, not sick and empty. Or so lonely that she wanted to weep.

If she'd expected some kind of scratch meal because the master of the house was absent, she was soon proved wrong.

A rich chicken broth was followed by pasta, grilled fish, and a thick meaty stew with herbs and beans, and, after the cheese, there was a creamy pudding tasting of blackcurrant.

I won't want another meal for a week, thought Laura, reflecting wryly that Emilia must have heard about airline food.

She guessed that as soon as Alessio returned she would be leaving, and she wanted to be ready. So she used the siesta time to shower and wash her hair. Emilia, beaming, had told her that the electricity had been restored, but Laura still chose to dry her hair in the sun, sitting on the bench in the courtyard. Last time she'd done this, Caio had been here, she thought idly, then stiffened.

Paolo, she thought. Paolo and his awful mother down at Lake Trasimeno. She hadn't given them a single thought. But then she doubted whether either of them had spared much time to consider her plight either.

Whatever, she would have to leave a message with some excuse to explain her abrupt departure alone. Paolo would probably not be pleased, but that couldn't be helped. And she'd probably done enough to convince his mother that the Manzone marriage was a non-starter, so some good might come out of the bleak misery of this ill-starred visit after all.

But three long hours later she was still waiting. She tried to occupy some time at the piano, but was too irritated by her own lack of concentration to continue, so she put the music away, and closed the lid gently. Another goodbye.

She wandered restlessly round the heated stillness of the garden, trying not to look at her watch too often, and failing. She still had no idea what flight she'd be able to catch. Maybe there wouldn't be one until the next day, now, and she would have to spend the night at the airport, but even that could be endured.

Anywhere, she thought with sudden passion. Please, God, anywhere but here. I can't be with him for another night. I can't...

The sun was setting when she at last heard the sound of the Jeep. She'd been curled up in the corner of the sofa, but now she stiffened, sitting upright, her eyes fixed painfully on the open doorway. She heard his footsteps, his voice in a brief exchange with Guillermo.

Then he came into the room and stood looking at her, in silence, a strange intensity in his dark gaze that parched her mouth and made her tremble inwardly.

She found words from somewhere in a voice she barely recognised as hers. 'The road—is it ready now? Can we go?'

'Sì,' he said quietly. 'It is open.'

She touched the tip of her tongue to her dry lips. 'Then—I'd better get—my things.'

He said something soft and violent under his breath, then came to her, his long stride swallowing the distance between them. He took her wrists, pulling her to her feet in one swift, almost angry movement.

Then he bent his head, and kissed her on the mouth with a searing, passionate yearning that made her whole body shake.

'Forgive me.' The words were forced from him hoarsely as he looked deeply, hungrily into her eyes. 'Laura, forgive me, but I cannot live one more hour without you.'

She should stop this now, a small sane voice in her head kept repeating as Alessio kissed her again. Stop it, and step back, out of harm's way. Anything else was madness.

Madness, she thought as coherent thought spun out of control, leaving nothing but this terrifying frenzy in her blood that demanded to be appeased.

Madness, she told herself on a small sobbing breath as she slid her arms round his neck, and let him carry her out of the room.

CHAPTER ELEVEN

THE whole villa seemed hushed, its only sound his footsteps as he strode swiftly with her along the shadowed corridor to his bedroom.

Alessio kicked the door shut behind him, then crossed the vast room, putting Laura down on the canopied bed. For a long moment he looked down at her, then he bent and quite deliberately took the neckline of her dress in both hands, tearing the thin cotton apart like paper.

She gasped, her eyes dilating in sudden uncertainty, and saw his swift, crooked smile.

He said softly, 'Do not be frightened, *carissima*. I have wanted for so long to do that, but now I will be gentle, I promise.'

He released her from the tangle of fabric, tossing it to the floor behind him, before stripping off his own clothing with unhurried purpose. Then, at last, he lay down beside her, framing her face in his hands as he kissed the lingering doubt from her wide startled eyes, then moved down to her mouth, his lips moving almost languorously on hers until he felt the tension leave her, and her slender body relax trustingly into his arms.

He let the kiss deepen, opening her mouth so that his tongue could seek the moist heat of hers, while his fingertips stroked her face and throat, and the vulnerable angles of her slender shoulders, his touch light and almost undemanding. Almost—but not quite.

He felt the growing tumult of her breathing as he began gently to caress her small, eager breasts.

Her rosy nipples were already hard with desire when he freed them from their lace cups, and bent to adore them with his lips and tongue. She gave a tiny whimper, her head moving restlessly from side to side, colour flaring along her cheekbones.

152

Her shaking hands went to his body, seeking his hardness, driven by the harsh flowering of her own need, but Alessio stopped her, clasping her fingers, and raising them swiftly to his lips.

'Not yet, my sweet one,' he whispered. 'It is too soon for us to enjoy each other as lovers should. This time, *mia cara*, these first moments must be for you alone.'

His hands traced a slow golden path down her body, brushing away her last covering as if it had been a cobweb. And where his hands touched, his lips followed, warm and beguiling. Luring her on.

Telling her—promising her that, this time, there would be no turning back. That the passionate covenant of his nakedness against hers would be fulfilled.

Laura's breathing rasped fiercely in her throat as her aroused senses responded with renewed delight to his caresses, to the physical fact of his nearness, and the warmth of his bare skin brushing hers.

His mouth returned to her breasts, suckling them tenderly as his hand slid between her thighs. She gasped a little in mingled excitement and apprehension, remembering that first time, but discovered at once there was to be nothing painful or threatening in this delicate exploration of her most intimate self.

She found herself sinking into a state of almost languid relaxation, aware of nothing but his fingertips moving on her softly and rhythmically at first, then increasing the pressure into a pattern of deliciously intense sensations. His thumb was stroking her tiny silken mound, coaxing it to heated tumescence, while, at the same time, the long, skilful fingers eased their way slowly into her moist inner heat, forcing the breath from her lungs in a sigh of totally voluptuous pleasure.

His lips moved back to hers, kissing her unhurriedly, his tongue stroking hers, thrusting softly into her mouth, mirroring the frankly sensual play of his hands.

Her earlier languor had fled. There were small flames dancing now behind her tightly closed eyelids. She could not hear, or make a sound, her whole being concentrated on this relentless, exquisite build of pleasure that he was creating for her.

Her body was writhing against his touch, begging mutely for some surcease from this incredible, unbearable spiral of delight that had become almost an agony.

She heard a voice she barely recognised as hers crying out hoarsely as he brought her at last to the peak of consummation, and held her there for an endless moment, before releasing her, and allowing the first uncontrollable spasms of rapture to shudder fiercely through her body, devastating her innocence for ever as she confronted, for the first time, her own sexuality, and his power to arouse it.

And as the first harsh glory of her climax softened into quiet ripples of satiation, there were tears on her face.

Alessio kissed the salt drops away, holding her close, soothing her, murmuring endearments in his own language.

At last she murmured huskily, 'You should have warned me.'

'Warned you of what, *carissima*?'

'How you were going to make me feel.'

She felt him quiver with laughter. 'You do not think, *mia bella*, that might have sounded both conceited and presumptuous?'

She buried her own smile in his shoulder. 'Well—maybe—a little.' She hesitated. 'But I don't expect you've had many failures,' she added with a touch of wistfulness.

There was a silence, then he said gently, 'Shall we agree, *mi amore*, to allow the past to remain where it belongs?' He paused, altering his position slightly but significantly, making her gasp soundlessly. 'The immediate future should concern us more.' He slid his hands under her, lifting her slightly towards him. 'Or I think so—don't you?'

His dark eyes were questioning, his faint smile almost quizzical as he looked down at her, and she felt the hardness of him between her thighs, pressing at the entrance to her newly receptive body.

Laura was suddenly aware of a pang of physical desire so strong—so incredible—that she nearly cried out. Suddenly, she knew that she could not allow herself time to think—to become afraid. To doubt her own capacity to absorb all that male size and strength, and return the pleasure he'd gifted to her only moments before.

Instead, she found herself reaching for him, forgetting her instinctive shyness as she caressed the powerfully rigid shaft with fingers that shook a little, making him groan softly, pleadingly. And then, with a total certainty she barely understood, guiding him into her. Surging almost wildly against the initial restraint of his first thrust to welcome him deeply—endlessly. To defy once and for always any discomfort that might still linger for her in this complete union of their bodies.

But this time there was no pain, only the heated, silken glide of him possessing her—filling her completely over and over again.

Making her realise, with shock, as she clung to his sweat-dampened shoulders, her slim hips echoing his own driving rhythm, that her body had not yet finished with its delight.

That his urgency had captured her too, lifting her, all unaware, to some other unguessed-at plane with heart-stopping speed, showing her that the pinnacle of rapture was there, waiting for her if only—if only she could reach...

Then the last remnants of reality splintered, leaving nothing but the primitive agony of pure sensation. And as she moaned aloud in the final extremity she heard Alessio's voice, hoarse and shaken, saying her name as his sated body crumpled against hers in sheer exhaustion.

The warm scented water was like balm on her sensitised skin, at the same time soothing the frank, unexpected ache of her muscles. Laura lay in Alessio's arms in the deep sunken bath, her head pillowed dreamily on his shoulder as his lips caressed the damp silk of her hair.

There was no point, she thought, in trying to rationalise what had just happened between them. It defied reason or coherent thought. It just—was.

And now nothing would ever be the same again. Or, at least, not for her.

For him, she thought with sudden unhappiness, it was probably just routine. Another eager girl to be taught the art of sexual fulfilment by a man who was undoubtedly ardent and generous—but also diabolically experienced.

He said, 'Where have you gone?'

She glanced up at him, startled. 'I don't know what you mean,' she parried.

'A moment ago you were here with me, and happy. But no longer. So what happened?'

'I'm fine.' She sent him a deliberately provocative look under her lashes. 'Perhaps you're better at reading bodies than minds, *signore*.'

But his glance was thoughtful rather than amused. 'And perhaps you do not always tell the whole truth, *signorina*.'

She turned, pressing her lips passionately against the smooth skin of his shoulder. 'Alessio, I am happy. I swear it. I—I never dreamed I could feel like this. Maybe I'm a little—overwhelmed.'

'And maybe you also need food.' He was smiling now as he reached forward to drain the water. 'I think we must forget dinner, *mia bella*, but maybe I can coax Emilia to provide us with a little supper, hmm?'

'Oh, God.' Laura groaned as he helped her out of the bath. 'What is she going to think?'

He grinned. 'That we have the rest of the night to enjoy, *carissima*, and need all our strength. She will feed us well.'

And so she did, although, to Laura's relief, Emilia allowed Alessio, who had gone on his quest wearing only a pair of jeans, to bring the basket of food from the kitchen himself.

Laura, having ruefully examined the ruin of her dress, had put on his discarded shirt. Now she pirouetted self-consciously for his inspection.

'What do you think?'

The dark eyes glinted. 'I think perhaps supper can wait.'

She laughed, and skipped out of range. 'But I'm starving, *signore*. You wouldn't want me to faint.'

He slanted a wicked grin at her. 'Well, not through hunger, certainly.'

The basket contained cold chicken, cheese, red wine and warm olive bread, which they ate and drank outside in the courtyard, while the goddess Diana stared over their heads with her cold, remote smile.

Laura said, 'I don't think she approves of us.'

'According to the old stories, she approved of very little,' Alessio said lazily as he refilled her glass. 'My grandfather originally commissioned the statue, but I think he was disappointed in the result, and I know my parents were planning to have it replaced at some point.'

'Yet they didn't?'

He was silent for a moment. 'They did not have time,' he said eventually, his voice expressionless. 'My mother was killed on the *autostrada* when I was sixteen. A lorry driver fell asleep at the wheel, and his vehicle crashed through the barrier. And my father never recovered from her death. Within the year, he had suffered a fatal heart attack, which his doctors always believed was triggered by his grief.'

'Oh, God.' Laura sat up, staring at him, shocked. 'Oh, I'm so sorry. I shouldn't have said anything...'

He touched her cheek gently. '*Carissima*, I have not been sixteen for a very long time. And I was looked after with infinite kindness by my godfather, the Marchese D'Agnaccio, and his wonderful wife, Arianna, so I was not left to mourn as a lonely orphan.'

Oh, but I think you were, she told him silently. However well you were looked after. And I think, too, that this explains some of the contradictions I sense in you. The way you seem to retreat to some remote fastness where no one can reach you. The emotional equivalent, perhaps, of this house.

He said, 'You have left me again.'

She bent her head. 'I was thinking of my own father. He died of a heart attack too. He'd liquidised all his assets, remortgaged the house to start up an engineering business with an old friend. He came back from a business trip with a full order book to find the place empty, and his partner gone, taking all the money with him. He must have been planning it for ages, because he'd covered his tracks completely. We were going to lose everything, and Dad collapsed on his way to the creditors' meeting.'

Alessio drew her into his arms, and sat with her, his lips resting gently against her hair.

After a while, he said, 'Would you like to sleep a little, *mia cara*?'

She found her eyes suddenly blurred. 'Yes,' she whispered shakily. 'Yes, Alessio, please. That would be good.'

He took her hand and led her back to the shadowed bedroom. Gently he unbuttoned the shirt, and slipped it from her shoulders, then put her into the bed and drew the sheet over her.

As he came to lie beside her Laura turned into his arms, and heard his voice murmuring to her softly, soothingly, in his own language until drowsiness prevailed, and she drifted away into oblivion.

It was very dark—some time in the small hours—when she awoke to his mouth moving gently, persuasively on hers, calling her senses back to life, and her body to renewed desire.

She yielded, sighing in sensuous acceptance as she fitted herself to him, waiting—eager once more to be overwhelmed—to be carried away on the force of his passion.

But he was, she soon discovered, in no hurry to enter her. No hurry at all.

Instead, she found herself shivering—burning in response as his fingertips stroked and tantalised every warm inch of her, awakening needs that, yesterday, she had not known existed.

His lips caressed her breasts, tugging gently on the hardening nipples until she moaned faintly, then kissed their way down her body, until he reached the joining of her thighs to demand a different kind of surrender.

She was beyond protest, unable to resist him as his mouth claimed her, and she experienced the intimate sorcery of his tongue working its dark magic upon her.

The breath sobbed in her throat as her body writhed helplessly beneath him, torn between shame and exaltation.

He was smiling against her skin, saying that she must speak—must tell him what she liked—what she wanted him to do to her. And was it this? And this? And—most of all—this? And as she was swept away into the maelstrom of anguished pleasure he had unleashed for her she heard her own drowning voice whispering an endless, 'Yes.'

It was almost dawn before they'd finally fallen asleep in each other's arms, and the next time Laura opened her eyes it was full morning, and sunlight was pouring through the slats of the shutters. For a moment, she lay still, savouring her memories, then she turned her head to look at the sleeping man beside her. Only the bed was empty.

She sat up bewilderedly in time to see Alessio emerge from the bathroom, pushing a white shirt into the waistband of his jeans.

She said, 'You're dressed,' and was ashamed of the open disappointment in her voice.

He was laughing as he knelt on the bed beside her, and kissed her mouth. 'I have to wear clothes sometimes, *carissima*. People expect it. Besides, I must go out. It seems that Fredo has recovered consciousness, and is asking for me.'

She stretched delicately, watching the sudden flare in the dark eyes as the sheet slipped down from her body. 'Shall I come with you?'

He glanced swiftly, regretfully at his watch. 'Next time, *carissima*. Now I really must go.' His hand tangled in her hair, drawing her head back for another kiss, longer, slower, deeper than the last, and she slid her arm round his neck, holding him to her.

'Stay here, and get some rest,' he told her softly, detaching himself with open reluctance. 'Because you will need it when I return.' He paused. 'I shall tell the servants you are not to be disturbed.'

Laura groaned. 'I don't think I shall ever be able to face them again.'

He grinned at her. 'Ah, but you will, *Madonna*. Now go back to sleep and dream about me, and I will return very soon.' At the door he turned. 'And then we must talk.' He blew her another kiss, and was gone.

She lay quietly for a while. She had never thought much about her body, except as something to be fed and clothed. Had found the physical facts of passion and consummation faintly ludicrous, and the prospect of actually finding herself in bed with a man— submitting to him—as both awkward and embarrassing.

And she'd never imagined herself as anyone's sex object either. She'd always supposed she was too thin, and her breasts were too small, to make her the focus of a man's desire.

And yet in one terrifying, rapturous night all her ideas had been overturned, and her principles swept aside.

She belonged body and soul to Alessio Ramontella. And every nerve ending she possessed, each muscle, and inch of skin, was providing her with a potent reminder of his total mastery. And of how much he had, indeed, desired her.

She realised she was blushing and pushed the sheet away, swinging her legs to the floor. Too late for blushes now—or even to remember her own careful taboos about casual sex. Although those hours of lovemaking could hardly be described as casual.

And, she thought, she didn't regret a thing. How could she?

She quickly straightened the bed, plumping the crumpled pillows and smoothing the covers flat, then wandered into the bathroom to take a long, luxurious shower. As she soaped herself she recalled other hands touching her, sometimes tantalising, sometimes almost reverent, and felt her heartbeat quicken uncontrollably.

I want him here, she thought, pressing a clenched fist against the tiled wall. I want him now.

As she emerged from the shower and reached for a towel she glimpsed herself in one of the many mirrors and paused, all her earlier doubts about her lack of glamour confirmed.

She turned away, sighing. She still had nothing to wear, and frankly she didn't fancy traversing the house to collect a change of clothing from her room, so she borrowed Alessio's black silk robe instead, rolling up the sleeves and tying the sash in a secure double bow round her slender waist.

The faint fragrance of the cologne he used still lingered in the fabric, she discovered with ridiculous pleasure as she stretched out on top of the bed to wait. She could almost pretend that he was here with her, his arms around her.

And the fantasy became even more real if she closed her eyes. She hadn't meant to doze, but the room was warm, the bed soft, and the shower had relaxed her, so the temptation was irresistible.

As she pillowed her cheek on her hand she remembered how Alessio had kissed her awake only a few hours before, and exactly what it had led to. And she wriggled further into the mattress, smiling a little as her eyelids drooped.

It was the sound of the dog barking excitedly that woke her.

Laura propped herself up on an elbow, and stared around her, momentarily disorientated. Caio, she thought, trying to clear her head. Caio in the courtyard outside her room, wanting her to come out and join him. Except he wasn't here—he was at Lake Trasimeno with the Signora. And—this wasn't her room either. It belonged to Alessio.

Just, she thought slowly, just as she did herself.

And, with that nosedive into reality, she suddenly became aware of something else. The sound of women's voices arguing, not far away. One of them was Emilia's. But the other...

Oh, God, Laura thought, transfixed with horror. It's the Signora. She's back. I have to get out of here.

But she was too late. The door was flung wide, and the Signora came stalking into the room, brushing away the volubly protesting Emilia as if she were a troublesome insect.

'So.' She stared at Laura, still huddled on the bed, and her smile was gloating. 'Just as I expected.' She turned. 'Paolo, my poor son, I grieve for you, but you must come and see this slut you brought here. This *puttana* you thought to honour with our name, and who has become yet another of your cousin's whores.'

Paolo followed her into the room, his expression sullen and

inimical. The look he sent Laura was enough to freeze the blood. 'Fool,' it said plainly.

'Sì, Mammina,' he said curtly. 'You were right about her and I was wrong. She has totally betrayed me, and now I cannot bear the sight of her.' He spat the words. 'So, get rid of her. Make her go.'

I'm still asleep, thought Laura. And this is a nightmare. A bad one. He couldn't still intend to keep up this ludicrous pretence, surely?

The situation was fast slipping out of control, and somehow she had to drag it back to reality. It was hard to be dignified when wearing nothing but a man's robe, several sizes too large, but she had to try, she thought, scrambling off the bed and facing them both, her head held high.

She said coldly and clearly, 'Paolo, I do not appreciate having my privacy invaded, or being insulted like this. So, please stop this nonsense, and tell your mother the truth.'

'And what truth is that, pray?' the Signora enquired.

Laura sent Paolo an equally fulminating glance. 'That your son and I are not involved with each other—and never have been.'

'And nor will we ever be,' he flung back at her. 'You faithless bitch. Do you think I would want my cousin's leavings?'

Laura felt as if she'd been punched in the midriff. She said, 'But that's insane—and you know it.'

'I know only that I want you thrown out of this house.' He turned to his mother. 'Arrange it, Mammina. I wish never to see her again.'

He stalked from the room, slamming the door behind him. Leaving Laura and the Signora looking at each other.

The older woman sent her a grim smile. 'You hear my son. Pack your things, and go. As the matter is urgent, my car will take you to the airport at Rome.'

Laura swallowed. 'This is not your house, signora. You do not give orders here. And I am going nowhere until Alessio returns.'

'You are over-familiar, signorina.' The Signora's tone was ice.

'Or do you imagine some sordid romp gives you the right—a nobody from nowhere—to refer to the Count Ramontella by his given name?'

She paused derisively. 'You mentioned the truth just now. So, hear it. I arranged this little comedy, and I am now ending it. Because I have achieved what I set out to do. I have separated you from my son. With the assistance, of course, of my dear nephew.'

There was a silence, then Laura said slowly, 'What—what are you talking about?'

'I am talking about you—and your host.' She snorted. 'You think my nephew would have laid a finger on you of his own free will? No, and no. I simply made it necessary for him to—oblige me. And he has done so.'

Laura was very still. 'I don't know what you mean.'

The Signora laughed. 'But of course not. You did not know—how could you?—that my nephew has been conducting a disreputable affair with a married woman—the worthless wife, unfortunately, of an old friend's son.' She sighed. 'So sad—and potentially so scandalous. But I agreed not to make this shameful episode public if Alessio would, in his turn, use his powers of seduction to win you away from my son.

'At first, he was reluctant. You are not the type to whom he would naturally be drawn, and very much his social inferior. But he decided that his mistress's dubious honour must be protected at all costs.' She picked up Laura's torn dress from the floor, and studied it. 'And it seems that, in the end, he—warmed to his task.'

Her malicious smile raked like rusty nails over Laura's quivering senses. 'He promised me he would send you home with a beautiful memory, *signorina*. I gather that his ability to do so is almost legendary, so I hope he has kept his word.'

'You mean I was—set up?' Even to her own ears, Laura's voice sounded husky—uncertain. 'You're lying.'

'Ask him,' said the Signora. 'If you are still here when he returns.' She gave a delicate yawn. 'I advise you go quickly and spare him the obvious recriminations. They will do no good. Alessio is, and will always be, a law unto himself.

'Besides,' she added, shrugging, 'it is clear he wishes to avoid a confrontation. As you see, when he learned I was returning, he immediately contrived to be absent. He may feel it is wiser to stay away until you have finally departed.'

'He—knew?' The words stuck in her throat.

'But of course. I telephoned earlier.' The older woman sounded mildly surprised. 'I needed him to make sure you would be found in his bed. That was our agreement.'

She nodded. 'Alessio has fulfilled his part of the bargain, and can now resume his liaison with that pretty idiot Vittoria Montecorvo in perfect safety, as long as he is discreet.' She smiled again. 'As you have found, *signorina*, he prefers fools. And variety.'

She added more brusquely, 'Your services are no longer required, *signorina*. You have amused my nephew for a short time, but anything else is only in your imagination.'

Did I imagine it? Laura asked herself numbly. Did I imagine the murmurs and laughter? The peace and sense of belonging? Was it really—just sex all along?

The Signora turned and opened the door. 'So, please go quietly without embarrassing scenes.'

Laura said quietly, 'Do you really think I'd want to stay?' She brushed past the older woman, and walked quickly away down the passage towards her room, stumbling a little on the hem of the robe.

In the courtyard, the goddess Diana still smiled with that chill serenity. But then, thought Laura as the first slash of pain cut into her, she was accustomed to having love torn to pieces in front of her. So this was the place where she truly belonged.

She ran the rest of the way, just making it into the bathroom before she was violently sick, retching into the toilet bowl until the muscles of her empty stomach were screaming at her, and the world was revolving dizzily round her aching head.

Eventually, she managed to drag herself back to her feet, to rinse her mouth and wash her face somehow. The light golden tan she'd acquired had turned sallow, she thought, wincing at her reflection, and her eyes looked like hollow pits.

While beating like a drum in her tired brain were the words, 'I have to get out of here. I have to go. Before he comes back. I have to go.'

Alessio parked the Jeep in front of the villa and sprang out, humming to himself. He had assured himself that Fredo was going to make a full recovery, then made his excuses and left, intent on returning as fast as possible to his warm, beautiful girl.

He had felt totally relaxed and serene on the homeward journey, but his mind was clear and sharp as crystal, visualising the whole shape of his future life laid out in front of him like a golden map.

He strode into the house and went straight to his room, but it was empty. He shrugged off his faint disappointment that Laura was not there, waiting for him, and went in search of her.

As he walked through the hallway Caio advanced out of the *salotto* barking aggressively, halting Alessio in his stride. His brows snapped together as he realised with sharp dismay the implications of the dog's presence, and, as if on cue, his aunt appeared in the doorway of the drawing room.

'*Caro,*' she purred. 'I did not expect you back so soon.'

'And I did not expect you at all, Zia Lucrezia.' His tone was guarded. 'The road has only just opened again.'

'So Guillermo informed me when I telephoned. He seemed to feel I should not take the risk, but my driver is a good, safe man.' She paused. 'You will be pleased to hear that our little conspiracy was entirely successful. Paolo was cured of his foolish infatuation as soon as he saw the English girl sprawling half naked on your bed.' She added brightly, 'And soon, she will be on her way to the airport and out of our lives for ever. *Bravo*, nephew. You have done well.'

Alessio had a curious sensation that it was suddenly impossible to breathe.

He said hoarsely, 'What have you done? What have you said to my Laura?'

She shrugged a shoulder. 'I simply—enlightened her as to the real reason for her presence here—and for being honoured with your attentions. Did I do wrong?' She smiled maliciously, adding, 'She seemed to accept the situation quite well. No weeping or hysteria. I was—surprised.'

He said on a groan, '*Santa madonna,*' and began to run.

Laura had taken out the clothes to wear to the airport, and put them on the bed. She went back into the bedroom to fetch her toothbrush and wash-bag, and when she emerged Alessio was standing there.

She recoiled instantly, with a little incoherent cry, and saw him flinch.

He said with shaken urgency, 'Laura, *carissima.* You must let me talk to you. Explain.'

'There's really no need, *signore.*' There was a terrible brightness in her voice. 'Your aunt has already told me everything.'

'No,' he said. 'Not everything.'

'Then at least all I needed to know,' she flashed. 'Which is— I got screwed. Several times and in several different senses of the word.'

His head went back. He said icily, 'How dare you describe what happened between us in those terms?'

'Too vulgar for you, my lord?' She dropped a curtsy. 'I do apologise. Blame my social inferiority.'

He drew a deep breath. 'We shall get nowhere like this.'

'I shall get somewhere,' she said. 'Rome airport, to be precise. After which I shall never have to see anyone from your lying, treacherous family again. And that includes you—you utter bastard.'

There was a tingling silence, then Alessio said quietly, 'I do not blame you for being angry with me.'

'Thanks for the gracious admission,' she said. 'And now perhaps you'll go. I have to finish up here, and your aunt's driver is waiting.'

He said curtly, 'My aunt will need her driver herself. She and Paolo are leaving.'

She lifted her chin. 'Your aunt didn't mention it.'

'She does not yet know. If you wish to go to the airport, I will drive you.'

'No.' She almost shouted the word. 'No, you won't, damn you. Can't you understand? I wouldn't go five yards with you. In fact, I don't want to breathe the same air.'

He looked at her wearily. '*Dio*, Laura. You cannot believe what you are saying.'

'Oh, but I do,' she said. 'And I also believe your aunt. Or are you going to deny that you had me brought here so that you could seduce me?'

He bent his head, wretchedly. '*Mia cara*, it may have begun like that, but—'

'But that's how it ended as well,' she cut across him. 'If memory serves. Now, will you please get out of this room?'

'Not until we have talked. Until I can get you to understand...'

'But I do. It's all perfectly clear. You have a mistress who is married. Your aunt threatened to make the affair public. You took me to bed to keep her quiet.' Her glance dropped scorn. 'You really didn't have to go to those lengths, *signore*. If you thought I was dating your loathsome cousin, then you only had to ask me to stop.'

'Laura—listen to me. I—I wanted you.'

'Please don't expect me to be flattered. What was I—your practice round? Keeping you in shape for your married lady?'

'Your memory does not serve you very well,' he said. 'You know it was not like that.'

'My most recent recollection,' she said, 'is being found by that unholy pair in your bedroom, and having to listen to their insults. Because you set me up. Your aunt telephoned you and said she was on her way.'

'I received no such call,' he said. 'And if I had, then you would have left with me.' He paused. 'If you still insist on going to Rome, then Guillermo will take you. But stay with me, *bella mia*, I beg you. Let me try and make amends.'

'There is nothing you can say, or do.' Her throat ached uncontrollably. 'You tricked me, and I shall always hate you for it. I just want to leave—and never see you again.'

There was another dreadful silence, then he said, slowly and carefully, 'Unfortunately, it may not be that simple for either of us. Last night, I failed to protect you as I should have done, a piece of criminal stupidity for which I must ask your forgiveness. However, it is a fact that you could be carrying my child.'

'Well, don't worry too much, *signore*.' Her voice bit. 'If I am, I'll take appropriate action to deal with it—and it won't cost you a red cent. So you can return to your mistress without a backward glance.'

'Vittoria is not my mistress.' His voice rose in exasperation. 'She never was. It was wrong, and I admit that, but it was only a one-night stand—nothing more.'

'And so was I,' she hit back at him. 'They seem to be your speciality, *signore*.' She saw his head jerk back as if she had struck him, and took a steadying breath. 'Now, if you have nothing more to say—no more lame and meaningless excuses—then, perhaps, you'll finally get out of this room, and leave me alone.'

She could feel his anger like a force field, and braced herself for the explosion, but it did not come.

Instead, he looked her over. 'There is one thing.' His tone was almost conversational. 'My robe. I would like it back, if you please.'

'Of course. I'll leave it—'

He held out a hand. 'Now.'

There was a silence. At last she said quietly, 'Please—don't do this.'

His brows lifted. 'What is your objection, *signorina*?' His tone mocked her. 'I am asking for nothing but the return of my property. Or do you wish me to take it from you?'

Her lips silently formed the word 'no'. She undid the double bow, fumbling a little, then took off the robe, which she rolled into a ball and threw at him. It landed at his feet. She stood her ground, making no attempt to cover herself with her hands. Trying to tell herself that it did not matter. That he already knew everything there was to know about her.

And at the same time, desperately conscious that it mattered terribly. Because the lover who'd adored her the previous night was gone for ever, and in his place was a stranger who had no right to look at her.

But Alessio was not even glancing at her naked body. His impenetrable dark gaze was fixed on her eyes—on the anger and fierce contempt in their stormy depths.

He said softly, 'You know, do you not, that I would only have to touch you?'

Yes, she knew, and the shame of it was like an open wound in her flesh. Somehow, she had to retrieve the situation. Somehow...

She said in savage mimicry of his intonation, 'And you know, *do you not*, that I would rather die?' She paused. 'So will you please get out of my life? Now.'

'*Naturalmente*. And I will give Guillermo his instructions.' He gave a curt inclination of the head. '*Addio, signorina*. I wish you—happiness.'

Then he was gone, closing the door behind him, leaving the discarded robe still lying on the floor.

Laura reached down, and picked up the mass of crumpled silk, carrying it to her face and holding it there. Breathing the scent of his skin for the last time.

'It's over,' she whispered. 'Over. He's gone. And I shall never see him again.'

CHAPTER TWELVE

ALESSIO was in his study with the door shut, but he still heard the car drive away taking Laura to the airport, and he sat for a long moment, his head buried in his hands, fighting for self-command.

He had been blazing with anger as he'd walked out of her room earlier, furious at her refusal to listen to reason, and outraged at the way she had spoken to him. Dismissed him so summarily.

Never, he'd raged inwardly, had he been treated like that before by any woman. But, then, honesty compelled him to ask, when had he ever behaved as badly before to any woman?

And the acknowledgement that he'd deserved every contemptuous word she'd hurled at him did nothing to soothe his temper.

But now his anger was beginning to cool, leaving in its place a bleak and echoing emptiness. He was stunned by his own wretchedness. And by his total failure to win her round, or reach her in any way that mattered.

And now she was gone from him, he thought starkly. How could he have allowed it to happen?

More importantly, how could he have stopped her?

Well, there was no way. She had made that more than clear, her words lashing him like a whip. And at least he had not suffered the ultimate humiliation of falling on his knees, as he'd been desperately tempted to do, and begging her to stay. Or committed the folly of telling her he loved her—something he had never said to anyone before—and having that rejected too.

He pushed his chair back impatiently, and rose. There was no point in brooding, he told himself. He could not change what had just happened. She'd left—hating him. But he could and would deal with the fallout, as he'd sworn he would.

170

On his way to the *salotto*, he was waylaid by an unhappy Emilia. 'I am so sorry, *Excellenza*, but we tried to keep the *signora*, your aunt, away from your room—and the little one—but we could not stop her. Is this why the Signorina Laura has gone away?'

He said gently, 'The blame is mine alone, Emilia. And the *signorina* had her own reasons for wishing to return to England.'

'But she will come back?'

He found he was bracing himself. Avoiding her concerned glance. 'No,' he said. 'I do not think so.'

He found his aunt ensconced on a sofa, glancing through a fashion magazine and drinking coffee.

'Alessio, *caro*.' She barely glanced up. 'Now that our unwanted guest has departed, I thought I might invite Beatrice Manzone and her father here for a short stay.' She smiled smugly. 'She and Paolo seemed to enjoy each other's company at Trasimeno so much. Maybe, even without your intervention, he might have come round to my way of thinking. Yet it was probably better to be safe.'

'I am sure you would think so.' His voice was harsh. 'However, I must decline to entertain any more guests of yours, Zia Lucrezia. Nor do I wish you or your son to spend another night under my roof.'

There was a silence, then she said, 'If this is a joke, Alessio, it is a poor one.'

His gaze was unswerving. 'Believe me, I have never been more serious. I do not wish to have anything more to do with you. Ever.'

'But Paolo and I are your closest living relatives.' There was a shake in her voice. Uncertainty in the look she sent him. 'Your father was my brother.'

He said icily, 'As I am ashamed to acknowledge. And for most of his life, you and he were strangers—at his wish.' He shook his head. 'I should have ordered you to leave my apartment as soon as you mentioned Vittoria,' he added grimly.

'Yet you did not,' she reminded him swiftly. 'You agreed to

my terms, and you carried them out to the letter, because you did not wish your liaison with her to become known.'

'No,' he said, after a pause. 'I did not. But, on reflection, I think I agreed for Fabrizio's sake, rather than hers. He is a fool, but he is a fool in love, and I cannot blame him for that.' His mouth tightened, then he went on levelly, 'Nor does he deserve public humiliation because his wife does not return his affection.' He shrugged. 'One day he may discover the truth about her, but it will not be through me.'

He gave her a cool, hard glance. 'Guillermo is driving Signorina Mason to Rome, so your own driver is free to take you wherever you wish to go. I would be glad if you would leave as soon as possible.'

The controlled, controlling veneer was beginning to crumble. She said, 'I cannot believe you mean this. You are hardly a saint, Alessio, to trouble yourself over the bedding of one stupid English girl.'

'That is enough.' His voice rang harshly through the big room. 'Believe that the matter is closed, and my decision is final.' He made her a swift formal bow. '*Addio*, Zia Lucrezia.'

She called after him, panic in her tone, but he took no notice.

He was in the library, forcing himself to look through his emails in an attempt at normality, when the door opened and Paolo came in.

He said uneasily, '*Mammina* says you have ordered us from the villa. There must be some misunderstanding.'

'No.' Alessio rose and walked round the desk, leaning back against it, arms folded across his chest. 'This is simply a day for departures—for finally severing damaging connections.' He looked icily at Paolo. 'As you yourself have done, cousin.'

'You mean the little Laura?' Paolo shrugged. 'But consider— if I had pretended to forgive her for sleeping with you, *Mammina* would never have believed it. So what else could I do but get rid of her?'

Alessio considered him, his mouth set. 'You do not seem distraught at her loss,' he commented.

'On the contrary, it is damned inconvenient,' Paolo said sourly.

'Until your intervention, I had *Mammina* nicely fooled. Another few days, and she would have admitted defeat over the Manzone girl.'

'How little you know.' Alessio's eyes were coolly watchful. 'And how was Signorina Mason involved in this—foolery?'

Paolo shrugged. 'There's no point in keeping it secret, any longer. The truth is, I picked her up in London. *Mammina* was right about that. Offered her a free holiday, plus cash, if she pretended to be in love with me.'

He gave a lascivious grin. 'I must say she threw herself into the role. Under all that English cool, she was a hot little number—as you must have found out last night.

'But I'm surprised she didn't tell you herself—during pillow talk,' he went on. 'But perhaps you didn't give her time, eh? I've been there myself, cousin, and I'm sure you had much better things for that pretty mouth to do...'

There was a blur of movement, and the odd sensation that he'd collided head-on with a stone pillar.

He found he was lying on the floor, his jaw aching, with Alessio standing over him, flexing his right hand.

He said softly, dangerously, 'That is a filthy lie, and we both know it. You never touched Laura Mason, and you will never speak of her in those terms again.' He paused. 'When you return to London, it will be to clear your desk. You no longer work for the Arleschi Bank. Now get out.'

He strode from the room, leaving Paolo to scramble to his feet, unaided and cursing violently.

'You will be sorry for this, cousin,' he whispered silently, gingerly feeling his jaw as Alessio's tall figure disappeared. 'And so will your little bedmate. Oh, yes, I know how to make her very sorry.'

Laura sat down at her desk and switched on her computer. It was almost a relief to find herself back at work, she thought, sighing. At least it would mean she would have something else to think about—during daylight hours, anyway. At night, it was not so easy to control her thoughts or dreams.

The long drive to the airport had been conducted pretty much in silence, although she'd been aware of Guillermo sending anxious glances in her direction.

Once they'd arrived, he had asked her quietly if she was sure— quite sure—she wished to do this, and she had said yes—yes, she was. And he had taken her to the desk, and arranged to have her ticket transferred to the next available flight in four hours' time. The transaction had taken place in Italian, and she was sure she heard him mention the Count Ramontella's name, but it had seemed wiser not to ask or protest. She was getting out of there, wasn't she? And more easily than she could have hoped?

The actual means had no longer seemed important.

'You have no message for me to take to His Excellency?' His voice was sad as he bade her goodbye.

'No,' she said, past the agonising tightness in her throat. 'No, thank you. Everything necessary has been said.'

On the plane, she pretended to sleep while the events of the past twenty-four hours rolled like a film loop through her weary mind, tormenting her over and over again. Telling her how gullible she'd been. The worst kind of fool.

The time since her return had not been easy for her either. Gaynor had naturally wanted to know why she'd come back earlier than expected, and didn't seem wholly convinced by Laura saying evasively that things hadn't worked out exactly as expected.

Her friend was also astute enough to read the signs of deep trouble behind Laura's attempt at a brave face.

'Please don't tell me you ended up falling for this Paolo after all?' she asked, dismayed.

'God, no.' Laura's voice was vehement with disgust. She'd encountered him briefly just as she'd been leaving the villa, and he'd called her an ugly name and told her she wouldn't get a cent of the money he'd promised. And for a second she'd stared at him, almost dazedly, wondering what he was talking about. Because it had all been such a long time ago, their arrangement, and now everything had changed, so that nothing—nothing mattered any more, least of all money...

'Well, that's a relief.' Gaynor gave her a shrewd glance. 'But, all the same, I'm sure there was someone. And when you want to talk, I'll listen.'

But Laura knew she would never want to discuss Alessio. The pain of his betrayal—of the knowledge that she'd been cynically seduced for the worst of all possible reasons—was too raw and too deep. She simply had to endure, somehow, and wait for time and distance to do their work.

However, at least she knew she wasn't pregnant. She'd had incontrovertible proof of that only two days after her return, and, for a long, bewildered moment, she'd not known whether to be glad or sorry. Just as there'd been times when she'd found herself wondering if he would—come after her...

But that was just a stupid lapse into unforgivable sentimentality, she told herself strongly. And never to be repeated. She wasn't having his baby, and he hadn't followed her to England. So, she'd been fortunate to be spared even more regret—more heartbreak. Nothing else.

And now she had to concentrate on things that really mattered, like her work. Because this was a big day for her. Her trial period at Harman Grace was complete, and she was about to receive her final appraisal and, hopefully, a permanent job offer, which would give her tottering confidence a much-needed boost.

So, she went into Carl's office for her interview with her shoulders back, and a smile nailed on.

But she'd no sooner sat down than he said, 'Laura, I'm afraid I have some bad news.'

She looked at him, startled. 'My appraisal?'

'No, that was good, as always. But, things are a bit tight economically just now, and we're having to make cuts, so there's only one job on offer instead of two as we planned.' His face radiated discomfort. 'And it's been decided to offer it to Bevan instead.'

'Bevan?' Her voice was incredulous. 'But you can't. He's struggled from day one. We've all had to pick up the pieces from his mistakes. Everyone knows that. My God, you know it.'

He did not meet her gaze. 'Nevertheless, it's the decision that's been reached—and I'm personally very sorry to lose you.'

Laura looked down at her hands, clenched together in her lap. She said half to herself, 'This cannot be happening to me. It can't.'

There was a silence, then Carl leaned forward, speaking quietly. 'I should not be telling you this, and it's strictly non-attributable. But the decision came from the top. One of our big new clients has put in some kind of complaint about you. Alleged you were incompetent, and impossible to work with, and that they'd take their business elsewhere unless you were fired. Times are hard, Laura, and the directors decided they couldn't take the risk.'

Laura gasped. 'They didn't even ask me for an explanation? It could be some terrible mistake.'

Carl shook his head. 'I'm afraid not.' His glance was compassionate. 'Some way, and only God knows how, you've managed to make an enemy of the head of the Arleschi Bank, honey. Alessio Ramontella himself. I've actually seen his personal letter to the board. And that's about as bad as it gets. No further explanations necessary.' He paused, saying sharply, 'Laura—are you OK? You look like a ghost.'

She felt like one too, only she knew she couldn't be dead, because she was too hurt, and too angry. It wasn't enough for Alessio to destroy her emotionally, she thought. He'd deliberately set out to ruin her career as well. She supposed it had to be revenge for their last encounter. After all, his anger had been almost tangible. He must have acted at once, to punish her for the things she'd said.

She thought, 'But that's impossible. He doesn't even know I work here,' and only realised she'd spoken aloud when Carl stared at her in disbelief.

'You mean there's something behind all this. You really know this guy?'

She lifted her chin. 'No,' she said quietly and clearly. 'I don't know him, and I never have done. Thankfully, he's a total stranger to me, and that's how he'll remain.' She rose. 'Now, I'll go and clear my desk.'

Alessio glanced at his watch, wondering how soon he could make a discreet exit from the reception. Attendance had been unavoidable, but now his duty was done and he wanted to leave. Not least because the Montecorvos were there, and he had been aware all evening of Vittoria's eyes following him hungrily round the enormous room.

If I'd known, he thought, wild horses wouldn't have dragged me here.

Since his return to Rome, Vittoria's letters and phone calls had returned in full force, although he'd responded to none of them. But she was clearly not giving up without a struggle, he realised, caught between annoyance and resignation.

He was on his way to the door when a slender crimson-tipped hand descended on his arm, and he was assailed by a waft of perfume, expensive and unmistakable.

He halted, groaning silently. 'Vittoria,' he offered insincerely. 'What a pleasure.'

She pouted, standing close to him, offering him a spectacularly indiscreet view of her cleavage. 'How can you say that, *caro mio*, when you know you have been avoiding me? Is it because of your aunt?' She lowered her voice, shuddering. 'She made my visit to Trasimeno a nightmare, the old witch, dropping hints like poison. But now she is no longer in the city. She has moved to her house in Tuscany, and Fabrizio's mother says she has no plans to return. So, we are safe.'

He began, 'Vittoria—' but she interrupted.

'*Caro*, I have good news. A friend of mine has an apartment not far from the Via Veneto, only she has been sent to Paris on business.

'And I have the key. We can meet there, without danger, whenever we wish.'

She smiled up at him, showing him the tip of her tongue between her lips. 'And you do wish it, don't you, *carissimo*? Because you are not seeing anyone else. I know that. Since you came back from Umbria over a month ago, you have been living like a recluse. Everyone says so.'

'Then, I am obliged to everyone for their concern,' he said icily. 'Unlike most of them, I have work to do.'

'But you cannot work all the time, *mi amore*.' Her low voice was insinuating. 'Your body needs exercise as well as your mind. And you cannot have forgotten how good we were together, Alessio *mio*. I shall never forget, and your Vittoria needs you— so badly.'

He met her gleaming, greedy gaze, and, with a sudden jolt of renewed pain, found himself remembering other eyes. Grey eyes that had smiled up at him in trust, then turned smoky with desire, before shining with astonished rapture as her body had yielded up its last sweet secrets. And all for him alone.

All that warmth and joy—and the small wicked giggle that had entranced him—and which it almost broke his heart to remember.

Laura, he thought with yearning, and sudden passion. Ah, *Dio*, my Laura—my beloved.

And suddenly Alessio knew what he had to do, just as surely as he'd done when he'd driven back to the villa on that last morning, only to find his plans—his entire future—wrecked by the disaster that had been waiting for him.

He took the hand that was still clutching his sleeve, and kissed it briefly and formally.

'You flatter me,' he said with cold civility. 'But I fear it is impossible to accept your charming invitation. You see, I have fallen deeply in love, and I hope very soon to be married. I am sure you understand. Feel free to tell—everyone. So, goodnight, Vittoria—and goodbye.'

And he strode away, leaving her staring after him, with two ugly spots of colour burning in her face.

It had been raining all day, and the air felt cool, promising a hint of autumn to come as Laura arrived back at the house and went slowly upstairs to her room.

She had been suffering from stomach cramps for most of the

evening, and, as the wine bar was quiet, Hattie, the owner, had dosed her with paracetamol and sent her home early.

She didn't usually have painful periods, but supposed wearily that her symptoms could be caused by stress. Because she still hadn't found another agency to take her on. Carl had given her a good reference, but prospective employers always wanted to know why she'd left Harman Grace after only three months. And they did not like the answer they were given.

So she was fortunate that Hattie could offer her full-time waitressing. But the money wasn't good, and there was little to spare once the rent was paid.

Her room felt damp and cheerless as she let herself in, and she shivered a little. She decided a shower might be comforting, but soon discovered that the water was only lukewarm in the small chilly bathroom. She sighed to herself. It seemed she would have to settle for the comfort of a hot-water bottle instead. She put on her elderly flowered cotton pyjamas and her dressing gown, and trailed off to the kitchen, carrying the rubber bag with its Winnie the Pooh cover.

She found Gaynor there ahead of her, taking the coffee jar from the cupboard, the kettle already heating on the stove. She swung round, starting violently, as Laura came in.

'My God, what are you doing here?'

'I live here.' Laura stared at her. 'Is something wrong?'

'No, no. But you're usually so much later than this. I wondered.'

'It's that time of the month again.' Laura grimaced. 'Hattie let me finish the shift early.' She held up the hot-water bottle. 'I just came to fill this.'

'Oh, hell.' Gaynor looked dismayed. 'I mean—what—what a shame. Poor you.' She gave Laura a smile that on anyone else would have looked shifty. 'Well, you go ahead. Your need is greater than mine, so the coffee can wait,' she added, backing to the door. 'I mean it—really. I—I'll check on you later.'

Laura turned to the stove with a mental shrug. There were two beakers on the small counter, she noticed, so clearly her friend had company. But what was there in that to make her so jumpy?

She carefully filled her bottle, and carried it back to her room, pausing first to tap at Gaynor's closed door and call, 'The kitchen's all yours.'

She'd taken two steps into the room before she realised that she was not alone. Or saw who was waiting for her, tall in his elegant charcoal suit, his dark face watchful and unsmiling as he looked at her.

He said quietly, *'Buonasera.'*

She clutched her bottle in front of her as if it were a defensive weapon. 'Good evening be damned,' she said raggedly. 'How did you get in here?'

'Your friend, who took pity on me when she heard me knocking, told me you had returned, and the door was open. So I came in.' He paused. 'It is good to see you again.'

She ignored that. 'What—what the hell are you doing here?' she demanded shakily. 'How did you find me?'

'The postcards you wrote that day in Besavoro, and I mailed for you. They had addresses on them.'

'Of all the devious...' Laura began furiously, then stopped, and took a deep breath. 'What do you want?'

'I want you, Laura.' His voice was quiet. 'I wish you to return with me to Italy.'

She took a step backwards, glaring at him. 'Is that why you had me fired—to offer me alternative work as your mistress?' She lifted her chin. 'I don't regard sharing your bed as a good career move, *signore*. So I suggest you get out of here—and I mean now.'

Alessio's brows lifted. 'Is that what you mean?' he asked with a kind of polite interest. 'Or what you think you should say?'

'Don't play word games,' she hit back fiercely. 'And before you ask, by the way, there's no baby.'

'So I gather.' His tone was rueful. 'Your friend has already informed me I have chosen the wrong time of the month to visit you.'

The hot-water bottle fell to the floor as Laura said hoarsely, 'Gaynor—said that—and to you?' She shook her head. 'Oh, God, I don't believe it. I—I'll kill her.'

For the first time, he smiled faintly. 'Ah, no, I was grateful for the warning, believe me. My friends who are already husbands tell me that sometimes a back rub can help. Would you like me to try?'

She stared at him in outrage, then marched to the door and flung it open. 'I'd like you to go to hell.' Her voice shook. 'Just—leave.'

'Not without you, *carissima*.' Alessio took off his jacket, and tossed it over the back of her armchair, then began to unbutton his waistcoat.

'Stop,' Laura said furiously. 'Stop right there. What do you think you're doing?'

He smiled at her. 'It has been a long and interesting day, and it is not over yet. I thought I would make myself comfortable, *cara mia*.'

'Not,' she said, 'in my flat. And don't call me that.'

'Then what shall I say?' he asked softly. 'My angel, my beautiful one? *Mi adorata?* For you are all these things, Laura *mia*, and more.'

'No.' She wanted to stamp in vexation, but remembered just in time that she was barefoot. 'I hate you. I want you out of my life. I told you so.'

'*Sì,*' he agreed. 'I am not likely to forget.'

'Nor did you,' she threw at him. 'In fact you wrote a stinking letter to Harman Grace, telling them to sack me as a result.'

'A letter was certainly written,' he said. 'I saw it today. But it did not come from me.'

Her jaw dropped. 'You—went to the agency.'

'It was during working hours,' he explained. 'I expected you to be there. I hoped you might be more welcoming when others were present. Instead I spoke to your former boss, who eventually showed me this ridiculous forgery.'

'It was on your notepaper,' Laura said. 'Signed by you. He told me.'

'I replaced my letterheads a few months ago. Those at the villa, I only use as scrap now. Paolo of course would not know this. And his imitation of my signature was a poor one, also.'

She blinked. 'Paolo? Why should he do such a thing?'

'He was angry and wished to revenge himself on me—on us both. And, to an extent, he succeeded.'

'But—he didn't care about me—about what had happened.'

'Ah,' Alessio said softly. 'But he cared very much when I knocked him down.'

She gasped. 'You did that? Why?'

'It is not important,' he said in swift dismissal. 'And his own troubles are mounting rapidly. He now works for Signor Manzone, and I am told his wedding is imminent.'

He paused. 'And you would have had to give up your job in any case, *mi amore*,' he added almost casually. 'You cannot live in Italy and work in London. The commuting would be too difficult.'

She lifted her chin. 'I think you must have lost your mind, Count Ramontella. I have no intention of living in Italy.'

He sighed. 'That makes things difficult. I have already had the statue of Diana removed from the garden, and had drawings commissioned so that we can choose a replacement. Also work has begun on the swimming pool to provide a shallower end until you get more confidence.

'And Caio is inconsolable without you. He howls regularly outside your room. At times, I have considered joining him.'

'Caio?' Laura lifted a dazed hand to her forehead. 'How does he feature in all this? He's your aunt's dog. Is she still at the villa?'

'No,' he said with sudden grimness. 'She is not. She left shortly after you, and I have no wish ever to see her again.

'But Caio did not wish to go in the car when she departed, and bit Paolo, who tried to make him. Then my aunt unwisely intervened, and he bit her too. She announced she was going to have him put down immediately, so Emilia quite rightly rescued him and brought him to me.'

He smiled at her. 'But we all know the one he truly loves.'

She said passionately, 'Stop this—stop it, please. I don't understand. I don't know what's happening. Why you're talking like this.'

He said gently, 'If you closed the door, and sat down, I could explain more easily, I think.'

'I don't want you to explain.' Her voice rose almost to a wail. 'I want you to go. To leave me in peace. It's cruel of you to come here like this. Saying these things.'

'Cruel of me to love you, *carissima*? To wish to make you my wife?'

'Why should you wish to do that, *signore*?' She didn't look at him. 'To make it easier for you to go on with your secret affair with that—that woman?'

He came across to her, detached her unresisting fingers from the handle, and closed the door firmly, leaning against it as he looked down at her.

He said quietly, 'Laura, I did a bad thing, and I cannot defend myself. Nor do I wish to hurt you more than I have done, but I must be honest with you if there is to be any hope for us.

'I am not having an affair with Vittoria Montecorvo. I never was. But we had met several times, and she had let me see she was available. After that our paths seemed to cross many times. I think someone must have hinted to my aunt that this was so, and she decided to have me watched.'

Laura stared up at him. 'Your own aunt would do that?'

He said grimly, 'You have met her. My father told me once that since childhood she had enjoyed observing other people's misdemeanours, and discovering their secrets, so that she could use them to gain unpleasant advantages, like a spider keeping dead flies in a web to enjoy later. Oddly, I never thought she would do it to me.

'Unfortunately, her need for a favour coincided with Vittoria's brief incursion into my life, and as I did not wish to cause the breakdown of Vittoria's marriage, or even see her again after my one indiscretion, it seemed I had no choice but to do as I was required, however distasteful.'

He sighed. 'And then I saw you, Laura, and in that moment everything changed.' He tried to smile. 'Do you remember how Petrarch spoke of his Laura? Because you too went from my eyes straight to my heart, *mi adorata*, and I was lost for ever.

Although I did not realise that immediately,' he added candidly. 'Which is why my original intentions were not strictly honourable.'

'No,' she said in a low voice. 'I—realised that.' Lost for ever, she thought. I felt that too.

He took her hand. Held it.

'You see—I am trying to be truthful,' he said quietly. 'I thought that once you belonged to me that everything would be simple. That I would take you away where my aunt could not reach us, and you would never need to know about that devil's bargain I had made with her. I even told myself it no longer mattered, because I wanted you for myself—and myself alone. And that justified everything. Only, I soon found it did not.

'When I realised—that first time—that you were a virgin, it almost destroyed me. Because I knew that you did not deserve to surrender your innocence for such a reason. That I could not— would not do what my aunt demanded, and to hell with the consequences.'

'Yet you did—eventually.' Her voice was small and strained.

'*Mi amore*, as I told you, I took you only because I could not live without you any longer. And I thought you felt the same.' He looked deeply—questioningly—into her eyes. 'Was I so wrong?'

'No,' she admitted, with reluctance. 'You were—right.'

'I was also certain that news of the landslide would keep my aunt at bay for another twenty-four hours, at least,' he went on. 'And that would give me time.'

'Time for what?'

'To tell you everything, *mia bella*, as I knew I must, if there was to be complete honesty between us. So, I drove back from Besavoro to make my confession, and beg absolution before I asked you to become my wife. But, again, it was too late. Once more, I had underestimated my aunt.

'And when you looked at me—spoke to me as you did—I thought I had placed myself beyond your forgiveness for ever. That, hurting you as I had done, I could hope for nothing. That I had ruined both our lives.'

He took her other hand. Drew her gently towards him. 'Is it true, Laura *mia*? Is all hope gone? Or can you try to forgive me, and let me teach you to love me as I think you were beginning to? As I love you?' His voice sank to a whisper. 'Don't send me away, *carissima*, and make us both wretched. Try to forgive—and let me stay with you tonight.'

She said jerkily, 'But you can't—stay. You know that.'

He sighed, and kissed the top of her head. 'Do you think I am totally devoid of decency or patience, *mi amore*? And do you also intend to turn me out of our bed each month when we are married? I don't think so.' He paused. 'I want to sleep with you, Laura. To take care of you. Nothing more. Don't you want that too?'

'Yes, I suppose—I don't know,' she said with a sob. 'But I still can't let you stay. I just—can't.'

'Why not, my angel?' His voice was tender. 'When it is what we both want.'

There were so many sensible and excellent reasons for sending him away for ever, yet she couldn't think of one of them.

Instead, she heard herself say crossly, 'Because I'm wearing really horrible pyjamas.' And then she burst into tears.

When she calmed down, she found that they had somehow moved to the armchair, and she was sitting curled up on Alessio's lap.

'So,' he said, drying her face with his handkerchief. 'If I promise to buy you something prettier in the morning, may I stay?'

'I can hardly throw you out,' she mumbled into his shoulder.

'And will you marry me as soon as it can be arranged?'

She was silent for a moment. 'How can I?' she asked unhappily. 'We hardly know each other. And I don't belong in your world, Alessio. If I hadn't been forced on your attention, you'd never have given me a second glance.'

'You are my world, Laura,' he said softly. 'Without you, there is nothing. Don't you understand that, my dear one?

'I want yours to be the face I see when I wake each morning. I want to see you smile at me across our dining table. I want to teach you to swim so well that you will dive off the side of our boat with me. I want to be with you when our children are born, and to love you and protect you as long as we both live.'

She said with a little gasp, 'Oh, Alessio—I love you too, so very much. I wanted to stop—I tried hard to—and to hate you— but I—I couldn't. And I've been so lonely—and so terribly unhappy. And I'd marry you tomorrow, if it was possible. Only it isn't. I—I can't just disappear to Italy with you.' Her hands twisted together. 'There's my family to consider. That's why I needed a decent job, so that I could help my mother with my brother's education.'

She swallowed. 'I only agreed to help Paolo because he was going to pay me, but then he didn't.'

'Good,' he said. 'Because I have no wish for you to be obliged to such a creature.' He stroked her hair back from her face. '*Mia cara*, I am going to be your husband, and I shall look after your mother and brother as if they were my own. How could you doubt it?'

'But I don't know that she'll accept that.' Laura's face was troubled. 'She has her fair share of pride.'

'We will go and see her tomorrow,' he said. 'After all, I have to ask her permission to marry you. And I will talk to her— persuade her that it will be my pleasure to care for you all. I am sure she will see reason.'

Laura raised her head from his shoulder, and looked at him in quiet fascination. 'I bet she will at that,' she said, her lips twitching in sudden amusement. 'Are you always going to expect your own way, *signore*, once we're married?'

'Of course,' he said softly, and wickedly, drawing her close again. 'But I will always try to ensure that your way and mine are the same, my sweet one.'

He bent his head and kissed her, his mouth moving on hers with a gentle, almost reverent restraint that made her want to cry again. But she didn't. And they held each other, and kissed again, whispering the words that lovers used. And were happy.

Much later, Laura was sitting up in bed finishing the *tisana* he had made her from Gaynor's herb tea when Alessio came back from the bathroom, her refilled hot-water bottle dangling from his lean fingers.

She looked at him with real compunction. 'Darling, I'm sorry. It's all so—unromantic.'

'Then maybe we should put romance aside for a while,' he said gently. 'And think only about love.'

He undressed quickly, and slid into the narrow bed behind her, wrapping her warmly and closely in his arms. Making her feel relaxed and at peace for the first time in weeks.

She was almost asleep when a thought came to her. 'Alessio,' she whispered drowsily. 'Will you promise me one more thing?'

'Anything, *mia bella*.'

She smiled in the darkness. 'Will you still teach me to play strip poker?'

'It might be arranged,' he returned softly. 'On some winter night, when we are safely married, and the fire is warm and the candles are lit.' He paused. 'But I must warn you, *carissima*. I cheat.'

Laura turned her head and aimed a sleepy kiss at the corner of his mouth.

'So do I, my darling,' she murmured in deep contentment. 'So do I.'

IN THE
MILLIONAIRE'S
POSSESSION

CHAPTER ONE

HELEN had never been so nervous in her life.

The starkness of her surroundings did not help, of course.

This was, after all, the London headquarters of Restauration International—an organisation supposedly devoted to historical conservation projects.

She'd expected panelled walls hung with works of art, antique furniture, and possibly a Persian carpet. Something with the grace and charm of the past.

Instead she'd been greeted by a receptionist with attitude, and dumped in this glass and chrome box with only a water cooler for company as the long, slow nerve-racking minutes passed.

And although she had to admit that the arrangement of canvas slats that formed her chair was surprisingly comfortable, it couldn't make her feel at ease mentally.

But then, in this life or death situation, what could?

Her hands tightened on the handle of her briefcase as she ran a silent check on the points she needed to make once she came face to face with the directors of Restauration International.

They're my last hope now, she thought. Every other source has dried up. So I need to get it right.

Suddenly restless, she walked across to the cooler and filled a paper cup. As she moved, she saw the security camera become activated, and repressed a grimace at the idea that unseen eyes at some control point might be watching her.

'Look businesslike,' her friend Lottie had advised her. 'Get out of those eternal jeans and put on a skirt. Remember you're making a presentation, not mucking out the ruins. You've had a lot of help over this,' she added with mock sternness. 'So don't blow it.'

And Lottie was quite right, Helen thought soberly. So many people had rallied round with quite amazing kindness. Checking the draft of her written report and making suggestions. Providing quick facelifts to the outside buildings and grounds with painting and weeding parties, in case the committee came to see the place for themselves. And even offering films of various events held at Monteagle over the past couple of years to use in the video, itself the result of a favour that had been called in by Lottie.

But now, at last, it was all down to her. She'd taken her friend's advice and put on her one good grey skirt, teaming it with a demure white cotton blouse and her elderly black blazer. Hopefully they wouldn't look too closely and see the shabbiness of her attire, she thought.

Her light brown hair—which badly needed cutting and shaping, when she had the time and the money—had been drawn back severely from her face and confined at the nape of her neck by a black ribbon bow, and there were small silver studs in the lobes of her ears.

Not much there for the hidden spectator to criticise, she thought, resisting the impulse to raise her cup in salute.

She made the trip back to her chair look deliberately casual, as if she didn't have a care in the world and there was nothing much riding on the coming interview.

Only my entire life, she thought, as her taut throat accepted the cool water. Only everything I care most about in the world now at the mercy of strangers.

Apart from Nigel, of course, she amended hastily.

Somehow I have to convince them that Monteagle is worth saving. That I'm not going to give up the struggle like my father and Grandpa and watch the place slide into total oblivion. Or, worse still, into the hands of Trevor Newson.

She shuddered at the memory of the fleshy, complacent face awaiting with a smile the victory that he thought was inevitable. Counting the days until he could turn Monteagle into the gross medieval theme park he'd set his heart on.

It had been those plans, as outlined to her, that had sent her on this last desperate quest to find the money for the house's urgently needed repairs.

All the other organisations that she'd doggedly approached had rejected her pleas for a grant on the grounds that Monteagle was too small, too unimportant, and too far off the normal tourist trails.

'Which is why it needs me,' Trevor Newson had told her. 'Jousting on the lawns, pig roasts, banqueting in the great hall…' His eyes glistened. 'That'll put it on the map, all right. The coach parties will flock here, and so will foreign tourists once I get it on the internet. And don't keep me waiting too long for your answer,' he added. 'Or the price I'm offering will start to go down.'

'You need not wait at all,' Helen said with icy civility. 'The answer is no, Mr Newson.'

'And now you're being hasty,' he chided in the patronising tone she so resented. 'After all, what choice have you got? The place is falling down around you, and it's common knowledge your father and grandfather left little but debts when they died.'

He ticked off on his fingers. 'You've got the rent from the grazing land and a bit of income from the handful of visitors who come when you open the place up each summer, and that won't get you far. In fact, it's a wonder you've hung on as long as you have.'

He gave a pitying shake of the head. 'You need to sell, my dear. And if you really can't bear to leave and move away I might even be able to offer you some work. These tournaments used to have a Queen of Love and Beauty presiding over them, apparently, and you're a good-looking girl.' He leered at her. 'I can just see you, properly made-up, in some low-cut medieval dress.'

'It's a tempting offer,' Helen said, controlling her temper by a whisker. 'But I'm afraid the answer's still no.'

'Ghastly old lech,' Lottie had commented. 'Better not tell Nigel, or he might deck him.' She'd paused. 'Is he going with you to confront this committee?'

'No.' Helen had resolutely concealed her disappointment.

'He's incredibly busy at work right now. Anyway,' she'd added, 'I'm a grown up girl. I can cope.'

As Nigel himself had said, she recalled with a pang. And maybe she'd simply taken too much for granted in counting on his support today. But they'd been seeing each other for a long time now, and everyone in the area presumed that he'd be fighting at her side in the battle to save Monteagle.

In fact, as Helen admitted to no one but herself, Nigel had been pretty lukewarm about her struggles to retain her home. He wasn't a poor man by any means—he worked in a merchant bank, and had inherited money from his grandmother as well— but he'd never offered any practical form of help.

It was something they would really need to discuss—once she got the grant. Because she was determined to be self-sufficient, and, while she drew the line at Mr Newson's theme park, she had several other schemes in mind to boost the house's earning power.

Although lately they hadn't had the opportunity to talk about very much at all, she realised with a faint frown. But that was probably her fault in the main. Nigel's work had kept him confined to London recently, but she'd been so totally engrossed in preparing her case for the committee that she'd barely missed him.

What a thing to admit about the man you were going to marry!

But all that was going to change, she vowed remorsefully. Once today was over, win or lose, it was going to be permanent commitment from now on. Everything he'd ever asked from her. Including *that*.

She knew she was probably being an old-fashioned idiot, and most of her contemporaries would laugh if they knew, but she'd always veered away from the idea of sex before marriage.

Not that she was scared of surrender, she thought defensively, or unsure of her own feelings for Nigel. It was just that when she stood with him in the village church to make her vows she wanted him to know that she was his alone, and that her white dress meant something.

On a more practical level, it had never seemed to be quite the right moment, either.

Never the time, the place, and the loved one altogether, she thought, grimacing inwardly. But she couldn't expect Nigel to be patient for ever, not when they belonged together. So why hold back any longer?

She was startled out of her reverie by the sudden opening of the door. Helen got hurriedly to her feet, to be confronted by a blonde girl, tall and slim, with endless legs, and wearing a smart black suit. She gave Helen a swift formal smile while her eyes swept her with faint disparagement.

'Miss Frayne? Will you come with me, please? The committee is waiting for you.'

'And I've been waiting for the committee,' Helen told her coolly.

She was led down a long narrow corridor, with walls plastered in a Greek key pattern. It made her feel slightly giddy, and she wondered if this was a deliberate ploy.

Her companion flung open the door at the far end. 'Miss Frayne,' she announced, and stood back to allow Helen to precede her into the room.

More concrete, thought Helen, taking a swift look around. More metal, more glass. And seven men standing at an oblong table, acknowledging her presence with polite inclinations of their heads.

'Please, Miss Frayne, sit. Be comfortable.' The speaker, clearly the chairman, was opposite her. He was a bearded man with grey hair and glasses, who looked Scandinavian.

Helen sank down on to a high-backed affair of leather and steel, clutching her briefcase on her lap while they all took their places.

They looked like clones of each other, she thought, in their neat dark suits and discreetly patterned ties, sitting bolt upright round the table. Except for one, she realised. The man casually lounging in the seat to the right of the chairman.

He was younger than his colleagues—early to mid-thirties, Helen judged—with an untidy mane of black hair and a swarthy face that no one would ever describe as handsome. He had a beak of a nose, and a thin-lipped, insolent mouth, while eyes, dark and impenetrable as the night, studied her from under heavy lids.

Unlike the rest of the buttoned-up committee members, he looked as if he'd just crawled out of bed and thrown on the clothing that was nearest to hand. Moreover, his tie had been pulled loose and the top of his shirt left undone.

He had the appearance of someone who'd strayed in off the street by mistake, she thought critically.

And saw his mouth twist into a faint grin, as if he'd divined what she was thinking and found it amusing.

Helen felt a kind of embarrassed resentment at being so transparent. This was not how she'd planned to begin at all. She gave him a cold look, and saw his smile widen in sensuous, delighted appreciation.

Making her realise, for the first time in her life, that a man did not have to be conventionally handsome to blaze charm and a lethal brand of sexual attraction.

Helen felt as if she'd been suddenly subjected to a force field of male charisma, and she resented it. And the fact that he had beautiful teeth did nothing to endear him to her either.

'Be comfortable,' the chairman had said.

My God, she thought. What a hope. Because she'd never felt more awkward in her life. Or so scared.

She took a deep breath and transferred her attention deliberately to the chairman, trying to concentrate as he congratulated her on the depth and lucidity of her original application for a grant, and on the additional material she'd supplied to back up her claim.

They all had their folders open, she saw, except one. And no prizes for guessing which of them it was, she thought indignantly. But at least she wasn't the object of his attention any longer. Instead, her swift sideways glance told her, he seemed to be staring abstractedly into space, as if he was miles away.

If only, thought Helen, steadying her flurried breathing. And, anyway, why serve on the committee if he wasn't prepared to contribute to its work?

He didn't even react when she produced the videotape. 'I hope this will give you some idea of the use Monteagle has been put to in the recent past,' she said. 'I intend to widen the scope of activities in future—even have the house licensed for weddings.'

There were murmurs of polite interest and approval, and she began to relax a little—only to realise that he was staring at her once again, his eyes travelling slowly over her face and down, she realised furiously, to the swell of her breasts against the thin blouse. She tried to behave as if she was unconscious of his scrutiny, but felt the betrayal of warm blood invading her face. Finally, to her relief, the dark gaze descended to her small bare hands, clasped tensely on the table in front of her.

'You plan to marry there yourself, perhaps, *mademoiselle*?' He had a low, resonant voice which was not unattractive, she admitted unwillingly, still smarting from the overt sensuality of his regard. And his English was excellent, in spite of his French accent.

She wondered how he'd taken the section of her report which stated that the fortified part of Monteagle had been built at the time of the Hundred Years War, and that the Black Prince, France's most feared enemy, had often stayed there.

Now she lifted her chin and met his enquiring gaze with a flash of her long-lashed hazel eyes, wishing at the same time that she and Nigel were officially engaged and she had a ring to wear.

'Yes,' she said. 'As a matter of fact, I do, *monsieur*. I thought I might even be the first one,' she added with a flash of inspiration.

Of course she hadn't discussed this with Nigel, she reminded herself guiltily, but she didn't see what objection he could have. And it would make the most wonderful setting—besides providing useful publicity at the same time.

'But how romantic,' he murmured, and relapsed into his reverie again.

After that questions from the other committee members came thick and fast, asking her to explain or expand further on some of the points she'd made in her application. Clearly they'd all read the file, she thought hopefully, and seemed genuinely interested in what she had to say.

The door opened to admit the tall blonde, bringing coffee on a trolley, and Helen was glad to see there was mineral water as well. This interview was proving just as much of an ordeal as she'd expected, and her mouth was dry again.

When the blonde withdrew, the Frenchman reached for his folder and extracted a sheet of paper.

'This is not your first application for financial assistance towards the repair and renovation of Monteagle House, *mademoiselle*. Is this an accurate list of the organisations you have previously approached?'

Helen bit her lip as she scanned down the column of names. 'Yes, it is.'

'But none of your efforts were successful?' The low voice pressed her.

'No,' she admitted stonily, aware that her creamy skin had warmed.

'So how did you become aware of us?'

'A friend of mine found you on the internet. She said you seemed to be interested in smaller projects. So—I thought I would try.'

'Because you were becoming desperate.' It was a statement, not a question.

'Yes.' Helen looked at him defiantly. Her consciousness of her surroundings seemed to have contracted—intensified. There might just have been the two of them in the room, locked in confrontation. 'By this stage I will explore any avenue that presents itself. I will not allow Monteagle to become derelict, and I'll do whatever it takes to save it.'

There was a silence, then he produced another sheet of paper. 'The surveyor's report that you have included in your submission is twenty years old.'

'Yes,' she said. 'I felt that the recommendations made then still apply. Although the costs have obviously risen.'

'Twenty years is a long time, *mademoiselle*. Having commissioned such a report, why did your family not carry out the necessary works at that time?'

Helen's flush deepened. 'My grandfather had every intention of doing so, but he was overtaken by events.'

'Can you explain further?' the smooth voice probed.

She took a breath, hating the admission she was being forced to make. 'There was a crisis in the insurance industry. My grandfather was a Lloyds' name in those days, and the calls that were made on him brought us all to the edge of ruin. He even thought Monteagle might have to be sold.'

'That is still a possibility, of course,' her adversary said gently, and paused. 'Is it not true that you have received a most generous offer for the entire estate from a Monsieur Trevor Newson? An offer that would halt the disintegration of the house, *mademoiselle*, and in addition restore your own finances? Would that not be better than having to beg your way round every committee and trust? And deal with constant rejection?'

'I find Mr Newson's plans for the estate totally unacceptable,' Helen said curtly. 'I'm a Frayne, and I won't allow the place that has been our home for centuries to be trashed in the way he proposes. I refuse to give up.' She leaned forward, her voice shaking with sudden intensity. 'I'll find the money somehow, and I'll do anything to get it.'

'Anything?' The dark brows lifted mockingly. 'You are a most determined champion of your cause.'

'I have to be.' Helen flung back her head. 'And if achieving my aim includes begging, then so be it. Monteagle is well worth the sacrifice.'

And then, as if a wire had snapped, parting them, it was over. The Frenchman was leaning back in his chair and the chairman was rising to his feet.

'It has been a pleasure to meet you, Miss Frayne, and we shall consider your proposals with great care—including the additional information and material you have supplied.' He picked up the video, giving her a warm smile. 'We hope to come to our decision by the end of the month.'

'I'm grateful to you for seeing me,' Helen said formally, and got herself out of the room without once glancing in the direction of her interrogator.

In the corridor, she paused, a hand pressed to her side as if she had been running in some uphill race.

What in hell had been going on there? she asked herself dazedly. Were they running some good cop/bad cop routine, where the upright members of the committee softened her up with their kindly interest so that their resident thug could move in for the kill?

Up to then it had been going quite well, she thought anxiously, or she'd believed it had. But her audience might not appreciate being regarded as the very last resort at the end of a long list of them, as he'd suggested.

God, but he'd been loathsome in every respect, she thought vengefully as she made her way back to the reception area. And to hell with his charm and sex appeal.

Quite apart from anything else, she knew now what it was like to be mentally undressed, and it was a technique that she did not appreciate. In fact, she thought furiously, it was probably a form of sexual harassment—not that anyone whose spiritual home was obviously the Stone Age would have heard of such a thing, or even care.

All the same, she found herself wondering who he was exactly and how much influence he actually wielded in Restauration International. Well, there was one quick way to find out.

The blonde was in the foyer, chatting to the receptionist. They both glanced up with brief formal smiles as Helen approached.

She said coolly, 'Please may I have a copy of the organisation's introduction pack?'

Brows rose, and they exchanged glances. The blonde said, 'I think you'll find you were sent one following your original enquiry, Miss Frayne.'

'Indeed I was,' Helen agreed. 'But unfortunately it's at home, and there are a few details I need to check.' She paused. 'So—if it's not too much trouble…?'

There was another exchange of glances, then the receptionist

opened with ill grace a drawer in her large desk, and took out
a plastic-encased folder, which she handed to Helen.

'One per application is the norm, Miss Frayne,' she said.
'Please look after it.'

'I shall treasure it,' Helen assured her. As she moved to put
the pack in her briefcase, she was suddenly aware of footsteps
crossing the foyer behind her. And at the same time, as if some
switch had been pulled, the haughty stares from the other two
girls vanished, to be replaced by smiles so sweet that they were
almost simpering.

Helen felt as if icy fingers were tracing a path down her
spine as instinct told her who had come to join them.

She turned slowly to face him, schooling her expression to
indifference.

'Making sure I leave the building, *monsieur*?'

'No, merely going to my own next appointment,
mademoiselle.' His smile mocked her quite openly. He glanced
at the pack she was still holding. 'And my name is Delaroche,'
he added softly. 'Marc Delaroche. As I would have told you
earlier, had you asked.'

He watched with undisguised appreciation as Helen struggled against an urge to hurl the pack at his head, then made
her a slight bow as upbringing triumphed over instinct and she
replaced it on the desk.

She said icily, 'I merely wanted something to read on the
train. But I can always buy a paper.'

'But of course.' He was using that smile again, but this time
she was braced against its impact.

'*A bientôt,*' he added, and went, with a wave to the other
two, who were still gazing at him in a kind of dumb entrance-
ment.

'See you soon', Monsieur Delaroche? Helen asked silently
after his retreating back. Is that what you just said to me? She
drew a deep breath. My God, not if I see you first.

She was disturbingly aware of that same brief shiver of ice
along her nerve-endings. As if in some strange way she was
being warned.

*   *   *

Marc Delaroche had said he had an appointment, but all the same Helen was thankful to find him nowhere in sight when she got outside the building.

She'd thought her nervousness would dissipate now that the interview was over, but she was wrong. She felt lost, somehow, and ridiculously scared. Perhaps it was just the noise and dirt of London that was upsetting her, she thought, wondering how Nigel could relish working here amid all this uproar.

But at least she could seize the opportunity of seeing him while she was here, she told herself, producing her mobile phone. Before she got her train back to the peace of the countryside and Monteagle.

He answered at once, but he was clearly not alone because she could hear voices and laughter in the background, and the clink of glasses.

'Helen?' He sounded astonished. 'Where are you ringing from?'

'Groverton Street,' she said. 'It isn't too far from where you work.' She paused. 'I thought maybe you'd buy me lunch.'

'Lunch?' he echoed. 'I don't think I can. I'm a bit tied up. You should have told me in advance you were coming up today, and I'd have made sure I was free.'

'But I did tell you,' Helen said, trying to stifle her disappointment. 'I've just had my interview with Restauration International—remember?'

'Oh, God,' he said. 'Yes, of course. I've been so busy it completely slipped my mind.' He paused. 'How did it go anyway?'

'Pretty well, I think—I hope.' Helen tried to dismiss the thought of Marc Delaroche from her mind.

One man, she thought. One dissenting voice. What harm could he really do?

'They seemed interested,' she added. 'Sympathetic—for the most part. And they said I'd know by the end of the month, so I've less than ten days to wait.'

'Well, I'll keep my fingers crossed for you,' Nigel said. 'And maybe—under the circumstances—I could manage lunch after all. Celebrate a little. It's certainly the most hopeful result you've had.' He paused again. 'I'll need to pull a few strings, change things around a little, but it should be all right. Meet me at the Martinique at one clock.'

'But I don't know where it is,' she protested.

'But the cab driver will,' he said with a touch of exasperation. 'It's new, and pretty trendy. Everyone's going there.'

'Then will we get a table?' Helen asked, wondering, troubled, whether she could afford the price of a taxi.

He sighed. 'Helen, you're so naïve. The bank has a standing reservation there. It's not a problem. Now, I must go. See you later.'

She switched off her phone and replaced it slowly in her bag. It sounded rather as if Nigel had gone to this Martinique place already. But then why shouldn't he? she reminded herself impatiently. Entertaining the bank's clients at smart restaurants was part of his job. It was all part of the world he inhabited, along with platinum cards, endless taxis, and first-class tickets everywhere.

Yet she'd travelled up on a cheap day return, needed to count her pennies, and most of her entertaining involved cheese on toast or pasta, with a bottle of cheap plonk shared with Lottie or another girlfriend.

Nigel belonged to a different world, she thought with a pang, and it would require a quantum leap on her part to join him there.

But I can do it, she told herself, unfastening the constriction of the black ribbon bow and shaking her hair loose almost defiantly. I can do anything—even save Monteagle. And nothing's going to stop me.

Her moment of euphoria was brought to a halt by the realisation that lack of funds might well prevent her from completing even the minor mission of reaching the restaurant to meet Nigel.

However, with the help of her *A to Z* and a copy of *Time Out*, she discovered that the Martinique was just over a mile away. Easy walking distance, she decided, setting off at a brisk pace.

She found it without difficulty, although the search had left her hot and thirsty.

Its smart black and white awning extended over the pavement, shading terracotta pots of evergreens. Helen took a deep breath and walked in. She found herself in a small reception area, being given a questioning look by a young man behind a desk.

'*Mademoiselle* has a reservation?'

'Well, not exactly—' she began, and was interrupted by an immediate shake of the head.

'I regret that we are fully booked. Perhaps another day we can have the pleasure of serving *mademoiselle*.'

She said quickly, 'I'm joining someone—a Mr Nigel Hartley.'

He gave her a surprised look, then glanced at the large book in front of him. 'Yes, he has a table at one o clock, but he has not yet arrived.' He paused. 'Would you like to enjoy a drink at the bar? Or be seated to wait for him.'

'I'd like to sit down, please.'

'*D'accord.*' He came from behind the desk. 'May I take your jacket?' He indicated the blazer she was carrying over her arm.

'Oh—no. No, thank you,' Helen said, remembering with acute embarrassment that the lining was slightly torn.

'Then please follow me.' He opened a door, and what seemed like a wall of sound came to meet her, so that she almost flinched.

Nigel had not exaggerated the restaurant's popularity, she thought. She found herself in a large bright room, with windows on two sides and more tables crammed into the rest of it than she would have believed possible. Every table seemed to be occupied, and the noise was intense, but she squeezed through the sea of white linen, crystal and silver after her guide and discovered there were a few remaining inches of space in one corner.

She sank down thankfully on to one of the high-backed wooden chairs, wishing that it were possible to kick off her shoes.

'May I bring something for *mademoiselle*?' The young man hovered.

'Just some still water, please,' she returned.

She had no doubt that the Martinique was a trendy place—somewhere to see and be seen—but she wished Nigel had chosen something quieter. She also wished very much that it wasn't a French restaurant either. Too reminiscent, she thought, of her recent interrogation.

She wanted to talk to Nigel, but the kind of private conversation she had in mind could hardly be conducted at the tops of their voices.

He clearly thought she'd enjoy a taste of the high life, she decided ruefully, and she must be careful not to give him a hint of her disappointment at his choice.

Besides, they would have the rest of their lives to talk.

He was already ten minutes late, she realised, and was just beginning to feel self-conscious about sitting on her own when a waiter appeared with a bottle of mineral water and a tumbler containing ice cubes. The tray also held a tall slender glass filled with a rich pink liquid, fizzing gently.

'I'm afraid I didn't order this,' Helen protested, as he placed it in front of her. 'What is it?'

'Kir Royale, *mademoiselle*—champagne and *cassis*—and it comes with the compliments of *monsieur*.'

'Oh,' she said with relief. Nigel must have phoned through the order, she thought, as a peace offering for his tardiness. It was the kind of caring gesture she should have expected, and it made her feel better—happier about the situation as a whole.

She drank some water to refresh her mouth, then sipped the kir slowly, enjoying the faint fragrance of the blackcurrant and the sheer lift of the wine.

But she couldn't make it last for ever, and by the time she'd drained the glass Nigel still hadn't arrived. She was beginning to get nervous and irritated in equal measure.

She beckoned to the waiter. 'Has there been any further message from *monsieur* to say he's been delayed?' she asked. 'Because, if not, I'd like another kir.'

He looked bewildered. 'There is no delay, *mademoiselle*. *Monsieur* is here at this moment, having lunch. Shall I consult him on your behalf?'

Helen stared at him. 'He's *here*? You must be mistaken.'

'No, *mademoiselle*. See—there by the window.'

Helen looked, and what she saw made her throat close in shock. It was Marc Delaroche, she realised numbly, seated at a table with two other men. He was listening to what they were saying, but, as if he instantly sensed Helen focussing on him, he glanced round and met her horrified gaze. He inclined his head in acknowledgement, then reached for his own glass, lifting it in a swift and silent toast.

She disengaged from him instantly, flushed and mortified. She said, 'You mean he—that person—sent me this drink?' She took a deep breath, forcing herself back to a semblance of composure, even though her heart was racing unevenly. 'I—I didn't know that. And I certainly wouldn't dream of having another. In fact, perhaps you'd bring me the bill for this one, plus the water, and I'll just—leave.'

'But you have not yet had lunch,' the waiter protested. 'And besides, here comes Monsieur Hartley.'

And sure enough it was Nigel, striding across the restaurant as if conducting a personal parting of the Red Sea, tall, blond and immaculate, in his dark blue pinstripe and exquisitely knotted silk tie.

'So there you are,' he greeted her.

'It's where I've been for the past half hour,' Helen told him evenly. 'What happened?'

'Well, I warned you I was busy.' He dropped a cursory kiss on her cheek as he passed. 'Menus, please, Gaspard. I'm pushed for time today. In fact, I won't bother with the *carte*. I'll just have steak, medium rare, with a mixed salad.'

'Then I'll have the same,' Helen said. 'I wouldn't want to keep you waiting.'

'Fine.' He either ignored or didn't notice the irony in her tone. 'And a bottle of house red, Gaspard. Quick as you can. Plus a gin and tonic.' He glanced at Helen. 'Do you want a drink, sweetie?'

'I've already had one,' she said. 'Kir Royale, as a matter of fact.'

His lips thinned a little. 'Rather a new departure for you, isn't it? Did the waiter talk you into it?'

'No,' she said. 'But don't worry. One is more than enough.'
She was ashamed to hear how acerbic she sounded, and it was
all the fault of that—that *creature* across the room. But she
was sharing precious time with the man she loved, and she
wouldn't allow it to be spoiled by anyone or anything.

She made herself smile at Nigel, and put her hand on his.
'It's so great to see you,' she said gently. 'Do you realise how
long it's been?'

He sighed. 'I know, but life at work is so hectic just now I
hardly have any time to spare.'

'Your parents must miss you too.'

He shrugged. 'They're far too busy planning Dad's retirement and giving the house a pre-sale facelift to worry about
me.' He shot her a swift glance. 'You did know they're moving
to Portugal in the near future?'

'Selling Oaktree House?' Helen said slowly. 'I had no idea.'
She gave him a blank look. 'But how will you manage? It's
your home.'

'Off and on for the past ten years, yes,' Nigel said with a
touch of impatience. 'But my life's in London now. I'm going
to stop renting and look for somewhere to buy. Ah, my drink
at last. My God, I could do with it. I've had a hell of a morning.' And he launched himself into a description of its vicis-
situdes which was still going strong when their food arrived.

Not that Helen was particularly hungry. Her appetite, such
as it was, seemed to have suddenly dissipated. Nor was she
giving her full attention to the vagaries of the financial markets
and the irresponsible attitude of certain nameless clients, as
outlined by Nigel. Her mind was on another track altogether.

Something had happened, she thought numbly. Some fun-
damental shift had taken place and she hadn't noticed.

Well, she was totally focussed now, because this involved
her life too. She'd assumed that Nigel would live with her at
Monteagle once they were married, and commute to London.
After all, she couldn't move away, use Monteagle as a weekend
home. Surely he realised that.

But there was no way they could talk about it now. Not with

Nigel glancing at his watch every couple of minutes as he rapidly forked up his steak.

Eventually she broke into his monologue. 'Nigel—this weekend, we have to talk. Can you come over—spend the day with me on Sunday?'

'Not this weekend, I'm afraid. It's the chairman's birthday, and he's celebrating with a weekend party at his place in Sussex, so duty calls.' His smile was swift and light. 'And now I have to dash. I have a two-thirty meeting. The bill goes straight to my office, so order yourself a pudding if you want, darling, and coffee. See you later.' He blew her a kiss, and was gone.

Once again she was sitting alone, she thought as she pushed her plate away. A fact that would doubtless not be lost on her adversary across the room. She risked a lightning glance from under her lashes, and realised with a surge of relief that his table was empty and being cleared. At least he hadn't witnessed her cavalier treatment at Nigel's hands. Nor would she have to grit her teeth and thank him for that bloody drink. With luck, she would never have to set eyes on him again. End of story.

She'd wanted this to be a great day in her life, she thought with a silent sigh, but since she'd first set eyes on Marc Delaroche it seemed to have been downhill all the way.

And now she had better go and catch her train. She was just reaching for her bag when Gaspard arrived, bearing a tray which he placed in front of her with a flourish.

'There must be some mistake,' Helen protested, watching him unload a cafetière, cups, saucers, two glasses and a bottle of armagnac. 'I didn't order any of this.'

'But I did,' Marc Delaroche said softly. 'Because you look as if you need it. So do not refuse me, *ma belle, je vous en prie.*'

And before she could utter any kind of protest, he took the seat opposite her, so recently vacated by Nigel, and smiled into her startled eyes.

CHAPTER TWO

'I THOUGHT you'd gone.' The words were out before she could stop herself, implying that she took even a remote interest in his actions.

'I was merely bidding *au revoir* to my friends.' He filled her cup from the cafetière. 'Before returning to offer you a *digestif.*' He poured a judicious amount of armagnac into each crystal bowl, and pushed one towards her. 'Something your companion should consider, perhaps,' he added meditatively. 'If he continues to rush through his meals at such a rate he will have an ulcer before he is forty.'

'Thank you.' Helen lifted her chin. 'I'll be sure to pass your warning on to him.'

'I intended it for you,' he said. 'I presume he is the man you plan to marry at Monteagle with such panache?' He slanted a smile at her. 'After all, it is a wife's duty to look after the physical well-being of her husband—in every way. Don't you think so?'

'You don't want to know what I think.' Helen bit her lip. 'You really are some kind of dinosaur.'

His smile widened. 'And a man with a ruined digestion is an even more savage beast, believe me,' he told her softly. 'Just as a beautiful girl left alone in a restaurant is an offence against nature.' He raised his glass. *Salut.*'

'Oh, spare me.' Helen gritted her teeth. 'I don't need your compliments—or your company.'

'Perhaps not,' he said. 'But you require my vote on the committee, so maybe you should force yourself to be civil for this short time, and drink with me.'

Smouldering, Helen drank some of her coffee. 'What made you choose this restaurant particularly?' she asked, after a loaded pause.

His brows lifted mockingly. 'You suspect some sinister motive? That I am following you, perhaps?' He shook his head. 'You are wrong. I was invited here by my companions—who have a financial interest in the place and wished my opinion. Also I arrived first, remember, so I could accuse you of stalking me.'

Helen stiffened. 'That, of course, is just *so* likely.' Her tone bit.

'No,' he returned coolly. 'To my infinite regret, it is not likely at all.'

Helen felt her throat muscles tighten warily. 'Why are you doing this? Buying me drinks—forcing your company on me?'

He shrugged. 'Because I wished to encounter you when you were more relaxed. When you had—let your hair down, as they say.' He leaned back in his chair. 'It looks much better loose, so why scrape it back in that unbecoming way?'

'I wanted to look businesslike for the interview,' she returned coldly. 'Not as if I was trading on my gender.'

'Put like that,' he said, 'I find it unappealing too.'

'So why are you ignoring my obvious wish to keep my distance?'

He lifted his glass, studying the colour of the armagnac. He said, 'Your fiancé arrived late and left early. Perhaps I am merely trying to compensate for his lack of attention.'

She bit her lip. 'How dare you criticise him? You know nothing at all about him. He happens to be working very hard for our future together—and I don't feel neglected in any way,' she added defiantly.

'I am relieved to hear it, *ma mie*,' he drawled. 'I feared for your sake that his performance in bed might be conducted at the same speed as your lunch dates.'

She stared at him, shocked into a sudden blush that reached the roots of her hair.

Her voice shook. 'You have no right to talk to me like that— to speculate about my private relationships in that—disgusting way. You should be ashamed of yourself.'

He looked back at her without a glimmer of repentance. 'It was prompted solely by my concern for your happiness, I assure you.'

She pushed back her chair and got to her feet, fumbling for her jacket. She said jerkily, 'When I get the money to restore Monteagle I shall fill the world with my joy, *monsieur*. And that is the only affair of mine in which you have the right to probe. Goodbye.'

She walked past him and out of the restaurant, her face still burning but her head held proudly.

It was only when she was outside, heading for the tube station, that she realised just how afraid she'd been that he would follow her—stop her from leaving in some unspecified way.

But of course he had not done so.

He's just a predator, she thought, looking for potential prey and testing their weaknesses. He saw I was alone, and possibly vulnerable, so he moved in. That's all that happened.

Or was it?

If only I hadn't blushed, she castigated herself. I just hope he interprets it as anger, not embarrassment.

Because she couldn't bear him to know that she didn't have a clue what Nigel or any other man was like in bed. And she'd certainly never been openly challenged on the subject before—especially by a man who was also a complete stranger.

She knew what happened physically, of course. She wasn't that much of a fool or an innocent. But she didn't know what to expect emotionally.

She hoped that loving Nigel would be enough, and that he would teach her the rest. It was quite some time since he'd made a serious attempt to get her into bed, she thought remorsefully. But she couldn't and wouldn't delay the moment any longer. It was long overdue.

Perhaps it was the fear of rejection which had kept him away so often lately. She'd been so wrapped up in her own life and its worries that she hadn't truly considered his feelings.

I've just been totally insensitive, she thought wearily. And the tragedy is that it took someone like Marc Delaroche to make me see it.

But from now on everything's going to be different, she promised herself firmly.

*　　*　　*

I still can't believe you're back already,' Lottie said, as she put a shepherd's pie in the oven. 'Your phone call gave me a real jolt. I wasn't expecting you until tomorrow at the earliest.' She threw Helen a searching glance over her shoulder. 'Didn't you meet up with Nigel?'

'Oh, yes,' Helen said brightly. 'We had an amazing lunch in one of the newest restaurants.'

'Lunch, eh?' Lottie pursed her lips. 'Now, I had you down for a romantic dinner *à deux*, then back to his place for a night of seething passion. Supper with me is a pretty dull alternative.'

Helen smiled at her. 'Honey, nothing involving you is ever dull. And, to be honest, I couldn't wait to get out of London.'

Lottie gave her a careful look as she sat down at the kitchen table and began to string beans. 'Your interview with the committee didn't go so well?'

Helen sighed. 'I honestly don't know. Most of them seemed pleasant and interested, but perhaps they were humouring me.'

'And is this Marc Delaroche guy that you phoned me about included in the 'pleasant and interested' category?' Lottie enquired.

'No,' Helen returned, teeth gritted. 'He is not.'

'How did I guess?' Lottie said wryly. 'Anyway, following your somewhat emotional request from the station, I looked him up on the net.'

'And he was there?'

'Oh, yes,' Lottie nodded. 'And he's into buildings.'

'An architect?' Helen asked, surprised.

'Not exactly. He's the chairman of Fabrication Roche, a company that makes industrial buildings—instant factories from kits, cheap and ultra-efficient, especially in developing countries. The company's won awards for the designs, and they've made him a multimillionaire.'

'Then what the hell is someone from that kind of background doing on a committee that deals with heritage projects?' Helen shook her head. 'It makes no sense.'

'Except he must know about costing,' Lottie pointed out

practically. 'And applying modern technology to restoration work. The others deal with aesthetics. He looks at the bottom line.'

Helen's lips tightened. 'Well, I hope the ghastly modern eyesore we met in today wasn't a sample of his handiwork.'

'I wouldn't know about that.' Lottie grinned at her. 'But I've printed everything off for you to read at your leisure.' She paused. 'No photograph of him, I'm afraid.'

'It doesn't matter,' Helen said quietly. 'I already know what he looks like.'

And I know the way he looked at me, she thought, remembering her sense of helpless outrage as his gaze had moved over her body. And that glinting smile in his eyes...

She swallowed, clearing the image determinedly from her mind. 'But thanks for doing that, Lottie. It's always best to—know your enemy.'

'Even better not to have an enemy in the first place,' Lottie retorted, rinsing the beans in a colander. 'Especially one with his kind of money.' She went to the dresser to fetch a bottle of red wine and a corkscrew. 'Did you tell Nigel how your interview went?'

Helen hesitated. 'Some of it. He was really pushed for time, so I couldn't go into details.'

'And you'll be seeing him this weekend, no doubt?'

'Actually, no.' Helen made her voice sound casual. 'He's got a party to go to. A duty thing for his chairman's birthday.'

Lottie stared at her. 'And he hasn't asked you to go with him?' She sounded incredulous.

'Well, no,' Helen admitted awkwardly. 'But it's no big deal. It will be a black tie affair, and Nigel knows quite well I haven't anything to wear to something like that.' She gave a little laugh. 'He probably wanted to save me embarrassment.'

'For the same reason he might have considered buying you an evening dress,' Lottie said with a touch of curtness. 'He can certainly afford it.'

Helen shrugged. 'But he didn't,' she said. 'And it really

doesn't matter.' She paused. 'Of course it will be different when we're officially engaged.'

'I hope so,' Lottie agreed drily, filling their glasses.

'And what about you?' Helen was suddenly eager to change the subject. 'Have you heard from Simon?'

Her friend's face lit up, her blue eyes sparkling. 'The dam's nearly finished, and he's coming home on leave next month. Only two weeks, but that's better than nothing, and we're going to talk serious wedding plans. He says from now on he's only accepting contracts which allow accompanying wives, so I think he's missing me.'

Helen smiled at her teasingly. 'You can't leave,' she protested. 'How are the locals to give dinner parties without you to cook for them?'

'I promise I won't go before I cater for your wedding reception,' Lottie promised solemnly. 'So can you please fix a date?'

'I'll make it a priority,' Helen returned.

She was in a thoughtful mood when she walked home that night. There'd been a shower of rain about an hour before, and the air was heady with the scent of damp earth and sweet grass.

She was delighted at Lottie's obvious happiness, but at the same time unable to subdue a small pang of envy.

She wished her own life was falling so splendidly and lovingly into place.

Yet Nigel seems to be managing perfectly well without me, she thought sadly. If only we could have talked today—really talked—then maybe we'd have had Lottie's romantic kind of evening—and night—after all. And he'd have bought me a ring, and a dress, and taken me to Sussex. And he'd have told everyone, 'This is my brand-new fiancée. I simply couldn't bear to leave her behind.'

She'd started the day with such optimism and determination, yet now she felt uneasy and almost frightened. Nothing had gone according to plan. And miles away, in a glass and concrete box, her fate had probably already been decided.

I need Nigel, she thought. I need him to hold me and tell me everything will be all right, and that Monteagle is safe.

She walked under the arched gateway and stood in the court-yard, looking at the bulk of the house in the starlight. Half-seen, like this, it seemed massive—impregnable—but she knew how deceptive it was.

And it wasn't just her own future under threat. There were the Marlands, George and Daisy, who'd come to work for her grandfather when they were a young married couple, as gar-dener and cook respectively. As the other staff had left George had learned to turn his hand to more and more things about the estate, and his wife, small, cheerful and bustling, had be-come the housekeeper. Helen, working alongside them, de-pended on them totally, but knew unhappily that she could not guarantee their future—specially from Trevor Newson.

'Too old,' he'd said. 'Too set in their ways. I'll be putting in my own people.'

You'll be putting in no one, she'd told herself silently.

I wish I still felt as brave now, she thought, swallowing. But, even so, I'm not giving up the fight.

Monteagle opened to the public on Saturdays in the summer. Marion Lowell the Vicar's wife, who was a keen historian, led guided tours round the medieval ruins and those parts of the adjoining Jacobean house not being used as living accommo-dation by Helen and the Marlands.

Her grandfather had been forced to sell the books from his library in the eighties, and Helen now used the room as her sitting room. It had a wonderful view across the lawns to the lake, so the fact that it was furnished with bits and pieces from the attics, and a sofa picked up for a song at a house clearance sale a few miles away, was no real hardship.

If the weather was fine Helen and Daisy Marland served afternoon teas, with home-made scones and cakes, in the court-yard. With the promise of warm sunshine to come, they'd spent most of Friday evening baking.

Helen had been notified that a coach tour, travelling under the faintly depressing title 'Forgotten Corners of History' would be arriving mid-afternoon, so she'd got George to set up wooden trestles, covered with the best of the linen sheets, and flank them with benches.

Placing a small pot of wild flowers in the centre of each table, she felt reasonably satisfied, even if it was a lot of effort for very moderate returns. However, it was largely a goodwill gesture, and on that level it worked well. Entries in the visitors' book in the Great Hall praised the teas lavishly, particularly Daisy's featherlight scones, served with cream and home-made jam.

For once, the coach arrived punctually, and as one tour ended the next began. Business in the courtyard was brisk, but evenly spaced for a change, so they were never 'rushed to death', as Mrs Marland approvingly put it. The weather had lived up to the forecast, and although Monteagle closed officially at six, it was well after that when the last visitors reluctantly departed, prising themselves away from the warmth of the early-evening sun.

The clearing away done, Helen hung up the voluminous white apron she wore on these occasions, today over neatly pressed jeans and a blue muslin shirt, kicked off her sandals, and strolled across the lawns down to the edge of the lake. The coolness of the grass felt delicious under her aching soles, and the rippling water had its usual soothing effect.

If only every open day could go as smoothly, she thought dreamily.

Although that would not please Nigel, who had always made his disapproval clear. 'Working as a glorified waitress,' he'd said. 'What on earth do you think your grandfather would say?'

'He wouldn't say anything,' Helen had returned, slightly nettled by his attitude. 'He'd simply roll up his sleeves and help with the dishes.'

Besides, she thought, the real problem was Nigel's mother Celia, a woman who gave snobbishness a bad name. She liked the idea of Helen having inherited Monteagle, but thought it should have come with a full staff of retainers and a convenient treasure chest in the dungeon to pay the running costs, so she had little sympathy with Helen's struggles.

She sighed, moving her shoulders with sudden uneasiness

inside the cling of the shirt. Her skin felt warm and clammy, and she was sorely tempted to walk round to the landing stage beside the old boathouse, as she often did, strip off her top clothes and dive in for a cooling swim.

That was what the thought of Nigel's mother did to her, she told herself. Or was it?

Because she realised with bewilderment that she had the strangest sensation that someone somewhere was watching her, and that was what she found suddenly disturbing.

She swung round defensively, her brows snapping together, and realised with odd relief that it was only Mrs Lowell, coming towards her across the grass, wreathed in smiles.

'What a splendid afternoon,' she said, triumphantly rattling the cash box she was carrying. 'No badly behaved children for once, and we've completely sold out of booklets. Any chance of the wonderful Lottie printing off some more for us?'

'I mentioned we were getting low the other evening, and they'll be ready for next week.' Helen assured her, then paused. 'We have had a good crowd here today.' She gave a faint grin. 'The coach party seemed the usual motley crew, but docile enough.'

Mrs Lowell wrinkled her brow. 'Actually, they seemed genuinely interested. Not a hint of having woken up and found themselves on the wrong bus. They asked all sorts of questions—at least one of them did—and he gave me a generous tip at the end, which I've added to funds.'

'You shouldn't do that,' Helen reproved. 'Your tour commentaries are brilliant, and I only wish I could pay you. If someone else enjoys listening to you that much, then you should keep the money for yourself.'

'I love doing it,' Mrs Lowell told her. 'And it gets me out of the house while Jeff is writing his sermon,' she added conspiratorially. 'Apparently even a pin dropping can interrupt the creative flow. It's just as well Em's got a holiday job, because when she's around the house is in turmoil. And it's a good job, too, that she wasn't here to spot the coach party star,' she went on thoughtfully. 'You must have noticed him yourself during tea, Helen. Very dishy, in an unconventional way, and totally unmissable. What Em would describe as "sex on legs"—but not, I hope, in front of her father. He's still getting over the navel-piercing episode.'

Helen stared at her, puzzled. 'I didn't notice anyone within a hundred miles who'd answer to "dishy"—especially with the coach party. They all seemed well struck in years to me.' She grinned. 'Maybe he stayed away from tea because he felt eating scones and cream might damage his to-die-for image. Perhaps I should order in some champagne and caviar instead.'

'Maybe you should.' Mrs Lowell sighed. 'But what a shame you missed him. And he had this marvellous accent, too— French, I think.'

Helen nearly dropped the cash box she'd just been handed. She said sharply, 'French? Are you sure?'

'Pretty much.' The Vicar's wife nodded. 'Is something wrong, dear?'

'No—oh, no,' Helen denied hurriedly. 'It's just that we don't get many foreign tourists, apart from the odd American. It seems—strange, that's all.'

But that wasn't all, and she knew it. In fact it probably wasn't the half of it, she thought as they walked back to the house.

She always enjoyed this time after the house had closed, when they gathered in the kitchen to count the takings over a fresh pot of tea and the leftover cakes. And today she should have been jubilant. Instead she found herself remembering that sudden conviction that unseen eyes had been upon her by the lake, and it made her feel restive and uneasy—as well as seriously relieved that she hadn't yielded to her impulse by stripping off and diving in.

Of course there were plenty of French tourists in England, and their visitor might well turn out to be a complete stranger, but Helen felt that her encounter with Marc Delaroche in the Martinique had used up her coincidence quota for the foreseeable future.

It was him, she thought. It had to be...

As soon as Mrs Lowell had gone Helen dashed round to the

Great Hall and looked in the visitors' book, displayed on an impressive refectory table in the middle of the chamber.

She didn't have to search too hard. The signature 'Marc Delaroche' was the day's last entry, slashed arrogantly across the foot of the page.

She straightened, breathing hard as if she'd been running. He might have arrived unannounced, but his visit was clearly no secret. He wanted her to know about it.

She simply wished she'd known earlier. But there was no need to get paranoid about it, she reminded herself. He'd been here, seen Monteagle on a better than normal working day, and now he'd gone—without subjecting her to any kind of confrontation. So maybe he'd finally accepted that she wanted no personal connection between them, and from now on any encounters they might have would be conducted on strictly formal business lines.

And the fact they'd been so busy today, and their visitors had clearly enjoyed themselves, might even stand her in good stead when the time came for decisions to be made.

At any rate, that was how she intended to see the whole incident, she decided with a determined nod, then closed the book and went back to her own part of the house, locking up behind her.

Helen awoke early the next morning, aware that she hadn't slept as well as she should have done. She sometimes wished she could simply turn over and go back to sleep, letting worries and responsibilities slide into oblivion. But that simply wasn't possible. There was always too much to do.

Anyway, as soon as the faint mist cleared it was going to be another glorious day, she thought, pushing aside the bedcover and swinging her feet to the floor. And, as such days didn't come around that often, she didn't really want to miss a moment of it.

She decided she'd spend the day in the garden, helping George to keep the ever-encroaching weeds at bay. But first she'd cycle down to the village and get a paper. After all, they might finish the crossword, earn some money that way.

George was waiting for her as she rode back up the drive. 'All right, slave driver,' she called to him. 'Can't I even have a cup of coffee before you get after me?'

'I'll put your bike away, Miss Helen.' George came forward as she dismounted. 'Daisy came down just now to say you've a visitor waiting. Best not to keep him, she thought.'

Helen was suddenly conscious of an odd throbbing, and realised it was the thud of her own pulses. She ran the tip of her tongue round her dry mouth.

'Did Daisy say—who it was?' she asked huskily.

He shook his head. 'Just that it was someone for you, miss.'

She knew, of course, who it would be. Who it had to be, she thought, her lips tightening in dismay.

Her immediate impulse was to send George with a message that she hadn't returned yet and he didn't know when to expect her. But that wouldn't do. For one thing it would simply alarm Daisy and send her into search-party mode. For another it would tell her visitor that she was scared to face him, and give him an advantage she was reluctant to concede.

Surprised, cool, but civil, she decided. That was the route to take.

Of course there was always an outside chance that it could be Nigel, returned early from Sussex for some reason—because he was missing her, perhaps. But she couldn't really make herself believe it.

In a perverse way she hoped it wasn't Nigel, because she knew what she looked like in old jeans, with a polo shirt sticking damply to her body and her hair bundled into an untidy knot on top of her head and secured by a silver clip, and knew that he disliked seeing her like that.

But, no matter who was waiting for her, she owed it to herself and no one else to make herself slightly more presentable, even if it was only a matter of washing her face and hands and tidying her hair.

She supposed reluctantly that she'd better sneak in through the kitchen and go up the back stairs to her room.

But he'd forestalled her—the intruder—because he was already there in the kitchen, sitting at the table and tucking into a bacon sandwich with total relish while Daisy fussed round him, filling his cup with more coffee.

Helen halted abruptly. 'What are you doing here?' She heard the note of aggression in her voice and saw Daisy glance at her, her lips pursed.

Marc Delaroche got to his feet. In casual khaki pants and a short-sleeved black shirt, he looked less of a business tycoon and more of a tough from the back streets of Marseilles.

'As you see, *mademoiselle*, I am having some breakfast.' He slanted a smile at Daisy. 'Your housekeeper is an angel who has taken pity on me.'

Helen forced herself to amend her tone slightly. 'I meant surely you saw everything you needed to yesterday, so why are you still around?' She pushed a dusty strand of hair back from her face. 'After all, a village is hardly your kind of place.'

'I still had some unfinished business here,' he said softly. 'So I decided to spend the night at the Monteagle Arms.'

She raised her brows. 'They don't do breakfast?'

'Of course,' he said. 'But after the dinner they served last night I was not tempted to try the *petit dejeuner*.' He gestured at his plate. 'May I continue?'

'Coffee, Miss Helen?' Daisy placed another mug on the table and waited, coffeepot poised, her expression indicating that her employer had breached quite enough of the laws of hospitality already.

'Please.' Helen gave her a swift conciliatory smile, and subsided unwillingly on to the chair opposite him.

She was bitterly aware that she'd neglected to put on a bra that morning—a fact that would not be lost on her unwanted guest, she thought angrily, burning her mouth on an unwary gulp of coffee.

'You mentioned unfinished business?' she said after a pause. 'I presume it's something to do with the house?' She forced a smile. 'After all, why else would you be here?'

'Why indeed?' he agreed cordially.

'So…' Helen gestured awkwardly. 'If I can help…?'

'I was not able to see all the rooms in the house during the tour yesterday, because your charming guide told me they are the private living quarters of yourself and your staff.' Marc Delaroche paused. 'Perhaps you could show them to me presently?'

Helen put down her mug. 'Is that strictly necessary?'

'It is,' he said. 'Or I would not have asked. Your application to the committee covered the entire building, not merely selected sections, as I am sure you understand. And your accommodation includes rooms of historic importance—the library, I believe, and the Long Gallery, and also the State Bedroom.' He gave her an enquiring look. 'Is that where you sleep, perhaps?' He added gently, 'I hope you do not find the question indelicate.'

'I have never slept there,' Helen said coldly. 'It was last occupied by my grandfather, and I wasn't planning to make it available to the public.'

'Even though one of your kings used it for a romantic rendezvous? Charles the First, I think?'

'Charles the Second,' Helen corrected. 'He's supposed to have come here to seduce the daughter of the house, who'd fled from court to escape him.'

His brows lifted. 'And did he succeed in his quest?'

'I haven't the faintest idea,' Helen said shortly. 'And, anyway, it's just a legend. I don't believe a word of it even though I was named after her!'

'Quel dommage,' he murmured.

'Well, Sir Henry always said it was true,' Daisy interposed from the stove.

'My grandfather liked to tease people,' Helen said stonily. 'He said the room was haunted, too, if you remember.'

'And you thought if you slept there you might wake to find a ghost in your bed?' The dark eyes were dancing.

'Not at all,' Helen denied. 'I simply prefer my own room.'

'Until you are married, *hein*?' Marc Delaroche said carelessly. 'When you have a living man beside you at night, *ma belle*, there will be no room for ghosts.'

'Thank you,' Helen told him, biting her lip. 'You paint such a frank picture.'

He shrugged. 'Marriage is a frank relationship.' He paused.

'But, legend or not, the State Bedroom and its romantic associations should be available to your public. I hope you will allow me to be its first visitor.'

Helen finished her coffee. 'Just as you wish, *monsieur*. Would you like to begin now?'

'Pourquoi pas?' he said softly. 'Why not?'

Oh, Helen thought wearily as she led the way to the kitchen door, I can think of so many reasons why not. And having to be alone with you, Monsieur Delaroche, heads the list every time.

And, heaven help me, I'm not even sure whether it's you I don't trust—or myself.

CHAPTER THREE

HELEN was still recovering from that unwelcome piece of self-revelation when they entered the library together. She pushed her hands into the pockets of her jeans, trying to compose herself for the inevitable inquisition, but at first there was only silence as Marc Delaroche stood looking round with a frown at the empty oak shelves that still lined the walls.

'It was a valuable collection?' he asked at last.

'Yes—very.' She hesitated. 'My grandfather was forced to sell it in the eighties, along with a number of pictures. It almost broke his heart, but it gave Monteagle a reprieve.'

He shook his head slightly, his gaze travelling over the motley collection of shabby furniture, the peeling paintwork, and the ancient velvet curtains hanging limply at the windows. 'And this is where you spend your leisure time?'

'Yes, what there is of it,' she returned. 'There's always some job needing to be done in a place like this.'

'You do not find it—*triste*? A little gloomy.'

'In winter it's quite cosy,' she retorted defensively. 'There's plenty of wood on the estate, so I have an open fire, and I burn candles most of the time.'

'Certainly a kinder light than a midsummer sun,' he commented drily. 'Shall we continue?'

She supposed they must. The truth was she felt totally unnerved by her physical consciousness of his presence beside her. Although he was deliberately keeping his distance, she realised, and standing back to allow her to precede him through doorways, and up the Great Staircase to the Long Gallery. But it made no difference. The panelled walls still seemed to press in upon them, forcing them closer together. An illusion, she knew, but no less disturbing for that.

She thought, I should have made some excuse—asked Daisy to show him round.

Aloud, she said, 'This is where the family used to gather, and where the ladies of the house took exercise in bad weather.'

'But not, of course, with holes in the floorboards,' he said.

She bit her lip. 'No. The whole floor needs replacing, including the joists.'

He was pausing to look at the portraits which still hung on the walls. 'These are members of your family? Ancestors?'

She pulled a face. 'Mostly the ugly ones that my grandfather thought no one would buy.'

Marc Delaroche slanted an amused look at her, then scanned the portraits again. 'Yet I would say it is the quality of the painting that is at fault.'

She shrugged, surprised at his perception. 'No, they're not very good. But I guess you didn't pay the fees of someone like Joshua Reynolds to paint younger sons and maiden aunts.'

'And so the sons went off, *sans doute*, to fight my countrymen in some war,' he commented, his mouth twisting. 'While the aunts had only to remain maiden. My sympathies are with them, I think.' He paused. 'Is there no portrait of the beauty so desired by King Charles?'

'Yes,' she admitted reluctantly. 'My grandfather wouldn't part with it. It's in the State Bedroom.'

'I cannot wait,' he murmured. *En avant, ma belle.*'

'Do you mind not calling me that?' Helen threw over her shoulder as they set off again. 'What would you say if I greeted you with, Hey, good-looking?'

'I should advise you to consult an eye specialist,' he said drily. 'Tell me something, *mademoiselle*. Why do you object when a man indicates he finds you attractive?'

'I don't,' she said shortly. 'When it's the right man.'

'And I am by definition the wrong one?' He sounded amused.

'Do you really need to ask? You know already that I'm engaged to be married.'

'Of course,' he said. 'But where is your fiancé?'

'He couldn't come down this weekend.' Helen halted, chin lifted in challenge. 'Not that it's any concern of yours.'

'This weekend?' he said musingly. 'And how many weekends before that? It is a matter of comment in the village, you understand.'

'The public bar of the Monteagle Arms anyway,' Helen said tersely. 'You really shouldn't listen to idle gossip, *monsieur*.'

'But I learned a great deal,' Marc Delaroche said gently. 'And not merely about your missing lover. They spoke too about your fight to keep this house. Opinion is divided as to whether you are brave or a fool, but none of them thought you could win.'

'How kind of them,' she said between her teeth. 'That must have done my cause a lot of good.' She paused. 'Did they know who you were—and why you were here?'

'I said nothing. I only listened.' He shrugged. 'They spoke of your grandfather with affection, but not of your parents. And you do not mention them either. I find that strange.'

Helen bit her lip. 'I hardly knew them. They left Britain when I was still quite small, and my grandfather brought me up with the help of various nannies. That's why we were so close.'

Marc Delaroche frowned swiftly. 'My father's work took him abroad also, but I travelled with him always. He would never have considered anything else.'

'My father didn't work—in the accepted sense.' Helen looked past him, staring into space. 'He'd been brought up to run Monteagle and the estate, but after the financial disasters we'd suffered that no longer seemed an option. Also, he knew he would never have a son to inherit what remained. My mother, whom he adored, was very ill when I was born, and needed an immediate operation. The name was going to die out.'

'He had a daughter. Did he not consider that?'

Helen's smile was swift and taut. 'I never had the chance to ask him. There's always been a strong gambling streak in our family—fortunes won and lost down the centuries—and my father was a brilliant poker player. He had a load of friends among the rich and famous, so he travelled the world with my mother, staying in other people's houses and making a living from cards and backgammon.' Her mouth twisted wryly. 'At times he even earned enough to send money home.'

'But then his luck ran out?' Marc Delaroche asked quietly.

She nodded, and began to walk along the corridor again. 'They were in the Caribbean, flying between islands in a private plane with friends. There was some problem, and the aircraft crashed into the sea, killing everyone on board. My grandfather was devastated. Up to then he'd always believed we would recoup our losses somehow, and carry out the restoration work he'd always planned. That we'd be reunited as a family, too. But after the crash the fight seemed to go out of him. He became—resigned. Instead of winning, he talked about survival.'

She stared ahead of her, jaw set. 'But Monteagle is mine now, and I want more than that.'

'Has it hurt you to tell me these things?' His voice was oddly gentle.

'It's all part of Monteagle's history.' She hunched a shoulder. 'So you probably have a right to ask. But that's as far as the personal details go,' she added, giving him a cool look. 'You're here on business, and I feel we should conduct ourselves in a businesslike manner.'

Oh, God, she groaned inwardly. Just listen to yourself. Miss Prim of the Year, or what?

'Ah,' he said. 'And therefore all matters of gender should be rigorously excluded?' His grin was cynical. 'How do you do that, I wonder?'

She bit her lip. 'That is your problem, *monsieur*. Not mine.'

She reached the imposing double doors at the end of the corridor and flung them open. 'And here, as you requested, is the State Bedroom.'

The curtains were half drawn over the long windows, and she walked across and opened them, admitting a broad shaft of dust-filled sunshine.

It was a big room, the walls hung with faded brocade wallpaper. It was dominated by the huge four-poster bed, which had been stripped to its mattress, although the heavily embroidered satin canopy and curtains were still in place.

'As you see,' she added woodenly, 'it has not been in use since my grandfather died.' She pointed to a door. 'That leads to a dressing room, which he always planned to convert to a bathroom.'

Her companion gave it a cursory glance. 'It is hardly big enough. One would need to include the room next door as well.'

'Just for a bath? Why?'

He grinned lazily at her. 'A leading question, *ma mie*. Do you really wish me to enlighten you.'

'No,' she said. 'Thank you.'

Marc Delaroche took a longer look around him, then walked over to the fireplace and studied the picture hung above it. The girl in it looked steadily, even a little shyly back at him, a nimbus of warm-toned ringlets surrounding her face. She was wearing pale yellow satin, cut decorously for the fashion of the time. There was a string of pearls round her throat, and she carried a golden rose in one hand.

He whistled softly. 'I wonder how long she fought before she surrendered to your king?' he said, half to himself.

'You think she did surrender?'

'Eventually. As all women must,' he returned, ignoring her small outraged gasp. 'Besides, there is no question. You have only to look at her mouth.' He held out an imperative hand. *'Viens.'*

In spite of herself, Helen found she was crossing the worn carpet and standing at his side. 'What are you talking about?'

'She is trying hard to be the virtuous lady, but her lips are parted and the lower one is full, as if swollen from the kiss she longs for.'

'I think you have a vivid imagination, *monsieur*,' Helen retorted, her voice slightly strained.

'And I think that you also, *mademoiselle*, are trying much too hard.' His voice sank almost to a whisper.

Before she could guess his intention and move away, out of range, Marc Delaroche lifted a hand and put his finger to her own mouth, tracing its curve in one swift breathless movement, then allowing his fingertip delicately to penetrate her lips and touch the moist inner heat.

In some strange way it would have been less intimate—less shocking—if he'd actually kissed her.

She gasped and stepped backwards, the blaze in her eyes meeting the mockery in his. Her words became chips of ice. 'How dare you—touch me?'

'A conventional response,' he said. 'I am disappointed.'

'You're going to have more than disappointment to deal with, Monsieur Delaroche. You'll live to regret this, believe me.' She drew a deep breath. 'Because I, too, shall be making a report to your committee, informing them how you've abused their trust while you've been here, conducting enquiries on their behalf. And I hope they fire you—no matter how much money you have,' she added vindictively.

'I am desolate to tell you this, but you are in error, *ma belle*,' he drawled. 'The committee is not concerned with my visit. It was my decision alone to come here.'

She looked at him, stunned. 'But—you've asked all these questions…'

He shrugged. 'I was curious. I wished to see this house that means so much to you.'

The breath caught suddenly, painfully in her throat. She turned and marched to the door, and held it open. 'And now the tour is over. So please leave. Now.'

'But that was not all.' He made no attempt to move. 'I came most of all because I wanted to see you again. And ask you something.'

'Ask it,' Helen said curtly. 'Then get out.'

He said softly, 'Will you sleep with me tonight?'

Helen was rigid, staring at him with widening eyes. When she could speak, she said hoarsely, 'I think you must have taken leave of your senses.'

'Not yet,' he drawled. His eyes went over her body in lingering, sensuous assessment. 'For that I shall have to wait a little, I think.'

She pressed her hands to the sudden flare of hot blood in her face.

'How dare you speak to me like this?' she whispered jerkily. 'Insult me in this way?'

'Where is the insult? I am telling you that I desire you, and have done since the first moment I saw you. And please do not insult me by pretending you did not know,' he added silkily, 'because I did not hide it.'

It seemed altogether wiser to ignore that. Helen struggled to control her breathing. 'You—you seem to have forgotten that I'm about to marry another man.'

'He is the one who has forgotten, *ma belle*,' he said, a touch of grimness in his voice.

'And you imagined that because he's not here I would turn to you for—consolation?' Her voice rose. 'Oh, God—how dare you? What do you take me for? I love Nigel, and I intend to belong to him and no one else. And I'll wait for him for ever if necessary. Not that someone like you could ever understand that,' she added, her voice ringing with contempt.

There was an odd silence as he studied her, eyes narrowed. Then, 'You are wrong, *ma mie*,' he said softly. *'Parce que, enfin, je comprends tout.'* He gave a brief, harsh sigh. 'I see I shall have to be patient with you, Hélène, but my ultimate reward will make it worthwhile.'

'Damn you,' she said violently. 'Can't you see I'd die rather than let you touch me again?'

He reached her almost before she had finished speaking, and pulled her against him, crushing the breath from her as his lips descended on hers.

Nothing in her life had prepared her for the heated relentlessness of his kiss, and he took all the time he needed, exploring deeply, draining every drop of sweetness from her startled mouth.

Tiny fires were dancing in the dark eyes when, at last, he released her.

'You see,' he told her ironically, 'you still live. So learn from this, and do not issue ridiculous challenges that you cannot hope to win.' He took her hand and raised it to his mouth, palm uppermost, and she cried out in shock as his teeth grazed the soft mound beneath her thumb.

'*Au revoir, ma belle,*' he said softly. 'And remember this— on my next visit I shall expect to spend the night.'

And he left her standing there, mute and shaken as she stared after him, her tingling hand pressed to her startled, throbbing mouth.

A lot of those weeds you're pulling out are plants, Miss Helen,' George told her reproachfully.

Helen jumped guiltily, looking at the wilted greenery in her trug. 'Oh, Lord,' she said dismally. 'I'm sorry.'

She'd hoped that some intensive gardening would calm her down and restore her equilibrium, but it wasn't working out like that.

The thought of Marc Delaroche was interfering with her concentration at every level, and this infuriated her.

She had tried to call Nigel and beg him to come down, even if it was only for a couple of hours, so she could talk to him. But his mobile phone was permanently switched off, it seemed.

And even if she had managed to contact him, what could she have said? That she needed him to hold her and kiss her and take away the taste of another man's mouth?

The only other man, in fact, who had ever kissed her in passion.

Her mouth still seemed swollen and faintly tingling from the encounter, but maybe she was just being paranoid. Someone had made a pass at her, that was all. The sort of thing that she should have been able to take in her stride if she'd possessed an ounce of sophistication. She could even have laughed about it, telling Nigel, You'd better stake your claim, darling, because I'm being seriously fancied by someone else.

And he would have laughed too, because he knew she'd never looked at anyone but him since she was thirteen, and that they belonged together.

Anyway, her best plan would be to put the whole thing out of her mind. Marc Delaroche had simply been amusing himself, she thought, and he probably had his next target already lined up. Quite apart from his admittedly diabolical attraction, he was rich enough to ensure that he didn't get many refusals. And he wouldn't waste time repining over any of the few women who resisted him. Or risk another rejection by returning.

He'd called her *'ma belle'*, but that had to be just a seduction ploy, because she wasn't beautiful at all. Moderately attractive was the best she could honestly claim, and he knew it. He'd probably thought she would fall into his arms through sheer gratitude, she told herself, viciously slicing her trowel through a dandelion root.

All the same, she wished desperately that he hadn't sought her out and forced this confrontation on her.

She might not like him, and she certainly didn't trust him, but she could have done with him on her side when the committee came to make their decision.

No chance of that now, of course. And she still couldn't understand what had possessed him. Yes, she'd been aware of him too, she admitted defensively, but only because she'd had no choice. During the interview he'd hardly taken his eyes off her. But she certainly hadn't offered him any encouragement to—pursue her like this. Quite the opposite, in fact.

At the same time she felt oddly depressed. She absolutely didn't want him as a lover. She probably wouldn't choose him as a friend, but she surely didn't need him as an enemy either, she thought, and sighed without quite knowing why.

The sun went down that evening behind a bank of cloud, and the following day brought grey skies and drizzle and the temperature dropping like a stone.

Outside work had to be halted, and if the miserable conditions persisted to the weekend, the tourists would stay away too, Helen fretted.

She caught up on the household accounts—a depressing task at the best of times—helped Daisy bake for the freezer, and waited feverishly for the mail van to call each day. The committee chairman had said she would hear before the end of the month, and that was fast approaching. All she could hope was that no news might be good news.

Thankfully, Marc Delaroche had made no attempt to contact her again. Maybe he'd decided to cut his losses and retire from the fray after all. But the thought of him still made her uneasy, and her attempts to blot him from her memory did not appear to be working too well.

It would have made things so much easier if she'd been able to talk to Nigel, she acknowledged unhappily. But there'd been no reply from his flat after the weekend, so she'd gritted her teeth and made the unpopular move of phoning him at work—only to be told that he was working in Luxembourg all week. And when she'd asked for the name of his hotel, she'd been told briskly that the bank did not give out that sort of information.

Back to square one, she realised without pleasure. Unless he called her instead, of course, and how likely was that?

She stopped herself right there. She was being critical, which was only one step removed from disloyal. Especially when she knew from past experience that these trips were often landed on him at ridiculously short notice. And he was bound to be home at the weekend, she told herself, because this time it was his mother's birthday.

Helen didn't know what kind of celebration was being planned, but she'd managed to find a card with a Persian cat on it that was the double of the bad-tempered specimen occupying its own special chair in Mrs Hartley's drawing room. She'd signed it 'Best wishes' rather than 'Love from', in tacit acknowledgement that her relationship with Nigel's mother had always been tricky. That was one of the reasons they'd delayed making their engagement official.

'She'll be fine,' Nigel had said. 'She just needs a bit of time to get used to the idea. And to you.'

But she's known me since I was thirteen, Helen had thought, troubled. And even then I don't think I was ever on her A-list.

Thought it—but hadn't said it.

Still, Mrs Hartley's sensibilities couldn't be allowed to intrude any longer—or any further. Helen suspected she was the kind of mother, anyway, who believed no girl would ever be good enough for her only son. Nothing useful would be achieved by putting off the announcement any longer.

Because, whether the committee's decision was for or against the restoration of Monteagle, she was going to need Nigel's love and support as never before. And surely, in spite of the demands of his career, he would understand that and be there for her—wouldn't he?

It irked her to realise that Marc Delaroche, however despicable his motives, had actually taken more interest in the house than Nigel had ever shown. And he was right about the State Bedroom, too. Her grandfather wouldn't have wanted it left untouched, like some empty shrine.

Instead, it should be top of her refurbishment list and opened to the public. She might find the Charles the Second legend distasteful, but a lot of people would think it a romantic story, and let their imaginations free on the use that giant four-poster had been put to during the King's visit.

She went up there with a notebook and pen and took a clear-eyed look round. The ornamental plaster on the ceiling was in urgent need of restoration in places, and there were timbered walls waiting to be exposed underneath layers of peeling wallpaper. The ancient Turkish carpet was past praying for, but it was concealing wooden floorboards that the original surveyor's report had declared free of woodworm or dry rot, and she could only hope that was still the case.

The silk bed hangings and window curtains were frankly disintegrating, and couldn't be saved, but their heavy embroidery was intact, and still beautiful.

Helen recalled that Mrs Stevens at the village post office, who was a skilled needlewoman, had told her months ago that if the elaborate patterns were cut out carefully they could be transferred to new fabric. She'd suggested, too, that the embroidery group at the Women's Institute, which she chaired, might take it on as a project.

First catch your fabric, Helen thought, doing some rueful calculations. But at least she knew now what her first priority should be, even though it was galling that she'd been alerted to it by Marc Delaroche.

But if I get the money from the committee I might even feel marginally grateful to him, she thought. Maybe.

She was sitting at the kitchen table on Friday evening, going over some of the estimates her grandfather had obtained and trying to work out the inevitable percentage increases for the intervening period, when Lottie arrived with the new batch of guidebooks.

'Hey, there.' She gave Helen a quizzical glance. 'Got any good news for me?'

'Not yet.' Helen gave a sigh. 'And I was so sure I'd hear this week.'

'Actually,' Lottie said, 'I was thinking of something more personal than the grant application.' She looked around. 'All on your own?' she enquired, with clear disappointment.

'Not any more.' Helen pushed her papers aside and got up to fill the kettle. 'Who were you expecting?'

'I thought Nigel might be here and had my speedy exit all planned,' Lottie explained. 'So—where is he?'

Helen shrugged as she got down the coffee jar. 'Arriving tomorrow, I guess. I haven't heard yet.'

Lottie frowned. 'But his car was in the drive at his parents' place earlier. That's when I put two and two together about the party.'

Helen stared at her. 'Lottie—what on earth are you talking about?'

'Oh, hell,' her friend groaned. 'Don't tell me I've put my foot in it. I was so sure…' She took a deep breath. 'It's just that Ma Hartley rang me this afternoon, all sweetness and light, wanting me to quote for catering a 'very special buffet' next month. She was so pleased and coy about it that I jumped to the obvious conclusion. I'm so sorry, love.'

Helen spooned coffee into two beakers with more than usual care. 'Nigel's probably planning it as a big surprise for me,' she said calmly, ignoring the sudden churning in her stomach. 'Although I can't really imagine his mother turning cartwheels over it. She must like me better than I thought,' she added, without any real conviction.

'I shouldn't have said anything,' Lottie said ruefully as she stirred her coffee.

'No, it's fine,' Helen assured her. 'And when I do see him I swear I'll be the world's most astonished person.'

That would be an easy promise to keep, she thought, when Lottie had gone. She was already bewildered and disturbed by his failure to contact her when he must know how she was longing to see him.

Well, she could do something about that at least, she thought, and she dialled the number of his parents' home.

She'd hoped Nigel himself would answer, but inevitably it was his mother.

'Oh, Helen,' she said, without pleasure. 'I'm afraid this isn't a terribly convenient moment. You see, we have guests, and we're in the middle of dinner.'

'I'm sorry,' Helen said. 'But I do need to speak to him.'

'But not this evening.' There was a steely note in Mrs Hartley's voice. She sighed impatiently. 'Oh, well. Perhaps if there's something particular, he could call you tomorrow?'

Oh, nothing special, thought Helen. Only the rest of my life.

'Thank you,' she said quietly. 'I look forward to hearing from him.'

But it wasn't true, she realised as she put down the phone. She had a feeling of dread, not anticipation. And once again Nigel's mother had succeeded in making her feel excluded— as if she had no place in their lives.

When she and Nigel finally managed to talk, Mrs Hartley's attitude was going to be one of the topics of conversation, she thought grimly.

When she awoke next morning, it was to intermittent sunshine and scudding clouds driven by a sharp breeze.

Unpredictable, she thought as she dressed. Rather like my life. But a good day for touring historic houses rather than going to the beach, so let's hope the queues start forming like they did last week.

Well, not quite, she amended hastily. At least this time Marc Delaroche would not be part of them.

She was on her way to the kitchen when she saw the post

van disappearing down the drive. At the door she paused, and drew a deep, calming breath before entering.

'Any phone calls for me?' she enquired, making her tone deliberately casual.

'Nothing so far,' Daisy told her, putting a fresh pot of tea on the table.

'What about mail?'

'A couple of bills,' Daisy said. She paused. 'And this.' She held out an imposing cream envelope embossed with the committee's logo.

Helen's stomach lurched frantically. She wiped her hand on her jeans and took the envelope, staring down at it. Reluctant, now that the moment had come, to learn its contents, slowly she pushed the blade of a table knife under the flap and slit it open.

The words 'We regret' danced in front of her eyes, making it almost unnecessary to read on. But she scanned them anyway—the brief polite lines that signified failure.

George had come into the kitchen and was standing beside his wife, both of them watching Helen anxiously.

She tried to smile—to shrug. 'No luck, I'm afraid. They try to help places that have suffered some kind of terrible devastation, like earthquake sites. It seems that rising damp, leaky roofs and dry rot aren't quite devastating enough.'

'Oh, Miss Helen, love.'

She sank her teeth into her lower lip at the compassion in Daisy's voice, forbidding herself to cry.

'Does this mean you'll have to sell to that Mr Newson?' George asked, troubled.

'No,' she said. 'I'm not going to do that. I'm never going to do that.' There was something else in the envelope, too. A note in the chairman's own hand, she discovered, wishing her well. 'Mr VanStratten and Monsieur Delaroche argued very persuasively on your behalf,' the note added, 'but eventually it had to be a majority decision.'

Her hand clenched round the paper, crushing it. That—lecherous hypocrite, speaking up for her? she thought incredulously. Dear God, that had to be the final blow.

Aloud, she said, 'There'll be something else I can do. Someone else I can turn to. I'll call Nigel. Ask for his advice.'

'He hasn't been so helpful up to now,' George muttered.

'But now the chips are down,' Helen said with more confidence than she actually felt. 'He'll find some way to rescue us.'

Rather than run the gauntlet of his mother's disapproval again, Helen rang Nigel's mobile number.

'Yes?' His voice sounded wary.

'Nigel?' she said. 'Darling, can you come round, please? I really need to see you.'

There was a silence, then he said, 'Look, Helen, this isn't a good time for me.'

'I'm sorry to hear that, but please believe that it's a far worse one for me,' she told him bluntly. 'Something's happened, and I need your advice.' She paused. 'Would you prefer me to come to you instead?'

'No,' he said hastily. 'No, don't do that. I'll be about half an hour, and I'll use the side gate into the garden. I'll meet you by the lake.'

'Bringing your cloak and dagger with you, no doubt,' Helen said acidly. 'But if that's what you want, then it's fine with me.'

She'd spoken bravely, but she rang off feeling sick and scared. Suddenly her entire life seemed to be falling in pieces, and she didn't know why, or how to deal with it.

Whatever, facing Nigel in working clothes wasn't a good idea. She dashed upstairs and took another quick shower, this time using the last of her favourite body lotion. From her scanty wardrobe she chose a straight skirt in honey-coloured linen, with a matching jersey top, long-sleeved and vee-necked.

She brushed her hair loose and applied a touch of pale rose to her mouth.

War paint, she thought ironically, as she took a last look in the mirror.

Nigel was already waiting when she arrived at the lakeside. The breeze across the water was ruffling his hair and he was pacing up and down impatiently.

'So there you are,' he greeted her peevishly. 'What the hell's the matter?'

'I think that should be my question.' She halted a few feet away, staring at him. 'You don't tell me you're coming down, and then you avoid me. Why?'

His eyes slid away uncomfortably. 'Look, Helen—I know I should have spoken before, but there's no easy way to say this.' He paused. 'You must know that things haven't been good between us for quite a while.'

'I've certainly realised we don't see as much of each other, but I thought it was pressure of work. That's what you told me, anyway.' She clenched her shaking hands and hid them in the folds of her skirt.

'And what about you?' he asked sharply. 'Always fussing about that decrepit ruin you live in—scratching round for the next few pennies. You've had a good offer for it. Why not wise up and get out while it's still standing?'

She gasped. 'How can you say that—when you know what it means to me?'

'Oh, I know all right,' he said bitterly. 'No one knows better. I discovered a long time ago I was always going to play second fiddle to that dump, and you took it for granted that I'd settle for that. No doubt that's what you want to talk about now. What's happened? Deathwatch beetle on the march again?'

'I do have a serious problem about the house, but that can wait,' she said steadily. 'What we obviously need to discuss is—us.'

'Helen, there is no 'us', and there hasn't been for a long time. But you refuse to see it, for some reason.'

Her nails dug painfully into the palms of her hands. 'Maybe because I'm in love with you.'

'Well, you've got a weird idea of what love's about,' Nigel commented sourly. 'Frankly, I'm sick and tired of this 'hands off till we're married' garbage. I've tried everything to get you into bed, but you've never wanted to know.'

She bit her lip. 'I—I realise that now, and I—I'm sorry.' She looked at him pleadingly. 'I thought you were prepared to wait too.'

'No,' he said brutally. 'Men only beg for so long, then they lose interest.' He shook his head. 'There's only ever going to be one passion in your life, Helen, and that's Monteagle. No guy stands a chance against a no-win obsession like that.'

She said carefully, 'You mean—you don't want me any more?'

He sighed. 'Let's be honest. It was a boy-girl thing at best, and it certainly didn't make it into the grown-up world. Although I hope we can stay friends,' he added hastily. 'Face it, you've never been interested in sex—or even curious. A couple of kisses have always been enough for you. But now I've met someone with a bit of warmth about her and we're getting married. I brought her down this weekend to meet my parents, so I really don't need you ringing up every five minutes.'

'I see.' Helen swallowed. 'You know, I had the strangest idea I was engaged to you myself.'

He shrugged. 'I know we discussed it,' he said awkwardly. 'But there was nothing definite. For one thing, I'd have had a hell of a fight on with my parents.'

'Oh, yes,' Helen said unevenly. 'I always knew they didn't like me.'

'It wasn't that,' he told her defensively. 'They felt we were wrong for each other, that's all. And they didn't want me tipping everything I earned down that money pit of yours, either.'

He paused. 'I have ambition, Helen, and I'm not ashamed of it. I want a wife who can help with my career—someone who likes entertaining and can provide the right ambience. Let's face it, you'd hate that kind of life.'

The wind was cold suddenly—turning her to ice.

She said quietly, 'And I haven't any money—to make up for my other deficiencies. Isn't that part of it?'

He gave her an irritated look. 'Money matters. Are you pretending it doesn't?'

'No,' she said. 'Particularly when I've just been turned down for my grant.'

'Well, what did you expect? Clearly they don't want to

throw good money after bad,' he said. 'That's not good business practice.'

She winced painfully. 'Nigel,' she said urgently, 'I—I'm trying to save the home I love. I thought you might be able to suggest something—someone who could help. Who might be prepared to invest in the estate...'

'This is a joke—right?' His tone was derisive. 'I suggest you look round for a rich husband—if you can find someone as frigid as you are yourself. And how likely is that?'

The pain was suddenly more than she could bear. She took a step towards him, lifting her hand, driven by a half-crazy need to wipe the sneer from his face.

Nigel retreated, throwing up an arm to ward her off, his smart brogues slipping suddenly in the mud created by the recent bad weather.

Helen saw his face change from alarm to fury as he overbalanced, teetering on the edge of the lake for a moment before he fell backwards into the water with a resounding splash.

He was on his feet instantly, dripping and crimson with rage. 'Bitch,' he shouted hoarsely, as Helen turned her back and began to walk, head bent, towards the house. 'Bitch.'

She was trembling violently, her breathing an agony, every nerve in her body striving to continue putting one foot in front of another so that she could reach sanctuary before she fell on her knees and howled her hurt and misery to the sky.

She was too blinded by his cruelty even to see that someone was standing in front of her until she collided with a hard male body and recoiled with a cry.

'Tais toi,' Marc Delaroche said quietly. 'Be calm.' His arm round her was like iron, holding her up. 'I have you safe. Now, walk with me to the house.'

And, too numb to resist, Helen could only obey.

CHAPTER FOUR

HE'D said 'walk', but Helen was dazedly aware she was being half-led, half-carried into the house. Warmth surrounded her, and a feeling of safety as its walls closed round her.

She heard Daisy's shocked exclamation, and his quiet reply.

When she could think clearly again she found she was sitting on the sofa in the library, with a mug of strong, hot tea clasped in her icy hands.

Marc Delaroche was standing by the fireplace, an elbow resting on the mantelshelf, looking contemplatively into the blue flames of the small twig fire that she supposed he'd kindled in the grate.

He was wearing jeans and a matching blue shirt, its top buttons undone and the sleeves rolled back, revealing the shadowing of dark hair on his chest and forearms.

He turned his head slowly and met her accusing gaze.

She said huskily, 'You knew, didn't you? I mean about Nigel. Somehow, you knew.'

There was a pause, then reluctantly he nodded. 'I regret, but, yes.'

'And is that why you're here—to gloat?' She took a gulp of the scalding brew in her beaker.

'No,' he said. 'Why should I do that?'

'Who knows,' she said, 'why you do anything? Yet here you are—again.'

'Among other things, I came to warn you. But I was too late.'

'How can this be?' Helen said, half to herself. 'How can you have guessed that Nigel didn't love me when I was still in the dark about it?'

He shrugged. 'You were in the dark, *ma mie*, because you had closed your eyes to what was happening—perhaps delib-

56

erately. Also,' he added, 'I had an advantage, because you were not sitting in the window of the Martinique that day when your supposed fiancé arrived. He came by taxi, not alone, and his companion was most reluctant to let him go. That was how I came to notice him—because their leavetaking was quite a spectacle. Each time he tried to say *au revoir* she wound herself round him the more. She behaved with *une ardeur etonnante*,' he added with a faint whistle. 'I almost envied him.'

He paused. 'And then I watched him join you at your table, and realised who he must be, and it was no longer so amusing.'

'So you took pity on me,' Helen said bitterly.

'Perhaps,' he said. 'But for a moment only. Because I could see that you were strong and would survive your disappointment.'

'Disappointment?' she echoed in angry incredulity. 'My God, I've just been dumped by the man I've loved all my life. The only man I'll ever love. And you talk about it as if it were a minor inconvenience.'

She paused. 'Why didn't you tell me there and then?'

'Because I already knew that the committee's decision would go against you,' he said. 'I did not wish to overburden you with bad news.'

'So instead you let me stew in my fool's paradise,' she said. 'Thank you so much.'

'Shall we agree it was a no-win situation for us both?' he suggested.

'I don't believe this,' Helen said raggedly. 'My life's in ruins, I'm falling apart—and you sound so bloody casual.'

She gave him an inimical look. 'And, for the record, there is no ''both''. There's myself alone, and no one else.'

'Are you so sure of that?'

'What are you saying? That he'll dump this new lady too, and come back to me?' She shook her head. 'I don't think so. And do you know why that is, Monsieur Delaroche? It's because I lack the necessary social skills. Also, I'm frigid—and she isn't,' she added, her voice cracking. Then stopped, horrified at what she'd let him see.

'He told you that?' Marc Delaroche raised his eyebrows. 'But how can he possibly know?'

She stared at him in silence, almost paralysed with shame as she interpreted what he'd just said to her. Oh God, she thought, he—he *knows* I'm still a virgin. And I wish I'd died before he told me so.

But you, were the one who told *him*, said a small cold voice in her head. You let it slip the last time he was here. And *he* said he'd be patient. How could you have forgotten that?

She'd tried to block out every detail of their previous encounter, but that was something she should have remembered. Because it spelled danger.

'I understand now why you pushed him into the lake,' Marc added.

'I didn't push him,' Helen said icily. 'He slipped.'

'*Quel dommage,*' he murmured. 'And, no—he will certainly not come back,' he went on calmly. 'But for a reason far removed from the ones you have given.'

She said, 'Oh?' her voice wooden.

The dark eyes studied her. 'He did not tell you, *peut-être*, the identity of his new fiancée? Then I shall. Her name is Amanda Clayburn.'

'Clayburn?' Helen repeated, bewildered. 'You—you mean she's related to Sir Donald Clayburn, the chairman of the bank?'

'His only daughter.' His grin was cynical. 'Your Nigel is an ambitious man, *ma mie*. He has chosen money and the fast track to the boardroom.'

'No,' she said. 'He couldn't. He *wouldn't*. And, anyway, he doesn't need to do that. He has money of his own.'

'Which he prefers to keep, *sans doute*.' He bent and added another handful of twigs to the fire. 'But it is all true. I have a colleague with contacts at the bank, and he informs me their *affaire* has been an open secret for weeks. She is wild and spoiled, this Amanda, and her father, they say, is glad she is marrying before she disgraces him openly.'

'Obviously a marriage made in heaven.' The words cut at her, but she refused to wince. Instead, she threw back her head.

'Monteagle and Nigel—the two things I care most about in the world—I've lost them both.'

'I notice,' he said, 'you place the house before your fiancé.'

'Yes,' she said. 'Nigel said that too. He said that because of Monteagle I would never be capable of loving anyone properly. All in all, it was a pretty comprehensive condemnation. And do you know the worst of it, Monsieur Delaroche? You—you were here to watch it happening.' She almost choked on the words. 'You—of all the people in the world. You're like some terrible jinx—do you know that?—because each time you appear in my life, everything goes wrong.'

She punched her fist into the palm of her other hand. 'Well, you've had your fun, *monsieur*, if that's what you came for, so now you can go. I need to be on my own. Even you should be able to appreciate that,' she added burningly.

His own glance was cool. 'You have a strange idea of how I choose to amuse myself, *ma chère*,' he drawled. 'And, although I am desolate to grieve you further, I must tell you I have no intention of leaving yet. Because I came not just to warn you, but also to offer my help.'

'Oh, of course,' she said. 'You spoke up for me at the committee—you and your Dutch colleague. I—I suppose I should thank you.'

'If we had succeeded, perhaps,' he said. 'But as matters stand I do not expect you to torture yourself with an attempt to be grateful.'

'But why should you do that?' she asked. 'When you knew what the verdict would be? You don't look like someone who supports lost causes.'

He shrugged. 'Perhaps I felt you did not deserve to lose yet again.' He gave her a measured look. 'So—what do you plan to do now? Will you take advantage of Monsieur Newson's offer—if it still stands?'

'I'd rather burn the place to the ground.'

'The insurance company might find that suspicious,' he murmured.

'Probably—if we were insured,' Helen said shortly, and for the first time saw him look taken aback.

'You like to take risks,' he said.

'Sometimes I don't have a choice in the matter. I found my grandfather had let the premiums lapse.' She drank the rest of her tea and put down the mug. 'And now please leave. I've answered enough questions, and you have no further excuse to be here.'

'Except my own inclination,' he told her brusquely. 'And I ask again—what will you do next?'

'I shall open the house up for visitors, as I do every Saturday.' Her smile was swift and hard as she rose to her feet.

'I think no one would blame you if, for once, the house remained shut.'

'I'd blame myself,' she said. 'Because Monteagle needs every penny I can earn. And, anyway, I'd rather have something to do.' She paused. 'Please don't feel you have to take the tour again, or pay any more visits here,' she added pointedly. 'I'm sure you have places to go and people to see, so let's both of us get on with our lives. Shall we?'

But he ignored that. 'Is that truly how you see your future?' His brows lifted. 'Welcoming crowds of the curious and the bored *pour toujours*? Serving them tea?'

She met his gaze. 'Yes,' she said. 'If I have to. I told you— I'll do anything to save Monteagle.'

'Will you?' he asked softly. 'I wonder, *ma mie*. I very much wonder. For example, will you have dinner with me this evening?'

Her lips parted in sheer astonishment. She said unevenly, 'My God, you never give up, do you? Do you think I'm in any mood to listen to another of your insensitive—tasteless invitations? Can't you understand that I've just lost the man I love?'

'You are planning to starve to death as an act of revenge?' He had the gall to sound faintly amused.

'No,' Helen said stormily. 'But I'd rather die than have dinner with you.'

He was laughing openly now, to her fury. 'A fate worse than death, *ma belle*? I always thought that involved far more than simply sharing a meal.'

She marched to the door and held it open. 'Just get out of my house and don't come back.'

'Your house,' Marc said softly, unmoved and unmoving. 'And how much longer will you be able to call it that, unless you find financial support—and quickly? You said you would do anything to save Monteagle. So, can you afford to reject my offer of assistance unheard?'

There was silence in the room, broken only by the crackle of the burning wood and the swift flurry of her own ragged breathing.

She felt like a small animal, caught in the headlights of an approaching juggernaut. Only she'd been trapped, instead, by her own words, she realised bitterly.

She said thickly, 'What—kind of help?'

'We will not discuss that now. Your mood is hardly—receptive. Also,' he added silkily, 'you have work to do. We will speak again later.'

He walked past her and she shrank backwards, flattening herself against the thick wooden door as she remembered, only too well, his last leavetaking. The hardness of his body against hers. The touch—the taste of his mouth.

He favoured her with a brief, sardonic smile. *À tout à l'heure!* he told her quietly, and then he was gone.

Did you take an order from the people in the far corner, Miss Helen?' asked Daisy, entering the kitchen with a stacked tray of dirty dishes. 'Because they're playing up at having to wait.'

Helen, lost in thought at the sink, started guiltily. 'Oh, Lord,' she muttered. 'I forgot all about them. I'll serve them next,' she added hurriedly, collecting one of the larger teapots from the shelf.

'Your mind's not on it today, and no wonder. You should have gone for a nice lie-down in your room,' Daisy said severely. 'I'd have got George to do the waiting on.'

'I'm fine,' Helen said untruthfully. 'And I really prefer to be busy,' she added placatingly.

Daisy sniffed. 'There's busy and busy,' she said. 'You've just put cream in the sugar basin.'

Swearing under her breath, Helen relaid the tray and carried it out into the sunshine.

Once again she'd been astonished at the number of visitors, but they hadn't been as easy to handle as last week's selection.

'You don't see much for your money,' one man had complained.

'We're hoping to extend the tour to other rooms in the house quite soon,' Helen had explained, but he'd glared at her.

'Well, that's no good to me,' he'd said. 'I've already paid.'

And a large family party had demanded why there were no games machines for kiddies, or even a playground, and why they couldn't play football in an adjoining field.

'Because my tenant wouldn't like it,' Helen had said, in a tone that brooked no further argument.

It had been an afternoon of moans and niggles, she thought wearily, and from the look of strained tolerance she'd glimpsed on Marion Lowell's face at one point, she wasn't the only sufferer.

Altogether, this was the day from hell, she thought. And she still couldn't decide what to do about Marc Delaroche and his dinner invitation.

Instinct told her to refuse. Reason suggested that if Monteagle's welfare was involved she should at least give him a hearing. But not over dinner, she thought. That was too much like a date rather than a business meeting.

'And about time.' Helen was greeted truculently by a red-haired woman as she reached the corner table and set down the heavy tray. She and her glum-looking husband peered suspiciously at the plates of scones and cakes. 'Is this all we get? Aren't there are any sandwiches? Ham would do. We've got a growing lad here.'

Growing outwards as well as upwards, Helen noticed with disfavour, as the child in question dug a podgy finger into the bowl of cream.

She said quietly, 'I'm sorry, it's a standard tea. But everything is home-made.'

The little boy glared at her. 'Aren't there any crisps? And where's my drink?'

'He doesn't like tea,' his mother explained in a tone that invited congratulation. 'He wants orange squash.'

Helen repressed a sigh. 'I'll see what I can do.'

Back in the kitchen, she halved oranges from the fruit bowl, squeezed out their juice, and put it in a glass with a pinch of sugar and some ice cubes.

Improvisation, she told herself with mild triumph as she took the drink outside.

'What's that?' The boy stabbed an accusing finger at it. 'I want a real drink. That's got bits in it.'

'They're bits of orange—' Helen began.

'Yuck.' The child's face twisted into a grimace. 'I'm not drinking that.' And he picked up the glass and threw the contents at Helen, spattering her with the sticky juice.

She gasped and fell back, wiping her face with her hand, then felt hands grip her shoulders, putting her to one side.

'Go and get clean,' Marc directed quietly. 'I will deal with this.'

She hadn't even been aware of his approach. She wanted to tell him she could manage, but she wasn't sure it was true.

She turned away, walking quickly back to the house, stripping off her ruined apron as she went, her colour rising as she became aware of sympathetic smiles and murmurs from other customers.

She looked back over her shoulder and saw Marc talking to the husband. Noticed the other man rise uncomfortably to his feet, his face sullen, gesturing to his family to follow.

When she reached the kitchen she found Lottie waiting, her face grave and troubled. 'Honey,' she said, 'I'm so sorry.'

Helen bit her lip. 'I see you've heard the news.' She ran cold water into a bowl and put her stained apron to soak.

Lottie nodded unhappily. 'It's all round the village. I still can't quite believe it.'

'It's perfectly true.' Helen lifted her chin. 'Nigel is being splendidly conventional and marrying his boss's daughter. I haven't worked out yet whether he ever meant to tell me to my face, or if he hoped I'd simply—fade away and save him the trouble.'

'Bastard,' said Lottie, with some force. 'But it certainly explains the special buffet episode.' She snorted. 'Well, I've rung his poisonous mother and told her to find another caterer.'

Helen smiled wanly. 'It's a lovely thought,' she said. 'But it's also the kind of gesture you can't afford any more than I could.' She glanced round her. 'Where's Daisy?'

'She said she had something to do upstairs and that she'd ask Mrs Lowell to collect the tea money. She probably thought we'd want to talk in private.'

'I don't think I have much privacy left,' Helen said ruefully. 'Not if the whole village knows.' She paused. 'I also found out this morning that I'd been turned down for that grant.'

'Oh, no,' Lottie groaned. 'That's really evil timing.' She gave Helen a compassionate look. 'Well—they say bad luck comes in threes, so let's hope your final misfortune is a minor one.'

Helen bit her lip as she refilled the kettle and set it to boil. 'No such luck, I'm afraid. It's happened—and it's another disaster.'

Lottie whistled. 'Tell me something—is there some gruesome family curse hanging over the Fraynes that you've never thought to mention?'

'If only.' Helen grinned faintly. 'Good business, a family curse. I'd have given it a whole page in the guidebook.'

Lottie started to laugh, and then, as if some switch had been operated, the amusement was wiped from her face, to be replaced by astonishment bordering on awe.

Helen turned quickly and saw Marc in the doorway, completely at his ease, arms folded across his chest and one shoulder propped nonchalantly against the frame.

He said, '*Je suis désolè*. I am intruding.'

'No,' Lottie denied with something of a gulp, getting quickly to her feet. 'No, of course not. I'm Charlotte Davis—Lottie—a friend of Helen's from the village.'

He sent her a pleasant smile. '*Enchanté, mademoiselle.* And I am Marc Delaroche—*à votre service*.'

To her eternal credit, Lottie didn't allow herself even a flicker of recognition.

Helen swallowed. 'What—what did you say to those people just now?' she asked a little breathlessly.

'I suggested only that they might prefer the Monteagle Arms. They accepted my advice.' He walked across to the table and put down some money. 'They also paid,' he added laconically. He paused. 'Tell me, *ma mie*, are many of your customers like that?'

'Not usually.' She went over to the stove and busied herself with the kettle. 'I'm just having a generally bad day, I think.' She hesitated. 'Would you like some coffee?' she offered unwillingly—as he instantly detected.

'*Merci.*' He slanted a faint grin at her. 'But I will leave you to talk in peace to your friend.' He added softly, 'I came only to say that I have reserved a table for eight o'clock at the Oxbow. I hope you will feel able to join me.'

He gave them both a slight bow and walked back into the sunshine, leaving a tingling silence behind him.

It was broken at last by Lottie. 'Wow,' she said reverently. 'Don't pretend even for a moment that he's your third disaster.'

'Oh, you're as bad as Mrs Lowell,' Helen said crossly, aware that her face had warmed. 'She was rhapsodising about him last week.'

'You mean this is his second visit?' Lottie's brows shot skywards. 'Better and better.' She eyed Helen. 'So, what are you going to wear tonight?'

'Nothing!'

Lottie grinned wickedly. 'Well, it would certainly save him time and effort,' she said. 'But a little obvious for a first date, don't you think?'

Helen's colour deepened hectically. 'I didn't mean that—as you well know,' she said, carrying the coffee back to the table. 'And it's not a date. In fact, I have no intention of having dinner with Monsieur Delaroche—tonight or any other time.'

'Nonsense,' Lottie said briskly. 'Of course you're going. Why not?'

Helen sank limply on to the nearest chair. 'You seem to have forgotten about Nigel.'

'Unfortunately, no,' said Lottie. 'But I'm working on it, and

so should you.' She gave Helen's arm a quick squeeze. 'And
what more could you ask than for a seriously attractive man to
wine and dine you?'

'You really think that a meal at the Oxbow could console
me in any way for Nigel?' Helen shook her head. 'Lottie—I'm
really hurting. He's always been part of my life—and now he's
gone.'

'Helen—be honest. You had a crush on him when you were
thirteen and decided he was the man of your dreams. He went
along with it for a while, but he's spent less and less time here
for over a year now. Some love affair.'

'No,' Helen said, biting her lip. 'It never was. That's the
trouble. I—I wanted to wait. So it wasn't an affair at all, in
the real meaning of the word.'

'Oh,' said Lottie slowly. 'Well—that's one less thing to regret.'

'But I do regret it,' Helen told her miserably. She sighed.
'Oh, God, what a fool I've been. And I've lost him. So do you
see now why I can't go out tonight? It would be unbearable.'

'Then stay here and brood,' Lottie told her robustly. 'And
why not have ''victim'' tattooed across your forehead while
you're about it?'

Helen gave her a bitter look. 'I didn't know you could be
so heartless. How would you like to face people if you'd been
dumped?'

'Darling, I'm trying to be practical.' Lottie drank some coffee. 'And I'd infinitely prefer to be out, apparently having a
good time with another man, than nursing a broken heart on
my own. Who knows? People might even think you dumped
Nigel rather than the other way round. Think about it.' She
paused. 'Anyway, why did you say it wasn't a date with Marc
Delaroche?'

'Because it's more of a business meeting.' Helen still looked
morose. 'He's got some plan for helping Monteagle now the
grant's fallen through. Or he says he has.'

'All the more reason to go, then.'

'But I don't want to feel beholden to him,' Helen said passionately. 'I—I don't like him. And I don't know what you all see in him,' she added defiantly.

'Helen—' Lottie's tone was patient '—he's incredibly rich and fabulously sexy. You don't think that you're being a mite picky?'

Helen said in a low voice, 'It's not just that. I—I think I'm frightened of him.' Her laugh cracked in the middle. 'Isn't that ridiculous?'

Lottie's expression was very gentle. 'A little, maybe. But there's not much he can do in a crowded restaurant.' She frowned. 'I wonder how the hell he managed to get a table at the Oxbow, it being Saturday and all.'

Helen shrugged listlessly. 'He's someone who likes to have his own way. I don't suppose he gets many refusals.'

Lottie gave her a wry grin. 'Then meeting you might be good for his soul.' She paused, then added thoughtfully, 'Or he might even be good for yours.'

She picked up her beaker and rose. 'Now, let's have a quick scan through your wardrobe and see what might be suitable for the best restaurant in miles.'

This is still such a bad idea, Helen thought a few hours later as she looked at herself in the mirror.

The dress she was wearing was in a silky fabric the dark green of a rose leaf, and made in a wrap-around style, with a sash that passed twice round her slender waist and fastened at the side in a bow.

It made her skin look exotically pale, and her newly washed hair glint with gold and bronze lights.

Lottie had spotted it at once, of course. 'So, what's this?' she'd asked, taking it from the rail. 'Clearly never worn, because it's still got the price tag. How long have you had it?'

'Not that long.' Helen moved a shoulder restively, her voice slightly husky. 'I—I bought it for my engagement party.' She forced a smile. 'Counting my chickens again. Stupid of me, wasn't it?'

'Not at all.' Lottie's tone was comforting. 'And you can put it to good use tonight instead,' she added, spreading it across Helen's bed.

'No,' Helen said sharply. 'I got it for Nigel. I won't wear it for anyone else. I can't.'

'What will you do with it, then? Wrap it in lavender and shed tears over it, like a latter-day Miss Havisham?' Lottie gave her a swift hug. 'Babe, you can't waste the only decent thing you've got—especially when you need to make a good impression.'

'And why should I want to do that?' Helen lifted her chin.

'Monteagle, of course,' Lottie told her with a cat-like smile. 'Did you get shoes as well?'

'Green sandals.' Helen pointed reluctantly. 'They're in that box.'

'You'll have to paint your toenails too,' Lottie mused. 'I'd better pop home and get my manicure stuff, because I bet you haven't any. And you'll need a wrap. I'll lend you the pashmina Simon sent me. But don't spill vintage champagne all over it.'

The promised wrap was now waiting on the bed, together with the small kid bag that matched the sandals.

I was so sure, Helen thought, her throat muscles tightening. So secure in my dreams of the future. And so blind...

And now she had to work towards a totally different kind of future.

She'd had plenty of time to think after Lottie had completed her ministrations and departed.

Lying back in a scented bath, she'd reviewed her situation and come up with a plan. She could not afford to pay for the restoration of the entire house, of course, but perhaps Marc Delaroche might help her raise sufficient capital to refurbish the bedrooms at least, so that she and Daisy could offer bed and breakfast accommodation. Possibly with a few extra refinements.

Spend the night in the haunted bedroom! she'd thought, with self-derision. See the ghost of the first Helen Frayne, if not the second.

I could even rattle a few chains outside the door.

Joking apart, the scheme had a lot to recommend it, she told herself. It could supply her with just the regular income she needed.

And if she could prove herself, even in a small way, the conventional banking system might be more ready to back her.

But first she had to persuade Marc that it was a workable plan, and an alternative to whatever assistance he was prepared to give.

And therefore it was—just—worth making an effort with her appearance.

Only now the moment had come. Daisy had tapped on her door to say that he was waiting downstairs, causing all her concerns and doubts to come rushing back.

Because she was taking a hell of a risk. She'd said it herself—Marc Delaroche was a man who liked his own way—so what on earth made her think she could manipulate him into doing what she wanted?

Besides, she already knew he had his own agenda. *On my next visit I shall expect to spend the night.*

She'd tried to block that out of her mind—as with so much else that had passed between them.

But now the words were ringing loud and clear in her head, especially as she'd spent some considerable time getting herself dressed and beautified for him—like some harem girl being prepared for the Sultan's bed, she thought, and grimaced at the analogy.

Her skin was smooth and scented. Her eyes looked twice their normal size, shaded, with darkened lashes, and the colour of her dress had turned them from hazel to green. Her mouth glowed with soft coral, as did the tips of her hands and feet.

She picked up her wrap and bag, and went along the Gallery to the broad wooden staircase.

Marc was below her, in the entrance hall, pacing restlessly, but as he looked up at her he checked suddenly, his entire attention arrested and fixed on her, his eyes widening and his mouth suddenly taut.

She felt a strange shiver of awareness rake her body, and for

a moment she wanted to turn and run—back to her room, to
safety. Back to the girl she really was.

Because for the first time it occurred to her that she was not
simply scared of Marc Delaroche.

I'm frightened of myself, she whispered silently. And of the
stranger I've just become—for him.

She drew a deep shaking breath, then very slowly she walked
down the stairs to meet him.

CHAPTER FIVE

THE restaurant was just as crowded as Lottie had predicted. Apart from their own, Helen could see only one vacant table, and that was reserved too.

She was conscious of a surprised stir as they entered, and knew that she'd been recognised by at least half the people in the room, and that the rumour mill had been functioning well. She tried to ignore the speculative looks and whispered comments as, with Marc's hand cupped under her elbow, she followed the head waiter across the room.

But a shock wave was preferable every time to a ripple of sympathy, she thought, straightening her shoulders. Lottie had been right about that too.

And it was difficult to feel too humiliated over Nigel when she'd been brought here in a chauffeur-driven car and was now being seated at a candlelit table in an alcove where a bottle of Dom Perignon on ice and two glasses were waiting for them.

And also when she was being accompanied by the most attractive man in the room, she acknowledged reluctantly.

Tonight, as she'd noticed in the car, he was freshly shaven, and the dark mane of hair had been combed into a semblance of order. Close-fitting dark pants set off his long legs, and his well-laundered white shirt was enhanced by a silk tie with the colour and richness of a ruby. The light tweed jacket, slung over his shoulder, shouted 'cashmere'.

Certainly there'd been no escaping the frank envy in some of the female eyes as they watched her progress.

Oh, God, she thought, swallowing, I must be unbelievably shallow to find all that even a minor comfort.

'It has a good reputation, this place,' her companion commented as the champagne was poured and the menus arrived.

'Yes,' Helen agreed, glad of a neutral topic. 'Lottie reckons

71

it's the best food in miles. And they do rooms as well,' she added, her mind returning to Monteagle and its problems.

'*C'est vrai?*' he queried softly. 'You wish me to reserve one for later, perhaps?'

Her head lifted from the menu she was studying as if she'd been shot, her mouth tightening indignantly as she saw the wicked amusement in the dark eyes.

She said between her teeth, 'Will you—please—not say things like that?'

'Forgive me,' he said, showing no obvious signs of repentance. 'But you are so easy to tease, *ma mie*, and you blush so adorably. Calm yourself with some champagne.'

'Is there something to celebrate?' She picked up her glass.

'Who knows?' He shrugged. 'But, anyway, let us drink to Monteagle—and its future.'

'Actually,' Helen began, 'I've been giving that some thought and—'

He lifted a silencing hand. 'Later, *cherie*,' he told her softly. 'You must learn how the game is played. And also accept that a man rarely grants favours on an empty stomach,' he added drily.

'But it's not a game,' she protested. 'Not to me.'

'*Quand même,*' he said. 'We will eat first.'

His rules, Helen thought resentfully, transferring her attention back to the list of food. A man who likes his own way. And just how far is he prepared to go in order to achieve it? she wondered, and shivered slightly.

But in the meantime she might as well enjoy the food, as this would probably be her first and last visit. She chose potted shrimps for her first course, following them with a rack of lamb, roasted pink, with grilled vegetables.

Marc ordered *tournedos* of beef, with *foie gras* and dark-gilled mushrooms, served with a Madeira sauce.

The Burgundy he picked to accompany the meal seemed to caress her throat like velvet.

'Will you tell me something?' Helen said, once they'd been served and the waiters had departed.

'If I can.'

'Why did the committee bother to hear me if they meant to turn me down?'

'We interview every applicant, or those that represent them. Mainly we concentrate on projects that will revive the tourist industry in former trouble spots, or attract it to areas entirely off the beaten track.' He shrugged. 'Your application was thought to be interesting, but not particularly deserving. Unluckily for you, *cherie*, you do not have to walk ten miles to find water each day, and your home is lit by the flick of a switch,' he added drily.

'Only,' she said, 'if I can afford to pay the bill.'

They ate in silence for a moment or two, and she was just nerving herself to mention the bed and breakfast idea when he said, 'Hélène—in an ideal world, what would you wish for Monteagle?'

'That's simple. I'd like it to be my home again, but with the money to maintain it properly, of course.' She sighed. 'No tour parties, no cream teas. Just peace, comfort and privacy. The way it once was. And the way a home should be, don't you think?'

'I would not know,' he told her drily. 'I have an apartment in Paris and a hotel suite in London. When I was a child my father never settled in any place for very long,' he added with a faint shrug. 'Only when he retired did he find somewhere— a vineyard in Burgundy with a small dilapidated château, close to the village where he was born. He planned to live there and make wine, but he died very suddenly before it was even habitable.'

'What happened to it?' she asked.

'I sold it to an English family in search of *la vie douce*.' He smiled faintly. 'Only God knows if they ever found it.'

'You weren't tempted to live there yourself?'

'And tend my vines in the sun?' He shook his head. 'I have factories to produce, and a world to travel in order to sell them.'

As he spoke he looked past her, and Helen saw him stiffen slightly, the dark brows snapping together. 'Ah,' he said softly. '*C'est complet.* The last table is now occupied—and by people you know, *ma belle.*'

She said, bewildered, 'People…?' And then stopped, staring at him, appalled.

'Oh, God,' she said unevenly. 'It's Nigel, isn't it? And his new lady?'

'And an older couple—*ses parents, sans doute,*' Marc drawled. Then, as Helen began to push her plate away, he reached across the table and captured her hands in his, holding them firmly. *'Doucement, cherie,'* he ordered softly. 'You are going nowhere.'

'But I must,' she whispered frantically. 'I can't stay here and see them together. I can't…'

'But you do not have to,' he said. 'It is all quite simple. You just look at me instead.' He lifted her hands to his lips, brushing light kisses across her white knuckles, nibbling gently at the tips of her trembling fingers, while she sat as if mesmerised allowing it to happen.

His eyes smiled into hers. 'Think, Hélène,' he urged quietly. 'If you run away, then they will know they have the power to make you suffer—and so they win. Better that you remain here—with me—and we finish our meal, *hein?*'

He released her hands and refilled her glass, wincing slightly as she took an unguarded panicky gulp of the precious wine.

She said huskily, 'Have they seen me?'

'I notice a certain *chagrin*, yes.' His mouth twisted. *'La mère*, I think, wishes to go, but her husband—*c'est un homme inflexible*, and he will get his way.'

'And Nigel?' She swallowed. 'How—how does he look?'

He shrugged. 'He seems to have survived his wetting in the lake.'

'Oh, God,' she said miserably. 'He'll never forgive me for that.'

'Perhaps,' he said. 'But that can no longer be allowed to matter to you.' He paused to let that sink in, then nodded at her plate. 'Now eat, *ma mie*, and take your time. After all, we still have the dessert to come. The apricot soufflés, I think, which have to be cooked to order, and will prove, therefore, that we are in no particular hurry.'

He cut off a sliver of beef and proffered it to her on his fork. 'In the meantime, try this, and—smile at me a little.'

'It's all right for you.' Unwillingly she did as she was told. The fact that he was talking sense made his advice no more palatable. 'You're not the one whose heart is being broken.'

He gave her a sardonic look. 'And nor are you, *cherie*, although you may not believe it at this moment.'

'How can you say that? How can someone like you possibly understand?' Helen asked passionately.

His brows lifted. 'You speak as if I was something less than human. Yet, *je t'assure*, I share all the normal emotions.' He smiled at her coolly. 'You wish me to demonstrate?'

'*No!*' Her face warmed. 'I meant that you've obviously never loved someone all your life as I've loved Nigel.' She shook her head. 'Why, I've never even looked at another man.'

'Perhaps because you have never had the chance to do so,' he said, unmoved. 'And your life is far from over. Now, eat something, *ma belle*, before your lack of appetite is noticed.'

Helen shot him a mutinous look from under her lashes, then reluctantly complied.

As they ate, Marc chatted to her lightly, asking mainly questions about the history of Monteagle, encouraging her to expand her monosyllabic replies into real animation as she warmed to her subject.

Making it almost possible, she realised with a sense of shock, for her to believe that she was there with him because she wished it, and not as a matter of expedience.

But she had to convince him of her enthusiasm, and her will to work, she thought, if she was to persuade him to lend her the money for the guest house scheme.

If only Nigel hadn't been there she'd have been able to outline her plan by now—have a proper business discussion, she thought with vexation. As it was, her companion had taken advantage of the delay while they waited for the soufflés, and taken her hand again, and was now playing gently with her fingers.

She glanced up, a muted protest already forming on her lips, but as their eyes met, and she saw the frank desire that smoked his gaze, she forgot completely what she was going to say.

She looked away swiftly, hating the involuntary colour that warmed her cheeks, trying unavailingly to release her hand from the caress of his long fingers.

She said haltingly, 'I—I don't know how you can—pretend like this.'

His faint smile was crooked. 'But I am not pretending, *cherie*,' he told her quietly. 'I want you. I have made no secret of it.'

She stared down at the tablecloth. 'Then you're due for a serious disappointment, Monsieur Delaroche. Even if I was in the market for an affair—which I'm not—you'd be the last person on earth I'd choose.'

'Then at least we agree on something,' Marc drawled. 'Because I do not want an *affaire* either. *Au contraire*, I wish you to become my wife.'

Helen was very still suddenly. She could feel her throat muscles tightening in shock. The blood drumming crazily in her ears.

'If—this is some kind of joke,' she managed hoarsely, 'then it's in very poor taste.'

'There is no joke,' he said. 'I am asking you to marry me, *ma belle*, and I am completely serious.'

She said, 'But you don't know anything about me. We've met three times at most.' She shook her head. 'We're strangers, for heaven's sake. You must be mad even to think of such a thing.'

'I do not suggest that the ceremony should take place next week.' He smiled at her. 'I intend to court you, Hélène. Give you some time to accustom yourself to the idea.' He paused. 'To all kinds of ideas,' he added drily.

He meant sleeping with him, she realised dazedly. She would have to face the prospect of him making love to her. With a sense of shock she found herself remembering their last encounter—the hard strength of his arms and the relentless heated urgency of his mouth on hers. Even though they'd both been fully dressed, she'd still been aware of every inch of his lean body against hers. And the thought of being held—touched—without the barrier of clothing, sent her mouth dry with panic.

He wanted her. He'd said so. Therefore he would not expect to be fended off—kept waiting until after the wedding.

Except there would be no wedding, she told herself with sudden fierceness. So why was she treating his outrageous proposal as if it was all cut and dried?

She said, 'You're wasting your time, *monsieur*. Did you think I'd be so terrified of being a spinster that you could catch me on the rebound?' She shook her head. 'You're wrong. Nothing on earth could persuade me to marry you.'

'Not even Monteagle?' he challenged. 'You wish it to become a home again. You said so.' He shrugged. '*Moi aussi.* Become my wife, and I will make funds available for the whole house to be restored in the way that you want.'

'No,' she said huskily. 'That's impossible. I couldn't—I can't.'

'Yet you said at the interview that you would do anything to save it.' He sat back in his chair, watching her from under half-closed lids. 'Clearly your devotion to your house is not as profound as you claim.'

'When I said that I was desperate.' Helen lifted her chin. 'But now I have a plan.'

'*D'accord,*' he said. 'A plan that you wish to share with me. But after we have finished our desserts,' he added calmly, apparently unfazed by her refusal, just as a waiter bore down on them with the soufflés, tall as chefs' hats, in their porcelain dishes.

She said unsteadily, 'You think I could eat anything else—after that bombshell?'

'*Mais, j'insiste.* One spoonful at least. To calm you,' he added, his mouth twisting wryly.

Unwilling, totally unnerved, she obeyed. The delicate flavour and texture melted deliciously on her tongue, and was impossible, she discovered, to resist.

So,' Marc said at last, putting down his spoon, 'what is this plan, and how will it save Monteagle?'

Helen took a breath. 'I want to restore and refurbish all the bedrooms so that I can offer bed and breakfast to tourists,' she said baldly.

His face gave nothing away. 'And you have costed this scheme? You have taken into your calculations the price of supplying each room with a bathroom *en suite*? Also refurbishing the dining room so that your guests have somewhere to eat this *petit dejeuner* without the ceiling falling on their heads? And, of course, there will be the updating of the kitchen to be considered, so that it meets the demands of Health and Safety regulations.'

'Well, no,' Helen admitted, disconcerted. 'Not entirely. Because I've only just thought of it. But I'll get proper estimates for all the work for you to approve first.'

'For me?' he queried, brows lifted. 'How does this concern me?'

She bit her lip, suddenly wishing that her earlier rejection of his proposal had been a little less forceful. 'I was hoping that—you would lend me the money.'

There was a silence. 'Ah,' he said. 'But you have forgotten that there is an offer already on the table, where I give you all the money you need and you become my wife.'

She said breathlessly, 'But if you gave me a loan we wouldn't need to be married. And I'd have thought you were the last man on earth in the market for a wife.'

The dark eyes glinted at her. 'It does not occur to you, *ma mie*, that, much like yourself, I might be deeply and irresistibly in love?'

Helen felt as if all the breath had suddenly been choked out of her lungs. She stared at him, her eyes widening endlessly.

She said in a small, cracked voice, 'I don't—understand…'

'No? But you have only yourself to blame, *ma chère*. If you had not written and spoken about Monteagle with such passion, then I would not have been tempted to come and see it for myself. *Et voilà*. The rest, as they say, is history.'

She clutched at her reeling senses. She said huskily, 'You—mean that what you really want—is Monteagle. *Monteagle?* That's what you're saying?' She shook her head. 'Oh, I don't believe it. It's impossible, besides being ridiculous—ludicrous. You *can't*...'

His brows lifted. '*Pourquoi pas?* Why not? Along with my lack of humanity, do you also claim that I have no feeling for history—or appreciation of beauty?'

'How do I know,' she said stormily, 'what you think—what you feel about anything? You're a complete stranger, and as far as I'm concerned you always will be.' She looked at him, her eyes flashing. 'But you're talking about *my home.* Mine.'

'At the moment, yes.' He shrugged. 'But for how much longer without serious investment? You say you will not consider the offer of Monsieur Newson, so I offer an alternative. One of its advantages is that you will be able to go on living in the house you prize so highly.'

'Except,' she said, quietly and clearly, 'I'd be obliged to live with you.'

'It's an uncertain world, *cherie*,' he said mockingly. 'And I travel to dangerous places. Think of this—I could be dead within the year, and you would be a wealthy widow.' He added sardonically, 'I might even die on our wedding night—of ecstasy.'

He saw her flinch, and laughed softly.

Helen sat in silence, her teeth doing yet more damage to her ill-used lower lip, as a waiter arrived with a pot of coffee and a bottle of cognac.

When they were once again alone, she said, 'Please reconsider lending me the money. I swear I'll work night and day, and repay you in full.'

'Yes, *ma belle*, you will,' he said softly. 'But in coin of my choosing.' He paused to allow her to absorb that. 'And my offer remains a gift, not a loan.' He smiled at her. 'A wedding present, perhaps, from the groom to his bride.'

Helen stared down at her hands, clenched painfully in her lap. 'Why are you doing this?' she asked in a low voice. 'You're forcing me to sell myself to you for Monteagle. What kind of man does something like that?'

'A rich one.' He sounded appallingly casual—even amused. 'If something I want is for sale, *cherie*, then I buy it.'

'No matter what the consequences?'

He shrugged. 'For me, they are good. I am gaining a house I want and a woman I desire. And maybe I have reached a time in my life when a home and children have become important to me.'

Her lips parted in a gasp. 'You think for one minute—you really expect me to have your baby?'

'Another consequence of marriage,' Marc drawled unsmilingly. 'If you still believe in the stork, *ma mie*, you have been misinformed.' He paused. 'But I am forcing you to do nothing, Hélène. Understand that. I merely offer you a solution to your most pressing problem. It is for you to decide whether you accept my proposal or deny me.'

He gave her a measuring look. 'And you have twenty-four hours in which to make up your mind,' he added coolly.

She picked up her glass and took a mouthful of cognac, feeling it crackle in her throat. At the same time she was conscious of a faint dizziness. It might be caused by the shocks of the past hour, but could also be ascribed to the amount of alcohol she'd unwittingly taken on board, she realised.

Well, there would be no more of that, at least. She wasn't accustomed to it, and she needed to keep her wits about her now as never before, she thought grimly.

She looked back at him defiantly. 'Is this how you usually propose marriage—by ultimatum?'

The hardness of his mouth relaxed into a swift, unexpected grin. 'Until this moment, *cherie*, I have never proposed marriage at all. Other things, yes,' he added shamelessly. 'But not marriage.'

She gave him a fulminating look. 'I suppose I should feel flattered,' she said icily. 'But I don't.' She reached for her bag. 'May we go now, please?'

He was still amused. *'D'accord.'* He signalled for the bill while Helen braced herself for the walk to the door, which would involve passing Nigel and his new fiancée.

But when she turned to leave she saw only an empty table, in the process of being cleared by the staff, and checked in surprise.

'They left about ten minutes ago,' Marc informed her quietly. 'They did not seem to be enjoying their evening.' He paused. 'Or perhaps your Nigel feared another dousing—from an ice bucket.'

Helen ignored that. 'Will you ask Reception to get me a taxi, please?' she requested with dignity.

She realised uneasily that she was having to choose her words, and her steps, with care, so the sooner she was rid of her companion, the better.

His brows lifted. 'My car and driver will be waiting,' he pointed out.

'But I really need to be alone,' she said. 'Surely even you can understand that?'

'"Even you,"' he repeated pensively. 'I see I shall have to change your low opinion of me, *cherie*.'

'By forcing me into marriage?' She shook her head. 'I don't think so.' She paused, lifting her chin. 'And now I'd really like to go home.'

He said lightly, 'As you wish,' and went to the reception desk.

'Your cab will be ten minutes,' he told her on his return. 'Shall I wait with you until it arrives?'

'No,' Helen said hastily, then added a belated, 'Thank you.'

She'd half expected a protest, but all he said was a casual, '*A bientôt,*' and went.

There was no avoiding the fact that she would be seeing him again—and soon, she thought wearily. After all, he'd given her only twenty-four hours in which to make up her mind—or rack her brains for a way out.

She still felt faintly giddy, so she made her way over to a high-backed chair in the shelter of an enormous parlour palm and sat down, leaning back and closing her eyes.

When she heard the main door open she assumed her cab had arrived early, but instead she heard Nigel's voice peremptorily addressing the receptionist.

'My mother seems to have mislaid her scarf. Could someone look in the cloakroom for me? See if it's there?'

Helen, transfixed, had a fleeting impulse to climb into the palm and vanish.

But it was too late. Nigel had seen her and was crossing the foyer. She got to her feet, her fingers tightening defensively round the strap of her bag.

'All alone?' he asked unpleasantly. 'Dumped you already, has he?'

She flushed. 'No, he hasn't,' she said, adding recklessly, 'On the contrary, I'll be seeing him again tomorrow.'

'Well, you're certainly full of surprises, Helen. I'll grant you that.' He scanned her insolently from head to foot. 'You do know who you're dealing with, I suppose?'

'Yes,' she said. 'I know.'

'So, what the hell's a high-flyer like him doing in this backwater?' Nigel demanded.

She shrugged. 'Perhaps you should ask him that yourself.'

'Oh, I don't know him that well,' he said. 'It's Amanda. She's met him at parties in London and she could hardly believe her eyes when she saw you together. You're hardly his usual kind of totty.'

Helen steadied her voice. 'I'm sorry if she's disappointed.'

'She's not interested one way or the other,' Nigel said rather stiffly. 'He's certainly not her type. Nor does he believe in long-term relationships,' he added waspishly. 'Just in case you were hoping. Apparently he has a very low boredom threshold where women are concerned. Two months is the top limit for his involvements. None of his girls are kept around for longer. He's notorious for it.' He grinned nastily. 'And you haven't even lasted the night, sweetie.' He paused. 'So how *did* you meet him—as a matter of interest?'

'I can't imagine why it should be any of your concern,' she said, 'but he happened to be on the committee that turned me down the other day and he was curious about the house. It's as simple as that.'

Oh, God, she thought with a pang. *If only it were...*

'Oh, the *house*,' he said disparagingly. 'That explains it.'

'Thank you.' Helen said coldly, wishing desperately that her cab would arrive—or that she would be abducted by aliens.

He flushed slightly. 'Believe it or not, I'm trying to warn you for your own good. Although why I should bother after the trick you played on me this morning, God only knows,' he added sulkily. 'Do you know how long it took me to come up with an excuse for being soaked to the skin?'

'Am I supposed to care?' Helen threw back at him.

He shrugged, giving her a faintly injured look. 'We've known each other for a long time. I assumed it might be possible to remain friends.'

'Difficult,' she said, 'when we don't even occupy the same planet. And here's my taxi.' She offered him a small polite smile. 'Goodbye, Nigel, and—good luck.'

'And you,' he said venomously, 'deserve everything that's coming to you. When your house has gone, and your French millionaire has used you up and spat you out, don't come to me for a handout.'

There wasn't even a fountain to push him into this time, Helen thought, let alone the preferred swamp. And that was her sole regret as she walked away from him and out into the night.

Nor was it because of this brief confrontation that she found herself trembling as she sat huddled in the back of the taxi taking her home through the darkness.

It was Marc Delaroche who occupied her mind, imprinting himself indelibly on her inner vision.

My first real proposal of marriage, she thought, fighting back the bubble of hysteria rising within her. And it's from him.

She looked down at the hand he'd caressed and found she was clenching it into a fist.

As they headed through the village towards Monteagle her driver slowed as a car approached them, travelling smoothly and swiftly in the opposite direction.

Helen recognised it instantly. Oh, God, she thought, as she shrank further into her corner. *His car.* On its way back to the Monteagle Arms, no doubt.

But where on earth could he have been up till then? she asked herself in bewilderment. He should have returned long before her. Had his chauffeur become lost in the twisting lanes?

Whatever, he was far too close for her comfort. But perfectly poised for tomorrow, just an hour or so away, when he would come for his answer.

His package deal, she thought bitterly, for which he was apparently offering a blank cheque. Her house and herself—not necessarily in that order—and no expense spared. Or so he wanted her to believe...

It was—almost flattering. But she wasn't fooled, Helen told herself with sudden, desperate decision. It wasn't a genuine offer—not in a civilised society. It couldn't be...

He was merely testing her resolve, and of course he expected her to refuse. He probably relied on it.

After all, why should he want to spend a fortune on a place he'd seen briefly a couple of times?

And, besides, even a marriage that was only a business arrangement had too permanent a sound for someone who counted his relationships in days rather than years.

It's a wind-up, she thought with an inward sigh of relief, as the cab turned into Monteagle's gates. It has to be, and unfortunately I fell for it. Let him see I was rattled. Big mistake.

But at least she had a whole day to decide how to deal with it.

She considered, and immediately discarded, the idea of trying to rattle him in turn. Of letting him think she was actually tempted by his proposition and allowing him to talk her out of it. It might be amusing, but it was also dangerous.

He was too unpredictable, and—which annoyed her even more—invariably several steps ahead of her.

The sensible plan would be to tell him unsmilingly that the joke was over and request him to leave her in peace—seriously and permanently.

Except that might not be as simple as it sounded. Marriage might not be in the equation, but Marc Delaroche still wanted her. Inexperienced as she was, Helen was unable to deny that. If she was honest, she'd recognised it from their first encounter, with a stark female instinct she'd never known she possessed until that moment. And he was determined for his desire to be satisfied, however fleetingly.

It was that knowledge which dried her mouth and set up that deep inner trembling when he was near, invaded her thoughts when he was far away.

Nigel had never looked at her with such hungry intensity, she admitted painfully. Had never touched her skin as if he was caressing the petals of a flower. Had never stirred her senses to the edge of fear.

That alone should have warned her, she thought, as she paid off the driver and turned to go into the house.

There was no sign of Daisy, but the kitchen was filled with the aroma of coffee and the percolator bubbled away cheerfully.

She still felt fuzzy round the edges. Daisy's rich brew would clear her head and hopefully remove the shakiness in her legs too. Because she needed to be in total control, able to think positively. To plan tomorrow's response to Marc. Convince him once and for all, and with some force, that both she and Monteagle would remain forever beyond his reach.

She locked the back door, then took a mug from the big dresser and carried it, with the percolator, along to the library. She had some heavy decisions to make, so why not in comfort?

The lamps were lit, and a small fire was burning briskly in the hearth. God bless Daisy, she thought gratefully, and took one step forward into the room, only to halt in startled disbelief as she realised suddenly that she was not alone.

As she saw, with stomach-lurching shock, who was rising from the sofa to greet her.

'So, you are here at last,' Marc said softly. And his smile touched her in cool possession.

CHAPTER SIX

HER heart was beating like a stone being thrown against a wall.
She stared back at him, her eyes widening endlessly in dismay.
His jacket and tie had been discarded, tossed over the arm of
the sofa, and his shirt was unbuttoned almost to the waist, the
sleeves rolled back over his forearms.

He could not, she thought numbly, have announced his intentions any more clearly.

Her voice, when she finally found it, was hoarse. 'We—we
said goodnight earlier. I saw your car on the way to the village—the hotel. So, what are you doing here?'

'You have a short memory, *ma belle*. It was my unfortunate
chauffeur you saw going to the hotel.' The dark eyes glinted
at her. 'I told you that on my next visit I intended to spend the
night here in this house.'

'Yes, but I never thought...' She stopped, biting her lip,
struggling for dignity. For some kind of rationality. Most of
all, for some way of keeping him at arm's length—or an even
greater distance. 'I prefer my guests to wait for an invitation.'

'I feared I might be made to wait for ever.' His mouth curled
sardonically. He walked across and took the percolator from
her wavering hand. 'Before you damage yourself, Hélène,' he
added drily. 'Or me. Now, come and sit down.'

If she turned and ran he would only follow her, she knew,
and she didn't want to demonstrate that kind of weakness—let
him see that she was scared in any way.

So she moved on legs that did not seem to belong to her to
the sofa, and sank down, grateful for its sagging support. A
small table had been drawn up, holding a tray with cups, a
cream jug and sugar bowl, plus a decanter of brandy and two
glasses.

She said shakily, 'You certainly believe in making yourself at home—in every way.'

He shrugged. 'Perhaps because I believe that very soon this will be my home.' He sat down at the other end of the sofa and began to pour out the coffee.

She gave him a swift, wary glance. 'Isn't that a premature assumption?' She tried to keep her voice toneless. 'After all, you said you'd give me twenty-four hours to answer you.' She paused. 'And I also thought you'd have the decency to allow me to consider your proposition in private,' she added, with a touch of hauteur.

'But I decided I would pay court to you instead, *cherie*,' he drawled. 'Decency has always seemed to me such a dull virtue.'

His words, and the amused glance which accompanied them, were like an icy finger on her spine. Her hands were clamped round each other in an attempt to conceal the fact that they were trembling.

But she lifted her chin. 'Virtue?' she echoed cuttingly. 'I'm surprised you even know what the word means.'

'What a low opinion you have of me, *ma chère*,' Marc drawled, pouring measures of brandy into the glasses. 'But at least it releases me from any obligation to behave well.'

He leaned towards her and Helen flinched instinctively, realising too late that he was simply putting her coffee and brandy within her reach on the table. She saw his mouth tighten with sudden harshness, but when he spoke his voice was casual.

'And I made you a proposal, not a proposition. Perhaps you would like me to demonstrate the difference?'

'No,' Helen said too hastily. 'I wouldn't.'

'To hear you,' he said softly, 'one would think that your namesake in the portrait had been a Vestal Virgin and that you were following her example.' His gaze rested fleetingly on her mouth. 'Yet all the evidence denies this.'

'I dislike being railroaded,' Helen told him, flushing. She was searingly aware of the lean body lounging so casually beside her—and alarmed by her awareness. 'That does not, however, make me a prig.'

'I am glad of the assurance.' His tone was faintly mocking. 'So,' he went on after a pause, 'what did Nigel say to you that has put you so much on edge?'

Avoiding his gaze, she picked up her glass and drank some brandy. 'I don't know what you mean.'

'But you don't deny that there was another *rencontre*, I hope.' He spoke pleasantly enough, but she was aware of a faint, harsh edge in his voice. 'You are not the only one to take note of passing traffic, *ma mie*. I saw his car returning to the restaurant. You must still have been there. Also,' he added judiciously, 'you are paler than before, and your eyes look bruised. Was he angry, perhaps, at your attempt to drown him?'

Helen took another restorative gulp of brandy. 'It was mentioned,' she said shortly. 'But he seemed more interested in bad-mouthing you.'

His brows lifted. 'I was not aware I had the pleasure of his acquaintance.'

'But you know—his new lady.' She had to struggle to say the words. 'Apparently you've met—at parties in London.'

'Ah,' Marc said softly. 'But I meet a great many people at a great many parties, *cherie*. She made no particular impression on me at the time.'

'Well, she remembers you very well,' she said, adding recklessly, 'And your reputation.'

He laughed. 'Do I have one? I was not aware.'

'You're said to be anti-commitment.' Helen stared down into her glass. 'You never continue any of your love affairs longer than two months.' She paused. 'Can you deny it?'

'*Certainement.*' He was still amused. 'I can assure you, *ma mie*, that love has never entered into any of my *affaires*.'

She bit her lip. 'Now you're playing with words. But then you like to do that, don't you, Mr Delaroche? Proposal versus proposition, for example. Not that it matters,' she added, 'because we both know that it's just some private game for your own amusement, and that you haven't the slightest intention of getting married to me—or to anyone.'

She drew a breath. 'So, can it stop right now, please? I'm getting bored with the joke.'

He reached for his jacket, extracted something from the pocket, and put it on the table. Helen saw it was a jeweller's velvet covered box, and nearly choked on the brandy she was swallowing.

'This is not the moment I would have chosen,' he said quietly. 'But perhaps this will finally convince you that I have indeed asked you to be my wife. And that I am quite serious.'

The diamonds in the ring were a circle of fire surrounding the deeper flame of an exquisite ruby. Helen's lips parted in a silent gasp that was part wonder, part horror.

'So, do you believe at last?' His smile was grim. 'Now all you need do, *ma belle*, is make your decision.'

She said huskily, 'You—make it sound so easy.'

'Yes, or no,' he said. 'What could be simpler?'

She shook back her hair in a defiant gesture. 'You seem to forget that I'm being asked to choose between freedom and a life sentence—with a stranger.'

'And what does this freedom allow you, *ma mie*?' His voice was hard. 'The right to struggle, to work endlessly while the house you adore crumbles around you? Never to be able to indulge your beauty—your joy in life?'

He paused. 'Besides,' he added cynically. 'If your informants are correct, the maximum term for you to serve would be only two months. Is that really such a hardship?'

Helen stared at him, aware of a strange icy feeling in the pit of her stomach. Yes, she realised, with sudden paralysing shock. Yes, it would be—if, somehow, I started to care. If, however incredible it may seem, you taught me to want you— to love you—and then you walked away.

Because that would be more than hardship. It would be agony. And it could break my heart for ever...

She said in a small taut voice, 'I suspect, *monsieur*, that even one month of your intimate company might be more than I could bear.' She took a steadying breath. 'Is there really nothing else you would agree to—for Monteagle?'

'You are brutally frank.' His mouth twisted. 'So let me be the same. My answer to that is nothing. I take the house and you with it, Hélène. Or you will be left to your—freedom. The choice is yours.'

Her fingers played with a fold of her dress. 'I—I'll give you an answer tomorrow.'

He glanced at his watch. 'It is already tomorrow. You are running out of time, *ma belle.*'

She said with sudden heat, 'I wish—I really wish you'd stop saying that. Stop pretending that I'm beautiful.'

He studied her for a moment with half-closed eyes. 'Why do you do this?' he asked quietly eventually. 'Why do you so undervalue yourself?'

'Because I'm a realist.' She finished the brandy in her glass. 'I loved Nigel and he chose someone else. Someone beautiful.' She paused. 'I didn't get a chance to look at her at the restaurant, so I assume she is—beautiful.' Her glance challenged him. 'You're supposed to be a connoisseur, Monsieur Delaroche. What do you think—now that you've seen her again?'

He was silent for a moment, then he shrugged. 'She has her charms. Dark hair, a sexy mouth and a good body. And a tigress in bed, I imagine,' he added sardonically. 'Is that what you wanted to hear?'

Colour flared in her face, and her own completely unsexy mouth didn't seem to be working properly.

She said thickly, 'That's rather—too much information.'

'You hoped I would say she was plain and undesirable and that her only attraction is her father's money?' He spoke more gently. 'I wish it was so.'

'Don't pity me,' she said raggedly. 'Just don't—bloody pity me.'

He watched her for a moment, his expression wry. 'I think, Hélène, that you have had enough brandy.'

'Well, I don't agree.' She held out her glass defiantly. 'In fact I'd like some more—lots more—if you don't mind.'

Marc lifted the decanter. 'As you wish. But it is really too good to be used as an anaesthetic, *ma mie.*'

Helen tilted her chin. 'Maybe I want to be…' She tried the word 'anaesthetised' under her breath, but decided not to risk it. The room seemed very warm suddenly, and her head was swimming. 'Drunk,' seemed a safer alternative, and she said it twice just to make sure.

'I think you will achieve your ambition,' he told her drily. 'And sooner than you believe.'

She hoisted the refilled glass in his direction, aware that he seemed to have receded to some remote distance. Which was all to the good, of course. Perhaps, in time, if she went on drinking, he might disappear altogether.

'Cheers, *monsieur*,' she articulated with great care, and giggled at her success. Fine, she told herself defiantly, swallowing some more brandy. I'm—perfectly fine.

'*Salut, petite.*' His voice sounded very close. She felt the glass being removed from her hand, gently but firmly. Felt herself drawn nearer so that she was leaning against him, her cheek against his shoulder.

She knew she should resist, and swiftly, but her senses were filled with the warm male scent of him, and she was breathing the musky fragrance of the cologne he used. An odd weakness seemed to have invaded her body, and she wasn't sure she could get to her feet even if she tried, or stand upright if she did.

She was suddenly aware, too, that his hand was stroking her hair, softly, rhythmically, and she was shocked by this unexpected tenderness from Marc of all men. Because it seemed as if he had, in some strange way, become her sole rock in an ocean of desolation.

But that, she knew, was impossible. The complete opposite of the truth. Because he was danger, not comfort. Her enemy, not her friend. The predator, with herself as prey.

She moved suddenly, restlessly, trying to free herself, but the arm that held her was too strong, and the caressing hand almost hypnotic as it moved down to smooth the taut nape of her neck and the curve of her shoulder.

'*Sois tranquille.*' His voice was gentle. 'Be still, Hélène, and close your eyes. There is nothing to fear, I swear it.'

And somehow it was much simpler—almost imperative, in fact—to believe him and obey. To allow herself to drift endlessly as her weighted eyelids descended. And to surrender her own body's rhythms to the strong, insistent beat of his heart against hers.

She was never sure what woke her, but suddenly she was back to total consciousness, in spite of her aching head and her eyes, which some unfeeling person had filled with sand.

She took a cautious look round, then froze, all self-inflicted wounds forgotten. She was still on the sofa, but stretched out full-length in the arms of Marc, who was lying asleep beside her, his cheek resting on her hair.

She was so close to him, she realised, alarmed, that she could feel the warmth of his bare, hair-roughened chest through the thin fabric of her dress.

One arm was round her shoulders and the other lay across her body, his hand curving round her hipbone, and her movement was further restricted by the weight of his long leg, which was lying slightly bent over both of hers, imprisoning her in an intimacy as disturbing as it was casual.

Dear God, she moaned silently. How did I let this happen?

Her only small comfort was that apart from their shoes, which were on the floor, they were both dressed. But she could hardly have felt more humiliated if she'd woken up naked.

And just how long had this been going on anyway? she wondered miserably.

The lamp was still burning, but the fire was a pile of grey ash covering just one or two glowing embers.

Moving her arm carefully, she glanced at her watch and saw that it was nearly four a.m.

She took a steadying breath. I have to get out of here, she thought. Right now.

It didn't appear as if anything untoward had happened—in fact, she knew it hadn't—but she felt totally vulnerable like this, in his embrace. She certainly couldn't risk his waking and finding her there with him, in case he decided, after all, to—take advantage of the situation.

With the utmost caution she pushed his leg away, then slid,

inch by wary inch, from beneath his arm, putting down a hand to balance herself before lowering herself slowly to the floor.

She sat motionless for a moment, listening intently, but he did not stir and there was no change in his even breathing.

In spite of the pounding in her head, she managed to get to her feet. Then, sandals in hand, she tiptoed to the door and let herself out into the dark house. She knew every step of the way, every creaking floorboard to avoid as she fled to her bedroom. Once safely inside, out of breath and feeling slightly sick, she turned the key in the lock, and for good measure pushed a small wooden chair under the handle.

Then she stripped, letting her clothes lie where they fell, and crept into bed, pulling the covers over her head.

All that damned brandy. She groaned, fighting her nausea and praying for the bed to keep still. I must have been insane. Why, anything could have happened while I was unconscious.

Only to her own bewilderment it was apparent that nothing had. Instead, Marc had let her sleep, peacefully and comfortably.

So he can't have wanted me that much, after all, she thought, turning over and burying her face in the pillow. It's the house—just the house. And found herself wondering why that particular realisation should sting so much?

She certainly didn't need to be desired by a serial womaniser, she reminded herself forcefully.

She had to think, clearly and rationally, she told herself. Find a watertight reason for turning him down and dismissing him from her life, whatever the consequences for Monteagle's future.

But her mind was still teeming with images and sensations, and it was difficult to focus somehow. To stop wondering what form his promised wooing of her might have taken. And to forget, as she must, the way he'd looked at her, the things he'd said, and—his touch. That, dear God, above all else.

Once he'd gone she'd be able to put him out of her mind, and devote herself to the on-going struggle to make Monteagle financially viable. She wouldn't have time to think about anything else—especially ludicrous might-have-beens.

She stayed awake, her brain going in weary circles, until sunlight penetrated the curtains, then dressed and went downstairs to go for a walk round the lake. Every movement was a penance, but the fresh air might help to clear her head, she told herself optimistically.

The door of the sitting room remained closed, and to her relief she had the kitchen to herself too, as she made some strong black coffee and drank it, wincing.

She stood by the water, looking across at the grey mass of Monteagle's half-ruined keep, wondering how much longer she could keep it standing without a substantial cash windfall.

Football pools, she thought. The Lottery. Quiz shows paying out thousands. What hadn't she considered in her efforts, however forlorn the hope? And now no other avenues suggested themselves.

However, she looked at it, Helen thought wretchedly, she was between a rock and a hard place.

Time was running out, and she still couldn't figure how to frame her refusal to Marc Delaroche.

With most men a simple 'I don't love you' would be enough. But he didn't want her love anyway. He wants Monteagle, she thought, her throat tightening, and maybe a son to inherit it. And a wife who'll pretend not to notice when he becomes bored and starts to stray. Or when he stops coming back altogether.

And, if I'm truly honest with myself, that's what really scares me—that I'll begin to love him because I can't help myself. That last night I felt safe and secure, for the first time in months, with his arms round me. And that in the end I'll be left alone and lonely, because that's what he does.

And I know now I couldn't bear that. It would kill me.

And that's something I can never let him guess—which is why I have to say no, once and finally.

She walked slowly back to the house. She would bathe, she thought as she went upstairs, and change. Put on a brave face.

She gave herself a little heartening nod, then flung open the bathroom door and marched in.

'*Bonjour,*' Marc said softly from the depths of the tub. He picked up the sponge and squeezed water over his head, letting it run in rivulets down his face and chest. 'Have you come to say that you will marry me? If so, you could begin your wifely duties by washing my back.'

'Oh, God,' Helen said, appalled, and backed out into the passage, slamming the door behind her to shut off the sound of his laughter.

Daisy was at the sink in the kitchen, dealing with the cups and glasses from the previous night, when Helen arrived, flushed and breathless from her headlong dash downstairs.

'Why,' she demanded, 'is Marc Delaroche still here? And what is he doing in my bathroom?'

'My guess would be—having a bath.' Daisy gave her a disapproving look. 'I dare say he could do with a bit of pampering—after last night.'

'And what's that supposed to mean?'

Daisy turned, hands on her hips, her gaze deepening into real severity. 'The very idea, Miss Helen—making the poor young man sleep on that wretched sofa when there was a perfectly good bedroom all ready for him upstairs. And Sir Henry always was such a hospitable man too. He must be turning in his grave.'

Helen took a deep breath. 'It's not a question of hospitality—' she began, but Daisy was firm.

'He told me when I saw him this morning that you were expecting him, Miss Helen. Isn't that so?'

Helen abandoned the struggle. 'Yes,' she acknowledged wearily. 'I suppose it is. I—I just wasn't sure when it would be.'

'Ah, well,' Daisy said comfortably. 'That's all right, then.' She hesitated, giving Helen a shrewd glance. 'I get the idea we'll be seeing more of Mr Marc in future.'

Helen murmured something non-committal.

I saw more than I needed just now in the bathroom, she thought, filling the kettle and placing it on the stove.

She was just making coffee when the bell at the front entrance jangled with two imperative bursts.

'Now, who on earth's calling at this time on a Sunday?' Daisy wiped her hands and moved towards the door. 'Have you invited anyone else, Miss Helen?'

'Not that I know of.' Helen attempted lightness. 'But maybe we'd better make up another room, just to be on the safe side.'

Of course it could be Lottie, curious to know how the previous evening had gone, so she turned, beaker in hand, prepared to be welcoming when Daisy returned. But the housekeeper was alone, her face set and stony. 'It's that Mr Newson,' she said shortly. 'He insists on having a word with you, so I've put him in the library.'

'Oh.' Helen abandoned her coffee and went reluctantly to join him, wishing that she looked tidier, more like the lady of the house instead of the hired help.

The room looked neat and cheerful in the sunlight pouring through the window, and her unwanted visitor was standing with his back to the empty fireplace, looking round him with his usual narrow-eyed appraisal.

She said icily, 'Is there something I can do for you, Mr Newson?'

'Yes,' he said. 'You can tell me that you've seen sense at last over this house and are prepared to sell to me. My team are all ready to go. I only need to say the word.'

'But I've already said the word.' Helen lifted her chin. 'And it's no. I thought I'd made that clear.'

'But that was when you thought you could get your hands on some money.' The fleshy face gloated at her. 'It's all round the village that you've been turned down for that grant you pinned your hopes on. You've nowhere else to turn, and you know it. So if you've got any sense you'll reconsider my offer, minus a small discount for the inconvenience you've put me to, and be quick about it. I'm planning to open next Easter.'

'Well, I hope you haven't spent too much on preliminaries,' Helen returned, with total insincerity. 'Because Monteagle is still not for sale.'

'I'm a tolerant man, Miss Frayne. Anyone will tell you that. But you're beginning to try my patience. Get it into your head, my dear. You've fought well, but you've lost. I hold all the cards, and I'm about to collect.'

Except, Helen thought, she held a final ace—if she chose to

play it. And what real choice did she have—if Monteagle was to be saved?

She heard the creak of a floorboard behind her. Knew without turning who had entered the room—and what he was waiting to hear. Her fight was over at last, and her choice made for her—whatever the consequences.

She took a deep breath, aware that she was shivering, her stomach churning as she faced Trevor Newson.

She said huskily, 'I'm afraid not. You see, I'm going to be married—very soon—and my future husband plans to restore the house completely—as our family home.' She paused. 'Isn't that right—darling?'

Marc's hands descended on her shoulders. His skin smelled cool and damp, but the lips that touched the side of her throat in a lingering kiss were warmer than the blaze of the sun.

He said softly into her ear, 'It will be one of my many pleasures, *mon amour.*'

He came to stand beside her, his arm circling her body, his hand on her hip in a gesture of possession as casual as it was disturbing. He was barefoot, bare-chested, a pair of shabby jeans his only covering.

'When I woke you were gone, *cherie.*' He clicked his tongue in a kind of amused reproach. 'And here you are, entertaining another man.'

'I don't think Mr Newson is particularly entertained,' Helen said coolly. 'Besides, he's just leaving.'

The older man's face was unpleasantly flushed. 'So this is your saviour?' He nearly spat the word. 'He doesn't look to me as if he's got two pennies to rub together, but I'm sure you've had him checked out.' He glared at Marc. 'She's a fast worker. I'll give her that. Up to yesterday she was supposed to be engaged to someone else, only he's dumped her. Now here she is with you.' Trevor Newson gave Helen a smile that made her skin crawl. 'So, where did you find this one, love?'

'She did not,' Marc said curtly. 'I found her. And you are offending my fiancée, *monsieur.* Perhaps you would like to go, before I throw you out.'

'You and whose army?' Trevor Newson blustered. He was

more heavily built than his opponent, but he was flabby and out of condition when compared with Marc's toned muscularity. 'But I'm leaving anyway.' At the door, he turned. 'This is going to cost you a fortune, my friend. I just hope you find she's worth the expense. Not many women are.'

As soon as he had gone Helen eased herself from Marc's arm and walked over to the window.

She said, 'Do you usually come downstairs half-dressed?'

'I had just finished shaving. You have some objection?' He sounded amused again.

She shrugged. 'It's—not very dignified.' She paused. 'And it made that awful man think…'

'That we had slept together?' Marc supplied cordially, as she hesitated again. 'But you can hardly deny that you spent most of the night in my arms, *ma mie*.'

'No,' Helen said between gritted teeth. 'I—can't.'

'But you wish so much that it were otherwise, *hein*?' He walked over to her. Turned her to face him, a hand under her chin, so he could look down into her eyes. 'So,' he said softly, 'you have agreed, after all, to make the ultimate sacrifice to save this house. For a while I thought your aversion to me might prove too strong.'

She bit her lip and stared down at the floor. 'So did I.' Her voice was bitter.

'I think I owe Monsieur Newson some thanks,' he said reflectively. 'If he had not come here this morning, your answer to me might have been different.'

'Yes,' she said. 'It would.' She took a deep breath. 'Don't you have any compunction about what you're doing—what you're forcing me to do? And all for a whim.' She shook her head. 'If you really want a house, there are so many others you could buy. So many women probably falling over each other to marry you.'

'But you are unique, *cherie*,' he said lightly. 'You do not profess undying love. You make it clear that you want only my money. I find that—refreshing.'

'And I,' she said in a low voice, 'find it degrading.'

He tucked an errant strand of hair behind her ear. 'Nevertheless, Hélène,' he said quietly, 'the bargain is made between us, and it will not be broken.' He dug a hand into the pocket of his jeans and produced the little velvet box. 'Now, give me your hand.'

She watched numbly as the ruby slid over her knuckle into its symbolic resting place. So beautiful, she thought, watching the slow fire that burned in its depths, and yet so totally meaningless.

He said, 'Will you give me a kiss, or do I have to take it from you?'

Swallowing nervously, she raised her mouth to his with reluctant obedience. But instead of the passionate onslaught she'd expected—and feared—Marc was gentle with her, his lips moving on hers with a strange, almost mesmerising sweetness, the tip of his tongue probing her defences softly and sensuously. Coaxing her, she thought, her mind reeling, to a response that she dared not risk—even if she wished...

She stood rigid in the circle of his arms, shakily aware of the heat of his naked skin through her clothes. Willing the kiss to end. Praying that she would escape unscathed.

At last, with a rueful sigh, he lifted his head, watching her through half-closed eyes.

'You lack warmth, *cherie*,' he told her wryly. 'But that will change once you have learned a little about pleasure.'

She stepped back from him, wrapping defensive arms round her body. 'Is that really what you think?' She invested her tone with scorn.

He laughed then, running the back of his hand teasingly down the curve of her stormy face. 'Yes, *petite innocente*, I do.' He paused, glancing at his watch. 'And now, *hélas*, I must dress and tear myself away from you back to London.'

'You're leaving?' She was genuinely astonished. 'Now?'

'*Pourquoi pas?*' He shrugged. 'After all, I have what I came for—and I have to prepare for an early meeting tomorrow.' He took the hand that wore his ring and kissed it. 'But I shall return next week. In the meantime my architect will be here, with his team, to begin restoration work on the house.'

His tone was brisk and businesslike, making her see the dynamism that drove him. See it, and resent it.

Monteagle, she thought, doesn't belong to you yet, *monsieur*.

She bristled defiantly. 'I have my own local people, thank you.'

'And now you will also have Alain.' He grinned at her. 'So, don't give him a hard time, *cherie*. He might wound more easily than I do.' He paused. 'One more thing,' he added casually. 'The number of your bank account, if you please.'

She gasped. 'Why should I give you that?'

'So that I can transfer some money for you.'

She said coldly, 'I have funds of my own, thanks. I don't need any charity.'

'And I am not offering it. But there will be incidental expenses once the work starts that you cannot be expected to meet.' He smiled at her. 'Also you have your trousseau to buy. I intend to begin the arrangements for our wedding tomorrow. I suggest a civil ceremony before witnesses at the end of next month.'

Helen's heart was thudding again. 'But you said there was no hurry,' she protested. 'That—that you'd wait...'

'I think,' he told her softly, 'that I have been patient enough already. And last night has kindled my appetite, *ma mie*.' His smile widened as he looked down into her outraged, apprehensive eyes. 'So, be good enough to write down your account number for me, and I will go and leave you in peace.'

Quivering with anger, she obeyed, handing over the slip of paper with open resentment.

Marc walked to the door, then turned slowly, letting his eyes travel down her body.

'On the other hand,' he said softly, 'I still have the memory of how you felt in my arms last night. And I could even now be persuaded to stay.'

He watched her eyes widen in sudden shock, and went on silkily, 'But it is a matter entirely for you to decide, *mon amour*. Although I promise you would find the bed in my room more comfortable than that penance of a sofa.'

The words were thick in her throat. 'I'll have to take your word for that, *monsieur*. Goodbye.'

She turned back to the window, hardly daring to breathe until she heard the door close quietly behind him.

Monteagle is safe, she whispered to herself. And that's all that matters. All that I can allow to matter, anyway.

The cost to herself—well, that was different, and she would have to find some way to endure it.

God, but he was so sure of her, she thought, digging her nails painfully into the palms of her clenched fists. So convinced he could seduce her into passionate surrender. But he would have to think again.

'You may own Monteagle, *monsieur*,' she whispered under her breath, resolution like a stone in her heart. 'But you'll never possess me—and that I swear, by everything I hold dear.'

CHAPTER SEVEN

LOTTIE looked silently at the ruby lying on the table between them.

She said, 'That's costume jewellery, and this whole thing is a wind-up—right?'

Helen shook her head. 'Wrong.' Her voice was husky. 'I really am engaged to Marc Delaroche. He—proposed last night. I accepted this morning.'

Lottie stared at her open-mouthed. She said, half to herself, 'This can't be happening. Twenty-four hours ago you considered yourself engaged to Nigel.' Her voice rose. 'And now you're going to be married to someone you've known a matter of days?'

'You made me have dinner with him,' Helen defended. 'You practically twisted my arm.'

'Yes,' said Lottie. 'Because I thought it would do you good to go out with someone lethally attractive who clearly fancied you. But that was when I thought you were both sane.'

She sat back in her chair, her worried gaze resting on Helen's pale face. 'Are we talking serious rebound from Nigel, here? Or are you telling me that love at first sight actually exists?'

'Love has nothing to do with it.' Helen drew a deep breath. 'The truth is that he's absolutely crazy about Monteagle and is willing to spend whatever it takes to restore the place to its old glory. Only it can't be completely his—unless, of course, I'm part of the package.' She shrugged. 'And that's it.'

'Oh, my God,' Lottie said helplessly, and relapsed into frowning silence. At last she said, 'Helen—just sell him the place, and save yourself a lot of heartache.'

'I'll never sell Monteagle, and he knows it. I made it clear enough at that damned committee meeting. He also knows I'm desperate.' Helen shrugged again, aiming for insouciance. 'I—

102

can't afford to refuse.' She hesitated. 'It's a business arrangement. What they call a marriage of convenience, I suppose.'

'Ah,' Lottie said blandly. 'Then presumably, as you're still virtual strangers, the deal does not include sex.' Her gaze drilled into Helen's. 'Or does it?'

Helen looked down at the table. 'We—we haven't settled the final details yet.'

'Now I know you're kidding,' said Lottie derisively. 'I saw him look at you, remember? And, while Simon and I may have been apart for a while, I still recognise old-fashioned lust when I see it. And, as you're not in love with him, how will you deal with that when payback time arrives? Are you really that sophisticated?'

Helen stared at the burn of the ruby lying between them. She said, half to herself, 'I—I'll cope somehow. Because I have to.' She forced a smile. 'What would you do in my place?'

'Sell,' said Lottie. 'And run.' She paused. 'Or you could try closing your eyes and doing exactly what you are told. That could be interesting.'

'You mean lie back and think of England?' Helen's laugh had a hollow ring. 'Or Monteagle?'

'I doubt whether Marc Delaroche will let you think about anything but him,' Lottie said drily. 'Don't say you weren't warned.'

After Lottie had gone, Helen lingered in the kitchen, washing the cups and glasses they'd used, and recorking the barely touched bottle of wine.

Daisy can use it to cheer up tomorrow's chicken casserole, she thought.

The housekeeper had taken Helen's halting news in her stride. 'So, Mr Marc, is it?' she'd said thoughtfully. 'Well, I wish you happiness, my dear. Things often turn out for the best.'

Mrs Lowell was the only other one on Helen's need-to-know list, because she'd have to explain why there'd be no more guided tours.

I'll go round to the Vicarage tomorrow, she told herself.

As she walked through the hall the telephone rang, and in spite of the lateness of the hour she found herself reaching for it.

'Hélène?' His voice reached her huskily across the miles, making her start.

She steadied herself, trying to ignore the frantic drum of her heart. 'Marc? What do you want?'

'All the things I cannot have, because you are so far from me.'

She could hear the smile in his voice and stiffened, loading her tone with frostiness. 'I mean why are you calling so late.'

'To wish you *bonne nuit*,' he said. 'And sweet dreams.'

'Oh,' she said, nonplussed. 'Well—thank you.'

'And to tell you that, to my sorrow, I will not be with you next week after all. I have to fly to New York.'

'I see.' She knew she should feel relieved at the news, if not be dancing in the streets. Instead, suddenly, there was an odd flatness. 'It was—good of you to let me know.'

There was a pause, then he said softly, 'You could go with me.'

'To New York?' An unbidden quiver of excitement stirred inside her, and was instantly quelled. She said stonily, 'Of course I can't. It's quite impossible.'

'Why? You have a passport?'

'Somewhere, yes.'

'Then I suggest you look for it, *ma mie*,' he told her drily. 'You will certainly need it for our honeymoon.'

'Honeymoon?' She was beginning to sound like an echo, she told herself with exasperation. 'But surely there's no need for that,' she protested. 'It—it's not as if it is a real marriage…'

'You will find it real enough when the time comes, *cherie*.' His words were light, but she thought she detected a note of warning. 'And we are certainly having a honeymoon—although it can only be brief because of my work commitments.'

He paused. 'An old friend has offered us his villa in the South of France. It stands on a headland above St Benoit Plage, and all the bedrooms have views of the Mediterranean. What do you think?'

'You seem to have made up your mind already,' Helen said. 'So what does it matter?'

She thought she heard him sigh. 'Then consider again about New York, Hélène. After all, how long is it since you had a holiday?'

'I went skiing with the school in my last spring term,' she said. 'That's what the passport was for.' She paused. 'But I can't just leave here. I have things to do—responsibilities. Besides...' She halted awkwardly.

'Besides, spending time alone with me in America, or anywhere, is not your idea of a vacation?' His voice was faintly caustic. 'Is that what you were about to say?'

'Something of the kind, perhaps,' Helen agreed woodenly.

'I suppose I should find your candour admirable, *ma mie*,' he said, after a pause. 'However, one day soon—or one night— we shall have to discuss your ideas in more detail.'

His tone sharpened, became businesslike. 'In the meantime, I suggest you use some of the money I shall deposit in your account to begin recruiting extra staff for the house and grounds.'

'But there's no need,' Helen protested. 'We can manage quite well as we are.'

'It is not a question of managing, *ma chère*,' Marc told her crisply. 'Monsieur and Madame Marland are no longer young, *bien sûr*, and at some point will wish to retire. In the meantime they will be glad of help, especially when there is entertaining to be done or when you are away.'

'But I'm never away,' she protested.

'Until now, perhaps,' he said. 'But that will change. You will be my wife, Hélène, not merely my housekeeper. Perhaps I have not made that sufficiently clear. When my work takes me abroad there will be times when I shall require you to go with me.'

Her voice rose slightly. 'You expect me to be your—travelling companion?'

'My companion,' he told her softly, 'and my lover. Sleeping with you in my arms was so sweet, *cherie*, that I cannot wait to repeat the experience.'

'Thank you.' She kept her voice stony, telling herself that the faint quiver she felt inside was anger. Hating the fact that she was blushing.

She took a steadying breath. 'Have you any more orders for me, or may I go now?'

He laughed. 'If I gave orders, Hélène, you would be coming with me to New York.' He gave her a second to consider that, then added more gently, 'Sleep well, *mon ange*—but think of me as you close your eyes, *hein*?'

She murmured something incoherent, and replaced the handset.

His unexpected call had shaken her, and raised issues she'd not wanted to contemplate. Questions of autonomy, among others.

It was disturbing that he seemed to want her to share his life at all kinds of levels she hadn't imagined. Starting with this— this honeymoon in the South of France. Exercising his power by taking her from her own familiar environment to his own domain, she thought, and shivered.

Slowly, she went up to her room. She took off his ring and placed it in the box which also housed her grandmother's pearls—bestowed on her for her eighteenth birthday, and the only other real valuable that she possessed.

Jewellery like the ruby didn't go with her lifestyle, and its non-stop cleaning and gardening. Nor would she take on extra staff, as he'd decreed. The arrival of his tame architect and his work crew was quite enough of an invasion of privacy, making her feel as if her personal hold on Monteagle was being slowly eroded.

But that wasn't all of it, she thought, looking down at her bare hand. There was still part of her in rebellion against the decision that had been forced on her. And she didn't want to admit to anyone, least of all herself, that both she and Monteagle would soon belong to Marc completely. Or display the symbol of that possession.

Think of me. His words came back to haunt her as she slid into bed and pulled the covers over her.

Oh, but he'd made sure of that, she thought bitterly. Turned it into an essential instead of a choice. Placed himself at the forefront of her mind each time she tried to sleep, making himself impossible to dismiss.

And when sheer fatigue overcame her, her sleep was restless and patchy, scarred by dreams that she burned with shame to remember in the morning. Dreams so real that when she woke she found herself reaching for him again across her narrow bed, before shocked realisation dawned.

She turned over, furious and humiliated, burying her heated face in the pillow.

'Damn him,' she whispered feverishly. 'Oh, damn him to hell.'

She got up, late and listless, and searched for distraction. With Daisy's assistance she finally removed the fragile bed and window hangings from the State Bedroom, folded them carefully into plastic sacks, and took them down to the village to deliver to Mrs Stevens at the post office.

The post mistress accepted them with a workmanlike glint in her eye. 'Now, this will be a real pleasure,' she said. 'We'll start on the cutting-out at once, while you decide on the new fabric.' She gave Helen a kind smile. 'So you're courting, then, Miss Frayne—that French gentleman who stayed at the Arms a while back, I hear. Met him then, did you?'

The village grapevine, Helen realised, was in full operation already.

'Oh, no,' she said with perfect truth, aware at the same time that she was blushing. 'It was before that—at a meeting in London.' *Just don't ask how long before, that's all.*

Mrs Stevens nodded with satisfaction. 'I knew it must be so,' she said.

And I wish it had been. The thought came to Helen, unbidden and shocking in its implication, as she made the short trip to the Vicarage.

'Oh, my dear girl.' Marion Lowell hugged her ebulliently. 'How amazing—a whirlwind romance. And such a gorgeous man.' She turned to her husband. 'Jeff, darling, now we have an excuse to drink that champagne we won in the Christmas tombola. I'm so glad we didn't give it back.'

'I hope none of the parishioners call,' Jeff Lowell said, grinning as he passed round the fizzing glasses. 'They'll probably have me defrocked.'

'Will you be getting married here in the church?' Mrs Lowell asked, after they'd drunk to her happiness, and Helen shook her head, flushing.

'I'm afraid not. It will be at the registry office in Aldenford.'

The Vicar looked at her quietly. 'I'd be delighted to hold a short service of blessing afterwards, if you'd like that. Perhaps you'd mention it to your fiancé.'

'Yes, of course,' said Helen, hating herself for lying.

She felt sombre as she walked home. They were so kind, so pleased for her, as if she and Marc had really fallen headlong in love.

Thank goodness they had no idea of the soulless—and temporary—bargain she'd struck with him. His words still echoed in her mind. *You do not profess undying love... I find that— refreshing.*

And that, she thought wearily, seemed to say it all.

As she rounded the bend in the road a lorry carrying scaffolding poles went past her, and carefully negotiated its way between Monteagle's tall wrought-iron gates.

She watched it bewilderedly, then began to run after it up the drive.

In front of the main entrance chaos confronted her. There seemed to be vans and trucks everywhere, with ladders and building supplies being briskly unloaded.

As she paused, staring round uncertainly, a man came striding towards her. He was of medium height, with brown hair and rimless glasses, and his face was unsmiling.

He said, 'I'm sorry, but the house is no longer open for visitors.'

'Where did you get that idea?' Helen demanded coldly.

'From Monsieur Marc Delaroche,' he said. 'The owner of the property.'

'Not yet,' Helen said with a snap. 'I'm Helen Frayne, and

the house still belongs to me.' She paused. 'I presume you're the architect?'

'Yes,' he acknowledged slowly. Behind the glasses his eyes had narrowed, as if he was puzzled about something. 'I'm Alan Graham. It's a pleasure to meet you, Miss Frayne,' he added, with no particular conviction.

'Marc mentioned you'd be coming—but not all this.' She gestured almost wildly around her. 'What's going on?'

He shrugged. 'He wants work to start as soon as possible.'

She said, 'I can see that. But how? You can't have arranged all this in twenty-four hours—it simply isn't feasible.' She stopped, dry-mouthed. 'Unless this was all planned some time ago, of course,' she added slowly. 'And you were just waiting for his word to—swing into action. Is that it?'

Alan Graham fidgeted slightly. 'Is it important? The house needs restoring, and we're here to do it. And time is of the essence,' he added with emphasis.

His tone implied that there was no more to be said. 'Is there a room I could use as an office, Miss Frayne?' He paused. 'Marc suggested that your late grandfather's study might be suitable, but any decision must be yours, naturally.'

Helen bit back the angry words seething inside her. Marc must have made his decision and given his orders almost as soon as they'd met, she realised with incredulity. As if he'd never had any doubt that she would ultimately accede to his demands.

How dare he take her for granted like this? she thought stormily, grinding her foot into the gravel in sheer humiliation. Oh, God, how dare he?

But it was done now, and she could see no way to undo it.

She took a deep breath. 'My grandfather's study has been unoccupied and unfurnished for some time,' she said expressionlessly. 'But you may use it if you wish.' She hesitated, still faintly stunned by all the activity around her. 'May I ask where all these people are going to stay?'

'That's not a problem. Accommodation has been arranged for them in Aldenford, and I've got a room at the Monteagle Arms.'

'Oh.' Helen digested this. She gave the architect a small cold smile. 'I'm afraid you won't be very comfortable there.'

'So Marc has told me.' For the first time Alan Graham's face relaxed a little. 'But it won't be for long. My wife is joining me today to look for a cottage to rent for the duration.'

'I see,' Helen said woodenly. 'And meals?' She had a horrified vision of cauldrons of soup and platters of sandwiches to be prepared daily.

'Packed lunches will be delivered.' He paused. 'Perhaps you'd direct me to the study, so that I can unpack my papers and drawings?'

'Of course,' Helen said, turning and leading the way to the house.

It seemed that Mr Graham shared Lottie's disapproval of this lightning marriage, she brooded over a mug of coffee a little later, having left the architect sorting out his workspace with chilling efficiency.

'Well!' Daisy exclaimed, bustling into the kitchen. 'You could have knocked me down with a feather when all those men started arriving. Mr Marc certainly doesn't waste any time.'

'No,' Helen agreed through gritted teeth. 'None at all.'

'They're starting on the State Bedroom,' Daisy informed her with excitement. 'The Helen Frayne portrait is being sent to London to be cleaned, and they're turning the little dressing room and the room next door as well into a lovely bathroom, with a wardrobe area.' She gave Helen a knowing look. 'Seems as if Mr Marc intends to use the room when you're married.'

'Does he, indeed?' was all Helen could find to say.

The master bedroom, she thought, her stomach twisting into nervous knots, being lavishly created for the master—and his bought bride.

When Marc telephoned that night, she was ready for him.

'You had this planned all along,' she stormed across his polite enquiries about her welfare. 'Even before you came here and saw the place you knew you were going to take on Monteagle's restoration. Why?'

'I found your application for help—intriguing. Then I saw you, *ma belle*, and my fascination was complete.' He had the gall to sound amused. 'But it seemed I had a rival, so I decided to offer you an interest-free loan in the hope that my generosity might ultimately be rewarded.'

'Then why didn't you?' Her voice was ragged.

'Because I realised that Nigel was betraying you and soon there would be nothing to prevent me claiming you for myself. It seemed unlikely that you would become my mistress, so I offered the money as a wedding gift to you instead. Do you blame me?'

'Blame you? Damned right I do,' she flung at him. 'I asked you to loan me that money—you know that. I begged you...'

'But we are both getting what we want, *mon coeur*,' he said softly. 'And that is all that matters. Why question the means?'

'Because you've deceived me,' Helen said hotly. 'You've behaved with a total lack of scruples. Doesn't that trouble you at all?'

'It is not of major concern to me, I confess,' he drawled. 'Particularly when it involves something—or someone—I desire. But if you wish it I will practise feeling ashamed for five minutes each day.'

Helen struggled to speak, failed utterly, and slammed down the phone.

He did not call her the following night, or the one after it. Gradually a week passed, and there was still silence.

And, Helen realised, she had no idea how to contact him. How ridiculous was that?

She presumed he was still in New York, and found herself wondering how he was spending his time, once work was over for the day. But that was a forbidden area, she reminded herself stonily. How Marc passed his evenings, or his nights, was none of her business. Or not until he spent them with her, of course.

Her only concern was, and always would be, Monteagle—not this ludicrously small, lost feeling that had lodged within her over the past days. There was no place for that.

All around her was a welter of dust, woodchips and falling plaster, as damp was eradicated and diseased timber ripped out amid the thud of hammers and the screech of saws and drills. Her dream was coming true at last, and Monteagle was coming slowly and gloriously back to life.

Alan Graham might still be aloof, but he knew his job, and his labour force were craftsmen who loved their work. No expense was being spared, either. Marc was clearly pouring a fortune into the project.

And that, as she kept reminding herself, was all that really mattered. She would deal with everything else when she had to.

She watched almost with disbelief as the State Bedroom was beautifully restored to its seventeenth-century origins, and, discreetly hidden behind a door, a dressing room and a glamorous twenty-first-century bathroom were created out of the adjoining room, all white and silver tiles, with a state-of-the-art shower stall and a deep sunken bathtub. Big enough for two, she noted, swallowing.

Members of the village embroidery group were already stitching the designs from the original hangings on to the pale gold fabric she'd chosen for the bed and windows, and had also promised a fitted bedcover to match.

Without the dark and tatty wallpaper, and with the lovely ceiling mouldings repaired and cleaned, and the walls painted, the huge bedroom looked incredibly light and airy, she thought. Under other circumstances it could even have been a room for happiness…

She stopped, biting her lip. Don't even go there, she told herself tersely. Happiness is a non-word.

Particularly when there had still been no contact from Marc. Clearly he was enjoying himself too much in America to bother about a reluctant bride-to-be in England.

But on the following Wednesday, while she was standing outside watching, fascinated, as the new roof went on, she heard the sound of an approaching vehicle.

She didn't look round because there always seemed to be cars and vans coming and going, until she suddenly heard Marc's voice behind her, quietly calling her name.

She turned sharply, incredulously, and saw him a few feet

away, casual in pale grey pants and a dark shirt. He held out his arms in silent command and she went to him, slowly and uncertainly, her eyes searching the enigmatic dark face, joltingly aware of the scorch of hunger in his gaze.

As she reached him he lifted her clear off the ground, and held her tightly against him in his embrace. She felt her body tremble at the pressure of his—at the pang of unwilling yearning that pierced her. Her throat was tightening too, in swift, uncontrollable excitement.

All those lonely nights, she thought suddenly, shakily, when she'd been able to think of nothing else but his touch—and, dear God, his kisses… All those restless, disturbing dreams that she was ashamed to remember.

Suddenly she wanted to wind herself around him, her arms twined about his neck, her slim legs gripping his lean hips. And realised, swiftly and starkly, the danger she was in.

As Marc's mouth sought hers she turned her head swiftly, so that his lips grazed only her cheek.

'Marc.' She tried to free herself, forcing a laugh. 'People are watching.'

He looked down into her face, his mouth hardening. 'Then that is easily remedied,' he told her softly. He lifted her effortlessly into his arms and began to carry her towards the house.

Colour stormed her face as she heard faint whistles and laughing applause from the workmen, but common sense warned her that to struggle would only make her look even more ridiculous.

Once inside, she expected to be put on her feet, but Marc carried her straight up the main staircase and along to the State Bedroom.

She said breathlessly, 'What the hell are you doing? Let me down at once.'

À votre service, mademoiselle.' His voice was cold, almost grim, as he strode across the room to the bed. Gasping, Helen found herself carelessly dropped in the middle of the wide bare mattress.

She fought herself into a sitting position, glaring at him as he stood over her, hands on hips. 'How dare you treat me like this? If you imagine I'm impressed by these—caveman tactics—then think again.'

'I should not say too much,' he told her with ominous quietness. 'It is nothing to what I would like to do to you. And will,' he added harshly, 'if you refuse my kisses again, in public or in private, no matter what grudge you may be harbouring.'

She bit her lip, avoiding the starkness of his dark gaze. 'You—you took me by surprise. I wasn't expecting to see you.'

'Évidemment,' he said caustically. 'Is that why you are not wearing my ring?'

Of course he would have to notice that!

'I'm living on a building site,' Helen returned a touch defensively. 'I didn't want it to get lost or damaged.'

He gave her a sceptical glance. 'Or did it remind you too much of how soon you will be my wife?'

She bit her lip. 'What do you expect—eager anticipation?'

'No,' he said softly. 'But if not a welcome—a little co-operation, perhaps?'

Before she could move she felt his hands on her shoulders, pushing her back on to the mattress again. Then, lifting himself lithely on to the bed beside her, he pulled her close, and his lips began to explore her mouth with cool, almost languorous pleasure.

Taking, she realised, all the time in the world.

Her hands came up against his chest, trying to maintain at least some distance between them, but that was all the resistance she dared attempt. His warning still rang in her mind, and she knew she could not afford to provoke him again. She would have been wiser to offer him her lips in front of everyone just now rather than risk this.

She was too vulnerable, she thought, shut away with him here in this room they'd soon be sharing. And, because they were known to be together, no one would be tactless enough to come looking for them. No one...

The midday sun was pouring in through the high windows, lapping them in heated gold.

She seemed to be sinking helplessly, endlessly, down into the softness of the bed, her lips parting in spite of herself to answer the sensuous pressure of his mouth, to yield to the silken invasion of his tongue.

Inside her thin shirt, her breasts were suddenly blossoming in greedy delight as his kiss deepened in intensity. Her hardening nipples seemed tormented by the graze of the lacy fabric that enclosed them, aching to be free of its constriction.

As if she'd moaned her yearning aloud, she felt his hand begin gently to unfasten the buttons on her shirt.

She lay still, scarcely breathing, the sunlight beating on her closed eyelids, her pulses frantic, waiting—waiting…

Marc was kissing her forehead, brushing the soft hair away from her temples with his lips, discovering the delicate cavity of her ear with his tongue, then feathering caresses down her arched throat to the scented hollow at its base, where he lingered.

His fingers slid inside the open neck of her shirt, pushing it and the thin strap beneath away from her shoulder.

Then he bent his head, and she experienced for the first time the delicious shock of a man's lips brushing the naked swell of her breast above the concealing lace of her bra, and knew that she wanted more—so much more that it scared her.

She made a small sound, half-gasp, half-sob. For a moment he was very still, then suddenly, unbelievably, she felt him lift himself away from her.

When she had the power to open her dazed eyes she saw that he was standing beside the bed, almost briskly tucking his own shirt back into the waistband of his pants.

'*Je suis désolé,*' he said. 'But I have arranged to see Alain for his progress report, and I am already late.'

Helen felt as if she'd been hit by a jet of freezing water. She scrambled up on to her knees, feverishly cramming her shirt buttons back into their loops. Restoring herself to decency with a belated attempt at dignity.

Her voice shook a little. 'I apologise if I've caused you any inconvenience.'

'Au contraire,' he said, his smile glinting at her. *'Tu es toute ravissante.'*

Anger began to mingle with shock inside her as she met his gaze. The victor, she thought stormily, with his spoils. And she'd nearly—nearly—let him...

She should have been the one to draw back, not him, she realised with shame. Oh, God, how could she have been such a fool?

He paused, glancing at his watch. 'But the report should not take long,' he went on softly, outrageously. 'Perhaps you would like to wait here for my return?'

'No,' Helen said between her teeth. 'I would not.'

One of her shoes had fallen off, and she began to search for it with her bare foot.

'Quel dommage,' he commented. 'I hoped you would show me round the rest of the house. Let me know what you think of the work that has been done so far and of any changes you would like to make.'

'I'm sorry,' Helen said icily, 'but we no longer provide guided tours. And the only change I want is never to see you again.'

He had the gall to grin at her. 'How fickle you are, *cherie*. When only a moment ago...' He shrugged and gave an exaggerated sigh.

'But your mention of tours has reminded me,' he added more slowly. 'As I drove here I met Madame Lowell in the village. She asked if you had told me of her husband's offer to bless our marriage. I said you had not been able to contact me, but that it was a great kindness of Révérend Lowell, which we would be delighted to accept.'

'You said *what*?' Helen abandoned the hunt for her shoe and stared at him, bright spots of colour flaring in her pale face. 'How could you do that? How could you? The Lowells are a sweet couple, and they really believe in marriage. Genuine marriage, that is,' she added, her voice stinging. 'It's sheer hypocrisy to involve them in our—sordid little bargain.'

His mouth tightened. He said harshly, all trace of amusement fled, 'Perhaps, *ma mie*, I feel that in spite of what has taken place between us here our—bargain needs all the help it can get.'

He took her by the shoulders, jerking her off the edge of the bed towards him, and his mouth was hard on hers in a kiss which bore no relation to his earlier tenderness.

It was, Helen thought, her mind reeling, almost a punishment.

When he released her, his eyes were glittering as they studied her startled face. Her hand went up mechanically to cover her tingling lips.

He said, 'So, understand this, Hélène: our marriage will be as genuine as anyone could wish—in all the ways that matter.' His voice was ice. 'On that, *ma belle*, you have my solemn word.'

He walked away from her across the big room, opening a space like an abyss between them. And left, slamming the door behind him.

CHAPTER EIGHT

HELEN stood, her hand still pressed to her mouth, as she tried to calm her flurried breathing.

She heard herself whisper raggedly, 'I—should not have said that.'

But she could not deny she'd wanted to make him angry— even to hurt him. She'd wanted revenge for his staying away in silence—for her dreams and her loneliness—and most of all for the way his hands and mouth had made her feel. Only revenge hadn't been so sweet after all.

Nor had he been angry enough to call off the marriage. And for Monteagle's sake she should be thankful for that.

She pushed her tangled hair back from her face and walked slowly to the door.

It might be politic to make some kind of amends, however. Not go to the lengths of an apology, of course. But perhaps if she prepared his room herself—put flowers in it?

She got sheets and pillowcases from the linen cupboard and carried them to the room he'd used briefly before. She opened a window to let in the sunlight and the faint breeze, wrinkling her nose at the sound of the building work, then quickly made up the bed, the pillows plumped and the sheets immaculately smooth.

She was coming back from the garden, her hands full of roses, when as she rounded the house she heard Alan Graham say, 'What are you going to do about Angeline Vallon?'

Helen halted, puzzled, then realised his voice was coming from the open window of her grandfather's study, just above her head.

Marc, she thought, shrinking against the cover of the wall. He must be talking to Marc. And felt her whole body tense.

118

She strained her ears, but couldn't catch the quietly spoken reply.

Then the other man spoke again. 'Marc—she's not a problem that will simply vanish. And she's bound to have heard by now that you're to be married. There could be trouble.' He paused. 'And your *fiancée* might find out.'

'Then I shall take care she does not.' Marc must have come to the window too, because, for her sins, she could hear him clearly now. And regretted it with all her heart.

'You worry too much, *mon ami*,' he went on. 'I will deal with Angeline—and that jealous fool she is married to if I have to. And Hélène need know nothing.'

Helen felt frozen. She was terrified in case Marc glanced down and saw her there below—eavesdropping—and knew she could not risk staying where she was a moment longer. Besides, she couldn't stand to hear any more.

I ought to be glad that there's another woman in his life. Relieved that our marriage is of such little importance to him, she told herself brokenly. But I'm not—*I'm not...*

Slowly and carefully, she tiptoed back to the house, pausing only to thrust the roses into one of the bins by the back door.

Some of the thorns, she saw, had drawn blood from her hands. But what she'd just overheard seemed to be draining the blood from her heart.

Because she realised she could never let him see how much this painfully acquired secret knowledge was hurting her. Nor dared she ask herself why this should be so. Her instinct told her that the answer she sought might be beyond all bearing.

The dress wasn't white, Helen told herself defensively. It was ivory. A major difference when it came to symbolism. But it was still her wedding dress, and in little more than an hour she would wear it as she stood in Aldenford registry office and became Marc Delaroche's wife.

Time had run out at last, and she was frightened.

Her hair, which had been skilfully layered and highlighted, framed a face that looked pale and strained in spite of the best efforts of the beautician who'd just left.

Also reflected in her mirror was the set of elegant matching luggage on the bed, containing the trousseau that Lottie, once she'd become convinced that Helen would not turn back from her chosen course, had relentlessly forced her into buying.

Including, of course, this slim-fitting dress in heavy silk. The skirt reached just below her knees, and the bodice was cut square across her breasts with slender shoestring straps, now hidden discreetly under the matching jacket, waist-length, mandarin-collared, and fastened with a dozen or more tiny silk-covered buttons.

It was beautiful, thought Helen, and in truth she hadn't needed much persuading to buy it.

Lottie had approved of the evening and cocktail dresses, the casual day clothes and beachwear that Helen had reluctantly se-lected.

'Don't be such a Puritan,' she'd urged. 'You're marrying a multimillionaire and going on honeymoon to one of the smartest resorts on the Riviera. Marc will expect you to dress—and un-dress—accordingly.'

'Why are you on his side all of a sudden?' Helen had asked, flushing.

'I'm on your side.' Lottie had given her a swift hug. 'Which is why I'm determined that you'll do yourself credit.'

She'd pulled a face at Helen's choice of lingerie, in crisp white cotton and broderie anglais, and raised her eyebrows at the nightgowns too, demurely simple in pale silk, and cut se-verely on the bias.

'Expecting fire to break out?' she'd teased, probably puzzled that there was no lace, no chiffon. Nothing sheer or overtly sexy.

But for that, thought Helen, wincing, Marc had someone else.

Even if she hadn't heard that betraying snatch of conversation she would have guessed as much by now. Because since those brief delirious moments she'd spent in his arms, and their angry aftermath, Marc had not made the slightest attempt to be alone with her, or to touch her—apart from a formal brush of his lips across her cheek on greeting or leavetaking. And sometimes not even that.

Nor had he spent a single night at Monteagle in the room

she'd made ready for him, choosing instead, on his flying visits, to stay with Alan and Susan Graham at Lapwing Cottage.

But that would end tonight. In a matter of hours they would be alone together in a starlit room overlooking the Mediterranean. And she supposed that in spite of the coldness between them he'd expect her to share his bed, submit to whatever demands he made of her.

Although that same chill might spare her the seductive persuasion he'd used the last time she was in his arms. There had been little defence she'd been able to summon against that, she thought, her throat tightening as she recalled her body's naïve response—and his almost amused rejection.

But tonight she would be on her guard, fighting ice with ice.

For the sake of her emotional sanity she had to try, anyway. Because this was the price she had to pay for Monteagle, and there was no escaping it.

Unless Marc himself let her go. And she could always hope—couldn't she?

Helen was shocked to find the parish church full as she walked up the aisle, her hand reluctantly in Marc's.

A lot of people were there, she knew, because they were simply curious to take a look at the French millionaire who'd swept young Helen Frayne off her feet. Probably quite a few were disappointed because she wasn't wearing a white crinoline with a veil. But the majority had just come to wish her well. She could feel the waves of goodwill rolling towards her as she stood at the altar with her bridegroom, and she felt the colour deepen in her face.

Oh, God, she thought. The blushing bride. What a cliché.

She wanted to turn and tell them, Don't be fooled. I'm a total fraud and this marriage is strictly business.

Up to that moment things had passed almost in a blur. The formal phrases uttered by the registrar in Aldenford a short while before had hardly impinged on her consciousness. But now the gleam of Marc's wedding ring on her hand was a cogent reminder that the deed was done.

She was aware that Marc had turned slightly to look at her,

and kept her own gaze trained on Jeff Lowell's kind face. She
didn't want to see what might or might not be in her new husband's eyes.

When they'd met at the registrar's office, he had told her
quietly that she looked very beautiful. He looked amazing too,
she thought with a pang, the elegant dark suit doing more than
justice to his tall, lean body. But naturally she hadn't said so.
Instead she'd thanked him with equal politeness for the cream
and yellow roses he'd sent her.

She'd been aware of Lottie looking anxious, and of Alan
Graham's tight smile as they stepped forward to act as witnesses
for the brief ceremony.

Now she stood taut as wire, the Vicar's serious words on
God's gift of love reaching her from some far distance. She
found herself wondering what he meant—questioning what rel-
evance his words bore to her confused and panic-stricken situation.

This is wrong, she thought, her throat tightening. What we're
doing is so wrong...

She knelt at Marc's side to receive the blessing, and realised
with surprise that he had made the sign of the cross as it was
pronounced.

As they rose, Marc took her hand and turned her towards him.
He said quietly, *'Ma femme.'*

She knew he was going to kiss her, and that this time there
could be no protest or evasion. Silently she raised her mouth to
his, allowing his lips to possess hers with a warm and lingering
tenderness she had not expected. And if she did not respond he
was the only one who knew it.

At the same time Helen was aware of a faint stir in the con-
gregation. No doubt they were pleased to see the romantic myth
fulfilled, she thought, torn between irony and bleakness.

Still clasping her hand, Marc led her down the aisle, courteously acknowledging the congratulations and good wishes from
all sides.

And then Helen, halfway to the sunlit doorway, understood
the reason for that sudden restlessness behind them. Because

Nigel was there, leaning against the wall at the back, smiling thinly as he watched them approach.

For a moment she thought she was having a hallucination—a waking nightmare. Because he was the last person she wanted to see—and what was he doing there, anyway? What could he possibly want?

She cast a fleeting glance up at Marc and saw his face become a coolly smiling mask just as his fingers tightened round hers.

Their car was waiting at the lych gate to take them to the airport, and suddenly she wanted to run to it. To be inside it and away without any further leavetaking or good wishes from anyone.

But there was no chance of that. People were pouring out of the church around them, and a lot had cards and lucky silver horseshoes to bestow, while even more seemed to have cameras.

Helen stood, smiling composedly until her facial muscles felt stiff. At some moment Marc must have relinquished her hand, because they'd become separated. Looking round for him, she saw he was standing a few yards away with Alan, enigmatically receiving rowdy advice from some of the local men.

'Do I get to kiss the bride?' Nigel's voice beside her was soft and insinuating, but the arms that pulled her into his embrace held no gentleness. Nor was there any kiss. Instead, his cheek pressed against hers in a parody of a caress as he whispered into her ear, 'If the conversation flags tonight, sweetie, why not ask him about Angeline Vallon? And see if he tells you.'

She pulled herself free, pain slashing at her. I don't need to ask, she wanted to scream at him. I already know.

But Nigel had already gone, melting into the laughing crowd. Instead, she saw Marc coming towards her, his face granite-hard.

He said curtly, 'I think it is time we left, Hélène. *Allons.*'

And silently, shakily, she obeyed.

Their silence during the ride to the airport had continued during the flight to the South of France.

Marc had apologised briefly for having work to do. 'But once it is completed I shall be able to devote myself to you,' he'd added, slanting a coolly sardonic smile at her before becoming immersed in papers from his briefcase.

Helen's heart had lurched uneasily, but she'd made no reply. Instead she sipped the champagne she was offered, and stared out of the window.

The flight should have provided some kind of respite from the stress of the day, but not when the name Angeline Vallon was buzzing in her brain.

The fact that she was Marc's current mistress must be common knowledge if Nigel was aware of it. Common sense suggested that she should confront her husband on the subject, letting him know she was not the innocent dupe he clearly imagined.

Yet some instinct told her that she had reached a threshold she should not cross. After all, Marc had never promised to be faithful, she reminded herself painfully. And it might even make her life easier if his physical demands were being satisfied elsewhere and she became simply his official wife, to be produced in public when required and left to her own devices in the country at all other times.

All she really needed was—somehow—to make her life bearable again.

Although her immediate concern, she realised, dry-mouthed, was to get through the week ahead of her—and particularly the next twelve hours of it.

She sat tensely beside Marc in the back of the chauffeur-driven car which had met them at the airport. It was already sunset, and lights were coming on all along the Promenade des Sables at St Benoit Plage, illuminating the marina, with its plethora of expensive yachts, and the up-market boutiques, bars and cafés that lined the other side of the thoroughfare.

Behind the promenade terraces of houses rose steeply to be crowned by a floodlit pale pink building with a dome, which Helen thought was a church until Marc informed her with faint amusement that it was the town's casino.

'Would you care to go there one evening?' he asked. 'There is an excellent restaurant, and you could try your luck at the tables.'

'Thank you, but, no,' she refused curtly. 'My father was the gambler of the family. I don't want to follow in his footsteps.'

He shrugged slightly. 'As you wish,' he returned. 'Then I shall go alone.'

The Villa Mirage occupied its headland in splendid isolation and was reached by a narrow snaking road. It was large and rambling, built on two storeys, and surrounded by a broad terrace at ground level. The first floor rooms were served by communal balconies, each with a flight of steps that led down to the luxuriant gardens, and bougainvillaea tumbled over the white walls.

In other circumstances she'd have been entranced. Now she was just scared.

The owners, Thierry and Nicole Lamande, were abroad on an extended business trip, Marc had told her, and they would be looked after by the staff, Gaston and Elise.

'I hope,' he'd added ironically, 'that you will not find it too secluded.'

Gaston turned out to be a taciturn man with a grave smile—in direct contrast to his wife, who was small and ebullient with a mass of greying hair. Chattering volubly, she conducted Helen upstairs to a large room at the back of the house, overlooking the swimming pool, with its own dressing room and elegantly appointed bathroom.

Gaston followed with her luggage, but, to her surprise, Helen realized that Marc's bags, brought up by the chauffeur, were being placed in an identical room just across the passage. And presumably by Marc's own order.

So the immediate pressure seemed to be off, she thought, suppressing a gasp of relief.

All the same, she tried to ignore the wide bed, with its immaculate white-embroidered linen, as she walked across to the long windows that led to the balcony and opened the shutters. The air was warm and still, carrying a faint fragrance of lavender from one of the local flower farms, while the rasp of cicadas filled the gathering dusk.

She took a long, luxurious breath, trying to calm herself. 'It's going to be all right,' she whispered. 'Everything's going to be fine.'

She turned to re-enter the bedroom, and halted with a stifled cry. Because Marc was there, leaning in the doorway, arms folded as he watched her.

She said unevenly, 'You—you startled me.'

'You seem easily alarmed, *ma mie*.' His mouth twisting derisively, he came forward into the room. 'I have only been asked to say that our dinner will be ready in twenty minutes.'

'Oh,' she said, trying to sound pleased when she'd never felt less hungry in her life. 'Then I'll come down.' She turned away, beginning to fumble with the little satin-covered buttons on her jacket, trying to drag them free from their loops.

'Be careful,' he said. 'Or they will tear.' He walked over to her and removed her shaking hands from their task, dealing with the fastenings himself, deftly and impersonally.

She'd planned to take the jacket off, of course, but she felt absurdly self-conscious as she slipped it from her shoulders—as if, she thought, she was suddenly naked under his inscrutable dark gaze.

'Your dress is charming,' he said, after a pause that seemed to Helen's overwrought senses to have lasted fractionally too long. 'Perhaps we should give a party when we return to England, so that all your friends in the village can admire its true glory. What do you think?'

She shrugged as she walked past him towards the door. 'I'm sure people will want to see how the house is progressing, anyway,' she returned quietly. 'But won't you find a village party rather boring?'

His brows lifted. 'With you beside me, *cherie*?' he asked mockingly. 'Impossible. Now, let us go and eat our wedding supper.'

A table had been set for them under an awning on the terrace, bright with tiny bowls of scented flowers and candles in little glass shades. Gaston brought Helen the dry white wine she'd asked for, while Marc drank Ricard.

The food was wonderful, even though Helen was fully aware she was not doing it justice. A delicately flavoured vegetable terrine was followed by poached sole, then tiny chickens simmered in wine and grapes. After the cheese came *milles-feuilles*, thick with liqueur-flavoured cream.

Helen was sparing with the excellent Chablis offered with the meal, and, to Marc's open amusement, resolutely refused the brandy that arrived with the tall silver coffeepot.

'Afraid that it will send you to sleep again, *ma chère*?' His brows lifted. 'I promise it will not.'

Her heart lurched. 'Did Elise do all of this?' she asked, keen to change the subject. 'She's a miraculous cook.'

'A lot of people would agree.' He smiled faintly. 'And many attempts have been made to lure her away, but she remains faithful to Thierry and Nicole.'

She said stiltedly, 'It was kind of them to lend you this beautiful house.'

'And I am sorry we have only a week, instead of the month they offered,' he returned. 'But it may be that we can go on a longer trip later in the year—to the Caribbean, perhaps, or the Pacific islands.' He paused. 'Would you like that?'

She didn't look at him. 'It—it sounds wonderful.'

Oh, stop pretending, she begged silently. *Please, stop pretending.*

It was growing very late, she realised. The deep indigo of the sky was sparked with stars, and a slight breeze had risen, carrying with it the murmur of the sea.

She suddenly realised she was going to yawn, and tried desperately to mask it with her hand. But he noticed.

'Tu es fatiguée?'

'No—not at all.' Her denial was too swift—too emphatic. 'It's so lovely here,' she added, forcing a smile. 'I'm trying to take it all in.'

'That may be easier in daylight. And I am glad that you are not tired.' Marc finished his brandy and rose. He came round to her and extended his hand. 'It is time for bed, *ma femme*,' he said softly. *'Viens.'*

Shakily, Helen got to her feet and let him lead her into the house, across the shadows of the *salon* and up the stairs beyond.

At her door, Marc paused, running a rueful hand over his chin. 'I need to shave,' he told her. 'So I will join you presently.'

Swallowing, Helen backed into her room and closed the door. The lamps had been lit on either side of the bed, and the covers were turned down. One of her nightgowns—the white one—was waiting for her, fanned out over the foot of the bed.

So she was not to be spared after all, she thought numbly. Even though there was another woman in his life, Marc was still not prepared to forego the novelty of possessing his virgin bride.

It had been bad enough when she'd only had the danger of her own responses to fight, she thought. But now she had the added humiliation of knowing that she would be sharing him. That even on their wedding night she'd be denied the small comfort of knowing that, for a brief time, he'd been hers alone.

A laugh like a sob escaped her. 'My God,' she whispered. 'And I thought I could fight him.'

She went over to the dressing table and sank down on the padded stool. In the lamplight she looked pale, her eyes wide and almost bruised.

She thought, How can I bear this? What shall I do? And sat motionless, her face buried in her hands.

She did not hear the door open, but some deep instinct warned her when she was no longer alone. She raised her head and met his gaze in the mirror. He was standing behind her, wearing a robe of dark silk which she knew would be his only covering.

He had showered as well, she realised. The clean damp scent of his skin filled her senses, and she took a swift breath of helpless longing.

He said quietly, 'I thought you would be in bed, *ma belle*.'

'My dress,' she said, snatching at an excuse. 'I—I couldn't reach…'

'You could have come to me, Hélène. Asked me to help you.' His hands closed on her shoulders, urging her gently to her feet. 'Like this,' he whispered.

Helen felt the tiny hook on her bodice give way, and the faint rasp of the zip as he lowered it. She felt his mouth touch the nape of her neck, then move with sure gentleness to her shoulder, pushing away the thin strap, baring the soft skin for his lips.

She felt the dress begin to slip down her body, and clutched it with both hands as the first dangerous and uncontrollable tremor of need quivered through her body.

He turned her slowly to face him, his mouth seeking hers. He said softly, *'Mon ange.'*

Angel, she thought dazedly, her pulses swimming. My angel. My—Angeline… Was that what he called her too—*mon ange*? Were these the caresses he used to seduce his mistress—and countless others?

Marc's women—so easily interchangeable. So soon forgotten.

But only if she allowed it, she told herself, anger building on wretchedness.

As he kissed her she turned her face away sharply, so that his mouth grazed only her cheek. In a voice she didn't recognise, she said, 'No—no, Marc, please.'

He paused, frowning, but more in surprise than annoyance. His hands cupped her face, making her look at him. *'Qu'as tu?'* His tone was still gentle. 'What is the matter?'

'I can't do this.' She swallowed. 'I thought I—could. But it's impossible.'

He put his arms round her, his hands slipping inside the loosened dress, gently stroking the naked vulnerability of her back, making her shiver and burn.

'Mon amour,' he murmured, as if he sensed her body's confusion. 'There is nothing to fear. Do you think I would hurt you? I promise I shall not.'

But she was in pain already. She screamed at him soundlessly. She occupied an agonising wasteland where need fought with reason and heartbreak and humiliation waited to devour her like hungry tigers. And if she turned to him now, she would be lost.

'Please—you have to let me go.' Her voice cracked. 'I—I can't be what you want—do what you want. You—you said you'd be patient…'

'Patient,' he repeated, almost incredulously. 'You dare to say that to me? *Mon Dieu!* When have I not been patient? Even when your body was mine for the taking, I held back. Waited for the moment when you would be my wife in honour.'

'There is no honour,' Helen said, her voice a shaken breath. 'We—made a deal. That's all.'

Grim-faced, he stepped back from her. *'Mais, oui,'* he said. 'We had a deal—that sordid little bargain of ours, to which you agreed, *ma chère*, however much you may regret it at this moment.'

She faced him, her arms wrapped round her body. 'You threw me a lifeline,' she said. 'And I was grateful. I didn't let myself consider—the personal implications. At least, not until now.'

'Not even when you were in my arms, *ma belle*?' His laugh was harsh. His words seared her to the core. 'I think you are lying.' He paused. 'But here is something else for you to consider. Why should I continue to keep to the terms of our agreement if you do not?'

There was a silence. At last she said hoarsely, 'You mean you'd—abandon Monteagle? Stop all the work because I—I won't…'

She stared at him pleadingly, but found she was looking into the narrowed angry eyes of a stranger.

She said, stammering slightly, 'But you couldn't do that, surely? You—you love it too much. Besides, you promised…'

'And you,' he said, 'made a vow also. Just today. And, whatever I feel about the house, I hate being cheated far more, *ma petite trompeuse*. And if you can break your word so easily, then so can I.'

He paused. 'Or maybe you would prefer to—reconsider, my beautiful wife. After all, we still have the rest of the night. And surely for the sake of your beloved Monteagle you can endure this—minor inconvenience. But do not make me wait too long for your decision,' he added coldly, turning away. 'And this time, *madame*, you will come to me.'

Helen stood motionless, hardly breathing as she watched the door close behind him.

After a while she unclasped her arms and let the dress slide to the ground. She stepped out of it and went into the bathroom, running water into the tub as she took off her underwear and put it in the linen basket.

Then she climbed into the bath and lay back, closing her eyes, trying to be calm—rational.

All over the world, she thought, women were having sex when they didn't want to. That was nothing new. She couldn't, of course, fake an orgasm. Even if she knew how she guessed Marc would not be deceived for a moment. Instead, she would have to feign the frigidity that Nigel had once accused her of. Maintain some kind of integrity by her indifference, no matter what the cost—and instinct told her it would be high.

This minor inconvenience, he'd said, his mouth twisting cynically.

Oh, God, she whispered wretchedly. How little he knew.

She could only hope he would soon become bored by her passive resistance. But until then...

She dried herself, cleaned her teeth and brushed her hair. Calming herself with the usual routine of bedtime.

She went over to the bed, picked up the pretty, fragile thing that lay there, and slipped it on over her head. She supposed he would want her to take it off. Supposed, but did not know. Not for certain. Nothing for certain.

It's ludicrous, she thought, swallowing a small, fierce sob. My first time with a man and I haven't a bloody clue.

Except, of course, the remembrance of his hands weaving their dark magic on her skin only a short time before. The magic she'd always known could be her downfall.

The white silk rustled faintly above her bare feet as she went slowly out of the room and across the passage. The door of his room was ajar, and she pushed it open and stepped into the lamplit silence.

CHAPTER NINE

MARC was lying propped up on an elbow, facing the door. Waiting, she realised, without one solitary doubt for her to appear. Savouring his victory in advance. The enjoyment he so confidently expected.

Yet there was no triumph in the brief, bleak smile he accorded her.

He pulled back the cover, indicating without words that she should join him. Helen obeyed, lying rigid and awkward beside him, aware of the painful thud of her heart, but even more conscious of his naked warmth and the grave dark eyes studying her face.

Still propped on his elbow, Marc lifted his other hand, stroking the hair back from her temples with his fingertips, then moving down to trace the arch of her eyebrows. His touch was as light as the brush of a butterfly's wing as it followed the hollows of her cheekbones, then hovered at the corner of her mouth.

'Hélène.' His voice was oddly gentle too. 'Do you know how I have longed for this moment—and for you?'

He bent his head and kissed her, his lips moving coaxingly on her unresponsive mouth while his hand slid down to the demure neckline of her nightdress, brushing its straps off her shoulders.

'C'est très jolie, ça,' he whispered. 'But I think you would be even lovelier without it.'

She was shaking inside as the silk slipped down her body, and she heard his soft murmur of satisfaction as his fingers cupped her bare breast. No matter how determined she might be to withstand him, she found with dismay that she could not prevent her nipple hardening in excitement at his caress, or deny the sudden languorous melting between her thighs.

132

Marc bent towards her again, his mouth closing on the rounded softness he'd uncovered, his tongue laving its engorged peak with passionate finesse.

He was lying beside her now, his arm round her shoulders, holding her against him, leaving her in no doubt that he was fiercely aroused. His hand drifted slowly downwards over her body, exploring each curve and contour through the thin fabric of her nightdress, creating a delicate, enticing friction against her skin.

She felt his fingers linger on her hipbone, then move inwards across the flat plane of her stomach with unmistakable purpose while his mouth sought hers with renewed intensity.

She moved then, swiftly, frantically, both hands capturing his and dragging it away from her body. 'Don't,' she said hoarsely. 'Don't touch me.'

He was still for a moment, then she heard him sigh.

'Ah, mon amour.' He took her hand and raised it to his lips, caressing her palm softly. 'Don't fight me, *je t'en supplié.* Relax. Let me make this beautiful for you.'

'Beautiful?' She echoed the word with bitter incredulity. 'You bought me for sex, *monsieur*, so how can it possibly be beautiful? Not that it matters. I—just want it to be over.'

He was suddenly tense, his fingers gripping hers almost painfully. At last he said quietly, 'Hélène, you do not know what you are saying.'

'Yes—yes, I do.' The words tumbled out of her, heartsick and wounded. 'I'm sick of this hypocrisy—this pretence that I'm anything more to you than just another girl in another bed, marriage or no marriage. And I can't bear to be touched— kissed,' she added quickly. 'So just—do it and let me go. Because I don't want you and I never will.'

His sudden harsh laugh made her flinch. He released her and sat up, the sheet falling away from his body, his mouth grim. 'And what now, *madame*? I am expected, perhaps, to admit defeat and send you back to the virgin sanctity of your room. Is that it? To be followed by a swift, discreet annulment back in England?'

He shook his head. 'Well, you may dream on, *mon coeur.*

Because you will go nowhere until I have made our marriage a reality.'

Before she even realised what was happening he had lifted himself over her, his hand pushing back her nightgown and parting her thighs with ruthless determination.

She felt his fingers discover the moist silken heat that he'd created, in spite of herself, heard him laugh softly, and could have died of shame.

'You'll make me hate you,' she stormed, trying to twist away from him and failing totally.

'That is your privilege,' he said. 'This—is mine.' And, poised above her, slowly, skilfully, he guided himself into her.

She lay beneath him unmoving, hardly able to breathe, her eyes closed and one fist pressed against her mouth, waiting for the pain but determined that she would not cry out.

Yet there was no need. She had not expected consideration. Probably did not deserve gentleness. But he offered them to her just the same. In spite of the unyielding tautness of her body, his possession of her was deliberately leisured and totally complete. Also utterly determined.

Yet at the same time it was a curiously sterile performance. Sexually naïve as she was, Helen could still recognise that. And although she'd stipulated no kisses or caresses she'd not expected him to listen. But it seemed that he had, because apart from that one supreme intimacy of his body joined to hers there was no other physical contact between them. His weight was supported by his arms, clamped either side of her on the bed.

When he began to move, it was also without haste. The drive of his body was controlled and clinical, expressing an almost steely resolve, and when Helen risked a scared, fleeting glance upwards at his face she saw that it was set and expressionless, his gaze fixed on the wall above the bed. As if he had withdrawn behind some silent, private barricade.

And even as she realised with anguish, This is not—*not* how it should be…she felt, deep within her, at that moment, a small stirring, as if the petals of a flower were slowly unfurling in the sunlight. But as her shocked mind acknowledged it, tried with a kind of desperation to focus there, it was gone.

At the same time she heard his breathing change suddenly, and felt his body convulse violently inside hers as he reached his climax.

She heard him cry out something that might almost have been her name, his voice hoarse and ragged, as if that unyielding wall of reserve had suddenly crumbled, and for an instant she felt his weight slump against her, pressing her down into the bed.

But he released himself almost at once and rolled away from her, burying his face in his folded arms so that she was free.

For a while she lay still, adjusting to the slight soreness between her thighs and knowing at the same time that it did not compare with the vast ache of loneliness and frustration that now filled her bewildered body, making her want to moan aloud.

She moved away a little, towards the edge of the bed. She said, dry-mouthed, 'May I go now—back to my own room?'

For a long moment there was silence, then slowly he raised his head and looked at her, his face wearily sardonic. '*Pourquoi pas?* Why not? I assume you do not wish to sleep in my arms and have me kiss you awake in the morning. So go back to your sanctuary, my little cheat.'

His words stung, especially when she knew that even now, if he reached for her—held her—she would not be able to resist him.

She lifted her chin. 'I hardly cheated. I did what you expected.'

'Did you?' His mouth twisted. 'How little you know, *cherie.*' He shrugged a sweat-slicked shoulder. 'And I still say you are a cheat. Because your victim is now yourself. You have defrauded your own body of the warmth and passion of being a woman. And you did it deliberately. Or did you think I would not know?' he added with contempt. 'So sleep with that, *hein*?'

Somehow Helen got back to her own room. Somehow she stripped off her crumpled nightdress, kicking it away, and turned on the shower, letting the warm water rain down on her in a torrent, mingling with the sudden tears on her face.

She whispered brokenly, 'It could have been worse. It could have been so much worse…'

And knew that she was lying.

It was late when Helen came back to full consciousness the next morning. She'd eventually fallen into an uneasy sleep around dawn, but now the sunlight was burning through the shutters, she realised, shading dull eyes with her hand as she peered at the window.

And somehow she had to shower, dress, and go downstairs to face Marc, she thought, uttering a soft groan at the prospect.

Yet at least she'd woken alone, and not been roused by his kisses, she told herself, remembering with a pang his soft-voiced taunt of the night before, as she pushed away the tangled sheet and swung her feet to the floor.

His accusation that she'd cheated herself of fulfilment still rankled bitterly, however, and her body was haunted by a feeling of numb emptiness that almost amounted to desolation.

Inexperienced as she was, her inner desolation was not helped by the recognition that her husband had subjected her to a possession without passion—a disciplined and calculated exercise for his own satisfaction. Nor was it alleviated by the knowledge that she'd deliberately instigated this bleak and untender consummation.

Was this a foretaste of what she could expect each night of this caricature of a honeymoon? she wondered. If so, at least it would make it marginally easier to withhold herself, as she knew she must.

She had to be careful too, she thought, remembering that brief instant when simply the stark rhythm of his body inside hers had been enough to provoke that strange flicker of desire, as unwelcome as it was unexpected, but no less potent for that.

She could only hope that, caught between boredom and anger in this war of attrition between them, Marc would be keen to put the whole wretched episode behind him and return to his former way of life—and the women who shared it. Once this painful pretence of a marriage was finished in any significant way, she might be able to attain some peace.

After all, she thought, swallowing, Marc still had the house, which was and always had been his main concern in all this. She'd only ever been intended as a bonus in the transaction. His personal perquisite. He would simply be forced to write her off as a loss. Well—he was a businessman. He would understand that, and shrug.

And although she would be freed from any kind of sexual partnership with him, and ultimate and inevitable heartbreak, she would make sure she was nothing less than the perfect chatelaine for Monteagle. He would have no complaints about the way his home was run, or her behaviour as his hostess.

She sighed, and trailed across to the dressing room. In the meantime she'd have to pretend that this was the first day of a normal marriage and find something appropriate to wear.

Much as she might wish it, she could hardly go for the full covered-up blouse and skirt look when the temperature was clearly in the high eighties. Besides, Marc might even regard that as some kind of challenge, and that was the last thing she wanted.

It was probably better to attempt the role of radiant bride, she thought. And her pride demanded that she should behave as if the previous night had never happened, even if she was still weeping inside.

Eventually, as a concession to the climate, she picked out a black bikini that wasn't too indecently brief, topping it with its own filmy mid-thigh shirt.

But, in spite of her fears, it was only Elise who was waiting for her as she apprehensively descended the stairs half an hour later.

'*Bonjour, madame.*' Her eyes were twinkling. 'You 'ave sleep well, I think? Your 'usband say to let you rest as long as you desire. But now you like *un petit dejeuner*?'

'Just coffee, please,' Helen said, self-consciously aware that her watch was saying it was long past breakfast-time. She glanced around her. 'Er—where is *monsieur*?' she ventured.

''E 'as go for drive into the 'ills,' Elise informed her. 'But 'e will come back soon. For the lunch. It is my fish soup, which 'e does not miss.' She nodded with satisfaction, then bustled off to get the coffee.

Well, she was being allowed a brief respite at least, Helen thought. Given a breathing space to decide how she should behave and what she should actually say when she encountered him at last.

Elise's coffee was a dark and vibrant brew, and it managed to rid Helen's head of the last unhappy wisps of mental fog and enable her to think clearly.

It was vitally important not to give Marc the idea that she cared too much about the bleak conclusion to their wedding night.

Perhaps she should give the impression that it was no more than she'd expected. Or maybe she should wait, she thought. Judge his mood when he returned. Leave it to him to dictate the scenario.

In the meantime, this was a wonderful house, with beautiful grounds and the luxury of a swimming pool. At least she could allow herself a little enjoyment.

She finished her coffee, then set off. The pool was sited in a sunken area of the garden, surrounded by flower-filled shallow terraces. At the deep end of the azure water was a diving board, while a small hexagonal pavilion had been built at the opposite end for changing purposes, and to house a comprehensively equipped refrigerator.

Cushioned loungers, each with its own parasol, had been set round the surrounding tiled area.

Helen applied some high-factor sun lotion and lay down, sighing gratefully. There was a paperback book in her canvas bag, but, for a while anyway, she preferred to close her eyes and drift, blocking out the dark fears and uncertainties that plagued her, her head full, instead, of the distant wash of the sea and the busy hum of insects among the flowers.

She almost slept.

The sudden instinctive awareness that she was no longer alone brought her back to full consciousness, her eyes flying open to see Marc standing at the foot of the flight of shallow steps. He was wearing black swimming briefs, and, apart from the thin cotton shirt flung over one shoulder, the rest of him was tanned skin.

For one shocked, unguarded moment, she was pierced by a shaft of yearning so strong it seemed to penetrate her bones.

And he was looking at her too, his mouth unsmiling, his eyes masked by his sunglasses.

He said laconically, *'Ça va?'*

'Fine,' she said, jack-knifing herself into a sitting position too swiftly and defensively. It had suddenly occurred to her that apart from last night, this was the nearest to naked Marc had ever seen her, and the realisation made her feel disquieted and uncomfortable.

'I regret this intrusion,' he went on. 'But Elise was insistent that I needed a swim before lunch.' He tossed the shirt on to another lounger. 'She feels, I think, that I am neglecting my bride,' he added, his mouth twisting. 'I could hardly tell her that I am merely obeying your wishes.' He paused. 'Unless, of course, you would like to join me in the pool?'

Helen swallowed. 'Another time—perhaps.'

'Why pretend?' Marc asked derisively. 'Why not say no?'

She turned away. She said in a stifled voice, 'Isn't it a little late for that?'

'Perhaps that is something we should discuss.' He walked across and sat down on the end of her lounger. He'd discarded his sunglasses and his expression was searching—sombre. She watched him, her own eyes wary, her body tensing instinctively at his proximity.

She said, 'You mean to apologise—for last night?'

'Apologise?' His brows lifted. 'No. Let us say instead, *ma mie*, that neither of us was very kind—or very wise—in our treatment of each other, and put last night far behind us.'

'How can we do that?' Helen asked stiffly.

'By agreeing that it is the present—and our future together—that should concern us more.'

Her small workmanlike hands were gripped tightly together. 'What future is that?'

He sighed, his mouth tightening. 'I have taken you as my wife, Hélène. How can we live as strangers?'

She lifted her chin. 'Because that's what we are—as last night proved.'

'It proved nothing,' Marc said shortly. 'Except that you had decided for some reason that you no longer wanted me.'

'No longer?' Helen echoed indignantly. 'When did I ever?'

His brows rose sardonically. 'You wish me to list the times, perhaps?' There was a pause then he added, 'I regret that I did not seduce you when I had the chance, *ma belle*, instead of waiting to offer you the security of marriage first.'

'Perhaps,' Helen said stonily, hating the colour that had flared in her face at the unforgivable truth of his words, 'perhaps even then you wouldn't have found me as easy as you seem to believe.'

'I never expected to find you easy, Hélène,' he returned softly. 'Merely—infinitely rewarding.' He smiled faintly. 'As your beautiful mouth promises, *mon coeur*. The mouth you would not allow me to kiss last night in case you melted for me as your ancestress once did for the King,' he added quietly.

The breath seemed to catch in her throat. 'You—flatter yourself, *monsieur*,' she said. 'And you're quite wrong, too. They were different people in a different age. No comparison.'

He shrugged, his mouth wry, '*Bien sûr*, I am not a king, but a good republican—and I am your husband as well as your lover. But are we really so far apart? She fled him and he followed, just as I am here with you now, in spite of all that has happened.'

'We're a world away.' Her voice sounded thick and strained. 'And you are *not* my lover.'

For a moment his head went back as if she'd struck him, and he was silent.

'Then may we not begin again?' he asked at last, his voice deepening huskily. 'You are my wife, Hélène, and I want you—I long to show you how it should be between us. How it can be. If only...'

He reached for her hand, but she snatched it away.

'*Ah, Dieu.*' Marc shook his head. He was silent for a long moment, then said gently, 'Don't fight me any more, *cherie*. Let me come to you tonight and make love to you, as I wish to do. If you would only allow it, I know I could make you happy.'

'I think you're more concerned with your own satisfaction,' Helen flung at him. 'And the fact that your masculine pride's been damaged. In spite of your fantasies, last night can't have been particularly *rewarding* for you.'

'Or for you,' he said with sudden harshness.

It was her turn to shrug. 'Nevertheless,' she said, 'that's as good as it gets. Come to me—stay away—it makes no difference.'

She saw the dark eyes flare and his mouth harden.

He got to his feet in one lithe movement and stood over her, reminding her suddenly of the previous night, his body poised above hers. Forcing her to remember that piercing instant of need...

She went rigid, her eyes almost blank with fright, and saw his mouth move in a faint smile that was almost a sneer.

'*Sois tranquille,*' he said coldly. 'I shall not ask again.'

He turned away and walked to the edge of the pool. His body cut the water in a clean dive.

Heart hammering, she scrambled off the lounger, cramming on her shirt and picking up her pretty embroidered beach bag.

She went hurriedly up the steps, not looking behind her. Back to the house, she thought shakily. Out of harm's way.

Yet she knew at the same time that it was not that simple. *She fled him and he followed.* That was what Marc had said. And, in spite of that icy parting assurance from him, Helen knew she would never feel completely safe again while they were under the same roof.

She made herself go down to lunch when Elise came, clearly puzzled, to call her. For one thing she needed to repair the damage done by that moment of recoil at the pool. She'd shown Marc too clearly that he had the power to disturb her, and then, even more stupidly, she'd run away.

Also, more prosaically, she was hungry.

He was already waiting at the table that had been set for them in the shade of the terrace, and rose formally as she approached, his eyes skimming over the pale green sundress with its halter strap that she'd changed into, although he refrained from the comment she'd expected as she seated herself opposite him and unfolded her napkin.

He had changed too, she realised, into dark blue linen trousers and a matching polo shirt, and his still-damp hair was combed back from his face. As Elise arrived with the tureen he smiled up at her, said something teasing in his own language, and the force of his attraction made Helen catch her breath.

Concentrate on the food, she adjured herself silently. It's safer that way.

The fish soup was delicious, aromatic and filling, forcing her to eat sparingly of the platter of cold meats and salad that followed, and choose just a peach from the bowl of fresh fruit that ended the meal.

She declined any coffee, and was rising to her feet when he said crisply, '*Un moment, madame.*'

Helen halted, startled and reluctant.

'We need to reach a certain level of agreement.' Marc did not look at her as he filled his own cup. 'Whatever our private arrangements, we should try to behave in front of others as if we were truly *les nouveaux mariés. Par chance*, we do not have to stay here for very long, but we need to spend some time together each day—and in public.'

Helen bit her lip. 'Is that really necessary?'

'By now the news of our marriage will have reached the newspapers, and the gossip columnists will know we are here.' He shrugged. 'They will wish to take photographs of us together—being happy. We should indulge them. What happens at night is the business of no one but ourselves,' he added coldly.

Helen bit her lip. She said, 'I suppose—if we must. What—what do you suggest?'

'You overwhelm me.' His tone was barbed. 'To begin with, I propose we go down to St Benoit. The car and driver have been placed at our service, so I have ordered him to come round in half an hour. With Louis at the wheel, you do not even have to be alone with me.' He paused, allowing that to strike home. 'Also I intend to work for part of each day,' he went on. 'There are matters that require my attention even on honeymoon, so I recommend you use the pool area during those times, in case the sight of you in a bikini arouses me beyond bearing.'

Unhappy colour rose in her face. 'Please—don't talk like that.'

'Tes conditions sont trop rigoureuses, ma mie,' he told her mockingly. 'I cannot sleep with you—I may not even swim with you—and it is obvious you would prefer to eat alone. These I accept. But I refuse to censor my words—or my thoughts. *D'accord?'*

There was a silence, then Helen nodded jerkily. 'As you wish.'

'I recommend you treat your time with me like medicine, *cherie.'* Marc swallowed the remainder of his coffee and re-placed the cup on its saucer. His eyes were hard. 'To be taken quickly and as soon forgotten.' He rose to his feet. 'Half an hour, then. And try, if you can, to smile for the cameras as if you were happy. This week will soon pass.'

By the time they came back to the villa that evening Helen had already reached at least one conclusion.

In the sunlit hours, she thought, she could—just—play the role assigned to her. But it would be an entirely different matter when the velvety darkness descended. That was altogether too intimate an ambience, and if she was to survive, as she must, her evenings had to be her own.

So when Marc turned to her after dinner and invited her to go with him to the Yacht Club, for coffee and brandies, she refused, saying mendaciously she had a headache.

'Pauvre petite.' His mouth curled with faint irony. 'Do you wish me to remain here and cherish you?'

'No, thank you,' she returned coolly. 'I'm not chained to your wrist. You're free to go out alone whenever you want.'

'How sweet you are,' he drawled mockingly. 'And how un-derstanding.' He paused. 'I shall try not to disturb you on my return.'

Elise, who was clearing the table, sent them a look that said louder than words that such a new wife should *expect* to be disturbed by her husband, and should, *en effet*, actively welcome it, headache or not.

Marc walked over to Helen, dark and devastating in his tuxedo, and bent, his lips swiftly brushing her hair.

He said quietly, 'Sleep well,' and went.

There was a silence, then Elise said dourly, 'I will fetch you a powder, *madame*, for ze 'eadache.'

She not only fetched it, she stood over Helen while she swallowed the foul-tasting thing. 'Now you will be restored for the return of *monsieur*,' she said with a firm nod.

But Helen wasn't so sure. The tension of walking round St Benoit Plage all afternoon, hand in hand with Marc, was threatening her with a genuine headache. It had been quite an ordeal for her, however impersonal his touch.

The villa was equipped with a state-of-the-art audio system and an eclectic mix of music. Helen curled up on one of the giant hide sofas in the *salon* and put on some slow sweet jazz. But the music alone couldn't stop her thinking, her mind replaying all the events of the past twenty-four hours. Above all she found herself wondering what Marc was doing—and who he might be with.

She'd been aware all afternoon of the predatory glances being aimed at him by tanned and sexy women keen to get closer regardless of her presence. And now she'd turned him out on the town alone...

But then what choice did she have? she argued defensively with herself. She certainly had no right to expect physical fidelity from him.

Sighing, she picked up one of the glossy magazines arranged on the low table in front of her and began to flick over the pages. She paused to glance at a double-page spread showing people attending a charity performance at the opera. The name 'Angeline Vallon' seemed to leap out at her.

She looked at the accompanying picture, her heart beating slowly and unevenly.

She saw a tall, beautiful woman, with a mane of dark auburn hair tumbling down her back, standing beside a much smaller man with a beard and a faintly peevish expression, described as 'her industrialist husband Hercule'.

Madame Vallon was wearing a very low-cut evening gown that set off her frankly voluptuous body, and a magnificent diamond necklace circled her throat.

She didn't look like someone who had to ask more than once for what she wanted, thought Helen, trying not to wince. Nor someone who would be easily persuaded to let go.

And you're quite right to opt for self-preservation, she told herself stoically. Because you're no competition for her. No competition at all.

She closed the magazine, replacing it with meticulous exactitude on the table, and made her solitary way up to bed.

But not to sleep. Not until much later, when she eventually heard quiet footsteps passing her room, without breaking stride even for a moment, and then the sound of Marc's door closing.

Helen turned on to her stomach, pressing her burning face into the pillow.

I shall not ask again. That, after all, was what he'd told her. And apparently he'd meant every word.

Somehow she had to be grateful for this one mercy at least.

But, dear God, how painfully, grindingly difficult that was going to be for her. And she found herself stifling a sob.

CHAPTER TEN

MARC had told her the time would pass quickly, but to Helen the days that followed seemed more like an eternity. Yet under other circumstances she knew they could have been wonderful.

From that first afternoon in St Benoit Plage she seemed to have stepped through the looking glass into a different and totally unreal world, peopled only by the beautiful and the seriously affluent.

To her astonishment, Marc had been right about the photographers, and Helen had been chagrined to find herself described in the local news sheet as 'charming but shy', under a picture of her with her mouth open, clinging to her husband's hand as if he was her last hope of salvation.

Not shy, she'd thought wryly. Just shocked witless at all this unwonted attention.

'Relax, *ma mie*,' Marc had advised, clearly amused. 'They will soon focus on someone else.'

In the days that followed he took her to Cannes, Nice and Monte Carlo, until her mind was a blur of smart restaurants and glamorous shops. She had learned early on not to linger outside the windows of boutiques, or admire anything too openly, otherwise the next moment Marc would have bought it for her. It was heady stuff for someone who'd existed up to now on a skeleton wardrobe, but she found his casual generosity disturbing.

No doubt he treated his mistresses equally lavishly, she thought unhappily, but at least they deserved it. Whereas she, patently, did not.

Not that he cared, she told herself defensively. After all, when this pathetic honeymoon had stumbled to its close he had Angeline Vallon waiting for him. And life would return to normal for them both.

She had to admit that Marc had kept his word about their own relationship. He'd made sure from the first that they were rarely alone together. In the car, with Louis as unwitting chaperone, they exchanged polite but stilted conversation, and at the villa, as he'd suggested, they pursued a policy of positive avoidance, under the frankly disapproving gaze of Gaston and Elise, who were clearly baffled by these strange newlyweds.

She had no idea where or how Marc spent his evenings, although she was always courteously invited to accompany him and had to struggle to invent excuses. She only knew that she lay sleepless, listening for his return, however late it happened to be. And how sad was that?

There were times when she longed to confront him—tell him to his face that she knew he had a mistress. But that would only betray to him how much it mattered to her, and she couldn't risk that. Couldn't admit that he had the power to hurt her.

Also, he might ask how she knew. And she could hardly confess that she'd been eavesdropping.

It was far less humiliating to simply keep quiet and count her blessings that she still had Monteagle, if nothing else.

She halted, startled, aware that she'd never regarded the situation in that light before. Always her home had been paramount in her thoughts. She'd said openly that she would do anything to save it, yet now, for the first time, she was counting the cost and finding it oddly bitter.

It will be easier when I go home, she promised herself. When I get back to the real world again.

And yet, as she at last began packing for the return journey, she found herself feeling oddly wistful—even empty. And for once she had a genuine headache. The sky had become overcast towards the end of the afternoon, and she wasn't surprised to hear a faint rumble of thunder from the hills.

When she arrived downstairs for dinner, she found that Gaston had prudently laid the table in the *salle à manger* instead of the terrace. 'It makes to rain, *madame*,' he told her lugubriously.

Elise came bustling in with a dish of home-made duck pâté.

'*Monsieur* begs you will commence,' she announced. ''E is engaged with the telephone.'

It was over ten minutes later when Marc eventually made his unsmiling appearance. 'I regret that I have kept you waiting.' The apology sounded cursory, and he ate his meal almost in silence, his thoughts quite evidently elsewhere.

Eventually, when coffee was served and they were alone, he said abruptly, 'We will be leaving for the airport in the morning, *à dix heures*. Can you be ready?'

Helen put down her cup. 'Has the flight been changed?'

'We are not catching the London plane,' he said. 'We shall be spending a short time in Paris instead.'

'Paris?' she echoed. 'But where will we stay?'

'I once told you that I have an *appartement* there,' he said.

'Yes,' she said. 'And a hotel suite in London.'

His faint smile was twisted. 'The *appartement* is larger, *je t'assure*. To begin with, there is more than one bedroom,' he added pointedly.

She flushed dully, annoyed that he should read her so accurately. 'All the same,' she said stiffly, 'I'd prefer to go straight home.'

He glanced at her meditatively. 'You are my wife, Hélène,' he said quietly. 'It might be thought that wherever I am your home is with me.'

'We don't have that kind of marriage.' She didn't look at him. 'And, anyway, I need to be at Monteagle. I want to see what progress has been made there. Besides, what would I do in Paris—apart from cramp your style?' she added recklessly.

Marc's brows lifted. 'Cramp my style?' he queried, as if he'd never heard the phrase before. 'In what way, may I ask?'

Helen bit her lip. 'Well—you have things to do—people to see,' she offered nervously, backing away from his challenge. 'And I'd be in the way.' She poured herself some more coffee. 'Anyway, I think we both need—breathing space—from each other.'

'You think so?' His tone was mocking. 'Shall I calculate for you, *cherie*, exactly how many hours we have spent together this week? Not that it matters, of course. Monteagle calls, and you obey.' He paused. 'So, I will go to Paris alone, and arrange to have you met at the airport in England.'

He swallowed the rest of his coffee and rose. 'And now you will excuse me. I intend to try my luck at the casino again tonight.'

'Is that where you've been spending your evenings?' Helen asked the question before she could stop herself. 'I didn't realise you were such a gambler.'

'And nor did I, *ma belle*,' Marc said softly, 'until I met you. And I find the turn of a wheel or the fall of a card infinitely kinder, believe me.' He kissed the tips of his fingers to her. *'Au revoir.'*

Helen hated thunderstorms. But she was almost grateful to this one for giving her something more to worry about than her immediate problems. After all, she'd won a victory over her return to Monteagle, she thought defensively. So why did it feel so much like a defeat? And Marc's absence so soon after the honeymoon would excite the kind of local comment she most wished to avoid.

But anything was better than accompanying him to Paris, like a piece of extra luggage.

And he certainly hadn't tried too hard to persuade her, either, Helen told herself defiantly.

She spent a restless evening trying to read, while lightning played around the hills, making the villa's electricity flicker. Eventually she gave it up as a bad job and went to bed.

Perhaps it was the prospect of going home that made her feel more relaxed, but tonight she found herself drifting into a doze almost at once.

When she awoke, everything was pitch-black and completely silent. The storm, it seemed, had rolled away at last, leaving the room like an oven and the bedclothes twisted round her. Clearly she hadn't been sleeping as peacefully as she'd thought. She struggled out of the shrouding covers and got out of bed, treading across to the window and opening it wide to step out on to the balcony, planning to cool off a little.

But the air outside was just as stifling. Helen leaned on the balustrade and inhaled, but the garden smelled raw and thirsty, and possessed by a strange stillness, as if it was waiting in anticipation of—what?

A moment later she found out. As if some cosmic tap had been turned, the rain began to fall in huge, soaking drops, and by the time Helen made it back into her room she was already wet through, her nightgown sticking in clammy dampness to her skin.

Grimacing, she peeled it off and dropped it to the floor. She discarded the coverlet from the bed, too, and slid back under the single sheet, listening to the heavy splash of rain on the balcony tiles, hoping it would have a soporific effect.

She had to train herself not to lie awake listening for Marc, she told herself wearily, because there would be so many nights when he would not be there. Starting with tomorrow.

She turned on to her side, facing the window, and stiffened as a tall shadow walked in from the balcony and moved soundlessly towards her. She wanted to scream, but her throat muscles didn't seem to be working.

Then the heavily shaded lamp at the side of the bed clicked on, and she realised it was Marc, his hair hanging in damp tendrils, water glistening on his dinner jacket.

She said hoarsely, 'What are you doing here?'

'I came to tell you that I won tonight.' He reached into his pocket and took out a packet of high denomination euros. 'Every table I sat at yielded gold.'

'I'm very pleased for you,' Helen said tautly. 'But the morning would have done for your news.'

He smiled down at her. His black tie was hanging loose, and several of the buttons on his dress shirt were unfastened. 'But it is the morning, *ma mie*. And besides, I have something else I wish to share with you.'

'Can't it wait?' She tried unobtrusively to raise the sheet to chin level. 'I—I'm very tired.'

'And I,' he said, 'have waited long enough. On our wedding night you accused me of buying you for sex. If so, Hélène, I made a poor bargain. And it occurred to me, as I came back tonight, that perhaps I had not yet paid enough for the privilege of enjoying your charming body. So—'

He scattered some of the banknotes across the bed. 'How much will this buy me, *mon coeur*? A smile—a kiss, *peut-être*? Or even—this.'

He reached down and took the edge of the sheet from her, stripping it back to the foot of the bed, leaving her naked.

'Oh, God,' Helen said, with a little wail of shock. She tried to curl into the foetal position, covering what she could of herself with her shaking hands. 'You said—' she accused breathlessly. 'You told me you wouldn't ask again.'

'But I am not asking,' he said gently. 'This time I am taking.'

'But why?' There was a sob in her voice. 'Weren't there any women at the casino you could have chosen—with all that money?'

'Dozens,' Marc told her pleasantly. 'And all of them more eager and welcoming than you, *ma chère*. But I decided I preferred a little—domestic entertainment.' He paused. 'And you can always close your eyes—pretend that I am someone else.'

Quietly ruthless, he unpeeled her arms from her body, one hand closing on both her slender wrists and lifting them above her head. Holding them there. Helen cried out in startled protest as his other hand grasped her ankles, straightening her body and drawing it gently but inexorably down the bed, leaving her with nowhere to hide from the insolent hunger in his dark gaze.

'Marc,' she whispered imploringly. 'I beg you—please don't do this.'

Marc lifted himself on to the bed and knelt over her, trapping her legs between his knees while he studied her.

He said quietly, '*Tu es vraiment exquise, Hélène.* And this is what your body was made for.' Then he bent his head and began to kiss her, his lips cool as the rain as they touched her.

Helen tried to resist, her mouth clamped shut, her head twisting frantically on the pillow. But he was not to be denied.

His tongue was like a flame against hers, teasing her slowly and sensuously, demanding that her lips yield him their innermost secrets. At the same time his hand found one small, pointed breast, his fingertips delicately stroking its soft curve, wringing a response that urged the nipple to bloom sweetly and helplessly into his caressing palm.

Helen found herself almost unable to breathe—to think. He was still clasping her wrists—but so loosely that she could have pulled free at any time, at least tried to fight him off. Instead, she realised she was sighing into his mouth, her body gradually slackening under the sensuous insistence of his lips and fingers.

When he had finished with her she would die of shame at her own weakness, she told herself dazedly. But for now...

His mouth moved down to her throat, making the pulse there leap and flutter. He explored the soft hollows at its base, then trailed kisses down to her breasts, his lips suckling each excited peak in turn, piercing them with sensations she'd never dreamed of.

When at last he raised his head she stared up at him, her eyes wide with bewilderment, her lips slightly parted.

He touched them lightly with his own, then released her wrists, turning her slightly so that the long, supple line of her back was at the mercy of his mouth instead, while his hands still stroked and pleasured her tumescent breasts.

He brushed the soft strands of hair away from the nape of her neck with his mouth, and she felt her whole body quiver in helpless response to the caress.

His lips and tongue travelled slowly, almost languidly, between her shoulderblades and down her spine, as if he was counting each delicate bone with kisses, while his fingers pursued their own erotic path across her ribcage to the flat plane of her stomach, coming to rest on the slender curves of her hipbones.

As he caressed the sensitive area at the base of her spine she gave a muffled moan and her body arched involuntarily, vulnerably. He drew her back against him, his arm across her breasts. At the same moment his other hand moved, cupping the soft mound at the parting of her slackened thighs with terrifying intimacy.

'No—please.' Helen's voice splintered as his fingertips began their first silken journey of discovery into the moist, scalding heat of her most secret self.

Marc kissed the side of her throat and she felt him smile against her skin. 'No?'

His hand moved, delicately, subtly, and she cried out, her body writhing helplessly against his enfolding arm.

Suddenly, unexpectedly, he turned her on to her back, and she caught a dazed glimpse of the heated glitter in his eyes. But she had no idea of his real purpose as he bent to her, his hands sliding under her flanks, lifting her towards him. The next instant, before she could move to prevent him, his mouth had taken possession of her, and the powerful glide of his tongue had sought and found the tiny hidden bud, continuing its exquisite arousal.

Helen's entire being tensed in shock, followed immediately by an agony of guilty, terrified delight. She tried once more to say no. To find the strength, somehow, to push him away and stop this shameful, delicious pleasure before it carried her away beyond all the barriers she'd tried to build against him.

But the only sound that came from her throat was a small sob. She closed her eyes in a desperate attempt to distance herself—to hang on to some kind of self-control. But it was already too late.

Her awareness had shrunk to the distant splash of the rain, her own jagged, fevered breathing, and the hot, beautiful semi-darkness that surrounded her—invaded her. She knew nothing but the response that Marc was forcing from her trembling body, the alchemy of his experienced caresses, seducing her bewildered senses and sweeping away her innocence for ever.

The pleasure began slowly, at first little more than a breeze rippling across still water, then building with irresistible, quivering urgency into a great wave, gathering force and speed as it lifted her, all control gone, to some unimagined peak of rapture and held her there.

Then the wave broke, and she crashed with it, helpless, whimpering, torn apart by the spasms of ecstasy that possessed her.

She lay dazed and trembling, unable to speak or move, or

even to comprehend what had just happened to her. She was no longer certain where she was, or even who she was.

A strange euphoria was spreading throughout her body. Every bone, muscle and skin cell was utterly relaxed, tingling with this new delight, as if she was floating in some beatific dream, drained and weightless.

She was dimly aware that Marc had moved away from her, and found herself reaching out a bereft hand, searching for him blindly across the empty bed.

'*Sois tranquille, mon amour.* I am here.' His voice was a whisper. He'd used his brief absence to strip, she realised, as he drew her to him, and she gasped silently as she felt the warmth of his aroused and powerful nakedness against her body.

Instinctively, she arched towards him, thrilling again at his touch, her arms circling his neck, the tips of her breasts grazing his hair-roughened chest, and heard him groan softly. His hands took her gently, positioning her, then he entered her with one strong, fluid thrust.

Her yielding was total, immediate. Almost languidly she lifted her legs, locking them round his hips, her own movements mirroring the smooth, almost voluptuous drive of his loins, drawing him deeper still into her body.

'Tell me.' His voice was a hoarse whisper. 'Tell me if I hurt you.'

'I want you.' Her reply was hardly more than a breath. 'I want—everything…'

She'd thought after that previous implosion of ecstasy that still lingered, suffusing her with its joy, she would find herself exhausted, emptied of sensation, incapable of anything but compliance. But she was wrong.

The controlled force of his possession was evoking a response that went far beyond mere surrender. Suddenly her body was coming unexpectedly, ardently to life again, and as his rhythm increased, became fiercer, she found she was being carried away with him, striving with him on some long, sweet spiral of such intensity that it frightened her.

Pleasure hovered on the verge of pain, and she heard herself crying out, crushing her mouth against his shoulder as the long, shuddering convulsions of her climax pulled her over the edge into Paradise. Seconds later he followed her, wildly groaning her name as he reached the white heat of fulfilment in his turn.

Afterwards they lay quietly in a tangle of sweat-soaked limbs, his arms holding her as she pillowed her head on his chest, both waiting for the storm of their breathing to subside.

But for Helen the descent to earth was swift, and soon unhappy.

Because now she knew there was no more room for pretence. She had taken as completely as she had given. And by so doing she'd sacrificed her self-respect, and any forlorn hope of feigning her indifference.

However it might have begun, Marc had given her a night she would remember always. But soon he would be lying with his lips against someone else's hair, his long fingers drowsily caressing another woman's breast. And she'd allowed herself to forget that for the sake of a few hours of total ravishment.

A little domestic entertainment. The coolly jeering words came back to haunt her. Because that was all he wanted—to ensure that when he came to Monteagle she'd be waiting for him with passionate eagerness, ready to give him anything he wanted. A perpetual honeymoon, Helen thought, biting her lower lip, still swollen from his kisses. Until, of course, her sexual education was complete, by which time her novelty for him would probably have worn off.

And all this pain—this heartbreak—she had brought upon herself.

I shall have to learn not to think, she told herself, as Marc's soft, regular breathing informed her that he'd fallen asleep. Not to wonder what he's doing when he's away, or who he might be with. No scenes and no accusations.

If I can manage to turn a perpetually blind eye, and he is reasonably discreet, then maybe our separate lives can be made to work.

She leaned across and switched off the lamp.

And now, she thought, she would try to sleep.

* * *

She opened her eyes to sunshine and birdsong, and Marc bending over her, clearly about to kiss her—and not for the first time, she thought, blushing, assailed by a vivid memory of him kissing her awake in the early dawn, and making love to her with such tenderness and grace that afterwards she'd found herself weeping in his arms.

'*Bonjour.*' He propped himself on an elbow and smiled at her. 'You awaken very beautifully.'

Her blush deepened. At some point during the night he must have retrieved the sheet, she realised, and covered her with it, because she now had a shield against the over-bright light of day. And, more importantly, against his eyes.

'Good morning,' she said, a touch awkwardly. 'Has—has the rain stopped?'

'You are a true Englishwoman, *cherie.*' He was laughing. 'You wish to discuss the weather even when you are in bed with your lover.'

But you're not my lover, she thought with sudden pain, even as her body clenched once more in unwilling yearning. Last night had nothing to do with love. It was simply a vindication of your own prowess in bed, because I rejected you. You needed to prove that you could make me want you against my own will and judgement. And against all reason—because I'm not the only woman in your life, and we both know it.

'I'm sorry,' she said stiffly.

'No, you must not be. It is charming.' He leaned down and kissed her mouth softly. 'And I wish very much that we could stay here for ever, but we have a plane to catch. Besides,' he added, stroking her cheek, 'there will be tonight.'

'Two planes,' Helen corrected, remembering the resolution she'd made last night and how badly she needed to keep it. He only had to look at her, she thought. Or smile. Or touch her lightly with a fingertip, and she was dying to melt in his arms. But she could not allow him to do this to her. Could not—would not—live this lie with him. 'We—we're on different flights.' She took a steadying breath. 'And yours, if you remember, is the earliest.'

'Different flights?' Marc repeated slowly. 'What are you

talking about? We will be travelling together. You are coming with me to Paris, *naturellement*.'

'No,' she said. 'I'm going back to England and Monteagle, as we agreed.'

Marc sat up abruptly, the sheet falling away from his body, and she looked away swiftly. Oh, God, she needed no reminders...

He said, 'But that was yesterday—before...'

'Before we had sex, you mean? You feel that should make some difference?' She kept her voice light. 'I don't see why.'

'I had hoped,' he said very quietly, 'that perhaps you would want to be with me. Now that we have found each other at last.'

But not in Paris, she wanted to scream at him. Never in Paris—at this famous apartment of yours, in the bed where you make love to your mistress. Don't you see that I *can't* go there? And that I won't—ever?

'But I shall be with you,' she returned instead. 'That is whenever you choose to come back to Monteagle.'

'Which may not be for some time,' he said. He looked at her steadily. 'That does not concern you?'

'You may come and go as you please. It's not up to me to interfere in your life—your decisions.' The rawness in her heart gave her voice an edge.

'I believed,' he said with sudden bleakness, 'that I had given you that right. So why do you refuse me?' He paused, and his voice hardened. 'Is it because there is some other one involved in our relationship? Has that come between us? Answer me.'

'You seem to know already.' She felt her heart give a sudden jolt. She hadn't intended this, she thought wretchedly. She hadn't thought he'd want to discuss Angeline Vallon or any of his women with her. She'd assumed he'd prefer her to ignore the rumours which would no doubt reach her. That he'd expect gratitude for Monteagle to keep her silent.

Why, she asked herself desperately, wasn't he playing according to the rules? But then, when had Marc ever done so?

'*Ah, Mon Dieu.*' He almost groaned the words, then was silent for a moment. At last, he said unevenly, 'Hélène—you are being a fool. Yet in spite of all this we can make our marriage work—I know it. This—other thing—it will not last. It cannot. And you cannot allow it to matter. To damage what we might have together.

'*Cherie.*' His voice deepened. 'You must not do this to yourself—to us.'

Us, Helen thought. There is no 'us' and never can be. Because even when Angeline Vallon is history, as you suggest, there'll be someone else in her place. There'll always be someone else—for a month or two...

'But I can't pretend it doesn't exist either,' she said raggedly. 'That wasn't part of the deal. So I shan't be going with you to Paris.' She took a deep breath. 'But Monteagle is yours too, of course, and when you choose to be there I'm prepared to reach some—compromise with you.'

'As you did last night?' The words slammed at her.

'Yes,' she said defiantly. 'Exactly like that.'

He said something under his breath—something harsh and ugly—then threw himself off the bed, grabbing for his discarded clothing. But he made no attempt to dress himself.

Instead, he reached into the pocket of his dinner jacket. 'Then allow me to congratulate you on your performance, *madame.*' His voice seared her like acid. 'You learn quickly—and, as I explained, I would not wish you to go unrewarded for your efforts.'

He tossed the roll of money into the air, and watched the banknotes flutter down on to the bed around her.

'Consider yourself paid in full, *ma femme,*' he added. 'Until the next time—wherever and whenever that may be.'

And he left her, white-faced and stricken, staring after him, as he strode to the door and vanished.

CHAPTER ELEVEN

'YOU mean it?' Lottie's face lit up. 'You'll let me have my wedding reception in the Long Gallery? Oh, Helen, that's wonderful.'

Helen returned her hug. 'Well, you can't squeeze everyone into your cottage—not without appalling casualties and structural damage anyway,' she added drily. 'And the Gallery looks terrific now it's finished. It really needs to be used for something special.'

Lottie hesitated. 'And you're sure Marc won't mind?'

'Why should he?' Helen asked with a light shrug. *As he's so rarely here...* She thought it, but did not say it aloud.

'I only wanted a tiny wedding,' Lottie said mournfully. 'A few close friends and family.' She sighed. 'But that was before our respective mothers presented us with their final guest lists, and a string of other instructions as well. I've had to rethink all my catering plans, for one thing, as well as dashing off to the wedding hire place in Aldenford for some ghastly meringue and veil.'

Helen patted her consolingly. 'You'll look wonderful,' she said. 'And I guarantee Simon will be secretly thrilled.' She paused. 'Shall we get some music laid on for dancing? Really test the Gallery's new floor?'

'Why not?' Her friend shrugged lavishly. 'In for a penny, in for a pound. The whole nine yards.' She gave Helen a speculative glance. 'Does Marc like dancing? I mean, he will make it to the wedding, I hope? Or will he be in Bolivia or Uzbekistan?'

'I—really don't know,' Helen admitted uncomfortably. 'But, wherever he is, I'm sure he'll do his best. I'll ask Alan to remind him. After all, he seems to see much more of him than I do,' she added, with attempted nonchalance.

There was another silence, then Lottie said fiercely, 'Oh, this is all so wrong—such a mess. Simon and I are so happy—so crazy about each other—and you're so damned miserable. And don't argue with me,' she warned, as Helen's lips parted in protest. 'Even a blind person could see it.'

'I have what I asked for,' Helen said quietly. 'And so has Marc.' She tried to smile. 'He seems quite content—and you have to admit the house is looking terrific.'

'I don't have to admit anything.' Lottie picked up her bag and prepared for departure. 'In fact there are times when I wish you'd sold Monteagle lock, stock and barrel to bloody Trevor Newson. So there.'

And there are times when I wish that too, Helen thought with sudden wry bitterness. The shocked breath caught in her throat as she realised what she had just admitted to herself.

She managed to keep a smile in place as she waved her friend off, but her stomach was churning and her legs felt oddly weak.

How can I suddenly feel like this? she asked herself as she made herself turn, walk back into the house she loved. The home she'd always considered worth any sacrifice.

Monteagle's been my life all this time. My lodestar. And so it should be still—because I have nothing else. Nothing...

She found she was making her way up the stairs, breathing the smell of paint, plaster and wood as she'd done for so many weeks. But, as usual, she encountered no one. The restoration team were busy at the other end of the house, and she was able to enter the State Bedroom once again unnoticed. Where she paused, staring round her, drinking in the room's completed beauty. And its strange emptiness.

The embroidery from the old bed curtains had been transferred exquisitely to its rich new fabric, and it gleamed in the mellow sunlight that poured in through the mullioned windows. While above the fireplace the other Helen Frayne looked enigmatically down on her descendant.

And, dominating the room, that enormous bed—made up each week with fresh linen, yet still unused.

Helen had stood in this room grieving after her grandfather's funeral, knowing that she was entirely alone. She'd tried with a kind of desperation to convince herself that it wasn't true. That she would spend her future with Nigel and find happiness and fulfilment—but only if she could save her beloved home and live there. That had always been the proviso.

No guy stands a chance against a no-win obsession like that. She found herself remembering Nigel's petulant accusation.

But it wasn't an obsession, she cried inwardly. It was a dream—wasn't it? Only now the dream was dead, and she didn't know why.

Except that she was lying to herself. Because it had begun to fade six weeks ago, when she came back from France.

Without Marc. Without even saying goodbye to Marc. Because he'd already left for the airport when she arrived downstairs that last morning at the Villa Mirage.

Later, on her own homeward journey, she'd asked Louis to stop at a little church she'd seen on the way out of St Benoit Plage, and she had filled the poor box to bursting with the euro notes that Marc had scattered so scornfully across her shocked body, hoping that by doing so she could somehow exorcise the stunned misery that was choking her.

All the way back to Monteagle she'd told herself over and over again that it would all be worth it once she was home. That somehow she'd even be able to survive this agony of bewildered loneliness once she could see her beautiful house coming back to life.

Only it hadn't been like that. Not when she'd realised that she was actually expected to move into this room—that bed— alone, and had known that she couldn't do it. That it was impossible. Unthinkable.

An unbearable solitude—worse than any imagining.

So she'd informed Daisy quietly that she'd prefer to sleep in her own bedroom for the time being, and the housekeeper, noting her pale face and tearless eyes, had tactfully not argued with her.

And there the matter rested. In distance and estrangement.

She'd explained, charmingly and ruefully, to anyone who asked that Marc was in serial business meetings and would join her as soon as he was free. But it was an excuse that sounded increasingly thin as a week had passed and edged into a fortnight without a word from him.

She'd found this lack of communication unnerving, and eventually swallowed her pride and approached Alan Graham.

'I was expecting Marc here this weekend,' she had fibbed, fingers crossed in the pockets of her skirt. 'But I've heard nothing—and I've stupidly mislaid his contact number in Paris. Do you know what's happening?'

'I certainly know that he's not in Paris,' Alan returned with a touch of dryness. 'He left for Botswana several days ago, and is going on to Senegal. He's unlikely to be back in Europe until next week, but even then I don't think he has any immediate plans to visit the UK.'

'I see.' Another lie. She forced a smile, but the architect's face remained impassive. 'Well, perhaps his secretary could supply me with a copy of his itinerary—or let me know if there's an opening in his schedule.'

She expected him to offer an address, a telephone extension and a name, but he did none of those things.

He hesitated perceptibly. 'Marc is incredibly busy, Mrs Delaroche. It might be better to leave it to him to get in touch—don't you think?'

In other words, if Marc had wanted her to make the first contact he'd have supplied her with the means, she realised, mortified. And Alan Graham—not just her husband's friend, but also his employee—had been instructed to block her, to keep her at a safe distance where she could not interfere with the way he lived his life.

'Yes,' she said, her voice stumbling over the word. 'Of course.'

As she turned to leave she saw an odd expression flicker in his eyes—something, she thought, which might have been pity. And her humiliation was complete.

Even now she could remember how she'd gone out of the house and walked round the lake, struggling to come to terms with the fact that her marriage was already virtually over.

Yes, she'd made him angry that last morning. But she'd been

upset, and desperately hurt. So how could he behave as if he was the only injured party in all this? If he cared for her at all, wouldn't he have been concerned more for her feelings and less for his own convenience?

Suggesting she should accompany him to Paris had been an act of brutal cynicism. Surely he must have realised that admitting there was another woman in his life had robbed her of any chance of peace and happiness whenever he was away from her?

Even now, when they were miles apart, she was still racked by jealousy and wretchedness. That last passionate, overwhelming night in France had done its work too well, creating a hunger that only he could assuage. But she was no longer a priority on his agenda.

She'd turned and stared at the bulk of the house through eyes blurred with tears. Her kingdom, she'd thought, where she ruled alone, just as she'd wanted. Her kingdom and her prison.

But even if Marc didn't want her, his plans for the house were clearly still foremost in his mind.

His team of craftsmen were still working flat out, over long hours, and she could only guess at the size of the wage bill being incurred. Also, the extra staff he'd insisted on were now in place—pleasant, efficient, and taking the pressure from George and Daisy. Far from feeling resentful, they were now talking cheerfully about the prospect of retirement on the pension that Marc had also set up for them.

'But what would I do without you?' Helen had asked, startled and distressed. 'I rely on you both totally. You're my family.'

Daisy had patted her gently. 'Everything changes, my dear. And you'll be having a new family soon—a proper one, with Monsieur Marc.'

Which, thought Helen, was almost a sick joke—under the circumstances.

She'd tried to keep busy, to stop herself from thinking, but apart from arranging the flowers and deciding what food to eat, there was little to occupy her at Monteagle, she had to admit. The place seemed to run like clockwork. Instead, she spent two days a week helping in a charity shop in Aldenford, and another afternoon pushing round the library trolley at the local cottage hospital.

So she'd been out when the longed-for telephone call had come to say Marc would be arriving the next day.

But her initial relief and elation had been dealt an immediate blow when Alan had informed her with faint awkwardness that this was simply a flying visit, to check on the progress of the house, and that Marc would be leaving again after lunch.

She'd managed a word of quiet assent, then taken herself up to her room, where she'd collapsed across the bed, weeping uncontrollably.

The next day she had departed early for a ceramics auction in a town twenty miles away. It had been purely a face-saving move. She had no particular interest in porcelain and pottery, and no intention of bidding on any of the lots.

She'd arrived back at Monteagle just before lunch was served, and returned Marc's cold greeting with equal reserve before eating her way through salmon mayonnaise and summer pudding as if she had an appetite, while Marc and Alan chatted together in French.

The meal over, she had been about to excuse herself when Marc detained her with an imperative gesture. Alan quietly left them alone together, standing on opposite sides of the dining table.

'The new staff? You find them acceptable?' he'd asked abruptly.

'Perfectly, thank you.' She hesitated. 'Of course it helps that they're local people.'

'And the house? The work continues to your satisfaction?'

'It all looks wonderful,' she said quietly. 'But naturally I shall be glad when it's over.'

There was an odd silence before he said, 'Then I hope for your sake, Hélène, that they continue to make the same progress and you are soon left in peace from all of this.' His brief smile did not reach his eyes. *'Au revoir,'* he added, and was gone.

And that, Helen thought unhappily, had set the pattern for

his two subsequent visits—except that Alan's wife had been invited to join them for lunch. But, as Susan treated her with the same polite aloofness as her husband, it couldn't be described as the most successful social experiment of the year.

There had never been any hint that he wished to spend the night here. In fact he didn't even want to touch her, she admitted, swallowing a desolate lump in her throat. It seemed that the beautiful Angeline was supplying all his needs, and that she herself was excluded from any intimate role in his life, however temporary.

Why did he do it? she asked herself. Why did he take me and make me want him so desperately that every day and night without him makes me feel as if I'm slowly bleeding to death?

But she already knew the answer. Because he could, she thought. And how cruel was that?

As unkind as the way he'd suddenly ended that brief interlude on the bed over there, she reminded herself. Her whole body had been singing to the touch of his mouth and hands when he'd stepped back, apparently unaffected by her response—except to be amused by it.

How silly and futile all her subsequent protests must have seemed to him—and how easily they'd been overcome, she thought bitterly. And she knew still that, in spite of everything, if he so much as beckoned to her she would go to him.

Her body was aching—starving for him. Demanding the surcease that only he could give, but which he chose to deny her.

Making it clear that there was no place for her even on the margins of his life.

Perhaps, she thought, wincing painfully, Angeline Vallon doesn't like sharing either, and has enough power to issue an ultimatum.

Sighing, she walked over to the portrait and stood staring up at it.

'How did you cope?' she asked softly. 'When your royal victor became tired of his spoils and moved on? How many days before you stopped hoping? How many long nights before he ceased to feature in your dreams? And what else must I endure before my sentence is served and I can get out of jail?'

On the other hand, if she did escape somehow, then where would she go?

Her mouth twisted wrily. Bolivia, she thought. Uzbekistan— or any of the places that Marc had been flying between over these long weeks. She'd always secretly yearned to travel, to get to the heart of cities and countries that were only names in an atlas, but she'd given up all hope of that for the sake of Monteagle.

If she could turn back time, she knew now she would have followed Marc downstairs that last morning, held out her hand and said, Take me with you. Because half a life at his side would have been better than no life at all.

A fly had appeared from nowhere, and was grumbling vainly against one of the windows. Helen walked across the room and opened the casement to allow it to escape, and stood suddenly transfixed, staring across the lawns below.

A woman was standing, a hand shading her eyes as she looked up at the house, her long red hair gleaming in the late summer sunlight.

No, Helen thought with disbelief. And, as the anger began to build in her, *No*.

Has Marc allowed this? she asked herself. Has he dared to let her invade my territory? And is she going to spend time here—with him—forcing me to move out for the duration? Why else would she be here, spying out the land?

Oh, God, she thought. How could he hurt me—insult me— like this?

She closed the casement with a bang and ran from the room, and down the stairs, almost flinging herself out into the open air.

As she reached the grass she saw the other woman walking rapidly towards the side gate.

She is not getting away with this, Helen told herself grimly. She'll stand her ground and hear what I have to say.

'Wait!' she called, cupping her hands round her mouth. '*Attendez, madame!*'

The other woman paused, turning as if surprised, then waited awkwardly, hands thrust into the pockets of her cream linen trousers, as Helen came running towards her.

She only stopped, breathless and shocked, when she realised that, apart from hair colour, her quarry bore no resemblance at all to the woman whose magazine picture still haunted her mercilessly.

She was considerably older, and thinner, and her face was pleasant rather than beautiful—although at the moment she looked embarrassed and wary.

'I'm sorry,' she said. 'The house isn't open to the public any more, is it? And I'm trespassing.'

'Yes, I'm afraid so.' Helen struggled to control her breathing. 'Did you want anything in particular?'

'Not really.' The other woman shrugged. 'Just a final glimpse, really. I went round with the guided tour a few times before the restoration work started, and I was curious to see if much had changed.'

Helen stared at her. 'You're quite a devotee.'

'I feel I've known the place all my life. You see, my great-grandmother was in service here years ago, and my grandmother too, and they loved it. I grew up with all these stories about Monteagle—felt as if I was part of them. Daft, I know, but we all have our dreams.'

She paused. 'You're Helen Frayne, aren't you? But you confused me when you called out in French. I thought that was your husband's nationality.'

'It is. I—I thought you were someone completely different. I'm sorry.' Helen hesitated. 'May I know who you really are?'

'Why not?' Another almost fatalistic shrug. 'My name's Shirley—Shirley Newson. You know my husband, I think?'

Helen said slowly, 'Yes—yes, I do.'

'And wish you didn't, I dare say.' Shirley Newson's smile was affectionate, but wan. 'Trevor's a good man, but when his heart's set on something he turns into a bull in a china shop. I know full well he ruined any chance we had of buying the place. All those stupid ideas about theme parks and the like.' Her eyes flashed. 'As if I'd have allowed that.'

She sighed. 'But I suppose he thought he could make my

dream come true, bless him, and turn a profit at the same time. It's what he's always done, so I can hardly blame him. But all I wanted was to live here quietly, doing the repairs bit by bit. Making it just like it was years ago, when my family worked here. Loving it, I suppose.'

She looked at Helen, biting her lip. 'Now I guess you'll call your security and have me thrown out.'

'Actually,' Helen said gently, 'I was going to offer you a cup of tea, Mrs Newson. And another guided tour—if you'd like that.'

It had been an oddly agreeable couple of hours, Helen decided when her unexpected guest had left. Shirley Newson had spoken no more than the truth when she'd said she knew the house. She was as accurate about its history as Marion Lowell, but she was also a fund of stories—amusing, scandalous and poignant—about the Fraynes and their guests, which her relations had handed down to her, and which Helen, thoroughly intrigued, had never heard before.

Perhaps, she thought wryly, if the wife had come to conduct negotiations a year ago instead of the husband there might have been a different outcome. Perhaps…

Anyway, she thought, it was all too late now. And she sighed.

'You did give Marc my message—about Lottie's wedding?' Helen tried to hide her bitter disappointment as she spoke. 'Because it starts in just over an hour, and he's cutting it incredibly fine if he intends to be here.'

'Mrs Delaroche.' Alan Graham's voice had an edge to it. 'Does it occur to you that there could be—circumstances which might make it difficult for Marc to leave Paris right now?'

Helen bit her lip. 'Meaning Madame Angeline Vallon, I suppose?' she challenged, too hurt and angry to be discreet.

Alan stared at her in open bewilderment. 'You know about that?' he asked incredulously.

'Yes,' she acknowledged curtly. 'After all, it's hardly a secret.'

'You know?' he repeated slowly. 'And yet you carry on with your life as if it didn't matter?' He'd never been friendly, but now he sounded positively hostile.

Riled, Helen lifted her chin. 'Marc makes his own choices,' she said. 'They have nothing to do with me. My world is here.'

His laugh was derisive. 'And so as long as it's looked after you don't give a damn about anything else. I'd hoped that, all appearances to the contrary, you might actually care.'

Care? she thought. *Care?* Can't you see I'm in agony here—falling apart?

She said freezingly, 'You may be my husband's friend, but that gives you no right to criticise me like this.'

'Mrs Delaroche,' he said, 'you are perfectly correct about that, and you can have me removed from this project any time you like. I have other more worthwhile proposals in the pipeline.'

He paused. 'I'm sure Marc will be at this wedding if it's humanly possible. No matter what it may cost him. Because you've asked him to do it. Is that what you want to hear?'

And with a final scornful glance at her, he walked away.

Helen wasn't sure if she had the power to fire him, but she knew she shouldn't let the matter rest. That she should go after him—demand an explanation for his extraordinary behaviour.

Except she had a wedding to dress for, she thought, pushing her hair back from her face with an angry, restless hand. And if she had to attend it alone, she would do so looking like a million dollars.

Because no one was going to accuse her of wearing a broken heart on her sleeve.

She'd decided, after a lot of consideration, to wear her own wedding outfit again. After all, Marc had once suggested that she should do so at a party of their own, she remembered unhappily, and under the circumstances Lottie's wedding reception was probably as good as it was going to get.

But once today was over, she told herself grimly, she would develop some attitude of her own—and deal with Alan Graham.

*　　*　　*

The service had already begun when she was aware of whispering behind her, and at the same moment Marc slipped into the pew beside her. She turned to look at him, lips parted, delight churning inside her—along with an almost savage yearning.

'I—I didn't think you'd be here,' she breathed.

'I had an invitation.' His whispered reply was cool and unsmiling.

Helen sank back into her seat, her heart thumping painfully. What had she been hoping? That he'd kiss her, murmuring that he could not keep away when all the evidence was to the contrary?

She hadn't been to many traditional weddings, and she'd almost forgotten the timeless resonances of the Prayer Book ceremony. Now they came flooding back with a kind of desperate poignancy, making her hands clench together in her lap and her throat tighten.

She watched Simon and Lottie with painful intensity—his unhidden tenderness, her glorious serenity—knowing that was how it should be when you were safe and loved.

If only Marc had looked at her like that, adoring her with his eyes, when they'd stood together to receive the same blessing the Vicar was pronouncing now, she thought passionately. And if only she'd been free to whisper the oldest vow of all—*I love you* as he bent to kiss her.

Because she knew now with terrible certainty that this was the truth she'd been fighting since she met him. That it wasn't simply the beguilement of sexual union that she'd feared, but the deeper spiritual and emotional commitment that she'd tried to reject. The recognition that in this man—this stranger—she'd somehow met the other half of herself.

Everything else had been a blind—the bargain they'd made, even Monteagle itself.

But only for me, she thought, pain lancing her. Not for Marc. To him it was never more than a deal, and now he has what he wants he's moved on.

She sent him a swift sideways glance from under her lashes,

silently begging him to turn towards her—take her hand. But Marc sat unmoving, his profile like granite, his expression as remote as some frozen wasteland.

And she knew that if there'd been a moment when she might have captured his heart it was long gone. All she was left with was loneliness, stretching out into eternity.

CHAPTER TWELVE

NOT long now, Helen promised herself wearily. The bride and groom had departed for their honeymoon in an aura of radiance, and the usual sense of anticlimax had immediately set in, so the party would soon be breaking up. And just as well, because she was almost at the end of her tether.

She could admit it now. She hadn't felt well all day—tired and vaguely sick. And it had been the same for the past week or more, if she was honest. Stress, she supposed. And sheer uncertainty about the future.

Not that the reception hadn't been a great success. The Long Gallery had looked wonderful, its mellow panelling gleaming in the late sunlight while Lottie's delicious food had been eaten and the toasts drunk, then later assuming an atmosphere of total romance once the candles were lit and the music began.

And Helen couldn't fault Marc. Wherever else he might wish himself to be, he'd behaved like a perfect host. He had danced with practically every woman in the room—bar one. He'd even stood beside her, his hand barely touching her uncovered shoulder, as Simon and Lottie thanked them lavishly for their hospitality and called for their health to be drunk.

'Marc and Helen—who saved our lives.'

And Helen had stood mutely, smiling until her face ached, determined to overcome the churning inside her and trying also to ignore the fact that Marc had not danced with her. Other people had, of course. She'd hardly been a wallflower. But she and her husband had been on parallel lines all evening—never meeting, never touching until that moment. Hardly speaking. And that was clearly the way he wanted it.

Wearing her wedding outfit had been a mistake too. As she'd removed the jacket, her nervous hands struggling once again with those tiny slippery buttons, she'd sensed him near

172

her, and glanced up, wondering if he remembered—if he would come to her rescue this time too. But Marc's dark gaze had swept over her in total indifference, and then he'd turned away, his mouth hardening. And deliberately kept his distance ever after, she realised forlornly.

But when the guests had finally departed and they were left alone—what then?

She'd learned from Daisy that he'd brought a travel bag, which had been put in the State Bedroom. So it seemed he was planning to stay the night at least. But Helen had no idea whether or not he intended to sleep alone, or if, in spite of everything, he would expect her to join him in that vast bed.

The warmth of Lottie's farewell hug and her fierce whisper, 'Be happy', still lingered, taunting her with its sheer impossibility.

Because even if she went to Marc tonight, and he took her, it would mean nothing. Just a transient usage of his marital rights, which she knew she would not have the power to resist. Because she wanted him too badly.

His arms around me, she thought sadly, on any terms. Any terms at all. No pretence. No defence.

And above all she needed to talk to him—to ask him to give their ill-conceived disaster of a marriage another chance. Even if she had to resort to the self-exposure of confessing how much his infidelity was hurting her.

But when she returned from saying goodbye to the bride and groom's parents, and the other departing guests, awash with gratitude and good wishes, the Long Gallery was empty and dark. Daisy and the staff were not scheduled to begin the big clear-up until the morning. But there was no sign of Marc either.

He hadn't even waited to wish her goodnight, let alone offered the chance of the private conversation she needed.

So I'll have to go to him instead, she told herself, taking a deep breath.

The door to the State Bedroom stood slightly ajar, and Helen paused before tapping lightly at its massive panels.

'Entrez.' His voice was brusque, and not particularly welcoming.

When she went in she saw that he'd changed into jeans and a sweatshirt, and was packing the elegant dark suit he'd worn for the wedding into a clothes carrier, his movements swift and economical.

She halted, the breath catching in her throat. 'You're leaving already? You're not staying the night?'

'As you see,' he returned unsmilingly. 'I am expected elsewhere.'

'Where this time?' She tried to speak lightly. 'Kabul? Rio de Janeiro? I can hardly keep pace with your travels.'

'I have to return to Paris.'

'Of course.' Helen lifted her chin. 'Another place that occupies much of your time and attention. But couldn't you delay your trip just a little—please? Go back tomorrow, perhaps, or the next day? I think we need to spend some time together—and talk. Don't you think so?'

'Yes,' he said slowly. 'That will probably be necessary very soon. But not quite yet.' For a long moment he looked at her, the dark eyes scanning her slender body in the pale silk dress, but he took no step towards her.

He added quietly, 'It is essential that I go tonight. Accept my regrets.'

But she was not quite beaten. Not yet. She braced herself for a last throw of the dice.

She said huskily, 'Marc, you—once asked me to go to Paris with you, and I refused. But I could pack very quickly—if you'd consider asking me again.' She stared at him across the space that divided them, her eyes shining with sudden tears. She whispered, 'Please don't leave me again. Take me with you. Keep me with you.' She paused, swallowing. 'Or couldn't you just—forget Paris altogether and stay here?'

She saw a flash of something like pain cross the dark face.

'I am sorry.' His voice was harsh. 'But that is not possible. Please do not ask me to explain.'

But no explanations were necessary, she thought, knifed by desolation. She already knew why there would be no second chance for them. For her. Why he'd decided to shut her out of his life. Angeline Vallon had won, and she was no longer wanted.

Her marriage was over almost before it had begun.

She said quietly, 'I—I'm sorry to have embarrassed you.' And turned to go, praying that she would not break down completely in front of him.

He caught her before she reached the door. 'Hélène.' His voice was low and urgent. 'Ah, *Dieu*. I did not mean it should be like this. Forgive me, if you can.'

Then his mouth was on hers, and he was kissing her with a kind of stark desperation, his lips plundering—bruising—as if he intended to leave his mark on her for ever.

His hands were in the small of her back, pulling her against him, and she was gasping, trembling, her body grinding against his hardness in open longing as desire scalded her. Her arms wound round his neck as her lips parted in trembling, passionate response.

Stay with me…

But he was already detaching himself, putting her away from him. He said hoarsely, 'I cannot do this. I have to go.' There was a kind of agony in his eyes. 'One day, perhaps, you will understand.'

She leaned against the massive frame of the door, listening to the sound of his retreating footsteps.

What was there to understand? she wondered drearily. Only that she'd humbled herself totally to try to win him and been rejected. And now she had to live with the shame of it, she thought. And began to weep very softly.

Helen came out of the doctor's surgery and stood for a moment, as if she wasn't sure which direction to take. She was shivering a little, but whether it was because of the autumnal feeling in the air or the news she'd just received she couldn't be certain.

Why didn't I realise? she asked herself numbly. How could I not have known?

At first she'd attributed her feeling of malaise and the disruption of her monthly routine to the strain imposed by the last turbulent weeks. But this morning she'd been swiftly and comprehensively sick as soon as she'd got up. And her immediate shocked suspicion had just been cheerfully confirmed by the doctor who'd known her all her life.

'Another page in Monteagle's dynasty,' he'd congratulated her. 'Your husband must be thrilled.'

'I—I haven't mentioned anything to him.' Helen had looked at her hands, twisted together in her lap. 'Not yet. I wanted to be sure.'

He'd said once, in a distant past that was somehow only a few weeks ago, that he wanted children. But since then everything had changed, and she could be certain of nothing.

She had received a keen look. 'I gather this wasn't planned?'

Her lips had formed themselves into a soundless 'no'.

'Then it will be a marvellous surprise for him,' Dr Roscoe had said confidently, and dismissed her with sensible advice about the morning sickness and instructions to make another appointment.

Now, somehow, she found herself outside again, taking great gulps of air and wondering when exactly this had happened. She could only hope it had not been during the brief nightmare of her wedding night, but on that other never-to-be-forgotten time, when Marc had ravished her body and her senses, unaware or uncaring that her heart was already reluctantly his.

But how would he react when he learned she was pregnant? she asked herself wretchedly. He had not wanted to stay with her for her own sake. Would he come back for the baby she was carrying?

Slowly, she turned and began to head back to Monteagle, her mind treading wearily round the same questions and coming up with uncomfortable answers.

She was so deep in her own thoughts that she hardly realised where she was, until a familiar voice said, 'You're looking glum, darling. Trying to figure out where you'll find your next millionaire?'

Her head came up instantly, defensively, and she met Nigel's derisive grin. His car was parked on the other side of the road, outside his parents' empty house with the 'Sold' board in the garden. And he was here, standing in front of her, the last person she wanted to see.

Strange, she thought, that worrying about Mrs Hartley's good opinion had once been her major problem.

She said, 'What are you doing here?'

He shrugged. 'Mother thought she might have left some things in the roof space, and asked me to check.' He paused. 'I saw you walking past and thought I'd say a last goodbye.'

'Thank you,' she said. 'And—goodbye.'

'I also wanted to say—hard lines.' Nigel detained her, his hand on her arm. 'It looks as if you'll have to sell that expensive heap of yours after all,' he added with a sympathetic whistle.

'I'm sorry,' Helen said coldly, 'but you're not making any sense.'

'No?' He started artistically. 'Then maybe Monsieur Delaroche hasn't told you the bad news. There's been a boardroom revolt in his company—too much going wrong, drop in profits, et cetera—and he's going to be out of a job very soon. Out of money too. He's wasted any fighting fund he might have had pouring money into Monteagle. And there'll be no golden handshake either—not if Hercule Vallon has anything to do with it.'

She said scornfully, 'I don't believe you.'

'Maybe you should take more interest in your husband's affairs,' Nigel drawled. 'His business ones, that is. The board's voting to replace your Marc some time this week, and as his company's his only asset, you're going to need another backer to keep Monteagle. Because he can't afford to.'

He grinned insolently into her shocked face. 'The beautiful Madame Vallon will have her revenge at last. But then you know all about that,' he added insinuatingly. 'You told me so at your wedding.' His smile widened. 'Maybe you should have considered the implications more carefully. You wouldn't have rushed into marriage with such indecent haste if you'd known your millionaire would soon be broke.'

Her heart was hammering and her mouth was dry, but she

managed to say with icy pride, 'I'd have married Marc if he'd been penniless.'

'You married him for Monteagle,' Nigel sneered. 'We all knew that. And once he loses everything do you really think you'll be able to afford to keep the place on? I don't.'

'No,' Helen said quietly. 'Nor do I.' She paused, lifting her chin. 'But I know a woman who will.'

As the taxi took her into the centre of Paris the following day Helen felt strangely relaxed. The calm after the storm this time, she thought.

She had wrung Marc's private address and the whereabouts of his company's head office out of a patently unwilling Alan Graham.

'This is Marc's battle,' he'd kept saying as she had confronted him. 'He didn't want you to know—to be involved.' He gave her a bitter look. 'After all, you only cared about this great white elephant of a house. You never displayed the slightest interest in his work—or his life, for that matter. Why start now?'

'Because I am involved,' she told him. 'I'm his wife, and I'm going to be the mother of his child.' She paused, allowing him to digest that. 'If he's fighting for our lives, then I should be with him.' She paused again. 'Especially as you seem to hold me entirely to blame,' she added drily.

'You came into his life at just the wrong time,' he said bluntly. 'Marc owed his success very much to instinct. He could almost smell political instability—knew when there was trouble brewing. But when he met you he took his eye off the ball. Even when things started to go wrong he thought the company's problems could wait a little while he made sure of you.'

He shrugged. 'But like most successful men he had enemies, and they were soon circling, smelling blood in the water. Given the chance, he could pull things around, and that's what he's been trying to do for the past weeks. But the odds are stacked against him.'

She said, 'And Angeline Vallon? Wasn't she—his mistress? I—I heard—rumours.'

'Angeline Vallon,' Alan said carefully, 'is a self-obsessed bitch, married to a man who's mega-rich and mega-stupid, who lets her do pretty much as she wants. A couple of years back what she wanted most was Marc, but he wasn't interested, and he made the mistake of letting her see it. So she started stalking him—letters—gifts—phone calls. She rented an apartment near his, boasted that they were lovers, tipped off the gossip columns. Turned up at any social event he was attending.

'In the end, he had to take legal action. She was turning his life into a nightmare. And for a while, admittedly, it went quiet. But that was just while she was thinking what to do next. And, of course, she came up with the alternative idea of taking his company away from him. He'd turned her down, so he had to be punished in a way that would hurt him most.

'She made her husband believe—God knows how—that she was the injured party—that Marc had been pursuing her, frightening her with his sexual demands. And, urged on by Angeline, Hercule got together with some of the board who thought they could make a better job of running the company than Marc. All they needed was a window of opportunity.'

He shook his head. 'And when Marc saw you, he left that window wide open.'

She said fiercely, 'Why didn't he tell me any of this?'

His mouth twisted ruefully. 'Because he thought that you only cared about the money—and saving this house. That if he lost the company he'd also lose what little he seemed to have of you.'

His voice deepened harshly. 'We've been friends for years. He always seemed—invincible. Until he met you. You made him vulnerable. And you didn't seem to give a damn about him either.'

He shook his head. 'When I saw him after the honeymoon he was like a stranger—so withdrawn, so wretched. Naturally he wouldn't talk about it, and I couldn't ask. But he no longer seemed to have the will to watch his back, just when he needed to most. And now it's probably too late.'

'No,' Helen said, swiftly and clearly. 'I don't accept that. Oh, why didn't he tell me what was happening?'

Alan was silent for a moment. 'Perhaps because he didn't want you to see him lose?' He hesitated. 'It might be better to wait until he sends for you.'

'But if he loses he may never send for me,' she said. 'And I'm not risking that. Because if he has to start all over again, I intend to be with him.'

It was late afternoon when she reached the Paris offices of Fabrication Roche, only to find the main entrance locked. She rang the bell and a security guard appeared.

She said in her schoolgirl French, 'Where is everyone?'

'They have been sent home, *madame*, following the meeting today.'

Her heart sank like a stone. 'And Monsieur Delaroche?'

'He is still here, *madame*,' the man admitted. 'In the boardroom. But he has given orders not to be disturbed.'

She said briskly, 'I am his wife—Madame Delaroche. Please take me to him at once.'

He gestured helplessly. 'But I have my orders, *madame*, to admit no one.'

Helen stared at him tragically, allowing her lip to tremble convincingly. 'But I have travelled all the way from England, *monsieur*. And I am *enceinte*. These rules cannot apply to me.'

She could never be sure whether it was her announcement that she was pregnant or the threat of tears that did it, but next minute she was in a high-powered lift, travelling to the top floor.

At the end of the short passage a pair of double doors confronted her. She opened them and slipped inside.

Marc was standing by the huge picture window at the end of the room, silhouetted against the fading afternoon light. His bent head and his arms folded tautly across his body spoke of a weariness and tension almost too great to be borne. And of a loneliness that tore at her heart.

She put down her travel bag. 'Marc,' she said softly. 'Marc, darling.'

He turned abruptly, his eyes narrowing in disbelief. 'Hélène—what are you doing here?'

She walked towards him. 'I made myself homeless this morning,' she said. 'I was hoping you might offer me a bed for the night. Or for quite a lot of nights. The rest of our lives, even.'

His mouth tightened. He said, 'Is this some game?'

'No,' she said. 'I'm deadly serious. You see—I've sold Monteagle.'

'Sold it?' His hands gripped her arms. He stared down into her face. 'But that is not possible. It is your home, the centre of your life.'

She said steadily, 'Marc, you're the centre of my life. Nothing else matters. So Monteagle now belongs to Trevor Newson—every brick, every beam, every blade of grass. All except the portrait of Helen Frayne,' she added. 'And Alan's taking care of that for us.'

He let her go, stepping backwards, his face a mask of consternation. 'You sold to Trevor Newson—to that man? But you loathe him—and his plans for Monteagle. You have always said so.'

'Yes,' she agreed. 'But I don't think his schemes will be as bad as I thought. He's buying the house primarily for his wife, and I suspect she won't let him go too far. Besides,' she added, shrugging, 'I won't be there to see what happens. I'll be with you, if you want me. And if you don't hate me too much for selling the place you loved so much.'

'I loved it for your sake, Hélène,' he said quietly. 'Because I adored you, *mon amour*, and I wanted only to make you happy.'

'And now perhaps I can make it up to you in turn, for losing Fabrications Roche.' She took an envelope from her jacket pocket. 'Marc, darling, this is for you. It's in your name.'

'Comment?' He was frowning as he tore open the envelope, then he stopped, his lips parting in a gasp of sheer astonishment as he saw the amount on the bank draft it contained. *'Mon Dieu!* He paid you this much?'

'Without a murmur,' she said. 'Egged on by the wonderful

Shirley. Alan and the bank manager advised me what to ask, and I think I could have got more.' She paused. 'But it's enough, isn't it?' she asked almost diffidently. 'Enough for us to start again—together? Begin a life—a real marriage? Because I love you, and I don't think I can live without you.'

He stared at her in silence and she tried to laugh, the memory of his last rejection burning in her. 'Marc—please. Haven't you got anything to say?'

He said unsteadily, 'I think I am afraid to speak in case I awake and find that I have been dreaming.'

Helen moved to him, sliding her arms round his waist under his jacket, pressing herself close to him. She whispered, 'Do I feel like a dream?' His body quickened and hardened against hers. 'Because you feel incredibly real.'

'Ah, mon ange.' He sank down to the floor, pulling her with him to the thick carpet. Their hands tugged and tore at each other's clothing, made clumsy by haste and need. She returned his kisses eagerly, moaning faintly as his hands uncovered and caressed her naked breasts, then lifted herself towards him, sobbing with acceptance as he entered her.

He said thickly, *'Hélène—je t'aime—je t'adore.'*

'Yes,' she whispered, her voice shaking as she began to move with him, their bodies blending hungrily. 'Oh, my love—my love…'

It was not a prolonged mating. Their mutual desire was too fierce, too greedy for its satisfaction. As the soft, trembling pulsations deep within her reached their culmination she cried out, and heard him groan his pleasure in turn.

When she could speak again, Helen said faintly, 'Thank heaven I packed some stuff. You've wrecked this dress completely.'

'I hope you do not want me to apologise.' He wrapped her closely in his arms, his lips against her hair. 'Perhaps you should stop wearing clothes altogether.'

'With winter coming?' Helen pretended to shiver. 'Besides,' she added, trying to sound casual, 'the baby might catch a chill.'

His caressing hand abruptly stopped its ministrations. 'Baby? What are you saying?'

'Yes, darling,' she told him softly. 'That's the other thing I came to tell you. It seems you're going to be a father.'

'*Ah, Dieu.*' He lifted himself on to an elbow, staring at her in a kind of anguish. 'What have I done?'

She looked back at him, her throat tightening in shock. 'You—don't want our baby? I admit the timing isn't ideal, but—'

'Want it?' He seized her hands, covering them in kisses. '*Mon coeur*, I cannot believe such happiness. But we should not have made love,' he added grimly. 'It could be dangerous when you are only just *enceinte.*'

'Well, the baby will just have to cope.' She smiled up at him. 'We have to make up for lost time, my love.'

'Then I shall have to learn to be gentle. You have to be kept safe, even if I have to wrap you in silk,' Marc told her softly.

'Safe.' She sighed the word. 'The first time you made me feel safe was when I'd had too much to drink and you slept with me on the sofa.' Her eyes widened. 'I think that was when I realised I was falling in love with you.'

He framed her face between his hands. 'And yet you ran away,' he reminded her teasingly. 'Why didn't you awaken me, Hélène, and tell me how you felt—what you wanted me to do?' he added, kissing her mouth softly and sensuously.

'Because Nigel had told me you exercised a two-month limit on your affairs, and I was frightened,' she said frankly. 'Scared to love you, or let you make love to me, in case you broke my heart.'

'But with you, it was never to be an *affaire*,' he said quietly. 'It was to be a lifetime. Because you were the one I had been waiting for, *cherie*. The girl of my heart. With the others before you—' he shrugged '—I can say only in my defence that I tried to be honest—to make no promises I would not keep, nor offer commitment I would not fulfil. When they knew there was no future in the relationship, most of my girlfriends walked away.'

She said in a low voice, 'But with me, you always said it was the house you wanted. And I was just part of the deal.'

'I said that to protect myself. And to stop you running away from me. You see, *mon amour*, at that time I thought you still cared for Nigel.'

'Nigel!' Helen sat up indignantly. 'Oh, you couldn't have done.'

'I saw you together at the wedding,' he said, his mouth twisting. 'You seemed quite happy in his arms.'

She said flatly, 'I think I was temporarily paralysed. He was telling me to ask you about Angeline Vallon. He—he implied she was your mistress.'

'And you believed him?' His voice was incredulous. 'But why did you not ask me?'

'Because I couldn't guarantee what your answer might be,' she said. She took a deep breath. 'I'm afraid I'd heard you talking to Alan about her, and I'm not proud of that. Nigel appeared to confirm what you'd said. So heartbreak seemed to be right there, waiting for me.' She paused. 'Anyway, why didn't you ask me about Nigel?'

'Because I told myself that once we were married, and in bed together, I could make you forget him,' he said huskily. 'That I could persuade you to fall in love with me. I was that arrogant—that stupid. I should have known that with you it could never be that simple.'

'I fought you for my own sake,' she said quietly. 'No one else's. But I still could not stop myself wanting you.' She was silent for a moment. 'That money—I gave it to the poor in St Benoit.'

His smile was crooked as he drew her back into his arms and lay down again, her head pillowed on his chest. 'How estimable of you, *cherie*.'

'I wish I hadn't now,' she said regretfully. 'After all, we need every penny we can get.'

He laughed. 'Things are not that bad, *ma petite*.'

'Marc—don't pretend. Alan told me you stood to lose everything.' She stirred uneasily. 'I don't suppose we should even be here—especially, my goodness, like this,' she added, recognising their joint state of *dishabille*. 'The security men might come to escort you from the building. Isn't that what happens? And don't you have a desk to clear? Because I could help...'

'Hélène,' he said gently. 'Do not upset yourself. There is no need, I promise.'

'I'm bound to be upset,' she protested. 'You've lost Fabrication Roche, and I know what it meant to you. How difficult it must be...'

'*Mon coeur,*' he said patiently, 'I did not lose. It was close, but I won. I still have the company.'

She stared up at him, open-mouthed. 'But Alan said—'

'Alan is a realist. He knew the odds were against me. But I had suspected a long time ago that someone might be planning a boardroom *coup*. We were suddenly encountering problems where there had been none before.' Wryly, he counted them on his fingers. 'Sabotage, strikes, accusations of racism, key workers abducted and held to ransom.'

He shook his head. 'Someone wished to acquire Fabrication Roche, and cheaply, but I did not at once see that Angeline Vallon might be involved. I thought that difficulty was behind me—that she had seen the error of her ways. But I was wrong.

'However, I knew that I had not been her only target. Not all of them had resisted, *naturellement*, but they had all found it was not easy to escape her talons, even when the relationship had palled and they wished it to end. She had a capacity for revenge, that one.'

Helen's eyes were like saucers. 'But her husband...'

'He worshipped her,' Marc said briefly. 'And she dominated him. He decided that her beauty made her the prey of other men's lusts, but that she was always innocent. I had insulted her, therefore I must be punished. He has a simplistic mind, *le pauvre* Hercule.'

His mouth twisted. 'And, as Alan saw, I had allowed my attention to wander a little. But what could I do, once I had seen the woman I had been waiting for all my life? I had to make you mine.'

She nestled closer. 'You were certainly persistent.'

He kissed her again. 'I was in love. So much so that I could almost understand poor foolish Hercule. That day when I sat beside you at Charlotte's wedding I knew I would give anything to have you look at me as she did at her husband, but it seemed hopeless. And I was afraid, too, that if I could not afford Monteagle I might lose you for ever.'

'But I came to you,' she said. 'I offered myself. You know that.'

'I did not know, however, what I could offer in return.' He stroked the curve of her cheek. 'I was scared that if it was a choice between Monteagle and myself, I would lose. So it seemed best to fight on alone, until I knew what kind of life I could lay at your feet.'

'And I thought you preferred Angeline Vallon and couldn't wait to get back to her,' she confessed.

'In a way, you were right. My legal advisers had contacted me to say that they had finally drawn up a dossier of her affairs, with testimony from her other victims. So I was able to present it to Hercule before the final meeting today and watch him collapse. It was not pleasant, and I felt,' he added quietly, 'like a murderer.'

'But his bid for Fabrication Roche collapsed with him, along with his allies on the board.' His smile was grim. 'They were the ones who found themselves being escorted from the building. Now there will be some restructuring and—voilà—life goes on.'

'So you didn't actually need the money I brought you.' There was a touch of wistfulness in her voice.

'Ah, but I needed the love that came with it.' His arms tightened round her. 'And the look in your eyes I had prayed for. A far more precious gift, mon amour.' He paused, his hand caressing the curve of her body that sheltered his child.

'Although,' he added. 'We could use the money, if you wish, to try and repurchase Monteagle.'

She shook her head slowly. 'No, that's all in the past, and I'd rather let it go—invest in our future. Find a new home for us both, and our children.' She hesitated. 'Marc—when I came in, you didn't look like someone who'd just won a famous victory. You looked—sad.'

'I was thinking of you,' he said quietly. 'And all the mistakes I had made. Wondering how soon I could go to you—to explain and ask you to forgive me. To try once more to persuade you to let me share your life—to love me. It seemed at that moment my real battle was still to come. Until you spoke, and smiled at me, and I realised that, little as I deserved it, I had been offered a miracle.'

He bent and took her mouth, gently and reverently.

'And now,' he told her, 'I must get you dressed and fed, my wife. But the only bed I can offer is in my apartment,' he added ruefully. 'And you have never wished to go there.'

'I thought I had my reasons,' she said. 'But I was wrong. About so many things.' She allowed him to lift her to her feet, and slid her arms round his neck, her eyes shining into his with joy and trust. 'Please, Marc—take me home.'

MILLS & BOON®

Why not subscribe?
Never miss a title and save money too!

Here is what's available to you if you join the exclusive **Mills & Boon® Book Club** today:

* *Titles up to a month ahead of the shops*
* *Amazing discounts*
* *Free P&P*
* *Earn Bonus Book points that can be redeemed against other titles and gifts*
* *Choose from monthly or pre-paid plans*

Still want more?
Well, if you join today we'll even give you
50% OFF your first parcel!

So visit **www.millsandboon.co.uk/subscriptions**
or call **Customer Relations on 0844 844 1351***
to be a part of this exclusive Book Club!

*This call will cost you 7 pence per minute plus your phone company's price per minute access charge.

SUBS_2016